TEMPEST OF WRATH AND VENGEANCE

THE LEGACY SERIES
BOOK THREE

MELISSA K. ROEHRICH

ALSO BY MELISSA K. ROEHRICH

LADY OF DARKNESS SERIES (COMPLETE)

Lady of Darkness

Lady of Shadows

Lady of Ashes

Lady of Embers

The Reaper (A Lady of Darkness Novella)

Lady of Starfire

Unrelenting Winds (A Lady of Darkness Novella)

Treasures of Darkness (A Lady of Darkness Compilation)

THE LEGACY SERIES

Rain of Shadows and Endings

Storm of Secrets and Sorrow

Tempest of Wrath and Vengeance

Book Four (Final Book)- coming August 28, 2025

Tempest of Wrath and Vengeance- 1st Ed.

Copyright © 2024 Melissa K. Roehrich

Editing Services: Megan Visger

Cover Design: Covers by Jules (www.coversbyjules.crd.co)

Rights and Representation by Katie Shea Boutillier: ksboutillier@maassagency.com at Donald Maass Literary Agency.

ISBN:

978-1-960923-11-0 (*Hardcover*)

978-1-960923-12-7 (*Paperback*)

❈ Created with Vellum

A COUPLE THINGS & CONTENT INFORMATION

taps mic and clears throat

Friends. Sweet Readers. Beloved Lovers of the Chaos—

I've been clear in the past, but I'm going to say it again: This is a DARK fantasy romance series. The characters? They're ALL morally grey. They're all walking, talking red flags who make questionable decisions, and in true dark fashion, they're probably going to stay that way. There's redemption. There's growth. But it's still Devram. They're still villains. If you are at all concerned about where this book is going or how relationships might end up (I don't do love triangles, friends), you need to check the content information provided on my website (www.melis sakroehrich.com). There you can find all the tropes, tags, and triggers. I put it there because I can easily update it if needed. If any of those things are not for you, it's okay! We give you this information so you can set your own boundaries and protect your mental health. However, please do not go in blind and then message me in disappointment or anger when things happen that were outlined in that information that has always been available to you. Yes, it's happened. I did my part; now I need you to do yours.

Okay, now that we got that out of the way, welcome back to Devram. Thank you for trusting me and for trusting the process. This book was a whirlwind from start to finish, and the twists and turns among the chaos certainly don't change. We finally get to some of the big reveals I have been so excited about from the beginning of this series. I promise you the same big feelings as before, and I promise we see our babies grow. I promise emotional whiplash, some swooning, and some redemption. I promise to have you holding your breath and to leave you wanting more. Don't complain. We have one more book after all.

A quick reminder until I am blue in the face: *The Legacy Series* takes place in the same universe as the *Lady of Darkness* series, but this is an entirely new world with brand new characters. You do NOT need to read the *Darkness* series to understand *The Legacy Series*. This series can be read separately. This story will have its own conclusion by the end. However, you WILL come across spoilers for the *Darkness* series and some dragon eggs along the way, even if you don't recognize them as spoilers at the time. Some of our favs have found their way to Devram, and we get to see them from a different perspective. I promise I reveal none of the big things from *Darkness*, but there will be minor spoilers.

You might need something stronger than wine this time. So grab that, strategically place padding for when you throw objects, and enter the Chaos. Welcome back to Devram.

XO- Melissa

PLAYLIST

I adore when books come with playlists that follow along with the story. You feel everything more. It immerses you more. It brings everything to life. If you find this to be true for you too, here you go! I spend a good chunk of time meticulously picking a song for each chapter (usually when I'm avoiding writing, haha!) Enjoy!

If you don't have Spotify, the full playlist can also be found on my website: https://www.melissakroehrich.com under Book Extras!

For those who are still trying to find their place in this world, it's okay. Take your time. It will be worth the wait.

LEGACY SERIES REFERENCE GUIDE

I know. There's a lot to remember and keep straight as you dive into Devram.
So here's a little reference guide to help you out!

OUR MAIN PLAYERS

Tessalyn Ausra:
Tes-uh-lin Ah-sruh
~~Fae. Legacy~~ Listen, no one knows
Source of the Arius Heir...sort of
A little (or a lot) wild and impulsive

Theon St. Orcas:
Thee-on Sānt Or-kus
Legacy, Heir to the Arius Kingdom,
A morally grey, walking, talking red flag
Source to...Tessa? Maybe?

Luka Mors:
Loo-kuh Morz
Sargon Legacy, Theon's Guardian
and advisor

Axel St. Orcas:
Ax-ul Sānt Or-kus
Legacy, Second-in-Line for the Arius
Kingdom, Theon's brother, was
involved with Katya
No one knows where he is

OTHERS OF NOTE

Dex: Dex
Wind Fae, Tessa's best friend?
Claimed by Achaz Kingdom

Oralia: Or-āl-eeuh
Water Fae, Tessa's Friend?
Claimed by Achaz Kingdom

Corbin: Kor-bin
Water Fae, Tessa's friend, involved
with Lange, claimed by Arius
Kingdom

Lange: Lāng
Wind Fae, Tessa's friend, involved with
Corbin, claimed by Arius Kingdom

Brecken: Brek-in
Wind Fae, Tessa's friend?
Claimed by Achaz Kingdom

Katya: Kat-ya
Fire Fae, Tessa's friend, claimed by
Arius Kingdom, was involved with
Axel

Tristyn Blackheart:
Tris-tin Blak-hārt
~~Mortal,~~ Legacy, owns Lilura Inquest

~~Penelope:~~ Pen-el-ō-pee
Fae, personal servant of Theon & Axel

Cressida St. Orcas:
Cres-ee-duh Sānt Or-kus
Legacy, Theon & Axel's mother

Eviana: Eve-ee-on-uh
Earth Fae, Source of the Arius Lord

LEGACY SERIES REFERENCE GUIDE

OTHERS OF NOTE

Felicity Davers: Fel-i-sit-ee Dav-ers
Gracil Legacy, Theon's prospective
Match

Cienna: Cee-en-uh
Banished to the Underground

Auryon: O-ry-un
Listen, we don't know what she is

Ford: Fōrd
Fae, Pen's replacement

Pavil: Pah-vil
Sleazy Legacy that works for Valter

Metias: Meh-tī-us
Sleazy Legacy that works for Valter

Julius: Jool-ee-us
Sleazy Legacy Advisor to Valter

Mansel: Man-sell
Sleazy Legacy Advisor to Valter

Razik: Ra-zick
A stranger who looks remarkably
like Luka

Eliza: Ee-lie-zuh
A Fire Fae stranger

Xan: Zan
A prisoner in Achaz Kingdom

Bree DelaCrux: Bree Del-uh-crū
One of the four coven leaders of the
Night Children who lead the
Dispensary District in the
Underground

Desiray: Dez-i-rā
A Sirana Legacy who oversees
Rosebell and the Sirana Villas

Elowyn: El-ō-win
A priestess in Achaz Kingdom

Gia: Gee-uh
A Witch in the Underground, Cienna's
lover

Nylah: Nī-luh
A wolf that guards Tessa

Roan: Rōn
A wolf that guards Tessa

LEGACY SERIES REFERENCE GUIDE

THE GODS

THE FIRSTS

Achaz (Ā-kaz)
God of light and beginnings

Serafina (Sār-uh-fee-nuh)
Goddess of dreams and stars

Anala (Uh-nall-uh)
Goddess of sun, day, and fire

Arius (Ar-ee-us)
God of death and endings

Falein (Fā-leen)
Goddess of wisdom/cleverness

Celeste (Sel-est)
Goddess of moon and sky

THE LESSERS

Zinta (Zēn-tuh)
Goddess of magic and sorcery

Sirana (Seer-an-uh)
Goddess of love and fertility

Sargon (Sar-gon)
God of war and courage

Pax (Pax)
God of peace and serenity

Silas (Sī-lus)
God of earth and land

Rai (Rā)
God of seasons

Saylah (Say-luh)
Goddess of night and shadows
Daughter of Arius and Serafina

Nith (Neeth)
God of creativity

Anahita (On-uh-hee-tuh)
God of sea, water, and ice

Reselda (Rez-el-duh)
Goddess of healing

Sefarina (Sef-uh-ree-nuh)
Goddess of winds and air

Gracil (Grah-sil)
God of empathy

Temural (Tem-oo-rall)
God of the wild and untamed,
Son of Arius and Serafina

LEGACY SERIES REFERENCE GUIDE

THE KINGDOMS

ACHAZ KINGDOM

- Ruling Lord: Rordan Jove (Ror-dan Jō-vā)
- Heir: Dagian Jove (Dāj-ee-un Jō-vā)
- Heir's Source: Sasha (Sah-shuh)
- Responsibilities: upholding Devram's laws and accords, ruling the realm
- Loyal Lesser Bloodlines: Zinta and Sirana

ARIUS KINGDOM

- Ruling Lord: Valter St. Orcas (Vall-tār Sānt Or-kus)
- Heir: Theon St. Orcas. (Thee-on Sānt Or-kus)
- Heir's Source: Tessa (Tes-uh)
- Responsibilities: Underground
- Loyal Lesser Bloodlines: Sargon

SERAFINA KINGDOM

- Ruling Lady: Maya Isleen (My-uh Iz-lēn)
- Heir: Lealla Isleen (Lee-all-uh Iz-lēn)
- Heir's Source: Maxson (Max-sun)
- Responsibilities: artists and architects
- Loyal Lesser Bloodlines: Anahita and Nith

FALEIN KINGDOM

- Ruling Lady: Raye Farhan (Rā Far-han)
- Heir: Prudence Farhan (Prū-dens Far-han)
- Heir's Source: Dade (Dād)
- Responsibilities: scholars and healers
- Loyal Lesser Bloodlines: Reselda and Pax

ANALA KINGDOM

- Ruling Lady: Kyra Aithne (Kī-ruh Āth-nee)
- Heir: Tana Aithne (Tan-uh Āth-nee)
- Heir's Source: Gatlan (Gat-lan)
- Responsibilities: food and agriculture
- Loyal Lesser Bloodlines: Silas and Rai

CELESTE KINGDOM

- Ruling Lady: Luna Candra (Lū-nuh Can-druh)
- Heir: Mahina Candra (Muh-he-nuh Can-druh)
- Heir's Source: Jasper (Jas-per)
- Responsibilities: running the Selection
- Loyal Lesser Bloodlines: Sefarina and Gracil

DEVRAM

EKAYAN
ISLAND

ORINTHIA   FAE ESTATE

SU
FO

FAE ESTATE

RAGHNALL
MOUNTAINS

ANALA
KINGDOM

FALEIN
KINGDOM

CAELAN RIVER

DOLION
WOODS

ACROPOLIS

TERRARUN RIVER

CELESTE
KINGDOM

NISHA
FOREST

ACHAZ
KINGDOM

LAKE
MOONMIST   FAE ESTATE

SIRAN

AROBELL

UNDERGROUND
ENTRANCE

OZUL
MOUNTAINS

ARIUS
HOUSE

CASTLE PINES

ROCKMOOR

SINVONS
LAKE

DARK
HAVEN

ARIUS
KINGDOM

SHADE PLAINS

FRACTURED
SPRINGS

NIGHT WATERS

RAVEN HARBO

RIVER OF ENDINGS

RIVER

SERAFINA
KINGDOM

DREAMLOCK
WOODS

FAE ESTATE

SANAL

ASTOWN PORT

ASNING
SEA

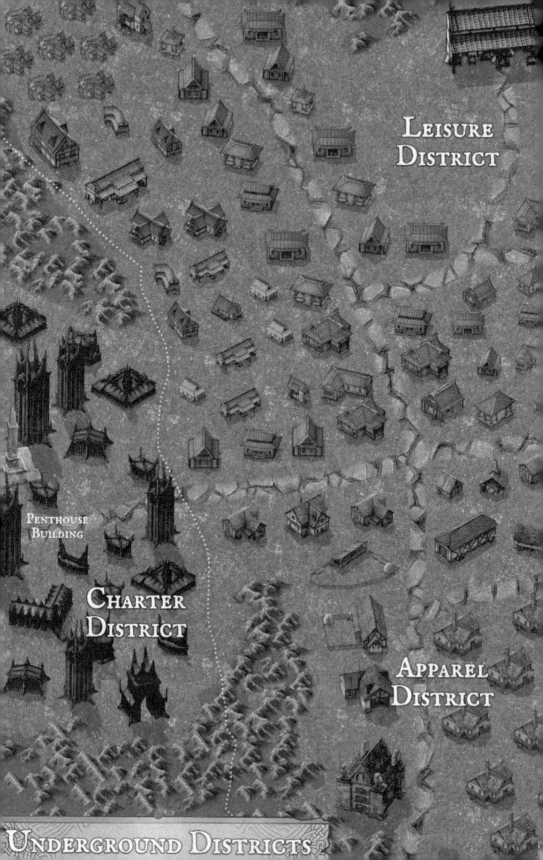

LEISURE
DISTRICT

PENTHOUSE
BUILDING

CHARTER
DISTRICT

APPAREL
DISTRICT

UNDERGROUND DISTRICTS

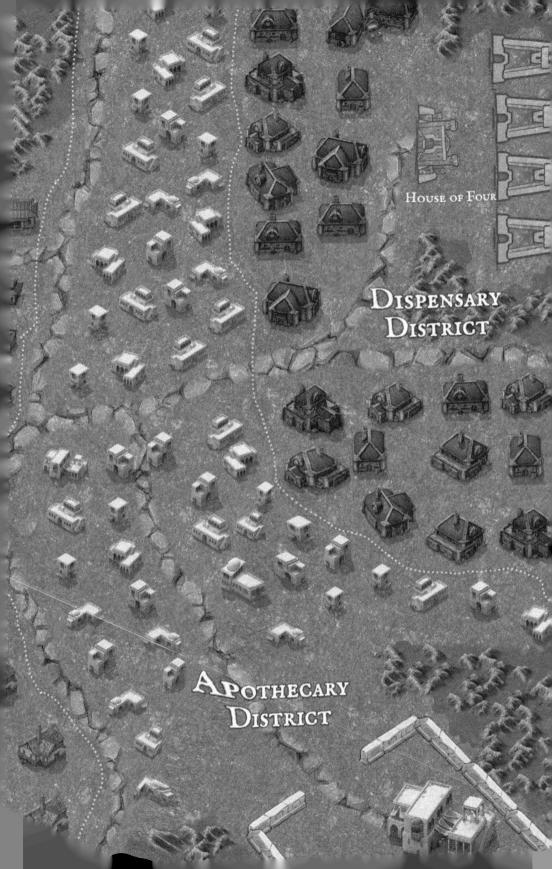

HOUSE of FOUR

DISPENSARY
DISTRICT

APOTHECARY
DISTRICT

STORM OF SECRETS AND SORROW QUICK RECAP
AS TOLD BY CYRUS

Hi, Darling! Welcome back. I get to give you a quick rundown of all the chaos that happened in *Storm of Secrets and Sorrow* even though I didn't actually go there.

Scarlett, *groaning*: By the gods, Cyrus. It's too early for your tantrums.

Cyrus: Tantrums? You tell me I can't go with you and Sorin, and then you *send* Eliza and—

Cassius, *sighing and rubbing at his brow*: Cyrus, can we just get on with this?

Fine, fine. We hop back into Devram and find Theon preparing for a hearing with the Tribunal, which is basically a council of the six rulers. The hearing is to determine if Theon is able to keep Tessa as his Source. *(Brow furrows.)* That's ridiculous. The only way to break a Source bond is if one of them dies. They can't just *decide* that.

Anyway, Theon is given a deadline to figure out Tessa's lineage by the Winter Solstice. This agreement comes with a few other contingencies, but he is able to keep Tessa at his side for the time being. I'm sure that will go really well for him, especially when his father tells him to figure out how to sever the bond so Tessa can be Matched with Luka, and Theon can take Katya as a new Source. On top of all that, Valter reveals to Tessa that Theon has signed a Match contract with Felicity Davers. In other words, Theon is kind of fucked, but he's going to give it his all to fix this, and we have to admire that tenacity.

Speaking of Katya, Axel is inexplicably enamored with her, and they end up sharing his room. Which...isn't exactly ideal since he is having a hard time controlling his craving for Fae blood. (*Looking up at Scarlett.*) What is with these guys and setting themselves up for failure?

Scarlett: If you only knew the half of it. Wait until Tessa gets her second Source Marking.

Cyrus: That's not a thing.

Scarlett: That's what I said! But the mother hen over here wouldn't let me say more.

Sorin: Talk to your sister about that, Love.

They take Tessa to a river to let her siphon off some power because she still has bands on that suppress her magic, and that makes anyone go a little crazy. While there, they are attacked by The Augury, a group of radicals who think Tessa is the center of a prophecy that will end Devram. Shortly after, Tessa gets her second *Source Mark*.

Cassius: Don't say it like that.

Cyrus: Are you doing this recap, or am I?

Cassius: By the gods.

So she gets this second Source Mark that's supposed to let them feel each other's emotions, except it doesn't go as planned. Theon isn't strong enough to overpower her, and Luka has to help. That is definitely going to complicate matters, but they are optimists apparently and decide to ignore that until they have to deal with it. I am sure that won't bite them in the ass. Tessa sleeps as she adjusts to another Mark, and her dreams continue to change. When she wakes up, she's curled between both Theon and Luka... Well, fuck. Good for her. Cass—

Cassius: Not a single word, Cyrus.

The crew goes to the Underground to visit Cienna, who tells them cryptic and confusing things. They end up being attacked by vampyres, and Tessa is gravely wounded. Theon and Axel get into an argument. Axel leaves with Katya and ends up kissing her in an alley. While Luka stays to watch over Tessa, the St. Orcas brothers go visit the Night Children clan leaders to find out why they were attacked.

They return to the kingdoms in time for a traditional feast where there's chitchat with the other Sources, lots of couples dancing, and Tessa runs into Tristyn. She ends up giving into the call of her magic, which is dangerous for everyone. While Theon and Luka are trying to bring her back, they are again attacked by the Augury, and—

Lifts his eyes to find Scarlett smirking.

Scarlett, *innocently batting her lashes*: And?

And a silver-haired queen and her husband show up to help. We learn the silver-haired queen is Tessa's cousin, and that she is also an obnoxious and annoying brat.

Scarlett: Rude.

Cyrus, *seriously*: I have been given this very important task rather than going there myself. I am obligated to recap this story accurately.

Scarlett, *rolling her eyes*: For fuck's sake. I still say it's too early for this.

Cassius, *dryly*: It's after high noon.

The silver-haired queen throws a fit—

Scarlett: I did not throw a fit!

Stop interrupting this essential job I have been entrusted with. Some information and knowledge are exchanged, and the silver-haired queen reveals that Tessa is the granddaughter of Arius and Serafina. Because she's exceptionally dramatic and likes being the center of attention, she also shares that Tessa's father is Temural among other things. Theon and Tessa share a moment together before she goes to Faven for a week, as per the agreement with the Achaz Lord.

Axel continues to battle his blood cravings, and Valter continues to manipulate him by withholding his weekly rations. He continues to grow closer to Katya, despite knowing it puts her in danger.

Tessa hangs out in Faven for a week, learning about her power and spending time with Dex. While there, her dreams become more intense. While she's away, Theon throws himself into researching her lineage with Katya's help, and they discover Tristyn knows far more than he's letting on. Another mysterious female shows up with black hair, who is skilled with a bow and moves among ashes— Wait, really?

Cassius: No, Cyrus. Keeping going.

But... Fine. This new female's name is Auryon, and she helps them fight off some Augury members. Tessa returns from Faven only to find the townhouse empty except for Felicity. Who she finds in the bedchamber Tessa shares with Theon. *What the fuck is this female doing in there?* That drives a wedge between Tessa and Theon, and rightfully so, even if it does appear to be a set up. Auryon becomes Tessa's new private instructor, replacing Mother Cordelia, and thank the gods for that because Mother Cordelia is a bitch.

Luka continues to train Tessa in self-defense, while everyone continues to try and figure out what she is before they run out of time. Katya is wounded, and Axel loses his mind. He refuses to leave her side as she heals. That sounds familiar, huh, Sorin?

Sorin: Wrap this up, Cyrus. We have a meeting to get to.

Okay, okay. The crew get permission to visit Ekayan Island to research in their vast libraries. They make some discoveries about Fae, and

Theon agrees to claim Lange and Corbin for the Arius Kingdom. Tessa's dreams continue to assault her, and she is attacked by the Augury again, only to find Mother Cordelia is an Augury member. Wolves come to Tessa's rescue, along with Auryon, and Tessa lets her power free. Luka finds her and takes her somewhere to release her fury, and we learn Luka can Travel. That is quite the secret to keep for years and years. Tessa also discovers she is bonded to both Luka and Theon, and they've been keeping it from her. Tessa receives the third Mark, both Luka and Theon being involved, and now they can hear each other's thoughts.

Axel and Katya are summoned by Valter, and Axel panics, knowing his father plans to use Katya in horrific ways. He kills Metias and Pavil, and sends Kat with Tristyn to hide her. He has no idea where Tristyn takes her, making him unable to tell his father when he's questioned or tortured for the information. In his fury, Valter hides Axel away, and no one knows where he is. Which is terrible for everyone.

Meanwhile, another hearing has been held. Having failed his task, Tessa is taken from Theon. Tessa is again attacked by the Augury, only this time we learn that Valter has been leading them this whole time. Tessa summons Hunters to protect her... They do that? Because here they just—

Cassius: For the love of Sargon, Cyrus!

Would you relax? Auryon and Tristyn show up to fight for her, and Tessa discovers they've been keeping secrets from her too. With everyone betraying her, she orders her Hunters to kill all the Legacy and capture Valter.

She goes to Theon, where she gives herself the fourth Source Mark while also branding him with the Achaz Mark. (*Snickering.*) She's clearly had enough, and who can blame her? She leaves him on his knees and goes to the Achaz Kingdom. Theon sends Luka to her, instructing his Guardian to tell him nothing. Tessa explores the Faven Palace where Valter is being held captive along with another who has sapphire eyes and brown hair and looks an awful lot like— Is *this* why you sent them there?

Scarlett, *with a sly smile*: I always have a reason, Darling. Surely you know this by now.

Cyrus: Clever. I stand by my dramatic comment though.

Scarlett flips him her middle finger.

In the end, Tessa vows to destroy the Arius line, and she chats with the mystery prisoner. Tristyn heads to the Underground to see his...sister. Huh. That's interesting considering she's a Witch. Eliza and Razik get to go on an adventure, while the rest of us are forced to stay here and sit around on our asses.

Cassius: Cyrus, drop it.

Cyrus: I absolutely will not.

Scarlett: You don't want to go there, Darling. You'd be treated like... (*Lips pursing.*) You don't want to go there.

Cyrus: Did you at least try this...pizza while you were there?

Scarlett: No, but I may have lifted some lull-leaf from Tristyn.

Cyrus, *in outrage*: And you're just now telling me this?

Scarlett, *smirking*: Now who's being dramatic?

ALWAYS MEANT TO DESTROY ONE ANOTHER

"Tessa, stop," Theon rasped, blood seeping from beneath his hand where it was pressed to his side.

Tessa stood over him with a gold dagger in her hand, and she twirled it between her fingers.

"Tessa," Theon tried again. "It doesn't—"

"Have to be this way?" she interrupted. "You mean it should be me on the ground preparing to cross the Veil?"

"No, Tessa. I—"

But he was cut off by a shuddering breath that turned into a cough followed by curses.

"Fuck," he muttered, lifting his palm to look at his wound before immediately applying pressure again. "Where the fuck is Luka?"

She smiled, and she could tell by the look on Theon's face that the smile looked as wicked as it felt. "He's a little...caged right now."

"You're fulfilling the prophecy if you do this, Tessa."

She whirled to the source of the voice, seeing Tristyn on the ground nearby, light binding his hands and ankles.

"It's what they want. Don't you see?" the male pressed now that he had her attention. "You will be the—"

"You had plenty of chances to tell me what you know," she said, power flaring through the light that held him and making him wince as it coursed through his being. "And even when you did tell me, it was shrouded in half-truths and motivations that only served you."

"No—" he gasped out, but she was already turning back to Theon.

"As for Luka, once you are gone, he can become my Guardian," she continued as though they hadn't been interrupted. "That's what he was always meant to be, isn't it? Auryon said so herself."

"You killed Auryon," Theon rasped, his darkness swarming around the wound. Trying to heal him. Trying to save him.

A pointless effort, but she'd let him waste that power of his. It wasn't as if she needed him as a Source anyway.

"I didn't kill Auryon," she scoffed.

"Your Hunters did," Theon amended. "At your command."

"Because she was trying to keep me from my destiny."

"Little storm, I was wrong. So very wrong."

She shot forward, gripping his hair and yanking his head back. The tip of her dagger pressed beneath his chin. "Your apologies are too late. They fall on deaf ears."

"I know, Tessa, but it changes nothing of how I feel about you."

"Stop it," she snarled as she felt his emotions flood down the bond. Then she felt Luka's emotions merge with them.

The three of them bound to one another.

Connected in a way that was never meant to be, but couldn't possibly be any other way.

Unless sacrifices were made.

"Stop it," she said again, releasing Theon and stepping back. "We don't have a choice."

Wind swept through the clearing, stirring dead grass and scorched earth from a battle that had left hundreds dead. Fae and Legacy alike had fought in a war that should have been reserved for the gods.

Too many sacrifices had already been made.

Corbin.

Lange.

Auryon.

Cienna.

"Breathe, my light," Luka coaxed down the bond. "We'll figure this out."

But they wouldn't figure this out.

Axel was gone.

Katya was missing.

And everyone who should have cared had betrayed her.

Thunder rumbled at the thought, the skies breaking open and raining its own wrath to the ground.

"It doesn't have to be like this, little storm," Theon tried again.

"We don't have a choice," she said, echoing words he'd said to her so often in her dreams. *"It's more than a bond, and it cannot be."*

Emerald eyes fell closed, acceptance filling features she had once thought she could love.

For so long, she had wished for death, and now, in this moment, she didn't want it. She'd found something to fight for, and then she was forced to sacrifice it. And now? Now she felt nothing but the fury that had consumed her.

"You're wrong," Tristyn rasped, trying to inch closer across the earth that had quickly turned to mud. *"Have you learned nothing over these past months? We've tried, Tessa. We've brought you aid—"*

"Once again to seek your own ends," she snapped.

"To save you," Theon said, clearly trying to keep her attention on him. His hair was plastered to his brow, rain mixing with the steady stream of blood from his wound. *"I tried to change it. I did everything I could."*

"But destiny beckons and sacrifice demands," she said in a mocking tone as she crouched before him once more. *"Those that came to this world unbidden learned that truth."*

"Their queen will seek her vengeance, Tessa. Make no mistake."

"We are counting on it."

"Her vengeance will know no bounds."

"Then she will know my wrath, just as you have."

"And I'd ask for it again and again if it is all you will let me have, clever tempest," Theon replied, a shaky hand coming up to cup her cheek. *"But I understand we are out of time. Once again, I am out of time."*

She got a little lost in dark emerald eyes and black hair. In a small dimple and lips she'd kissed more times than she could count. Then she was kissing him. Deep and lovely, just like it always should have been.

"I'm sorry I failed you, Tessa," Theon said when they broke apart, sorrow filling in his features. *"I tried. I tried to save you."*

"I understand," she whispered. *"I'm sorry I couldn't give you all of me. Every piece of me."*

And she sank that gold dagger into his chest.

"But only one can be left standing when Chaos comes to reign."

PART ONE
DESTINY BECKONS

1

THEON

"Fucking son of Achaz," Theon cursed when he slammed a drawer shut on his fingers.

He was in his father's study at Arius House trying to find any possible clue as to where Axel could be. Not that he hadn't searched it a dozen times already in the last two weeks. He'd combed through the study, his father's private office in the other wing of the house, his father's private rooms—much to his mother's disapproval— and anywhere else his father had told him never to enter. He'd scoured the rooms beneath Arius House. Rooms where prisoners were sometimes held, and torture was handed out freely. Theon had spent plenty of time in those rooms himself—both as the victim and the one doing the torturing. Then he'd gone through other rooms that seemed too obvious. He'd gone to the Underground, searching all the known properties there, but there was nothing. Not a single indication of where he could have hidden Axel away. It was as though he'd simply disappeared.

His father's advisors were no help, mainly because he couldn't find them either. This entire situation was murky and unprecedented. Was he truly the Arius Lord if his father still lived? Apparently, most believed that was not the case. His mother tittered around the house, saying he would be back soon, and the nobles of the kingdom chose to ignore any and all communication. But even though he was not viewed as the reigning Arius Lord, it sure as fuck was enough to fulfill the Bargain he'd made with Tessa. A Bargain he'd made thinking he'd gained the upper hand only to have her flip the whole godsdamn thing upside down.

Again.

His gaze cut to the Mark on the back of his hand. Three interconnected triangles. The exact opposite of the Arius Mark he'd drawn on her skin months ago. She'd been vicious and spiteful, and he'd known she hated him. There was no going back. She'd made that perfectly clear when she'd taken everything from him and left him with half a title and no one to share the burden. Axel was missing. She was gone. He'd sent Luka to her and told him not to tell him a word. Axel had Katya hidden away. Blackheart wouldn't answer his calls. All he was left with were two Fae, Lange and Corbin, and the-gods-only-knew if he could trust them.

And this fucking bond.

It was pining for Tessa in a way he'd never experienced. They'd never been apart this long, but this was more exaggerated than merely being separated by distance and time. The bond seemed to know they were irreparable at this point, and it was in utter agony.

Or maybe that was him.

Theon dropped into his father's chair, eyeing a tablet he'd found in a desk drawer. He was assuming it was a backup of some sort, but he hadn't been able to get into it. He was close to asking Corbin for help. Everyone kept saying he was adept at technology, despite being a Fae. But again, he was back to this trust thing. He only trusted two people implicitly, and both of those people were inaccessible to him right now.

With another sigh, he pulled Axel's mirror from his pocket. He'd found it in his room at the townhouse in the Acropolis. It had fallen in between the couch cushions. He didn't know how to use the thing like Axel did. Or rather, Cienna didn't respond to him like she did to Axel. So he was left waiting, with nothing to do but search this stupid house and the estate manor near the Acropolis.

He'd never felt so alone in his entire life.

He'd also found Axel's phone, his earbuds, and a book written in an old language. It would take Theon months to translate, and he could only assume Katya had been working on it. Why Axel had kept it, Theon wasn't sure. Of course, he had no way of getting in touch with Katya either because, again, Blackheart wouldn't answer his godsdamn calls.

A knock on the door had him spinning the chair to the sound. When the door didn't immediately open, it took him a minute to remember his father would have punished someone for not waiting for permission to enter.

"Enter," Theon barked, not bothering to stand.

A Fae male entered. Not Ford. That fucker was locked in a cell beneath the manor, where Theon had immediately escorted his father's personal servant. He knew where the male's loyalty lay, and it was to his father, not the Arius Kingdom as a whole. The male standing here now was another member of the house staff.

"You have a visitor, my Lord," the Fae said, his head bowed.

"I do not have any appointments, nor am I seeing anyone right now," Theon replied, already turning away.

"I understand, my Lord. He did say—" He flinched when Theon spun back to face him again.

Theon couldn't blame him. His father would have already had Eviana hurting him for continuing to speak.

"Who is here?" Theon asked, trying to sound reassuring, but gods, he was not in the mood to see anyone.

The male swallowed thickly before trying again, his voice trembling. "He refused to give his name, but said that when you refused him, I was to tell you 'salvation or destruction is your choice.'"

Tristyn. Fucking. Blackheart.

The male couldn't bother to answer his phone, but he could show up here whenever he wished and demand to see him.

Theon stood, the male flinching back at the movement. He slipped the mirror back into his pocket before shoving the tablet back into a desk drawer. Brushing past the male, he made his way down the hall to the foyer where Blackheart was indeed waiting.

Tristyn's hands were shoved into the pockets of his dark jeans as he studied a portrait on the wall while he waited. His brown hair was a little disheveled. Theon was used to it being clean-cut and styled impeccably. Russet-colored eyes lifted to meet his as he approached.

"Arius Heir," the male drawled, looking Theon up and down. "Or is it Lord now?"

"What are you doing here?" Theon asked, stopping a few feet away. His darkness appeared, pooling at his feet and drifting closer to the Legacy before him. Tristyn glanced at it, but didn't appear bothered in the least.

"I am here to bring you to those who can help with your...predicament," he finally answered.

Theon scoffed. "As if you know anything of my predicament."

Tristyn's eyes seemed to flash, the russet color almost glowing for a second before it receded. "I was there when Tessa chose her side. I tried to bring her back to you that night. I tried..." He gritted his teeth. "I suppose it doesn't matter what I tried. I failed. And now I am here to offer assistance."

"You tried to bring her back to me? What the fuck does that mean?"

"Exactly what I said. I tried to bring her back to you. Well, both of you. Do you want my help or not?" Tristyn asked.

Theon studied him. He looked tired and worse for wear. His button-down shirt was untucked, and the buttons were mismatched. He wore a worn brown leather jacket over the top that seemed decades out of style. It didn't even smell right.

"Fine. Where are we going?" Theon finally said, standing straighter.

"The Underground."

"I'll need to bring Lange and Corbin with us."

"Bring whoever you want," Tristyn replied. "Just be quick about it."

Theon glared at him, but he turned to the Fae who'd come to announce Tristyn's arrival and asked him to fetch Lange and Corbin. As they waited, he said to Tristyn, "It will take at least a full day of driving to get to the Underground."

"I can Travel."

Theon blinked once. Twice. "How is it you can Travel?"

"The same way Luka can. I wasn't born in this realm. Therefore, the enchantments and safeguards put in place do not entirely affect me," Tristyn replied.

"How convenient," Theon deadpanned.

"Quite," he agreed as the sound of footsteps reached them.

Corbin and Lange looked wary as they approached, and Theon couldn't blame them. They'd been shuffled around from the Fae dormitories to the townhouse and now here. Only now, they didn't have Tessa or Katya to help guide them. Fuck, even Axel had seemed to be able to put them at ease.

Without a word, Theon motioned them forward. Tristyn made sure they were all touching, and then he felt a pull at his navel he'd never experienced. Luka had certainly never Traveled with him because Luka had kept that particular skill a secret for godsdamn decades.

"I cannot Travel directly into the Underground," Tristyn said as they appeared near the main gates. "Most areas in Devram are not warded against Traveling because it is not an expected ability, but the Underground has always been different."

"You know a lot of things, Blackheart," Theon muttered, trying to swallow down the nausea. He'd had enough vomiting to last a lifetime after Tessa had tricked him with that last Source Mark.

Tessa.

The bond immediately strained at the mere thought of her, and Theon closed his eyes for a moment, tamping down on that desire too. But he could still picture her in that thin, floor-length skirt of navy blue that was so dark it was nearly black. Her hair loose around her and her light banded around her arms. Violet eyes full of malice and rapture as she tipped her head back, riding him and taking her pleasure.

Clever and exquisite.

Brutal and malevolent.

Salvation and destruction.

"While you have lived nearly three decades, I have lived well over three centuries. Too many of them spent in this godsforsaken realm. I should know a lot of things," Tristyn answered as they ventured into the Underground passages.

"Then why not share what you know?" Theon countered. "This could have all been avoided."

"Why do you keep your knowledge secret?" he countered, and Theon couldn't argue with that. "But aside from secrets being currency, messing with fate is a dangerous game. I reveal too much, and it could be seen as me playing with free will in an effort to obtain a specific outcome. It is safer to not say anything at all."

"But you have," Theon argued. "You revealed pieces here and there. Why take the risk?"

Tristyn stopped, turning to face him. His eyes flared again, and he held Theon's gaze when he said, "Because some things are worth the risk and more."

They said nothing else as they traversed the tunnels of the Underground. He glanced back to make sure Corbin and Lange were still with them. They were quiet, hand in hand and keeping up. Theon wasn't entirely sure why he'd brought them with, but he didn't trust leaving them at Arius House. It wasn't that he didn't trust *them*. It was that he didn't trust anyone else. Tessa would be livid if something happened to her friends, and the last thing he needed was to give her yet another reason to hate him.

Not that it really mattered anymore.

"Since I am with you, I assume this is not your unaccompanied visit you bartered for?" Theon said as they turned down another passage. Theon didn't know where they were going, and he was beginning to wonder how Tristyn knew how to traverse the Underground so well.

Tristyn glanced at him with a smirk. "Consider that debt paid, *my Lord.*"

Theon was about to snap something back in reply until they stepped into a spacious cavern he immediately recognized. Three work tables were in the center of the space, multiple shelves with herbs and ingredients lined the walls. There were three hearths, one with a cauldron steaming atop a fire.

"You know Cienna," he said in understanding, looking around for the Witch, but she was nowhere to be found.

"Something like that," Tristyn answered, walking over to a table and tossing some type of powder into a pot.

"I wouldn't mess with her things," Theon warned, knowing full well what it was like to be on the Witch's bad side.

"I can handle her," Tristyn answered.

As if his words summoned her, Cienna's voice carried from a side tunnel. "Never useful when I need you, and now you are messing with my potions."

Theon felt his entire face go slack as Cienna and Gia, her lover, entered the cavern with two others. One was a female with red-gold hair braided into a plait over her shoulder. Definitely Fae, she had a sword at her back and more weapons strapped to what appeared to be some kind of leather armor. But the male?

He looked just like Luka.

His brown hair wasn't nearly as long, but it was shaggy and curled around his ears. His skin tone was a little darker, as if he spent more time in the sun. But the square jaw and facial features? The sapphire blue eyes? The build and stature? It was impossible for them not to be related, but that also meant that this male was a dragon shifter.

How many siblings do you have?

Those had been her taunting words. That arrogant silver-haired queen had known even then.

"Is she here then?" Theon asked.

"Who?" Cienna replied, shoving at Tristyn to get him out of the way before peering into the pot.

"Scarlett," he answered.

"No," the new female said. "She has been...forbidden to interfere here."

"So she sent you two?"

The male sighed, as if he was utterly annoyed with everything happening. "She is incredibly adept at finding loopholes. It is both brilliant and irksome."

"Must run in the family. Her cousin is the same," Theon muttered, crossing his arms and leaning a hip against the table. "Are you her Guardian then? She mentioned one."

The male made a face that told Theon he would rather swallow glass and bleed out of his eyes than be Scarlett's Guardian. "No, but I am her brother's Guardian."

Theon nodded. "She mentioned a brother." Glancing at the female, he asked, "Are you the sister that tried to kill her?"

Her brows knitted in confusion for a brief moment before understanding seemed to don. "No," she said with a huff of laughter. "I wish I could call myself a Wraith of Death, but that would be Nuri. I am the general of the Fire Court."

"Fire?" Theon said. "You are a fire Fae then?"

She nodded, eyeing him before her gaze slid to the others.

"This is Eliza," the male said, stepping subtly closer to her. "I am Razik Greybane."

"You are certainly more forthcoming with information than Scarlett is," Theon answered.

"Scarlett doesn't tell anyone anything," Razik replied.

"That's not true," Eliza scoffed.

Razik sent her a frank look before turning back to Theon.

"You do not like Scarlett?" Theon asked.

"No," he answered.

"Raz," Eliza snapped, elbowing him in the gut hard enough to make him suck in a breath.

"I see no point in lying about it," Razik replied, stepping aside when she tried to elbow him again. "Stop, *mai dragocen*. It is not as if this is a new revelation to you."

Eliza rolled her eyes, crossing her arms before her grey gaze settled on Theon. "I am assuming you are the Arius prince or whatever?"

"Arius Heir. I mean, Lord." He sighed, shoving a hand through his hair. He wasn't entirely sure what he was at this point.

Eliza eyed him another moment before saying, "I am not very confident in your ability to lead a kingdom if you do not even know your title."

"That is rude, Eliza," Razik chided, but the twitch of his lips told Theon he was goading her.

Luka did the same godsdamn thing.

Eliza tsked under her breath, tossing a hand in Theon's direction. "We were sent here to help him, and he doesn't even know who he is, Raz. How are we supposed to work with this?"

"What, exactly, did she send you here to do?" Theon asked, glancing at Cienna and Tristyn who had gone noticeably quiet.

"That's what you were supposed to tell us," Eliza retorted sharply.

Theon's brows rose at the address. "Do you always speak to Legacy in such a manner?" Then he glanced at Razik. "You *allow* her to speak to Legacy in such a manner?"

The female's lip curled up, baring her teeth, and her hand inched toward a dagger at her hip. Those were definitely flames in her eyes as she replied in a voice that was lethally calm, "He does not *allow* me to do anything, and if you ever speak to him about *my* actions again, you will find yourself bleeding."

"Do you remember how I was trying to explain how the Fae are treated differently here?" Tristyn interrupted, stepping back as Cienna pushed him away from her work tables again.

The female looked like she was about to say something else, but Razik stepped in. "She does not care and neither do I, but let's discuss something else before she becomes violent." Eliza glared up at him, crossing her arms again with a huff. He glanced down at her. "I did not say I would stop you if you chose to stab him, *mai dragocen.*"

The female muttered a curse under her breath, but she looked away, apparently done with the conversation.

"Now that that's settled," Razik said, bringing a hand to Eliza's lower back. She immediately seemed to calm a little, some of that tension leaving her shoulders. Then her head tipped a little as if she heard something, and Theon narrowed in on the action. That seemed an awful lot like—

"Perhaps we should discuss the female who should not exist," Razik went on, and the words made Theon's attention snap back to him.

"If you are referring to Tessa, I will be the one doing the stabbing,"

Theon snarled, a short sword appearing in his hand from a swirl of darkness.

"I would assume so," Razik drawled, looking as worried about the weapon as Tristyn had about Theon's power earlier. "Isn't that what this entire prophecy is about?"

"What prophecy?"

"For fuck's sake," Eliza groused. "Fae are treated as less than here, but the Legacy don't know shit. How the fuck does that work?"

"That is not—"

"He knows plenty. He simply knows falsehoods and inaccurate history," Cienna cut in, and the room went silent at her interruption.

"I still do not understand how that is possible for how advanced this world appears to be," Razik said. "Who are they?"

Theon followed his line of sight and turned. Corbin and Lange were standing quietly by, taking everything in.

"They are Fae in service to the Arius Kingdom," Theon answered.

Eliza's eyes narrowed, and he could swear there were embers drifting through her red-gold hair, but he'd had enough of this.

Turning back to Tristyn, he said, "If this is the help you spoke of earlier, I'm afraid it has fallen flat. Unless you have information that is actually useful, do not contact me again."

He was already striding for the exit. He didn't know exactly how he'd find his way back through the network of the Underground, but he'd figure it out.

"Theon St. Orcas, you will sit and listen to what needs to be said," Cienna called after him. "She told you of her dreams, didn't she? Of you killing her?"

He went still, turning slowly back to face the Witch. "How do you know of them?"

Her smile was sharp and grim when she answered, "I think you should be more worried about those visions becoming reality because if something is not done, that will be the only way to stop her."

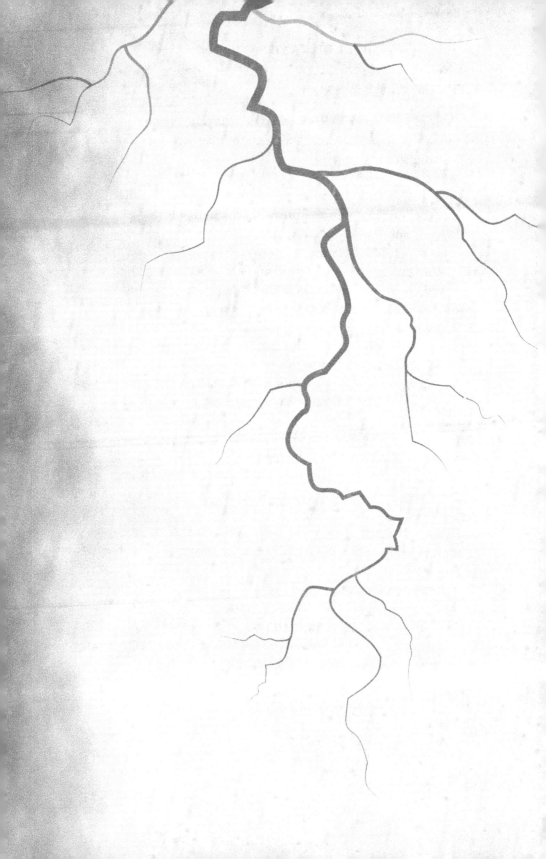

2

TESSA

Tessa dragged her fingers along the railing. She was in the loft overlooking the Tribunal Hearing room. The last time she'd been here, she'd been down there. The Achaz Lord had told Theon that she was no longer his. She had been given her freedom. Taken away from the Arius Heir who had forced her to her knees and taken and taken and taken from her.

And yet here she was, staring at the Arius seat below, wondering if he was going to be the one to take it when the Lords and Ladies of Devram entered.

The other Heirs and Sources were milling about below. None of them had noticed her. Or rather, none of them were acknowledging her. Except Gatlan. The Fae was the Source of the Anala Heir. He glanced up at her and winked with a nod of his head.

"You didn't have to attend this today, Tessie."

She went rigid at Dex's voice, having forgotten he'd come up here with her.

"Why would I stay behind?" she asked, gaze still fixed on the others below.

"There is no need for you to be here. It is politics and pointless arguing."

"You think I will not understand?"

After a pause, his tone was carefully neutral when he said, "That is not what I meant."

She only hummed a response.

"I only mean I cannot stay up here with you," he added.

"Then don't," she answered, finally turning to face him. "I am perfectly capable of being alone."

Dex's lips thinned, clearly unhappy with how the conversation was going. His dark eyes swept over her as he debated what to say.

Finally, he said, "Just stay up here, all right?" She felt the corner of her lips tilt up, and that obviously only made him more worried as his mouth turned down in a frown. "Are you…"

"All right?" Tessa supplied. "Does it matter?"

She didn't wait for an answer, turning back to look down at the Tribunal room. She heard Dex leave, his footfalls slowly fading as he descended the stairs. Her fingers curled around the railing once more, and her gaze fell to the bands of light around her wrists. It never wavered. She never felt like her power was running out, and Rordan never once mentioned putting the bands on that would suppress her magic. It was the opposite actually. He constantly encouraged her to use it, siphon it off, learn about it. He'd arranged for her to train daily with her magic, and she did so with the same instructor from her week in Faven when she'd been separated from Theon. The problem was, she was more powerful than the instructor, and it was becoming increasingly difficult not to harm her while training. More than once, a Healer had needed to be summoned.

The sound of a door opening below drew her attention, and she watched as the Falein and Anala Ladies emerged first. Lady Aithne's golden eyes flicked up to her, a brow arching before she returned her attention to the Falein Lady, nodding at whatever she was saying. Next to emerge were the Celeste and Serafina Ladies. Lady Isleen didn't bother to acknowledge her, but Lady Candra, the Celeste Lady, immediately looked up at her. Tessa had wondered if her presence would be made known beforehand, and clearly Rordan had informed them all.

Lady Candra's eyes narrowed, her lip curling into a sneer, and Tessa held her stare the entire time as she leaned on the railing, resting her chin in her hand. The light around her wrists flared brighter, and she knew there was lightning flickering in her eyes. The sneer fell from Lady Candra's lip, something akin to nervousness replacing it.

And Tessa smiled.

She liked that.

She liked that they feared her. Liked that they didn't know what to expect from her.

Liked that they knew they couldn't control her.

She was in control now, and everyone below her knew it.

Lady Candra broke the stare first, her eyes dropping, and Tessa slid her attention to the door where Lord Jove was entering the room. His Source, Dysani, was a step behind him. The female's hands were clasped in front of her, gaze fixed on her Master.

Rordan glanced up at Tessa, a warm smile filling his face as he dipped his chin in greeting before settling into his chair on the raised dais. Six chairs looked out over the rest of the room; all of them were now occupied but one.

Tessa straightened as the bond stirred. It shouldn't be doing that. But more than that, this wasn't the stirring of *him* being near. She'd been learning to differentiate between the two during her last days with them. The bond with Theon was insistent and demanding, but this was different. This was coaxing and left her wanting. This was—

"My apologies for my late arrival," came a male voice that had her stumbling back a step.

What was he doing here? He wasn't supposed to be here. This was not how today was supposed to go.

"Luka Mors," Rordan said from his seat. "To what do we owe the pleasure?"

Tessa watched as Luka paused for only a moment to bow to the Lords and Ladies before he stepped *onto* the dais without invitation. He lowered into the Arius seat as if he had every right to be there. His legs were sprawled, and he leaned back in the chair as though he would rather be anywhere else. No one said a word, and Tessa couldn't take her eyes off him.

His brown hair was pulled back, tied in a knot on top of his head, and he was in a three-piece suit, all of it black. It fit him like it'd been custom tailored to fit his muscular frame, and it likely had been. And she knew he hated wearing the thing. She'd only seen him in a suit a handful of other times. He usually opted for suit pants and button-down shirts, just formal enough to keep Valter off his back. But Valter wasn't an issue anymore, and yet here he was, looking like a Lord himself.

A Sargon Lord, she realized, if such a thing were allowed to exist.

It wasn't until Rordan spoke again that Tessa realized she was clutching the railing so tightly her knuckles were white, and her magic was flaring once more. But Luka never looked at her. For all he appeared to care, she may as well not exist in this room at all.

"I would suggest you explain your actions, Mors," Rordan said, sitting straighter in his chair. A faint flare of power flickered at his fingertips.

"Theon was unable to attend on such short notice," Luka said. "As I am sure you are aware, Valter is currently unavailable."

"Everyone is aware that Lord St. Orcas is handling some pressing matters in the Underground," Rordan answered.

"Which is why we expected an Arius Heir to be here," the Serafina Lady cut in with a questioning look to Luka.

She knew Rordan had fed the ruling Ladies some lie about Valter. That was not what surprised her about this whole exchange, and she now had the same question as Lady Isleen. She had been prepared to see Axel. All morning she had been preparing herself to see him. Theon *couldn't* come here. Not with the bargain they'd made. If he intentionally entered the same space she was in, it would break that deal, and he would incur a curse of some kind. Axel was supposed to be here, not Luka.

"Unless Axel St. Orcas is no longer the next in line?" Lady Isleen continued.

"What are you implying?" Luka asked, his eyes narrowing on the Serafina Lady.

"Theon does have a Match contract," the Falein Lady mused as if this made perfect sense. "It would stand to reason he could have an heir of his own at this point."

The entire room went still as thunder rumbled, and Tessa felt the floor beneath her shudder with the sound.

That was when Luka finally deigned to look at her.

Sapphire eyes connected with hers, and her heart was beating too wildly. She shouldn't care. She'd walked away from him. She'd finally won. Finally taken her freedom, leaving nothing but blood and desolation in her wake.

Because that was what monsters did.

It was the only way to survive in a realm full of villains.

Luka's attention had already returned to the room as he said, "There is not another heir that I am aware of. Axel is also unavailable. Therefore, as Theon's advisor and second, for all intents and purposes, I was sent to report back whatever is discussed."

"This is absurd," the Celeste Lady scoffed. "You are not of the Arius bloodline. You cannot sit in that seat."

"Then who do you propose should be in this seat?" Luka countered.

"The next most powerful Arius Legacy," she retorted.

"Are you saying the most powerful Legacy of a bloodline should have a kingdom seat?"

"That is how things have always been done," Lady Candra snapped. "You know this."

"Then why is *she* up there?"

Everyone turned to look up at her now. Heirs shifted uncomfortably in their seats. The Sources tensed, elements stirring around them as they prepared to protect their bonded.

"*She* should not even be here," the Serafina Lady finally said, breaking the silence that had descended.

"You believe she should be in my seat?" Lord Jove asked, his power slithering out from him.

While Tessa's power wound around her like a lover, the Lord's power seeped out like Theon's darkness did. It slowly made its way in Luka's direction, and Tessa tensed. Her own power pressed at her, and she couldn't tell if it was seeking out its own likeness or if it was seeking to protect.

Luka, however, didn't seem fazed. He never did, and it drove her mad. The gods themselves could come back to Devram, and Luka Mors would act as if he didn't have two fucks to give.

"Is she not more powerful than you?" Luka asked.

"No," Lord Jove answered immediately.

Luka only shrugged.

A godsdamn shrug to the Achaz Lord, the unofficial ruler of the realm.

"I assure you she is not," Rordan added, his power still growing.

"You are certain?" the Anala Lady asked, her red-gold hair glimmering in the light of Rordan's power.

"Of course," he answered.

"Then you have ascertained her entire lineage?" Lady Aithne pressed.

"She is clearly an Achaz Legacy," the Celeste Lady snapped.

"Is she?" the Falein Lady asked. "The powers we have witnessed suggest she is more than that, and we have been told repeatedly that Rordan does not know her full lineage. Has that changed?"

"I have told you I am making progress on that front," the Lord retorted, his power pausing in its path to Luka and now veering towards Lady Farhan.

"And yet you have not shared any new information since convincing us she should be separated from the Arius Heir," the Anala Lady cut in. "Is that not why we are here, Rordan? The Arius Heir was making more progress than you are."

"No one has given me a chance to speak. We have only just taken our seats," Lord Jove bit out.

"Then speak," Lady Aithne said, her voice too calm with the flames that flickered in her golden eyes.

They seemed to have forgotten Luka and why he was here instead of Axel, but Tessa hadn't. Now she was more annoyed than ever that he was here because he had put the focus directly on her. It likely would have found its way to her eventually. The purpose of this meeting, from what she understood, *was* to discuss her remaining in the Achaz King-dom. But Luka had wasted no time in reminding everyone she was not what she was supposed to be.

Too wild.

Too impulsive.

Too much of a hassle.

Uncontrollable.

Tessa pushed off the railing, Mother Cordelia's words finding her even here. She'd heard no word of the Estate Mother since the female had tried to turn her over to the Augury. She was never mentioned in the conversations she was a part of or overheard. It was as if she had just...disappeared.

"How can you be sure it is her mother's line that is Achaz blood? Do you know the identity of her mother?"

The Falein Lady's voice carried up to her, and Tessa stilled, only just now realizing she was pacing. Her bare feet were quiet on the marble floor, her shoes discarded on a nearby chair. The gown she wore was a gold velvet, the winter months having finally come in full force, leaving snow on the ground that stuck. But the fitted bodice and long sleeves of the dress were making her hot up here on the balcony. She hadn't even wanted to wear this thing today. It was impractical. Leggings and a sweater sounded divine, but Oralia had claimed this would be the wiser option if she insisted on attending this hearing. The female had made it as clear as Dex had what her opinions were on Tessa being here today. For some reason known only to the gods that hated this realm, Oralia had been appointed to serve her.

A *Fae* was serving *her*.

The mere idea made her want to vomit, but Oralia insisted it was the best assignment she could have been given.

Tessa begged to differ.

She should be paying attention to what was being said, absorbing every word. It was all she'd been doing for months. That was how she'd been able to turn the tables on Theon. She already knew everything that was being said anyway.

Lord Jove had been the one to tell her of her mother's bloodline. That her mother was a descendant of Achaz, but he didn't know how far down the line. Closer than he was, that much was certain. He claimed he was still more powerful than her. She didn't think that was the case, but she hadn't trained enough with her own power to know.

Yet.

The Lord may be full of confidence and poise in front of the other realm rulers, but she knew he was observing her more than anyone else.

He couldn't summon the Hunters.

He didn't have wolves that answered to him and him alone.

He wasn't both beginnings and endings, light and dark.

And he didn't know that her grandfather was Arius, the god of death and endings himself.

She wasn't stupid. She'd kept that card close, and apparently so had Theon. Outside of those who had been in the room when Scarlett had shared that truth, she was sure no one else knew her paternal lineage.

Secrets were currency after all.

It was the reason Lord Jove shared just enough truth to show he was working with the others. The other rulers had to know he was withholding information. They had secrets of their own, and Tessa had collected so much currency as of late, she might very well be the wealthiest being in Devram.

Tired of the velvet rubbing against her skin with every step, she dropped into a chair. She could still hear everything being said. Arguments about where she should be housed, as if Lord Jove would let them remove her from the Achaz Kingdom where she belonged. But he entertained their arguments, and she tipped her head back, her eyes falling closed. She hadn't had a good night's rest in weeks. Not since the last night she'd slept between Theon and Luka.

And when she did sleep, her dreams were...not dreams at all.

That thought alone had her lurching to her feet. She could not fall asleep here. If she had a vision, she never knew what her mental state would be when she woke. She felt more chaotic away from them, and that was saying something considering she'd been told she was chaos her entire existence.

Slipping her socks back on, she picked up the heeled, black ankle boots she'd worn so they wouldn't click against the stairs as she made her way down. The entry of the Tribunal building was bustling with all the Lords and Ladies here, and she cursed under her breath when she spotted Dex and Oralia standing off to one side. Of course Dex was positioned to see her only exit. It was as if he suspected she would make an attempt to leave.

Scowling, she debated what to do for only a few seconds before climbing halfway back up the stairs and conjuring a portal. The gateway flared brightly, making her squint as she stepped through directly into an alleyway beside the building.

"Neat trick," came a male voice that Tessa knew all too well, and she turned to find Brecken leaning against the wall.

The male was dressed like Dex was in black pants and a white button-down shirt. As he lifted a cigarette to his lips, the sleeve pulled up, revealing his markings— Celeste Estate, air element, and in service to the Achaz Kingdom.

"What are you doing out here?" she demanded, dropping her boots to the pavement and sliding her now damp feet into them. Great. As if socks weren't bad enough, now they were wet socks.

"Smoking," Brecken answered, taking a drag off the thing. "Your turn."

"Sneaking away from Dex," she retorted.

Brecken grinned. "Usually we're sneaking *with* you, Tessie."

She was about to say something in response when the scent of his smoke hit her. "Are you... Is that lull-leaf?"

He lifted a dark brow before he took another drag and extended the roll to her. "Is that you asking for a hit?"

Tessa glanced at it, worrying her bottom lip. It *did* sound nice. She knew it would ease her nerves, but...

She'd only smoked lull-leaf with Tristyn Blackheart.

And he'd only been using her.

And Auryon had betrayed her.

And Dex and Oralia were lying to her. She just hadn't figured out what they were lying about yet. If she couldn't trust them, she certainly couldn't trust Brecken.

Seeming to take her non-answer as a rejection of his offer, Brecken shrugged, bringing the roll back to his lips. "Where are you off to then?"

"Need to report back to Dexter?" she sneered.

Brecken huffed a laugh, tipping his head back against the wall and closing his eyes. "Your whereabouts have always been his concern, not mine."

"Obviously. You are rarely around," she muttered, growing restless. She couldn't simply stand around in a back alley.

"Katya, however..." Brecken went on, ignoring her comment.

"Kat is fine. She is safe and protected," Tessa answered.

"With an Arius Legacy?" Brecken mused. He huffed another derisive laugh. "Doubtful."

"Axel is—" But she cut herself off. She couldn't defend an Arius Legacy. Not with her destiny laid out before her. Clearing her throat, she said, "Katya will be fine. I'll see to it."

Brecken only hummed, dropping the last of the lull-leaf that was left to the ground and squishing it beneath his shoe. "What am I to tell Dex then?"

"Tell him whatever you want," she retorted, turning away. "Rordan does not limit my movements, so Dex is in no position to be doing so either."

"So much *freedom*," he crooned, pushing off the wall.

"Fuck off, Brecken," she snapped, feeling her power coiling as sparks of energy skittered along the ground at her feet.

He slipped his hands into his pockets, sauntering past her, but he stilled for a breath when he was beside her. "Be who you were meant to be, Tessalyn," he said, his voice low. "*My* freedom depends on it."

Before she could ask what that meant, he was turning a corner, leaving her alone all over again.

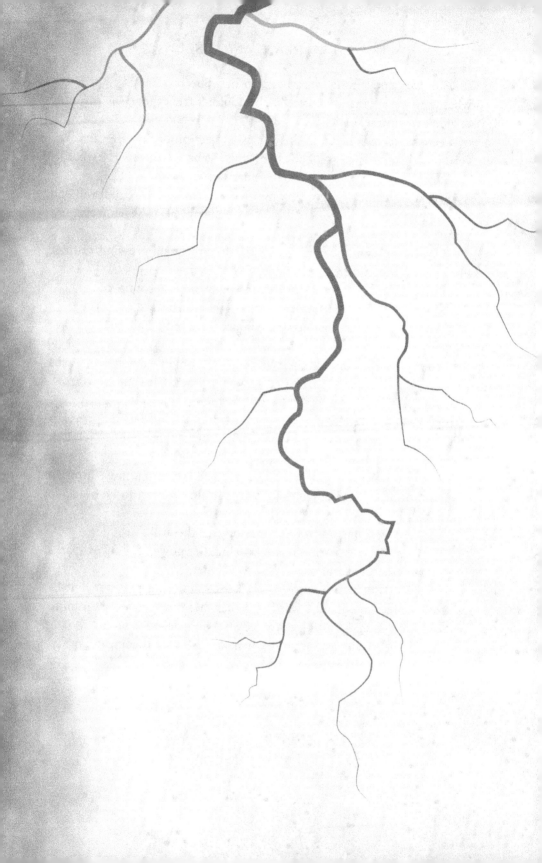

3
TESSA

She may have been alone, but she didn't mind. For the first time ever, she wandered around the Acropolis unaccompanied. She was being watched, of course. It was hard not to be noticed with a giant silver wolf at her side, but Roan had appeared the moment she'd stepped from the shadows and onto the street. Snow was gently drifting to the ground, and Tessa wrapped her arms tightly around herself. In her need to get out of the Tribunal building, she'd left her coat.

There was a large fountain in the center of the Acropolis, various enchantments keeping the water from freezing, and she stopped to watch it flow. A glittering sculpture of blacks and golds was in the center, water pouring from various locations. There was no rhyme or reason. It was just chaos feeding into the pool that had been sectioned off into six distinct areas, one for each kingdom.

Slowly, she circled it, her fingers dragging through the snow that was piling up on the lip of the fountain. A mosaic of what it was thought each god or goddess looked like was built into the bottom. Anala with her bright red-gold hair and golden eyes. Serafina with her silver hair and crown of white flames. Falein with her warm skin and black curls. Arius with his dark hair and emerald eyes and—

Tessa gasped when she ran into someone. She started to splutter an apology and ask for forgiveness, the habit to take the blame for anything still ingrained in her being, but the words died on her tongue when she looked up.

The being she'd run into was wearing a cloak, the hood up and features hidden. They were tall, but the hand that had steadied her was unmistakably feminine. Before she could get a look, the figure stepped back, her fingers disappearing into the sleeve of the cloak once more. There was no pearlescent mask beneath the hood, and Roan wasn't growling at her side. In fact, the wolf was sitting. His attention was pinned on the figure, but he was calm, clearly not sensing any danger.

Because this person wasn't a member of the Augury.

This was the Keeper.

But that wasn't possible because the Keeper who had awakened her power, who had spoken to her, who had called those around her fools, had been unmistakably male. It was said no one truly knew who or what the Keeper was. That the use of glamours and spells kept their identity ever changing, but the Keeper was also never seen outside the Pantheon.

"Who are you?" Tessa demanded, stepping back from the figure.

They only tilted their head, and she could feel them studying her.

She lifted a hand, lightning sparking between her fingers. She was past the days of not protecting herself, of blindly trusting, and of giving someone the benefit of the doubt. No, at this point she just assumed everyone wanted to use her, cage her, or sacrifice her. Perhaps all three.

"You will cause a scene," the figure said, her voice as feminine as her touch had been.

Tessa slowly lowered her hand because she knew that voice. Definitely female, but harsh and unyielding.

"You are not the Keeper," Tessa said, taking another step back.

"Am I not?"

"I… How are you here?"

"The same way you are here," she answered.

"But I do not know how *I* am here."

The female tsked from beneath her hood. "You know where your answers lie, daughter of wild and fury. You simply do not wish to have them."

"That is not true," she snarled, lurching forward as light arced from her palms. She directed it to the side a second before it could collide with the female, cracking the edge of the fountain.

"He has your answers," the female replied calmly.

"He will not answer my questions," Tessa argued.

She nodded. "He will not until he knows where you stand."

Tessa growled in frustration, causing Roan to get to his feet and place himself between them.

"And still they guard you," the female murmured so low Tessa barely heard her. "Perhaps all is not lost yet."

"Perhaps everyone still underestimates me," Tessa countered, a gust of wind blowing through the courtyard. Her golden hair blew across her face, snowflakes getting caught in the strands. She brushed them out of the way as a golden mist started floating up from the crack in the fountain lip. Seconds later, a Hunter stood beside her. Roan was growling now, but the female was backing up.

"You stand on the precipice of salvation and destruction, Tessalyn. Choose wisely."

Then she was gone, disappearing into the very air. Tessa wasn't remotely surprised she could Travel. It appeared one of Theon's first actions as the acting Arius Lord was to rescind the banishment placed on Cienna that had been keeping her confined to the Underground to avoid Valter's death sentence. But that meant everyone who believed the Keeper was one person was wrong. There was more than one, and as of this moment, she was perhaps the only one who knew that secret.

She smiled to herself as she filed that information away with all the other secrets she'd collected. She'd figure out who the other Keepers were. She already had ideas and would be able to test those theories in time. Brecken had let secrets of his own slip in that alleyway. And the Lords and Ladies? The tension between them was already growing. She could have stayed and witnessed more of that, but this information regarding the Keeper was worth missing out on that.

"You called, your grace?" the Hunter asked, his voice raspy and unearthly as it always was. She'd come to love it. It was as icy as her own soul had become.

He glided in front of her, his pale skin as white as the falling snow.

"You suggested visiting the Pantheon last night," Tessa answered. "Is that still necessary?"

"He will see you, but you must find your way to him."

"Then let's go."

"And the Arius blood I taste in the air?" the Hunter asked.

She shook her head, making her way to the Pantheon. "Not today. I cannot draw any more attention, especially once we're inside."

"Understood, your grace."

There was a flash of light before he passed her a golden sword with a sheath that buckled across her chest. The sword settled between her shoulder blades as if it had always been a part of her. Always hers. Since the dawn of time.

People scattered, veering down side streets as she approached, and gods, it felt so good. She'd take the terror over the sneers and condescension. The guards at the Pantheon tried to bar her entrance as she approached, but as soon as her lips tilted up and her head canted to the side, they scrambled aside moments before her power struck where they'd been standing. These people would have turned her over solely for existing. She didn't have it in her to care about morals anymore.

Then again, that wasn't true either.

It wasn't true as she strolled through the halls of the Pantheon, going deeper and deeper where no one was allowed but the priestesses. It wasn't true as she came upon two of those priestesses with a male Fae who clearly didn't want to be there. It wasn't true when she didn't hesitate to send her light arching and wrapping around their slender throats. It wasn't true when the Hunter tried to tell her they were Zinta Legacy, and she silenced him with a single look before her power fed on the death she bestowed. It certainly wasn't true as she bent to retrieve the male's clothing and handed it to him, his trembling fingers closing around the fabric and his eyes staying fixed to the floor.

She crouched before him, tipping his head up with a single finger beneath his chin. "You can access the deepest parts of the Pantheon?" she asked, holding his hazel stare.

The Fae shook his head. "I can only go where the priestesses can. The deepest parts are reserved for the—"

"Keeper," Tessa interrupted. "Take me as far as you can go."

He nodded, and Tessa stood, turning away while he got dressed. It wasn't until he was leaving them at a passage that he stammered, "Thank you for... Just thank you...your grace."

"Tell whoever you will of this," she answered. "And let them know that should anyone else touch you in such a manner, I will return to bestow the same fate."

The Fae's face paled, but she was already striding down the narrow passage, the wards crackling against her skin but ultimately doing nothing to stop her.

Wards had never been an obstacle for her.

The Hunter was silent as they made their way deeper into the Pantheon, Roan having stayed outside. They'd had to avoid priestesses in the halls the Fae had led them down, but these passages were completely deserted. It wasn't until they started winding downwards that her breathing grew shallow as she realized they were descending underground.

"Your grace?" the Hunter asked, pausing when she did.

She ignored him, breathing deep. She could feel them. They had felt her sudden spike in emotion, and both of them were pacing on the other side of that bond she was blocking. With another deep breath, she bent and removed her socks and boots, leaving them in the passage. Her toes curled against the cold stone beneath her, and she brought her hand to the wall, dragging her fingertips along the uneven surface.

One step in front of the other. Just focus on the next step.

Luka's words from the Underground echoed in her mind, and she inhaled once more before she took that next step and the next and the next. The coolness of the stone kept her grounded, but she became so focused, her mental shields slipped.

That's our girl.

She hissed out a curse as Luka's voice clanged in her mind once more, and she realized her shields had slipped the moment she'd known she was going below ground. Those words hadn't been memories, but *him*.

How do you even know where I am? she retorted down the bond. These were the first words she'd spoken down the thing since she'd left Theon on his knees in his room. Actually, the last time she'd exchanged words with Luka, they'd been coaxing her along as Augury members had led her through damp tunnels.

How fitting.

I don't know where you are, Luka replied. *But I do know when you are panicking, Tessa.*

I don't need either of you.

Ignoring that comment, he said, *I do need to speak to you though. In person. Where are you?*

I am not going to see you.

Tessa, it's important.

No.

And with that, she hauled her mental shields back into place, blocking him out once more. It wasn't lost on her that Theon hadn't said a single word. She'd felt him there the entire time though. So had the bond. She'd spent these last weeks becoming so accustomed to the longing of the thing that it was more of a constant ache now. Something she'd become numb to, but she felt it now. Which was annoying.

Looking around, she found the passage they'd been following had emptied into a large chamber, and with another start, she realized she'd been here before.

No, wait.

Not here, but somewhere similar.

The Augury members had led her through a chamber like this, only there had been an altar in the middle. This circular chamber was much smaller and empty. There was nothing in here except for a large mirror.

Large probably wasn't accurate.

It was taller than a doorway and arched along the top. Bordering it were various markings. As she ventured closer, she recognized some of them as the symbols of the gods, but there were other symbols she didn't know.

"This is what the Keepers guard so heavily?" Tessa mused. "A mirror?"

"Things are not always what they appear," the Hunter said, gliding forward.

"That is true," she conceded, stepping closer still. Theon claimed he'd seen Scarlett in a mirror after all, but that mirror had been in the Underground from what she understood. She ran her fingertips along a few of the symbols, tracing them.

"Blood calls to blood," the Hunter whispered in her ear when she reached the Achaz symbol of three interlocking triangles.

"What?" Tessa asked, turning to him. His pure white eyes glowed faintly. She'd grown used to the fact they didn't have pupils. Or names, apparently. She'd asked once, but none of them responded. Considering they all looked exactly the same, it hadn't surprised her.

"Blood calls to blood," he repeated, pulling a gold dagger from the air that matched the sword at her back.

"I'm keeping this," she said, taking the blade and weighing it in her hand.

"Of course, your grace," he replied with a bow of his head. "But allow me."

Taking the dagger back, he moved quickly, swiping the tip along her palm. She gasped, jerking her hand back as blood dripped to the stone floor.

"Blood calls to blood," he said again, icy fingers clasping her wrist and tugging her hand towards the etched symbols.

She understood then, and the Hunter seemed to sense that, releasing his grip on her. She wasn't entirely sure how they appeared to know what she was thinking or feeling. Studying the symbols, she hesitated for the briefest of moments when her eyes landed on the Arius symbol. He was her grandfather. Maybe she was more closely related to Arius than Achaz.

She had no idea what this was going to do. The gods were forbidden to interfere in Devram. Blood calls to blood could mean anything. She could summon another Arius or Achaz Legacy to the mirror from another realm. Maybe it would summon Scarlett. The queen was her cousin, after all.

Or maybe it would summon her father.

Or her mother.

The thoughts had her stepping back from the mirror. Her hand closed into a fist, blood seeping between her fingers.

But this might be her only chance to use this mirror. Could she call it a mirror? That seemed too simplistic for what it actually did.

"He will answer your call," the Hunter whispered, those icy fingertips brushing along the nape of her neck. "He waits for you."

With a surge of determination, she lurched forward, slamming her bleeding palm atop the Achaz symbol. This is what she wanted. This is what she *needed*. Answers. And if no one here would give them to her, then she'd go directly to the sources themselves.

Something began swirling in the mirror, images flashing among shadows and silvery light. They moved so quickly, they were blurs she couldn't make out as she stepped back and watched.

"Does it always take this long?" Tessa asked after several minutes, the gash on her palm having long since healed.

But the Hunter didn't answer, his attention fixed on the mirror as well.

Growing bored, she ventured closer again, studying some of the other symbols. She knew the main kingdoms and those of the other Legacy in Devram, but so many of these were foreign to her. A triangle inside a circle. A crescent moon atop a circle. One she could only describe as a tangled knot.

That was the one she was reaching to touch when a male voice said, "Not that one, child."

Tessa lurched back, tripping on the skirt of her gown and landing hard on the stone floor. Her light flared, lightning bouncing across the floor as a golden shield erupted around her.

That was new.

But all thoughts left her mind as she lifted her eyes back to the mirror to meet blue eyes with brilliant flecks of gold. His entire being seemed to glow, light swirling around him the way it wound around her arms. He had a tanned complexion, and his golden hair—hair that matched her own—reached nearly to his chin. And gods, he was tall. There was no question that she was looking upon a god.

The god of light and beginnings.

Achaz.

"Well done, Hunter," the god said. "You have managed to find what no one else has been able to."

The Hunter bowed deeply. "My purpose is to please you, my king."

Tessa had managed to get back to her feet, and she fidgeted, fighting every impulse to drop to a knee before the god. She wasn't a Legacy, but she sure as fuck wasn't a goddess. And Achaz was *the* ruler of the gods.

As though he could read her thoughts, Achaz said, "You do not bow? Has such consideration truly been lost in that realm?"

"Perhaps such *consideration* was lost when the gods abandoned the realm and left it to its own demise," she retorted.

Regret immediately surged through her at the impulsiveness. So typical of her, and to a god of all people. But she'd already said it, and even if she'd wanted to apologize, she couldn't force the words to pass her lips.

Achaz was staring at her, the gold flecks in his eyes luminous with pure power. His lips were pressed into a thin line, and it was only then that she noticed the golden hilt of a sword peeking over his shoulder. His entire being was elegance and grace, from the fine clothing to the way his power took on the faint shape of wings behind him.

When he'd appeared to finally accept she would not offer an apology or ask for forgiveness, he said, "I see." Then he added, "Such arrogance comes from your father's side."

She doubted that. Tessa had a feeling all the gods were born with such arrogance.

Still she said nothing, waiting for him to speak first. She'd found if she waited long enough, others tended to reveal their secrets without her having to do much of anything.

Watch. Listen. Learn everything you can about the people in this room.

Theon had taught her that, and she'd be lying if she said it hadn't served her well these past months.

"The tenacity, however," Achaz said after another long minute of watching her, "you get from my line."

"I imagine so if you have held a grudge for centuries," she quipped.

"You know nothing of what you speak," he replied coolly.

Tessa shrugged. "I know you need me more than I need you."

"And what makes you believe such a thing?"

She stepped up close, rapping her knuckles against the glass. "I'm not stuck on the other side of a mirror."

"A mirror? Is that what you think this is?" Achaz asked, a thread of amusement in his voice. "These are vessels of power. They were not always this, but it's what they have become over time."

"How?"

"I am not here to give you history lessons," he snapped, growing agitated.

By the Fates, his moods were more fickle than Theon's.

"Then why are you here?" she asked, for once not matching his tone, but sounding calm and bored as she idly began tracing the etchings around the mirror again.

"To make sure you understand your purpose."

The words made her pause for the briefest of moments as her fingers hovered over the Arius symbol.

"My purpose is to correct the balance," she said, her tone taking on an eerie ring.

"That it is," Achaz agreed, and she could hear just how pleased he was with that answer. "And tell me, granddaughter, what does correcting the balance mean?"

Granddaughter.

The familial term did something to her, and she couldn't decide if it made her want to draw closer to a blooded relative or shrink away from a god. But more than any of that, it was a confirmation she'd been seeking.

Tessa stepped back from the mirror, clearing her throat softly. "You wish for the Arius line to be eradicated for breaking laws of old."

"Very good," he praised.

"But did you not do the same? Should I even be standing before you?"

The approval on the god's face quickly morphed into annoyance. "When Arius broke the laws, I had no choice but to follow."

"And if his line is erased, what of your own? Would it not stand to reason that the balance would then be tipped in the other direction?"

"You forget who I am, child," Achaz replied, his voice going dangerously low. "You think I have not already thought of these things? Arrangements have already been made to correct such a balance." Before she could speak the question forming on her tongue, he added, "You are not privy to the dealings of gods and chaos."

She snapped her mouth shut, familiar fury starting to build.

It's not your place to know.

Same words, different meaning. She was still a vessel being used. She wasn't stupid.

"And my mother?" Tessa asked, trying to sound nonchalant, but she was desperate to put these final pieces of her lineage together. To *know* where she came from, and what she was, and *why* this was her purpose.

Achaz's head canted to the side. "What of her?"

"Who is she?"

The smile that filled the god's face immediately told her she'd revealed too much. He saw right through her false indifference.

"Fulfill your purpose, granddaughter, and I will bring you to her," he said.

"What?" Tessa stammered. "How... You cannot come here."

"No," Achaz agreed. "Not at this time anyway. But you, blood of my blood? You have the power to change that, don't you? And beyond that, even if I can never step foot in Devram, you can certainly *leave* the realm."

"How?"

"Fulfill your destiny. Find me again when it is done," was all he said before his image started fading.

"Wait!" Tessa cried, lurching forward once more and pressing her hands to the glass.

But he was gone, and she was left alone all over again.

It took her a few minutes, her brow pressed to the cool glass as she worked to stifle the fury and power pressing at her soul. But when she stepped back from the mirror, she smoothed her hands down her dress and made her way back out of the Pantheon. She needed to get back to the Tribunal building anyway.

Roan was waiting for her, falling into step beside her as the three of them wound their way through the Acropolis streets once more. Every footfall was filled with renewed determination.

Fulfill her purpose.

Collect more currency.

Correct the balance.

All of this was reckless and impulsive and wild. But that was exactly what she needed to be if she expected to survive.

Because she'd stopped playing the games of the Legacy and had entered an arena with gods, and if she failed, her only purpose was death.

4
LUKA

"This is fucking stupid, Theon," Luka griped as he yanked his tie off and threw it across the room. His phone was on speaker, sitting on the coffee table before his sofa.

"It's not stupid, Luka," Theon replied. "What's stupid is you calling me right now. I told you not to contact me. Not to tell me anything."

"What exactly have I told you? You felt her emotions as much as I did," he answered, shrugging out of the suit jacket. He hated wearing all this, but he'd had no choice in the matter when he was meeting the rulers of the realm as the representative of Arius Kingdom.

"Then why are you calling me right now? To tell me what I already know?"

A frustrated growl escaped him as he started working the buttons of his shirt. When he finished undoing the final one, he sank onto the sofa, his shirt falling open as he swiped up his phone and brought it to his ear. "She was there."

"Where?"

"At the Tribunal hearing."

"Again, why are you telling me this?"

Luka sighed, pulling the band from his hair and letting the strands fall around his face. "Because you told me to go to her, to find out where Axel is, and she won't talk to me. I figured you had experience with... Well, you know."

A long pause greeted him before Theon said, "Are you trying to say I have experience with Tessa completely shutting me out?"

"Don't act offended," Luka said, toeing off his shoes before removing his socks.

"And now you are asking me for *advice* on how to handle her?" Theon continued, unfazed. "The one she fucked and then left on his knees?"

"Well, when you say it like that," Luka grumbled, calling his power forth and letting black flames linger.

For so long they'd kept his true lineage quiet. Most had assumed he was an Arius Legacy, and it was second nature to keep his power hidden just as he'd kept his dragon form and Traveling abilities hidden. This was one of the few places he felt at ease and able to drop all his shields and pretenses, even with the truth out in the open now.

There was an exasperated sound on the other end. "You want to know how I got her to finally talk to me when she was actively ignoring me?" Theon asked. "I pushed her, Luka. I pushed her too godsdamn far when the rest of you warned me not to. I told her to get herself under control, and then I pushed her to the point of losing it. I'm not the one to give you advice on this. That's why I sent you to her. *You* are the one she asks for. You are the one she likes to be able to see. You are the one..." He trailed off for another long moment before saying, "You're the one who has always known she wasn't the one for this, and now I know why."

"What does that mean?" Luka asked, extinguishing the flames in his palm.

"It's nothing I can explain now."

Suspicion immediately blossomed because the only time Theon told him that was when he was trying to work something out, which usually meant he'd discovered some new information.

"With everything going on, this is not the time to keep secrets, Theon. If you learned something new, you need to tell us," Luka said.

"Us? We don't even know where the fuck Axel is right now," Theon retorted.

"Then what's the plan?"

"There is no plan, Luka. You're the one who repeatedly said the plan was fucked."

"The *original* plan was fucked," he argued. "We can't just move forward without a plan. That's just...chaos."

"The plan right now is for you to talk to Tessa and see if she knows where Axel is. I'll keep searching on my end while also trying to run an entire godsdamn kingdom."

"You should probably start by showing up for the Tribunal meetings," Luka replied dryly.

"I told you I couldn't get there this time. Not when they call a meeting last minute like this. I'm tied up with something else."

"Right. Something you can't explain now."

"For fuck's sake, Luka," Theon sighed. "Just tell me what happened."

"Now you want me to tell you things?"

"Gods, you're broodier than usual. When was the last time you went flying? Or went to your cave?"

"I'm there now," he answered, looking around at the place he'd claimed as his own.

He'd spent an exorbitant amount of money to make it not so cave-like. The floors had been sanded smooth, and he'd paid an Anahita Legacy to enchant pipes so he had running water throughout the caverns that branched off from the rest of the space. He even had a high-end kitchen installed, which was ridiculous because he never cooked. But here, no one taunted him about how he liked his giant bed in another cavern room to be a mess of pillows and blankets. Here it was quiet, and he could think. Here there weren't expectations and demands constantly being made of him. Here there wasn't a need to prove he was worthy of the blood that ran in his veins.

And here, no one touched his godsdamn things.

"Just tell me about the meeting," Theon said. "Then go fly for a bit."

"There's a lot of tension among the rulers right now," Luka offered, tucking the hair tie into a bronze tin and picking up one of the rings inside it.

"When isn't there?" Theon replied.

"This was more than that," Luka said, rolling the silver ring between his fingers. "Tessa being there was a power play by Jove, whether she realizes it or not. It didn't matter that she left before things really got under way. The others saw her."

"Wasn't that the point of the meeting? To discuss how to handle Tessa now that they know what she is?" Theon asked, shuffling sounds coming through his end before it quieted down again.

"They don't know though," Luka argued, placing the ring back inside the tin and snapping the lid shut. "They are all worried about her paternal line, and Jove keeps trying to play off her maternal line."

"Do you think he knows?"

"I honestly cannot tell. He insists she is not more powerful than he is, but merely being the granddaughter of Arius would make her more powerful."

He could practically see Theon rubbing his jaw as he said, "But she's hardly displayed any Arius gifts for being a direct descendant. All of her gifts have manifested as Achaz powers. That would suggest she's just as close, if not closer, to Achaz."

"Except the ability to summon storms. That is neither of them," Luka said, getting to his feet and moving to a wall of empty frames.

They both fell silent at his words because it put them back at the beginning of all this. They'd learned so much about her, yet still had no solid answers.

"I think that's ultimately the missing knowledge for Jove too," Luka finally said. "He knows she has Achaz blood, but does he know about her visions and Witch heritage?"

"There is no way they know she's essentially Achaz, Zinta, Arius, and Serafina. They would have already killed her," Theon said. "They would have never let her get this strong or this powerful."

"Unless Jove thought he could control her."

"Control the uncontrollable," Theon muttered. "It all goes back to that stupid prophecy."

"Tell me again what your theory about her maternal line is," Luka said. He should be writing this all down. Theon could keep facts straight in his head, but Luka had always been more visual.

"There are texts that suggest Achaz had a child with a daughter of Zinta. I don't think Tessa is that child because those texts were written centuries ago, and Tessa is obviously only twenty-four years. But beyond that, she could be anywhere in the line."

"So we know nothing," Luka said bluntly, running his fingers along an ancient gold frame.

"We know her paternal line, but the other things... Yeah, we know nothing," he answered, sounding utterly defeated.

"Theon, you keep trying to do this alone, and you don't have to. You know that, right?"

"It's my responsibility," he replied.

"No, it's—"

"Is there anything else?" Theon interrupted, his tone going hard.

Luka sighed, not wanting to push this during a phone conversation of all things. "Yeah. There's one more thing. When the meeting was concluding, it was reported that two priestesses were found dead at the Pantheon."

The pause on the other end was deafening.

"Like the Arius Legacy that have been turning up dead?" Theon finally asked.

They'd been finding bodies all throughout the Acropolis for the last two weeks. It was another reason the emergency meeting had been called. It didn't matter if they were full-blooded Arius Legacy or if they simply had Arius blood somewhere in their ancestry. Every single victim had some type of Arius lineage.

Until the priestesses.

"These were Pantheon priestesses, Theon," Luka answered.

"So full-blooded Zinta Legacy," Theon replied.

"The Celeste Lady was furious considering the Pantheon is part of her responsibilities in correlation with Selection duties," Luka replied. "They are demanding Tessa be detained until her lineage is determined and until it is proven she is not responsible."

"Why would she be responsible for this? Wasn't she at the Tribunal building?"

"I told you, she disappeared shortly after it started. That's when we felt her panicking."

"Are you saying Tessa killed the priestesses?" Theon asked.

Raking a hand through his hair, he said, "I don't know, Theon. But all the evidence is pointing to her. Not the Augury."

"She can't... She wouldn't..." But Theon trailed off, and Luka knew he was cataloging all the evidence in his mind.

He had sat there and listened as the rulers of Devram had done the same. Lord Jove hadn't even tried to argue any of the points. Luka had tried, but he'd quickly realized the error of that because of course he would defend the Arius Heir's chosen Source. He'd suddenly found himself being questioned about the Arius Kingdom's intentions in Selecting her.

To put it bluntly, all of this was a fucking mess.

"What was the outcome?" Theon asked.

"Rordan swore he had things under control and that she would be confined until all their questions could be answered."

"Maybe that's for the best."

"Can you repeat that? Because it sounds like you just said locking up the female who shattered wine bottles and has powers no one can identify is a good idea," Luka said in disbelief. "You, of all people, know what happens when someone tries to confine her."

"If she's confined and more bodies show up, it will prove her innocence. Not only that, they'll be the bad guys as much as we are because she thinks they're giving her freedom," Theon reasoned.

"By the gods," Luka muttered. "Are you listening to yourself?"

"You called me, remember?" Theon retorted.

"Fuck all that has done."

Theon made an annoyed sound. "Go flying. Then maybe you won't be such a broody ass."

"Get in touch if you get any leads on Axel."

"Don't call me again, Luka."

He didn't bother answering, instead disconnecting the call and tossing the phone aside. While he understood the thought process behind having no contact, that was impossible when the three of them were bonded. Mental conversations between them were not private, and when emotions became too much, they all felt them. Theon would have heard the entire conversation he'd tried to have with Tessa, but Theon had stayed quiet, as if he weren't there at all. But he was there, and Tessa would have known that. She would have felt him down the bond.

He had no other way of contacting her though. She didn't have the phone Theon had given her. Short of just showing up at the Achaz Lord's doorstep, he wasn't going to see her, let alone talk to her. Theon had pushed and pushed, forcing his way into the very air she breathed, but at least she'd spoken to him.

Removing the remainder of his clothing, he made his way down a short passage that emptied onto a ledge overlooking the Ozul Mountains. It was well hidden, and even if someone managed to find it, he'd paid ungodly amounts for wards from, ironically enough, Lilura Inquest.

With a flash of pale blue light, he shifted into his dragon form. Scales rippled as he stretched his neck and wings. He hadn't been in this form in weeks. Claws scraped on stone when he moved to the edge, and yet all he could think about was the look on Tessa's face when she'd seen him in this form the first time. Awe and wonder had filled her features as she'd reached out and run her hand along his scales, her fingers gentle and cool against his hot skin.

He shook his head, trying to shake off the memory before he leapt into the darkening sky.

He was standing in the city center of Rockmoor, the capital city of the Arius Kingdom, and he was standing among carnage.

Bodies were everywhere. The streets were red, and the cries of the dying filled the air. Phantoms glided among them all, gold weapons in their hands that silenced the cries. Luka had never fought in a war, but he knew that was what this was. It was a battle, and one side had lost terribly because these weren't warriors dead on the ground. These were common Legacy— males, females, and younglings.

And standing in the center of it all was Tessa.

She was fury incarnate as she held a golden sword of her own, blood glistening on the blade. She looked as she had the day he'd found her stabbing wildly with an arrow. Blood was splattered across her face and in her hair. There was nothing of the female they'd found at the Pantheon all those months ago. There was only cold wrath and wickedness on her features when she crouched beside one of the dying. There was no pity, no mercy, as she said something softly to the person before pulling a golden dagger from a flash of light and slamming it into their chest. Her power followed, arcs of crackling light making the male scream as he arched off the ground.

The silence that followed was deafening, but it also allowed his enhanced hearing to pick up on the low conversations happening.

Luka shifted his eyes, his pupils turning to vertical slits so he could see farther and more clearly when one of the phantom figures glided closer to Tessa. It was then he realized they weren't exactly phantoms. Not as the being reached out with a hand and swept Tessa's hair over her shoulder. Luka clamped down on the growl that swelled in his chest as his dragon snarled at someone else touching her.

"Are you pleased, your grace?" the figure asked, his voice icy and eerie. Tessa didn't even react though, as if she was used to conversing with them.

"It is what must be done," Tessa replied tonelessly, violet eyes sweeping over the chaos around her.

"This realm is yours, your grace," he replied, circling around her.

Where were her wolves?

"The realm is Rordan's, not mine," she answered, reaching to sheath her sword down her back, the gold glinting in the gloomy day. "I want nothing to do with this godsforsaken world."

"You wish to go home?" the being asked.

"I have no home."

"But you do, your grace, and you would be welcomed," he purred, a semi-corporeal hand skimming along her lower back, and Luka couldn't hold in his growl at that touch.

Violet eyes snapped to his, but she appeared to be the only one who heard him. The beings did not react, and the dead did not stir. But her eyes narrowed, and even from here, he could see the lightning flashing in them. Her head tipped to the side, the gold dagger still gripped in her hand.

She was a godsdamn vision.

Golden hair flowed around her, and her entire being was humming with a faint glow. Her white dress was cut low in the front, reaching to her bare feet with deep slits up the side. She had some type of leather armor strapped along her torso with vambraces on her forearms. All of which was splattered with blood. She looked almost as if she'd stepped from another world, standing among the ruin.

Actually, she looked like another version of Auryon, only with blades instead of arrows and light instead of dark.

"You are not supposed to be here," a voice hissed, moments before he was yanked backwards by one of the beings.

Luka whirled to find a gold dagger at his throat and a female standing beside the phantom being. These had to be the Hunters Tristyn had warned them about. The female was beautiful in a haunting sort of way. Tall and lithe, her raven hair was stark against her pale skin. It was woven into a simple plait, strands of gold interspersed among it. Her gown was gold, and so were the bangles on her wrists. Her eyes, though, were bright violet as they glared at him.

"Did she call to you? Or were you sent?" the female demanded.

"I don't know what that means," Luka replied.

"We shall see, young warlord," she sneered, before her hand shot out, slamming into his chest.

Luka lurched to his feet, tripping over the mess of blankets and pillows as he looked around wildly, blinking sleep from his eyes. He was still at his cave. It was still dark. His black flames still cast a low glow over the space. He was still alone.

But somehow, he'd also just been in one of Tessa's visions, and he didn't know what the fuck to do with that.

5
AXEL

He was dying.

That was all he could think as he sat in the dark room, alone and chained.

Well, that and he needed a drink. Something warm and coppery would do. Something full of power and heat. Gods, he could practically taste it. Practically taste *her*. She would taste like smoke and fire, and the magic would be all-consuming. Where would he drink from? Her wrist? Her thigh? Her throat?

Perhaps all three?

He'd heard it was more intoxicating to drink it straight from the source rather than a glass. He wondered how true that was...

"Fuck," Axel rasped, shifting against the hard wall he was leaning against. Sharp rock dug into his spine, and every movement ripped open wounds that weren't being allowed to heal. The wound in his thigh was searing. There was no doubt it was becoming infected because Julius wouldn't let it close. He could feel his blood already trickling down his back, but the pain and sensations brought him back to this place and kept him from thinking about blood, particularly her blood.

He didn't know exactly where he was. The only light he was ever granted was when the door to the room was opened. Otherwise, he was kept in the pitch black, the room so dark he couldn't see his own hand in front of his face.

Of course, he also couldn't bring his hand to his face with the shackles on his wrists.

And the broken arm. That was an issue too.

But the biggest problem was it was so godsdamn quiet in here. There was no music to distract him, and no tasks to keep him busy. He was just left to sit here and think about how thirsty he was, and how empty he felt, and how he would rather be dead than feel like *this*.

Out of control.

Deranged.

Powerless.

He raked the fingers of his good hand across the stone floor. His fingernails had been broken and torn from repeatedly doing this, but the pain was the only thing that distracted him from the overwhelming *need*.

His shadows gave a feeble twitch in his soul, but there was nothing else. They were as dead as he felt. His power wells couldn't even begin to replenish naturally with these bands on his wrists.

He tipped his head back against the wall, a warm-skinned Fae with black curly hair and amber eyes filling his mind.

And he wondered what her blood would taste like.

He knew her name. It was there, in the back of his mind, but that was second to the craving. He knew her name, but all he cared about was that she was Fae.

A powerful Fae.

So much power just there for the taking. Why wasn't anyone taking that? She was just walking around. There for anyone to have.

No, not anyone.

His.

She was his.

His to have.

His to take.

His to make bleed…

"Fuck!" Axel yelled again, knowing this wasn't right. It couldn't be right. He knew she meant something to him, but he didn't need it all. Just some of her and he'd be fine. It would be enough to take the edge off.

Something in his soul shuddered at the idea, and that was the only thing he could cling to that reminded him this wasn't right. He wasn't supposed to want this, but he was supposed to want her. It was confusing, and he didn't understand, and he couldn't think in all this godsfor-saken silence.

But it did allow him to hear the footsteps some time later, which in turn allowed him to brace for the brightness of the light when the door was thrown open. It still stung as the light filtered through his eyelids and made him squeeze them shut even tighter. He assumed this was the same guard that always came in here, spoon-feeding him food and having him drink warm water from a straw. Wisely, the guard was a Night Child. At least his father hadn't been lying about taking him to the Underground. Granted, there were a few Night Children employed outside of the Underground, but they tended to stay in the kingdoms that paid them their coin and supplied them their blood.

Maybe they'd had it right all along. Get paid in extra rations rather than coin...

"Do you think anyone has noticed you're gone yet?"

That voice was not a Night Child though, and Axel cracked his eyes open, squinting through tiny slits at the male Legacy who stood before him. His auburn hair was cropped short, and his mossy green eyes sparkled with some kind of sadistic amusement as he stood over him. He still wore a three-piece suit, even here, as if the mere act of wearing the garment made him better than everyone else.

"What do you want?" Axel asked, tipping his head back once more.

"The same thing we've wanted from the beginning," Mansel replied, moving closer.

Mansel was one of his father's closest advisors. A distant cousin of his mother, he was a Nith Legacy, a descendant of the god of creativity. It had been his idea to chain Axel's wrists to the floor with only a few links for movement. Having them also connected to his ankles was a special kind of torture as was being left in his undergarments. The cold of the room had seeped into his bones. He didn't know how long he'd been down here, but it was long enough to have grown numb to the chill.

So yesterday they had bathed him in ice cold water. His teeth had still been chattering when he'd finally fallen asleep.

Fingers snapping in front of his face had him focusing on the Legacy again.

"Stay awake, Arius Heir. You've got a dinner date," Mansel said, slapping this cheek a few times.

"I don't think I'm dressed for such an occasion," Axel replied, turning his chin away.

"That's what these are for."

It was only then that Axel realized he was holding clothing in his hand.

"You're kidding, right?" Axel said. "How do you expect me to get dressed? Or did you forget you broke my fucking arm?"

"I did not forget that at all," Mansel replied. Then he threw the clothing at him, the fabric falling into Axel's lap. "I'm sure you can manage a pair of pants."

He produced a key, unlocking the wrist shackles from his ankles and the bolts keeping the ankle chains secured to the floor. Then the fucker stood back and watched Axel struggle for the next ten minutes to get the loose pants on over the ankle shackles. Mansel grinned at every hiss from Axel when his broken arm was bumped or when the fabric rubbed along the open stab wound. Blood immediately seeped into the thin material, but apparently that was fine for this dinner meeting.

He limped after Mansel, taking his time as he was led down an unfamiliar hallway. If they were indeed in the Underground, he had never been in this place. He was arguably one of the most knowledgeable about the Underground, but even he didn't know all its secrets.

The stairs were the hardest part of the trek, and he was out of breath when he reached the top. The floor was uneven, and his bare feet were constantly assaulted with cuts and nicks as he went. He knew this was just more punishment from his father, and he assumed there were about to be more demands made of him at this so-called dinner.

He also knew when he refused, the pain and torment were going to become unbearable, so he was stealing these small moments of discomfort knowing there was much worse to come.

The low lighting of the dining room eased the aching of his temples, and Axel swallowed down a curse. That pain had kept him distracted from his craving, and now all he could think about once again was how dry his throat was and how empty his power wells were.

That was why it took him longer than it should have to realize there was someone already seated at the dining table that was set for four.

Bree DelaCrux— one of the four Night Child clan leaders that ruled the vampyres in the Underground.

She was the oldest of the four, an original, whereas the other three clan leaders had risen to power later. But Bree had been here from the beginning, one of the first to be banished when the Underground was created. Axel had always had a good relationship with her, so to find her here could go one of two ways. Seeing her with his father's closest advisors, however, did not make him feel warm and fuzzy inside.

"Hello, Axel darling," Bree greeted in her usual seductive lilt. Her onyx hair was half up, the rest curled and flowing over one shoulder. Honey-colored eyes sparkling with a trace of mirth watched him, a slight frown pulling at her red-painted lips. "They have truly done a number on you this time, haven't they?"

This time?

"Come sit," Bree continued, gesturing to the chair at her right.

He made his way to the closest chair, though, pulling it out with his good arm, and easing into it. Gods, the cushioned seat felt amazing after sitting on a stone floor for the-gods-knew-how-long. Bree didn't comment on his seat selection. She only slid him a glass of water.

"It's not what you really want, but it's better than nothing," she said with a small, knowing smirk.

Mansel had taken a seat across the table from Bree, sitting back comfortably in his chair without a care as another vampyre appeared and placed a plate of food in front of him.

"I have clearly missed something," Axel said, unable to keep his mouth shut. "What the fuck is going on here? Where am I?"

Bree planted her elbow on the table, a manicured fingernail tapping her chin. "One would think you, of all people, would recognize the Underground."

"Obviously," he snapped. "Where, exactly, in the Underground has my father hidden me away?"

At that, her smile grew into something dark. "Oh, you were moved after your father was...detained."

Axel lurched forward; then he barked out a curse as pain shot up his arm. "What do you mean he was detained? What has happened?"

"It appears Theon's little Source has plans of her own," Bree sighed dramatically, reaching for a bowl of fruit that had been placed on the table. Picking up a strawberry, she added, "She has daddy locked up somewhere, and your brother is now the acting Arius Lord."

Axel blinked, trying to comprehend what she was saying, but all he could come up with was, "How long have I been here?"

"With me?" Bree asked, her tongue darting out to lick at the strawberry juice on her lips. "Nearly two weeks."

"How long since I was brought to the Underground?" he demanded.

"A few days more than that."

"You have had me for *days* and kept me in the dark?"

Bree shrugged, sifting through the bowl some more. "I needed some time."

"For what?" Axel asked, dumbfounded at this turn of events.

A cunning smile filled her lips. "For the craving to begin to become unbearable."

As she said it, another entered the room, and Axel immediately straightened. His injuries and wounds were an afterthought as a Fae he'd never seen before walked across the room, a Legacy Axel knew at his side.

Shoulder-length blond hair. Blue eyes. Tall and thin. Julius strolled with his hands in the pockets of his suit pants. On instinct, Axel flinched, conditioned to expect pain whenever this male was near him. The corner of his lips turned up into a small, cruel smirk, but he strode past Axel. When he rounded Bree's chair, his hand came up, fingers dragging along her bare shoulders, while the Fae came to a stop beside her and held out his arm. With a wicked grin, Bree sank her fangs into the Fae's arm.

The scent of blood immediately flooded Axel's senses. It became his entire world. All he could think about. All he could smell. He could taste it, and it wasn't until the pain of his arm became too extreme that he was pulled from that bloodlust.

It was only then that he realized he was on his knees, with sweat on his brow and his entire body shaking with want and need and pain. The three feelings were so intertwined, he couldn't differentiate them. They may as well be the same thing at this point. But Mansel was there too, a hand on his shoulder holding him back. Julius watched him with sadistic delight as he toyed with a strand of Bree's hair while she continued to drink deeply from the Fae.

"You are both traitors," he gritted out, holding Julius's stare.

His voice was smooth and beguiling as he said, "We are simply realists."

"How long have you been in her bed while sucking my father's cock, Julius?" Axel sneered before hissing as another wave of pain wracked his body.

"Now, now," Bree chided, leaning back from the Fae. "We don't need any of that." She stood, her heels clicking when she made her way over to Axel. With her thumb, she wiped at the blood lingering on the corner of her mouth. Bending down, she swiped that blood along his lips as she whispered into his ear, "Just a taste, Axel darling."

He shook his head, but it was useless. He would have lapped blood off the floor at this rate. There was no resisting it on his lips. His tongue darted out, and he groaned at the taste.

"Good boy," she crooned, patting his cheek as he licked his lips again, searching for any bit of it he may have missed.

It was everything he'd imagined and more, only this was earthy instead of the fiery taste he wanted. His shadows stirred as his eyes locked on the Fae who still stood by Bree's vacated chair. He would certainly do until he could find what he truly wanted. He could give him back enough of his power so he could heal and find her.

"Yes, you *could* have more," Bree agreed as though he'd spoken his thoughts aloud.

Maybe he had. He didn't know. All he knew was there was a Fae mere feet from him that had everything he needed to fix all of this.

"We have some things to discuss first," Bree continued, waving a hand in dismissal.

The Fae took one step, and the growl that ripped from Axel had the male pausing. It also had more pain ripping through him as Julius used his magic to keep him on his knees before Bree. The only sound then was his ragged breathing as the Fae left the room, leaving him once again empty and on the edge of insanity from this craving.

"What do you want from me?" Axel asked.

She couldn't want the fire Fae. His father wanted her, but Bree would have no use for her outside of feeding off her. But that Fae was *his*.

"Come and eat, Axel darling," she replied, gripping his good arm and helping him to his feet and then to his chair. Once he was seated again, a plate of food was placed before him. Steak. Potatoes. Bread. Roasted vegetables. A glass of liquor.

He wanted none of it.

Shaking his head to clear his thoughts, he forced himself to focus on Bree, but her red dress was the color of blood itself, which only made him think of the Fae that was supposed to be his. Amber eyes. Ample curves. Power. A pulse he'd felt beneath his thumb.

Fuck, fuck, fuck.

A faint clunking sound drew his attention back to his place setting where a goblet had been placed beside the liquor glass. A clear goblet with red liquid.

He wasted no time, drinking down the blood in two gulps. It wasn't enough—not even close—but it was enough to let him collect his thoughts and focus on what was happening before him. Not that he had any idea what was actually going on.

With a shuddering breath, he picked up his fork. The band on his wrist was loud as it scraped against the tabletop, but he scooped up a bite of mashed potatoes, ignoring how it tasted like ash on his tongue. He needed this sustenance as much as he needed the blood.

No, he didn't *need* the blood.

He just needed these bands off. Then he could recover his power wells naturally. More blood would only serve to drive him closer to an edge he didn't want to go over because...

He actually couldn't remember why he didn't want to go over that edge; he just knew it was something he *shouldn't* want.

Clearing his throat, he brought another bite of food to his mouth before focusing on Bree. The Night Child was watching him with a gleam of amusement in her eyes. She was eating another strawberry, clearly waiting for him to initiate the conversation now.

"I want to speak to you alone," Axel said, stabbing at tender carrots.

"Leave us," Bree said without taking her eyes off him.

He didn't break her stare either as the sound of chairs scraping and footfalls leaving filled the air. It wasn't until the doors to the room had shut that he said, "I'm a little offended here, Bree. I thought we were on good terms."

Her amusement grew as she took a bite of her fruit. "You have done well these last years, Axel. I will give you that."

"So what has this been? You've helped me. I've helped you. This tit for tat has been for nothing? Has only been for you to betray us?"

"Us or you?" Bree countered.

"What?"

"I feel as though you are taking this personally."

"I am," he answered, setting his fork down and reaching for the bread. "I have worked hard to make sure you and all the clans are taken care of."

"Is that what Theon was doing when he ripped out Henry's heart?" she asked conversationally.

"Henry was a problem. You cannot deny that. Theon simply took care of it."

"It was not his place," Bree said, her tone growing icy.

"Is it not our place to take care of the Underground? To aid you? Is that not what I have promised you?"

She clicked her tongue, sitting back in her chair and crossing her slender legs. "You are like your brother in so many ways. Always knowing the right words to say. I was worried for a while there, you know."

"Worried about what?" Axel asked, setting his bread aside and settling back in his own chair.

"Theon is too…suspicious of everyone. He trusts no one. You, however… You are the younger heir who is trying to find his place in this world," Bree said, picking up a goblet of her own that Axel hadn't noticed.

"What do you want?" Axel snapped, growing irritated by the conversation that seemed to keep going in circles.

"Why, the Underground, of course."

"Fuck off," Axel said in disbelief. "You want the Underground?"

"For starters," she replied, sipping on her glass of blood.

"Oh, I cannot wait to hear this," he muttered, swiping up his glass of liquor. It wasn't enough for him to be stuck here, injured and on the brink of destruction. Now he needed to deal with someone clearly staging a coup. What the fuck was he supposed to do with this? It wasn't like he had any way of contacting Theon or Luka right now. All he could do was gather information and hopefully have time to do something with it.

"The Arius Kingdom seems to be under the illusion the Underground is theirs," Bree went on.

"It is in the Ozul Mountains which lie in our kingdom," Axel answered. "We have relations with all the people here. We take care of them. They are our allies."

Bree only smiled. "Are they?"

"Yes," he snapped. "I have spent the last few years making sure that is the case."

"You have had a couple of years, Axel St. Orcas," Bree replied. "That is a blink compared to my *centuries*. Do you forget I did not take my power? I was one of the first to be banished here. I have lived in the dark for longer than even your father has lived. The Underground is *my* kingdom that I have let you all believe you control."

"Let's say that is the case," Axel said. "To what end?"

"To that of me ruling Devram as it should have always been."

Axel couldn't help the laugh of disbelief. "The Legacy rule. The gods decreed it."

"The gods sent their offspring here and left them with lies," Bree sneered.

Axel paused, his glass halfway to his lips. "Where were you born, Bree?"

"Not here," she simpered. "I was sent after the realm was created. The gods may not be able to interfere, but you already know that has not kept them from sending others to do just that."

"And what were you sent here to do?" he asked casually, taking a drink of his liquor.

"You truly are becoming so clever," she said with a breathy laugh. "But you forget I have been playing these games longer than this world has been breathing. I will not offer you all my secrets right now, but I will offer you something else."

His brows shot up at the prospect, and she let out another breath of laughter.

"Not blood, Axel darling. Although, if you accept my proposal, you can have all that you'd like."

"Color me intrigued, Bree," he replied, sipping on his liquor and wishing to any god or Fate or being that it was blood.

"There is division among the kingdoms of the realm, and Theon's Source is creating cracks that will become irreparable."

"What does that have to do with me? As you so eloquently reminded me, I am merely the spare heir."

"Division among the kingdoms weakens them," Bree went on. "They are so focused on maintaining their own individual power, and they are so worried about Tessalyn and what she is, that they are leaving themselves vulnerable. They forget we even exist."

"You want to take on the realm?" Axel said in disbelief. "You are mad. You cannot win."

"While we have been left to rot in the dark, they have forgotten what we are. Shifters and Witches. Fae who are treated as less than by those who rule. Night Children banished solely for existing unless they need our skills for their own ends," she said, her tone growing colder and colder with each word. "And then there are the Legacy. Those who questioned. Those who didn't agree with the way things were being run. Those who tried to stand against them. The kingdoms forget there is wrath brewing here as they worry about the fury walking among them."

"You cannot win," Axel repeated.

"We can. We will," Bree countered, getting to her feet again.

"And what does this have to do with me?" Axel asked again as she came to a stop beside his chair.

A red-painted nail skated lightly through the thick stubble that had grown along his jaw. "You are right, Axel darling. You have been good to me, so I would like to return the favor."

"How?"

"A spot at my side," she answered.

The sound that came from him was somewhere between a choke and a laugh. "You cannot be serious."

"Think about it," she said, resting her ass against the table. "I have the loyalty of the Underground, and you're right. You have been building those relations here. You have more respect here than your father or brother. More than that, you are an Arius descendant. You have connections I do not have outside the Underground. We can lead the Underground. The kingdoms are going to destroy themselves from within, and then we will be there."

Axel shook his head, too dumbfounded to know what to say. "And if I refuse?"

A small frown formed, and she reached out to run her hand through his hair. "Axel, darling, you have no idea how...debilitating bloodlust can be."

"I think I have a pretty good idea," he said dryly.

"Not yet, but you will," she replied, pushing off the table. "I'll give you some time to think about it, but know that should you decline, these last two weeks will be a dream compared to what will come."

6

THEON

Theon eyed the two Fae who were seated stiffly on a sofa across from him. After spending an entire day in the Underground a few days ago, everyone had come back to the Arius Estate just outside the Acropolis. He didn't want to go back to Arius House because his mother was there, and frankly, he didn't trust half the staff. More than that, even with all the chaos going on, the Selection Year was still proceeding as normal. The townhouse would not have been big enough because when he said everyone had come back here, he meant *everyone*.

He'd been able to rescind the death order on Cienna, freeing her from the Underground, but the enchantment had taken hours to undo. It was why she'd never been able to leave, even with her magic and skills. Had she left, his father would have been immediately alerted along with several dozen of his sentries. The complicated network of tunnels and passages in the Underground, along with her own spells, were what had kept her hidden all these years. Even when she and Tristyn were sure they'd all been lifted, she still insisted on a glamour from Tristyn the first time she stepped outside, and Theon could have sworn there were tears shimmering in her eyes before Tristyn had Traveled them all here.

All of them: Lange, Corbin, Cienna, Gia, Eliza, and Razik. The only one Tristyn had refused to bring here was Katya. In fact, he'd refused to even tell Theon where Katya was, saying he'd sworn to Axel he'd keep her safe. The male had insisted on putting up his own spells and enchantments around the Arius manor and estate before bringing her here, and it wasn't as if Theon was in any position to argue. He was finally the godsdamn Arius Lord, and he was more powerless than ever before.

With a sigh, he raked his hand through his hair. "Are you comfortable in your room?" He asked Corbin and Lange.

They both shifted under his stare, but Corbin was the one to say, "The room is more than adequate. Thank you, my Lord."

"You don't—" But Theon stopped himself because in what world was a Fae not supposed to be thankful and respectful to a Legacy?

"I swear to Anala, Raz, if you say one more word about that bowl, I'm going to throw it against the wall," came a female voice.

"Eliza, if you intentionally break something that valuable, I'm going to—"

"What, Razik?" she drawled as they entered the sitting room. She looked wholly annoyed and utterly unconcerned with his threats. "What, exactly, are you going to do?"

The Fae didn't acknowledge any of them as she flopped down onto an overstuffed chair, but Razik was right on her heels. His hands landed on the armrests on either side of her, and he brought his face close to hers when he said, "I will haul your ass into the sky."

Her grey eyes narrowed. "You wouldn't dare."

"Of course I would," he scoffed, but his lips twitched into the smallest smirk that was clearly meant to infuriate the female.

And it worked, but not in the way Theon was expecting.

Eliza went still for a moment before she leaned forward, holding his stare. Whatever passed between them had Razik's eyes shifting to vertical slits and glowing blue.

Theon cleared his throat as Eliza settled back in her chair, but she didn't look at him. Instead, her attention turned to the two Fae on the sofa. "Do you two know Katya?"

"Do *you* know Katya?" Theon demanded.

She slid her gaze to him before looking pointedly back at Lange and Corbin. The latter shifted, clearly uncomfortable, as Lange said, "Yes, but not well. We were raised on the same estate, but I never interacted with her there. I didn't interact with her at all until we were moved to the Celeste Estate."

"Why were you moved?" Eliza asked, shifting her legs so Razik could sit on the arm of the chair.

How were they just...fine now? After what had clearly been some kind of argument and power struggle?

"We don't really know," Lange answered.

"Who would know?" she pressed.

Lange shrugged. "The Estate Mothers, I suppose."

Eliza only hummed. Tristyn and Cienna had clearly briefed them on some of the inner workings of their realm, so they knew the bare minimum of what was being discussed.

"Katya mentioned theories. Does she have theories on this?" Razik asked.

Corbin rubbed at the back of his neck. "Kat and Axel are the ones with the theories. They're better at explaining them."

"But Axel is missing, correct?"

Lange glanced at Theon before looking away again and nodding.

"And your father has him?" Eliza asked, finally deigning to address Theon.

"Sort of," he answered.

Eliza's eyes rolled to the ceiling as if she was praying to the gods for patience. "How does someone *sort of* have a person imprisoned?"

"Tessa has my father, so I suppose, in a way, *Tessa* has Axel," Theon snapped, irritated with the way this conversation was going.

Razik straightened at his tone, his eyes narrowing on Theon, but it was Eliza who scoffed, "It is no wonder this realm is damned."

"It is damned because the gods didn't follow their own fucking rules," Theon spat. "It is damned because the balance was tipped long ago, and we are the ones paying for it."

Eliza *laughed*. An all out laugh of disbelief.

"Is that what you believe?" she asked. "From my understanding, you just learned of that supposed betrayal between Arius and Achaz. How do you explain the imbalance in this world since its creation?"

"What are you talking about?" Theon gritted out.

She didn't say a word, but her grey eyes flicked to the Fae who were watching the exchange.

"You cannot fault me for believing something to be true when that was all I'd been taught. All I have seen my entire life," Theon argued.

"You cannot recognize injustice?" she countered. "Because from what I understand, there are those in this realm who *can*, and have been working for decades to counter it."

"Please direct me to these referenced revolutionaries," Theon drawled because where the fuck did this Fae get off telling him all about this realm when she'd been here a handful of days?

But again her eyes flicked to the two Fae on the sofa, and Theon stilled.

"That is not entirely true," Lange interrupted. When Theon only arched a brow, he added, "I mean, how could it be? We're not even decades old."

"Then what is she talking about?" Theon said, and Corbin shifted so he was blocking Lange, but both of them swallowed thickly.

"I did tell you that you would find allies in unexpected places if you chose to fight back," Corbin answered.

Theon didn't have words as he stared back at the male. Hazel eyes held his stare, and Theon didn't miss how tense Lange was. He knew his power was there, just below the surface, and somehow he also knew that he would attack a Legacy to defend Corbin.

And he also knew that the other two people in this room would side with them. He might be the most powerful Arius Legacy, and he'd take at least two of them out with him, but he wouldn't win this fight with a dragon and three Fae of different elements before him.

Taking a deep breath, he stood, Lange and Corbin tensing even more, but Theon made his way over to the alcohol cart, pouring himself a measure of whiskey.

"We will discuss more of that in a bit," he said after swallowing the entire glass. Pouring a refill, he turned to Razik and Eliza and said, "Tell me of your Source bond."

Eliza's brows shot up as Razik said, "What of it?"

"You chose her as your Source?" Theon said.

Razik glanced at Eliza, who had pulled her legs up onto the chair. Her hands were in her sleeves, fingers curled around the edges.

"We have a complicated history," Razik answered. "But she offered to be my Source as a means to a different end. We discussed what that would mean after which I accepted her offer."

"So *she* chose to be your Source?" Theon asked in confusion.

"Yes, but it was not for my benefit."

"That doesn't make sense. Who else would it benefit?"

"We were in a war. My power was needed to win that war. I was needed for my power. She did it for the greater good, not for me."

Theon nodded, watching Eliza carefully as he said, "But you are more than that now? It wasn't a bond you necessarily wanted, but now you do? What changed? How did that happen?"

"There were other factors," Eliza replied, leaning slightly into Razik. Theon was sure she hadn't even realized she'd done that. It was just a natural thing that Tessa had done with him when she was too distracted to remember to hate the bond between them.

"Care to elaborate?"

"No," she snapped.

His fingers clenched around his liquor glass as he tried to keep his composure. He wasn't used to this. His entire life he had been taught to intimidate and silence those who questioned him. Resistance was met with a show of power. There wasn't cooperation, only domination.

It was a realm full of villains after all.

Even these last months of trying to build relations with some of the other kingdom heirs it had all been about gaining an upper hand. Great if they could be amenable, but find something to lord over them? Make them bow to his wishes as much as his Source was supposed to? That was always the real goal because that was where the power lay.

But there was none of that here. Razik and Eliza couldn't care less, and why would they? If things got too intense here, they could fuck off right back to their home world. The truth was, he needed them, and they knew it. Clearly Blackheart knew it too, or he wouldn't have sent for them.

So instead of pushing Eliza on this entire matter, he said tightly, "I am told our Source Marks differ from yours."

Eliza blinked, looking up at Razik once more. "Is this what Scarlett was talking about?"

"I'm presuming so," he answered, standing now. "She told me you believe there are four Source Marks."

"Because in Devram there are four Source Marks," he replied.

Razik's eyes slid down, narrowing at the hand that clutched the liquor glass. "That's not a Source Mark. That's the Achaz symbol."

He wanted to punch this male in the godsdamn face.

"I am aware it is not a Source Mark," Theon gritted out.

"Then what is it?"

"Vengeance."

"Our dearest Tessa bestowed that upon him," came a male voice, and they all turned to find Tristyn.

And with him was Katya.

Her black ringlets flowed over her shoulders, golden eyes scanning the room. She was wearing black pants and a cream tunic that was stunning against her dark skin. Her outfit vaguely reminded him of what Cienna would wear, which made sense since she'd been staying with her in the Underground from what he could gather. Axel had told Tristyn to keep her safe, and he'd taken her to Cienna, who was also wanted by his father. Theon couldn't deny the genius of the move.

Katya reached up, tucking her hair behind an arched ear. A small, sad smile tilted on her lips when she met Theon's gaze.

And then she started to drop to a knee.

"Don't," Theon said in a rush, lurching forward a step before he could stop himself. When she paused, her head tilting in question, he added, "It is not necessary here."

"Are you not the acting Arius Lord?" she asked, and gods, she sounded tired.

"I am, but it's not— You don't—"

"I have never known you to be this inarticulate."

"Really?" Eliza cut in. "Because that's all he seems to be since I met him."

"No," Katya said, moving deeper into the room. "Theon is actually quite academic and astute. He was simply never taught how to process his emotions."

Eliza huffed out a laugh, and by the gods, when had this day become about evaluating him and his strengths and weaknesses?

Kat stopped a few feet from him. Looking up into his face she said, "Thank you for rescinding the order to have me sent to Julius and Mansel. I am sure that would have been an unfavorable experience."

"It would have been more than unfavorable," he replied.

"I know," she whispered. "It's why he did what he did."

He hadn't even processed what he was doing when he thrust his liquor glass towards her and said, "Here. You need this more than I do."

Her gaze slid to the glass then back up to him before she tentatively reached for it. "Thank you, my Lord."

At no point in his nearly three decades of life had he thought he would ever hate hearing those words directed at him, but gods, did he loathe it in this moment.

She took a small sip of the liquor, not even wincing at the burn, before she asked, "Is there any news of him?"

Theon shook his head, unable to say the simple word.

Katya only nodded before her eyes swept the room again, searching for what, he didn't know. But she didn't seem to find it as she worried her bottom lip for the briefest of moments before straightening and appearing to shove aside whatever she'd been thinking about.

"What are we discussing?" she asked, holding the liquor glass at her side.

"Why Tessa gave him an Achaz Mark," Lange supplied, sliding down the sofa to make room for her, but she didn't move to join her friends.

"She did what?" Kat asked, her gaze immediately going to his hand.

"It was just her getting revenge. It means nothing," Theon gritted out, his hand clenching into a fist.

She blinked several times before she said, "I just told them you were intelligent, and here you stand, making me a liar. She may be impulsive, but even Tessa has intention behind her actions, Theon."

"This was anything but impulsive, Katya," Theon retorted. "This was a calculated move."

"Exactly," she replied, taking another sip of her liquor.

He didn't have time for this. Turning back to Razik and Eliza, he said, "Can I see what your Source Mark looks like? So I can compare it to ours?"

With an exasperated sigh, Eliza pulled back the sleeve of her shirt. Of course, the female made him come to her, and Razik stood far too close, as if he thought Theon would hurt her.

Eliza's Source Mark was on her forearm, and it looked... Well, it looked similar to the *last* Source Mark given in Devram, which only served to further their theory that the first three Source Marks weren't Source Marks at all.

"When Scarlett was here," Theon said, continuing to study the Mark on Eliza's arm, "she became upset when she saw Tessa's first two Marks."

"So I was told," Razik muttered. "Do you have Ash Riders here?"

"I don't know what that is," he murmured, seeing exactly how the Guardian Mark had been incorporated with their final Source Mark.

"They can move through ashes and smoke. Believed to be of the Anala bloodline," Razik went on.

Theon glanced up at him, finding his eyes narrowed across the room. "Are you talking about Auryon?"

"I don't know what that is."

"*That* is a she that can move through smoke and ashes, but it was random you brought her up now," Theon answered.

"Because she's here," Razik replied.

Theon whirled around. He hadn't seen the female since well before Tessa was taken from him, and he had so many questions for her, starting with why the fuck she'd kept her real motive for being here a secret.

"Where?" Theon demanded, looking around the room and not finding a trace of her.

"By the window," Razik answered.

"There is nothing there," Theon said.

"She's there," he replied. "I haven't seen her leave yet."

"But you saw her enter?"

Razik nodded. "Only because I am used to watching for them."

Theon hadn't felt her cross the wards though. He'd had to alter them for Tristyn, which he'd done begrudgingly, but it made the most sense. With his newly revealed Traveling abilities, he could come and go without others knowing. The gods-only-knew the turmoil it would cause if it was learned Tristyn Blackheart, founder of Lilura Inquest, was seen aiding and playing favorites with the Arius Kingdom. No, his involvement in all of this would need to be kept a secret just as the male had kept his identity a secret for decades.

The wards had never been designed to keep someone like Auryon out though. Because why would they? She wasn't a Legacy or Fae, and that was what these wards were designed to detect. The female had been able to access almost anywhere whenever she wanted in Devram. If she was here now, how many conversations had she listened to or encounters had she watched?

"Auryon," Theon seethed. "Are you too much of a coward to even face me now?"

His hand snapped up to catch the arrow he'd been expecting, the thing inches from his chest as the female stepped from smoke. Her long black hair had ashes drifting among the strands, and swirling grey eyes were glaring at him. Her leathers were in place over her black pants and top, ashy footprints left in her wake as she stalked towards him.

"Call me a coward again, Theon St. Orcas," she snarled, another arrow appearing from smoke. She had it nocked on her bow in the next blink.

"What else would I call someone who came to another world and hid her true motives?" he retorted, his own power rallying. Darkness writhed around him, tendrils reaching for the female while some of his magic wrapped around him, preparing to defend.

Luka and Tessa apparently felt it too. He felt both of them pause down the bond, but Luka didn't reach out, thank Arius. The last thing he needed right now was Tessa hearing them interacting. And Tessa? She was probably hoping whatever was happening would finally be his end.

"I owed you nothing, descendant of Arius," Auryon sneered. "You asked if I was here for her, and the answer was yes."

"Yet you came to me for permission to get to her," he countered. "You knew even then you needed my trust—"

"I wasn't here to gain *your* trust. I couldn't care less if you or your Guardian trusted me," Auryon said, lowering her bow. "I was here for her. It was her trust I needed, and I had it until the end."

"You lost that trust," he sneered.

"Then I guess we have something in common," she retorted.

The smirk that tipped up on the corner of his lips was nothing short of the darkness that ran in his veins. "She knew to expect it from me. I've never given her any reason to think otherwise, but you? Your betrayal was so much worse, wasn't it?"

Her features went just as dark as she glared back at him, her fingers tightening on her bow at her side.

"Tell me, Auryon, what will Temural do when he learns you failed your task to save his daughter?" he went on.

To his shock, Auryon tipped her head back and laughed. "How naïve of you to think it is only Temural you must worry about."

"Me?" Theon asked. "You are the one who failed."

"But you are the one who broke her."

The words hit their mark, and Theon felt himself wince as he stepped back from her.

"So instead of trying to shift blame and make me the bigger monster here," Auryon went on, the arrow disappearing as she looped her bow across her chest, "perhaps we should focus on what we are going to do to pull her back before it is too late. Because if we lose her completely, this will no longer be just a war between Arius and Achaz. If we lose her, wild *and* fury will come for you."

He rolled over in bed with a heavy sigh. He'd been tossing and turning for the last three hours. It didn't surprise him. Sleep had been hard to come by for weeks now. With both Tessa and Luka being gone, he wasn't even sure why he tried. To make matters worse, he could still smell Tessa on the sheets from the last time they'd stayed here. There was no way he was sleeping in the master suite that had been his father's. So he'd taken the room he'd always stayed in, but they hadn't stayed here since the night of the Emerging Ceremony.

The night that had led to the Bargain with his father.

With a frustrated grumble, he threw the blankets off and sat up, grabbing his phone from the nightstand. He cleared the messages from Felicity, ignoring them like he had all the other messages for the last two weeks. There was nothing else, and he wasn't sure why he'd expected there to be. The other people who would be trying to get a hold of him in the middle of the night were either locked up somewhere or didn't want to speak to him.

Tossing his phone aside, he made his way to the bathroom. Bracing his hands on the vanity, he lifted his head to look in the mirror. He looked as exhausted as he felt, and he knew there would never be a restful night's sleep without her. The bond strained at the thought of her, and because he was weak, he let himself remember a time when she would curl into him, her hand resting on his chest. He let himself think about how she would seek him out, whether for comfort or reassurance. For the briefest of moments, he'd glimpsed what it could have been like, and it'd all been a lie on her end.

Gods, he craved those lies.

Reaching down the bond, he pressed a palm along that wall that was keeping him out. He felt the shudder on her end, and he smiled despite himself.

Until she let him in and spoke.

What do you want, Theon?

Only you, Tessa. It's all I've ever wanted.

You mean my power.

Maybe in the beginning, but not anymore. You could be a mortal, and I'd still only want you.

There was a pause before she said, *Your lies are still pretty.*

I've never lied to you.

He felt her scoff before he felt something else.

Want.

Need.

Desire.

It will never be enough, beautiful.

What are you talking about?

You touching yourself right now.

A dark laugh skittered down the bond. *What makes you think it's my hand doing the touching?*

Theon gripped the counter harder, darkness seeping from his palms. *Tessa...*

Do you want me to tell you what he's doing?

Is it Luka?

There was another pause. *Why would Luka be here?*

He couldn't even respond as he thought of another touching her.

He's got two fingers in my cunt, and my breast in his mouth right now, and gods. It's so—

He didn't hear the rest as his fist slammed into the mirror. Glass shattered, raining down on the vanity. Shards were embedded in his knuckles, and he watched the blood stream. It dripped onto the dark countertop, but he couldn't feel it. He couldn't feel anything besides the fury and the envy and the *pain* of knowing she was finding pleasure with someone else.

You made me bleed. Now I make you bleed, Theon.

Then she shoved him out, putting that wall back up down their bond as her dark laugh echoed in his mind.

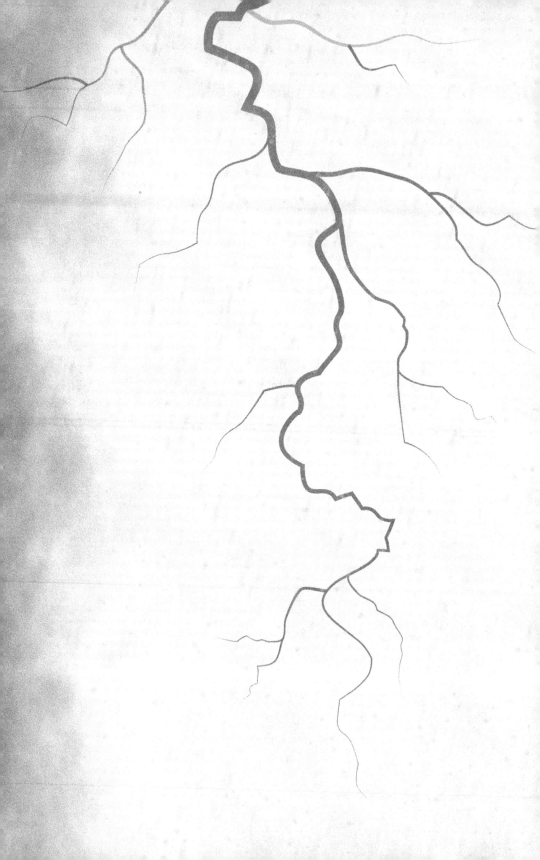

7
TESSA

"Get up, Tessa," came a voice that grated on her ears.

"Get out, Oralia," she retorted as the Fae threw open the room-darkening curtains. Light flooded the room, and it had Tessa burrowing deep into her covers to escape it, seeking the dark. Not that she'd been sleeping. She never slept anymore, but she'd made it worse by taunting Theon about someone else being in her bed. No one had been here, of course. It had all been to rile him up, and it had worked. She'd felt the slice of pain and his anger. It should have been satisfying to know she'd made him bleed the way he'd made her bleed, but it had been satisfying in an unexpected way.

She *enjoyed* feeling his jealousy at the mere idea of someone else touching something he considered to be his. Not because it hurt him or because she thought she belonged to him in any way, but because it made *her* feel valued.

And what did that say about her?

Probably that she was indeed the monster she claimed to be.

"I do not have time for your whining today, Tessa," Oralia chided. "Get up, and get dressed. We need to go."

"Go where?" Tessa muttered, still not moving.

"It appears the acting Arius Lord sent his guard dog to check on your wellbeing."

Tessa threw the blankets back, sitting up. "Luka is here?"

Oralia was in the large walk-in closet now, but her voice carried out as she said, "Not yet, but he will be shortly. He was spotted entering the grounds and felt crossing the wards."

Tessa hadn't felt him down the bond, which could only mean he was blocking it on his end. A dirty, clever move after her refusal to speak with him a few days ago, but to show up in the Achaz Kingdom? At Lord Jove's home?

That was a stupid move she'd never have expected from the dragon.

More than that, he was far too close to something she didn't want him knowing about.

That thought alone had her up and out of bed, rushing to the door.

"Where are you going?" Oralia demanded, darting in front of her and blocking her path.

Tessa skidded to a halt, her power crackling around her. "Did you not just tell me to get up?"

"Yes, and *get dressed*," she drawled, tossing some clothing onto the bed.

Tessa looked down at her nearly sheer night clothing that stopped mid-thigh. Oralia was probably right. She spun, hurrying back to the bed while simultaneously pulling the nightgown over her head. The thing was a golden cream color because all of her clothing was light now, but her gaze snagged on the black Marks on the back of her hands. A Mark claiming her as his, and a Mark that took everything from him.

"Tessa!" Oralia snapped, another piece of clothing landing on the bed. "Let's go."

"I don't understand why we're in a hurry. Luka isn't going to do anything to me," Tessa muttered, sliding on flimsy underthings and loose-knit white training pants. Then she reached for the sports bra and cropped top, the sleeves tight fitting on her arms.

She quickly brushed her teeth and slipped a hair tie onto her wrist. She'd have to put it up later for training with Odessa, the instructor who was helping her master her gifts. That was what she did most mornings, and judging by the clothing Oralia had laid out, that was the plan again today.

"Shoes, Tessa," Oralia called after her as she breezed through the door.

"Can you grab them?" she yelled back, loving the feel of the cool marble beneath her bare feet.

"Tessa, wait!"

But Tessa ignored her, moving along the hallways she was coming to learn well. Her fingers dragging on the wall, she was descending the grand staircase when she heard Dex.

"As I said, the Achaz Lord and his heir are out right now. You need to make an appointment to see them."

"And as I said, I won't be speaking with a *Fae*. Find me a Legacy to speak to," came a familiar drawl that had her heart skipping a beat and the bond vibrating in her chest. She put everything she had into blocking that stupid bond right now. Luka didn't need to know what she was feeling.

"That is not an option available to you," Dex retorted.

In the past weeks here, she still had not figured out how Dex had gained such a position in the Achaz Lord's household. It was one secret she had yet to uncover, but she would in time.

"It is the only acceptable option," Luka replied, crossing his arms and squaring off with Dex.

"Your options are to leave and make an appointment, or wait in the cells beneath this house," Dex sneered, straightening to his full height, but Luka still had an inch or two on him.

The tilt of Luka's lips was slightly terrifying when he said, "Try it."

Before Dex could answer, Tessa said, "He can stay with me until Rordan returns."

Dex spun in her direction, but Luka's eyes only flicked to her as though he'd known she'd been standing there the entire time.

Which he only confirmed when he said *'About time you use that voice of yours'* down the bond.

When had she dropped her shields?

You're an ass, she retorted, and to her annoyance, she saw his lips twitch.

"He can't stay with you, Tessa," Dex said in an exasperated tone as he turned away from her.

"Of course he can," she replied, drumming her fingers on the wall, energy flickering off them.

Dex sighed, turning back to her once more. "Where is Oralia?"

Tessa shrugged. "I assume I am going to train? Luka can come with me."

"We're not leaving you with an Arius Guardian," Dex snapped.

"What does he want anyway?" she asked, dropping down to sit on a step and resting her chin in her hand.

"To speak with the Achaz Lord," Dex answered.

"About what?"

"He won't tell me."

"Because you are clearly not the Achaz Lord."

"Tessie," Dex snapped again. "I don't know what I did to deserve your attitude this morning, but we can discuss this later."

Tessa arched a brow just as Oralia came rushing down the stairs. "Sorry!" she cried, and Tessa winced at the shrillness. The glare Dex shot Oralia told Tessa all she needed to know: Oralia's job had been to keep her busy while he'd dealt with Luka.

"Tessa, let's get going. Odessa is waiting," Oralia said, ignoring Dex and dropping shoes next to Tessa on the stairs.

"Great. Luka is coming with us," Tessa said, not bothering with the shoes as she stood.

"He is not," Dex said. "Lord Jove will have my ass, Tessie."

"I'll take the blame," she replied.

"That won't matter. I'll still bear the punishment. You'll subject me to that?"

Her gaze slid to Luka's, finding him watching her, his arms still crossed. "If you're that worried, put some bands on him."

"That's not—" Dex let out a frustrated sound.

"He doesn't think I'm going to hurt you, *Tessie*," Luka said, and she glared at him. "He thinks I am somehow going to talk you into coming back to the Arius Kingdom."

Tessa blinked a few times before sliding her attention back to Dex. "After all this, you think Luka can say some pretty words to me, and I'll go back to Theon?"

"No, but I—" Dex started.

"You really have such little faith in me?"

"That's not what I said—"

"You do not trust me to fulfill my destiny?"

"Stop, Tessa," Dex barked. "You know I only want to protect you."

"I do not need *protection* from Luka," she sneered, descending the final few steps and striding past him. "I will let Rordan know of the situation. You need not worry about your own wellbeing."

"Tessa, wait!"

But she was already out the front door. She didn't need to look to know that Luka was following her. She could feel it down the bond. Neither of them spoke as she led him across the grounds to a small training building. It was a miniature version of the training arenas at the

Acropolis, enchanted to contain the magic that was practiced within. She'd been told this was where Dagian had mastered his gifts, and Rordan before that.

Odessa was waiting for them. Her dirty blonde hair was tightly braided as always, and she wore the same attire Tessa was wearing. Well, almost. She had shoes on. Tessa was still barefoot, which was fine. She usually ended up barefoot by the end of training anyway.

"Who is this?" Odessa asked, faint light already emanating in her palms while she stared at Luka, her dark blue eyes narrowing.

"No one you need to worry about," Tessa said with a dismissive wave of her hand, calling forth her own power that flared far brighter than Odessa's.

"Did Lord Jove authorize him being here during your training sessions?"

"Rordan does not need to authorize anything for me," Tessa said, energy sparking within her light.

"Perhaps not for you, but for me, he does," Odessa replied. "He must leave, or I cannot proceed with our lesson today."

"He's not leaving."

"Then I will," the instructor countered.

"Then leave."

Odessa blinked in surprise, and it took a few moments before she hesitantly said, "I don't think that would be wise."

"Either proceed or leave," Tessa said.

"I..."

"Leave, Odessa."

"Of course," she said with a small bow before leaving the training building.

"Look at you," Luka said the moment the doors closed behind her. "Taking a stand against not one, not two, but *three* people."

"Shut up," Tessa snapped. "I still don't want to talk to you."

"Then why not let me pass the time in the cells like your Dex suggested?"

"He's not *my* Dex," she muttered, focusing on the power still pooling in her hands.

Luka only grunted a sound of acknowledgment, but she could feel him watching her. With an exasperated huff, she closed her fists, extinguishing her light as she said, "What?"

Luka raised a brow. "I didn't say anything."

"You don't need to. You're staring at me."

"If memory serves, you like it when you can see me."

Tessa pursed her lips, her power and the bond vibrating in her soul while she held his stare.

"So what now?" Luka asked, taking a few steps to the right.

She turned to keep him in her sight. "Now nothing."

"Nothing?"

She turned more as he kept moving. "Yes, nothing. What are you doing here, Luka?"

"I need to talk to you."

"No."

He nodded, still moving. "It's important, Tessa."

"I don't care."

"Clearly," he deadpanned. "Then I suppose we spar. If I win, you speak with me about some important matters. If you win, I sit quietly until Lord Jove returns."

"I'm not going to spar with you. You'll win," she argued.

"Yet you're already in a defensive stance."

"I..." She trailed off, looking down to find her feet planted in the same godsdamn position he'd made her stand in for hours during all their training sessions.

That was when she realized he'd been circling, and she'd done this naturally, preparing for an attack.

"You did this on purpose," she accused.

"Seemed like a waste not to utilize the space, and we have time," he said. "Glad to see you retained everything since you left."

"This isn't the type of training I do with Odessa," she said, still not breaking her stance for whatever reason. "She's teaching me to use my magic. It's not physical training."

"What a waste," Luka scoffed.

"It's not a waste," she retorted, resisting every urge to stomp her foot at his arrogance.

"No? Is she as powerful as you?"

"No."

"Then how is she training you?"

"Who do you suggest *should* be training me?" Tessa drawled.

"Someone at least *close* to your power level," he replied. "And they should be training you to use your magic and fight at the same time."

"Why do you care?"

"That's what you're doing here, isn't it? Starting a war? If you're going to start a war that will be the death of tens of thousands, you should at least have the common decency to fight in it," Luka said, taking a step towards her.

"I thought we weren't talking," she gritted out as he took another step closer.

"Only if you win," he replied. "You don't want to spar? Fine. We can train with our magic," he added, summoning his black flames.

She swallowed her gasp as her power surged, rushing to the surface, and she couldn't control it. Not as her light flared to life, a golden mist swirling around her. It tugged at her, reaching for Luka, and he fucking smirked at her.

Fine. He wanted to play? She would play.

"If I win this match, you speak with me about these important matters. If you win, I will not ask to speak of such things with you again. Do we have an accord?" Luka asked.

Before she could register what he said, she answered, "Yes."

Then she silently cursed him when she felt the telltale sensation of a Bargain Mark on her forearm.

Godsdammit.

She threw her power in his direction. There was no finesse. No art or direction. She'd never been able to control it, and Luka was right. Odessa had never been able to help her do so. How she'd trained Dagian or Rordan was beyond her. They were certainly more powerful, and yet she'd somehow taught them control.

Luka's black flames met her light, wrapping around it before snuffing it out, and she ground her molars as she summoned more magic.

"You can't simply throw your power around," Luka chided. "Have a purpose, Tessa."

"I do have a purpose," she snapped, energy crackling among the golden power this time. "To shut you up."

This time her power wasn't so much of a blind attack. There was some form to it as she sent it at Luka, tendrils branching off to try to pull his attention in different directions. But Luka had been doing this far longer than she had, directing his fire to circle around and chase hers.

"You're trying to do too much too soon," he said. "Don't separate your magic yet. Keep it centered and focused."

"But Odessa has been telling me the opposite," she argued, shaking out her arms as she pulled more power to the surface.

"Because they are trying to figure out just how powerful you are," he replied. "Don't move."

"What?"

But then he was behind her, having stepped through the air and appeared there. She jolted in surprise when a large hand landed on her forearm, and then he cursed when a jolt of energy went through him.

"Should have expected that," he muttered, but he didn't release her. He adjusted her wrist before pushing her other arm down to her side. "Focus on this one spot," he said, tapping her upturned palm. "And while you let your power pool there, think of where you want it to go. What you want it to do."

Then he was gone, appearing where he'd been before. And she wasn't focusing on the power in her palm, but on the sudden loss of heat on her arm where he'd been touching her.

Her magic took advantage of her momentary lack of focus, flaring bright and leaping for Luka once again.

"Focus, Tessa," Luka commanded.

"I can't when it's just me," she argued, putting her arm back in position and starting over.

"What does that mean? I've seen you fight. I know you can do this. I heard about what you did when the Augury tried to kill you. This is no different."

"Yes, it is."

"How?"

"It was fight or die!" she cried. "And it wasn't just me. Roan and Nylah were there. There were others fighting *for* me. It wasn't just me against them. It was—" She paused, her breathing coming too quickly now. "I don't know what it was."

Luka nodded as if he understood exactly what she was saying, and she didn't understand how he could possibly know.

"You had something to fight for," Luka said, unbuttoning his shirt cuffs and rolling his sleeves up his forearms. "I can work with that."

"This is ridiculous," Tessa said, throwing her hands up in frustration. "Let's just— *Luka!*"

His name was a cry of shock and pain as black flames singed the exposed skin of her torso. She looked down in disbelief, finding her pale skin red and splotchy.

Dragging her eyes back to him, she said, "You burned me." She didn't know what else to say. He'd actually fucking *burned* her.

"That fury I see burning in your eyes?" Luka said. "Channel it into your power and focus, Tessa. If you think I'm not going to burn you again, you're wrong."

"Luka, wait. I— *Stop!*" she snarled, feeling his fire lick at her again, this time along her ankles. A faint trace of smoke wafted from the light-weight pants where there was a definite hole with blackened edges.

"Your wolves aren't here. Your Hunters aren't here. No one is going to fight for you right now."

I will always fight for you, little storm.

"He's not here either," Luka said, clearly having heard the words she remembered coming from Theon's lips so many times. "It's just you, Tessa, and you can do this."

She cried out again as the sting of a burn blossomed along her collarbone and up her neck.

And then she was crying out a scream of rage.

The power in her palm grew and grew, and while it was chaotic, there was purpose to it. It swirled in her hand, flickering flecks of energy resembling sand in a whirlwind as it grew. Higher it rose, gusts swirling in the room and sending furniture flying into the walls.

"Look at what you can do," came a gruff voice in her ear. It was low, and she could feel the rumble of it in her bones. Not only that, she could feel an admiration mixed with desire, and she shoved it aside, pushing him out.

He didn't move though. Instead, he stepped imperceptibly closer, his front brushing against her back as he guided her hand. "*This* is what they are watching for, Tessa. They do not want you to control this power. They only want to control *you.*"

Her fury burned hotter making her magic flare. Drops of water landed on her brow, her cheek, her neck, causing the burn to sting more. This wasn't just light and energy anymore. This was wind and rain. This was a storm. *Her* storm.

And then it was gone, and she was letting out an *oomph* as she found herself on her back, the air knocked from her lungs. Her power exploded, shattering in every direction, but she was wrapped in a cocoon of black flames, Luka kneeling beside her. A hand was pressed to her stomach, directly atop the burn. His palm was hot, and she squirmed, trying to move away from him. But one warning look from him had her stilling. His eyes glowed that brilliant blue, vertical pupils never leaving her stare. It took a moment for her to realize he was soothing the burn, his power somehow lessening the damage he had caused.

Then she was squirming for an entirely different reason as his palm slid up her torso, between her breasts. It'd been weeks since she'd lost herself in any sort of physical release, and Theon had been right last night: her own hand was never enough. Nothing was ever enough unless it was him, but maybe it could be with—

She swallowed her gasp when Luka's hand slid up to her throat, fingers loosely clasping around her neck. There was no silencing the soft sigh that came from her as he soothed that last burn. He leaned over her, coming even closer, and she wanted— No, she *needed* this. But her lungs weren't working, and she couldn't suck in a breath. All she could think about was what it would feel like to feel his lips on hers. Anywhere on her body for that matter.

He hovered there, so close she could feel his words on her lips when he said, "I won."

Her eyes went wide, shock rippling through her. "What?"

"Our little sparring match," he added. "I won."

"You did not," she cried in outrage.

His mouth tilted into that smirk that made her want to become physically violent. "You are on your back. Your power is nowhere to be seen, while mine is still surrounding us. I think that's a pretty clear victory."

"You— I— You're an ass," she spluttered, shoving at his chest and pushing him away. She scrambled to her feet, glaring at the Bargain Mark on her forearm. The square around three intersecting arrows taunted her about her never-ending impulsivity.

"But a victorious ass nonetheless," Luka said, crossing his arms and watching her with amusement from where he stood a few feet away.

"Fine then," she snapped, her hands going to her hips. "What do you so desperately need to talk to me about?"

All the mirth faded, and her stomach did a weird tumbling sensation as unease crept in. She tried to shove it aside. She shouldn't care about anything he had to say. This was her purpose. This was her destiny. She had to correct the balance. She had to—

"Axel has been missing for weeks," Luka said. "And only you can help us find him."

She said nothing, only staring back at him.

"You have nothing to say to that?" Luka said in disbelief, but it quickly morphed into a calm rage. "Or have you known this entire time?"

"Don't be daft. Of course I didn't know," she retorted.

"No? Because the last one to see him was Valter, and *you* have Valter, do you not?"

Her fingers flexed where they still rested on her hips as she tried so fucking hard not to care. She *couldn't* care. Axel was still part of the Arius line. Her destiny still beckoned, and his sacrifice would be demanded just as much as the rest of the Arius descendants.

After several moments of tense silence, she said, "So you, what? Want me to go ask Valter where he is?"

"Yes," Luka said immediately.

"And then report back to you?"

"Yes."

"So you can report back to Theon," she stated.

Luka started to answer, but then pressed his lips together. He finally broke their stare, shifting on his feet as he clearly tried to think of how to respond.

He didn't need to bother.

"You have nothing to say to that?" she mocked, liking this feeling of having the upper hand once more. "I *left* the Arius Kingdom, Luka. I do not have to bow to his demands or answer his summons. I owe him nothing."

"He sent me to you," Luka said, meeting her gaze once more.

"Obviously," she replied, rolling her eyes.

"No," he said, shaking his head. "He *sent* me to you. Told me not to tell him anything that was spoken between us."

She clicked her tongue in annoyance. "You're his Guardian."

"I made the same argument. He sent me to you anyway."

"It's a ruse. It's always a game with him, but this is *my* game now," she sneered.

"And Axel is what? Collateral damage?" Luka countered.

"I can't trust you, Luka. Surely you understand that."

"And I can't trust you. Not after what you did."

Her hands dropped to her sides as she siphoned off some of her growing frustration with this entire conversation. Tiny bolts of lightning skipped across the floor.

"Then what is the point of this?" she finally asked.

"I just need you to find out where Axel is," Luka said. "He is not part of this thing between you, me, and Theon."

"No. He just held me down for a fucking Tracking Mark. He just sat and watched while Theon shoved me under a table. He just—"

"Gave you music," Luka interrupted, prowling towards her. "Brought you doughnuts. Gave you distractions and little things when you had control over nothing. He made you laugh, and he argued with Theon on your behalf far more times than you know."

She had backed up while he'd advanced, and she didn't stop until her back pressed to the wall. With nowhere else to escape, Luka's hands landed on either side of her, caging her in.

"Your war is with Theon. Your fight is with me. Axel is not part of this, and if you don't believe that, know that he is missing as punishment for saving Katya from the hands of males who would have taken everything from her," Luka said, black flames sparking in his sapphire eyes.

Again she said nothing, staring back at him with her lips sealed. He searched her eyes, and she locked down every emotion, focusing on keeping the bond blocked.

With a derisive huff of laughter, his arms dropped to his sides, and he stepped back from her. "*This* is what will make you a monster, Tessa."

"You think I don't know that?"

Another breath of disbelief came from him as he said, "You claim to hate the dark, yet the light is leaving you blind."

Then he left her standing in the training room, the doors clicking shut, echoing his retreating footsteps.

And she forced herself not to care.

8

LUKA

He stalked through the foyer of the training building, pushing open the doors that led outside harder than he intended. They slammed forcibly, bouncing back quickly as he made his way through them.

Only to come face-to-face with sentries in white and gold uniforms, the Achaz symbol embroidered across the chest.

Godsdammit.

The deal was that he'd stay with Tessa, and here he was, alone in a foreign kingdom.

"She'll be here in a minute," Luka said, lifting his hands in a placating gesture.

"The Achaz Lord has returned and is waiting for you," one of the sentinels said. "We are here to escort you to him."

Great.

He'd come here thinking if he could just tell Tessa about Axel, she would be as worried as the rest of them and immediately offer her assistance. Instead, she'd stared at him. Not a hint of worry or care crossed her icy features. Just a stone-cold indifference. And the thing was, he couldn't decide if it was real or not. She had made sure her emotions were locked down tight, and he could feel nothing down the bond. But all of them could feign indifference. He and Theon were professionals at it, and she was far more clever than anyone gave her credit for. She had watched them so carefully these last months, doing exactly what Theon had told her to do.

Watch.

Listen.

Learn everything you can.

"Come with us," the other sentinel said, making room between them for him to walk.

He couldn't blame them. He was bound to the Arius Heir. They were right to be suspicious.

"Should I get Tessa?" Luka asked.

"That isn't necessary," the first sentinel answered. "The Lord requested it be only you."

He nodded, stepping into the space between them and matching their pace as they made their way back to the sprawling Achaz palace. He could admit it was a little nerve-wracking to be summoned by a foreign Lord *without* the reason he was here with him. Why wouldn't he want Tessa there if he was as open with her as she claimed he was? He wasn't stupid. He knew the Lord was keeping things from her just as Theon had. Only Lord Jove had somehow convinced her he wasn't. That he was trustworthy, and this was the place she needed to be. What if he wasn't the only one waiting for him? Was Dagian going to be there? Some of the ruling Ladies?

What if Valter was there?

It took a lot to rile him, but Luka couldn't deny that his heart was beating a little too fast as he was led up a flight of stairs and to the end of a long hallway. Another sentinel stood guard outside the study, and he nodded to the other two before knocking twice on the door and pushing it open. There was no waiting for an entrance command. Valter would have had Eviana strangle someone within an inch of their life for that.

Luka entered, pushing the door open wider. He was immediately relieved to find only Lord Jove sitting behind an expansive cherry oak desk with his Source nearby. Two cream-colored armchairs were set before it. The rest of the space was minimalistic, which surprised him. Valter's dark office was filled to the brim with anything and everything that exuded wealth and status. Rordan's office was almost warm and inviting with its soft white walls, cream rugs, and a large glass fireplace with a roaring fire. Simple cream furniture was placed around the fireplace, and a tasteful alcohol cart sat off to one side. Artwork of various places around Achaz Kingdom lined the walls in gold frames. Behind his desk was a floor-to-ceiling bookcase full of books with no trinkets or clutter to be found, and sunlight poured in from the windows along the opposite wall.

He bowed at the waist to the Lord, straightening when he heard the door click shut behind him. Rordan settled back in his chair, bright blue eyes ringed with gold watching him as he said, "Here I assumed it would be Theon who showed up at my home demanding her back. This is an interesting turn of events."

All the tension eased from Luka's shoulders as he matched the Lord's casualness, strolling to one of the armchairs and taking a seat across from him. He'd learned long ago how to deal with the various personalities of the realm. It was why he appeared confident in every action, never allowing another to think they were above him. It made them nervous when he appeared aloof and unconcerned, even when he felt anything but. Every look, every mannerism, every word spoken was strategized and a chance to gain information or reveal too much.

"Theon is attending to other matters," Luka answered.

Rordan arched a brow as he steepled a finger along his temple. "More important than the female he has fought so desperately to keep these last months? I find that unlikely."

"He is a Lord now, is he not?" Luka countered. "That places more demands on his time, and while he would prefer to be the one sitting across from you, surely you know that is not always possible of a Lord."

"He has not been declared a Lord just yet," Rordan replied. "But I suppose with his father...indisposed, he does find himself more burdened these days."

"Indeed."

"And now that you are here, I imagine you wish to speak with Valter?" he continued.

Appreciating the male for dropping the pretenses, Luka said, "I don't want to see Valter. He's not going to talk to me or tell me anything of value."

"Then what is it you want?"

"To stay for a while," Luka answered.

Rordan chuckled in amusement. "Surely you are joking." When Luka only gave him a frank look, he added, "I would ask why you think I would agree to such a thing, but I cannot trust you. Therefore, I believe this conversation is over."

"That's fine. I'm sure a conversation with the Ladies about Valter would be more in my favor anyway," Luka answered with a shrug, but he made no move to leave.

He hadn't come this far just to be sent away. Where was he going to go anyway? Back to his cave? While that may be what he wanted to do, he had a task to complete, and he'd never failed an assignment. He wasn't about to start now. He needed Tessa's help with Axel. Nevermind the fact that now that he'd seen her, spoken to her, touched her, the dragon beneath his skin was agitated and wanting more. He'd almost kissed her in that training room, for fuck's sake.

Rordan was scrutinizing him, and Luka didn't move a muscle. There would be no uncomfortable shifting or diverting his eyes.

Finally, the Lord said, "Your point has been made, but there is still the issue of me being able to trust anything you say."

"Likewise," Luka replied.

"Then you are amenable to a truth agreement in the form of a bargain?"

"For the next hour."

"That seems acceptable. For the next hour, neither of us can lie to one another. Do we have an accord?"

"It's a bargain," Luka answered, once again feeling the unmistakable sensation of a bargain mark on his skin. This time it was on his shoulder.

"Now that that's settled," Rordan said, sitting forward and placing his palms on his desk. "Let me make one thing clear: should you endeavor to blackmail me again, this conversation *will* cease and you will be in a cell. Is that understood?"

Luka nodded, knowing the Lord would see it for the slight it was. Verbal responses were always expected to the rulers.

"Aside from the fact that it would be foolish to let an Arius bound guardian stay in my kingdom, it is clear Tessa also does not want you here," Rordan said.

"Is that so?"

"That's what was reported to me about earlier interactions today."

"I don't know what was reported, but Tessa never once told me to leave when I arrived. She knows I need to be here. We made an agreement that I would train her," Luka replied.

"You are telling me a bargain was made to that effect?"

Luka didn't answer. It would have been a lie. Tessa *had* asked him to train her, and he'd agreed, but a bargain had never been made. So he couldn't audibly answer with this truth agreement in place, but he nodded once more.

"And if I summon Tessa here, she would tell me the same thing?"

"Go ahead," Luka said, settling back in his chair, his legs falling wide. "Can I have a drink while we wait?"

Rordan mirrored his movements, his chair reclining some as he leaned back. "Show me this Bargain Mark."

His sleeve still rolled back from the interactions with Tessa, Luka showed the Lord the Mark from the bargain he'd made with her. If he actually called Tessa here to corroborate the story, he was truly fucked.

"And that Bargain Mark is from a bargain made between you and Tessa regarding training in some form?" Rordan asked.

"It is," he answered, thanking Sargon that he had worded that just vaguely enough to answer truthfully.

"Then answer me this: why would I *want* you to train her?"

Luka blinked, surprised by the question. "You do realize her current instructor can't possibly train her properly? She is not even close to Tessa's power levels. How do you expect her to train her?"

"I do not need her to be more powerful," Rordan answered. "She is handling matters just fine as things stand."

"Handling matters," Luka deadpanned. "Within minutes of me starting a training routine with her, her emotions overtook her, and she summoned a godsdamn storm indoors. She is not handling anything. Beyond that, power is only useful if it can be contained."

A cold smirk tilted at the corner of the Lord's lips. "Spoken like a true war lord, but what do you care? Why would you want her trained when she is no longer loyal to the kingdom you serve?"

"For the same reason I'm betting the ruling Ladies would want her trained," Luka answered. "She is a danger to the entire realm if she cannot get that power under control."

"And, of course, it is a layer of protection for your Ward as a Guardian," Rordan said.

"Yes, I must always work for what keeps him safe, but this is bigger than him. You're not a fool."

"That I am not," he agreed. "And because I am no fool, what do I get out of letting you train her? I have no stake in your bargain with her, and from what I understand, *she* will not suffer if your end is not upheld."

"Aside from me staying quiet about Valter?" Luka asked.

"You already showed your hand, Mors," Rordan countered. "I could have you caged below this manor and move on with my day. I'm going to need a little more incentive out of this deal."

"What do you want?" Luka asked, his eyes narrowing.

"Information about your lineage."

It was his turn to huff an amused laugh. "I know nothing of my lineage."

"You are one of your kind," Rordan countered. "Should I have questions about your bloodline, I would like them answered truthfully."

"Fine," Luka said, because Rordan likely knew more about his bloodline and the god he descended from than he did.

"You cannot end my life," Rordan went on.

"Why would I want to kill you? That is never something we have wanted," Luka said.

Rordan smiled pointedly. "I think the reason behind such a request is obvious enough."

Luka knew there was motive behind everything, but a basic insurance policy against him seemed reasonable enough.

"Agreed. Anything else?" Luka all but drawled.

Rordan rubbed at his chin, leaning back further in his chair. "Yes. While we're at it, let's add that onyx ring Theon always wears, just to prove your commitment to the cause."

The idea of giving that ring to him made his dragon huff in protest, but it was one ring. He had dozens hoarded back at his cave. Theon would understand why this was necessary, and Luka recognized it for what it was from the Lord: a show of dominance and a power move.

Everything in this realm was a game of moves and countermoves. He could concede to such a minor thing now in order to get what he needed. Small sacrifices now to secure victory in the future. That was what this was on his end.

"We have an accord," Luka said.

"So we do," the Lord agreed.

And when Luka left that office, the Bargain Mark on his shoulder was gone, but there was a new one just below where it had been on his bicep. A triangle with three horizontal lines through it now stood out against his tanned skin. One line for each of the Lord's demands.

Yet as he was led to the room he'd be staying in for the foreseeable future, he knew those negotiations with Rordan had been nothing compared to the storm he was going to face when Tessa found out about the deal that had just been made.

He knew before he opened the door who was on the other side, even without the bond and his dragon acting up at how near she was. He hadn't been sure if she would keep her distance and try to ignore him in the coming days, or if she would show up here. Apparently her impulsiveness had won out. Again.

Shirtless and wearing only loose, black knit pants, he made his way to the door. It was late, and well past midnight. He'd been trying to figure out when and how he was going to meet up with Theon to get this ring for Rordan, wanting to complete his side of the bargain as quickly as possible. He hated being indebted to another. It took too much of his control and created unnecessary vulnerabilities.

He'd scarcely touched the doorknob when a tiny thing of fury stormed into his room. She was wearing a gold sleeveless nightgown with a white silk robe open over the top of it. Her hair was a mess, the strands tangling down her back and around her shoulders, and her feet were bare as always.

"What is wrong with you?" she cried, already pacing in the space, moving back and forth between the end of the bed and the small sitting area.

Luka quietly closed the door before making his way over to the small desk and leaning back against it, crossing his arms.

"I tell you I don't want to speak with you, so you go to Rordan?" she continued to rant, her words coming faster with each breath. "What right do *you* have to go to a Lord and request to stay here? *How* can you stay here? You're supposed to be protecting Theon, not here in this space where I can hear you and smell you and see you all the fucking time."

His brow arched at that as her hands went through her hair, her feet still following the same path back and forth.

"And you told him we had an agreement that you would train me?" she went on. "We both know that agreement ended the moment I was granted freedom from Theon. No. The moment I *took* my freedom from Theon. I did that."

The words were turning to muttering now, and he watched, some-what fascinated, as she seemed to descend from frustration and anger into some kind of confused madness. She almost appeared to be arguing with herself as she continued her rant.

"He thinks if he stays here I will stop. I can't stop," she muttered. "I can't stop because this is my purpose. I have to correct the balance, and I can't do that when he's here. He can't be here." The bands of power on her wrists glowed, snaking up her forearms. "He's not part of the balance though. Yes, he is. No! No, he's not. Rordan would make him leave if I asked. Would he? No, no. There's a bargain between them now."

Her eyes flashed to him, and his entire body tensed when he found them glowing bright violet. Golden light ringed her irises, bolts of energy flashing through them like lightning. What the fuck had happened to her in the two weeks she'd been away from them? He'd been playing the game when speaking with Lord Jove, but this only confirmed what he'd said. She wasn't in control, and if she didn't figure this out, her power would ruin more than just Arius Kingdom.

She tugged at her hair, fingers getting caught in the strands. "Are you going to say anything?"

"No."

She paused. "What do you mean, no?"

He shrugged, keeping a close eye on that power that was swallowing her whole. "You seem like you have a lot to say, and—"

"Because you went to Rordan about staying here!"

"*And* it's rude to interrupt people when they are speaking," he continued, feeling the smirk trying to form as she went still, finally ceasing her pacing.

"Since when have you cared about being rude?" she demanded.

"I don't," he answered. "I was just waiting for you to get that all out of your system. Are you done?"

Her mouth popped open for a brief moment before her eyes sparked with fury once more. The uncertainty and confusion that had been present moments before was replaced with a cold wrath as she seethed, "What the fuck were you thinking?"

"I was thinking I needed to stay here until you agree to talk to Valter and find out where Axel is," he answered. "Besides, we *do* have a bargain."

"That you tricked me into. Either way, I already told you I cannot help you."

"I tricked you into nothing, and you told me you *will* not help me."

"Semantics," she scoffed.

"There is a difference," he said. "*Cannot* is a matter of inability. *Will not* is a choice you have made."

"You can't stay here, Luka," she cried again, fingers going back to her hair.

"It seems your Lord says I can."

Light flared as she snapped, "He's not my Lord."

He gave her a sharp smile. "My mistake."

"Always such an ass," she muttered, resuming her pacing.

And as she did, her power crept up her arms more and more, sparks of energy echoing each footstep.

"He'll see too much if he's here," she murmured. "It's distracting, but I want it. No, I hate it. We hate it. We can't have the things we want. No happy endings. Purpose and destiny, then I can leave the dark forever. I can do this. This is my game and my storm. I don't need them. Clever tempest. That's what he calls me."

"More like a temptress," Luka muttered.

She whirled on him. "What did you just say?"

"You heard me," he retorted. "You're more akin to a wild temptress than a clever tempest."

"How in the realm do you figure that?"

"Well, for one, you stormed into my room in that," he replied with a pointed look at her attire.

She looked down at herself before crossing her arms tightly over her chest.

Which only served to push her breasts up.

"That didn't help," Luka said dryly.

She tsked under her breath, rolling her eyes, but her power had stilled its movement around her, as if it was waiting to see what she was going to do. Her eyes dropped to her attire again, and she plucked at the sash of the silk robe.

"Everything is white or cream or gold here," she grumbled.

"Missing the dark, are you?"

"No," she snapped.

He hummed in response before he said, "Go get some rest. Sleep on all of this, and we can talk in the morning when you are...calmer."

"I can't sleep," she retorted. "There is no resting or peace. Not since—"

Her mouth pressed into a thin line, and she started pacing again, her magic immediately resuming its movements too.

With a sigh, he went into the closet. There was plenty of clothing in here, but he certainly would not be wearing the provided garments in whites and light greys and creams. She wasn't wrong about everything being those colors. He'd Travel to Rockmoor tomorrow and pick up other options, but he did have the clothing he'd been wearing earlier today.

Snatching the black button-down shirt from the hamper, he went back out to the bedroom, where he tossed it at her. With a startled gasp, she caught it, but not before it hit her in the face.

"Is this his?" she demanded.

"Why would I have Theon's shirt with me?"

"It smells like you," she muttered to herself, holding the shirt away from her body and studying it.

"Take it with you, and—"

But she'd already slid the robe down her arms and was reaching for the hem of her nightgown. It shouldn't have surprised him. She'd never cared about modesty or nudity, but by the gods.

That was his mouth going dry at the sight of bare skin.

That was his cock already half-hard as she slipped his shirt on.

That was his power pushing at him to go take as she worked the buttons of the shirt.

That was his dragon growling *'mine'* as his scent covered her.

Wild temptress, indeed.

Leaning against the desk once more, he forced out, "Go get some sleep, Tessa."

Her violet eyes darted to the bed, and a sense of satisfaction he had no right to filled his chest.

"What would your Lord say if they found you in my bed in the morning?" he asked with a quirk of his brow.

"I don't want to be in your bed," she snapped, bending to retrieve her nightclothes

Which caused his shirt to ride up with the movement, allowing him to glimpse the bottom of her ass.

Godsdammit.

"I'm not staying in here with you," she added, stalking to the door.

"I didn't ask you to," he retorted as she wrenched it open.

She said nothing else, slamming the door behind her.

He didn't move from his spot at the desk, waiting a full two minutes before he pushed off it and made his way to the door. Pulling it open, he found her standing there, nightclothes clutched to her chest. He said nothing. Only stepped to the side as she stomped back in.

"This is only because I need to sleep," she said, dumping the nightclothes onto the sofa.

"Naturally," he replied.

"Shut up," she grumbled, spinning and watching him pull the sheets back.

"Well?" he said, glancing from her to the bed.

She shifted on her feet, eyes darting from him to the bed. "You can't sleep naked," she blurted.

He sighed. "I won't, Tessa. Just get in the bed."

"I need a—"

But he was already reaching for the hair band he'd placed on the bedside table earlier that night.

As she piled her hair up in a messy knot on top of her head, he asked, "How'd you get in here anyway? Don't they have a guard outside your door?"

"They didn't until you made this deal with Rordan," she retorted, climbing onto the large bed and crawling to the other side before slipping under the sheets.

"And they just let you walk past them? You need a new guard."

"No. I created a portal to this floor, and in case you've forgotten, I *am* skilled at finding escape routes."

"Definitely didn't forget that," he retorted, sliding into bed beside her. "I'm assuming Rordan taught you how to create a portal since that's only something the Lords and Ladies can do?"

"The week I spent in Faven," she answered tightly.

Luka nodded, propping a hand behind his head. There was a long stretch of silence between them before he said, "When's the last time you truly slept, Tessa?"

"The night before the hearing," she whispered. Then, even quieter, she added, "I can't have this."

He didn't respond, and it wasn't long before she was muttering to herself again.

"I can't have this. I shouldn't want this. I *don't* want this. I don't want them, right? Right. We don't want them. We don't..."

He felt the bed shift as she rolled over to face him.

"I have to do this, Luka," she said softly.

He stayed quiet.

"It's bigger than me and Theon," she added.

Still, he didn't utter a word.

"We were always meant to destroy one another."

Silence.

"I can't help with Axel, and even if I could, it would be pointless. I don't..." She trailed off before she said, "Can you say something?"

"There's nothing to say, Tessa. You made your choice. Don't come to me seeking validation for it," he answered.

"I'm not," she snapped, her tone going icy as she rolled away from him.

He sighed again, staring up at the ceiling as he said, "You either want someone to make decisions and choices for you, or you don't, Tessa. You wanted control. You have it. That makes you responsible for the consequences. No one else. I'm not going to be the one to make you feel okay about those choices. Theon is the one to seek out when you need someone else to make decisions for you so you don't have to feel the ramifications. *He's* the one who's going to take on that responsibility so you don't have to, because he'd do anything to keep you from harm. He's the one who will protect you from yourself. I'm going to be the one who lets you decide whether you're going to crawl, run, or fly, and I won't catch you unless you ask me to."

"A balance," she muttered, shifting once more. "In all things, there must be balance."

The quiet grew between them, and he knew the moment she drifted off to sleep because she rolled into him, draping a leg over his thigh and nestling into his side. Her breathing was deep and tranquil, her hand resting lightly on his abdomen.

And he made a choice as he curled his arm around her and tugged her closer.

He made a choice knowing there was no one to catch him when the consequences came.

9
AXEL

He cupped his hands together, letting the warm liquid pool in them. Thick and sticky, it smelled like copper. He could practically taste it as it rained down around him.

At some point he'd been moved from the dark room they'd been keeping him in and shoved in here. Another day, another hour, another room. It didn't matter. The dark was the dark. He'd sank to the floor, finding his way to a wall to lean against. His hair was still plastered to his brow from sweat. He'd been lost to the need for what felt like years now. His entire body ached, and his mouth was beyond dry. His power was screaming in his soul. Then again, that might have been him screaming. Maybe that was why his throat was scratchy and raw.

They hadn't chained him again. There hadn't been a need to. Locked away in a place where he couldn't see, there was nothing he could do. Not that he hadn't tried. He'd stumbled around that room as though he was intoxicated, running his palm along the floor and every wall. He couldn't even tell where the door was. He had, however, found a small drain. That had been useful for taking care of his needs and for the vomiting. It'd done nothing for the smell though.

Eventually, he'd stopped noticing the stench.

Eventually, all he could think about was the insatiable need that would never be quenched. Not until he could find her.

He hadn't noticed the fresher air in this space when they brought him here, but he'd noticed when it started raining blood.

He was going to savor this. Every last drop. Just like he was going to savor it when he got out of here and found her. The red against her dark skin was going to be so fucking beautiful. He could already see it sliding down her neck. He'd lick it up with the tip of his tongue before going back for more. He'd take every last drop from her. She was all his anyway.

His to have.

His to take.

His to do with as he pleased.

That was what she was for.

He smiled, thinking of her lovely dark curls and those bright amber eyes. How could he take from her and watch them dim at the same time?

Droplets continued to splash onto his face, down his bare arms, his chest. It was almost time for him to feast, and he was going to savor it. Gorge himself on this blessing that had been bestowed upon him.

Until the liquid seeped through his fingers, and he panicked. He couldn't waste any of it! Lurching forward, he brought his cupped hands to his mouth, drinking it down and—

No!

No, no, no!

"No!" Axel cried, shoving his fingers into his mouth and sucking on them. This wasn't blood. This was water. Lukewarm water.

"No, no, no!"

He ran a palm across his face before licking it.

Water.

He did the same to his arm.

Water.

All of it was water, but he could smell it. He could taste it in the air. He could—

He cursed as brightness blinded him, someone turning on lights. So used to the dark, his vision was blurry, and he blinked several times, water continuing to cling to his lashes and drip down his face. It took him far longer than it should have to realize he was in a shower, and quite a grand shower at that. Beautifully tiled in black, the floor he was sitting on was the same color. It was large with gold fixtures, two rain-fall shower heads in the center and a bench on the other end that he'd clearly missed in his manic blind search. One wall was entirely glass, and that was when he saw her, perched on a vanity. Her long legs were crossed, the deep slit of her dark red dress reaching nearly to her hip.

There was amusement on her face as she lifted a crystal goblet to her lips, taking a sip that stained her lips redder than they already were.

"The craving can be such a bitch, can't it?" she simpered.

"Not as much of a bitch as you," he rasped out.

She tsked at him as she gracefully slid from the countertop. The clicking of her heels was sharp as she crossed the tiled floor before tapping her fingernails on the glass, making him wince.

"Your senses are so heightened it hurts, and everything reminds you of what you can't have," she replied in a sensual purr. "All other needs fade away. The need to eat, drink, clean up, fuck." She shrugged, taking another drink from her glass. "I am told it is worse for a Legacy on the brink of turning. Is that true?"

"I wouldn't know," he bit out. "I have nothing to compare it to."

"Fair point," she mused, tapping a single nail against the glass in thought. "Clean up and come have dinner with me. We can discuss your...situation further."

"No," he ground out.

"Axel, darling, you really have no choice," she replied. "Either clean yourself up, or I shall have Julius come and assist you."

Axel blinked, looking down at his exposed thigh to find it completely healed.

"Everything else fades to the background," Bree said again. "Even pain outside of the craving becomes trivial in comparison. It was silly to allow it to remain without a purpose. You can thank me by joining me for dinner."

With that, she turned and left the bathroom, each click of her heels making him flinch. His vision was still bleary as he cataloged his skin. All the wounds inflicted on his father's orders were gone. There were scratch marks on his arms, but he was fairly certain those were self-inflicted. If anything, maybe getting out of the dark would help him feel more grounded and help him regain some control over himself.

Using the wall for support, he managed to get to his feet, stumbling his way under the shower water. It was hot compared to the spray that had been reaching him along the wall. All he could do was stand there for a minute, letting the water beat down on him before he made the effort to remove his underwear.

He had to talk himself through every motion.

Reach for the shampoo bottle.

Open it.

Tip it over.
Use your fingers to squeeze the bottle.
Watch it spill into your hand like her blood will spill.
No!
Lather your hair.
Rinse it out.
Feel the water.
Water, not blood.
It's water.
Water.
Hot water.
Hot like fire.
Her fire.
Her fiery blood.
Fuck!

By the time he finally stumbled out of the shower and reached for a towel, he was exhausted, and he still needed to brush his teeth and get dressed. He found a pile of clothes on the vanity that he'd completely missed when Bree had been talking to him. Then again, he couldn't focus on much, even now.

Brush teeth.

That was what he needed to be doing.

Toothpaste onto toothbrush.
Brush.
Brush.
Brush.
Clean teeth to sink into her throat and stain them red.

"Godsdammit!" he spat, toothpaste spraying as he threw the tooth-brush at the mirror.

He braced his hands on the vanity, his head hanging between his shoulders. He didn't know how much longer he could do this. He just needed a taste. Something to curb the craving. Something to fill the aching emptiness of his power. Something to drown in that wasn't *this*.

He suddenly understood exactly why Tessa lost herself in a liquor bottle or in bed with another. Any type of distraction would do at this point, whether it be pain, pleasure, or inebriation.

As it happened, Mansel was even a welcome distraction when he came through the door and barked at him to "get fucking dressed."

In black pants and a black shirt he'd tried buttoning for a full minute before he gave up due to his shaking fingers, he followed Mansel through passageways he may have traversed before. He wasn't sure. However, he wasn't led to the same dining room. He was led up a few more flights of stairs and through a parlor. Pulling aside a curtain, Mansel gestured for him to go through, and he stepped onto a balcony.

They were underground, of course, so there was no sky or sun, but the air was still fresher out here than wherever they'd been keeping him inside. A small table for two was set with a light meal waiting, but Bree wasn't seated and waiting. Her back was to him where she stood at the railing, arms stretched out and hands resting atop it.

Slipping his hands into his pockets, Axel moved in her direction. The food wasn't even remotely tempting. It wasn't what he wanted, and it would taste like ash. He did pause when he noticed a small glass of red. It was no bigger than a shot glass, but he'd swiped it up and gulped it down before he'd even registered what he was doing.

There was a faint salty taste among the copper. A water Fae then. Still not what he wanted most, and the small taste only made the craving worse, not better. His shadows gave a feeble twitch that hurt his soul, his legs nearly giving out at the gnawing ache as his power demanded more and more.

Bree still hadn't turned to him, but a rustling sound had him spinning to find Julius there with a goblet and a smirk. The male said nothing as he held the silver chalice out to him. There was no hesitation when Axel grabbed it and drank the entire contents in three gulps. He could feel a drop run down his chin, and he swiped it up his thumb, sucking the digit clean. He knew in his bones there would be no more given to him this day unless he agreed to whatever Bree wanted to discuss with him right now.

Setting the goblet aside, he made his way to her. She glanced at him briefly, her honey-colored eyes flicking over him, before she looked back out over the Underground below her.

He knew then where he was. He could see the structure below that resembled the Tribunal building. One had to go through it before entering the House of Four that was built into the wall of the Underground. The House was as high as the cavern itself and branched off into four distinct wings, each painted with a symbol of the four clans. Bree's symbol was a triangle inside a circle, and this high up, he could see the entire Underground. He could even make out the tower that housed their penthouse suite in the Charter District on the other side of the Underground network.

"It is beautiful, isn't it?" Bree asked, her raven hair pulled over her shoulder.

Axel had never really thought of the Underground as *beautiful,* but he could admit there was something resilient about the people. They were survivors in a realm that wanted to forget they existed.

When he didn't say anything, she continued, "I hope you found the shower and subsequent sustenance refreshing?"

"Let's not play coy, Bree," he said, surveying everything below. "You know it wasn't nearly enough."

"No, but it was enough to let you focus on this conversation for roughly the next hour. Then I suspect it will overtake your thoughts once more," she replied simply.

"Sounds great," he muttered.

Bree said nothing else. She only continued to stare out over the Districts.

After what had to be no less than thirty minutes had ticked by, Axel said, "If I only have an hour, you might want to get to the point of this meeting while you still can."

"You are the first Legacy in a long time who has truly cared for those here," she replied. "Do you know that?"

"I..."

But he didn't know what to say to that.

"There have been many over the millenniums that have come in and laid down laws, established themselves as lords and kings. They come here to remind us who rules, and why it is them and not us. They send us their dark and depraved, the criminals and the monsters. They do not wish to look upon them or deal with them, so they send them here to rot and waste away, contained and forgotten. Every once in a while, one comes along who truly sees us for what we are, but they never survive long. And if they do, they soon find themselves one of us." She finally turned to look at Axel, dragging her fingers along the railing as she moved. "Much like you do now."

"I am not one of you," he retorted.

"Not yet."

"Not ever."

Her red lips pressed into a thin line before she said, "Perhaps you are no different from all the Legacy before you after all."

"You speak as if you never were one," he retorted. "Or has it been so long, you have forgotten what it was like?"

She huffed a humorless laugh, stepping closer to him. "Your smart mouth is always so amusing, but it betrays your own age. You are a child compared to me."

"And yet you want me at your side," he countered.

Her smile was sharp when she said, "Because of all my years, I see your potential. I know what we could be, and what this realm could be. You think you are a tortured soul here? You think that this craving, that turning into a Night Child is the worst thing that can happen to you? You know nothing of war and torture. You know nothing of fighting for a cause and failing. You see this life as a curse, while others found it to be a blessing."

"What did you just say?" he demanded because he'd heard those words before. But that itchy feeling in the back of his throat was starting up, and he couldn't recall where he'd heard it or who had said it. Not as the memory of how the blood had felt on his tongue less than an hour ago surged to the forefront.

Shaking his head to try to clear his thoughts, he said, "How long have you been a Night Child, Bree?"

She stepped closer still, her front brushing his as she reached up. Her hand slid along his jaw before her thumb swiped across his lips. "Longer than this world has been breathing."

But he barely heard her answer as something rich and coppery assaulted his senses. Every part of him turned predatory, and he spun to face the doorway where Julius stood with a Fae.

A bleeding Fae.

There was a long gash cut into her inner forearm that Julius was preventing from healing, and Axel lunged.

Or he tried to.

A hand was at his throat, sharp nails digging into his windpipe. He choked out a gasp as Bree pushed him to his knees.

"The thing about the bloodlust is that you become so focused on it, so overcome with want, you forget about your other needs. You ignore the necessities of food and water, but your body doesn't. You weaken, and still you don't care," she said as he tried to pry her hand from her throat.

But Night Children were just as strong as a Fae or Legacy, and he was powerless here. Weak, just as she said.

Julius drew closer, the Fae with him, and as she held him in place with a single hand, Bree sank her fangs into the Fae's arm. Axel thrashed, strangled cries of desperation coming from him. Not because she was holding him by the throat, but because all he could see was red. All he could smell was the metallic scent that came with a life force. All he could hear was the blood rushing in his ears, reminding him of what he needed with every pulse. All he could taste was the memory of when he'd once been whole and healthy and safe. All he could feel was the burn in his throat, his veins, his very soul at being denied this.

It felt like an eternity before she finally lifted her mouth from the Fae's arm, brushing her thumb along the corner of her lips. Red shimmered on the pad of her thumb, and she made him watch while her tongue darted out and licked it away. Tears stung the back of his eyes as his last hope of relief was led away.

Bree's hand slid up his throat and under his chin, tilting his head back. With him on his knees and her in her heels, his head was level with her stomach, and she stroked a hand through his hair.

"The Fates can be so cruel, can't they, Axel darling?" she murmured with faux sympathy. "You only need to say the words, and I will call her back."

But he found himself saying, "She's not mine."

Bree's head tilted, and she studied him for a long moment, an expression he couldn't read on her face. Then a small smile tilted on her lips. Her hand slid to his jaw now, her thumb sweeping along his cheekbone. "I know exactly what you need, darling. Just tell me her name, and I will find her for you."

"I don't know it," he answered.

Because it was always there, on the tip of his tongue but just out of reach.

Her thumb and forefinger gripped his chin, keeping his eyes on hers. "Tell me of her then," she coaxed.

He shook his head, trying to clear his mind, and her grip tightened, nails digging in sharp enough to make him wince. But it also let him focus.

"Black curls and warm skin. Golden eyes," he murmured.

"What else?" she pushed.

"She'll taste like fire and desire," he said, and gods, she would. Fiery and hot and his.

His to have.

His to take.

Bree released his chin, and he sat back on his heels, feeling as if he'd just run ten miles. His heart was racing, and his breaths were coming too quickly.

"I will find her for you," Bree said in a soothing voice.

He looked up at her again, hope blooming in his chest. "You will?"

She nodded, her smile growing.

"And until then?" he asked, already dreading going back to that pitch-black room to waste away.

"I won't put you back in the dark, Axel darling," she replied. "I will give you everything you need. All I ask is that you repay the favor when I have."

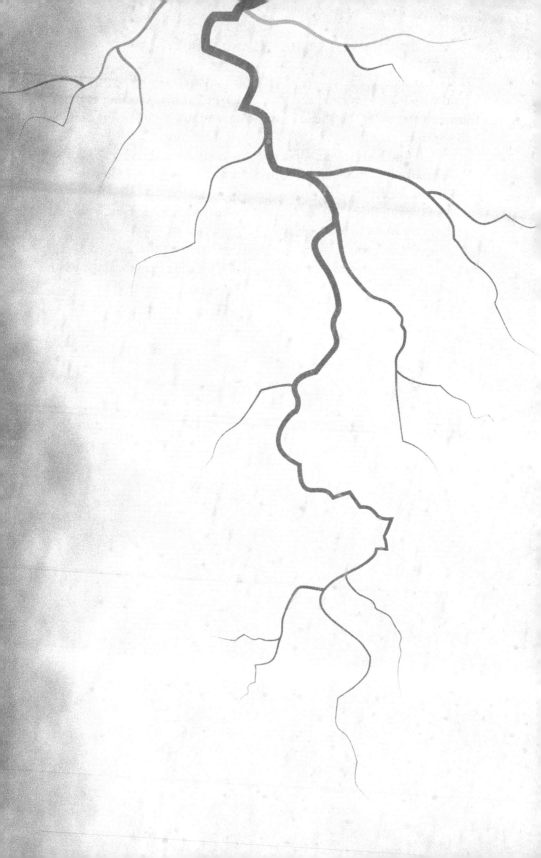

10

TESSA

She slipped from the bed without so much as a word or a backwards glance. She knew he was awake. He always woke before her and was usually up and busying himself around the room by the time she woke. But not this morning. He was still there, letting her curl into his side, and gods, she'd *slept*. A deep sleep with no dreams or visions. He had stayed in that bed for her, and she didn't want to think about why.

Or about how her stomach did unacceptable things if she thought about it for too long.

But she needed to get up and get back to her own room before Oralia showed up like she did every morning.

With a steadying breath, she summoned a portal and stepped through. Her chest tightened at the fact that he didn't even try to stop her, but she'd say that was the bond.

Because she didn't care.

Dropping the nightclothes to her floor, she pulled the band from her hair and ran a hand through it. She felt more centered. Less chaotic. More balanced.

She supposed a full night's rest would do that for a person.

She'd taken a whole two steps towards her bathroom when a voice made her jump and sent her heart to her throat.

"This is what you're doing now?"

She whirled, a hand on her chest. "Gods, Dex," she gasped. "What are you doing in here? And in the dark no less?"

"I was hoping I was going to prove Oralia wrong, but here you are," he answered from where he sat in an armchair. There weren't any lights on, but the fireplace was still on a low setting, casting dancing shadows across his features.

"What are you talking about?" she asked.

"You're wearing his shirt, Tessa," he said with a pointed look.

She looked down, suddenly remembering she *was* still wearing Luka's shirt. It stopped mid-thigh and was only half buttoned, just enough to keep her breasts covered.

Wrapping it tighter around herself, she pursed her lips, refusing to look at Dex.

"What are you doing, Tessa?" he demanded, pushing to his feet.

He rounded the sofa, stopping in front of her. His crisp, white shirt was paired with dark pants, and why was he dressed already? The sun wasn't even up yet.

"What are you doing?" he repeated.

"If you must know, I was going to use the bathroom," she answered, gesturing to the doorway across the room.

Dex rolled his eyes. "What are you doing with *him*? This is exactly why we didn't even want you to see him. Then you told him he could stay?"

"I didn't tell him anything," she snapped, jabbing her finger into his chest. "Rordan told him he could stay here. Not me."

"If you would have let me handle it when he showed up, none of this would have happened," he retorted. "How do you manage to mess with everything all the godsdamn time?"

A harsh laugh of disbelief came from her, and she took a step back from him. "You mean why do you always have to clean up after me, right?"

"That's not—"

"For your information, there's nothing to *clean up* here," she cut in. "I didn't fuck up anything. Unless there are things you haven't told me? In which case, that's on *you* for keeping those things from me."

"You're missing the point, Tessa," Dex growled, pinching the bridge of his nose.

"No, *you're* missing the point," she retorted. "How do I know if I'm messing with anything if I don't know there's anything to mess with?"

"You just need to trust us," he said, throwing his hands up in frustration.

"You know I don't blindly trust anyone."

"I'm not just anyone," he spat. "Or I wasn't just anyone until he came along."

"Theon has nothing to do with this, and neither does Luka."

A derisive scoff came from him before he said, "You're wearing his godsdamn shirt, Tessa."

"I needed to sleep, Dex! I haven't been able to sleep since I came here," she cried.

"Have you been drinking the tea that the Lord suggested?"

"I..." But she trailed off because she hadn't drunk it for several nights. Sure, she slept when she drank it, but it wasn't a restful sleep. In fact, she was almost *more* tired when she woke. Her dreams were more vivid, more intense, and she felt even more out of sorts afterwards.

"That's what I thought," Dex sniped. "We try to help, but you won't let us. Instead, you go back to them. You forget your purpose—"

"I've forgotten nothing," she spat, her palms landing on his chest and shoving hard. Her power poured from her, throwing Dex backwards. Except she wasn't in control, just like Luka accused her of, and she was thrown back with the force of it too. The sound of bodies hitting furniture echoed around them, and she sucked in a breath as pain shot up her spine and ricocheted down her arms. It took her a few moments before she rolled to her knees.

She found Dex already on his feet, making his way to her. His shirt was ripped from the surge of unexpected power, and his dark brown hair was mussed and askew.

"Tessie," he sighed. "Are you all right?"

He reached for her, helping her to her feet.

"I'm fine," she muttered, jerking her arm from his grasp and tugging down Luka's shirt.

He took her face in his hands, tilting her head back. She looked into dark eyes she'd once trusted with her world. When had that changed? When had she become more suspicious of him rather than believing he only wanted what was best for her?

"For the past several years I told you to be who they wanted you to be now so you could be who you were meant to be later," he said. "It's later, Tessie. You know your purpose. Focus on that. Let us worry about the rest."

"Did you always know?" she asked, her tone flat and monotone.

"Did I always know what?" he asked, reaching to tuck her hair behind her ear.

"About me?"

He paused, his fingertips still in her hair. "I always knew you were meant for more, Tessie. I just needed you to believe that too."

"But did you know about *me*?" she insisted. "My power. What I am. That I was Achaz blood and— That I was this."

His eyes narrowed. "Do you know your lineage, Tessa?"

"Do you?"

"Only what Lord Jove knows," he answered. "Did I always believe you were more? Yes. But I couldn't know how much until your power was allowed to emerge. And I was right, wasn't I?"

"I guess," she muttered.

"So focus on your destiny, Tessa."

"Right," she said, eyes darting to the side.

"It's not with them. I thought you'd accepted that."

"I did."

"Then start acting like it," he said, his tone hardening once more as he dropped his hands.

She glared up at him. "Get out, Dexter."

"Take a shower and get his scent off of you," he retorted, striding to the door. "I'll have breakfast waiting for you."

She watched him walk away, the back of his white shirt more shredded than the front had been. Once he'd slammed the door shut behind him, she made her way across the room to the off-white feather on the floor. Picking it up, she ran a single finger along the soft barbs. Once. Twice.

She carried it with her into the bathroom, turning it over in her hand and studying it. It wasn't until she was ready to get in the shower that she carefully set it aside on the countertop before undoing the few buttons of Luka's shirt. She folded it, tucking it into the back of a linen cupboard in her bathroom. Closing the cupboard door, she felt him down the bond. Not Luka, but Theon. The same hesitant caress she'd felt the night she'd taunted him.

For whatever reason—likely to be defiant of everything Dex had just berated her for—she answered.

What? she demanded

I felt you minutes ago. Are you all right?

It'd been a few days since she'd heard his voice, and the sound of it in her mind had the bond immediately stretching and aching in a way she hadn't experienced since that night. Sleeping beside Luka had soothed one part of it, but this other part? It would always want Theon unless she could figure out a way to sever their bond.

Tessa? Are you hurt? his voice came again, but all she could think about was Dex's accusing words and how he was right. She was losing focus.

Correct the balance.

Fulfill her destiny.

Leave this forsaken world behind forever.

Answer him, temptress, or I'll be banging on your door in minutes to see for myself you aren't dying, came Luka's rough growl down the bond.

Don't bother, she retorted. *I won't be here.*

So you're not hurt? Theon asked, and he sounded...distracted? What was he doing?

It didn't matter. She couldn't care.

No, I'm not hurt, but even if I was, I'm not yours to worry about anymore, she sneered in response.

The silence stretched on for so long, she thought he'd actually given up on her for once. But then—

You've forgotten, Theon said.

Forgotten what?

That I'll always fight for you. You'll forever be mine.

She made her way down the cool, white marble steps, her fingers dragging along the wall. The orbs of golden light lit her way, Roan and Nylah padding along at her sides. They were a comforting presence in the chaos of her world.

She'd showered and gotten ready for the day. Not in training clothes as would be expected of her, but in a pair of leggings and a soft grey sweater. For a moment, she'd contemplated putting Luka's shirt back on just to spite Dex at this point, but his scent would distract her from what she had to do today.

Oralia had never shown up in her room like she had every other morning. Tessa could only assume that Dex had told her not to. She hadn't missed the way he'd paused mid-bite when she entered the dining room, her bare feet soundless on the floor and her hair loose and still damp.

She also hadn't missed that he was sitting *at* the table, a premade plate for her beside him. Rordan wasn't there, but Dagian was. Sasha, his Source, was seated beside him, her eyes fixed on her food. The Achaz Heir didn't say a word the entire meal. No one did. The tension in the air had been thick, and when Tessa had excused herself after only a few bites of food, no one tried to stop her.

Training with Odessa was usually next in her new daily routine, but she wasn't about to go train with Luka this morning. She may have slept beside him all night, but she was still furious he'd gone around her to Rordan. If he thought she was just going to accept this arrangement that had been made, he was sorely mistaken.

Lifting her hand, she pulled the feather from a swirl of light, twirling the quill between her thumb and forefinger. She passed several of the glass cells, most of them empty, before coming to a stop in front of Valter's.

The Lord's hair was a little longer now, resembling his younger son more than his eldest. His dark hazel eyes glared at her from where he sat on a small cot. The bands on his wrists had made the skin around them red and raw, and her lips tipped up at the sight of it. He had a little more room to move about compared to the prisoner at the end of the passage. Valter could at least pace the length of his small space and have his piss bucket on the other side of the cell.

"Where is Eviana?" Valter demanded, still sounding like the Lord he no longer was.

"I already told you she is fine," Tessa replied, tilting her head as she continued to twirl the feather. "I know you can communicate with her."

"I want to see her," he replied.

She huffed a small laugh. "And draw from her in a useless attempt to try to get out of this cell? I think not."

"What I do with my Source is not your concern," he retorted.

"Apparently it is since I can control if you see her," Tessa said. "Do you know what this is?"

Valter's eyes darted to the feather she waved in front of the glass, but he said nothing.

"I suppose my question should be: do you know of any beings with feathered wings? Beings who can banish their wings like you can banish yours?"

He gave her a dark, dry look. "Surely you are not this stupid."

"Not at all," she replied with a simpering smile. "In fact, your son finds me quite clever."

"Then why in the realm would you expect me to answer a question when you will not let me see Eviana? This is about negotiations, Tessalyn," he said.

Nylah let out a low growl at his tone that was somewhere between menacing and conceited, and Roan pressed against her leg.

"Negotiations," she repeated, sending the feather away with her magic before placing a hand against the glass of the cell. It flickered, light and energy dancing across the pane, but she absorbed it, drawing it all to the space beneath her palm. "You would like something in return?"

"Yes," Valter sneered. "I would like to see Eviana."

"That's not possible," Tessa replied, faux sympathy in her voice as power continued to pool beneath her hand.

"What are you doing?" Valter asked, his gaze darting to the swelling magic.

"The thing is, I'm really not sure," she replied, her head tilting as she watched the power grow.

"Well, stop," he demanded.

"Is this the negotiating part?"

"What? No. This is…"

She smiled darkly as he trailed off.

"I don't know anything about the fucking feather," Valter said, his gaze fixed on where her hand was connected to the window.

"Oh, that's fine," she chirped. "I think someone else down here will be able to answer those questions. I need to know about Axel."

"Axel?" Valter repeated.

"Yes," she drawled. "You know, your other son?"

"What do you want with him?"

"I did not think you were a forgetful person considering the grudge you have held for decades," she mused.

She flexed her fingers against the glass, and the magic shuddered around the movement. Valter's eyes widened, the color draining from his face.

"Are you?" she pressed.

His gaze flicked to hers, but when it went right back to the glass, she pressed her other hand to the smooth surface.

"What are you doing?" he repeated.

"You truly are absent-minded, aren't you? I already told you I have no idea what this will do, just as I told you before that I would be the downfall of your entire bloodline. That includes Axel, and I'm told you have him hidden away somewhere," Tessa said, the power in her veins vibrating with the additional magic she was channeling into it.

"I will not tell you where he is just so you can kill him," Valter said, a slight tremor in his voice.

"Because you are such a loving and caring father," she said sarcastically, feeling the power that sparked in her eyes. "You only want him for leverage."

"Which is what I have right now," he replied, his chin lifting an inch with the words. "You just gave me the upper hand."

"No, my *Lord*," she said, her tone as icy as death and the darkness she hated. "I still have that."

With a push of power, the light and energy she'd been hoarding refracted across the glass and straight into his cell. Rays of magic burst forth, striking the Arius Lord from all angles as they bounced around the glass and marble cell.

Truthfully, she hadn't known what would happen when she placed her hand on that glass. She didn't know what she was doing; she never did.

Impulsive.

Uncontrollable.

Wild.

It was what was expected of her, so she continued to lean into it. Valter's screams of agony on the other side of the glass only fed her. Her heart was pounding with the adrenaline rush of having someone so powerful at her mercy. Someone who had demanded she be caged. Tamed. Someone who had suggested she be used for securing deals, and who believed her sole purpose was to serve at the feet of the Legacy.

When the enchanted cell absorbed the last of her power as it bounced against the glass, she saw him on the floor, curled in on himself. His clothing had holes, and there were dark spots splattered across the material of his pants and shirt from the various cuts on his visible skin.

Bringing her hand back to the glass, she drummed her fingers along the surface once. Twice. Three times before she placed her hand flat against it again, energy immediately surging towards it.

"Don't!" Valter gasped, pushing onto his hands and knees.

Even from here she could see his arms trembling with the effort.

Pulling her hand away, she asked in a calm, collected tone, "Where is Axel?"

"My advisors took him," he panted, his face taking on a greenish hue as though he may vomit.

"Took him where?"

"To the Underground."

"*Where* in the Underground?" she said tightly, dragging a single finger along the glass.

But Valter shook his head, spitting red onto the floor. "I don't—"

"Don't tell me you don't know," she snapped, a jolt of power ricocheting into the cell. It hit Valter in the side in the exact place she'd once witnessed him stab Theon. He collapsed onto his front again, his chin hitting the floor, and she heard his curse as his teeth sank into his lip. "You're going to tell me, *my Lord*. And do you know why?" She didn't give him a chance to answer before she continued. "Because you value your own comfort and safety over that of your son's. You will tell me because you would rather me find him, knowing full well it will be the end of his life, rather than endure discomfort to save him from that fate."

Valter shook his head again, struggling back onto his hands and knees.

"Oh, yes. Because you still think you will find a way out of this. You still think you can win. You sit in this cell all day and night, planning and scheming. But here's a secret for you, *Valter*," she purred. She stepped so close to the glass she could see her breath on it when she said, "I've become so numb, I can't feel anything anymore, and unlike you, I'm not afraid to die."

Tessa slammed her palms to the glass, letting her power free. The light in the cell now was so blinding, she couldn't see the Arius Lord, but she could feel her power feasting. She could feel it sinking into his soul, burrowing deep, and taking, taking, taking.

Roan and Nylah were on their feet, one growling and one letting out a soft, low whine.

It took mere seconds before Valter was screaming, and something in the back of her mind was telling her they couldn't kill him, not yet. They still needed him.

So she pulled her power back, leaving Valter panting in the middle of his cell. His shirt was nothing but scraps of fabric now, his torso riddled with deep cuts and burns.

"Do you have something to tell me?" she asked, tapping a finger on the glass.

Valter flinched with each tap, and each wince made her smile grow.

"I have a place in the Leisure District. I pay the Alpha and Beta enough to buy their secrecy. You'll have to pay them more for their betrayal," he answered. He turned then, eyes full of hatred as he added with a sneer, "Good luck."

"Thank you," she replied, trailing her fingers along the pane as she took a few steps away. "I'll see you again soon, *Valter*."

She left him there, not caring if and when he got aid for the injuries. The bands would prevent him from healing himself, so a Healer would be needed. That was someone else's problem to worry about.

Tessa, where are you? came Luka's growl down the bond.

Her shields must have slipped while she'd been...busy.

That's none of your concern, she replied, continuing down the passage.

Is this not your usual training time?

It is, but thanks to you, I no longer have a trainer.

Tessa...

The warning rumble in his tone had her nearly tripping over nothing and her stomach doing those unacceptable things yet again.

You said someone close to my power levels should be training me. Until that person is found, I have better things to be doing.

Tessa, when I find you—

But she shut him out, slamming the shield back in place as she stopped before the last cell on the left.

He sat where he'd been the only other time she'd come down here. His long brown hair reached well past his shoulders, still a mess of tangled knots. His facial hair was a little longer, but not by much. Shirtless, she could see the Marks that ran the entire length of his left arm. That large onyx ring on his finger was a stark contrast to the manacle of pure white stone at his throat, the flecks of gold shimmering in the faint light of his cell.

And his sapphire eyes were already pinned on her.

With an exaggerated flourish, she sank to the floor, sitting in the same place she had last time. The male arched a brow, his lips twitching as he clearly fought a smirk.

Just like another always did.

Roan settled down beside her, his head in her lap, but Nylah was pacing back and forth before the cell, her nose to the floor as if searching for something.

"How did you come to be in that cell?" she asked, stroking her fingers through Roan's fur.

The male watched her for a long time before finally saying, "I heard you torturing the Arius Lord, and now you come to me for casual conversation?"

"Is that a problem?" she challenged.

The male shrugged. "Depends on your motivations."

"I'm collecting currency," she replied, leaning back on her hands.

"And what have you learned?"

Tessa shrugged, lifting a hand to pull the feather from a swirl of golden mist. "Do you know what being might have feathered wings?"

The male stretched his legs out, crossing them at the ankles. "The Arius Lord was right. You know nothing of negotiating," he said, tipping his head back against the wall.

"The Arius Lord is currently bleeding and in agony at having some of his soul ripped from his veins by my light," she snapped, lurching forward. "I know how to negotiate just fine."

The male slowly lowered his chin, his gaze finding hers once more.

Tessa cleared her throat, running a fingertip along the feather barbs. "I am well aware that such methods would likely be ineffective with you."

"Because you are clever like her," he replied.

She paused at that comment, but forced herself to focus on her task.

"I believe we can come to…some sort of agreement," she went on.

"And why would I make an agreement with you?" he asked, eyes narrowing.

"Because unlike the Arius Lord and the conversation you so rudely eavesdropped on—"

"It is rather hard not to overhear things down here," he interrupted.

"Either way, I would venture to guess that unlike the Arius Lord, you are an honorable father," she continued, turning the feather over in her hand. But she saw it in her periphery. She saw the way the male went still. "I imagine that while Valter gave up his secrets to damn his son and save himself from a little pain, you will do the exact opposite." She lifted her gaze to his. "Am I right?"

The male said nothing, but the hard look in his eyes was answer enough. If she felt anything anymore, she'd probably shrink back from that look. Too bad she was as soulless as she'd just told Valter. This was as much a reminder to herself as it was to everyone else.

"Wonderful. I have your attention," she said, twisting so she sat on her knees. "But to make sure we understand each other, I sleep beside him. I kept him from being locked in one of these cells, albeit that was admittedly because I couldn't have him learning about you just yet. *I* am his protection in this place now."

"And if I tell you information, you will make sure no harm comes to my son?" the male said, his hands clenched into fists atop his thighs.

"If you tell me *accurate* and *truthful* information," she emphasized. "Then yes, I agree to keep harm from your son to the best of my ability. Do we have an accord?"

Sapphire eyes bored into hers. Nylah was still sniffing along the floor at the base of his cell, and Roan lifted his head, looking at the male.

"It's a bargain," the male said.

And Tessa felt the words imprint on her skin. Turning her wrist over, she saw the Mark on the inside of it.

"You are still on the path of destruction," the male said grimly, studying his own new Mark.

She sent him an icy smile, and her voice held that eerie ring to it as she said, "If this is my destruction, then I'll make sure the world burns with me."

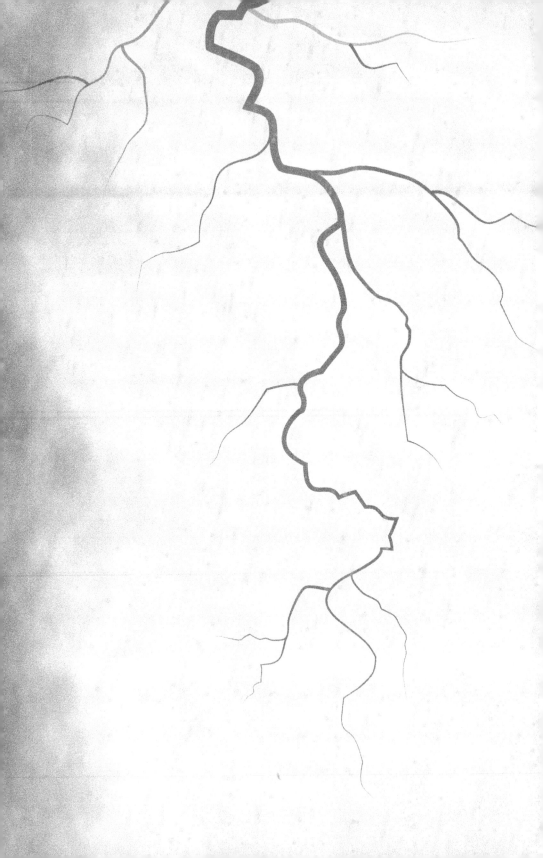

11

TESSA

"**Y**ou are so much like her," the male mused, sapphire eyes still watching her carefully. "Did you know she threatened to burn a realm to nothing for you?"

"How would I know that?" Tessa retorted, moving up to the glass. "And who is she?"

"Your mother."

Tessa went so still, she forgot to breathe.

Her mother?

Her mother had threatened to burn a realm to nothing for her?

Then where was she?

"You know my mother?" she asked.

"I do."

Tessa waited, but when he didn't elaborate, she said, "Well, who is she?"

The male smiled, and it was so much like his son's that she felt her stomach do that little flutter thing she hated so much.

"We made a bargain," Tessa said. "You must tell me."

"There were no timeframes specified," the male said. "It was only stated that I must tell you truthful and accurate information."

"I— You—"

A scream of frustration left her.

"She is impulsive when lost to her fury as well," he said knowingly.

Tessa slammed her palm to the glass, power skittering along the pane. "You and your son know how to manipulate us so we become reckless in our decisions."

"That is likely true," he said without concern. "We look for weakness to capitalize on. It is in our nature, both in what we are and in our bloodline."

"You will not tell me what I wish to know?" Tessa demanded, power hissing under her fingers.

"I didn't say that, but I will tell you in my own time." As an afterthought, he added, "And some things I will only tell you when you no longer side with the Light King."

"I will not go back to Theon," she snapped.

"I never asked you to."

"Then what do you want from me?" she said, and it was almost a cry.

Another person who wanted something from her.

But his answer was, "Nothing."

She hadn't realized her hand was in her hair until she paused, the strands wrapped around her fingers. "What do you mean nothing? You just told me you wanted me to not side with the Light King. Who is that? Rordan?"

"No."

"Achaz then?" He said nothing, and Tessa placed her palms on the glass once more. "How did you come to be in this cell?"

"I was detained for information."

"That you have refused to give. Glad to know it isn't just me you withhold information from," she drawled.

"But I withhold it for the same reasons," he replied.

"Yes, yes," she sighed. "Because we are loyal to Achaz."

"Not at all," he answered. "I made a vow to keep you safe, even at the cost of my own life." When Tessa only blinked in surprise, he added, "It is not only my son I have endured torture for."

She didn't know what to say to that because why would someone who didn't even know her be willing to suffer so greatly for her? Be imprisoned for years? Leave his own son?

"He thinks you are dead," she blurted.

A sadness flickered on his features. "I assumed that was the story he was told."

"The Arius— Valter said you brought me to this realm. Is that true?"

"Yes."

"Why?"

"To hide you from Achaz."

"In a world the gods could not go to," she murmured, pacing before his cell, fingers dragging on the glass.

The male nodded slowly. "But like so many others have discovered, one does not need to physically be in a realm to deliver chaos."

She stopped suddenly. "Everyone is always trying to protect me. They think they know what's best for me. But no one ever asks me. They just shove me into the dark and lock me in—"

"Tessalyn."

Her name was somehow both a command and a soft reminder, and his voice was so similar to his that it stopped her spiral into the madness that was slowly eating away at her.

"She loses herself to the chaos at times too," he said just loud enough for her to hear.

"You speak as if you love her," Tessa said, startling when Roan brushed against her legs. Always beside her, comforting her, keeping her grounded.

"Not in the way Temural does, but she is endeared to me, yes," he answered.

"Then don't you think I should know your name?"

"Ask me the next time you find your way down here."

Tessa rolled her eyes. "Or you could just—"

People are looking for you, Tessa, came a growl down the bond.

What people?

Does it matter? They are accusing me of hiding you away, Luka retorted.

That's not my problem.

Except that it was. Because she'd made the stupid bargain with the male in the cell that she would keep his son safe from harm.

So godsdamn reckless.

"I have to go fulfill my end of our deal," she said, the male watching her with a look of intrigue.

At her words, he arched a brow. "You can sense him in trouble?"

"No. I mean, yes, but I—" Tessa pursed her lips, her hands clenching at her sides. "If you will not answer my questions, I see no need to answer yours."

The male's head tilted, a newfound interest she didn't understand staring back at her. "An answer for an answer before you take your leave then."

She barked a humorless laugh. "I will not be making another bargain with you."

"No bargain," he said, shifting against the wall. "A trade. An answer for an answer."

"No."

His brows shot up. "No? But all you've wanted since the first time you spoke to me is answers."

"And you've either never provided them or tricked me into a deal."

"I didn't trick you—"

"Yes, yes. He said the same thing," she interjected, waving him off.

"You will not even hear my question?"

"No."

"Then I propose this," he said. "You ask your question first and get your answer. Then I will ask my question, and you can simply walk away if you do not wish to answer it."

"Just walk away," she repeated dryly.

"It's not as if I could stop you."

He had a point.

She stepped closer to his cell once more, debating her options. Her mother's name? Where she was? Where her father was? How they got here? But the question that came from her lips was none of those things.

"If you brought me here, and you were supposed to be protecting me, how did I end up at the Celeste Estate, alone and abandoned?" she asked, her tone harsh and accusing.

The male clearly hadn't been expecting that question. Not as he jerked back, then winced when the action caused some type of reaction inside the cell.

"I didn't abandon you," he replied.

"My time spent in dark places without food or companionship begs to differ," she retorted. "But that is neither here nor there. You did not answer my question."

"I did not know where you ended up," he answered, and she had to believe him because the bargain required him to answer truthfully. "At that time, the Achaz and Arius Lords were still working together. An Augury attack was planned. I was brought here. Valter took my son, and you were... Well, from what I've gathered, you were lost among the chaos. Both Lords spent the next two decades searching for you."

"That's what you believe?"

"Based on the information they've tried to torture out of me over these last years, yes. That's what I believe."

"What is your question?" she asked coldly.

"My son is here with you? Separated from his Ward?"

Tessa blinked in surprise. "That is your question?"

The male only nodded, his eyes never leaving her.

"Yes," she answered. "He said Theon *sent* him to me, but I do not know if I believe him."

"Either way, there is only one instance that would allow him to put another before his Ward."

"And what is that?"

The male tipped his head back, his eyes falling closed. She could swear a small smile played on his lips as he murmured more to himself than her, "She is going to hate this."

"What, exactly, is *this*?" Tessa snapped.

"I thought you had to go?"

She swallowed her scream of frustration before spinning on her heel and making her way back up the stairs, her wolves on her heels. She slipped through the door and into a deserted hall. There was truly nothing remarkable about the passage or the door. It was why she'd stumbled upon it by accident, but it was still odd to her there were no sentinels guarding this door. She could only assume it was warded, which was why she was able to pass without detection.

Nylah was in front of her as she often was, while Roan prowled at her side, always staying close. When the darker wolf paused, her ears perking up, Tessa paused too. Seconds later, Luka rounded the corner.

"Where have you been?" the dragon demanded.

She took her time looking him up and down. Which was a mistake because he was in black pants and a black button-down, both of which hugged muscles she didn't want to be looking at. And why the fuck was this suddenly such an issue? She'd spent months with this male. Sure, she'd noticed he was attractive, but it hadn't been like this, even once the three of them had been bonded. She hadn't been constantly drawn to him. Theon had always been there, demanding her attention.

"Tessa?" Luka snapped. His hand grabbed her wrist, spinning her so her back was against the wall.

Then he went still as deep growls reverberated through the space. Nylah was a few feet away, her paws planted, head down, and the hair on the back of her neck standing on end. Her teeth were bared, but

Roan was right next to them. His massive jaws were snapping, and he was already crouched, preparing to attack.

And Tessa smiled, something dark and serpentine. Her head tilted, waiting to see what Luka would do next. His eyes shifted to those vertical pupils, and he stared down Roan as he exhaled a stream of smoke. Tessa was kind of impressed.

Okay, she was more than *kind of* impressed as Luka held his ground against her wolves. It did things to her, and—

Gods-fucking-dammit.

If Luka felt any of her inner turmoil, he didn't let it show. His eyes were still on Roan, his muscles coiled tight as he gritted out, "Call them off, Tessa."

"Let me go," she sneered.

She felt him hesitate, his fingers flexing where they still held her wrist against the wall by her head. With another shuddering breath, he released her and took a step back. Roan immediately moved forward, putting himself between them.

"I didn't mean to— You get lost in your head sometimes," he finally said. "I was only trying to bring you back. That's all I'm trying to do."

"I don't get lost to fury," she said tightly.

Luka blinked, those vertical pupils studying her. "I didn't say you did," he said slowly, as if unsure if he should say anything at all.

"I can't— I don't— What do you want anyway?" she stammered, reaching for her hair. But when Luka tracked the movement, she buried her fingers in Roan's coat instead.

"People are looking for you," he said.

"Why?"

"I'm assuming they want to keep track of their unpredictably powerful possession."

"Fuck off, Luka," she spat, shoving past him and continuing on her way, but he easily caught up to her with his long strides.

"Come now, Tessa," he said, a hint of mocking to his tone. "You can't see this for what it is?"

"Theon viewed me as a possession. That's not how it is here. No one fucking *owns* me here."

Luka didn't answer as they turned another corner, and she winced when she spotted Dex, Oralia, and Brecken at the other end of the hall. It was a wince Luka clearly felt down the bond because he looked down at her with a sardonic curl to his lips.

"No one owns you?" he said, a questioning arch to his brow before he put a few steps of space between them.

"I hate you so godsdamn much," she muttered as the three Fae came towards them, a stern scowl already on Dex's face.

"We've been looking for you," Dex said before they'd even come to a stop. Then his attention shifted to Luka. "I thought you said you didn't know where she was?"

"I found her two minutes ago," Luka answered in his usual bored tone. "I told you she didn't show up for training."

"And yet we still find her with you," Dex sneered.

"You're welcome," Luka replied.

Dex's eyes narrowed, but Tessa said, "What do you want, Dex?"

"This bratty side of you is so becoming, Tessie. I think I like it," Brecken said, dark eyes holding mischief.

"Shut up, Brecken," Dex chided. "We don't need anything, Tessa. We're just a little more cautious with another kingdom's advisor here for the foreseeable future."

"If Rordan was that worried about it, he wouldn't have let him stay," Tessa countered.

"It seems there wasn't much of a choice because of a bargain *you* made."

She pursed her lips, knowing she couldn't counter that without letting it be known Luka had lied about the training. Even without this bargain she'd made with the male in the cell, she wouldn't have done it. She should. She should have told Rordan the moment she found out about the whole damn thing, but she'd wanted to talk to Luka first for some unknown reason. That had led to sleeping beside him, which had led to the lecture from Dex, and now here she was again.

"I don't need protection from Luka," was all she could think to say.

"Even if she did, protection follows her everywhere," Luka added, looking pointedly at Roan, who was still at her side. Nylah was sitting a few feet away, watching everything.

"No one knows where the wolves came from," Dex said, eyeing the beasts.

"It doesn't matter," Tessa said. "The point is there's nothing to worry about."

"That's where you're wrong, Tessie," Dex said. "I made the mistake of thinking there was nothing to worry about once. I won't be making it again."

"What is that supposed to mean?"

"My gods, Tessa," Oralia chided. "We all know how the Emerging Ceremony turned out."

"You still blame me for that?" Tessa asked incredulously.

"Of course not," Dex cut in before Oralia could answer. "We just don't want any more surprises, but it seems they are unavoidable with you. Anyway, we are being sent into Faven on some errands for Lord Jove. I thought you might like to join us. Get out of here for a while."

"Yeah, sure," she muttered, the bond already making her anxious at being separated from Luka.

Which is exactly why she didn't look back as she followed the Fae and left him behind.

"Is your meal to your liking, Tessa?"

"What?" she asked, startled from her thoughts at Rordan's question.

The Achaz Lord glanced at her plate, then back to her, smiling warmly. "You've scarcely touched your food, my dear."

Tessa looked down at her plate where the finest cut of meat sat, with garlic potatoes, a vegetable medley, and two buttery rolls. It was the type of meal she'd never been provided when everyone had thought she was Fae, and she found herself wondering if Theon would have let her eat it even now. As it was, she'd only managed to push her food around on her plate amid the few bites of meat she'd taken, and it had everything to do with the male seated at the table with them.

"The meal is lovely," she answered with a half-hearted smile, picking up her knife to cut another bite.

"I can have something else prepared if you prefer?"

She felt her eyes go wide at the mere idea of forcing a Fae to make her another meal. "That is not necessary," she said quickly, scooping up a bite of potatoes. "I am merely tired from the day."

"Did you not sleep well last night?" Rordan asked, holding Tessa's stare, and gods, she knew then that he knew she'd spent the night in Luka's bed. She felt her cheeks go hot, and she shouldn't care because caring meant Luka was right. This Lord owned some part of her to make her feel like this.

"Are we still planning the trip to the Sirana Villas?" Dagian asked after the uncomfortable silence stretched on too long.

"Yes," Rordan answered, taking a drink from his wine glass. "Desiray said she has some new information on that issue we've been having."

"I assume there are new younglings to sign off on?" Dagian continued.

"There always are," Rordan answered.

"How often do you go there?" Tessa interrupted.

Dagian dragged his gaze to hers as Rordan answered absent-mindedly, "Once a month."

"I would like to go with you."

The Lord didn't even look up from his plate as he waved her off. "It is a routine visit. Nothing exciting."

"Nevertheless, I would enjoy visiting a place that I've never seen before."

Rordan did pause this time, setting his silverware aside. He folded his hands, resting his chin atop them as he studied her. She did her best not to fidget, all the years of Mother Cordelia forcing her to sit for hours coming into play.

"There is nothing of interest in the Sirana Villas," the Achaz Lord finally said. "I fear you will find yourself incredibly bored, and your time may be better spent in training to fulfill your bargain."

Her eyes darted to Luka, who was feigning his usual boredom, but she knew he was cataloging this entire exchange. It would be one more thing for him to taunt her with. *Tell her how this was just another cage, and how they only want to control her.*

Those thoughts alone had her turning back to Rordan and saying, "I am sure a day or two without training will be fine."

"Well, then," Rordan said, picking his flatware back up. "I will let Desiray know to expect additional visitors for this visit."

"You can't be serious, Father," Dagian cut in with dismay.

"If Tessalyn wishes to go, who are we to stop her?"

"You are the Achaz Lord," he fumed.

"And *you* are the Achaz *Heir*," the Lord replied pointedly. "If you wish her not to go, you stop her, but we both know that's not possible based on recent performance in the training arenas."

Tessa watched as Dagian swallowed his retort. Valter would have physically tortured his son for not being the most powerful in a room. Rordan, it seemed, found other ways to torture his offspring.

A tense quiet settled over the dining room, the two Sources dutifully eating their food. Dagian's mother was rarely around. In fact, she'd only been present at their meals twice. Rordan said she preferred to take her meals in private. Dex and the others weren't at the table since they were Fae. They were, however, standing along the wall, while Luka sat across the table next to Dagian.

Tessa wasn't sure why Luka was dining with them in the first place. Not until Rordan spoke again, breaking the awkward silence.

"So, Luka," he said, taking a drink of his wine. "Is Theon going to be able to take time out of his busy schedule to attend the Sirana Gala?"

Tessa's fork was halfway to her mouth, and she stilled. She'd completely forgotten about the Gala.

The Gala was held at the mid-point between the Winter Solstice and Spring Equinox. It was just another grand affair for the Legacy, although they claimed it was to honor Sirana, the goddess of love and fertility. It never made any sense to her if the gods didn't care about this world, but it was an event she'd always looked forward to anyway. Not because Fae were allowed to attend, but because the Estates were often left to their own for a few nights. It was easier to sneak away, and she knew there wouldn't be any unexpected *lessons.*

Well, except for that one year Mother Cordelia went to the Sirana Gala and left her in that cupboard for those days, but still.

Luka finished chewing his bite of bread before he answered, but his eyes were pinned on Tessa. "I don't know what his plans are or if he will be *able* to attend."

Rordan made a sound of disapproval. "As his advisor, I would strongly suggest *advising* him that it would be wise to attend."

"I will take that under advisement," Luka said dryly, and Tessa had to stifle her snicker at the retort.

Rordan's eyes narrowed, and he pushed his empty plate to the side. "Continually shirking his duties is not a wise start for someone who has not officially been given his seat yet."

"With all due respect, he is tending to his people. His people are his duty. Or are you suggesting his priorities should lie elsewhere?"

"Do not get smart with me, Mors," Rordan said, his voice going low as light sparked at his fingertips. "How can we present a unified front if one kingdom refuses to be part of it?"

Tessa's head canted to the side as she studied his magic. She hadn't realized the subtle differences from her own. Her power sparked into something like lightning, chaotic and unpredictable. His light coiled and arched, the sparks like gold-flecked mist.

"Let's speak plainly, my Lord," Luka replied, sitting back in his chair, a hand resting on the table. "The unity you speak of is hanging on by a thread."

"And it will not get any better if he refuses to attend meetings and events," Rordan snapped, his light flaring. The Sources flinched back, but none of the Legacy did.

"I will be sure to pass along your concerns," Luka said, picking up his glass of wine and draining the last of it.

Rordan appeared to have regained some of his composure as he held out his glass to be refilled, a Fae immediately appearing with the wine bottle. "All of these young heirs are so eager to uproot their parents and take their seats, yet they have no godsdamn idea what they're doing. They think they are ready to rule. Have it all figured out and know how to do it better."

Tessa watched as Dagian scowled down at his plate, scraping vegetables into a pile.

"Yet when it comes to making the necessary sacrifices?" Rordan went on, sitting back so his dessert could be placed in front of him. "None of them are ready for *that*, are they? When sacrifice demands? Then we will see who is ready to have those thrones and make the hard decisions. Then they will understand the cost of the power they so desperately seek."

No one else spoke for the rest of the meal.

12

LUKA

"What?" came Theon's irritated voice when he answered the phone. Wherever he was at, it sounded loud and chaotic.

"I need your ring," Luka answered.

There was a long pause during which the background noise seemed to die down. Then Theon said, "Repeat that."

"The black onyx one. I need it."

"For what?"

"To give to the Achaz Lord."

Another bout of silence greeted him at that. "And *why* are we giving the Achaz Lord a ring?"

"Because it was part of my bargain to let me stay here," Luka answered.

"Why the fuck are you making bargains with the godsdamn Achaz Lord?" Theon demanded.

"Because *you* sent me to Tessa, and this was the only way he'd let me stay here. If you want to blame someone, blame yourself, but I'm going to need that ring," Luka replied, tipping his head back against the sofa.

He was in his room, a silencing enchantment pulled in tight around him to make sure this call wasn't overheard. It was nearly midnight, and he could feel her, restless and frustrated down the bond.

And that frustration wasn't just with not being able to sleep.

She'd been avoiding him, refusing to meet him during the regular training times. Needless to say, he was just as frustrated as she was.

In all the same ways.

"I take it things haven't been going well," Theon asked.

"You could say that. What is happening there?"

Theon's sigh was audible. "Nothing I can say over the phone."

"You know we could meet in person. It wouldn't be difficult for me to—"

"No," Theon cut in. "I'll find a way to get the ring to you. What do you think he wants it for?"

"He said it was to prove my commitment or some bullshit, but that's exactly what it is. Bullshit. I stole the ring once. I can do it again once I've fulfilled that part of the bargain," he answered.

"You and your penchant for rings," Theon muttered. But then he said, "Wait, *part* of the bargain? What else did you agree to, Luka?"

"Answering questions about my bloodline—"

"We don't know much," Theon interrupted.

"Exactly. And not to kill him."

Theon huffed a laugh. "A little arrogant of him to assume we even want to."

"Agreed," Luka said, stretching out his legs and crossing his ankles.

Silence fell between them, and in that quiet, Luka realized just how much he missed his best friend. They'd been separated before for longer periods of time, but this felt different. Theon was stepping into a new role. One they'd planned for and prepared for for years, and he should be there with him, godsdammit. At the very least to tell him when he was being too neurotic and making stupid decisions.

"How is she?" Theon finally asked.

"Do you really want me to tell you?"

"No. Yes." Another sigh before, "I feel her sometimes. When her shields slip, and she's... Are we too late?"

"I don't know," he answered truthfully. "I can't get her alone, and when I do see her, she refuses to acknowledge me."

"After all this time, everything still hinges on her," Theon murmured, and Luka could hear the exhaustion in his voice. It was the same exhaustion they were all feeling. At least he'd gotten a decent night's sleep when Tessa had slept in his bed five nights ago.

"Nothing on Axel?" Luka asked.

"No, and other matters are starting to become pressing. I can't ignore the rest of the kingdom much longer," Theon said.

"Let me leave here and go looking for him," Luka insisted.

"You're in the best place to find information, and she needs some-one," Theon said, those last words sounding full of an acceptance Luka rarely heard from him.

"There is no information to be found here if she will not speak to me," he argued.

"Keep trying. I promised her I'd always fight for her. This is the only way I know how right now. Keep trying," he repeated.

"How long?" Luka demanded.

"How long what?"

"How long are you going to make me stay here?"

"Is the Guardian bond becoming an issue?" Theon asked.

"Not like it has in the past," Luka said.

In the past when they'd been separated for more than a few days, the Guardian bond would become somewhat unbearable. The need to make sure Theon was safe and not in danger turned to paranoia the more time passed. In fact, Valter had used it as a means to control him in the same way he would use blood to control Axel. But that hadn't been an issue since he came here, which could only mean it was her. There was no other explanation, and gods, wasn't that a convenience he didn't want right now. Because every minute spent here, even with her not fucking speaking to him, was weakening a resolve he'd held firmly in place since the moment this girl had become a prospective Source. There was no way Theon understood what forcing him to stay here was doing, or he wouldn't be making him.

"How long?" Luka asked again.

There was an annoyed huff, and Luka knew his friend was raking a hand through his hair in irritation. "Another week, all right? Give it another week and if nothing has changed, we'll change tactics," Theon said.

Tactics. Strategies. This is what Luka liked to hear.

"Fine," Luka said. A muffled male voice sounded in the background, and Luka was immediately on high alert. "Who is that?"

"One of the things I can't discuss on the phone," Theon replied tightly. "I have to go."

"Yeah, all right," Luka muttered a second before the line went dead.

Letting the silencing enchantment drift away, Luka tossed his phone across the sofa. Maybe he'd just Travel to his cave tonight. He had a better chance of getting some sleep there. Yet he knew he wouldn't go. He had this same thought every night, and every night he stayed because if she happened to show up at his door again, he needed to be here. Just like Theon said, she needed to know someone had stayed for her.

And two hours later, when the bond lurched in his soul and his dragon lifted his head, he knew. She didn't knock on the door like she had last time. No, this time, she created one of those blinding portals directly into his room.

"You need to learn to Travel," Luka growled, shielding his eyes until the light faded.

He blinked a few times, readjusting to the dim lighting of the room to find her standing between the sofa and the bed. She was in an oversized Chaosphere sweatshirt that went to mid-thigh, and he had no idea where she'd gotten that thing from. The Whirlwinds logo was big and bold across the front, and for some unknown reason, he found himself wondering when the last time she'd even gotten to watch a game was.

It took him a minute to tear his gaze from her bare thighs to realize she was holding something in her hand: his shirt she'd worn his first night here. Dragging his gaze up her body to her face, he found her scowling.

Fidgeting in her irritation, she said tightly, "It doesn't smell like you anymore."

Elbow on the armrest, Luka steepled a finger along his temple as he arched a brow. He said nothing, waiting to see what she was going to do.

"Can I just...have a different one?" she finally asked after a long tense silence.

"You haven't bothered to show up to training sessions, hardly speak more than a few words to me, and avoid me at every turn. Now you show up here and want something from me?" Luka asked.

He watched her hand clench tighter around the fabric, her power flickering before she managed to snuff it out.

"I just need a different shirt," she said.

"Then get one from your own closet. I'm sure your Lord has provided plenty."

"Gods, Luka. Can you just not be an ass for one day in your entire godsdamn life?" she snapped.

"Can you not act like a brat for two minutes and have a godsdamn conversation?"

Her eyes flared violet. "I'll get it myself," she sneered, stalking towards his closet.

And he let her because he had too much on his mind to bother fighting with her tonight.

She emerged a minute later, the black shirt he'd worn that day now in hand, but she lingered in the closet doorway. Her eyes darted to his bed, the pillows and blankets all perfectly arranged in what others would call a mess. At least here, he wasn't deemed important enough to have his room tended to daily.

"No," was all he said when she opened her mouth to speak.

Her features hardened again. "You don't even know what I was going to say."

"Were you not going to ask to sleep in here tonight?" When she pressed her lips into a tight line, he said again, "No. If you can't bother showing up for training, I'm not going to let you sleep in my bed. You don't get to ice me out and still get what you want from me in the end. I'm not Theon."

She stared at him in disbelief, her mouth opening and closing a few times before she managed to find words again.

"How dare you," she seethed.

But he dared all right. Maybe he wasn't too tired to fight with her after all.

"You think I got what I wanted from Theon in the end?" she said, her fury igniting in those bands of light around her wrists. "I cannot wait to hear how you came to that conclusion."

"Are you still at his side?" Luka challenged.

"That is because of *me*, not him," Tessa retorted. "I did that."

"Did he follow?"

"He can't follow me, Luka. Not without breaking a bargain."

"That he made to make you happy."

"That he made because he thought he was outsmarting me." Then she added with a sneer, "Want to try again?"

Luka stood then, so suddenly it startled her, and she stumbled back a step as he approached. Her light had advanced, winding around her arms again, and he shifted his eyes, just to match her chaos because he could.

"You're right, Tessa. He took from you, manipulated you, and tried to cage you. But you did the same godsdamn thing. Call it revenge. Call it justice. Call it whatever you fucking want, but don't pretend you are the innocent victim in this. Maybe you started out that way, but not anymore," Luka said.

"Are you saying because I fought back, I, what? Deserved everything that happened?" Tessa fumed.

"No," he replied, leaning in closer. "I'm saying that it's a little paradoxical that you hated the monsters so much, you decided to become one only to employ the same tactics you hate. Who cares about the casualties as long as you get the ending you want, right?"

"*You* told me that the monsters take their happy endings and leave blood trails, Luka," she cried, throwing up her hands in frustration. "I am doing nothing different from you or Theon. You believe in your purpose and will sacrifice for it."

"You're sacrificing *Axel*, Tessa," he replied, his voice rising.

"Of course that's your argument," she scoffed.

His head tilted, a completely predatory move as his dragon paced, wanting to put her in her place but loving that she wasn't afraid of him. Not like she once was.

"What's that supposed to mean?" Luka asked.

"If it was someone you didn't know, if it was anyone else but Axel or Theon, would you even care, Luka?" she shot back.

He straightened, stepping back. Would he? Would he be this upset? Probably not, if he was being honest.

Her smile grew more wicked and confident. "I suppose that's the good thing about not having anyone, not *caring* about anyone," she mused. "I *don't* care if it's Axel or you or Theon. I don't care if it's Rordan or Tristyn—"

"Katya or Lange? How about Corbin?" Luka interjected, knowing full well it was stupid to keep pushing her on this tonight. Her magic was already teetering on an edge.

"What is your problem tonight?" Tessa demanded, and Luka could swear her skin was glowing faintly.

"My problem is you showing up here whenever you want," he sneered, trying to figure out when, exactly, he'd started throwing fits like the St. Orcas brothers.

She barked an incredulous laugh. "Are you forgetting that I don't even want you here? You are the one who made that deal with Rordan, Luka. Blame yourself for that one."

"And yet, you haven't told him it's all a lie. Why haven't you, Tessa? If you want me gone so damn badly, that's the easiest way, and yet you insist on being diff—"

"Call me difficult, Luka Mors," she interrupted. "I dare you."

Her voice was deadly and had that ring to it that always made him take pause. Her eyes were brilliantly violet, flecks of gold shimmering in them, and the power that wove around her arms was doing more than that now. Her feet were an inch off the ground. She hovered in the air, her golden hair floating on a phantom breeze, and what he could only describe as golden ashes were floating among the strands.

Gods, she was stunning with all that power and rage. If she could just learn to harness it, she would be unstoppable.

And before he knew what he was doing, he was back in front of her and taking her face in his hands. He *felt* her heart stutter at the action, and his dragon was pushing for more. She was right here, in his hands, and he knew she wouldn't stop him.

"You're not difficult, Tessa," Luka said, his power lurking just beneath his skin and ready if she lost the little control she still held. "But you're trying so hard to be the villain, you're walking right into the very thing you're running from."

"I have a purpose," she said, holding his gaze, but there was a thread of defeat in her tone. "I have a destiny I cannot deny."

"Says who?"

"What?"

"Who says you cannot deny destiny? Fuck, who says this *is* your destiny?"

She shook her head, his large hands still framing her face. "I wouldn't expect you to understand."

"You've never let us try."

Her eyes darted to the side, and he felt her reinforce her shields, blocking the bond.

"I told you that monsters take and leave blood trails," he said in a low growl. Her eyes flew back to his at the words. "But I also told you it didn't have to be like this, so right now, I'm calling bullshit on all of this. Everything you've just said. All the fuckery about destiny and promises, sacrifices and purpose."

"You can't call bullshit on fate, Luka."

"I just did," he answered, and before he could second guess the action, he closed the space between their mouths.

A small, surprised sound came from her, and she went still for a few seconds before she was kissing him back. This was so much better than their first kiss had been, when she'd barely been awake, let alone comprehended what was happening. She understood now. That was evident when her tongue slid out to touch his, apprehensive and unsure. Fire burned through his blood, and he was swallowing down the growl that was clawing at him.

One of his hands stayed on her cheek, cupping her jaw, while the other slid into her hair. His fingers twined into the golden locks, tugging just as he'd told her it would be if things had been different. A soft moan came from her in response, and that small growl slipped free from his throat.

He pulled back just enough to murmur onto her lips, "Let me train you, Tessa."

"No," she said. The response was breathy, but it was a firm rejection.

And it broke whatever had just happened in that kiss.

"Then you can't sleep here tonight," he said.

"Fine." She stepped back, his fingertips dragging along her jaw as she did, his other hand slipping free from her hair. Then she shoved the shirt at him that she still clutched in her hand.

"Take it," he said, trying to hand it back to her.

"I don't want it," she replied, that hardness back in her features. "I don't want anything from either of you."

Blinding light appeared behind her, making him wince and turn away. By the time it dimmed, she was gone.

Another choice where there was no one to catch him when the consequences came.

It took him several seconds to figure out where he was. This wasn't the Arius Kingdom, the Underground, or any other territory he knew intimately. No, he'd only been in this space a handful of times. This was a large lounge in the Pantheon where the ruling families gathered before a Selection Ceremony. Not the last time, of course. He'd been in the Grand Hall with Theon trying to talk him out of choosing Tessa.

But Tessa was here now. All the ruling families were. Anala and Falein. Celeste and Serafina. Rordan still headed Achaz. In fact, the only difference from the Selection five years prior was the absence of Valter.

Theon was here, clearly the ruling Lord now, and at his side was a very pregnant Felicity. Her chestnut hair fell down her back in waves, a Union Mark visible on her hand. Her eyes darted between Theon and where Tessa sat in an armchair. *Violet eyes were taking everyone in, and the air was thick with tension.*

"Axel and Brigid are the only two Selecting this year," Rordan was saying, *"so the Ceremony itself should be relatively short."*

"I still do not understand why she is here," Felicity said, looking up at Theon, *a hand resting protectively on her stomach. Her tone held nothing but disdain, and it was clear she was referring to Tessa.*

His eyes were on Tessa where they'd been this entire time. "We have been over this. There is a collective understanding."

"Is that what it is?" Tessa asked, shifting and stretching her arms above her head. Everyone tensed, and she smiled a sharp, pointed thing. The silver wolf lying at her feet didn't move, but his glowing eyes watched the room.

Theon sent her a look that would have made her cower the night he'd Selected her, but while Tessa still bore four Source Marks, Theon also still sported the Achaz Mark on the back of his hand too.

"It is more than you deserve after what you did to our kingdom. You should be in the Underground," Felicity spat.

"I wish I were," Tessa purred in response.

"Enough," Theon hissed, his darkness appearing and making his wife flinch back. Tessa, however, didn't even blink. "Unless you are suggesting you know better than the Lords and Ladies standing in this room with you, you will accept the consequences agreed to."

Tessa clicked her tongue as she said mockingly, "Someone forgot their place."

"Tessa," Theon warned.

But Felicity's smile turned as pointed as Tessa's when she replied with faux sweetness, "And yet my jewelry was a gift."

Tessa glared, and it was then that Luka realized Tessa had rings on six of her ten fingers. The type of rings that blocked power, keeping it trapped within. The same type Valter would use on them to keep them weakened during punishments. What the fuck had happened, and why would Theon agree to this?

"We all know you only have that ring because Theon needed to fulfill a bargain," the Anala Lady said. Her amber eyes went to Theon. "And Tessa is right. Your wife forgets her place."

Luka was still trying to wrap his head around everything that was happening when the doors opened, a sentinel letting them know it was time to proceed to the Grand Hall. Everyone started getting in order to get things underway, but Tessa stayed seated.

"You remember the arrangements, Tessalyn?" Rordan asked, turning and smiling at her.

Tessa's return smile was small and forced. "Of course," she replied, all her previous arrogance gone.

The Lords and Ladies filed out, and the moment the doors closed, she curled in on herself. She clearly didn't notice him standing in the corner of the room. She started tracing patterns on the chair with her finger while reciting song lyrics softly under her breath.

Exactly like she would do when she'd been locked away somewhere.

He cursed under his breath, and the wolf's head lifted, ears perking. Glowing eyes settled on him at the same time that muted violet ones lifted to him as well.

"You're not supposed to be here," she mused.

"Where am I supposed to be?" he replied.

She only hummed, returning to tracing the pattern on the chair.

He debated it for only a moment before cautiously moving forward until he stood beside the chair. The wolf gave a low warning rumble before he placed his head back on his paws.

"This feels different," she murmured.

"What feels different?"

"This dream or vision or whatever it is."

He crouched beside the chair. "How is it different, Tessa?"

"Lately they've been..."

"They've been what?" he pushed, trying to understand something. Anything.

She turned to face him, confusion coloring her features now. "I don't know how to explain it, but everything has felt different since..."

"Since you left," he finished for her.

"I had to leave," she retorted, that familiar fury flaring in her eyes.

"You don't have to do anything."

She huffed a harsh laugh. "Tell that to him."

"To Theon?"

She turned away from him again at the name, resuming her tracing. He was about to say more, but the wolf was suddenly on his feet, hackles raised and teeth bared.

"You again?" demanded a female voice.

And before he could turn around, he was yanked from the vision once more.

13

THEON

He jolted so violently his knee crashed into the table he was seated at in the manor library. Eliza glanced up at him. Razik didn't bother.

"What is wrong with you?" Eliza asked, annoyance heavy in her tone.

"Nothing," Theon replied, but she continued to stare at him. She had this unnerving way about her that always made him feel like he was this giant inconvenience solely for breathing. But she also made him feel like she almost cared in a strange way he couldn't explain.

"It's nothing," Theon repeated, getting to his feet. "I just need to take a walk and stretch my legs."

"All morning you went on and on about having to get some things done for your kingdom, leaving us to do the research as usual, and now you're going for a walk?" Eliza asked, a brow arching.

"I do not leave you to do all the research," Theon snapped. "The reason I am so behind on the 'kingdom things' is *because* I've been doing so much research."

The Fae rolled her eyes, but before she could say anything, Razik spoke first. "She is getting cranky being cooped up in this manor day and night."

"I am not getting cranky," she retorted, sitting back in her chair with a huff.

"You're right," Razik said, still not bothering to look up from the pages he was turning. "You've been cranky for days now."

Honestly, Theon had just assumed this was how she always was. Razik's constant broodiness made sense with his dragon heritage, but he didn't know why Eliza carried such a chip on her shoulder all the time. She made it well-known that the Fae were treated vastly different in her world. They ruled entire Courts for gods' sake. She led the armies of one of them and was clearly close with Scarlett. So what could she possibly have to be this upset about?

"I'm not holding you hostage here," Theon said, getting to his feet and swiping up his phone from the desk. "But if you do leave—"

"Yes, yes, I know," Eliza grumbled. "I'll need to blend in."

Theon couldn't imagine the Fae General ever blending in with the other Fae in Devram. On top of that, Razik would definitely be noticed as an unfamiliar yet familiar face. He still hadn't figured out how he was going to tell Luka about this, but like he'd told him, it wasn't something he was going to divulge over the phone either.

He jolted again as a buzzing started in his veins, his chest, his soul. The bond was straining in a way that could only mean one thing.

"I'll be back in a bit," Theon said.

But Eliza only waved him off and reached over to pull the book Razik was looking through towards herself. A smirk was playing on Razik's lips as his fingers started toying with the end of her braid. Theon still couldn't figure out how they worked together, and while he'd observed them whenever he could, he knew there was some piece he was missing. Every time he brought it up, Eliza was quick to move the conversation in another direction. Razik just flat out ignored the question.

Theon forced himself to keep a casual pace through the manor, the staff bowing their heads as he passed. Kat, Corbin, and Lange were at their daily lessons, being escorted to and from by Tristyn secretly Traveling them. Katya would have immediately figured out what was going on. She was clever and observant like that, but she'd been quiet and withdrawn since she'd returned. She'd never voiced it, but he knew the fact that Axel was still missing was weighing on her.

It was weighing on him too. He'd always protected Axel from the brunt of his father's wrath. Or he'd tried to. Another thing he'd failed at in the end, he supposed, but he'd been pouring all his time into trying to find him while simultaneously trying to initiate a smooth transition of power that was not going smoothly in the slightest.

Theon let his darkness out, releasing some of the tension coiled tightly in his muscles. The inky magic speared ahead of him, knowing what he knew too.

Tessa was here.

The bond didn't lead him to the rooms they'd shared. No, it led him to his father's study. Or his study now? He still didn't know. This was some kind of grey place that he imagined had never been seen in Devram before. Much like his entire Source experience had been.

He wiped his palms on his pants before he reached for the door. He had no idea how this was going to go. Why was she here? Did she need him? Was she going to draw from his power? What would that be like? Would there be a fight or just words exchanged? Was she by herself? Was Luka with her? Lord Jove? Someone else? The person who'd touched her when she'd taunted him down their bond?

Chiding himself for overthinking this entire thing, he turned the knob, pushing the door open.

And there she was, sitting on the edge of the desk, her legs crossed with one visible from the deep slit of her cream dress. Her bare feet were off the floor. She was so short and small, but the mighty power he could see crackling in her eyes made up for any of that. Her long, blonde hair was curled in soft waves, and she had it pulled over a shoulder. The dress had lace sleeves and a low neckline that showed off the Mark over her heart. Delicate gold thread was embroidered intricately throughout the bodice. The slightest movement made it glimmer in the low light of the room.

Leaning against the doorjamb and crossing his arms, all he could think to say as he stared at her was, "It's cold out, beautiful. You should dress warmer."

She didn't say anything in response. She only reached for the glass of amber liquid sitting beside her. Holding his stare, she took a sip, leaving red lipstick on the glass.

"I don't feel anything, so it doesn't really matter, does it?" she said, her forearm resting atop her knee, and the glass now dangling from her fingertips.

"So you're telling me if you dropped those shields you have mastered —exquisitely, I might add—I wouldn't feel anything down our bond, little storm?" he asked, pushing off the doorjamb and moving deeper into the room. He flipped a switch, the glass fireplace springing to life, and her eyes darted to the flames.

"Only loathing," she answered plainly.

He stopped a few feet from her. "I'll take whatever you'll give me."

Her head canted to the side. "And if all I am willing to give you is death?"

"You won't kill me, Tessa." But the tilt of her lips told him he was quite possibly wrong in that assumption. "Why would you when you need me?"

"I don't need you, Theon," she said in a too sweet tone.

His darkness was curling loosely around her ankle, and he was close enough to see the goosebumps appear on her flesh. From here he could also see the dark circles starting under her eyes that told him she was getting as much sleep as he was lately.

"You don't think you need me?" he countered. "Did you not make me your Source?"

Her laugh was an eerie lilt. "If I needed to replace a Source, I'm sure I could find one. Isn't that what is done in Devram?"

"You are powerful, Tessa. You need a powerful Source."

"Do I?"

"Why wouldn't you need a Source?"

That pointed smile returned as she uncrossed her legs. It was only then that he realized there was an equally deep slit up the other side of the dress, and he glimpsed the gold dagger strapped to her upper thigh.

"Did you really come here armed?" he asked, shock rippling through him.

"Don't act surprised," she scoffed. "I did tell you I was going to kill you. You are the foolish one for coming here *unarmed*."

He took a step forward on instinct. No one threatened him. It had been beaten into him for so long. All threats were met immediately with a show of power, and his hand was already coming up to reach for her throat.

Until he found he couldn't move it.

He looked down, finding a thread of light wound around his wrist.

In disbelief, he brought his eyes back to her, where her smile had turned coy. A vicious yank of her power wrenched his arm behind his back. When she did the same with his other arm, he gritted his teeth.

"You don't scare me, Tessa," he ground out.

She gave him a mocking pout. "I really, really should, Theon," she replied, and as she slid gracefully from the desk, her power yanked again.

Caught off guard, he fell to his knees. With their drastic height differences, he was still level with her torso from this vantage point, and when he looked up at her, he found she held that gold dagger in her hand.

"Is this the part where you kill me, clever tempest?" he asked, holding her stare. He couldn't read her emotions. He'd never been able to, and she still had their bond solidly blocked. He knew the only way to get those shields to slip was to make her lose a little control, and he knew all too well how to push her to that state.

"Silly boy," she chided, idly twirling the handle of the dagger in her fingers. "I can't kill you yet."

"And why is that?"

She reached out, sliding her fingers into his hair, and damn it all, he leaned into her touch, the bond leaping at the first physical contact with her in weeks. Then her grip tightened, yanking his head back. She leaned in so close he felt every word she spoke on his lips.

"I told your father I would be the downfall of his bloodline and that I would let him witness it all before I killed him. I keep my promises, Theon."

At his name, she allowed her lips the barest touch against his, and he jerked against his restraints, wanting desperately to pull her closer. Make that kiss harder. Remind her he was the only one who could give her what she needed.

But she released her hold on his hair, taking a step back and leaving him wanting more. Always wanting more from her.

"How's Felicity?" she asked casually.

He started at the sudden change in subject. "What? Why would I know that?"

"Because she's your Match," she said simply, moving around the desk. Her fingertips brushed along the surface, that dagger still in hand.

"That I never wanted."

She paused, looking over her shoulder at him. "How ironic."

And yeah, he could see the irony of that statement. That she had been forced into something she hadn't wanted, had resisted as much as he was resisting this Match arrangement.

"Tessa, I—"

"You know I could have this seat if I wanted it, right?" she interrupted, stabbing her dagger into the desktop before lowering into his father's chair. The thing was overly regal, like all his father's decor was, and she leaned back in it, running her hands along the arms. She looked like a queen more than his father had ever looked like a king.

"That seat's not yours, beautiful," he said, his darkness starting to drift around the light that bound him.

She didn't seem to notice as she said, "It could be if I wanted it."

"You can't handle the responsibilities of that seat."

She went still, violet gaze snapping to his. "What is that supposed to mean?"

"That job requires caring for those in the Arius Kingdom. I think you'd find that hard to do if your goal is to *kill* all the Arius Legacy." When she only narrowed her eyes, he pushed on. "I know you are the granddaughter of Arius, Tessa, but there's more to ruling this kingdom than merely being the most powerful. Why do you think I wanted to take the role from my father? I've never lied about that."

"No," she snapped. "You've only used *me* to try to reach that end."

"And you're any different?" he retorted, his magic gently winding into her light.

"Why does everyone keep berating me for this?" she seethed, and Theon stilled as her bands of light started rapidly winding up her arms.

The air around her stirred, charging with chaotic energy, and her next words were said more to herself than to him.

"They made me into this. They tried to make me small. Too wild. Too impulsive. And now when I join them? Become a monster? Be one of them?" Her gaze snapped back to him. "I am exactly what you wanted me to be," she said, a maniacal note to her voice. "Someone they fear as much as you."

"Together, beautiful. I wanted them to fear what we would be together," he corrected, every part of him going on high alert as what appeared to be flecks of gold and silver ashes—or maybe they were embers?—flickered in the air around her. "And not at the expense of my people. Not at the sacrifice of *Axel*."

"You made me what I am, Theon," she snapped, getting back to her feet. She wrenched the dagger from the desk, sparks of energy flitting down the golden blade. "You and Luka. Your father. Mother Cordelia. This entire fucking realm. You do not get to pick and choose the villains. You don't get to choose the sacrifices."

"And you do?"

"It is what fate demands of me," she replied sharply.

"Fate doesn't get to own you, Tessa."

"And you do?" she parroted.

"You saying this is fate is no different than the Lords and Ladies saying it is the destiny of the Fae to serve," he said, his darkness seeping into the light a little more.

Her laugh was a harsh sound. "Are you telling me you suddenly believe the Fae should have *choices*, Theon St. Orcas?"

Was he saying that? The days had been so busy and hectic, he'd hardly had time to speak with Corbin and Lange about what they knew, and when he did, they were vague. Which was infuriating in and of itself, but he was trying to... Build some trust maybe? He didn't know.

In all of this, he wasn't entirely sure what to believe anymore. But he knew he needed to protect his kingdom and the innocent people who had no idea they were about to be casualties in a war they didn't even know was playing out. He believed this as much as she believed it was her purpose to destroy it.

We were always meant to destroy one another.

He shoved the echo of her words aside, and switching tactics, he said, "I'm saying it seems a little cowardly to not care about someone who cared so deeply about you. And so we are clear, I'm referring to Axel here."

The quick clarification had that fury in her features stilling. "Do go on," she purred. "Tell me more about how *cowardly* I am."

He forced himself to rein in his own emotions just a little longer as he felt his darkness carefully prying her light from his wrists. "He fought for you, Tessa!" he snapped. "He gave you time to run from Pavil and Matias. He tried to save you the night of the Emerging Ceremony. He took you running, and— He fucking *cared*, and you clearly did not."

He got his hands free just in time to stop the explosion of power she threw at him.

Darkness met light.

He felt the force of that collision as it flared outward, but he managed to keep his feet planted. His darkness had immediately settled over him like armor. Tessa might be stronger than he was, but that didn't mean she could easily overpower him. He'd never truly fought back against her, and because of that, she seemed to think that overtaking him would require little effort. Her look of shock at him being free of her bonds was proof enough of that.

His darkness drifted along the floor, a thick, inky fog that was knee high. His shadow wings had appeared, spreading wide behind him, and he knew his eyes were more black than green right now. Orbs of black hovered near his hands, ready for him to pull weapons from a pocket realm, while his magic coiled in his palm, waiting for him to issue an order.

And Tessa was staring at him, eyes wide, but her shields had also dropped and he could feel her. There wasn't a trickle of fear. No, all he could feel was...want? That couldn't be right. But that was awe that stared back at him, as entranced as her magic seemed to be. Tendrils of light reached for his darkness. He let his power rise to meet hers, taunting and teasing. Her magic wanted as much as she did, and he wasn't surprised. Power would always be drawn to power, and despite her presence in this realm, he was still one of the most powerful Legacy in Devram. This was the first time he'd ever let her see the full extent of that.

"Like what you see, beautiful?" he asked knowingly, her power still seeking him out.

"No." But it came out breathy. Her eyes were still wandering, raking slowly over his body and lingering. That was definitely want and need coming down the bond. Her magic was in a vibrating frenzy he could feel.

"You were lying to me the other night, weren't you?"

"What?" she asked, enthralled by the magic all around her, and he realized if he didn't pull her out of it soon, he'd have bigger problems on his hands. Her magic would overtake her, and according to Luka, she still hadn't learned how to control it in the slightest.

He took a step towards her as he said, "No one else has touched you since me. There was no one between your thighs, no hands on your flesh, or lips on yours—"

"You're wrong," she said, and he felt the tug as she tried to pull her magic back to her.

"Am I?"

"Yes," she snapped, her eyes finally connecting with his. "Just last night I was kissing another. Isn't that what you *sent* him to me for?"

He went still. Luka had kissed her?

Her smile grew, and he felt her power surge in response.

And then he felt the yank on his power.

He tsked, sinking his darkness into her magic. "You think it will be that easy, clever tempest?"

She scowled, her magic surging again and her brow furrowing in concentration. She was so focused on trying to take his magic, she didn't feel his dark power winding around her. Not until it brushed along her throat like fingers.

"You might be stronger, Tessa. Your power might be greater, but make no mistake, this will not be easy for you," he said, his voice low and menacing. "But I will *always* give you what you need."

With those words, his power tightened around her throat, giving her just that— an outlet for that fury and desperation and need. Someone to challenge her because he'd come to realize that was what he needed too. He craved her defiance, pushing her to rebel, and then he'd punished her for it. It was dark and twisted, but it fed his need for control. He was seeing that now. How he'd forced her to become what he needed her to be. She wasn't wrong. They'd made her into this, and if he was too late to bring her back, he'd make sure to give her what she needed now, no matter the cost.

With a shriek of rage, her light sank its teeth into his power, and he ground his molars as a growl sounded from his chest. He wouldn't intentionally hurt her, but his power would still protect him. And *gods*, she *was* strong. If only she'd learn how to leverage that strength. She couldn't control it. She just let her power do what it wanted, letting it loose and hoping it would do what she needed it to. Sure, she'd held control for small increments of time, but she'd never hold it long enough to win a fight. She'd destroy everyone, allies and enemies. No one would be left standing if that chaos came to reign.

The power around her arms had wound along her chest and torso now, her hair a mess of chaos floating around her. With lightning at her fingertips, she dug them into the darkness at her neck, somehow *grabbing* it and ripping it from her throat.

She shoved hard at the air, and it hit him square in the chest, as if she'd physically struck him. The thing was, she'd flung his *own* power at him, and it sent him flying backwards. His wings kept him upright, but the burst of power flared wide, sending an end table crashing into the wall. It shattered, wood splinters going in all directions. Theon barely had time to get a shield up before another burst of magic was coming at him. This was *her* power though, and the charge of energy that slammed into his darkness didn't dissipate. It bounced around as if trapped inside, content to stay there, and he felt it vibrating throughout his being. Sharp jolts of power that stung, but those stings made his power angry.

A whip of lightning shot for him, and with a hand coated in inky power, he grabbed it the same way she'd grabbed his power. He tugged, and Tessa stumbled forward, her torso hitting the desk she still stood behind. He heard her soft grunt across the room, and when her eyes found his, he knew that fury was only growing. He pulled harder, and she scrambled atop the desk so it wasn't digging into her stomach, but she threw out a hand, forcing him to dodge another burst of light flecked with whatever-the-fuck those gold and silver embers were.

Keeping a firm hold on the light, he conjured a thicker shield around himself, hoping it would be enough for her magic to bounce off of rather than forcing him to go entirely on the defensive. It'd been a long time since he'd had to call on the full strength of his gifts like this because usually—

Black flames erupted between them. He heard Tessa's scream of surprise, but Theon took the moment to take a breath and readjust his grip on her magic. Luka was exactly the reason he rarely needed the full strength of his gifts. The Guardian bond always drove him to intervene.

The flames receded, Luka standing between him and Tessa, where she was still standing on the desk.

"What the fuck are you doing?" Luka demanded, gaze scanning Tessa before he turned to Theon.

"Just having a conversation," Theon answered, breathing hard. "What the fuck are you doing here?"

"I figured with the two of you in one place—"

He was cut off by Theon's darkness shoving him to the side to avoid yet another onslaught from Tessa, and she didn't stop this time. Apparently Luka's appearance had given her a moment to regain her composure too because light was followed by a burst of wind, and then came a streak of lightning that skittered along the floor, spearing out to the walls. It kept coming, and while he was busy getting Luka out of the way, he took a hit to the ribs.

"Motherfucker!" he growled, his power already converging and clawing at the power that was sinking into his bones.

She struck again, and he lifted a hand, a shield propelling her magic to the side. A window cracked and shattered, glass shards somehow spraying inward rather than outward.

"Tessa!" Luka barked, fire wreathing his hands as he took a step towards her.

"No!" Theon snarled, his power pushing his Guardian aside again. "This is our fight, Luka. Stay out of it."

"Stay out of it?" Tessa sneered. "Didn't you send him to interfere? Glad to see those double standards extend to more than just me."

"If you'd bother to listen to either of us, you'd know that's not the case," Luka retorted.

"I can't trust you!" she cried. "I can't trust anyone!"

"What in the name of Anala is going on in here?"

Everyone spun at the female voice. Eliza and Razik stood in the doorway, and fuck. Luka's face had gone slack in a rare show of emotion.

"Um, Raz...?" Eliza trailed off.

"I see, *mai dragocen*," Razik replied, his sapphire stare pinned on Luka.

The silence stretched on until Tessa started laughing, a maniacal thing of glee.

"What is so funny?" Theon gritted out.

"Everything," she mused. "Eventually, Theon, you're going to have to let others in on your plans, because all you ever seem to do is give people more reasons not to trust you."

"And what about you?" he retorted, noting that Luka had regained his composure but refused to look at him.

"I've told you from the beginning I was an excellent liar," she said, that insanity bleeding into her features as she looked around the room. "But you create just as much chaos as I do, don't you?"

She leapt from the desk, seeming to float to the floor before she was striding towards him.

Luka didn't try to intervene. He didn't even tense at the danger prowling towards his Ward.

Tessa stopped a few feet from Theon, her head tilting back slightly so she could look into his face. "Your father has a place in the Leisure District of the Underground. Speak with the Alpha and Beta, and bring a fair bit of coin."

Nothing about what she'd just said made any sense. His father didn't have any holdings in the Leisure District, and the Alpha and Beta who ran it were fickle and not to be trusted. They'd turn their back on an ally for a better offer in a heartbeat.

A portal burst to life behind her as she spun to leave, but she paused just before she stepped through it. Looking over her shoulder, she added, "To be clear, this favor is for him, not you. Because I did, in fact, care for him too."

And then she was gone.

"Luka, wait. Let me explain," Theon started, seeing his friend extinguish the flames that were still in his hands, almost as if he'd forgotten they were there.

"I need to go make sure she doesn't destroy anything," he answered before he disappeared into the air.

Theon pinched the bridge of his nose between his thumb and forefinger, squeezing his eyes shut. He inhaled deeply, holding the breath for several seconds before exhaling harshly.

"I'm going to assume that was Tessa," Eliza started carefully. "But the male was..."

"My Guardian," Theon said, opening his eyes and meeting Razik's shocked gaze. "And if your queen is to be believed, he's also your brother."

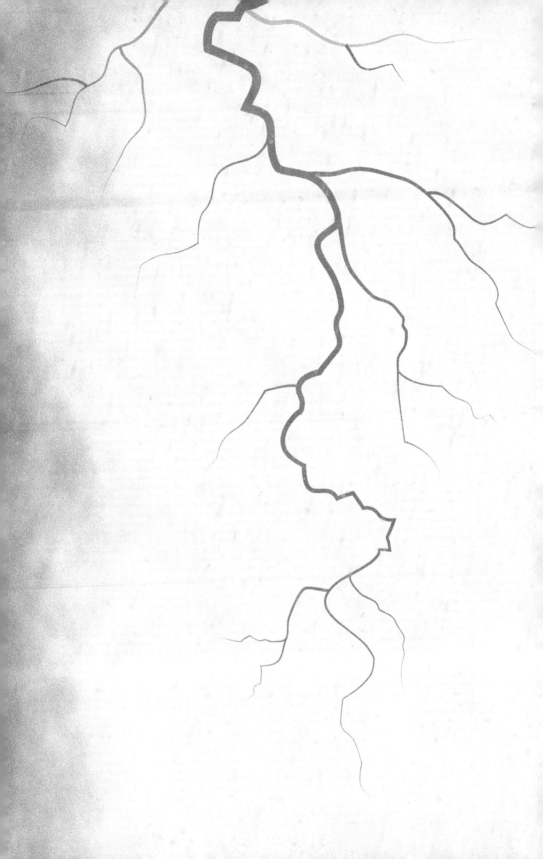

14

TESSA

She stepped onto the bank of the Wynfell River just outside the Acropolis in the Arius Kingdom. Tessa didn't know why she'd come here. Going back to Faven would have been the wise thing to do, but her power was still too restless and angry, and she couldn't get it under control.

Her bare feet sank into the snow that had accumulated, but she didn't feel the cold as it tried to seep into her bones. The hem of her dress was immediately soaked, wet fabric sticking to her shins and ankles. Threads of light still wound around the length of her arms, her chest, her stomach. Each footstep was echoed by lightning, and not that she had anyone she could admit it to, but she was becoming rather alarmed at the fact that she couldn't rein this power in.

Useless.

That was what she was with this power. Utterly useless.

Yes, she was stronger than Theon. Yes, she had a theory that she was the most powerful being in Devram, but she would have lost that fight with Theon in the end. All he'd done was defend himself. The little power he had used against her wasn't the full extent of what he could do. That was evident by the way he'd let it manifest around him, and that had been…intoxicating. It was the only word she could think of to describe how Theon had looked with his darkness drifting around him, shadow wings spread wide. She hadn't been able to tear her eyes away. And her magic?

Gods, her power had wanted as much as she had, and it had tried to take. It had lunged for him, snapping any leash she had on it. Theon had met it blow for blow, wielding his darkness with a precision and skill she couldn't even fathom having. It shouldn't have surprised her. His goal was to have control over everything. Of course he would have complete control over his magic before he'd even reached thirty years. He wasn't even that much older than she was. Five years at the most. She certainly couldn't use the excuse that it was because her power was more extensive when she had just witnessed what still couldn't have been the full extent of his. What would it have been like if he *had* eventually drawn from her?

Mud was squelching between her toes. She'd worn a path where she was pacing next to the partially frozen river. Her dress was now not only wet, but dirty. Her power was still tangled around her. She usually loved it when her magic did this. It made her feel safe and guarded. She didn't need to depend on someone else to protect her. She had her light. That was all she needed. But now she felt...chaotic.

Out of control.

Impulsive.

Wild.

And the urge to just give in, to let her magic have its way for good, was so strong as it writhed in her soul, demanding more and more of her. Taking what it wanted. She remembered Theon once telling her that if she let it, her magic would consume her until there was nothing left.

Nothing left didn't sound so bad...

That thought bounced around her head as she slowly turned to the river. The water near the banks was frozen, but the current in the middle was violent, breaking off chunks of ice as it moved. Could she even drown? How do you kill the daughter of a god?

No, Tessa, came a growl down their bond. At the same time a dark voice said, *Don't you dare, little storm.*

She shook her head, the sounds of their voices quieting her chaotic thoughts. She didn't want to cross the Veil. At one point in her life, maybe, but not now. Not most days anyway.

"What do we have here?" came a croon that had Tessa spinning. "A little Source where she shouldn't be?"

She watched as a tall, wiry figure slunk from the shadows, wearing some sort of long cape. It had a hood that was pulled up, keeping his face hidden from the sun. In fact, not an inch of flesh was visible, and that only confirmed to Tessa what she already knew: he was a Night Child.

"I'm not a Source," she retorted, her light converging in her hands, energy sparking.

"Maybe not to the Arius Lord, but you are a source of something," he answered, stalking closer.

"Who sent you?" she demanded, remembering how Theon had told her the vampyres were often hired as mercenaries.

The male tutted disapprovingly. "You know I cannot betray my employer. Even if I wanted to, a Secrecy Mark prevents me from uttering a single word."

The sound of snow crunching underfoot had Tessa turning to find another vampyre appearing. And another. And another. This was the Underground all over again, except this time, she was by herself.

Her heart hammered as they drifted closer, her power vibrating around her. She'd expended a decent amount with Theon, and now her magic was ready to feast and refill. She had no control over it, and a part of her didn't care. Her light flared out in a wide radius, the Night Children hissing and flinching back.

"He betrayed his own people by bonding with you," the leader of the group seethed. "For a decade they have preached to us of freedoms. They have told us they see us as more than the rest of the realm views us. Then he brings *you* to the Underground with all that godsdamn *light*, proving what we've always suspected."

"So you turned on him and partnered with another?" Tessa sneered.

"Clever little source," he crooned, daring to slink closer. "I still won't tell you who."

She gave him a simpering smile. "Then I guess my light will search your darkness for the answer."

She tried to direct her power where she wanted it to go, like that day in the training arena when Luka had popped up behind her and talked her through it. She turned her hand, trying to get the positioning just right, but when the power arced, it hit too far to the left.

The vampyre stared at the spot for a long moment, and then he laughed, the others joining in. "Here we were worried," he replied, pulling back his hood and baring teeth with canines that were too long. "But I know you're going to taste divine as I drain the life from you."

"You can't kill me," she retorted. "I'm not a Legacy."

"No, but you are the death of this realm," he returned, and then they attacked.

Any semblance of an organized defense evaporated as she descended into panic. Her magic took over, and it tugged at her, begging her to give in and let it have complete control. She tried. Gods, did she try to hang on, but when she didn't willingly give in, it yanked itself free.

And while it protected her, it was terrifying. The last time this had happened, she'd loved it. She'd loved that people now feared her, feared what would happen when she appeared, but her power did not seem to care who or what it was devouring. She was fairly certain it would take from friend and enemy at this point.

Shrieks of pain rang out as her magic moved. It didn't take them all at once. It was strategic, going after them one at a time and reveling in their misery as it took and feasted. And with each death, it strengthened. With each life it took, her hope of regaining any semblance of control lessened.

But if she called others to fight, maybe she could calm the storm in her soul.

She'd left her dagger at the Arius manor, and the sword seemed overkill. Bracing herself, she brought her wrist to her mouth, preparing to sink her teeth into it and draw blood. Her lips had just touched her skin when ashes swirled before her.

"Do not even think about summoning the Hunters and letting them loose here," Auryon said in a clipped tone, two arrows already flying through the air.

Moments later, howling sounded. Roan and Nylah burst from the surrounding foliage. Tessa didn't know how they always knew when she needed them or how they always managed to be *where* she needed them, but she was grateful as they took over the fight.

But that gratitude soon devolved into familiar feelings of inadequacy and disappointment. She was supposed to be this all powerful being, the strongest in Devram, and she still had to be fucking rescued.

A scream of frustration ripped from her throat, and her power followed suit, screaming from the sky. Lightning struck, but there was no rhyme or reason to it. Some of them struck true, killing a vampyre. Some hit the ground, the snow melting and smothering any flames that tried to ignite. One struck dangerously close to Roan, and Tessa cried out in worry as the wolf lurched to the side to avoid the hit.

Then she cried out in terror as a vampyre attacked him, his fangs sinking into Roan's throat. The wolf let out a snarling whine, twisting and trying to shake the vampyre free, and Tessa was running, *screaming*.

Her feet slipped in the snow more than once, but she was too terrified to try to use her power. With her lack of control and training, she could very well hit Roan instead of the Night Child.

She was, however, pulling that golden sword from a swirl of light. As she got closer though, she couldn't get a clear shot as the wolf and vampyre continued to roll, red staining the once pristine white snow.

"Auryon!" she screamed, unsure where she had gone or where Nylah was.

Useless.

That was how she felt as Roan let out another pained whine. The vampyre was strong and so incredibly fast. Anytime it looked like Roan was about to get the upper hand, the Night Child found another tender spot to sink his teeth into.

Until black flames wound their way around the vampyre. The fire moved like twisting snakes, singeing and burning as it wrapped tighter and tighter around the being. The screams were all his now as the black fire dragged him away from Roan.

Tessa didn't bother looking around for Luka as she stumbled to the wolf, dropping down beside him. His light coat was wet and matted with dark red, and she didn't know where to touch or what to do. She couldn't tell where the wounds were or how to even begin to stop the bleeding.

"Auryon!" she screamed again. "Auryon, help!"

This time there was a swirl of ashes before the female was crouching beside her.

"Shit," Auryon muttered, then she let loose a shrill whistle. It was answered by a howl, and moments later, Nylah was prowling forward.

"It was just a vampyre," Tessa said, her breaths coming too fast. "It was just— They can't kill him, right? They can't— It was just a vampyre."

Nylah nudged Roan with her nose, and the whine that came from him had a sob crawling up Tessa's throat. These wolves were hers. They were hers without question. Their loyalty to her had been freely given. She hadn't had to earn it or prove herself to them. They were a connection to a past she hadn't known she had, and she had done this to him. All he had ever done was protect her from harm, had been a steadfast companion, and she had done this because she couldn't control her godsdamn magic.

Her hands thrust into his fur, sticky blood covered her fingers. She looked up at Auryon. "A vampyre can't kill him, right?" she repeated. "He's not a normal wolf. He's not— Is he going to die?"

"The Night Children are predators by nature," Auryon said, her smoky magic drifting over Roan as if cataloging all his injuries. "While their magic was taken from them, they retained their enhanced senses and were given the means to survive."

Tessa shook her head, feeling the tears track down her face. "That didn't answer my questions," she cried. "Is he going to die?"

"It is possible," Auryon said. "And likely if something is not done in the next few minutes, but I do not know who can help him here."

She couldn't get a breath down. Any air she sucked in seemed to get caught in her throat, never making it to her lungs. Roan's breaths were shallow too, his ribs scarcely rising on an inhale.

"But he's not a— He can't— He's not a real wolf," she insisted as Nylah dropped to her belly. Her head rested between her front paws, glowing eyes fixed on Roan, and a soft whine sounded from her.

Tessa didn't notice the male that stooped beside her until large hands were taking her shoulders. She jolted, her magic lashing out, but he didn't release her.

"I know where we can take him, Tessa," Luka said grimly. "I can't make any promises he'll survive, but—"

"Yes," she said immediately. "Take us there. Now."

"But you should know—"

"This is me asking you to catch me, Luka!" she sobbed. "Please, Luka. Please!"

He nodded, glancing over her head at Auryon. "Make sure we're all touching."

A second later, Tessa felt the now familiar tug at her naval before they reappeared inside somewhere. She looked around, and it only took a moment for her to recognize where they were.

She lurched to her feet, frantic as a large black horse stuck his head over the top of his stall gate, huffing in irritation. Whirling to Luka, she demanded, "Why are we here?"

"Because you asked me to help, Tessa," he said calmly. "Theon keeps a Healer on staff specifically for his horses and hounds."

She hadn't known that. She'd avoided these areas as much as possible, mainly because the animals terrified her at first, but now...

Swallowing thickly, she glanced down at Roan. The wolf's eyes were closed, and her own welled with tears again just as the stable door swung open and Theon strode in.

He wore the same casual attire he'd been in a mere hour ago. His gaze connected with Luka for a moment, before he nodded and those emerald irises found her. He stayed back, shoving his hands deep into his pockets.

"Shea is on her way," he said.

Tessa nodded, her hands fisting in the sopping mess of her dress. She assumed that was the animal Healer.

"You don't have to do this," she murmured, unable to look at him. "I mean, I would understand—"

"Is it what you need?" Theon cut in.

She swallowed again, nodding once.

"I promised to always give you what you need, and I also keep my promises."

Ignoring what those words did to her, she turned her back on him, lowering to Roan's side once more. She stroked his head, tracing the edge of his ear with her finger. Leaning in close, she whispered in a strained tone, "I am so sorry. Please don't go. Please don't leave me here after we just found each other."

There were silent tears tracking down her cheeks now, and once again, Luka had to pull her back a minute later.

"Shea is here," he whispered into her ear. "We need to give her room to work."

Tessa nodded, letting Luka tug her to her feet. A Legacy with black hair pulled back in a bun was beside Roan now. She was smaller than Tessa had expected, maybe only an inch or two taller than she was, but she was already holding her hands over the wolf. A faint blue-silver light was emanating from them, her brow furrowed in concentration.

"What is she doing?" Tessa asked, only then realizing Luka had her loosely held to his chest, her fingers curled tightly into his shirt.

"In the simplest sense, she is seeing all the injuries. She is no different from the Healers for people," he answered.

"I've never seen a Healer work," she said tightly. "I'm usually unconscious for this part of the assessments."

Luka didn't say anything to that, but she could feel Theon's gaze on her and knew he was listening to everything being said.

"He is more than wolf? Like your hounds?" Shea asked, looking up at Theon.

"I don't know," he answered. "Auryon?"

The female's features were tight where she stood a few feet away, Nylah sitting beside her. "Yes," she answered.

"I am going to need more than that," Shea replied, pulling things from her bag.

"They are Trackers," she answered.

"You mean they are relatives of the Trackers," Theon clarified.

Auryon shook her head. "No. They are Trackers. From the god realms. Arius gifted a litter of Trackers to Temural as a gift when his powers emerged. These are from that litter."

"But that means a vampyre cannot kill him, right?" Tessa interrupted. "Because he is not a normal wolf?"

"Trackers can be killed," Auryon said, swirling eyes fixed on the injured wolf. "They are not invincible."

"What are the odds here, Shea?" Theon asked.

"I don't know," she answered. "I've never worked on a Tracker."

"I will send Cienna and Gia to help."

Tessa looked at him out of the corner of her eye. His eyes were studiously fixed on Roan and Shea, that muscle in his jaw twitching.

"Their knowledge would be appreciated. Is there somewhere we can move him?" Shea replied.

"You can't move him!" Tessa spluttered, shrugging out of Luka's grip and lurching forward. "You could make it worse."

"I'll help move them wherever they need to go, Tessa," Luka said.

"No," she snapped, the bands of light around her wrists that had dimmed flared faintly.

"Tessa, we need to listen to the Healer here. They are the knowledge-able ones."

"Here is fine," Shea said, glancing up at them. "We can move him if we can get him more stable."

"*If?*" Tessa demanded.

"Why don't you take Tessa up to get some fresh clothing," Theon said, addressing Luka. "I will stay with the wolf and Auryon. I'll let you know if there are any new developments." Finally, he met her gaze. "Is that agreeable to you?"

She didn't know. She was so torn because she needed to get out of this dirty sopping dress and clean the blood from her hands, but she didn't know if she could leave Roan's side. On top of all that, Theon was giving her a choice, and that was doing things to her she didn't even want to try to process right now.

So she did what she did best and shut it all down. Her thoughts. Her feelings. She shoved all of herself down deep to keep the world out, and she said in a monotone voice, "Yeah, all right."

"Are you sure, Tessa?" Luka asked, his tone low.

"Yes. I will be no help here."

She could feel him studying her, but after a moment, she felt his hand settle on her lower back. They'd only taken a few steps when Theon called out, "The others from earlier today are in my rooms."

She felt Luka stiffen, but he only said tightly, "Noted."

It was snowing when they stepped out of the stables and into the gardens. Big flakes were swirling on wind gusts that made the air sting against her flesh. Luka's fingers wrapped around her elbow, tugging her to a stop. "Now that we are away from Shea, I can Travel us."

"I can walk," she said flatly.

"You're not wearing shoes, and you are…" His gaze flicked to the sky, then back to her. "You're hardly wearing anything. Walking through this weather in wet clothing is not ideal."

"Fine," she said, the word as flat and clipped as the rest had been.

Seconds later they were standing inside a bedroom she had never been in before, but she immediately knew it was his. It had the same modern decor of Theon's rooms. Only rather than blacks and greys, this room had deep navy blues and dark browns. The bed wasn't quite as big as Theon's, seeing as how it wasn't made for three, but the plush comforter and nearly a dozen pillows took up a lot of the space. An overstuffed soft brown leather sofa was in front of a fireplace that Luka had switched on, and all she could think was how silly it was that he had a fireplace in his room when he could just make his own. More than that, he was always hot to the touch. What did he need a fireplace for?

Theon's rooms were always neat and tidy; everything had a purpose and a place. But Luka's space had the same odd trinkets scattered about like he had at the townhouse. Little gold statues, a strange assortment of random dishes, silver candlestick holders, and small bronze tins were throughout the room. Without thinking, she made her way to one. Lifting the lid of a larger tin, she found it inlaid with velvet, at least twenty different rings lying inside. Why did he have all these?

His throat clearing from behind her had her closing the lid before she turned to him. He'd lost his shoes somewhere, and the light from the bathroom was casting a warm glow onto the floor.

"You should shower, temptress. Get out of those wet clothes and warm up some," he said.

She rolled her eyes. "There is nothing tempting about me at this moment." She lifted her hands, dried blood caked to them, in emphasis.

Luka said nothing, but she felt something shudder down the bond. She was just too apathetic to think about it right now.

Without another word, she walked to the bathroom, shutting the door behind her. She peeled the dress from her body before stepping into a shower just as grand as the one in Theon's suite. Thankfully, that meant she already knew how to work the different knobs.

Hot water poured over her, and she watched as the pink-tinged water swirled down the drain at her feet. Eventually, she washed using whatever she found in the shower. Luka had more hair products than Theon used, likely because he kept his hair longer. When she stepped out of the shower sometime later, steam had enveloped the bathroom, the mirror fogged over with condensation.

Using a fluffy navy blue towel to dry off, she wrapped it around herself before stepping up to the vanity and swiping a palm along the surface. Violet eyes stared back at her, flecks of dull grey breaking through. Part of the second Mark was visible, peeking out from beneath the towel, and she traced a finger along it. She knew she should get back to Faven, but something about the familiarity of this place had her entire being settling after the events of the day. And could she really leave Roan here and go back without him? He'd been her companion since she'd gone to Faven to begin with. He had been her sense of normalcy there, had been what grounded her, and now he would be gone too.

Moving mechanically, she wandered through the doorway that led to a large closet. Suits and formal attire lined an entire wall, and she dragged her fingers along the sleeves until she came to the back wall. There was a larger dresser that spanned the entirety of it, an odd assortment of empty frames were meticulously displayed across the top. She pulled open a shallow top drawer only to find more rings. Silver and gold, copper and platinum. The variety was vast. Different gems, different sizes. She picked up a gold band inlaid with sapphires and emeralds, turning it over in her hand before putting it back.

Pushing the drawer closed, she moved to the next wall. It was a smaller selection of clothing, but seemed to be more casual, and when she came across a hooded Chaosphere sweatshirt, she tugged it off the hanger and slipped it on. Of course it was huge on her, oversized and reaching to her knees. And it was the Firewings. That team was terrible. Not nearly as good as the Whirlwinds, even if they had beaten her team the last time she'd watched them play.

Unwrapping her hair, she hung her towels up before rummaging through drawers to find a brush or comb. When she finally emerged from the bathroom, she found Luka on the sofa, one foot propped on his coffee table. He was scrolling through something on his phone, and he glanced up at the door opening. His eyes went back to his phone before they immediately snapped back to her.

She paused, fingering the hem of the sweatshirt. "I didn't have anything to wear."

It took him a few seconds before he said, "You can wear that."

"I still don't understand how you can like the Firewings," she added.

His lips twitched, some tension easing from his posture. "Theon sent a message that Shea is still working on Roan. Cienna and Gia are there now too."

Tessa nodded, swallowing down the fresh tears threatening to pool.

"Do you want me to take you back down there?" Luka asked.

"No," she said softly. "I think I am just in the way there."

"You are never in the way, Tessa."

She didn't have a response to that as she shifted on her feet. "I'm not ready to leave. Not until I know he'll make it."

"We don't have to leave until you're ready," he answered, setting his phone aside.

"Okay."

A silence fell over them that was awkward and strained until finally Luka said, "Come here and sit."

She moved stiffly, her body feeling as if she'd done some strenuous activity today when in reality she'd done nothing but endanger a friend she loved.

That was all she could think about as she settled onto the sofa next to Luka. She needed the comfort of the bond right now.

Staring into the flickering flames trapped behind the glass, she said, "Luka?"

"Yeah?"

"I want you to train me. To fight like you and Theon. To control this power." She paused before saying again, "I want you to train me."

His arm came around her shoulders, and a jolt of pleasure shot down her limbs at the sensation. Pulling her a little closer so she nestled into his side, her temple fell to his shoulder, resting there as he said, "That's my girl. We'll start tomorrow."

15

AXEL

He watched the drop of blood slide down the wall. It was slow, leaving a red smear in its wake.

It wasn't dark here, just like Bree had promised. He was curled on his side on a soft bed, the comforter stuffed with feathers and pillows everywhere. It reminded him of the way Luka always arranged his bed, but he didn't really care about the luxury or the comfort. Not as another drop of blood followed the first.

He'd gotten up plenty of times to taste it. Tried to catch it on his finger. He'd even gone so far as to lick the godsdamn wall. It always disappeared. A figment of his imagination. After numerous attempts, he'd stopped trying. Now he'd been lying here for hours, tortured by visions. Was this how Tessa felt? At least her visions eventually became real in some way.

Another drop of blood came. Another. Another. Another.

He was empty.

His power wells were empty.

His soul was empty.

Maybe Bree's request wouldn't be terrible. In fact, the longer he lay here, the more he had trouble remembering why he shouldn't take it. He wouldn't have to hide anymore. He wouldn't have to struggle with the cravings. His father wouldn't be able to use his weakness to control him.

Another drop of blood.

It was so pretty against the rich brown of the mahogany wall.

Her blood would be prettier.

Her hair was shinier with those ebony curls that reflected the light.

Why had he been avoiding this for her? Bree would find her, and she could come with him.

A kitten and a monster.

It was a perfect balance.

He smiled to himself as he watched another drop of blood trickle down the wall.

She would come to him, and he wouldn't be empty anymore.

Another drop.

Just a little longer.

That was what he told himself as he rose from the bed and tried to catch that drop of blood.

Again.

And again.

And again.

16

LUKA

Luka snatched his phone off the side table, looking to make sure the vibration that alerted him to the incoming message hadn't woken Tessa. She'd fallen asleep against his shoulder an hour ago, and he'd eventually eased her down to a pillow resting against his thigh. He'd let her sleep, knowing she likely hadn't slept decently since the last time she'd been in his bed. Idly, he wondered if now that she'd agreed to train with him, if that meant she'd be seeking out his bed more often. He ignored how much his dragon liked that idea as he flipped the phone over and saw who the message was from.

> **Theon:** Where are you?
> **Luka:** Bedroom. She's asleep on my sofa.
> **Theon:** On my way. Living room?
> **Luka:** Meet you there.

Despite the fact that they *could* communicate down the bond, neither of them chose to do so. There was something too intimate about it when it was just the two of them speaking. It was different when it involved Tessa, almost as if it needed to be the three of them for it to make sense.

Tessa's brow pinched in her sleep as he slid off the sofa, trying not to jostle her too much. He grabbed a plush blanket off the end of the bed and draped it over her before making his way to the living room. He left the door to the bedroom open. If she woke, he wanted to make damn sure she knew Theon was out here before she triggered the bargain. The bond would likely tell her, but he wasn't taking any chances.

The wards around his room alerted him a second before Theon came through the door. He looked as tired as Luka felt, and he assumed it was because no one was getting any sleep. He couldn't believe he was actually wishing they were all sleeping in that cramped small bed back at the townhouse.

"How is she?" Theon asked.

Luka shrugged. "She showered. She's getting some sleep. She agreed to train."

Theon arched a brow. "Really?"

"The wolf nearly dying really shook her up," Luka said, moving to his small kitchen. There wasn't much there though, considering he hadn't been staying here.

"I can order some food to be sent up," Theon said, already reaching for his phone. "I'm sure she'll be hungry when she wakes too."

While Theon busied himself with that, Luka got himself a glass of water, drinking the whole thing before placing the glass in the sink. The two of them had more to talk about than just Tessa, and he didn't know where to begin. How had things gotten so fucked up in such a short period of time?

"I suppose you haven't had a chance to substantiate what she said earlier today?" Luka asked when Theon came over and took a seat on a stool at the island.

"About the residence in the Leisure District that my father supposedly has?" Theon asked. When Luka nodded, he sighed and said, "No. I will need to go there. I doubt Kylian and Giselle would answer any correspondence, but if it's true, it's a brilliant place to hide Axel away."

The Shifter Alpha and Beta would likely demand an audience to answer any questions. They would feel snubbed with anything else.

"So you'll be going to the Underground then?" Luka asked.

"I guess."

"You're going to the Underground without me?" he clarified.

"She needs you more right now," Theon said, glancing at the open bedroom door.

"I am still your godsdamn Guardian, Theon," he snapped, his lungs burning a little as he exhaled a plume of smoke in agitation.

"I know you are," Theon retorted, his power appearing in his eyes and answering a challenge on instinct. "She's the most important thing right now. That's what I need you guarding."

Right. Because it was so easy to spend all this time away from him. It was still a godsdamn bond that apparently affected him more than Theon. Maybe he was just more focused on Axel right now, but this had never happened before Tessa.

"I'll take Tristyn with me," Theon supplied.

"Blackheart?" Luka demanded. "You cannot be serious."

Theon sighed again. "He's proven himself valuable a time or two, and he's been helpful as of late. He has standing with the elite of Devram, and he can access information with his company."

"So you trust him now?"

"Not implicitly, but he is trying to help with Tessa."

"Who are they?" Luka asked, done with the subject of Tessa right now.

"Razik Greybane and Eliza," Theon said, knowing exactly who Luka was referring to. "They are from Scarlett and Sorin's world. Eliza is his Source, but not like a Source here. I'm still trying to figure it all out. They are limited in what they can share so they don't tempt fate or whatever," Theon said. "But Razik is... I think Scarlett believes he is your brother, and this is why I couldn't tell you anything over the phone."

Because even if Razik wasn't related to him in some way, which was highly unlikely given how much they resembled each other, the implication was clear. The male *was* a Sargon Legacy.

"He can shift?" Luka asked flatly.

"I haven't seen his full dragon form, but he can isolate it. Like you," Theon answered.

"He believes we are related?"

"I don't know. After the encounter this morning, he and Eliza retreated to the rooms they are staying in. I didn't see him again until I had to ask him to Travel me here, and even if we'd had time, he wouldn't have discussed it with me. He doesn't speak much, is easily irritated, and... Well, he's..." Theon waved a hand in Luka's direction.

"Thanks," Luka deadpanned.

"It's not an insult," Theon replied. "He has the same qualities as you. The biggest difference is he's more knowledge driven rather than strategy driven like you are. The guy knows *a lot* of shit, and he can often interpret Cienna's nonsense that is never nonsense."

"Sounds like you have plenty of help then," Luka muttered.

Theon paused. "Are you—"

"No," Luka cut in, straightening from where he'd been leaning on the counter. "I'll keep Tessa busy while you handle...every other facet of the plans."

"Luka, you can't be serious. That's not what's happening here," Theon said.

He blew out an irritated huff. Luka understood his disbelief because when had he ever acted like this? He did what needed to be done to make sure their plans succeeded. Even when Valter sent him on his own errands to the Underground, he carried out orders because it was leading to something bigger, and suddenly here he was, throwing a fit like the St. Orcas brothers did. But he'd never felt so...inconsequential. The thing was, the Guardian bond made the need to protect Theon strong, and the dragon in him viewed Theon as *his* because of that bond. The bigger problem was that the dragon was also seeing Tessa as *his* these days, and Luka didn't know what to do with any of it. It was irritating, and it was making him irritable in return. They called Theon possessive, but when his dragon claimed something as his? Luka felt as out of control as Tessa often was.

And suddenly he was wondering if Razik experienced the same thing. Was it a normal trait for his bloodline? What about the instinct of knowing if objects were valuable? Would the male bother to sit down and talk with him? Did he even care they might be related? Might be *brothers*? Were there others like him? Or was he alone in his home world too?

"Luka?" Theon said, low and urgent. "You know that the reason I sent you to Tessa is because—"

The sound of a throat clearing had them both straightening and turning to the doorway. Tessa stood there, and Luka watched as Theon took her in, wearing his sweatshirt and little else.

"Tessa, how are you?" Theon asked, pushing off his stool and standing, but he'd taken all of one step towards her and she was stepping back. Glancing at Luka, her eyes narrowed into an accusatory glare.

"We were just talking, temptress," Luka said, coming around the island. She didn't step back from him, and Theon clearly noticed, judging by the way his mouth pressed into a thin line.

"About me," she clarified.

"Some," Luka admitted. "But not all of it."

"Right," she said doubtfully.

"Despite what you seem to think, not everything is about you," Luka replied dryly, stopping a few feet from her.

"Such an ass," she muttered under her breath. Her eyes darted to Theon. "How is Roan?"

"Stable from what I understand," Theon answered, his hands slipping into his pockets. "Auryon and I helped move him to a back room in the kennels. It is where I keep my females when they are close to birthing a litter."

Tessa nodded slowly. "Auryon is with him now? And Nylah?"

Theon glanced at Luka, and he could feel the trickle of hope down the bond. Tessa speaking calmly and rationally to him was not something they'd witnessed often. She'd also just experienced a near-devastating loss. Her heightened emotions usually made her hysterical, not... this.

"Yes, Auryon stayed with him along with the other wolf. Shea is also there monitoring. I told her to do whatever was necessary," he answered. "But Cienna agreed he should survive. The recovery period is unknown right now."

Tessa nodded again, fiddling with the hem of the sweatshirt and drawing both the males' eyes to her bare legs. "Auryon said they are not wolves. She said they are Trackers."

"She did," Theon agreed.

"And you believe her?"

Theon arched a brow. "You do not?"

At the question, the bands at her wrists sparked, the same flashing in her eyes. "She lied to me. For months. About who she is and what she is doing here. I trust no one."

"That's fair," Luka said. "But it doesn't negate the fact that she is knowledgeable."

"That we know of," Tessa countered. "She could be lying about everything for all we know."

Theon rubbed at his brow with his thumb and forefinger as he said, "Trackers are real, Tessa, and based on what I've seen between you and them, she speaks truth. I didn't know they still existed, or I would have put it together sooner. Or rather, I didn't realize they could enter Devram."

"What are they?" Tessa asked, moving closer to him, and Luka knew she didn't realize she was doing that.

"Trackers were—*are*—exactly what they are named for. They emerged from the Chaos bound to the Firsts. A pair for each of them," Theon explained.

"So they're like the gods?" Tessa asked, her head tilting with interest.

"No," Theon said, shaking his head. "They have gifts, but they are not nearly as powerful as the gods."

"Then they are like Guardians?"

Theon shook his head again. "Bound maybe isn't the best term. They are not driven to protect like a Guardian bond between a Sargon and Arius Legacy. They can choose not to, but their unique gifts allow them to always track the one they are tethered to. They can Travel, and have an immortal lifespan like the gods they emerged with. Strength and speed like the Night Children, but they don't need blood."

"But they can die?" Tessa asked.

She'd drifted so close now that Theon could reach out and touch her if he wanted to, and Luka knew he wanted to. He could tell it in the way his fingers twitched at his side. How he leaned closer the smallest amount. How his eyes went from her hair to her mouth to her eyes, as if he was memorizing every detail because he didn't know when he'd see her again.

"They can," Theon answered. "Many have."

"How?"

"That is something we would have to ask Auryon. I do not know the specifics."

Tessa went quiet for a minute, her attention darting around the space, and Theon dared to glance at Luka. He just shrugged in answer. She was utter chaos waiting to explode in this moment, and he didn't know how to prepare for that.

"But there are more? They...mated or whatever?" Tessa asked, drifting away from Theon and wandering around the living room.

Touching things.

Things that were *his*, and yet nothing stirred in his soul as she picked up an antique frame and turned it over in her hand. No, now his dragon slept peacefully, not even opening an eye.

Fucking useless thing.

"If what Auryon said is true, then yes," Theon was saying.

"She said they were mine," Tessa muttered.

"It would appear that is the case," Theon said. "That they are indeed tethered to you in some way."

"But how? If I have been here, unless—" She stopped abruptly, her gaze connecting with Luka's. He arched a brow in question, unsure why she'd suddenly sought him out.

Tessa turned away from him, setting the frame down and making her way around the room some more. He knew as soon as she reached for her hair what was coming next, and sure enough, her mutterings were to herself rather than to them.

"He knows. I need to go back. We have a deal. He has to tell me. I'm holding up my end of the bargain."

At those last words, Theon's attention snapped to Luka, accusation heavy in that one look.

"I have no idea who or what," Luka said in a low voice. Then he jerked his chin in her direction because they needed to be listening. She tended to reveal things when in this state. The things she said were as nonsensical as Cienna's words most of the time, but they always made sense later, when whatever she was speaking of came to pass. The difference was Cienna *knew* what she was speaking of; Tessa didn't understand any of this.

"He wasn't here, and I wasn't here. They were not here. No one belongs here. Fix the balance. That's what we need to do," she continued, that light of hers winding up her arms again.

She stopped so suddenly it was as though she'd hit an invisible wall.

"Can he return with me? Roan, I mean?" she asked Theon.

He hesitated, clearly trying to say whatever he needed to in a way that would not set her off.

"It was a risk to move him when we did," Theon ventured. "And that was only a short distance. But you can, of course, stay here until he can—"

"I can't *stay* here," she cut in.

Theon stiffened. "Of course you can."

"No. I can't," she repeated. "Is that why you helped?"

Theon took a step towards her, and she held her ground. There was no flinching. No keeping space between them. There was no nervousness or fear down the bond, and Luka found himself proud of her for this one act of standing up for herself. For once, she wasn't depending on someone else to do it for her.

"I already told you, little storm," Theon said, his voice rough in a way that had a visible shudder roll through Tessa. "I will always give you whatever you need. Roan is clearly important to you. Therefore, he is important to me."

He took another step, and still she did not move. But her throat bobbed with a swallow.

"If you wish to stay here, you can stay in our rooms. I will stay elsewhere," he added before she could object. "If you choose to go, I can send updates as often as you'd like."

"Such pretty words," she murmured.

"I've never lied to you, Tessa," he replied.

Luka knew Theon didn't realize he was doing it. It was an impulse, a natural reaction to the bond and her and everything they weren't supposed to be. But his hand came up. Tessa was so lost in his stare, she didn't notice it either. Not until the barest of touches when his fingertips brushed her cheek.

Then she jerked backwards, her bare feet tripping on the rug beneath them. Her power flared, lightning crackling around her, and Luka lurched forward to put himself between them. He still felt the sting of her power as it collided with his flames, and *now* the dragon beneath his skin was wide awake.

"I cannot stay here," Tessa sneered, any trace of vulnerability completely eradicated. "Keep Luka informed on Roan. I'm sure you call him for regular updates anyway."

"I don't—" Theon started, but he cut himself off before he finished whatever he was going to say. "I will keep Luka updated on Roan."

Turning to Luka, she said, "I need pants."

"You have plenty in the suite," Luka replied, gesturing to Theon.

Chewing on her bottom lip, she asked in a clipped tone. "Will you get them for me, please?"

"Yeah," Luka said with a sigh, knowing exactly why she didn't want to go in there. He wasn't sure if she'd ever step foot in those rooms again. "Just stay here, all right?"

"I know the rules," she drawled sarcastically.

"You also never care to follow them," he drawled in kind.

A knock on the door drew her attention, and she went rigid, her power immediately swelling around her.

"Easy, baby girl," Luka said, any trace of sarcasm gone. "It's food."

"Food?" she repeated in confusion.

"There's nothing here to eat since I haven't been staying here. Theon ordered food." At her sour face, he added, "Burgers and fries."

"It is not," she scoffed.

But sure enough, when the food was set on the island counter, it was three bacon cheeseburgers and fries that had Tessa drifting back to the kitchen. While Luka took a seat though, Theon did not.

"I will go grab some clothing from...my rooms," he said. He paused, watching her, but she was resolutely refusing to look at him now. "I will check in on Roan while I am gone too."

She nodded, still looking anywhere but at him. Luka felt his sigh of resignation down the bond before Theon turned and left the room. The male wasn't blocking anything, which meant Tessa was also feeling everything as long as she wasn't completely shutting them out, but she probably was.

After a couple bites of her food, she said sharply, "Don't do that."

Luka paused, his burger halfway to his mouth. "Don't do what?"

"Sit here and wait for me to apologize or whatever."

"What would you have to apologize for?"

She set her own burger down, wiping her fingers on her napkin as she turned on her stool to face him. Her knees bumped against his, and she didn't seem to notice since she didn't fucking move them.

Godsdammit.

"You think I should be...nicer to him," she accused.

"I did not say those words at any point in time."

"You don't have to," she groused, shoving her food away.

"By the gods, you have to eat something, Tessa," he growled, pulling her food back once more. "I know your power doesn't seem to require food to regenerate. Or blood." He went quiet for a minute when she looked anywhere but at him. "You know how your power refills, don't you?"

When she still wouldn't look at him, he reached out and took her chin, tipping her face up to his. Violet eyes finally connected, hard and unyielding. He couldn't blame her. They'd made her into this. They'd forced her not to trust them. He certainly didn't expect her to apologize to Theon for anything, but he could know all of that and still know she was choosing the wrong side in all of this. Know that they were all villains, but some were worse than others. He was just running out of ideas on how to prove that to her.

Releasing her chin, he sat back. "Eat up, baby girl. While your power might not need it, your body does. It's already been a long day, and it's barely past high noon."

She eyed him as though looking for a ruse in his words before she cautiously said, "You'll still train me?"

"Why wouldn't I?"

"Why *would* you?" she countered.

"That power is a danger to the entire realm if you can't control it, Tessa," he answered.

"But by training me, aren't you basically training me to..."

"Kill everyone in the kingdom I've worked my entire life trying to protect and free from a power-hungry Lord? Yeah, I guess I am. But at least it will be contained to just the innocent people here rather than the whole of the realm," he replied, picking up his burger and taking another bite.

Tessa was quiet after that, finishing her meal without another word. When Theon came back, he didn't come in. Luka met him at the door, where he handed over a few pairs of leggings, jeans, and tops, along with her phone and earbuds. He gave Luka a quick update on Roan, and then he slipped the onyx ring from his finger and handed that over too.

"I don't know when I'll see you again, so you may as well take this now," Theon said, his voice low. "I have to get back to the Acropolis. Razik and Eliza are waiting for me."

He paused, and Luka wanted to ask if the male had even asked to meet his possible relative, but he pushed down that impulse.

"The wolf is in the kennels if she wants to see him before you leave," Theon added.

"I know it goes against everything in you not to be with her, guarding her, keeping her sheltered and safe, but she needs to see for herself, Theon. All the things you've tried to protect her from? She needs to see to understand. Just like Axel had to," Luka said.

"That's why I sent you to her. Because I can't..." He trailed off, stepping back from the doorway. "I'm not the one for that. I wish I was, but that can't be me. I'll update you later tonight on the wolf."

Then he was striding down the hall, already scrolling through emails on his phone as he went.

Shutting the door behind him, he turned to find Tessa cleaning up their dishes and placing them in the sink.

"He didn't eat," she said, picking up his plate with the untouched burger and fries.

"Can you blame him?" Luka retorted, crossing the room in a few long strides. He took the plate and passed her the clothes. "Put pants on. We can go see Roan before we go."

She nodded, not bothering to go to the bedroom. She just placed everything on the sofa, slid on a pair of leggings, and left his giant sweatshirt on. While she did that, he went and found a bag. He shoved some of his own clothing into it before grabbing her extra clothes too. None of it was white or cream or light.

Gathering her still damp hair atop her head, Tessa started looking around for a hair tie. Luka sighed, opening a small wooden box on the table beside her and pulling one out.

"Thank you," she murmured, peering inside the box. Then she paused. "What are all those rings for?"

"Nothing," he muttered, slamming the lid shut.

"You're broodier than usual today," she grumbled.

"Yeah, well, I had to come break up a fight between you and Theon, rescue you from vampyres, and just found out—"

Her head canted to the side when he stopped talking abruptly. She didn't ask what he'd been about to say, but he suspected that was because she already knew.

"It's already been a long day," he finally finished.

She nodded slowly, but said nothing else. Shifting on her bare feet, she worried her bottom lip, and he wished they could just go back into the bedroom and sit on the sofa doing nothing for the rest of the day.

"We should go see Roan and get back," Tessa said.

"I know you have said you cannot stay here—"

"I can't, Luka," she interrupted. "This place holds... I can't."

"I understand that. You can't stay here, but you also do not have to go back *there*," he said.

"Where else would I go?"

"Anywhere else."

"There is nowhere else for me to go," she said, all of her features hardening once more. "Not until I fulfill my purpose. Then I can leave this place forever."

She brushed past him, pulling open the door and stepping into the hall, and as Luka followed her, he knew she hadn't been speaking about Arius House with that statement. He also knew Theon would never truly let her go.

The thing was, the more time he was forced to spend with her like this, the more attached his dragon was getting to the idea of keeping her too.

Because he never gave back things that were *his*.

17
THEON

Fifteen Years Ago

"Come on, Theon. Just play one game with me," his brother begged, tossing the chaosphere ball back and forth in his hands.

"I already said no, Axel," Theon gritted out, looking between his tablet and the open book in his lap and comparing the texts.

He checked the time again. Eighteen minutes. That was how much time he had before he needed to go back inside. He was due in his father's study in thirty minutes. That would give him plenty of time to make sure he was early.

"You promised, Theon," Axel said, and Theon could hear the irritation and disappointment. His tone was bordering on a whine at this point.

If Axel's power had emerged, he'd likely have shadows drifting around him with his growing emotions. At least, they all assumed his power would be shadows like the rest of the Arius line. There was no reason he wouldn't have the same gifts, and they would emerge when his emotions were heightened. Eight years was too early. It was more likely to happen around ten years. Axel was counting down, and Theon was hoping his magic showed up later than other Legacy. When power appeared, that was when their father sent them for more intense training.

"I promised I'd come outside," Theon corrected, grabbing a pen and underlining something in the book. "Here I am. Outside."

"You're an ass," Axel retorted.

"Don't cuss," Theon replied, only half-listening to him.

"You and Luka cuss all the time."

"We're older."

"Where is Luka anyway? He'll at least play a round with me while you read your stupid books," Axel grumbled, dropping the ball to the ground and kicking at it.

"You should read some stupid books," Theon retorted. "Term starts next week."

"I'll read books then. Where's Luka?"

"Not back yet."

Truth was, he didn't know where his best friend was. His father had started sending Luka to training camps that lasted days at a time. He was supposed to be home today, but Theon didn't know when. He didn't like it when he was gone. When they were together, he could at least try to keep things under control, but when he was gone...

"Theon, just one quick game," Axel whined, bending to pick up the ball again.

"No, Axel," Theon growled, his darkness snapping out and wrenching the ball from his brother's hands. He sent it flying across the makeshift chaosphere field.

"I liked you better before," Axel muttered, turning and wandering off to retrieve the ball.

Before what? Theon had no idea, but he didn't have time to worry about that. One day Axel would understand. One day his brother would realize that he was protecting him. One day he'd see that everything he was doing was to keep everyone he loved safe, and he really only loved a handful of people: his brother, Luka, Caris, and Pen. As long as they were safe, he didn't really care what it cost him. If it required disappointing them from time to time, so be it. Control the situation, and you control the outcome. That was what he was coming to learn. Do whatever it takes to keep control because control meant keeping everyone safe.

Which is why when he glanced at the clock again, he began gathering his things and placing them into his messenger bag. Book. Tablet. Pen. He checked three times to make sure his phone was still there. He'd only made the mistake of misplacing his phone once. His father had made sure of that.

Leaving Axel to kick his chaosphere ball around, Theon started the trek back to the house. As he went, he recited the names of all his father's advisors, where they lived, their bloodlines, their gifts, and what roles they played in his *father's kingdom. Then he started going through all the ruling Lords and Ladies, their heirs, and who they were watching as potential Sources. Then it was the history of Devram. All things a future Lord of the Arius Kingdom should know.*

All things he made sure to know so he wouldn't feel the sting of Eviana's vines full of thorns his father would use for lashings to help him "remember." Vines that wound around his limbs and throat, keeping him immobile. If he forgot anything this afternoon, those lashings would tear open the wounds still healing from this morning. Axel had left his messenger bag on the floor in the foyer rather than taking it to his room, but Theon had told his father it was his.

But that was just for now.

One day he'd be as powerful as his father. One day he'd have a Source of his own. One day he'd rule Arius Kingdom, his father would be a nightmare long past, and they could prosper whether or not the rest of Devram recognized them.

One day.

But that day was not today.

He paused when he reached the floor of his father's study, straightening his tie and adjusting the cuffs of his suit jacket. He was just lifting a hand to knock when he heard footsteps.

"When did you get back?" he asked when Luka came to a stop beside him, adjusting his own shirt cuffs. He didn't have a suit jacket on, but he did have a button-down shirt and tie.

"Just now," his friend replied. "Was summoned straight here."

The hair on the back of Theon's neck immediately stood on end. That was never a good sign.

"Ready?" he asked Luka after another few seconds.

Luka nodded.

"Enter," his father called after Theon had rapped his knuckles on the study door.

He went first, Luka right behind him. Eviana was in her usual chair, turquoise eyes flicking from him to Luka and back. Two of his father's advisors were also here—Julius and Mansel—and Theon shoved down the fear. He knew what their gifts could do.

"Take a seat," was all his father said.

Present Day

His phone ringing pulled Theon from the memory, and he sighed when he looked down at the screen to see who was calling.

"Hello, Mother," he answered, continuing to stare out the window. The skies were grey like they always were these days. They were already experiencing record snowfall this winter season thanks to a certain... Was she a goddess? He didn't know, but he did know she was responsible for the weather, even with her spending most of her time in Faven. Somehow the Acropolis was still experiencing the extent of her wrath.

"Theon? The help said you were here today," his mother said, worry and disappointment sounding in her voice.

He rubbed at his brow with his thumb and forefinger. Razik had Traveled them back to the manor outside the Acropolis, scarcely sparing him a glance before he'd Traveled somewhere else with Eliza. That was over an hour ago. He'd been standing in this same spot in the study since then.

"Yes, I was there," Theon answered.

"Was?" Cressida demanded.

"Yes. Sorry I didn't have time to visit."

"Theon St. Orcas, your father is missing. Your brother is missing. And you can't spare a minute to check on your mother when you come home?"

He winced because when she put it like that... But who was she kidding? She'd been anything but motherly during his childhood. More than that, Axel had clearly been her favorite.

"Do you have news of your brother? Your father?" Cressida continued.

"A few potential leads, but nothing concrete," he answered.

"Is that what you were doing here?"

"No. I was there to meet Luka and Tessa."

He was greeted by silence at that statement. It went on so long he pulled his phone from his ear to make sure the call was still connected.

"Mother?" he finally said.

"Tessa was here?"

Her voice was cold and more serious than he'd ever heard it.

"With Luka. Yes."

Whatever had come over his mother seemed to disappear, her voice back to its usual feminine lilt, but there was still an icy undercurrent to it. "Was she well?"

"What do you mean?"

"She appeared...unharmed?"

"Luka was with her. Of course she was unharmed. Why are you upset?"

"She wronged you, Theon. A mother has a right to be upset when her son is wronged," she admonished.

"She is still my Source, Mother," he answered, turning to the door when a knock sounded.

"Yes, but I do not believe for one second it is a coincidence that your father and brother disappeared shortly after her declaration of freedom. Do you think she did something to them?"

Theon rolled his eyes at the worry in his mother's voice, despite it being well-founded. Tessa *had* done something to his father, and he wished she'd finished the job.

"She wouldn't hurt Axel, Mother," he answered as the door opened, and Tristyn Blackheart walked in.

Theon held up a finger to signal he'd be a minute, and Tristyn nodded, turning to peruse the shelves of the study.

"And she can't hurt your father," his mother was prattling on. "He's the Arius Lord. She'll only be able to hurt him if the Achaz Lord helps. What are you doing about this, Theon?"

"I'm working on it," he gritted out.

"Where are you?"

"Back at the Acropolis."

"How did you get back there so fast?" Before he could figure out an answer to that, she said, "Oh! Have you learned to shadow walk? As wonderful as that is, Theon, you need to be careful until Tessa is dealt with."

"No one is *dealing with* Tessa but me," he retorted. "Unless you know something I don't?"

"Of course not," his mother tsked. "You are the Arius Heir, Theon."

But something wasn't sitting right with her questioning and her tone.

"Mother, if Father told you something—anything—I need to know."

He saw Tristyn slowly turn to face him, clearly eavesdropping on the conversation.

"All I know is that my son came home and couldn't be bothered to even look in on his mother," Cressida said, her tone bordering on hysterics now.

For the love of Arius.

"I will try to make some time to see you in the next few days," he replied, ignoring Tristyn's impatient gesture telling him to wrap things up.

"I should hope so," she replied.

"Goodbye, Mother." He hung up before she could reply. Slipping his phone in his pocket, he said to Tristyn, "Everything go all right today?"

The male usually just dropped the Fae off and left. He only lingered if he had information to share.

"As far as I know," Tristyn answered.

"Are you sticking around? Tessa was here this morning, and—"

"Tessa was here?" Tristyn interrupted. "How was she?"

Theon blinked at his concern. "I'd say she was channeling her Arius lineage this morning because she was the epitome of a death-seeking goddess. But shortly after that, she learned that being the most powerful doesn't always guarantee victory. It has been a long day, to say the least."

He gave him a brief rundown, and when he finished, Tristyn said, "Roan is stable, though?"

"Cienna was still there when I left."

Tristyn nodded, relief flashing in his russet eyes. "She will be able to keep him alive."

"Did you know they were Trackers?"

"Yeah," he admitted. "But there's only so much we can say before we are tempting fate."

Every time someone uttered those words, Theon wanted to punch something. Fate this and fate that. As far as Theon could tell, the Fates had abandoned their world as much as the gods had. If anything, the Achaz Lord was using the Fates to convince Tessa her purpose was to wipe out the Arius line.

But that was neither here nor there right now. He needed to talk to Corbin. He needed information about these supposed revolutionaries, and he was done playing games.

"I'm assuming you have news since you're still here," Theon said, heading for the door.

"Not so much news as a push in a direction," Tristyn said. "You're running out of time, Theon."

"You think I don't know that?" Theon snapped. "You know, you've never made it clear what stakes you have in this. Why does all this matter to you? You and Auryon pushed her to this state as much as I did."

For the first time that he could remember, the male didn't have a quick comeback. He was quiet as Theon led the way to the living area where the Fae usually congregated in the evening. When he got there, though, he only found Corbin and Lange.

"Where is Katya?" Theon asked.

"She didn't say where she was going," Lange answered. "But if I had to guess, she went to look through books. She was not herself today."

He was seated next to Corbin, who didn't look up from the computer he was typing away on. Theon had given him one to see if he could find his way into some databases and discover...well, anything really. But Katya hadn't been "herself" for some time now. She kept pushing forward, her determination never wavering, but even Theon could tell she was starting to break.

"I am going to go find her, but then I'm coming back here," he said to the males. "Tessa was here today and gave me some information, but you two need to start talking about what you know about the Underground."

The males glanced at each other, but neither said anything.

Theon turned, nearly running into Tristyn. He'd forgotten the male was still here.

Sighing, he said, "Say what you need to, Blackheart. I'll add your cryptic warnings to the list of shit I need to figure out."

"You know I'd be clearer if I could, right?"

"Would you?" Theon challenged. "Because from where I'm standing, you had *plenty* of time to interfere, to give your warnings, to do fucking anything, but you waited until Tessa appeared."

"What was I supposed to do, St. Orcas?" Tristyn demanded, and Theon could swear his eyes had a faint light green glow to them. "What would you have done if I'd shown up here and told you a godsdamn thing? Would it have changed your plans? Altered your course of action? Would you have let her be knowing what she is? Somehow I doubt that. This is bigger than you. Bigger than Devram. There are so many moving parts to all of this, you have no godsdamn idea. One misstep and this realm becomes nothing but a memory."

"What difference would it make?" Theon said. "That's all we are to the gods anyway."

"That's not—"

The soft sound of a throat clearing had them both turning to find Katya standing there, a book in her hand. It was the book Cienna had given her that Theon knew she had been painstakingly translating. Her curly black hair was piled atop her head, and Theon could see how tired she was in her amber eyes. He was positive that was Axel's shirt she was wearing with her training pants, and he didn't know where she'd found the chaosphere tee shirt she had knotted in the front.

"Sorry to interrupt," she said.

"You're not," Theon replied. "I was actually just coming to find you."

She nodded, tucking a stray curl behind her ear. "What can I help with?"

"It's not so much what you can help with, but that I think you'll want to be part of this conversation," he replied. "Tessa came to see me today."

That had all the Fae turning to him.

"But before we get into that, did you find something?" Theon asked, nodding at the book she held, a page marked with her finger.

"I don't know," she answered, shifting on her feet. "But I... This is going to sound a little crazy, but I don't think Axel is doing well."

"That doesn't sound crazy. I am sure he is suffering," Theon said, his brow furrowing.

"No, I..." She blew out a harsh breath. "It's more than that. It's like I can *feel* him sometimes. And then I found something. But I might have translated it wrong, and I—"

"Let me see," Theon said, moving closer.

"I'm sure I translated it wrong," she said hesitantly, letting him open the book to the page she still held.

Inside was a sheet of paper with her transcription on it, and Theon skimmed the words before glancing back to her. She was worrying her bottom lip, watching him.

"This refers to a bond. The Source bond?"

Katya shook her head. "I don't think that's what it is. It seems similar, but also different."

"Looks like I don't need to push in any direction after all," Tristyn said, and Theon turned to find the male with a small smile, his hands in his pockets. "And perhaps the Fates haven't abandoned this realm as much as you think."

"What are you talking about?" Theon asked. "What do you know about this?"

Tristyn appeared to debate the questions for a minute before he said, "I know some, but I believe your visitors would know far more than I do."

"Razik and Eliza?"

Tristyn nodded.

"They've been here this whole time and said nothing?" Theon said, his annoyance and frustration already rising.

"They have to be careful about what they say," Tristyn answered. "They do not know what is common knowledge here and what is not. Their purpose is singularly focused. They cannot deviate from it, or they risk—"

"Tipping the balance. I'm aware," Theon cut in. "At this point, I don't give a fuck if it tips as long as Tessa isn't the sacrifice for it."

Tristyn fell silent, but the look on his face told Theon he'd stumbled upon something profound.

"No," Theon snarled. "She will *not* be the sacrifice to correct this."

But Tristyn didn't speak another word.

"All this time she's hated me and accused me of trying to use her for her power, when it's been everyone else all along," Theon sneered, stalking from the room and barking orders to the Fae to follow him. He didn't stop until he was outside the suite that Razik and Eliza had been staying in, and darkness gathered around him as he pounded on the door.

"We need to talk about some things," Theon called out, pounding on the door again.

It was wrenched open, an irritated female on the other side. "You are incredibly needy today."

Theon didn't reply to the taunt. Instead, he held up the book, still open to the page Katya had translated, and showed it to Eliza. She skimmed the page for only a few seconds before she said, "Razik?"

He appeared immediately, glaring at Theon. "What do you want now?"

"Raz, look," Eliza said, pointing at the pages.

The male's eyes narrowed. "Where did you get that book?"

"That's not your concern at the moment. What do you know about this bond?" Theon asked.

"Can you read this?" Razik asked instead.

"Not fluently. It takes hours to translate, but I didn't translate this.

Katya did," Theon answered. "She says she can feel Axel at times, but that is something common between a Source and Master."

"Except it's not," Eliza said, pulling the door open wider. "You all should come in."

A tense silence settled over them as they filed into the sitting room off of the main bedroom of the suite. Tristyn was last, still conspicuously silent. Katya perched on the edge of an armchair while Lange and Corbin took a seat on the sofa. Theon remained standing, crossing his arms and waiting for Eliza or Razik to speak.

"When Scarlett was here, she started working some things out," Eliza started. "But none of us could figure out how it would be possible. Only certain bloodlines can create new Marks."

"Which ones?" Theon interrupted.

"Zinta and Taika."

"Scarlett is neither one of those, from my understanding."

"Yes, but her history is not black and white. She...attained other powers. She does carry some of that lineage and *can* create new Marks. That is not the point though. We keep telling you that your Source Marks are not Source Marks, but the Marks you do use..."

Eliza trailed off, looking up at Razik.

"There is more than one type of bond among the realms," Razik said with a sigh that said he found everyone in this room to be annoying for not already knowing this. "The Source bond you all have here is not what it was intended to be. Instead, someone, at some point in time, took a sacred bond and desecrated it."

"Could you be any more vague?" Theon asked, his irritation matching Razik's.

Razik shrugged. "Probably."

"Stop," Eliza cut in again.

She pulled her hand from the sleeve it was currently curled around and held it up for them to see. A Mark was on the back of it, tendrils of black branching out and winding around her thumb and first two fingers. She elbowed Razik in the stomach, and he sighed, holding up his left hand as well. The same Mark graced the back of his hand, tendrils winding around the same three digits.

"Scarlett and Sorin had a similar Mark," Theon said, stepping closer to study their hands.

"Not similar. The same," Eliza said. "Only theirs was complete."

"What does that mean? Complete?"

"There is a bond called a twin flame bond," Razik said, his arm coming around Eliza's waist and his hand resting on her hip. "The Mark is a twin flame Mark, and if both accept the Mark, it initiates something called the Trials."

"What are those?" Theon asked, still studying the Mark.

Scarlett had never let him get a good look at hers, and he'd been too busy trying to find Axel and figuring out everything about Tessa to really worry about the Mark on these two. And yeah, he felt foolish realizing a potential answer had been in front of him this entire time. But they could have said something. *Anything*.

"The Trials aren't particularly important here," Razik answered. "What *is* important is what twin flames can do. Once the bond is initiated, they can feel each other's emotions and speak to each other via their thoughts."

Theon slowly lifted his gaze to Razik's. "Repeat that."

He didn't.

Instead, Eliza said, "And once the bond has been completed, they can combine the strength of their power so one or the other can use it."

"I fail to see how this differs from the Source bond," Corbin cut in. "We simply call it something different, no?"

Eliza shook her head. "From what I can gather, the Fae here do not *choose* the Source bond, but that is not the most concerning part. Finding your twin flame is not particularly common. More than that, it is not limited to only the most powerful. Any Fae and Legacy could be twin flames."

"So this bond can only occur between a Fae and Legacy?" Theon clarified.

"Correct," Razik answered. "It is said the bond is a gift to the Fae from the gods as a thank you for being a source of power for their legacy."

"It is *not* something to be forced upon the Fae," Eliza cut in, her tone hardening. "If accepted by both sides, it is something to be revered. A twin flame is the one soul you are destined to be with, have been joined with since the beginning of time. It is believed the souls of twin flames recognize each other, somehow finding each other among the stars, and this godsforsaken realm has used it to force the Fae beneath them."

Theon had taken a step back as she'd spoken, flames igniting in her eyes and embers mingling with her red-gold hair.

"We didn't know," Theon said, the words almost a whisper.

"*Someone* knew," she retorted. "Someone did this."

Razik tugged her gently into his side, bending to brush a kiss to the top of her head. She nodded, and Theon understood then that all this time they'd been using their twin flame bond to communicate. Sorin and Scarlett had done the same. Eliza untangled herself from Razik, disappearing into the bedroom.

"She needs a moment," Razik said.

"We didn't know," Theon repeated, unsure of what else he could say.

"I gathered that," Razik replied dryly. "Scarlett told us her suspicions, but to be honest, we didn't believe her. To take something so sacred and use it to… We didn't believe it until we came here."

"And you're sure?"

Razik nodded, moving to the side table and retrieving a book. He flipped it open, and Theon immediately recognized the four Source Marks. Setting the book on the coffee table, Razik sat next to the Fae on the sofa, placing his hand beside the pages.

"It took a while to place it all, but it appears with your advancements in this world, they have somehow deconstructed the twin flame Mark," he explained, and Theon could see some resemblances.

"But the first Mark is just the symbol of a god," Lange said, leaning forward to see. Katya had done the same, Corbin looking over Lange's shoulder.

"That's the one I still haven't quite figured out," Razik said. "But I think that part is some of the Source Mark. When the actual Source Mark is given, one power has to overtake the other. The next one though." He tapped on the second Source Mark. "That one is this part of the twin flame Mark."

Razik traced a few lines on his hands.

"The third Mark is this portion," he went on, tracing another portion of the Mark on his hand. "The last Mark took me a little while to work out. There are small traces of the twin flame Mark, but it also has the actual Source Mark in it along with—"

"The Guardian Mark," Theon finished, looking between Razik's hand and the Source Marks. He was right. It was subtle in some ways, but he was still right.

And somehow Scarlett had seen this instantly when she was here.

"Your queen is clever," Theon muttered, still studying everything.

"She's not my queen," Razik retorted.

Theon glanced up at him. "I thought she was the High Queen of the World Walkers?"

"And I am not a fucking World Walker."

"But Eliza serves in her Court?" Katya asked, and thank the gods he wasn't the only one confused now.

"She is the general of the Fire Court. Technically, she serves under the Fire Prince," Razik said, withdrawing his hand and leaning back against the sofa.

"Whom Scarlett is married to," Theon said.

"Yes, but Scarlett's brother rules another continent. *His* wife is my queen," Razik answered. "Speaking of, where is Auryon?"

"What does Auryon have to do with anything?" Theon asked, returning his attention to the book before him. But then his gaze whipped to Katya in understanding. "You believe you and Axel are twin flames."

It wasn't a question, and he watched as a blush colored her cheeks.

"I didn't say that, but that thought may have occurred to me," she answered. "But after hearing everything about it, I don't think it was an accurate thought."

"Why not?" Lange asked. "You're Fae. He's Legacy. Isn't that the requirement?"

"It is," Razik answered.

Which meant Tessa couldn't be his twin flame, Theon realized. She couldn't be anyone's anything because she wasn't Fae or Legacy.

She couldn't be his, despite these Source Marks trying to force her to be just that.

"You said you could feel him, though?"

They all turned at Eliza's voice, finding her standing in the bedroom doorway.

"I can't say for sure," Katya murmured, her eyes fixed on her hands that were folded in her lap.

"Yes, you can," Eliza said, moving back into the room. Razik tracked her every move, already on his feet and meeting her halfway. He took her chin, tilting her head back. Again, they said nothing, but Theon could tell some silent exchange was happening.

That.

That was what he'd been wanting with Tessa.

Not the relationship he saw between his father and Eviana.

Not the bonds he witnessed between the other Legacy and their Source.

But *that*.

He just hadn't realized it, and now? Tristyn was right. He was running out of time, and he still had no idea how to get to... Well, *that*.

"You felt him?" Eliza said, coming to stand in front of Katya. "When?"

"I..." Katya started, her eyes darting to Theon, and he nodded for her to go on. "I don't know if I did."

"How well do you know him?" Eliza asked. "Did he send you into hiding to protect you?"

"Yes, but..."

"And the two of you were inexplicably drawn to each other?" Eliza pressed.

"Not right away," Katya argued.

"But Axel was," Theon interjected. "The moment he saw her at the Emerging Ceremony. He insisted we claim her for the Arius Kingdom. Did so before we could stop him."

Katya was blushing once more as Razik said, "A male usually feels the pull first."

"And when emotions are incredibly heightened—fear, sadness, agony —the other can sometimes feel it even before a Mark is taken," Eliza said. "If you think you felt him, there is a good chance you did."

Katya was staring at them as she whispered, "He is not well, and I..."

"You can find him," Eliza said.

"What?" Katya and Theon asked at the same time.

"Taking the Mark, if it is a true twin flame bond, will allow her to speak to him. He can tell her where he is. Or at the very least, give her a description of his surroundings. She'll be able to feel the bond as she gets closer to him," Eliza said.

Just like the first Source Mark.

"But what if they're not twin flames?" Corbin asked, everyone turning to them now.

Eliza pressed her lips together, her eyes flicking to Razik. He was the one to answer.

"As with any Mark, there is a cost. Taking the twin flame Mark is an offering of a piece of one's soul to another. If the two are true twin flames, their souls recognize one another, and the Trials are initiated. If they are not, the Mark fades after time, and the piece of the soul offered fades with it. Some believe they have found their twin flame but are too afraid to test it against the Marking, so they are content to simply be together without the bond," he explained.

"But if I take it and Axel does not, how would we know?" Katya asked.

"Taking the twin flame Mark without a companion is offering a piece of your soul up for anyone to find. It is drawn to its twin flame, but if it is not accepted, it continues to try to find its counterpart and drains its owner of their power. It weakens them until they have depleted their magical reserves or until something else finds it," Eliza said quietly.

"Something else?" Corbin interjected.

"There are plenty of beings in the various worlds. Some who gain their power from the souls of others," Razik said darkly.

"There is another way to find him," Theon cut in, not liking the sound of any of that for Katya.

"What do you mean?" Katya asked,

"It was what I needed to discuss with you. Tessa was here today and gave me information that might help us find him."

"Might?" she repeated skeptically.

"I don't know how true it is, but we can start there. She said my father has holdings in the Leisure District of the Underground. If that's true, I did not know such holdings existed," he replied.

"How will you know?"

"I need to go visit the Shifter Alpha and Beta. They control the Leisure District and would know."

"When will you go?"

"That's the thing," Theon said, rubbing at the back of his neck. "I've sent a formal request to see them, but I have to wait for their reply."

"You are the Arius Lord," Katya said, panic creeping into her voice as she pushed to her feet.

"I know, but it's best not to piss them off when I'm not officially appointed yet," he replied.

"It's been weeks, Theon," she insisted.

"I know, Kat. I know, but…"

But one misstep could throw his world off balance more than it already was.

She turned to Eliza. "I'll do it. Give me the Mark."

"Katya, no," Theon interjected. "Give me a day at least."

"And if they do not reply, that is a day wasted," she argued.

"It's one day, Kat."

"And he has been gone for too many days already!" she cried. "If I truly felt him... Theon, he is not well."

He stepped forward then, gently taking her shoulders. "What do you think Axel will do if I let you do this, and it is not what they say it is? Sacrificing a piece of your soul?"

"That will be my burden to bear," she answered, tears welling in her eyes.

"But he will blame me," Theon said.

She was quiet for a long moment, amber eyes never leaving his. Finally, she said, "He sacrificed everything for me. The least I can do is sacrifice a piece of myself for him. I am asking you to let me do the very thing you would do for Tessa without a second thought."

"I'm his older brother. It's my job to protect him, not yours."

"Theon, you can't protect us all," she said softly.

"Yes, I can. I just need a little more time," he insisted.

"I think we're living on borrowed time now, don't you?" When he didn't answer right away, she added, "You're one person, Theon. You can't save the world by yourself. You need him, and I... I didn't know I needed him until he found me."

"I can't let you do this, Kat," he said. "If something happens..."

A sad smile turned up the corners of her mouth. "I am doing this, Theon. Whatever the punishment is for disobeying you, I'll accept it. It'll be worth it."

"I won't *punish* you for trying to save Axel, Katya," he said in dismay.

But he should. Isn't that what he'd been taught his entire life? The Fae are here to serve? Except everything Eliza and Razik had just told him was in direct opposition to everything he knew. Again.

Kat was still staring at him in that way that said she knew exactly what he was working out. They'd spent so many hours together these last few weeks, it shouldn't surprise him she was learning to read him a little.

Another thing *he* would have been punished for if his father was still the Arius Lord.

But he wasn't.

Whether he was recognized by the other Lord and Ladies yet, it shouldn't matter. He'd worked his entire life to get to this position, where he could not only protect his own but his people as well. So had Luka. So had Axel.

Eventually, Theon, you're going to have to let others in on your plans because all you ever seem to do is give people more reasons not to trust you.

Her words echoed in his mind. He supposed if he wanted others to trust him, he needed to learn to trust them a little bit too.

"Fine," he finally gritted out, dropping his hands to his sides and straightening. "This is your choice. If you want to take the Mark, take it. I will give the Shifters a day to reply. If they haven't, I show up unannounced, and you'll come with me to see if you can...feel him."

"Thank you, Theon," Katya whispered.

"I still don't like this idea. If he's too far gone and doesn't take the companion Mark..."

"That is my burden to bear," she repeated.

"Not just yours," he answered. Looking over his shoulder, he found Tristyn, who was still silently watching everything play out. "When I go see Kylian and Giselle, I request you go with me."

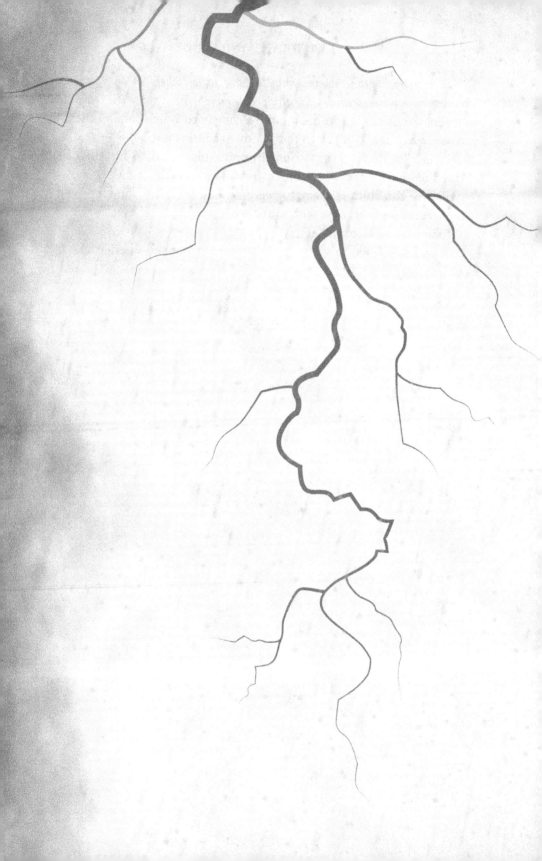

18

TESSA

The Sirana Villas were nothing like she'd thought they would be. That was all Tessa could think as she followed the others through Rosebell. Rordan had portaled them all here, and from what she was told, he'd taken them as far as they could go. The wards around the Villas prevented them from portaling directly inside. Which she found odd considering he was the Achaz Lord and unofficial ruler of Devram.

Rosebell was south of Faven and nestled right on the edge of the Dreamlock Woods. It was halfway between Faven and Sanal, the Serafina Kingdom capital, and Tessa was sure that wasn't a coincidence now that she had an inkling of what went on at the Villas. Granted, the Villas weren't the only part of Rosebell. In fact, if one didn't know the Villas were part of the city, you'd never know they were here.

The city itself had the feel of the rest of the major cities in Devram. Towering buildings. Bustling streets. It was also pristine. Flowers on all the street corners and potted around street lamps. Trees that were well tended to. Even the streets and sidewalks looked like they were swept of debris multiple times a day, and that was after any snow was removed.

Her shoes clicked against the pavement with every step. She hated them. They hurt her feet and squished her toes, and she still didn't understand why Oralia had insisted she wear these today. The black heels were ridiculous. And loud. How was she supposed to wander around without anyone knowing?

Although, she suspected that was exactly why Oralia had insisted.

The female, Dex, and Brecken all trailed behind their company. Tessa had stopped trying to figure out how they'd managed to become so trusted by Rordan. Now she just wondered why. Why would he put so much trust in Fae? It only furthered her suspicions that their heritage was as murky as her own. They probably weren't the children of gods, but Rordan only surrounded himself with the most powerful. That was something he and Valter had in common.

They'd left this morning after Tessa had finished her training session with Luka. It had only been her fifth one, but she'd already learned more from Luka than she had in all her sessions with Odessa combined.

Not that she'd ever admit that to him.

Luka spent the first half of their training sessions helping her control her magic. Which was always...somewhat uncomfortable. He was powerful, and her own magic recognized that. The first day Luka had given her a knowing look, and she'd gritted her teeth, refusing to acknowledge it. If he and Theon and all the other powerful beings of the realm could learn to control their magic, so could she.

The second half of their training time was still magic training, but he added physical training to it. Drills and routines designed to reinforce things he'd already taught her, making her practice over and over, just like he'd made her stand in that godsdamn position for hours. She wasn't entirely sure what he did the rest of the day, and every night she battled with whether she should go to his room. He said she could sleep in his bed if she agreed to train, but she didn't want to give him the satisfaction. It would only serve as a distraction anyway, and not the kind of distraction she was aching for. Because, gods, she hadn't been properly fucked since Theon, and until this bond was dealt with, she knew nothing would come close to satisfying that need.

So she spent her nights pacing her room, trying to keep busy by reading books and practicing with her power. Anything and everything to keep her focus elsewhere all while knowing they could feel her frustration and irritation and want, and that only made the need that much worse.

"Not the excitement you imagined, I assume?" Rordan said with a hint of amusement in his tone, drawing Tessa from her thoughts.

"Rosebell is quite beautiful," she replied with a smile. "I do enjoy seeing other parts of Devram."

"I imagine you do after being confined to the Estate for so many years," he said.

"Yes," was all she managed to say, her fingers curling in her gloves at her sides.

At least they let her wear pants, even if they were incredibly impractical. They were, of course, white. Everything was white and light and—

Gold.

Just like the large gate they'd stopped in front of.

Well, the gate itself wasn't gold. It was actually two large panels that had gold designs inlaid into it, all gleaming and glinting in the daylight. Symbols of the gods. Marks she knew and some she didn't. Without realizing it, she lifted a hand to trace one, but a hand clamped around her wrist, stopping her.

"They're enchanted," Dagian said tightly. "Touching them would end unfavorably for all of us."

"What happens?" Tessa asked, a frown pulling at her mouth.

"I've never had to find out," he answered.

She glanced over his shoulder where Sasha was dutifully a step behind him, her brown eyes holding a pleading warning for her not to push this. With a sigh, she pushed down her curiosity and shoved her gloved hands into the pockets of the long wool coat she was wearing.

That was also white.

She startled when the gates started sliding open, and Dex's hand was on her arm, steadying her.

"Relax, Tessie," he murmured quietly. "They're just letting us in."

She looked up, meeting his dark eyes. "Have you been here before?" Looking past him, she said to Oralia and Brecken, "Have you?"

None of them answered, maintaining their demeanor of servitude, but Brecken winked at her. When would they have been here? They hadn't been in service to the Achaz Kingdom that long.

"Your grace, it is a pleasure to welcome you once more," came a male voice that had her turning back to the now fully open gates.

A sentinel was bowing to Rordan and Dagian, and when he straightened, his gaze fell on Tessa. Uncertainty flickered across his features as he took her in, and Tessa sent him a cheeky smile with a wink of her own. Maybe she didn't need Theon after all. She just needed to find someone else. Or someones. She didn't really care.

"Put this on," Dagian said, holding out his hand. In his palm was a thin rose gold ring.

Looking around, she found everyone sliding identical rings onto their fingers, but she'd witnessed rings and bracelets and collars be more than just an adornment. She wasn't about to blindly put on a piece of jewelry.

"Why?" she asked, her hands still firmly shoved deep into the pockets of her coat.

"Do you have to question everything?" Dagian ground out, trying again to get her to take the ring.

"Is that an honest question?" she retorted, still eyeing the ring.

"The Sirana Villas are devoted to Sirana herself," Rordan cut in, taking the ring from his son. "Her presence is felt more strongly here because of that, and not even the strongest of us are immune to those effects."

"I still don't understand," Tessa said, taking a step back and bumping into a solid chest. Looking up, she found Brecken towering behind her.

"You're going to want to fuck, Tessa," Brecken said, taking the ring Rordan held out to him while tugging her hand from her coat pocket.

Her mouth dropped open. "You can't be serious. Just by stepping through the gates?"

But hadn't she just been entertaining the idea of finding someone to replace Theon?

"Sirana is the goddess of love and fertility," Dex said as though he was speaking to a child. "Her presence is felt strongly here."

That was the most ridiculous thing she'd heard. The gods had abandoned this realm. How could her presence be felt here?

"And the ring does what?" she asked as Brecken tugged her glove from her hand.

"They are spelled to make you immune to the effects," Dex answered. "Otherwise, you'll find yourself in a room with another within the hour. Probably faster for you."

Actually, that didn't sound *terrible*, even if Dex had just essentially called her a whore.

Her gaze wandered back to the waiting sentinel. Light brown hair just long enough to run your fingers through. Muscled from training for his position. A light layer of scruff along his jaw.

Put the fucking ring on, Temptress, came a growl down the bond and not from the male she'd expected it to come from.

These fucking shields.

And this fucking bond.

She snatched the ring from Brecken's hand, sliding it onto her pointer finger. Brecken arched a brow at her sudden change in demeanor, and she took her glove back, slipping it back on her hand.

"You'll be more comfortable with it on," Rordan said reassuringly. "Shall we?"

Tessa nodded, stepping through the gates at his side, while his Source followed a step behind.

A somewhat narrow path greeted them, only wide enough for three people to walk side by side. Towering trees kept them corralled on the path, and with a start she realized they were no longer on the edge of the Dreamlock Woods, but entering them. Why would they put the Villas *in* the Dreamlock Woods? Where it was said dreams became nightmares that hunted you? Where it was said creatures lived that couldn't be found anywhere else in the realm?

"It's fine, Tessa," Dagian murmured in a low tone, and it was only then she realized she'd drawn closer to him. "You're scarier than anything you'll find in here."

She wasn't entirely sure about that when Dagian had been the one to torture her in these woods during an assessment vision, but nevertheless, she straightened and let her power linger around her. She saw Dagian glance at her sidelong, but he didn't say anything else.

Staying close to the others, the path eventually emptied into a large courtyard, and she was able to take in the Villas around her. She nearly tripped over her own feet. Although, that was likely due more to the cobblestones they were walking on. Actual cobblestones. Stepping beyond those gates was almost like stepping into another realm.

There were no vehicles in here. Only people walking within the large courtyard. In the center was a tall statue of Sirana, her figure impossible to mistake with those curves, full breasts, and long hair. Of course, she was also nude. The Villas themselves surrounded the courtyard. They were three stories tall with open hallways. The arches, railings, and columns were ivory with pink roses climbing everything. There were four distinct Villas, all connected by walkways with the same arches and railings, but instead of entering any of them, they walked under one of the walkways, moving further into the woods.

When they emerged on the other side, Tessa stopped in her tracks. Because beyond the Villas was a sprawling manor house. Smooth ivory with the same pink roses everywhere, the doorways were all arched with gold detailing on the doors themselves that matched the gates. The manor was six stories tall, and from the balcony at the top, Tessa knew one would be able to see everything in the Villas.

A Legacy was descending the steps as they approached. Despite the winter season, she still wore a dress, her long legs visible from the deep slits up the sides with every step she took. The dress may have had long sleeves, but the wide scooping neckline still left golden tan skin on display with ample amounts of cleavage. Her shiny brown hair reached her ass, even with the loose curls. Her brown doe eyes were stunning, and her full lips even made Tessa wonder what it would be like to taste them.

"My Lord," she said in a sensual lilt that Tessa felt all the way to the tips of her toes. Bowing low, she added, "Welcome back."

"Thank you, as always, Desiray," Rordan answered warmly, taking the hand she extended in both of his and squeezing it. "As you are aware, we have an extra guest with us today. Tessalyn, this is Desiray. She oversees the Sirana Villas as well as Rosebell. Desiray, meet Tessalyn Ausra."

"The one the realm is all abuzz about," she purred, those big eyes sweeping over her. "Such a pretty thing you are. Your offspring will be stunning provided you have the right partner."

"Um...thank you?" Tessa said, resisting the urge to shift uncomfortably.

"And that power," she added, a thread of excitement in her tone as her eyes flicked to Dagian. "Do you have a Match contract, my dear?"

"All in good time," Rordan said with a chuckle, but his words had Tessa tensing. He'd never once mentioned a Match contract to her.

"When the time comes?" Desiray pushed.

"You'll be the first to know as always," he answered. "But that is not the purpose of this visit."

"Of course," she said, turning and sweeping up the steps. "Come with me. I had a light meal prepared while we discuss business."

"And the tour for Tessa?"

"Arranged per your request," she added.

Tessa's brows arched. Another thing she'd been unaware of.

"That isn't necessary," Tessa said, trying to make sure she didn't trip while walking up the stairs. "I am perfectly fine to join you for a meal."

"Don't be silly," Rordan said, gently taking her arm when she stumbled on a step anyway. "You said you wanted to see the Villas since you've never been here before. I arranged for that."

She couldn't exactly argue with that fact. That *had* been her argument for getting him to agree to her coming here.

"Well, in that case, thank you for doing so," she replied with a smile.

Rordan patted her arm before releasing her as they stepped inside the manor. It was much warmer in here, and several Fae instantly appeared to take their coats. Her soft gold sweater was almost too warm inside. She was hoping they'd take their shoes off, but she had no such luck there.

"I had some pastries and sandwiches wrapped for you to take on your tour along with some beverages," Desiray said while small bags were passed to Dex and Brecken. "My daughter, Larissa, will escort you."

A female appeared, nearly identical to her mother. She was a touch shorter, her hair a lighter shade of brown, but other than that, it was clear they were related. Tessa suddenly wondered who Desiray's Match was.

"I can show you around the manor first before we go to other areas of the Villas," Larissa said, her tone as sultry as her mother's.

"That would be great," Tessa said tightly.

It took nearly an hour before she was led back out to the courtyard and the surrounding four villas. Legacy came and went, Fae greeting them outside the villas before disappearing inside the buildings.

"Are we going to go indoors?" Tessa asked.

"Are you cold?" Dex asked. "There are gloves in your coat pockets."

"No. I am not cold," she retorted, fingers curling into the coat she had put on again before leaving the manor. "I simply wish to see inside them."

Larissa and Dex exchanged glances before Larissa said, "There is truly nothing exciting inside."

"I find that hard to believe."

"Tessa, remember we are guests here," Dex chided.

"And remember that I am no longer one of you nor beneath you," she snapped in response, her power shuddering in her bones, stretching and yawning.

"I wasn't implying that," Dex argued. "I was merely stating you are being rude, and you shouldn't be difficult."

Tessa rolled her lips, her magic doing more than stretching now.

"Not be so difficult," she repeated.

"Yes," Dex snapped.

"Not be so impulsive."

"Precisely.

"Not be so wild and uncontrollable."

"Yes, Tessalyn," he sighed in irritation.

"Dex, man," Brecken warned. "This isn't accomplishing what you think it is."

"Tell you what, *Dexter*," Tessa said. "You and Larissa can stay out here. I'll head inside and warm up a little."

"Tessa, wait," Dexter started.

"No," she said simply, the bands of light at her wrists flaring and sparks of energy flying in all directions.

"Tessa, this wasn't agreed to with Rordan or Desiray," Dex tried again, reaching for her but halting when his gaze dropped to her wrists.

"Rordan?" she repeated. "You are now on a first name basis with the Achaz Lord?"

"No, I..."

She sent him a sharp smile. "I'm better without you, Dexter."

"Don't be ridiculous, Tessa," Oralia chided, her voice grating. "Dex has saved your ass more times than you can count."

"Then maybe he should stop if it's such a hassle," she retorted before striding across the courtyard, heels clicking on the stones.

She heard voices murmuring, and she caught Dex telling Brecken to stay with her. She didn't care if anyone followed her, as long as it wasn't Dex. And she knew he wouldn't. He'd want to avoid a scene. Would likely run to Rordan.

The Fae at the doors bowed when she approached, neither of them questioning her as they opened the doors for her. Stepping inside was once again like being transported to another realm. If outside was quaint and welcoming, inside was dark and luscious. Dim lighting along the edges of the floor led her deeper into the villa until it emptied into a large room lined with booths, curtained areas, and a stage in the center.

A brothel.

This was a brothel.

"See anything to your liking, my lady?" came a male voice, and she looked up to find a Legacy standing beside her.

"I, uh..." She trailed off, watching a male and female Fae on the stage, wearing nothing.

"Not to worry. That's why I'm here. We'll find you what you like," he went on. "Do you prefer male? Female? Both? An element preference?"

She suddenly couldn't find her words. Not because she didn't know what to say, but because she was *angry*.

"She is looking for a private room. Second floor," Brecken cut in smoothly.

The Legacy straightened, looking down his nose at Brecken. "With you?" he said with a sneer.

"If the lady still desires," Brecken said, eyes fixed on the floor and playing the role they'd been trained to play for two decades.

Submissive.

Subservient.

Docile.

Meek.

Clearing her throat, Tessa said, "Yes. That is what I desire."

"Of course, my lady. Right this way," the male said, leading them past booths where Legacy had Fae on their knees and in their laps.

More Fae were being led to the curtained areas, glimpses of Legacy waiting for them as the curtains parted. Grunts of pleasure, soft whimpers, and more assaulted her ears. The more she heard and the more she saw, the more her fury built. A spiral staircase was in the corner, and she followed the Legacy up and along a hall overlooking the activities below. She forced herself to look. To see the tired Fae. The greedy Legacy. Gods, there were even *mortals* here. The villas apparently catered to every taste and desire.

Placing his palm on a door, she heard it unlock before the Legacy pushed it open and stepped to the side. A lavish bedroom lay beyond, and she couldn't make her feet move when the male asked, "How long, my lady?"

"What?"

"How long are you booking the room for?"

What was an appropriate answer? She didn't know. But she couldn't just stand here or they'd begin to suspect she shouldn't be here. So, much to her dismay, she thought about how she'd expect Theon to act in this situation.

Her light flared, golden arcs swirling around her. She knew lightning flickered in her eyes and echoed her footsteps as she swept past the male and into the room. "Until I'm done," was her response, cold and demanding.

The male's eyes widened a moment before he sputtered, "Of course, my lady," and hastily shut the door behind him.

The sound of slow clapping had her turning to Brecken.

"Nice job, Tessie," he said. "For a moment there, I thought you were going to fuck this all up."

"Shut up," she snapped, taking a single step towards him. Her entire being was vibrating with fury. "Are all the villas...*this*?"

He clasped his hands behind his back, rocking on his toes. "Are they all places for the Legacy to come and fuck? Yep."

"There are mortals here."

"Sure are," he answered, wandering around the room.

"And the Fae?"

"Are assigned to serve the Sirana bloodline," he answered, but she'd already known that. Jasper had told her exactly where she would have ended up if she hadn't been...whatever she was.

"And Legacy just..."

"Come here to fuck? Yep. Place orders for exactly what they want. Didn't you notice none of the Fae or mortals had these?" he asked, holding up his hand where the rose gold ring sat on his pointer finger. "Some of the Legacy even forgo them. They say it makes the experience more intense."

Her fingers curled into fists, her magic winding tighter around her arms, her chest, her middle.

"What's on the third level?" Tessa asked from between her teeth.

It was the first time Brecken's expression changed. This entire time he'd been frank and apathetic, but now something flickered in his dark eyes. "The Fae trying to conceive and those with child."

"How do you know all this?" Tessa demanded. The eerie ring to her voice had Brecken taking a step back.

"That's a long story we don't really have time for right now," he replied.

"You better fucking make time, Brecken," she spat, the air in the room stirring.

"I can either tell you a story or give you somewhere to release that fury, Tessa. Your choice," he answered.

A choice.

That had her pausing.

"Aren't you supposed to be..."

"Controlling you? I told you before, you were always Dex's concern. Never mine," he said, making his way across the room. He reached up, sliding a vase of pink roses on a decor shelf to the side, and a panel in the wall slid open. Looking over his shoulder, he said, "You coming? After your little display of power, they won't dare come check on you for at least a few hours."

"And the others?"

"I swore to Dex I'd keep an eye on you while they went to find Lord Jove and Desiray," he answered. "So I suppose you better come with me so I can keep my word."

She eyed Brecken, her power still needing a release. Or maybe that was her? "Where does that lead?"

"To some underground tunnels that take us to another villa beyond the manor," he answered.

"Underground?" she repeated.

Not to mention deeper into the Dreamlock Woods.

"The only way to overcome a fear is to face it," he said.

"I'm not *afraid* of going underground," she bristled.

Brecken arched a brow. "I suppose not. You're just afraid of being trapped down there. You're letting your fears become your limits, Tessa. Be who you were meant to be."

"Stop saying that," she hissed, making her way to him. "I don't want to be whoever I was meant to be. I want the freedom to be whoever *I* want to be."

"Then take it," he said before he disappeared into the passage.

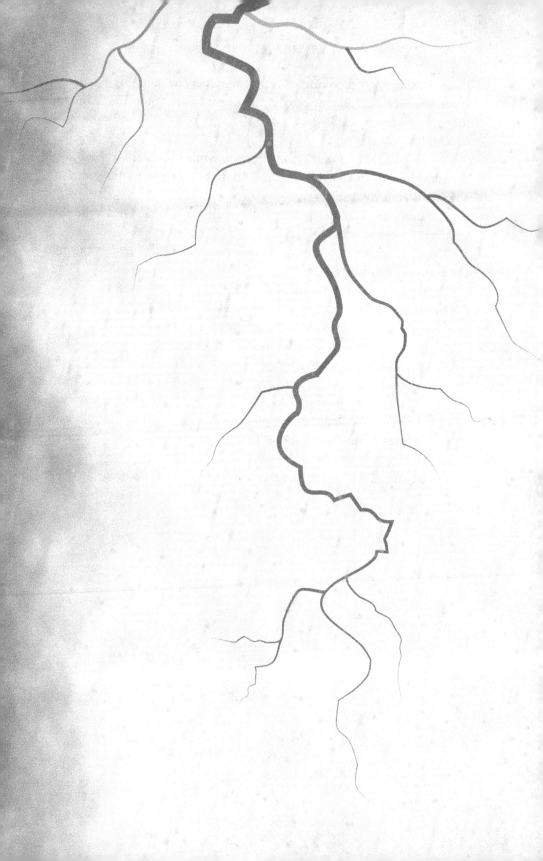

19
TESSA

"By the gods," Tessa muttered, following him inside. He was waiting, and while he did something to make the panel close behind them, she lifted a hand, letting light pool there.

Brecken eyed the magic when he slipped past her. "Don't lose control in here, Tessa. There's not much room for me to survive."

"Fuck off, Brecken," she sneered, kicking off her heels and leaving them by the door before she followed after him.

The first few minutes were fine, but the longer they were in the passage and the lower she descended, the more effort each step took. The more each breath was difficult to take. The more her heart raced. The more—

Breathe, baby girl, came Luka's voice down the bond.

Where are you? We can be there in seconds with Luka's Traveling, echoed Theon.

You can't just drop everything and come find me, she scoffed, letting them distract her with conversation.

Tessa, if you think I won't leave the meeting I'm in right now to find you and spill the blood of anyone who got in my way, you're underestimating what I mean when I say I protect what is mine, Theon answered.

I'm not yours.

The Mark on your hand says you are.

If that's your argument, then you belong to me, Theon, she retorted.

I never claimed otherwise, little storm.

Well, that was something she didn't want to think about right now.

Tell me about the Dreamlock Woods, she said, keeping her eyes fixed on Brecken's back as he led her along.

There was a long pause before Theon said, *Tessa, where are you?*

The Sirana Villas, Luka answered when she didn't.

No one asked you, she bit out.

I'm part of this now whether you like it or not.

For now.

There was another long pause before Theon said, *What does that mean?*

Exactly what I said. This is all for now. I'll find a way to free myself from you, from Luka, from the entire realm.

I'll always come for you, Tessa, Theon answered.

Until the day you can no longer find me.

With that, she shoved them out, stacking her mental shields back into place. Brecken had opened a door, daylight filling the passage and guiding her to the outdoors. He hadn't been lying. This was clearly behind the manor. The large house cast a shadow over the area where they now stood. Looking back, she found a small brick cottage where they'd emerged, and in front of them were two two-story villas nearly identical to the ones in the courtyard.

Except these didn't have the open arches.

These didn't have any windows at all.

They were just ivory buildings with climbing roses. She couldn't even see a door to enter.

"Brecken?" she asked uncertainly.

"This way," was all he said, setting off again.

She hurried along, her now bare feet feeling the sting of the cold cobblestones.

"Slow down, Brecken," she hissed.

"Can't. If we get caught, you better be ready with that power of yours."

A minute later, they were slipping in a side door that Tessa would have missed if Brecken clearly hadn't known it was there. She felt the wards ripple around her, but Brecken was clearly granted free access here. Suddenly, he grabbed her elbow and dragged her into a small closet, the door snicking shut behind them. There was barely enough room for the two of them to both fit with the random cleaning supplies and shovels stashed in here.

"No," she rasped, shaking her head and trying to push past him. "We cannot stay in here."

Brecken rounded on her, crowding her against a stack of boxes. He took her jaw in his hand, forcing her to look up at him, and when her power wound around his wrist in warning, he didn't even flinch.

"All those Fae and mortals you saw in those villas?" he said, his voice low and vicious. "They are *happy* there because it means they are not *here*."

She went still.

"What do you mean?"

"It means for once in your life, Tessalyn, I need you to not focus on yourself."

Her eyes went wide, anger immediately sparking back to life.

"Does that make you mad?" he went on, still holding her chin. "Piss you off a little bit? Good. It should. Because while you've had a shit life, those here have had it so much worse. If you weren't who you fucking are, this is exactly where you would have ended up. So I need you to listen closely, because if we fuck up even one part of this, more than the innocent people here will suffer for it. Do you understand?"

She held his dark gaze for one second.

Two.

Three.

Then a slow, dark smile curled on her lips that had Brecken's eyes going wide. She brought a hand up, curling it around his wrist. This time when he felt her power sink into his being, he tried to jerk back, but her power held. Seeking. Wanting. *Taking.*

"Tessa, stop," he said, panic creeping into his tone.

She took a step forward. Another. Forcing him to step back as she crowded *him* against the wall. She reached up, pushing onto her tiptoes, to take his chin in her hand, her nails digging in.

"I need *you* to listen very closely, Brecken, because if *you* fuck up even a little bit, *you* are the one who will suffer for it, and then you will not see the outside of this closet again. Do *you* understand?"

He had gone utterly still, but his throat bobbed as he gave the barest of nods.

"Do not *ever* speak down to me like that again," she said. "I did not walk away from Theon to be used by someone else. I am not Theon's Source. I am not Rordan's to use and command. I am not Dex's. I do not belong to Achaz or Arius or any other god. And I sure as fuck am not your pawn for some vendetta or vigilantism. You can tell me what you wish me to know, but rest assured, I'll find the truth as I have with everything else. So lie or don't, but know that whatever choice you make in this moment determines your salvation or destruction."

"So much fury," Brecken murmured, some of the tension bleeding from his being.

Tessa's head canted to the side, not understanding why that would put him at ease.

"You got it, Tessie," he said casually as her fingers slid from his jaw. He straightened his shirt, tugging at the cuffs. "I can't tell you everything that happens here because I'm bound by an Oath, but I can show you."

She eyed him, looking for the catch and trying to decide if she could trust him.

"But in order to do that, I'm going to need you to pretend to be what Cordelia raised you to be," he went on. "Just long enough for you to understand. Then you can be your own vigilante if you want."

Her eyes narrowed. "If you are playing me, Brecken, I will find a way to end you."

His smile was slightly maniacal as he replied, "I'm counting on it."

A mutual understanding seemed to pass between them before Brecken nodded once and pushed the door open. The moment they were in the hall, his hand clamped around her upper arm, and he led her around a corner to a much wider passage that led up a set of stairs. They passed a few Legacy on their way, but no one batted an eye at them. Not until they rounded another corner and came face-to-face with a male Legacy who stopped in his tracks. Light blue eyes raked over her, and there was no mistaking the hunger in them.

"A new one, Breck?" he asked, his tongue darting out and wetting his lips.

"Yep," Brecken answered in a bored tone.

"Element?"

"Wind."

That was definitely excitement that filled the male's features as he sauntered closer. It took everything in her not to react when he skated his fingertips up the column of her throat before sliding his thumb along her bottom lip.

"I suppose that means I'll be seeing you real soon," he said, his tone low and rough.

"She has to be processed first, Arlo," Brecken said.

"Where'd you find her?" the male asked, stepping closer still and twirling a piece of her hair around his finger.

"Falein Estate."

Arlo glanced up at him. "No luck with Anala yet?"

Brecken rolled his eyes. "Kyra has her Kingdom and Estate locked down tighter than the Keeper has the center of the Pantheon locked down."

Arlo snickered. "Supposedly they're making progress on that."

"Until then, I'll keep finding Raye's," Brecken said with a shrug. "But I've got to get going," he added, tugging on Tessa's arm.

She stumbled, and Arlo let out a huff of laughter, slapping her ass as she was dragged past him.

"Easy, Tessa," Brecken murmured out of the corner of his mouth. "Save it."

She curled her fingers, hiding the power sparking there. Thankfully, she was still wearing the coat so the bands on her wrists had been hidden from the Legacy.

A minute later, Brecken was ushering her into a decent-sized office.

An empty office.

The moment the door closed, he said, "Go find what you can. I'll stand guard."

"What?"

He jerked his chin at the desk. "I can't tell you where to look. Find what you can. I don't know how long we have. Could be minutes; could be an hour."

Uncertain of what exactly was happening, Tessa made her way to the desk. The office itself was fairly sparse. A map of the realm on the wall. A book detailing magic on the shelf. A tablet in the center of the desk.

She tapped it, the screen illuminating and asking for a password. She looked up at Brecken with a questioning look.

He rolled his eyes. "I don't know it, Tessa, but if you can get past wards you're not supposed to, surely you can break into a tablet, no?"

She'd never thought of it that way before.

Fingers hovering over the screen, she focused on letting out a sliver of her power. Too much and she would surely make the thing explode.

It took far more energy than it should have to make sure only a small amount of her power emerged, but she managed it. And to her utter shock, the home screen displayed.

"Holy shit," she muttered.

Brecken said something, but she didn't hear him as she picked up the tablet and clicked on the only program on the screen. It was labeled Hybrid. A list of names appeared she couldn't make any sense of, so she clicked on a random one.

- Name: Meera Koplin
- Lineage: Water Fae (M) x Water Fae (P)
- Element: Water
- Current Location: Hybrid Villas
- Pairings: Anahita Legacy (Rolf Alings) Result: Favorable (M-37y), placed
- Nith Legacy (Klayton Janiak) Result: Favorable (M), disposed
- Anahita Legacy (Rolf Alings) Result: Pending

Her brow furrowed as she backed out of the document and selected another name.

- Name: Jasper Dusak
- Lineage: Water Fae (M) x Anahita Legacy (P)
- Element: Water+
- Current Location: Serafina Heir Source
- Pairings: Water Fae (scheduled after Selection year)

"What the fuck?" Tessa muttered, exiting and scrolling the names more. Then she sucked in a gasp when she clicked on another name.

- Name: Eviana Perin
- Lineage: Earth Fae (P) x Silas Legacy (M)
- Element: Earth+
- Current Location: Arius Lord Source (replacement per request)
- Pairings: Nith Legacy (Mansel McKinlay) Result: Favorable (F-9y), Serafina Estate

Her breathing was too fast when she snapped her gaze up to Brecken again.

"Keep going," he said flatly, nodding at the tablet.

"Brecken, are these…"

"I can't say it."

"Are they forcing…" She couldn't say it either. Finally, she rasped out in a rush, "Are they breeding the Fae?"

"In the Villas, yes. But the Hybrid Villas are more than that. Keep going," he repeated.

Tessa was shaking. Not from shock or fear, but from pure and raw *fury*.

She scrolled, opening one name after the other. More of the same. Fae forced to fuck a Legacy to produce children. Some children were placed; some were labeled disposed, and Tessa could only assume what that meant. Some were kept here until they were of age, and then they were forced into the same. When she found another like Eviana, she nearly vomited. Lady Isleen had requested a specific *combination* for her Source.

She tapped the next name.

- Name: Lange Castellon
- Lineage: Wind Fae (M) x Unknown Sefarina Legacy (P) *unsanctioned*
- Element: Wind+
- Current Location: Arius Kingdom claimed (unplanned)
- Pairings: In negotiations

Tessa swallowed down her angry tears, clicking out of the document and scrolling specifically for another name.

She had just found it when Brecken hissed, "Put it away. We have company."

Tessa quickly exited out of the program, relocking the tablet before she placed it back in the center of the desk. Brecken was waiting for her in the middle of the room. She ran to his side, settling into place beside him and letting him grip her arm once more just as the door banged open.

A devastatingly handsome Legacy entered, his piercing eyes sweeping over them before he said, "Brecken, I wasn't expecting you today."

"Wasn't planned, Darius," he answered. "Stumbled upon this one. Figured I'd drop her off before I was sent on my next job."

The male settled behind the desk, picking up the tablet, and Tessa held her breath as he unlocked it, waiting to see if he discovered anything amiss.

"Ran into Arlo. He said you found her in the Falein Kingdom," Darius said.

"Yep. Was there for something else and found her working in an archive," Brecken answered.

The male tsked. "Raye will break at some point, and then we can put all our efforts into Kyra and the Anala Kingdom."

"And Arius?" Brecken asked.

The male let out a derisive laugh, his silvery-blond hair falling across his brow. "They're doing the job for us. It's imploding. Rordan and Maya are just waiting for the right time to finish the job. What's her name?"

"Alora," Brecken answered. "Wind element."

The male nodded, typing and clicking through his screen. "Any ideas on lineage?"

"No, but she's powerful. My guess is an unsanctioned pregnancy the mother tried to save," Brecken said, and Tessa was trying her hardest to follow along with this conversation.

"I can't find her files," Darius muttered. "I'll have to contact Lilura Inquest. See what's going on."

"You want me to take her to a room until then?"

"Yeah, yeah, that's fine," Darius answered, pulling his phone from his pocket and waving them off. "I'll deal with her once I know her history."

Brecken squeezed her arm in a signal for her to follow him, but she couldn't make her feet move. He tugged again, and she only dug her heels into the floor.

"There's quite a few people interested in my history," Tessa said, and even she could hear the slight mania in her voice.

Good.

Darius's head snapped up, ire flashing. "Did you just speak to me?"

"Simply stated a fact," she replied, slowly undoing the buttons of her coat.

He stared at her in disbelief, his cheeks flushing with fresh rage. "Which Estate were you raised at?"

"What does that matter?" she asked, reaching the last button.

"Because you clearly were not taught your place, and I need to have a discussion with the Mother there," he sneered, rising to his feet.

"My place? Beneath those more powerful than me?"

"Exactly," he snarled, rounding the desk.

"Serafina Legacy," Brecken muttered. He'd long since let go of her arm. "He can see your deepest dreams and desires and—"

"Impossible," Darius rasped before Brecken could finish. "You cannot exist."

"And yet I stand in front of you," she replied, slipping her coat off and handing it to Brecken. Her power was radiating now, swirls of light encompassing her arms, lightning crackling, and silver and gold ashes swirling around her.

Those were new.

But she didn't have time to think about it. She may have only had five training sessions with Luka so far, but it was enough to give her control in this moment. One on one? She had the upper hand, and Brecken appeared to realize that as he took several steps back.

"I can see your deepest desires. I can— He's been lying to all of us," Darius continued to splutter, his pretty face draining of color.

"You'll have to be more specific," Tessa said. "Everyone here is a liar."

"He said he didn't know your lineage. He said he was taking care of this. You— You're—"

Tessa struck, a whip of lightning in her hand before he could speak again. She snapped it out, wrapping the energy around his neck. He immediately dropped to his knees, fingers clawing at his throat. She yanked, and his palms hit the floor as he tried to suck in another breath.

She sauntered forward, dropping to a crouch beside the male and tilting his chin up with her nail. "*This* is how my Estate Mother disciplined me," she said coldly. "Took away my ability to breathe. Locked me in cupboards. Withheld food. And you're right. It still wasn't enough."

She moved quickly then, gripping his throat and letting her magic seep from her palm into the male. It flooded him, and she gritted her teeth as she kept it in line, making sure it stayed focused solely on him. It ripped his power from his veins, devouring and feeding. When she sent another bolt of energy into him, he screamed, rolling onto his back and arching off the floor.

And she smiled as she pushed to her feet and stood over him, watching him writhe in pain because all she could wonder was which of the Fae here had *he* fucked?

"Do you decide all the pairings, or is there another?" she demanded suddenly, giving him a reprieve.

He shook his head, tears and snot leaking from his eyes and nose.

Tessa lifted a hand, her fingers glowing as light pooled. "To clarify, that was me speaking to you."

Darius shook his head again. "She has final say."

"Who?"

"Desiray," he rasped, wiping his wrist across his nose and mouth.

Tessa looked at Brecken, who only nodded once in confirmation.

Then Tessa pulled her golden sword from a pocket realm and plunged it through the male's throat, blood spraying across her white pants.

The room went so silent, she could hear the clock ticking on the desk.

"You are kind of terrifying when upset," Brecken finally said.

She only held his stare as she went to slide her palm along the exposed blade still impaled in the male's neck.

"Wait!" Brecken cried, lurching forward.

But there would be no waiting. She would set her Hunters free here. Tell them to kill any full-blooded Legacy. She would fall asleep to the memory of their screams echoing in her mind. A lullaby to her soul.

Her blood dripped to the floor, and a moment later, one appeared, his white eyes fixed on her.

"You called, your grace?"

"First, I need a new dagger. I...lost mine," she said, still annoyed she'd left the thing at Arius House. "Actually, make it two."

"Of course, your grace," he said, two golden daggers appearing in his palms that he held out to her with a bow.

She took them, one in each hand, while she asked, "Can you tell the difference between a full-blooded Legacy and one with mixed blood?"

"We can, your grace."

"Good," she purred. "Then I have a job for you."

"Tessa, just listen to me for a moment," Brecken interjected again, stepping to her side.

The Hunter's head slowly turned to him. "You speak out of turn, light guardian."

Brecken ignored him, turning to face Tessa fully. "If you let them loose in here, they will know it was you."

"Good," she said again.

"And what about the innocent Fae? They have nowhere to go right now, Tessa. Worse, they may be blamed for this," Brecken went on.

That had her faltering. Where *would* they go?

"If you didn't want me to do anything about this, then why did you bring me here?" she demanded coldly.

"Because I wanted you to see so that you can help do something about it when the time is right."

"And until then I just...walk away?" She shook her head. "I can't do that, Brecken."

"I know it's hard. I do it every time I'm here, but I needed you to see so you can portal back when it's time. You'll be able to cross the wards without detection. As soon as we have some place for the Fae to go," he insisted.

"You find these Fae and bring them here, Brecken. I can't possibly trust you," she said, shaking her head and trying to decide what to do.

On one hand, he was right. The innocents would have nowhere to go. Sure, the Legacy here would be dead, but then what? On the other hand, Brecken was clearly part of furthering this.

"You would have brought Katya here?" Tessa asked tightly.

"They have been trying to get into Anala Kingdom for decades," Brecken answered. "She was the first fire Fae I found in all my time here. I was supposed to bring her here. She was never supposed to go to the Emerging," he answered.

"But you brought her to the Celeste Estate."

He nodded. "I knew what they'd do to her, and I couldn't... It was the only way I could protect her then."

"Why do you care?"

Brecken's gaze flicked to the Hunter, who stood eerily still, waiting for orders.

Tessa turned to him. "Find me a Sefarina Legacy. He answers to Arlo. Bring him to me alive."

"Yes, your grace," he said with a bow before gliding away straight through the solid door.

When he was gone, she turned back to Brecken expectantly.

"There is much I can't tell you, Tessa," he finally said. "But you are right not to trust anyone."

"But I should trust you?"

"I brought you here, didn't I?"

"All the times you left the Estate, where did you go?"

"I was sent to find the hidden Fae. Those who have Legacy blood, and they don't know it."

"How do you find them?"

He hesitated before saying, "I can sense power and the strength of it."

"How?"

"I cannot tell you."

She nodded because an Oath would truly be preventing that.

"I worked around it as much as I could, Tessa," he pleaded. "I slipped Darius's name into the conversation so you knew it. I lured him to reveal crucial information for you to work with."

She nodded again. "In two days' time, I am going to let the Hunters loose here. I am going to instruct them to kill every single full-blooded Legacy inside these gates."

Brecken nodded. "I will try to have some place for them to go."

"Do not try, Brecken," she said tightly. Before he could answer, her power struck, wrapping tightly around his throat. "If you are playing me, your death will be anything but short and painless."

"Understood, Tessa," he gasped out, but he wasn't struggling. He wasn't trying to draw a breath.

Submitting.

That was what he was doing as he stood before her.

The door opened, the Hunter herding Arlo into the office.

"And this one will die today," Tessa said, releasing Brecken from her hold.

Arlo immediately turned, trying to flee, but the Hunter was there, sword raised. "My grace requested your presence. Now bow."

Arlo slowly turned back to face her, and she smiled in delight. "Yes, Arlo," she purred. "Bow."

"You are not a Lady in the realm. I do not bow to you," he sneered, but she heard the faint tremble in his voice.

"No," she agreed, taking a single step forward. "In *this* realm, I am a goddess, but to you, I am your ending."

Energy crackled around her, and a glowing orb hovered in the air near her head. She knew she was pushing this too far. Any moment, her control was going to snap, and then there'd be no telling what would happen. That was when she became too wild and uncontrollable, and she could feel her magic straining, wanting to take. Always wanting more and more and more.

Which meant she needed to do this without her magic.

She shoved her power down, tightening her grip on the daggers as she stalked forward. To the Hunter she said, "Get him on his knees."

Tessa didn't know what he did, but a moment later, Arlo was screaming in pain as he sank to the floor.

"Stretch out his right arm," she said.

Again the male screamed as some phantom power yanked him forward on his hands, pulling his arm straight. Tessa was sure it had dislocated his shoulder.

She lowered to a crouch once more, slamming a dagger straight through his hand and into the floor.

His screams were a symphony she wished she could add to a playlist. She hummed along as she used the other dagger to sever his fingers from his hand, one by one. When she was done, she smiled sweetly at the male whose face was a pale mess of tears and drool as he continued to whimper before her.

"Wh-why?" he stuttered.

"Because you touched me as if you had the right to," she answered plainly. "So I assumed I had the right to take from you too." He whimpered when she twirled the bloody dagger in her hand, drops of blood splattering. "You looked at me like you had the right to do so as well. Shall I take your eyes next?"

"Pl-please don't!" he wailed.

"And when the Fae ask the same of you, do you stop?"

His only answer was another sob.

"How many young have you fathered within these walls?"

When he didn't answer, she yanked the dagger from his hand and drove it into his shoulder. Gods, his screams did something to her. Made her feel alive.

"They don't tell us," he wailed. "They call us when we're needed."

"And today?"

"I have an appointment tonight," he blubbered.

Tessa only hummed, yanking the dagger free again to another agonized wail. "Who?"

"I don't know!" he cried. "I swear it."

"But you would have come and found me, right?"

His answer was several shallow sobs.

This time she sank her dagger into his side. "Right?" she pressed. "And don't lie to me, Arlo. I'll cut out your tongue."

"Yes," he said on another sob.

"To take from me."

He didn't verbally answer, but he nodded several times.

Then there was only gurgling as she slashed her daggers across his throat, one after the other.

The male fell face-down to the floor, blood spilling and pooling around her bare feet. She frowned as she looked down at the daggers in her hands, unsure of where to store them. Shrugging, she bent and wiped the blades on the male's clothing, humming to herself. Then she sent them to a pocket realm before she moved to retrieve her sword still impaled in Darius's corpse. She did the same with the sword, bloody footprints marking her path.

When she was done, she turned to Brecken. "Should we go?"

He was staring at her, his mouth agape. "Tessa..."

She only smiled, her entire being buzzing from the adrenaline of taking.

Of being the most powerful.

Of rescuing herself.

It was another few seconds before he managed to say, "You have blood...everywhere."

She looked down, finding red sprayed across her white pants and gold sweater. With another frown she said, "Maybe I should just portal us back to Faven? Will I be able to do that if Rordan couldn't?"

Brecken nodded mutely, and she summoned a portal, both of them stepping through. She hadn't realized how much time had passed until she saw the twilight sky out the windows.

"I'm going to go. I'll send word to Dex and the others that you wanted to leave," Brecken said. "I have some things to get figured out."

"Two days, Brecken," she warned as he crossed her room to the door.

He said nothing else, but when he was gone, Tessa knew there was no way she could go to bed. She was too wound up. Felt too reckless.

Too impulsive.

Too wild.

So she summoned another portal and stepped through.

20

LUKA

He knew she was back. He could feel it down this godsdamn bond, and it was taking every ounce of self-control not to hunt her down.

Luka had felt her all afternoon. They'd finished their training session before she'd taken off to shower and get changed. They'd left for the Sirana Villas midafternoon. He'd been informed they were having a light dinner with Desiray, but he'd felt her anger, then her distress, then her renewed fury. Both he and Theon had tried to reach out to her, banging against the mental barrier that was keeping them out. That was the thing, though. Eventually, that barrier fell, and try as they might, they couldn't reach her. She was too lost to her wrath, and he had no idea what had triggered such a visceral reaction. Was she hurt? Did she need help?

His phone was buzzing on the bedside table, but he didn't need to check it to know it was Theon. He didn't have any answers for him, so he didn't bother responding. He'd spent the entire afternoon and evening doing anything he could to keep from thinking about Razik and the potential blood relation. What did it say that the male hadn't even attempted to reach out?

Then again, neither had he.

Luka had even gone so far as to Travel to Arius House to check on the wolf despite Theon's consistent updates. But now she was back, and his dragon was pressing at his soul. He hadn't felt this out of control with his magic and shifting since his power had first emerged.

He was almost grateful when bright light eclipsed the low flames keeping his room dim.

Almost.

He made a mental note to start teaching her to Travel in one of their next lessons because he was sick and tired of being blinded whenever she felt like showing up.

Those exact words were on the tip of his tongue when he turned back to face her, but then his mouth dried out at the sight that greeted him.

She was in white fitted pants and a gold top, and there was blood. All over her clothes. Her face. Her feet left bloody footprints on the floor when she took a single step forward. Her golden hair was down, speckled with red, and those violet eyes were glowing bright with a craze he didn't know what to do with.

"Tessa?" he ventured carefully, partly because he didn't know what was going on, but also because everything in him wanted to comfort her, claim her, and then end whoever had done this to her.

She didn't answer. Only watched him in a way that made him feel like he was somehow the prey in this situation, and it had his magic pushing even more.

"Tessa?" he said again, not moving. "Are you hurt?"

"I killed someone," she said, and fuck, her voice had that ring to it.

"Okay," he replied.

"Two people actually."

He nodded. "Okay," he said again. "Was anyone else hurt?"

"Do you know what they do at the Villas?"

"Yes, Tessa. I know what the Villas are."

Her features hardened. "The ones behind the manor house too?"

His brow furrowed. He didn't know there were villas behind the manor house. Whatever his expression told her, it had her relaxing the smallest amount.

"Tessa...who did you kill?"

"Two Legacy."

"Did they hurt you?"

"They wanted to. One touched me."

The growl that sounded was more dragon than male.

"I cut off his fingers before I killed him," she added.

"Good girl," he said, starting to understand what was happening. "Did you just get back?"

She nodded. "The others are still there. I came back."

"Alone?"

"With Brecken."

"And now?" he pressed, crossing his arms and leaning against the back of the sofa.

"Now I..." She shifted on her feet, her hands opening and closing at her sides before she reached up and brushed back hair from her face. Red smeared across her cheek. "My magic is— I can't—" She released a frustrated sigh. "Everything is heightened. I feel...out of control."

"It's the adrenaline," he said. "For mortals, it fades, but when you've just fought and come out on top, your magic wants more. You need to expel the energy."

"Just let my magic out?"

"Fuck, no," he balked. "Your magic will take until there's nothing left."

"Then what do *you* do?" she sneered.

Luka shrugged. "Something to distract me. An intense training session. Spar with Axel or Theon. Fuck."

He couldn't tell if that was a wince or a flinch of surprise.

Pushing off the sofa, he added, "Go clean the blood off, and I'll take you to the training arena."

"I don't want to *train*, Luka," she grumbled.

"Then what do you want to do?"

She shifted again, and he knew exactly what she was feeling. It was exactly how he felt every time he won a sparring match. Every time he'd completed a mission for Valter. Every time they fought Night Children. He knew Axel and Theon experienced it too, but he'd always thought his experience was heightened due to his Sargon blood. His post-fight high always seemed more intense and savage than theirs did, and apparently Tessa experienced it that intensely as well. He could see it in her rigid limbs and the inability to stay still. The way she couldn't process what was happening or put it into words. The way she was struggling to keep control of her magic, but he was so fucking proud of her for doing it. A week ago, she wouldn't have cared. She would have let her power have her because it was easier than fighting for control.

"I want... I need..." She trailed off, another frustrated sound coming from her, this time accompanied by a flare of her power. He straightened, his flames ready to meet hers, but she got herself back under control. "Just tell me what to do, Luka."

"If that's what you need, go to Theon," he replied.

"I can't go to Theon."

"Why not?"

"Because I can't," she spat, her power flaring again.

"Control it, Tessa," he ordered.

"That's just it," she cried. "I *can't*! It's too much. It's too wild. *I'm* too wild. I'm too impulsive. I'm too—"

He was in front of her before she could utter the next word. Taking her chin between his thumb and forefinger, he said, "You are none of those things. Do you understand me?"

She shook her head, silver pools of frustration welling in her eyes where gold flecks peeked out among the violet. He could *feel* her power vibrating beneath his fingers and see her entire being visibly trembling.

"Okay, here's what we're going to do," he said, his tone a low command. "We're going to get you cleaned up."

"That's not—"

"One thing at a time," he interrupted. "Since you came straight here, I'm assuming no one else knows you killed two Legacy today?" When she nodded, he said, "So we need to get rid of the evidence, which means washing away the blood, cleaning up the footprints, and burning this clothing."

"One foot in front of the other," she said tightly.

"Yes, Tessa. Exactly that."

She nodded again, taking in a deep breath as he took her hand and led her to his ensuite. He reached into the shower, adjusting the water temperature. Not sure how hot she'd want it, he left it on lukewarm, only to turn and find her already shedding her bloody clothing and tossing it in a pile.

"So much white," she muttered, toeing at the discarded fabric.

And it was his turn to take a deep breath as she stood there naked in his bathroom.

"Shower, Tessa," he ground out while internally fighting with his dragon. "I'll take care of the clothing and footprints."

He scooped it up, refusing to look back at her as he left the bathroom as quickly as possible. He held the clothes in his hand while he burned them, his black flames devouring every scrap of fabric and blood, and then he burned the ashes to nothing too. When that was done, he debated what to do about the footprints. If he burned them away, there would be scorch marks left behind. In resignation, he decided it would be good old-fashioned scrubbing with soap and water, but there was no way he was going back into his bathroom with her naked and wet in there.

He Traveled to her rooms, taking care of her suite first. There was a single set of footprints in here. She truly had appeared here with Brecken and then immediately came to him. He went to her bathroom to get a cloth and soap, and of course, all the towels were white. He'd have to burn that too unless they were going to somehow play it off as her cycle, but with their luck, the Achaz Lord would have the blood analyzed. Burning it would be.

He cleaned her floor before rinsing the cloth and soaping it back up. Then he Traveled back to take care of the floor in his room. After he incinerated it, he swiped up his phone, sending a message to Theon that she was back and fine.

Theon: What the fuck happened? Did she say?
Luka: Apparently she killed some Legacy who tried to hurt her.
Theon: Good.
Luka: That's what I said, but no one knows it was her.
Luka: And it happened at the Sirana Villas.
Theon: What the fuck was she doing there?
Luka: She insisted on visiting the Villas. But did you know there were more behind the manor house? She seemed relieved when I said I didn't know about them.
Theon: I had no idea. I'll look into it.
Theon: Is she all right?

It took him a second to answer that because Theon was going to know exactly what he was talking about when he told him what was going on.

Luka: She's going through the post-survival and victory high.

Then there was a long pause from Theon before another message popped up.

Theon: I trust you, Luka.

And that was it. Nothing else came in, and Luka cursed under his breath. What the fuck was he supposed to do with that?

With nothing left to keep him busy other than to go check on Tessa, he steeled himself for the encounter. He'd heard the shower shut off a bit ago, which meant she was either wrapped in a towel or naked. The girl's lackadaisical attitude towards nudity was becoming increasingly taxing. He'd never had a problem with nudity either until she'd started showing bare flesh all the godsdamn time.

His magic and his dragon, on the other hand, were pacing with excitement as he entered the ensuite. She was standing on the bathmat, dripping wet, but at least there was a towel wrapped around her.

Leaning his shoulder along the doorway, he glanced at the vanity. He should have grabbed her hairbrush while he was in her rooms. "What do you want to wear?" he asked.

"I can get my own clothing," she answered, an edge to her tone that told him she was still riding that high, but there was an undercurrent of ire there too.

"I know you can," he answered. "I was only offering to help."

"Help," she repeated, and the way she said it had him tensing.

"Yes," he gritted out. "Tell me what you need."

Her laugh was humorless and tinged with madness. "Why? So you can tell me to go to Theon to get it?" Before he could respond, she went on, "You won't even look at me. How are you going to give me what I need? Is it because I killed Legacy? Because I won't apologize for that, and—"

"I'm glad you killed those fucking Legacy, Tessa," he cut in, his gaze snapping to hers and holding her stare. "You defended yourself, and I'm godsdamn proud of you for that. Tell me how you did it."

The anger in her eyes faltered a fraction. "What?"

"You heard me. Tell me how you killed them. Did you use your power?"

"For one of them."

"Did you drag it out?"

He watched her throat bob with a swallow. "Yes. Forced him to his knees. Took away his air. Took his power."

"And then?"

"I shoved a blade through his throat," she said breathlessly.

"Such a violent temptress," Luka said, his voice all gravel. "And the other?"

"I didn't use any magic. Only blades."

"I would have liked to see that."

"Why?"

"Because I've seen you when you're vicious, and it's stunning to witness."

"Stop," she snapped.

He arched a brow. "Stop what?"

"Saying things like that."

He shrugged a shoulder. "You asked. I answered."

"No," she sneered. "You say things like that. Say you're going to give me what I need and then deny me. Unless you plan to just take from me like him?"

"I'm not going to take anything from you, Tessa. You're going to have to come over here and ask for what you want."

"Ask for it?" she scoffed.

"If you think I'm making this choice for you, think again. You want people to make the hard decisions for you and that won't be me."

"I never had to ask him," she retorted, clutching the towel at her chest. "He just *knew* what I needed."

"You think I don't know what you need?" he asked with a smirk that was all predator. "I know exactly what you need, but I don't think *you* know what you need. You accuse everyone of *taking* from you—when we both know that was one thing he never *took* from you—so now you need to ask for it."

"Ask for it," she repeated again, that fury sparking once more. "What? You want me to crawl across the floor and beg sweetly from my knees?"

"If that's what you want to do."

"Absolutely not," she snarled.

He shrugged again because now that image was in his head, which was just...fucking fantastic. He was already barely hanging on the way it was. His dragon loved the idea of her on her knees, and his magic loved the idea of... Well, just her. Because now that he was spending so much time with her—alone—the pull he'd been avoiding for years was only getting stronger. But these were thoughts he had no business entertaining.

Because she was Theon's.

Mine, his dragon growled so forcefully he knew his eyes shifted.

She clearly noticed because her features shifted to something sensual. "You wouldn't know what to do with me if I crawled to you, Luka," she purred, sauntering towards him.

"Baby girl, I know exactly what I'd do with you," he countered, immediately rising to the challenge because there was no way he would let her get the upper hand in this. No part of his being would allow it. "However this isn't about what I'd do with you, but what you need right now."

"And what is it I need?"

"To expel all that energy from the high of victory," he replied.

"By sparring?" she drawled, rolling her eyes as she pushed past him.

"No, you brat," he snarled, spinning her so her back was up against the wall of the bedroom now. A dismayed huff came from her lips as he braced an arm above her head. "Ask me."

Violet eyes full of wrath and heat and suspicion stared back at him. Her words were tinged with agony when she said, "Please don't be an asshole with this."

"Ask me," he repeated.

Her eyes fell closed for a brief moment as she clearly debated what to do. When she reopened them, she whispered, "I can't."

"Why?" The word was guttural as he waited for her explanation.

"Because I don't trust you," she admitted. "I can't trust you."

Something in his chest twisted at that admission, and his dragon reared back as if she'd struck him. In a way, she had because he was here, with her, and not where he wanted to be. He was training her to control magic that would destroy the kingdom he had sworn to protect. He was standing here, ready to give her what she needed, and she said she couldn't trust him?

His mouth was on hers before he knew what he was doing, and gods, he swore every time he did this, her mouth would be the death of him. Yet here he was, coming back for the torment again and again. Didn't she realize what this was doing to him? What he was going through for her? And she couldn't fucking trust him?

He hadn't meant for this to be a deep, soul-crushing kiss. Then again, he hadn't meant to kiss her at all. This was supposed to be soft with light flicks of tongue, but then her hands were slipping into his hair. Both of them. Which meant she'd dropped that towel.

That knowledge alone had him groaning into her mouth, and the sound seemed to spur her on. She arched her back, and his arm slid around her waist before his fingers moved, tracing up the length of her spine to grip the back of her neck and hold her in place. Her mouth was hot and hungry, needing more and needing it rougher, harder. Then it was her moaning into his mouth as he gripped her hips and hoisted her up. Her legs immediately wrapped around his waist, and he cupped her ass, never breaking their kiss as he walked her to the bed.

He lowered her to the mattress, but her hands fisted the collar of his shirt, keeping him close. She was desperation and desire. His hands skimmed up her side, and it wasn't until he took one of her full breasts in his hand that she finally released his mouth with a gasp.

"Yes," she rasped, arching into his touch. "More, Luka. Please."

Theon got off on the begging. He knew that from the times they'd shared a partner in the past, but Luka had always been drawn to *this*. A female asking him for what she wanted. Giving her what she needed fulfilled some deep-seated purpose of taking care of her.

He tweaked her nipple, the soft moan the sweetest reward he'd ever received. Then he was pulling that nipple into his mouth, sucking hard. Her moan became a gasp, and he was suddenly chasing a different kind of high than she was. Gods, she tasted good. Perfection and wildness. Light and dark. Sunshine and stormy skies.

One hand kept him held above her while the fingers of his other hand skated down her belly, over her hip, and straight to the wet heat between her legs. He dragged the pad of his thumb over her swollen clit, the whimper that came from her instantly becoming his favorite sound in the realm.

"More," she rasped, her breaths shallow and fast as she thrust her cunt into his hand.

He swiped his thumb over her sensitive nerves again and felt her whole body shudder as he kept rubbing. He took his time, teasing and exploring, until he skimmed his fingertips down to her opening. His dragon snarled in satisfaction to find her dripping. Or maybe that was him doing the snarling? He didn't know at this point. All he knew was he wanted to be inside her more than he wanted anything else. There would be no coming back if he did, and that thought alone might kill him because he couldn't do this.

I trust you, Luka.

Those were his words. She didn't trust him, but Theon sure as fuck did. That was where his loyalty was. So no, he wasn't going to fuck her. But he was still going to give her what she needed, and later tonight, he'd feel like a bastard because he was going to enjoy every moment of this.

He dipped two fingers into that sweet wetness, then slid them back up where he continued to rub slow circles over her clit. He kept his gaze on her face, not wanting to miss a moment as he played with her cunt. Her hips started rocking against his hand, and her features went hazier and hazier.

"I like you like this," he said. "Not so fucking mouthy."

She tried to scowl, but he took the opportunity to dip his fingers inside her cunt, and again her expression slipped back to rapture.

"More, Luka. Please give me more."

"What would you want?"

"Anything. Everything. Your mouth. Your hand. Your cock."

Fucking Sargon.

"I can't," he said, nearly choking on the words.

"You said you'd give me what I needed," she whined, panic filling her features.

"I will, baby girl," he replied before dipping his head to suck and lick at her breasts again.

A sigh slipped from her, one of her hands moving into his hair. Her fingers tangled in the strands as her legs wrapped around his waist. She was trying her hardest to pull him closer. He was wrong. *This* might be what killed him. Knowing she wanted it, needed it. Knowing that he could have her, and she would let him do whatever he wanted.

He slid a finger in deep, and she immediately clenched around it.

"By the gods," he breathed, adding the second finger again. Her groan was somewhere between rapture and pure relief, and it was all he needed to keep going. While his thumb continued its ministrations on her clit, he slid his fingers in and out, keeping the rhythm lazy and letting her climb higher and higher. Her eyelids grew heavier, and then the fingers she had tangled in his hair gave a sharp yank.

"If you're not going to fuck me, then at least kiss me," she panted out before her tongue found his again.

She'd gone from rapture and relief to pure desperation now, her fingers clawing at his shoulders. A frustrated sound came from her as she tugged at his shirt, clearly seeking bare skin, but she was still riding his fingers. Still trying to drive him closer with her heels. And that was when he finally let his magic free.

Wisps of black flames licked along her naked flesh, and the sound that came from her was pure sex as her light raced to chase it. Their power meeting was enough to make him nearly give in, but he forced himself to stay focused on her.

"Time to come, temptress," he ground out, his own breathing just as harsh as hers. His hand kept moving, fingers sliding in and out. He knew she was there, right on the edge. He could tell by the way she was squirming beneath him, clamping around him, and fisting whatever she could find. His hair. His shirt. The bedding. He plunged his fingers in deep once more before curling them and stroking firmly.

Tessa cried out, her words a mix of unintelligible syllables and curses as her climax rippled through her. He felt it all around his fingers, in the way her body shuddered beneath him, in the way her legs squeezed tighter where they were still wrapped around his waist. Then her tiny frame went utterly lax. Her legs fell to the side, a satisfied sigh falling from her lips as Luka watched her eyelids grow heavy for a different reason now.

He eased the pressure on her clit, slowly thrusting his fingers a few more times as she came down from the high of everything. The climax. The fighting. The killing. The victory. It wasn't until he slipped his fingers from her completely that her eyelids fluttered open, connecting with his.

"Can I sleep in here tonight?" she murmured.

As if he'd let her sleep anywhere else after that.

But he said gruffly, "Yeah. Just let me clean up."

He turned, heading for the bathroom, but he stopped in the doorway. "You good, Tessa?"

"So good," she answered, already sounding half asleep.

He nodded, kicking the door shut behind him.

Then he was removing his pants in record time and taking his cock in his hand, fingers still coated in her arousal. There was no godsdamn way he was going to be able to sleep beside her without taking care of this.

Making his way to the shower, he gripped his base, pumping his shaft. He was so godsdamn hard it was painful. He didn't even bother turning the shower on. Just stood there, his feet wet from the shower Tessa had taken, and his cock wet from her and his own precum he was using to glide his fist along his length.

It didn't take long before his balls were tightening and his legs were quivering. His head went foggy, and for the briefest of moments, he had no idea why he was jerking himself in a shower instead of burying himself between her thighs. Taking her. Worshiping her.

Claiming what should have always been his.

It took everything in him to swallow the groan so she wouldn't hear as he came all over the shower wall, his release shooting through him and nearly making his knees buckle. As he was catching his breath, his brow against the cool shower wall, he finally loosened his hold on the mental shields he'd held in place throughout all of that.

With his fingers still trembling, he undid the buttons of his shirt before tossing it out of the shower and turning on the water to quickly rinse off. When he returned to his room, sliding on a pair of loose linen pants as he went, he found her already nestled under the covers. He couldn't tell if she'd put clothing on or not, and he was equally hoping she had and hadn't.

Turning off the bedside lamp, he slipped into bed, and she turned to face him, her hand tucked beneath her cheek. "You told me you always sleep naked."

"I used to," he muttered, trying to get comfortable on his back. Which was pointless because all he really wanted to do was pull her against his chest and make sure she stayed there all godsdamn night.

"But you slept beside me naked before."

"That was different."

She went silent for a long minute before he felt her roll away from him.

"Roan is doing well," he said into the dark.

"Thank you," she answered.

There was another stretch of quiet before he said, "About the Legacy you killed."

"What about them?"

"Were they Arius Legacy?"

She took a few seconds before she said, "No."

"But that's still your plan?"

"I can't tell you that," she said, her tone both hard and tired. "I can't trust you, Luka. Your loyalty is to him, not me."

And he found himself asking the same question he'd asked her months ago. "Do you wish it was to you?"

The silence stretched on for so long that he thought she wasn't going to answer until finally she whispered, "Yes." Every part of his being twisted with both betrayal and satisfaction at the admission until she added, "But wishes and hope are for the innocent and the heroes, not the monsters and the villains, so I no longer bother with either."

21

THEON

Everything about this felt wrong.

That was all he could think as he walked towards the stone house that had been built into a northern wall of the Underground. The home of the Shifter Alpha and Beta had floor to ceiling windows on each of the three levels. It stretched along a good ways, easily three city blocks if not more. While the main floor was used for business and running the Leisure District they oversaw, the upper two floors were where they lived along with several of their family members, both immediate and extended.

Theon's shoes stirred the dust of the makeshift road, and he glanced to his right where Tristyn was keeping pace. He looked as formidable as any Arius Legacy, and Theon wasn't entirely sure why. It had taken quite a bit of convincing before the male had finally agreed to accompany him. But Theon needed someone with him because he didn't have Axel or Luka.

And that was why this all felt wrong.

A male he didn't fully trust was at his right, and to his left was Katya, a fresh Mark on the back of her left hand. He still didn't like that she'd taken the thing, especially when Kylian and Giselle answered his request the very next day. Granted, they'd made him wait an additional week for this meeting.

Katya had asked Eliza to tell her how to use the Mark to find Axel, but neither Eliza nor Razik could offer any type of instruction. They both told her that each pair was different, and it was something she would need to learn on her own. Theon knew it frustrated Katya to no end. It wasn't something she could read about and learn from a book. Theon understood that annoyance well. How many hours had he spent in books trying to figure out his own Source bond?

That had been eight days ago, and Katya still hadn't felt Axel again, if she even had to begin with. Guilt churned in his gut because if this twin flame thing wasn't real between them, Axel was going to hate him for allowing Katya to take that Mark. But there was fuck all he could do about it now. They could only move forward, and hopefully something good would come of it if this meeting turned out to be pointless.

A white owl was perched on top of a gate as they approached, a loud hoot sounding. Theon nodded to the shifter guard, knowing that hoot had been announcing their arrival. Several wide steps led them up to the house where two large snow leopards were lounging, golden eyes pinned on them.

"Zara. Nico," Theon greeted the siblings who were often on guard. They were a distant relation to the Alpha and Beta, and he couldn't recall a single visit where they hadn't been stationed here.

The large double doors were thrown open, a broad male staring stoically at them. His dirty blond hair reached past his shoulders and was braided back while the sides were shaved. Muscled and tall, the male was a wolf shifter and a mean fucker at that. Which was why he was the one who greeted all guests and escorted them to the Alpha and Beta.

He rarely said anything, but today was apparently the exception as dark blue eyes narrowed on Tristyn. "What the fuck are you doing here?"

Tristyn, in true arrogant fashion, pulled a roll of lull-leaf from his brown leather jacket. "It's been a while, Altair," he answered, lighting the lull-leaf. "Thought I'd drop by and catch up."

"That is not why we're here," Theon cut in, throwing a glare at Tristyn. "He's here because he's helping me with a confidential matter. The Alpha and Beta are expecting me."

"I know they are expecting *you*," Altair replied, his stare still fixed on Tristyn. "But I'm betting they are not expecting *him*. You are usually accompanied by your brother and Luka."

He wasn't wrong, which just circled back to all of this feeling wrong without them here, but he was also more than curious about what had happened between Blackheart and the Shifters. The Shifters were easily offended, but they were also not people you wanted to be on the wrong side of.

"Be that as it may," Theon said, letting his magic drift around him while he adjusted his shirt cuffs beneath his suit jacket. "Who does and who does not accompany me does not need to be monitored by anyone when I give you all such freedom here, wouldn't you agree?" Altair's stare slid to him, and Theon's smile was tight and sharp as he added, "This is also a pressing matter, so you can escort us to Kylian and Giselle now."

It was clear this was a dominant command. Altair's mouth pressed into a thin line, and he stepped aside to let them in.

The floor was laden with ornate rugs that muffled their footsteps as they were led past several of the windows and into a room that was situated deeper into the cave wall. There were no windows in this room. Only two overly large chairs at the front that were suspiciously similar to the chairs the Lords and Ladies sat on at Tribunal Hearings.

A male was seated on the one on the left. His brown skin appeared even darker in the low lighting of the room that cast shadows across them all. He was solidly built, his brown hair shaved on one side while the other was long, reaching nearly to his waist. His olive eyes watched them intensely, a stern look on his face as they approached.

On the other seat sat a female. The word beautiful wouldn't do her justice. Her wine red hair brushed her collarbones, while light grey eyes passed over them with an amused gleam. High cheekbones, full lips, and fuller breasts with curves that made both males and females stare, she was sipping from a golden chalice, one long leg crossed over the other.

The pair of them were mates, and they were also power shifters. While most Shifters only had one other form, power shifters could shift into any animal or anyone, and they were rare. So rare, Theon only knew of six of them in the Underground. They could also shift energy and matter, but they did each have a preferred form. Kylian favored a large, black jaguar, while Giselle often shifted into a giant python.

The doors thudded shut behind them, but Theon knew Altair stood just outside.

"Thank you for agreeing to see me," Theon said, his darkness still drifting around him both as a warning and as a reminder of who he was.

"Anything for the Arius Lord," Giselle said with a sensual purr that rolled over him like a physical caress.

"He's not the Arius Lord yet," Kylian said in a deep voice. "And bringing Tristyn Blackheart into our home is not the way to start this encounter. Did he not tell you he is not welcome here?"

"I did relay to him that this would likely not go well with my presence, but you know how the Lords and Ladies can be," Tristyn said with a mocking sigh as he took a toke of his lull-leaf. "No one can tell them what to do."

Theon slowly turned to him, but Tristyn didn't appear to notice as he blew smoke from his lips. Tamping down on his irritation, Theon returned his attention to the Shifters.

"Tristyn is not your concern here. He is accompanying me on another matter, but let's cut right to the heart of things," Theon said. "I am told my father has holdings in the Leisure District. As the new Arius Lord, those holdings now belong to me. I need to know their locations."

"I have no idea to what you are referring," Giselle said, and if Theon didn't know how cunning the Shifters were, he would have believed her. Maybe she was speaking the truth, but they could lie so smoothly, it was nearly impossible to take them at their word. He needed proof, but if there truly were no holdings, how would they prove that?

"Even if we did, as was already stated, you are not the Arius Lord yet," Kylian added.

"A technicality," Theon scoffed. "Either way, I am the acting Arius Lord. Even if that weren't fact, I would still be the Arius Heir, and it is still my kingdom that allows you to govern this District so freely. I'm sure that could be changed rather quickly if necessary."

His power thickened around him, black swallowing his emerald irises. Neither of the Shifters moved, but neither of them had a retort for him either.

"But now that such matters are settled," he went on, letting his magic wane as he pulled his darkness back to him, only letting wisps linger. "I am also prepared to pay what is necessary for the information."

"Are you?" Giselle asked, her chin resting in her hand as she swirled her chalice.

"Yes," Theon answered immediately.

"And if the price is not coin?

Not how he thought this was going to go, but he said, "I'm listening, assuming this price is within reason."

"Within reason?" Giselle asked with a small lilt of laughter. "What price is too high for this information you are desperate to have?"

He thought about lying about the desperation part, but who was he kidding? Axel had been missing for weeks. He *was* getting desperate.

Giselle's eyes flicked to Katya, who was standing quietly a step behind him, like a Fae had always been taught to do.

"She is not part of these negotiations," Theon said quickly.

"So possessive of your Fae," Giselle tsked.

"Not possessive, but protective of what is my responsibility to keep safe," he replied, his magic trembling with the desire to speed this along.

"Like your people," she commented.

"Yes, like my people."

"And your family."

"Yes," he gritted out.

"Glad you see it that way," she continued. "Because we are also very protective of what is *our* responsibility to keep safe. Like our people. And our family."

A small, knowing smirk pulled at the corner of her lips when Kylian spoke. "And what of your companions? Are *they* willing to pay such a price?"

"You negotiate with me," Theon said sharply.

Kylian's sharp smile had every part of him on high alert as something wild and predatory entered his eyes. His eyes shifted to feline pupils when he said, "A bargain then, young Legacy."

By the gods. All these fucking bargains being made left and right. Eventually, this was going to catch up to them.

"State your desired terms," Theon said.

"Find our missing Shifter Prince."

Theon once again blinked at him until all he managed to say was, "I was unaware one of your children was missing."

"My children are all accounted for," Kylian replied. Those feline eyes slid to Tristyn. "My sister's child, however, is not."

Theon turned to Tristyn, finding him staring at the Shifter Alpha in horror. Theon had never seen the male so unpoised.

"You never told me there was a child," Tristyn said.

"It wasn't your business to know," Kylian replied coldly. "But it seems we have also reached desperate times."

"I need someone to fill me in here," Theon said, looking between the two males before he turned to Giselle. "How and when?"

"I think Tristyn can fill you in on the how. As for the when, twenty-three years ago," Giselle said, her features hardening.

"And how, exactly, am I supposed to find him?" Theon asked.

The small smirk returned. "I suppose it is a good thing you brought Tristyn along after all. Between him and his sister, you should be able to come up with something."

"Sister?" Theon repeated, once again turning to Tristyn.

But he was glaring at the Shifters. "Thanks for that," Tristyn ground out.

"I would call it karma, but truly, it's just vengeance," Giselle replied sweetly.

The moment they reappeared inside the penthouse of the high rise, Theon rounded on Tristyn.

"You couldn't have said something *before* we came here?" Theon demanded, his darkness whipping out and latching onto the male. "Or, you know, *any* of the times we've had interactions."

Tristyn looked from him to the black threads wrapped around him then back again. There was no mistaking the way his russet eyes took on a sage green glow before Theon's power stuttered as if confused. It slowly loosened, despite Theon's hold on it, but his magic resisted, as though there wasn't a threat standing before them.

"Everyone believes the god of peace and serenity is just that. Peaceful. Calm. The god everyone would pray to in the midst of war and conflict," Tristyn said, his tone low and forceful. "The thing no one realizes is that he is just as cunning as any god. He can be just as cruel when he makes everyone around him feel serene and relaxed just so he can shove a blade into their back."

It took a minute to process those words, his brain feeling sluggish and lax, but when he did, he found Tristyn idly twirling a dagger between his fingers.

"You're a Pax Legacy," Theon sneered. "But that doesn't explain how *Cienna* is your sister because she is clearly a Witch."

That was what Tristyn had begrudgingly revealed to him after Giselle's little comment. There hadn't been time to dive into the specifics. No, instead Theon was sporting yet another Bargain Mark. This one was on the back of his shoulder. Theon would locate this lost Shifter Prince and only then would they reveal the location of his father's holdings within the District. At least they'd admitted that he did in fact have holdings, so Theon could try to locate them on his own.

"I am not a Pax Legacy," Tristyn said. "Pax is my father."

"Bullshit," Theon huffed, but even as he said it, he knew it was true. Why wouldn't it be?

"As for Cienna, yes. We are full-blooded siblings. Pax fell in love with one of Taika's descendants," he replied.

"So you are both Pax and Taika Legacy?"

"We are not Legacy at all. A direct descendant of a god makes us deities," Tristyn answered. "And before you ask, Tessa is more than that, despite being a direct descendant of Temural."

"Of course you know that," Theon muttered.

"Anyway, the magic of the witchcraft sisters favors females. I can access it, but it takes more effort on my end. She favors healing and potions; I favor enchantments and spell enhancements."

"All of Lilura Inquest's technological advances," Theon said in realization. "That's how you built your company."

"Something like that," Tristyn said with a sly smile, still twirling the dagger.

"If Pax is your father, you're not from this world."

"Has anyone ever told you how smart you are?" Tristyn asked mockingly.

"Fuck off," Theon snapped. "Everyone keeps berating me for not knowing things when I've been taught one thing my entire life. Even when I found books and texts that challenged the history I was taught, they were so sparse I couldn't substantiate anything. Then I come to find out you've been here this entire fucking time doing fuck all to change a godsdamn thing."

Tristyn moved fast, but Theon met his advance with a short blade pulled from a swirl of black. The male might be a deity, but Theon had been trained in the most ruthless of manners. Still, he could feel Tristyn's power weighing on him, coaxing his magic into passivity, and he found himself wishing Tessa or Luka were here. He could draw from either one of them because he would certainly weaken faster than Tristyn.

"You think I have been doing nothing for hundreds of years while I was waiting for her to get here?" Tristyn demanded, and there was no russet color left in them now. They were pure glowing sage green.

"Waiting for her to get here?" Theon repeated in confusion.

"You all whine and complain about being forgotten by the gods, when the reality is you all like it. There's no one here to correct you. The Lords and Ladies can keep everyone in the dark, and the gods that do manage to meddle here are never caught because everyone thinks they can't be here. You all have been isolated for so godsdamn long you forget that anything is possible if one is willing to pay the price."

Tristyn's breathing was harsh after his tirade, and Theon was still trying to wrap his mind around what he'd said. He was still stuck on the same question though.

"What did you mean when you said you've been waiting for her to get here?" Theon repeated, slowly lowering his blade when he was sure Tristyn wasn't going to lunge at him again. "How many years have you been here?"

"Four hundred fifty-nine years, seven months, and twelve days," Tristyn answered, his arm falling to his side.

"You know down to the day?" Theon said in disbelief.

"You'd know too if it was the last time you'd seen the one you'd sacrifice anything for," Tristyn replied.

Theon couldn't argue with that. He already counted how many days it'd been since he'd seen Tessa.

Eight.

Eight days with each day feeling longer and longer as the bond made everything that much more intense.

"You've been separated from your...wife? For over four centuries?"

"She's not my wife. Not yet," he answered. "But she will be."

"Where is she?"

Sadness filled his face, the glow in his eyes fading. "I don't know."

"You don't... I don't understand," Theon said.

"It's not for you to understand," he answered. "The point is, I'm here. Helping you. Because if Tessa continues on the path she's on, we'll have much bigger problems than the underhanded politics of Devram."

"Explain that," Theon said, his fingers clenching around the hilt of the short sword he still held.

"You know all this already," Tristyn said in annoyance. "Auryon told you if something happens to her, her parents will come for you."

"Because it will be my fault?"

Tristyn appeared to debate that for a minute before saying, "That's fair. They'll come for the realm."

Theon sighed, a faint throbbing starting at his temples. "We'll come back to…all of that. Right now, tell me what the fuck happened with the Shifters twenty-three years ago."

Tristyn shrugged out of his jacket, tossing it over a nearby chair. Pushing a hand through his hair, he said, "When Tessa was brought here, she became lost."

"Who brought her here?"

"I can't tell you that," he answered. "But we were trying desperately to find her. I went to the Alpha and Beta to ask them for aid. Shifters are excellent trackers. The next best thing to an actual Tracker. Outside of this realm, the Shifters favor Temural, as do most animals, and he favors them. I didn't give them details. Only that I was searching for a missing child. Kylian and Giselle wouldn't leave the Underground, but Kylian's sister, Khari, agreed to help.

"Every lead we found eventually led to a dead end, and after two years, we were both getting anxious. I was watching every request that came through Lilura's Inquest hoping for a new direction to go in, but Kylian was demanding that Khari return to the Underground. It was getting harder to keep my real identity a secret because I couldn't Travel or move around as freely with her. But more than that, about a year into our search, we had come across a Fae who was on the run, trying to make his way to a rumored safe haven for the Fae. Khari fell in love with the male, a water Fae. She didn't want to go back to the Underground. She wanted to stay with him."

"That's why they hate you?" Theon asked.

"No, they hate me because Khari was captured and held hostage for over a year. And apparently she had a child in that time," Tristyn answered. When Theon only waited expectantly, he went on. "We were in the Celeste Kingdom following a lead. Knowing what I know now, we were so close to finding her, but we were attacked. Not for me. Not even for the Fae, but for her. Somehow they knew she was a Shifter. Long story short, they killed the Fae, I was incapacitated, and she was taken."

Theon's brow furrowed. "Taken where?"

"The Sirana Villas," Tristyn said, looking anywhere but at Theon. "I don't know how much you know about what goes on there—"

"I know what happens at the Villas, but Tessa mentioned there are other Villas behind the manor."

Tristyn nodded. "They…" He pushed out a long breath, his hand going through his hair again. "They basically do experiments there. Force Fae to conceive with Legacy. Try to create stronger Fae."

"That's forbidden," Theon said automatically. Because it was. There were laws against it. It was why the Fae were given their contraceptive shots regularly.

Tristyn gave him a mocking look. "Because those who run this realm clearly follow their own laws. They're as hypocritical as the gods. The Sources of the Lords and Ladies? All of them have Legacy blood. No one else knows. They had them specially bred for this exact purpose."

"That can't be true," Theon said, but even as he spoke the words, he knew it was. It sounded exactly like something the rulers would do.

It sounded exactly like something his father would do.

"Anyway," Tristyn said when the silence lingered. "Khari was taken and housed there. Apparently they succeeded in forcing her to carry a child."

"Are you saying there is a half-Shifter, half-Legacy somewhere in Devram?" Theon asked. "That's who we're looking for?"

"I don't know who the father would be. Could be Legacy. Could be Fae. Could be another being," he replied with a shrug. "But to start, we should try to speak to Khari."

"Like that's an option," Theon scoffed. "They practically kicked us out of their home after I made the bargain with Kylian."

"I would be willing to speak to Khari if the Alpha and Beta are open to it."

They both turned to find Katya in the doorway.

"No," Theon said immediately. "It's too dangerous."

She gave him a small but challenging smile. "I think we're well past this, Theon, don't you?"

"Axel is already going to kill me for letting you take that Mark," he said. "There is no way I'm letting you speak to Khari on your own."

"Then send someone with me," she insisted. "I'm part of this, Theon. I became part of this long before I took this Mark," she added, lifting her left hand in emphasis. The Mark stood out, dark against her warm skin. "You can't do it all yourself. You have to let others help, especially with Luka and Axel not here."

"I'll think about it," Theon said tightly, this whole idea of compromising and conceding a foreign concept.

Katya nodded. "Please do. I'm going to make some food. Would you like something?"

"You don't have to do that," Theon said.

"But I am offering to. I'll see what I can find."

The kitchen would be sparse here, but he let her wander off. He knew it was more about her needing something to do rather than the need to eat. He'd learned that about her these past weeks. She kept herself busy to the point of exhaustion. He suspected it was to keep from thinking too much about Axel. If she let herself stop for even a moment, she felt like she was giving up on him.

At least that was how it felt when it came to Tessa and all of this mess.

"I think I remember this," Theon said.

"Remember this? You would have been, what? Four years?"

Theon nodded. "I was forced to sit in on his meetings from the time I was three years. I vaguely recall mentions of a missing child." When Tristyn only stared at him, he asked, "If you had found her, where would you have taken her?"

"To the Anala Kingdom," Tristyn answered, watching him carefully.

Theon only nodded as he made his way to the alcohol cart because of course that was where he'd take her. To the kingdom that kept everyone else out. To the kingdom that had been content to let the Arius Kingdom take the brunt of the hatred for centuries so they could go about their own agendas as unnoticed as possible.

"What's her name?" Theon asked, pouring the whiskey into glasses. "The one you haven't seen in over four centuries."

He watched Tristyn swallow thickly as Theon brought him a glass of liquor.

"Lilura," he answered hoarsely.

Before Theon could comment, both his and Tristyn's cell phones pinged with multiple incoming messages. The two glanced at each other, pulling their phones out. It was rare to get any kind of service in the Underground, but he suspected it had something to do with the male he was currently sharing a drink with.

"By the gods," Theon murmured at the same time Tristyn said, "Fucking Fates."

Urgent message after urgent message came in. Some were texts. Some were messages left after missed calls. But all of them said the same thing.

There had been a massacre at the Sirana Villas. All the casualties had been Legacy, and the Fae housed there were missing.

22

AXEL

xel? Axel, can you hear me?

He blinked as he watched the blood pool on the floor beside him, the puddle growing bigger and bigger the longer he stared at it.

Until he tried to dip a finger in it.

Then the fucking thing would disappear.

And now, apparently, this was a fresh level of fuckery. He could hear her. The one whose name he couldn't remember.

Axel? Axel, please answer me.

She sounded so desperate. Or maybe that was just his own voice manifesting in his head. Because he was fucking desperate.

He shoved his hands through his hair, pulling on the strands that had grown out longer than he liked. Bree had someone shave his face a few days ago, but there was now a layer of scruff along his jaw again.

Axel? Where are you?

Well, fuck it. May as well have a conversation with himself. What else was he going to do in here besides try to catch mythical blood?

Where are you? he countered.

The penthouse in the Charter District.

He paused at that because why would he conjure that type of response?

Axel? the voice came again.

You're at the penthouse?

Yes! Yes, I am. Where are you?

He reached out, trying to dip his fingers into the blood again, the puddle instantly disappearing as he scraped his nails against the floor. Another hallucination. That was all this was. Because if it was really her, she would be able to—

What's your name? he demanded. *What do I call you?*

There was a pause that had him smiling to himself. He wasn't falling for all these mind tricks of the bloodlust. He could still spot—

You call me kitten, the voice answered.

That seemed even more far-fetched. Why would he call her that?

And why was this door unlocked?

Wait. Better question. When had he gotten up and walked across the room?

He looked over his shoulder. The blood on the floor and the walls was gone. In fact, he was thinking clearer than he had in weeks.

Cautiously pulling the door open, Axel peered into the hall, finding it empty. Which was perfect. Because she was nearby. He could practically feel her. And if she was nearby, then he could finally—*finally*—have her.

He paid no attention to his surroundings. His entire being was narrowed in on finding her. Seeing her. Tasting her. Having her. His. She was his and no one else's. If anyone tried to stop him, he'd simply end them. He just had to get outside of these walls.

He continued wandering, taking several staircases down. Surely he must need to go down to find his way out. That was logical. He was already underground. How much deeper could he go? Okay, that was a silly notion. Obviously they could go deeper into the ground. There were earth Fae down here, but—

He went still when he entered a large room and found Bree lounging on a settee along one wall. She wore her usual red dress, her legs crossed and arms spread across the back of the furniture. He relaxed a fraction when she smiled at him.

"My room was unlocked," he said, suddenly wondering how he was standing. His legs were weak, and he could feel himself trembling.

"I know," Bree said. "I'm the one who unlocked it."

"Why?" he rasped out.

Slowly, she got to her feet, closing the distance between them. She reached up, brushing a lock of hair from his brow. "I told you I'd find her for you, didn't I?'

His brows pinched together. "You found her? Where is she?"

"Somewhere only you can go," Bree replied.

"And you're just...going to let me go? I won't come back."

She patted his chest before smoothing down his shirt. Then she stepped back from him. "I trust you'll find yourself exactly where you need to be. Fate is funny like that."

Then he watched her saunter off down a hall, leaving him standing in the middle of the foyer.

He wouldn't be coming back. Not if he truly was about to find her.

He'd find her and take and have and all would be well in the world again. His power at his fingertips. Back with his family. No more gods-damn hallucinations. No more mania.

He looked around at the shops that lined the road. Once again, he didn't remember leaving the foyer or walking out here. Looking back over his shoulder, the House of Four towered behind him. He was never stepping foot in there again. When this was over, if Theon needed something from the vampyres, he could go himself.

The penthouse.

That was where she said she was.

It became his singular focus as he made his way through the roads of the Underground. He passed others—Night Children, Shifters, Witches, and Fae. Oddly enough, he didn't even care about the Fae. Because she was getting closer. He could feel it.

The only time he paused was when he passed the turn for the Leisure District. The faint scent of jasmine and citrus caught his attention, that underlying smokiness and spices almost having him turning in that direction. But what would she be doing in the Leisure District? That was where people went for pleasure of all kinds. Opioids. Taverns. Sex.

Something inside of him went feral at the idea.

His.

She was his.

If she had gone there for any of their offerings...

No. Somehow he knew she wasn't there. Something in him was drawing him away from that path and towards the Charter District. That was where she'd said she was. Or the voice inside his head had said that. This...kitten.

Gods, maybe he was still hallucinating.

But even if he was, he was still free from the House of Four.

So he continued on, those scents growing as strong as the pull in his gut.

"Late night, huh?" the doorman said in a gruff voice as Axel drew near the building that housed the penthouse. He'd shown up here bloody and disheveled more than once, so his appearance wasn't out of the ordinary.

He nodded to the male, but didn't linger because she was here. He could feel it in his bones, in his blood, in the center of his soul.

The lift seemed to take hours to finally get to the top, and when he stepped into the living area, the space was dark. Everyone here was likely sleeping, and since the wards recognized him, they wouldn't have alerted Theon or Luka to his presence.

Somehow knowing exactly where she was, Axel climbed the stairs to the second floor. Luka's room was down the hall, and Theon would be on the third floor with Tessa. He stopped outside his room, fingers trembling as he reached for the doorknob. Feeling the surrounding wards unlock, he slipped inside, quietly closing the door behind him.

And there she was. Asleep in his bed. Waiting for him.

Except she wasn't asleep.

She lurched upright, a hand coming to her chest. Her amber eyes almost glowed in the dark room. Coils of black hair framed her face and fell around her shoulders. She blinked several times, that hand moving from her chest to her mouth as she stared at him.

"Don't be scared, kitten," he said, watching her while he leaned against the closed door.

"Axel? I... How are you here?"

She slid from the bed, but she didn't come any closer. One hand rested on her stomach, a black Mark on the back of it, while she twisted the fingers of the other into the sheets.

"You told me where to find you," he said in a low tone, every last shred of self-control going into keeping himself on this door. He'd been waiting so long for this moment. He was going to savor it.

"I did, but I didn't expect you to... You have been unwell," she said, her stare never leaving his.

"How would you know that?"

"I... We learned some things. Let me get Theon," she said, taking a single step.

Then she stilled when Axel straightened. There was no way she was leaving here. Not now that he finally had her in his grasp. Not until he'd tasted her, the warm blood on his tongue, feeding every part of him.

She swallowed, her throat bobbing. "Axel," she whispered. "Let me go get Theon. Please."

"Theon won't understand," he said, transfixed on the pulse point in her throat now. He could hear it beating wildly like the wings of a hummingbird. He could *feel* her, both relieved and terrified, but there was something else there. Something he couldn't place with the mania of being this close to her and her blood and blessed paradise when he finally got to take it from her.

But there was something off about her scent too, now that he was this close. Jasmine and citrus, yes. Smoke and underlying spices, but also...something woodsy? No. That couldn't be right. Unless—

"Were you in the Leisure District?" he snapped.

She took a few steps back. "Yes," she answered. "We were visiting the Alpha and Beta. Trying to find you."

He narrowed his eyes. "What else?"

Her brow furrowed. "What else? Nothing. What else would I do in the Leisure District?"

"Any number of pleasures and sins can be found there," he snarled, prowling forward. Each step amplified his need and craving. His body was buzzing with it. His ears were ringing with it. Gods, he could swear even his canines were tingling with anticipation.

"You cannot possibly be accusing me of—" She cut herself off mid-sentence, flames flickering in her eyes as a glimmer of irritation filled her features.

It made him pause for only a moment. He liked it when she was like this.

"We have been doing nothing for weeks but trying to find you. I have researched for hours while simultaneously fulfilling my obligations to *your* kingdom. I have hardly slept. Corbin and Lange make sure I eat. And all of this on top of—" She stopped speaking again when he came to a stop directly in front of her. Her next words were breathy, but still laced with anger. "How dare you accuse me of doing that when I would do anything for you."

"You smell different," he said, reaching out and wrapping a coil of black around his finger.

Something akin to surprise crossed her face, but she snapped, "You just plain old smell."

He smiled a pointed thing. "You would do anything for me?"

"Yes," she rasped as he released her hair and skated a fingertip along her jaw. Her eyes fluttered closed, and her entire body leaned into that single touch.

"Sacrifice anything?" he said, that finger sliding down along the column of her neck.

Her eyes flew open as she jerked back, but she wasn't nearly fast enough. His arm was already wrapped around her waist while his other hand clamped onto the back of her neck.

"Axel! Wait! I need to tell you—"

Her words dissolved into a strained whimper as his teeth sank into her throat. Warm and luscious, she tasted exactly like he knew she would. Hot and fiery. Sweet and citrusy. He groaned, sucking harder, and his power wells. *Gods.* His power wells stirred in excitement, thin wisps of shadows appearing. Her hands were on his chest, pushing and shoving against him, but she would never be able to overpower him. Even when her fire appeared, he had enough magic now that his shadows created a barrier, keeping him safe to feed, and it only strengthened with each pull.

He took, and he took, and he took.

Life must give, and death must take.

Every second made his shadows thicken. Every minute strengthened him. Every swallow had him only wanting more. The chase. The hunt. The victory. This was his prize. After weeks of waiting, weeks of agony, this was his to claim. His to have. His to make bleed.

He took another hard pull. Her fingers had curled into his shirt, but they loosened some, another strained cry coming from her lips.

Axel, stop.

Her voice was faint, a whisper in the back of his mind.

Relax, kitten, he crooned back. *It will all be over soon.*

All of him was focused on her. On how she tasted. How her blood felt sliding down his throat and how her skin felt beneath his fingers and tongue. That scent that still was off yet somehow right. Sounds were fuzzy and muffled because nothing mattered but this.

Until there were hands on his shoulders and darkness wrapped around him, dragging him away from what was his.

Axel snarled as his mouth was ripped from her, his canines scraping and tearing flesh. Blood ran down her neck. All that blood being wasted! Seeping between the fingers of another who had his hand pressed to the wound. She was lax in his arms, and the male was murmuring low, trying to wake her. Who was he to touch what was his?

He snarled again, baring his teeth, but when he tried to attack, he was yanked backwards again, so violently he fell, landing on his back. Another male was instantly on top of him. Inky black swirls obscured emerald irises as the male tried to pin him down. But he had his magic back, and he had just fed. He was just as strong, and with a roar of rage, he rolled the male, landing a punch to his side.

"Axel! Enough! You were going to kill her!" the male barked, grabbing his shirt. He pulled, the fabric ripping, and Axel landed another punch, this time to the male's jaw. He spat out blood, another wave of his magic throwing Axel to the side. "Don't make me do this, Axel," he pleaded. "I know you're experiencing blood lust, but I need you to—"

He was cut off when he went flying backwards as shadows picked him up and threw him. Axel didn't give a fuck what he needed. He only cared that this asshole had taken him from what was rightfully his and someone else had her. From a swirl of shadows, he pulled a dagger, advancing on the male who now had black wings.

"Are you fucking with me right now?" the male said, clearly annoyed as he conjured a blade of his own. "Axel. You have to stop. If you drink any more, you will undoubtedly trigger the curse."

"She is *mine*," Axel snarled, his shadows converging around him

"You're right," the male retorted, his sword raised in a defensive position. "She is yours, and you're hurting her instead of protecting her."

Axel lunged, steel meeting steel at the same time that shadows met darkness. The male met him blow for blow as they maneuvered around the room. That other male still held her in his arms, blood still dripping to the floor.

"No!" Axel cried, abandoning the fight and trying to get back to her again, but darkness latched onto him and forced him back to the ground. His shadows clawed and thrashed.

"Don't make me do this, Axel," the male muttered again, standing over him and breathing hard.

Axel kicked out, connecting with the male's shin and making him bark a curse. It was enough to loosen the grip of his magic, and Axel was back on his feet.

"Get a fucking band on him, St. Orcas! Now!" the other male yelled.

"I'm trying," the male he was fighting yelled back. "Focus on Katya."

"We need Cienna for this."

"Fucking Arius," the male muttered, tossing his sword to the ground, that inky magic thickening around him and spearing straight for Axel.

He tried to move. Leap out of the way. *Something.* But the magic jumped with him, encasing his feet and ankles and cementing them to the floor.

With another snarl of rage, Axel started pooling his shadows, letting them writhe around him until a giant feline stood beside him, snarling and snapping.

"For fuck's sake. Not you too," the male muttered, holding out a palm. A black band lay in the center of it, until it didn't. Until the male's magic engulfed it, and then it swirled around Axel's wrist, the band suddenly appearing.

His shadows sputtered out, the feline dissipating, but his fury didn't.

As the male approached, Axel took a swing.

"By the gods, Axel! Stop!" the male snapped, blocking the punch. "Do you want me to let you kill her?"

Axel, stop.

His head swung to her. Her eyes were open now, fixed on him. Her warm skin was pale, her face leeched of color. Blood still trickled across her throat, the shirt she wore now stained red around the collar, and all he could think about was needing more. He'd finally had her, and now she was being taken from him again. A trick. This had been a trick to lure him here and torture him some more.

"I won't go back there," he said, not sure who he was even talking to, but his eyes went back to the male. His eyes were wholly emerald now, the darkness gone. "I'd rather die."

"We're not taking you back there," the male said, his tone softening. "We're going to take you home."

"Home," Axel repeated, the word foreign on his tongue.

"Yes, brother. Home."

"Axel?" Her soft voice was scarcely above a whisper, ravaged and raw. "Axel, look at me."

He slowly slid his gaze back to her.

"I need you to come back. This isn't you. I need you to come back."

Each of her words were pained and clearly a struggle to get out, and something in his chest cracked as he stared at her.

Then it shattered when her voice echoed in his mind.

We need you to come back. Me and our babe.

Her hand slid to her stomach, resting atop it as her eyes fell closed again.

He lurched forward, needing to go to her, but he was still being held in place by Theon's magic.

Theon.

His brother.

"Let me go, Theon," Axel said, still straining against the magic.

"I don't think that's a good idea right now," Theon said, massaging his jaw where Axel had hit him. "We just had a decent brawl, and I know you would have stabbed me and then gone back to her."

Axel flinched. It was a full body reaction to his words. "I'm not going to… Thank you. For stopping me."

Theon's eyes narrowed as if he was debating if he was being honest or if this was all a ruse.

"You have this band on me. I can't access my magic," Axel tried, lifting his arm in emphasis.

"Your magic is the least of my concerns here, Axel," he said. "You look…"

Axel looked down at his ripped shirt and loose linen pants. He didn't even have shoes on. How had he not noticed he wasn't wearing shoes? He'd walked across the entire Underground barefoot. When he really thought about it, though, he didn't remember the walk here. It had to have been a good two hours, if not more, and he didn't remember it. He only remembered being focused on her, knowing where she was, and how he could finally have her.

And then he'd nearly killed her. Her and…

That couldn't have been true. That was a lingering hallucination from the bloodlust. There was no possible way because the Fae were given regular contraceptive shots. Sure, when he fucked around with other Legacy, he took a tonic beforehand to ensure there were no unwanted Arius heirs, but he hadn't bothered with Kat because of the seasonal Fae shots.

"Axel?" Theon said, his tone a touch softer but still a firm command. "I know you want to be near her, but after what just happened here—"

"It might not be a bad idea," the other male cut in, and it was only then that Axel registered it was Tristyn Blackheart who was lifting Katya's lax form to the bed. "I sent a message to Cienna. Gia is on her way, but having Axel near might ease discomfort until she gets here."

"Ease discomfort," Axel said with a disbelieving huff. "I did this to her."

"I understand," Tristyn said. "But you weren't in your right mind, and there's something you don't know."

"I know," Axel said tightly.

"You know about the bond?" Theon asked in surprise.

And that made two of them, because what fucking bond?

The confusion on his face must have been evident because Theon said, "If you weren't talking about the bond, what were you talking about?"

"Nothing," Axel muttered, running a hand through his too long hair. "What bond?"

"You know what? Let's not go into that here. Not until you're... thinking more clearly," Theon said, eyeing him.

"I'm not eight anymore, Theon," Axel sighed. "You don't need to protect me from the world. It already swallowed me whole and spit me back out to be fucked all over again."

"Axel—"

"No," he cut in. "If it will help her, just tell me what to do. Stay close by, and stop me if I try to... You know. Again," he said, refusing to meet his brother's gaze.

There was a long stretch of silence before he felt Theon's magic release him. He moved stiffly to the bed, sucking in a sharp breath at all the blood. Not because he wanted to taste it, but because what had he done to her?

"It's all right," Tristyn said. "We're here if you try anything."

"What should I do?" Axel asked hoarsely.

"Just touch her. A physical connection will help."

"A physical connection?" he repeated, his hand shaking as he reached for her. "That sounds like a Source bond."

Another few seconds of silence ticked by before Theon only said, "Sort of."

Axel skated the tips of his fingers along her arm, realizing now she was wearing his shirt. He eyed her stomach. Even with her curves, his shirt was too big on her, obscuring her belly. He traced the new Mark on the back of her hand before sliding his palm up, laying it flat over her torso and splaying his fingers wide. There was no possible way.

"We should get out of the Underground," Theon was saying. "Take her back to the Acropolis manor. Cienna can meet us there."

"Cienna?" Axel asked. "She can't leave the Underground."

"A lot has happened, Axel," Theon said, rubbing at his brow with his thumb and forefinger.

"Is that why Blackheart is here instead of Luka? And where is Tessa?"

He could swear Theon winced. "Yeah, that's why."

"Great explanation. Cleared up a lot of things," he replied dryly.

"I think we should wait until Gia checks her over. If Gia says we can move her, then we will," Tristyn cut in. "But there are only so many places I can Travel in the Underground. There are too many wards and enchantments down here that can cause unexpected complications."

"You can Travel?" Axel asked.

"Again, a lot has happened," Theon said. "So let's focus on Katya. Then get you cleaned up and your mind cleared. Once we're out of here, I'll explain everything."

"My mind clear. Right," Axel muttered, his hand still on Kat's stomach.

She couldn't be pregnant. The others would have sensed it. Some of the tension eased from his muscles at that thought. More than that, Kat shifted on the bed, her features twisting in pain, and that snapped him out of any remaining stupor. Despite being filthy, he climbed onto the bed, being careful not to jostle her too much as he pulled her against his chest. If physical contact would help, then that was what he'd do. Anything to fix this colossal mess.

He didn't know how long it was until Gia finally arrived, her chin-length dark auburn hair swaying around her sharp features. Her violet-blue eyes went straight to Katya, her lips pursing. Setting her leather bag down, she stepped forward, faint light flaring from her hands as she held them over Kat.

"You need to speak to Cienna," she said, her eyes closed in concentration while she worked.

"We will when we get back," Theon said from where he stood at the foot of the bed.

"Not you," Gia replied. She opened her eyes briefly, connecting with Axel's stare. "You."

He watched as her hands hovered over Kat's stomach, and in that moment, he knew.

He knew it hadn't been a hallucination. Katya had somehow spoken to him the way a Source and Master communicated. He could only assume it had something to do with the new Mark on the back of her hand.

But that also meant she was carrying a child.

His child.

He couldn't even protect her from himself, and now he was supposed to protect a child? A child that would be killed on sight if discovered because Fae and Legacy were not to procreate.

His stomach lurched at the thought of what his father would do when he learned of this. It was a death sentence for Kat and the child, and for him?

He'd likely find himself back in the dark for the rest of his days.

"You're breathing too fast, and I need to focus on her right now," Gia snapped. "Do not pass out or vomit."

"Okay," he rasped, as if he had any control over that.

"Axel, she's going to be fine," Theon said. "I'll make sure everything is fine."

Except not even his older brother could fix this or protect him from the fallout.

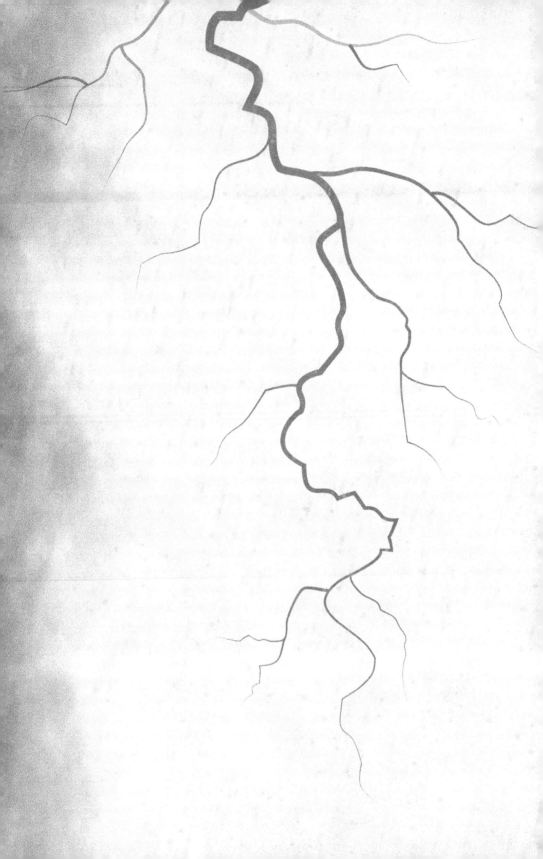

23

TESSA

"Did your training session go well?"

Tessa let out a small scream at the unexpected voice, her power appearing and striking out. She had just taken a shower after her morning training with Luka, and seeing Rordan sitting in an armchair in her room made her glad she'd put on a robe today. She was fine with nudity and all, but being bare in front of the Achaz Lord was not high on her list of things to accomplish in this life. And thankfully the robe was gold, not white, because white would have still shown everything.

"I wasn't expecting you," Tessa said, her heart rate slowly returning to normal.

Rordan only smiled, his hand still raised from where he'd intercepted her magic. She hadn't meant to attack him, of course. It had been an impulsive reaction.

When he didn't speak, Tessa fiddled with the sash of the robe, pulling it tighter. "Did we have a meeting I forgot about?"

"No," Rordan said casually. "Apparently you've kept yourself busy these days, and I thought we should discuss your extracurricular activities."

She went still at that, her entire body tensing and going on high alert. Two nights ago she'd gone back to the Sirana Villas and done exactly what she'd told Brecken she was going to do. The wards hadn't been an issue, just as they'd suspected, and Brecken had been there, waiting for her. She'd summoned the Hunters and told them to start at the front gates. With the sentinels out of the way, there was no one to let help in when the screams filled the night. There had been no way to shield the Fae without alerting the Legacy, but it hadn't taken long for them to realize they weren't the targets. Tessa had taken care of Desiray herself, enjoying every moment of draining her power and then her life. Watching as black lines webbed across her skin, sparking with energy. Her daughter, however, hadn't been killed, which was a surprise. A Legacy overseer without a full-blooded Legacy child was unheard of.

Brecken had reassured her that all of them would be screened upon arrival to the safe haven, and those with Legacy blood would be held until it was determined if they were a threat or not. When Tessa had asked where, exactly, they would be going and how they would get there, Brecken only led her back to the same brick cottage they'd emerged from that day. Standing there waiting for them was Gatlan, the Source of the Anala Heir. He'd given her a wink before a fire portal appeared and Tana Aithne, his Mistress, had stepped through.

"There are more than I anticipated," Tana had said, surveying the sea of Fae waiting to be told what to do next.

"But they will be safe?" Tessa had asked, immediately suspicious.

"We've been ferrying people into the Anala Kingdom for decades," Tana had said. Then she'd set her amber eyes on Tessa. "And if you breathe a word of this to Theon or Rordan, we will find a way to end you."

Flames had flickered in those amber depths, and Tessa had smiled sharply at the threat. "And if I hear anything has befallen any of these innocent people while in *your* care, I will destroy your entire bloodline."

She'd left the dead to be discovered. There was no way to know with certainty it had been her, but she'd been waiting for someone to ask her about it. Apparently, that was happening now.

"I'm going to get dressed before we discuss my daily schedule," Tessa said, not waiting for a response before she disappeared into her closet. She slid on a pair of jeans and a sweater. A light rose-colored one. Only because it was the darkest sweater she could find. Leaving her hair to air dry, she reinforced the bands of light around her wrists.

When she re-emerged still barefoot, Rordan hadn't moved from the armchair. He was rigid, more tense than she'd ever seen him. His shoulder-length golden hair wasn't tied back, hanging loosely around his face. Bright blue eyes ringed with gold were fixed on her, and all she could think as she stared back at him was he never wore white. Even now he was in his favored navy suit. Okay, he wore white shoes, and there was a white shirt beneath the suit coat, but still. She didn't have any navy in her closet. And yes, she recognized this wasn't what she should be focusing on right now. Not as power flickered in his eyes.

Her own power responded in kind, slowly winding up her arms, and on instinct, she moved into the defensive stance Luka had drilled into her. She could call to Luka down the bond. He would come help her. Or rather, she was fairly sure he would come help her. But she didn't want him here. This was between her and the Achaz Lord. Whatever this was about to be.

"I am sure you have heard the news of the Sirana Villas," Rordan said tightly.

"I have," Tessa answered. "So many tragedies there. I assumed that was why you haven't been at breakfast the last two mornings."

"Yes," he replied. "The Ladies and I have had to do damage control. Again. Of course, Theon hasn't bothered to show up and help."

He hadn't?

Tessa had no idea what he was up to. There had been a spike of surprise and panic down the bond a bit ago, but mostly she just felt anxiety and stress from him when she didn't have the bond completely blocked. He'd given her phone back to her, but she hadn't turned it on. It was tucked away in a drawer. He sent Luka updates on Roan twice a day, and Luka relayed them to her. She was planning to go see the wolf this afternoon, but this little conversation was getting in the way of that.

"I don't speak to Theon, so I have no insights for you," she replied, holding Rordan's stare. She didn't fidget. There was no shuffling of her feet.

"And his advisor?"

"Trains me. That is all."

Rordan tsked. "You expect me to believe you sleep in his room, but all he does is train you?"

"I sleep in there because he is the closest thing I have to Theon, and it lessens the strain of the bond," she retorted.

Not entirely true, but she couldn't exactly tell him she was bonded to both of them. And she certainly wasn't going to tell him about how she rode his fingers when she came back here covered in blood. She spent far too much of her time imagining how to get him to do that again. Or what his tongue would be like. His cock.

And these were things she didn't need to be thinking about with a Lord sitting mere feet from her. The look on his face told her he didn't believe her excuse in the slightest, and that sparked her irritation.

"Even if I was doing more than sleeping in his room, I was unaware my bedroom activities were your concern," she snarked.

She expected him to become angry. That's how Valter would have reacted. And Theon. But Rordan only arched a brow, the corner of his mouth quirking up. "What makes you think your bedroom activities *aren't* my concern?"

"Why would they be?"

"You think I will allow all that power to be passed down to just anyone?"

Something in her stirred at those words, his comment to Desiray echoing in her mind.

All in good time.

"Of course, the plans of *thousands* must now be altered because of what happened in Rosebell," Rordan continued, the gold in his eyes brightening.

"What does Rosebell have to do with anything?"

"I'm glad you asked," Rordan said, the fingers of his right hand curling into the upholstery of the chair.

Where was Dysani? The Lords and Ladies never went anywhere without their Sources, yet his was nowhere to be found at the moment.

"As you know, Sirana is the goddess of love and fertility. It has long been a struggle for Fae and Legacy alike to conceive children, which is why we keep our Sirana Legacy close and monitored. Their gifts make conception more likely. When two Legacy complete a Match Ceremony and are ready to try for a child, they go— Or rather, they *went* to see Desiray. The magic of the Villas increased chances of conception by over fifty percent," Rordan said tightly. "In addition to that, the Villas are located on the outskirts of the Dreamlock Woods. The power of Sera-fina Legacy lingers there. Those who dream of having a child find more success when trying to conceive in the Villas."

Okay, well, Tessa hadn't known any of that, but it certainly didn't negate the fact that those same powers and enchantments were used to force Fae to conceive children as well. That same magic that lingered in the woods and brought a Legacy's dreams to fruition brought a Fae's nightmares to life.

"And now the Villas have been destroyed, and Desiray is dead.

Numerous other Legacy were killed, and dozens of Fae are unaccounted for," Rordan said, rage seeping into his voice.

"It is truly a tragedy," Tessa said, trying her hardest to sound sympathetic.

"A tragedy that could have been avoided if you had simply asked a question," he snarled. He still sat motionless in that chair, and it was unnerving.

"What would me asking a question have changed?" she asked, the thing inside her sitting up straighter as Rordan clearly became more and more upset.

"Let's not dance around this," he snapped. "Few things can kill a Legacy. You went back there and murdered over a hundred Legacy because you misunderstood the purpose of the Villas."

Her brows shot up. "Misunderstood the purpose of them?"

"I've let you have your fun. Let you explore your power and test your limits. I've given you a freedom you'd only dreamed of in the past, and yet *this* is how you repay that?" he demanded, finally pushing to his feet. It took everything in her to hold her ground and not take a step back. "I have spent the last weeks *defending* those choices to the other ruling Ladies, and with this one act, you have made me a liar. What am I to say to them when they demand you be locked up for this? When they argue you are too uncontrollable to be left to your own devices?"

"If you or anyone else tries to lock me up, you will learn precisely what I am capable of," she snarled, her magic flooding out of her like a wave of light. Those gold and silver embers flickered among it, lightning crackling with the storm of power.

"You have a purpose, Tessalyn," he spat out. "And you forget it."

"You mean *you* have a purpose," she countered. "And you are using me to achieve it."

He struck then, his magic cutting a path through hers and wrapping around her chest, arms locked to her sides. She struggled, her own power latching onto his and sinking its claws in, ripping and tearing. But Rordan was strong, and while she might eventually overpower him, it would take time she wouldn't be afforded.

And his Source wasn't even here.

Slowly, she raised her eyes to his, a smug sneer on his lips. "Had I known this was all I needed to do to figure out your paternal lineage, I would have done this long ago." He came closer, his magic pressing down on her and forcing her to her knees. He took her chin in his hand, tilting her face up. "Only Arius had the power to drain another's magic. That whole god of endings thing. I've had my suspicions; now I need to figure out just how closely related you are."

She was still struggling against his power, but at his words, she stopped. She didn't want him to know just how strong she was or what all she was capable of. Those were secrets she needed to keep yet, so she stopped fighting, shoving it all down.

Just like she had so many other times.

"Very well," he said, releasing her chin and loosening his power. "Telling me would have been a good start at an apology for your actions—"

"I apologize for nothing," she spat, not moving because his power still hovered too near. "Forcing Fae to carry children, then taking those babes from them? Using Fae in attempts to create stronger Sources? Fae being assigned to *pleasure* the Legacy when the Legacy can already take whatever they want from us?"

"Us?" Rordan interrupted. "You seem to have forgotten you are not Fae."

"And you seem to have forgotten you are not a god," she retorted. "I'd do it again. I *will* do it again. Only I won't stop at the Villas. I won't even stop at Rosebell. Then I'll come for you all."

Rordan *smiled*. "I'm counting on it, Tessalyn. Until then, you do have debts to pay, don't you?"

Confusion crossed her features. "What debts?"

"You think I have allowed you to live in my home, eat my food, and do as you please for nothing? Freedom has a price, child, and it's about time you started paying it."

He turned on his heel, his power going with him. The door clicked softly shut behind him, and for the first time since she'd come here, she felt trapped. She'd known another monster lurked behind the warm smiles and pretty words. It had been an ongoing game of who would break the façade first. Once again, her impulsive actions had made her the loser rather than the victor, and yet she still couldn't bring herself to regret it.

She would do it again.

And she'd be the one to sink a golden blade into Rordan's heart too.

Tessa? came Theon's voice down the bond. *Are you... I don't understand what you are feeling right now. Do you need us?*

No, was all she managed to reply before she stacked her shields back where they belonged.

She needed no one.

Kindness was never free.

There was always a cost.

And she was done accumulating debts.

After getting herself together, she created a portal directly down to the hidden entrance of the cells beneath the Achaz Palace. Quickly slipping inside, she made her way down the stairs. It felt weird to be down here without her wolves. She'd grown used to them always being at her side, always seeming to know when she needed them. So she shouldn't have been surprised to find Nylah waiting for her when she reached the bottom. Her dark coat shimmered in the light of the sconces, and Tessa crouched down beside her.

"How is he?" she asked softly, stroking her fur and scratching behind her ears. The wolf leaned into her hand, a low whine sounding. "I miss him too," Tessa whispered. "Can you stay close?"

Nylah rubbed against her arm, then her legs as Tessa stood. Roan was always the one to stick close while Nylah went ahead of them. Swallowing the sudden lump in her throat, she strode down the passage. She had planned to completely ignore Valter, but she couldn't stop herself when she paused in front of his cell.

His hair was even longer and unkempt. A thick beard covered his face now, and hatred still shone in those hazel eyes. But she didn't miss the slight flinch when she pressed her palm to the glass of his cell, pulling a wicked smile to her lips. Bringing her back to herself. Reminding herself she wasn't weak. She wasn't a pet. She wasn't a means to someone else's end.

"What do you plan to do with Eviana's daughter?" Tessa asked casually, tiny sparks of energy flickering at her fingertips.

"What daughter?" he retorted, his voice hoarse from disuse.

Tessa only continued to smile. "That's fine. I can ask her instead."

That had Valter lurching to his feet, stopping just short of slamming his hands to the glass. "Where is she?" he demanded.

"That bond can be such a bother when apart for too long, can't it?"

she replied with mock sympathy before she turned away from him, dragging her nails along the glass.

"Get back here and answer me, you cunt," he snarled.

She would have let him be today.

Until he spoke those words.

In a flash of light, she spun back to him, both her hands on the glass. Light ricocheted into the cell, bouncing around. His screams filled the air, and the monster inside of her soul sat up and smiled too.

She left him whimpering in agony on the floor, making her way down the passage. She did need to go speak to Eviana, but that would have to wait for another day.

When she arrived in front of his cell, he was in his usual spot, gaze already fixed on her and waiting. She sank to the floor without preamble, Nylah pacing back and forth in front of the glass. Crossing her legs, she rested her chin in her hand and held his stare. She wasn't entirely sure why she was down here. Sure, she had questions, but part of her just didn't want to sit alone with her thoughts.

For once, he was the first speak.

"You are different today."

"You have another son," she replied without adornment.

The male's eyes went wide, his entire body jerking back before he was cursing in pain.

"How do you know that?" he demanded, and she could swear he was trembling.

"What is your name?"

He shook his head. "No. Tell me how you know I have another child."

"You told me to ask you your name the next time I found myself here."

"Tessalyn," he snapped.

But Tessa only arched a brow, leaning back on her hands. "Who would have the power to sense what gifts another has and how strong they are?"

"That is a power of Arius," the male answered. "That is the only question I will answer until you answer mine. How do you know I have another son?"

"An answer for an answer then?" she replied with a smirk.

"Done."

"I met him," she answered casually.

"Where?" the male demanded.

She clicked her tongue. "It's my turn. What is your name?"

He stared at her, clear displeasure filling those sapphire eyes. "Xan. My name is Xan Mors. Where did you meet my other son?"

Tessa hummed for a moment before she said, "Met probably isn't the right word, but he looks remarkably like Luka. I saw him at Arius House with Theon."

"He is here? In Devram?" Xan asked, color draining from his face.

"What is a light guardian?" she asked instead. It was her turn after all.

Xan stared at her, that familiar annoyance that often accompanied his son filling his features. "You should ask Rordan these questions."

"Rordan will lie to me. Or make me pay for an answer," she snapped.

Xan's stare turned piercing, as if he was seeing something in her she couldn't. "Your loyalty is wavering."

"My loyalty is to myself," she said sharply.

After another few seconds, he said, "The descendants of Sargon become the Guardians of the Arius bloodline. Achaz did not like this, so he created guardians of his own from beings known as seraphs. Some seraphs were given additional power, like the ability to Travel and banish their wings, but their primary magic must be stolen."

Tessa's face scrunched in confusion. "How can one steal magic?"

"My turn," Xan said in a smug tone. "Is my other son in Devram?"

"I saw him a few days ago, but yes. At that time, he was in Devram."

"Has he met Luka?"

"My turn," she simpered. "How can one steal magic?"

"When they reach a certain age, the light guardians select a being. Leading up to this point, they have been watching and observing count-less magical beings—Fae, Legacy, Shifters, Witches. They study them and try to determine which power would serve them best."

"Wait," Tessa cut in, sitting up straight. "They watch beings for years, and when they reach a certain age they...*select* one?"

Xan nodded. "Only they kill them and steal their magic."

"You can steal magic by killing someone?"

"No. Only the light guardians can do such a thing, and they can only do so once. Once they make their choice, they cannot kill another for a different power."

But...her Hunter had called Brecken a light guardian. So that meant...

Brecken had killed an Arius Legacy at some point to have the power that he did. And if Dex and Oralia were light guardians as well, then they had done the same somewhere along the line. It all fit. The feathery wings she'd thought she'd imagined surrounding Dex. Random feathers in her room.

But Brecken had displayed wind magic at the Emerging Ceremony. How could he have both?

"These light guardians are in Devram?" she asked.

"Not that I know of when I freely walked this realm," Xan answered. "But my other son wasn't here at that time either, so much has changed."

"And they can only have one gift?"

"Yes. I have now answered several of your questions. It is my turn," he said, shifting on the floor. "Has my other son met Luka?"

"They saw each other," she answered. "If they have formally met, I am not aware of it."

"And he is helping Theon?"

"I don't know what he is doing here. Theon and I were in the middle of...a disagreement when they appeared."

"They?"

"Your son and a female."

He nodded again, going quiet.

"How long has it been since you've seen him?" she asked, her head tilting with the question as she watched him.

"Centuries," he answered. "I left him in another realm with my brother centuries ago."

"You left him in another realm? Like my parents left me?"

He met her gaze again, pain and regret shining in his eyes now. "He was to be the Guardian of Arius's grandson. It is our duty, but also..." Xan trailed off, clearly debating if he should say more. "Our bloodline is hunted throughout the stars by Achaz, his light guardians, and more. The world we once called home is nothing but a requiem. We were forced to flee, so yes, I hid my son in a realm where I thought he would be safe. Just like your parents did with you."

Tessa nodded, starting to stand, but he called out, "Wait. I get a final question."

She sat back down and nodded for him to go on. "Should you see them again, will you forgive them? Your mother and Temural? Knowing they did it to protect you?"

She blinked several times, weighing her answer, before finally saying, "I would have rather been in constant danger with people who I knew cared about me than abandoned in a realm where I was alone and unwanted. I do not know if I can ever forgive them for that."

Xan nodded, his throat bobbing with emotion. She stood, and this time she made it all of three steps before he called out once more. "She loves you, Tessalyn. They both love you so much, they made unfathomable sacrifices for you. That has to count for something, right?"

Looking over her shoulder, she said, "I don't know, and I do not know if he will forgive you either."

Later that night, she crawled into Luka's bed without asking while he was in his ensuite. She felt terrible about it. After being forced to share a bed for months without a choice, she always asked Luka. Every single time. But tonight, she just...*needed*. It was selfish, and she shouldn't want anything from anyone. But tonight her soul was weary in a way it hadn't been in a while, and she was feeling all of it. If he told her to leave, she wasn't sure what she'd do. Go to Theon? No. But maybe for one night of comfort from the bond?

Luka emerged from the bathroom and paused when he saw her. She held his stare, allowing him to see it all. This day weighing down on her. The loneliness. The exhaustion. Gave him this rare moment of vulnerability in exchange for letting her have this one night.

He didn't say anything. Only pulled his shirt over his head and set it aside before he slipped into the bed. Tessa rolled into him, and he immediately pulled her into his chest, a large hand sifting through her hair. For an inexplicable reason, tears pooled in her eyes, but she refused to let them fall.

For several moments, that was it. The two of them in the dark. His fingers stroking her hair. Her head on his chest. Breathing in his scent and heat. The bond between them hummed in contentment, soothing her as much as his touch was.

She didn't know how many minutes had passed before he said in a voice that was just like his father's, "Even the monsters and the villains need others. We're not meant to do life alone."

She didn't reply, but a single tear slipped free.

She stood on a cliff, and Tessa immediately realized she'd been here before. There were no winged warriors attacking this time, and she took a moment to look around. There were trees, but they were grey and barren. The sky was much of the same, and with no one around, she carefully moved to the edge and peered over. As she'd suspected the last time she was here, they were floating on an island in the sky. Off in the distance, she could just make out another.

"I'd tell you not to stand so close to the edge without your dragon nearby, but I guess I don't need to."

Tessa spun to find the female with the red-brown hair watching her with violet eyes. She wore the same outfit as before— fitted black pants, black top, and black boots with a cloak around her shoulders.

And standing a few feet away was Luka.

Tessa had seen him in her last few visions, but she could never figure out how he fit in. How was he here?

Sliding her gaze back to the female, she said, "Lilura, right?"

Her smile was razor-sharp. "Did you deliver my message?"

"How do you know Tristyn?"

"We don't have time for such talk," she replied.

Then she took a step forward and pressed her palms to Tessa's temples.

"What the—" Tessa started, but before she could finish, Lilura was being pulled backwards and a warning snarl was coming from Luka.

Lilura looked up at him, unimpressed. "I know what she is to you, Son of Xan."

"You know Luka?" Tessa asked, startled.

Almost as startled as Luka looked at being addressed in this vision.

"I don't," Lilura answered. "But she does."

A second later, a purplish-black dragon soared up from beneath the island, sunlight glinting off her wings. The dragon let out a roar as she circled them, and Tessa was suddenly being yanked into Luka's chest.

"Where are we?" Luka hissed into her ear, his vertical pupils honed in on the dragon.

"I don't know," she retorted. "How are you here?"

"I don't know."

They watched the dragon circle lower and lower until there was a pale flash of purple light and a female was striding toward them. She was in black pants and a long-sleeve black shirt. More modern looking than Lilura. Her dark *purple hair reached just past her shoulders, swaying as she strode toward them in black boots, and her eyes were a shade of brown that made them look crimson.*

She stopped in front of them, her entire demeanor completely predatory, and it had Luka shoving Tessa behind him. Much to his annoyance, she peered around him to address the Shifter, "You know Luka?"

"Luka?" the female said. "That is not the name I knew him as, but we were scarcely walking the last time we saw each other."

"What are you talking about?" Luka demanded. "I've never seen you before."

She studied him, inching closer and inhaling deeply. "It was centuries ago, but—"

"Then it was not me. I am only twenty-nine years," he interrupted.

"Interesting," she said, her head cocking to the side. "But your father is Xan? Were you once called Razik?"

Tessa's mouth dropped open. This female knew Razik?

"No," Luka said tightly.

"Enough of this," Lilura cut in. "Before your Guardian intercepted—"

"I'm not her Guardian," Luka said at the same time Tessa said, "He's not mine."

"There is a sorceress altering your visions," Lilura said, ignoring them both.

"Like this one?" Tessa said, stepping out from behind Luka despite his grumbled protests. "Is that how Luka is here with me?"

Lilura eyed Luka once more. "That I do not know, but he protects you even here."

Another roar sounded, both Luka and Tessa looking to the sky. It took a minute to spot the silver dragon against the clouds, but his appearance had the female dragon cursing.

"I'll handle it," she said to Lilura. "Get them out of here."

Then she ran, leaping from the cliff and shifting to her dragon form in midair.

"You need to go, but be mindful of your visions. They are not all truth," Lilura said. "And tell him I'm still waiting for that dance."

24

AXEL

"You should drink some," Theon said, holding the bottle of blood out to him.

"No," Axel said tightly, looking anywhere but at the bottle. It simultaneously made him want to vomit and chug the whole thing.

When Gia had deemed Kat safe to move, Theon had carried her to a point where Tristyn said he could Travel. They'd taken her to Axel's room in the Arius manor where she'd apparently been staying. Corbin and Lange had a room across the hall, and two doors down from them was where Razik and Eliza were staying. He'd been given the barest of details on what had happened since he'd been gone, and quite frankly, he couldn't have processed more than that anyway. He'd showered, put on clean clothing, eaten proper food, and then he'd slept for nearly an entire day.

In another room.

Every part of him had rebelled at the idea, but he didn't trust himself enough not to wake up and immediately lunge for her.

Because warm blood, fresh from the source? That was far superior to the chilled blood Theon was currently offering him. It was intoxicating. A drug he wanted to lose himself in over and over again.

Axel squinted at the setting sun that was shining in the room. Walking over to the window, he pulled the curtains closed. He'd become so used to the muted light of the Underground, the sunlight physically hurt his eyes right now.

He'd been told Cienna had been here while he'd slept and checked on Kat. That had made him feel a little better, but he wanted to talk to the Witch personally. And not just about Kat. Gia had said he needed to speak to her.

"I need to go check on a few things at Arius House. Tristyn is taking me," Theon said, capping the bottle of blood. "Do you want to go along? Or am I still waiting to inform mother you've been found?"

"Don't tell her yet," Axel said, sitting back in the chair at the foot of the bed. Not too close, but close enough to be able to see her. He hadn't said a word to anyone about the possible child. Another thing he wanted to speak to Cienna about.

"I'll give it another day or two, but then you need to go see her," Theon said. "She's been beside herself with worry over you and father."

"Yeah, all right," Axel muttered.

"Then I'm going to go. You have your phone if you need anything, right?"

He looked up, startled. "What do you mean go? You can't leave me alone with her."

Theon blinked slowly. "I'm not, Axel. Corbin and Lange are downstairs. Razik and Eliza are down the hall. They stay holed up in their rooms unless we are researching something together, but they are a formidable pair."

"But someone else should be in here with me at all times to make sure I don't—"

He couldn't say the words. At least someone had helped her clean up and change into fresh clothing. They'd told him she'd only been awake for a few minutes here and there though, and that was his fault. So much blood. He'd taken far too much from her.

"The fact that you are sitting here worrying about this tells me you are in the right mind," Theon said. "Your power wells are replenished. Don't use your magic, and you'll be fine until I get back in a few hours. Tristyn will stop in, and Cienna will be checking in on Katya as well."

Axel nodded, but he wasn't fine with this in the slightest. Something dropped into his lap, and he looked down to find his earbuds.

"Listen to some music," Theon said. "Put together a new playlist, yeah? Only the very best songs you can find."

Axel nodded again, a part of him settling at the thought. It was Theon who had taught him to use music to stay calm and drown out the world when necessary. He'd said those same words to him when he was younger, on a day their father had been in a particularly nasty mood. Theon had given him his best pair of earbuds and told him to find him the very best songs. That was the first time he'd truly understood what Theon was protecting him from.

He slipped the earbuds in, flicking through songs on his phone, but he wasn't focused in the slightest. Bree had let him go. He knew he should be suspicious of that, but he hadn't told Theon any of that yet. He was too busy just trying to...survive? Wrap his mind around everything? Figure out what he was going to do about Katya and a child?

Axel bent forward, his elbows on his knees as he pushed both his hands through his hair before clasping them behind his neck. It wasn't until movement caught his eye that he realized he still had the earbuds in, music still flowing through them. But he hadn't heard her wake up because of it.

Katya was struggling to get out of bed, a hand clasped over her mouth.

"You shouldn't stand," Axel said, tossing the earbuds aside while he rushed to her. "Seriously, Kat. Stay in bed."

"You don't want that," she said in a rush. "Because I'll be sick all over the bedding."

"It's fine. I'll change it."

She shook her head, still attempting to get to her feet, and rather than fight her, he took her arm and helped her.

"I'm fine, Axel," she rasped, trying to shrug him off.

"You're clearly not fine."

"I've been doing this for a while now. I promise I'll be fine."

He knew she didn't mean it as a verbal jab, but it sure as fuck hit like one. Releasing her arm, he stayed close as she quickly made her way into the bathroom.

"Please don't follow me in here," she groaned, dropping to her knees before the toilet.

"Not going to happen," he answered, pulling her hair back as she retched. Not that there was much to vomit up.

After another round of heaving, she said, "Can you please go get Eliza?"

"Eliza?" he repeated in confusion.

"She's staying in the room down the hall."

"I know where she is staying. What I don't know is why I'm fetching her."

"She is one of five people who know about this child," Kat answered, still hovering over the bowl. "I guess six now that you know."

"But why—"

"Please, Axel."

And she sounded so utterly exhausted that he pushed to his feet, not wanting to argue with her.

Moving quickly through the room and down the hall, he stopped outside the door. While he knew *of* them, he hadn't actually *met* Eliza and Razik yet. This was going to be more than awkward.

He knocked twice before shoving his hands in his pockets and waiting. He heard the light footsteps a few seconds before the door opened. A female with flowing red-gold hair stood there, her grey eyes narrowing as they looked him up and down.

Leaning her shoulder against the doorframe, she said, "You must be the brother."

Unsure what to say to that, he rubbed at the back of his neck. "Uh, yeah. Axel. Eliza, right?"

She nodded, crossing her arms. A black Mark stood out on the back of her left hand, tendrils of the Mark winding down three of her fingers. She wore long-sleeves, but another Mark peeked out from the top of her shirt. Source Marks, maybe?

Yeah, so this was definitely awkward.

"Listen, Kat says you know about... She asked me to come get you," he finally said when the silence stretched on.

She straightened. "Is she all right?"

"She's vomiting, but—"

She was already shoving past him, down the hall, and into his room before he'd realized what was happening. Axel followed, the bathroom door shut when he entered the bedroom, and not knowing what else to do, he sat on the edge of the bed.

It had to be at least twenty minutes before the door opened, Eliza emerging. She left the door open, the sound of the shower running echoing her footsteps.

"She's fine," Eliza said.

"Should she shower by herself?"

Eliza gave him a confused look. "Why shouldn't she bathe by herself?"

"Because she's... She said you knew."

"She's pregnant, not an invalid," she said flatly. "She can do whatever she likes while carrying a child."

"I know, but I…" He cleared his throat. "Thank you. I don't know what you've done to help her, but thank you."

Eliza nodded, watching him. It was unnerving and made him feel like he needed to keep talking.

"Kat said only a handful of people know about the babe," Axel said.

Eliza nodded again. "Outside of us, only Razik, Cienna, and Gia know."

"Cienna and Gia know?" He wasn't even sure why he asked. Of course they knew.

"Yes," Eliza answered.

"And you know because…?"

"Because I was there when Katya realized it. We were in the Underground with Cienna for a period of time while Kat was staying there. That's where Tristyn hid her."

Well, that was smart. No one could find Cienna so they wouldn't be able to find Kat, but that meant that—

"Tristyn knows Cienna?" Axel asked.

"They're siblings."

"Shut the fuck up."

Eliza blinked at him. "I don't think I understand that saying from your realm."

"I'm just shocked is all," Axel muttered.

The awkward seconds continued to tick by until Eliza said, "Can you feel her?"

"What?"

"Can you feel her?" she repeated. "Her emotions or discomfort?"

"No," Axel said carefully. "We don't have a Source bond, so I wouldn't be able to feel her emotions or physical well-being."

"They haven't told you yet?"

Now he was getting irritated. "Sorry," he drawled. "I've been recovering from bloodlust-induced mania. I'm still getting caught up on the fuckery of everything that's happened since I've been gone."

She smirked at that, and a minute later, a male was entering the bedroom.

Axel had to do a double take before he said, "Holy Arius."

Because he looked remarkably similar to Luka.

"Yeah, yeah. We know," the male grumbled.

He was broody and irritable like Luka too.

"Razik, Axel. Axel, Razik," Eliza said, gesturing between the two. "Yes, we know they are likely related. No, we do not wish to discuss it right now. What we need to discuss is the fact that the female carrying your child took a Mark to find you, and if you don't take the same, she'll—"

"Calm down, *mai dragocen*," Razik cut in. "You're scaring him."

"He's one of the people who force the Fae to serve them," Eliza argued, gesturing angrily at Axel. "He needs to understand what she did to find him."

"Okay, first of all, I didn't force Kat to do anything," Axel cut in, his own irritation and anger growing. "In fact, I tried to talk her out of...all of this multiple times. I'll admit I shouldn't have let it get this far, but it was like we couldn't help it."

"Because you're drawn to each other," Eliza supplied.

"Because you're twin flames," Razik added.

Eliza slid her gaze to him, unimpressed. "You say 'let's not scare him,' then you just say *that*? By the gods, Razik."

Razik just shrugged before sitting in the chair Axel had been holding vigil in.

"Can one of you just tell me what a twin flame is?" Axel cut in. A bond had been mentioned before, but it was one of the things not yet explained to him.

Eliza held up her left hand with that Mark. "I'm assuming you saw the Mark on her hand?"

"Yes, but I haven't had time to talk to her about it."

But while Katya showered, Eliza and Razik told him all about twin flames. What the bond was. How it worked. How the Legacy of Devram had taken that bond and twisted it into something abhorrent. Katya emerged as they were explaining how she took the Mark in the hope it would help her find him, and all he could do was stare at her.

His mouth was dry, the words gravel as he said, "You took that Mark for me not knowing what it would do?"

She smiled weakly, but she looked better. There was more color in her cheeks. She was moving a little faster, and when she reached for a glass of water, he rushed to grab it for her.

After she took a drink, she said, "Look what you sacrificed for me. I could handle a Mark."

"A Mark that will slowly drain you if a companion Mark isn't taken," Axel argued.

She shrugged. "I guess I had to believe it would work. I had to believe I would find you, and you would take the Mark. Because you're a sliver of good in this world, Axel, and if I couldn't believe in that, then what is the point?"

Axel blinked back the moisture threatening to pool in his eyes before his gaze dipped to her stomach. "You are sure? About…"

Her soft smile was back. "Yes. Cienna confirmed it. Eliza has been helping me hide it from everyone."

"How?"

"There is a Mark that masks the scent of the child," Eliza offered. "It fades every few days though, so it must be reapplied. I am trained to draw Marks."

"Are you a priestess?" Axel asked, still staring at Kat's stomach.

"What's that?"

"We call them Witches in our world. Descendants of Zinta," Razik said.

"By Anala, no," Eliza said. "I can draw Marks because of my earth Fae lineage." Before Axel could question that, she added, "Don't ask. I'm not telling you my life story."

She was kind of…rude.

"And you knew of this particular Mark because…?" Axel asked, helping Kat back into bed now.

"I've used it in the past," she answered tightly. "Again, I'm not telling you my life story."

Taking the strong hint that the discussion was over, he said, "Then you can give me this twin flame Mark, right?"

"I gave Kat hers," Eliza answered.

"Then let's do that. Right now."

"Axel, you can think about it first," Kat cut in.

"There's nothing to think about, kitten," he answered, bending to press a kiss to her brow. "We'll figure the rest out later."

He turned back to Eliza, who was already holding a scion. "Left hand," she said impatiently.

Axel held out his hand, his eyes fixed on Katya the entire time. "So when this is done, I'll be able to feel her emotions and hear her thoughts?"

"And sense her physical location," Razik answered while Eliza worked. "The bond itself is pretty instantaneous, but it strengthens once the Trials are completed and the bond is Anointed."

"How long does that take?"

"Each pair is unique. Some complete the Trials within a year or two. Others take longer. The Fates decide," he said.

When he felt the scion pass over the same spot for the fifth time, Axel finally looked at his hand.

Where there was nothing.

"What's wrong?" Axel asked.

Eliza's brow was furrowed in concentration as she pulled the scion across the back of his hand again, Axel gritting his teeth against the burn. "I don't know," Eliza said. She looked over her shoulder at Razik. "Why isn't it working?"

He leaned forward to see before rubbing at his jaw. "I don't know. Twin flames are rare enough, we don't know everything about them. There's not a lot of texts about them, and certainly not in this realm. But I can see what I can find."

"Thank you, Razik," Kat said. When Axel started to protest, she reached out and squeezed his hand. "We have time, Axel. Let them see what they can find."

He didn't like it, but he didn't have much of a choice.

"We'll let you know as soon as we find something," Eliza said before she and Razik filed out of the room.

He turned to face Kat fully, taking her all in. Her dark hair already coiled tight as it dried. Her amber eyes, tired but bright. Her warm skin. He winced when his gaze slid to her throat. There was no scarring—not even a faint mark—but he knew what he'd done. That was enough.

"Will you sit with me?" she asked, noting his stare.

He should say no. He didn't know if it would set him off or not, but just like the moment he first laid eyes on her, he couldn't deny the pull. It was a need to touch her. To pull her close. To know she was safe.

His to have.

His to protect.

His to love.

He climbed onto the bed next to her, and she immediately snuggled up to him. Her head rested on his chest, her damp hair seeping into his shirt.

"Are you upset?" she asked quietly.

"Upset?" Axel repeated. "What would I be upset about?"

"The babe."

"Are you…" He paused, using his finger to tip her chin up. "Are you asking if I'm upset you are pregnant?"

"Yes."

"You know it took two to fuck and make that child, right?"

Her unimpressed glare had him huffing a laugh. Everything felt right as he relaxed more and more with each passing minute.

"Shocked, yes. Upset, no. I'm only upset that you've been going through this alone," he replied, pressing his lips to her temple. "Like I said, we'll figure this out. Theon will help us figure this out. He always knows what to do. He'll come up with a plan."

"I think I know how it happened," she said, tracing patterns on his shirt.

He huffed another laugh. "Me too, kitten. I was there."

She lightly smacked his chest. "Not that," she scoffed. "I mean, there was so much going on with Tessa and the Selection and all the other chaos, I wasn't given my seasonal contraceptive injection."

His fingers had been stroking up and down her arm, and now they stilled. "Gods, Kat. I'm so sorry."

"Why are you sorry?"

"Because I should have made sure that was done."

"So you are upset?"

"No, but I take responsibility for not making sure you were taken care of. How long after I sent you with Tristyn did you know?" Axel asked, resuming the soothing strokes down her arm.

"A week or so. It was probably the best place for me to find out. I was sick one morning. Gia took one look at me and went to get Cienna," she answered around a yawn.

"And no one else has suspected anything since you came back?"

"No," she murmured. "I always go off by myself. It wasn't out of the ordinary. Unless I was at classes or researching with Theon, I was in your room. Researching or resting. The sickness comes and goes. Eliza said that never really goes away."

"She's kind of terrifying," Axel mumbled.

"She is," Kat agreed, stifling another yawn.

"You need to rest," Axel said, pressing yet another kiss to the top of her head.

"Mhmm," she agreed in a sleepy murmur.

In less than five minutes she was fast asleep on his chest. He was a little chilled, and she was so warm with that fire in her veins. He didn't realize how much he'd missed just having her close. His hand slid to her stomach, and he pressed his palm to it, still unsure how there was a child —*his* child—growing in there. Well, he knew *how*, but it was still... Something he didn't have words for. He didn't care if this went against the laws of Devram. Theon would help them figure this out. He would get his blood cravings under control, and this, right here, would be his world.

The door opening and closing drew his attention, and a minute later, Cienna came into the bedroom. Her violet eyes went from him to Kat's sleeping form, and something akin to sympathy flashed across her face. It was something Axel had rarely, if ever, seen from the Witch.

"I'm told you've been tending to her for weeks," Axel said as she approached the bed. "Thank you."

She hummed an acknowledgment while she held her hands over Kat, faint light emanating.

"Is she healing all right? I took a lot of blood from her," Axel asked, the relaxation immediately replaced with anxiety.

"She will be fine," Cienna said tersely.

"And the babe?"

"Is fine as well."

He nodded, pushing out a breath of relief. "Is there anything I can do? What should I know? What can I do to make this easier for her?"

Cienna rounded the bed to his side. "Fae pregnancies are hard. Just like all magical being pregnancies are difficult. It is the cost for bringing more power into the worlds," she answered. "Katya is strong. She will be fine. Your job in this is to keep her safe and protected when she is vulnerable."

"Of course," he muttered while Cienna reached out and took his face in her hands, turning his head from side to side. Unsure of what she was doing, he went on, "They told me about the twin flame bond. Of course I will take that. Eliza said it will help to have the bond."

"It would," Cienna agreed, stepping back from him. She was rubbing the tips of her fingers together as she watched him, and to be frank, it was making him incredibly uncomfortable.

"She, uh, tried to give me the Mark, but it wouldn't work. Maybe because I'm still recovering? Razik was going to see what he could find, but I thought you might know something?"

"You can't take the twin flame Mark, Axel," Cienna said, a thread of sadness in her tone.

"What? Why not? They said it was a bond between a Fae and Legacy," he said, trying to keep his voice low to not wake Katya.

"Yes," Cienna said. "A twin flame bond can only be between a Fae and a Legacy. Twin flames also cannot physically harm each other. The bond does not allow it. But you were already on an edge and hadn't taken the Mark to initiate the bond. Even if you managed to take it, it would fade. Just as hers will."

He had harmed her.

He had nearly killed her.

"I told you it could not be undone," Cienna added.

He was shaking his head at the words. "No," he said. Then firmer he repeated, "No. This isn't— My *father* had me locked away. I was a prisoner. They wouldn't give me rations. I didn't do this."

"I know, Axel."

"I didn't *do* this," he said again. "I didn't do this!"

"I understand," she said calmly.

"I can't be— You're wrong," he said, lifting a hand and letting his shadows free. "I still have my magic."

"And it will slowly slip from your soul," she replied. "In a week, maybe two, you will no longer be a Legacy. Your skin is already cooler to the touch, and I would guess you find the sun a little too bright."

"No," he said, shaking his head again in fierce denial. "That's because I was locked in the dark for weeks. I'm still adjusting. Recovering. I'm not— I don't *feel* any different. I still have my fucking power!"

Katya stirred beside him, and he looked down at her. Perfect and soft. Innocent and *good*. Carrying his child.

His child.

"The babe—"

"Was conceived before this. He will be an Arius Legacy," Cienna said.

"He?" Axel repeated hoarsely.

She nodded once.

And he wouldn't be here for any of it.

He wouldn't be here to see him born.

Would he have his eyes or hers? A darker complexion like her warm skin or the perfect mix of both? Would he be studious like her, or love music and chaosphere like him?

He wouldn't be here.

He wouldn't be here to see his first steps and hear his first words. He wouldn't be here when his power emerged to help him learn to master it. He wouldn't be here to play chaosphere or give him music or watch him grow. He wouldn't be here to see what kind of person he became.

He wouldn't be here.

Because he would be a danger to his mother.

Forever.

There was no swallowing the emotion this time. Tears spilled over.

Hot and angry.

Sad and agonized.

Raw and brutal.

He couldn't stay here.

He couldn't stay with her.

He looked up at Cienna again, finding her still watching him.

"Many are on the receiving end of injustice every single day. A choice was taken from you. It's not right, and it's not fair. But you get to decide how to move forward. That choice is still yours. You get to decide how it shapes you. You will not be the same on the other side of this," Cienna said. "But you get a choice on who that person will be. Your path is not yet decided. Fate waits to make her final choice for you. Choose wisely."

With those parting words, the Witch left.

Choose wisely.

She'd said those same words to him months ago in the Underground caverns, and look where he was now. Exactly where he'd feared he'd be.

But he could make sure his worst fear didn't come true.

He could make sure he wasn't a threat to Kat ever again. That he never took from her in a moment of weakness. That he never watched the life dim from her eyes.

Happy, safe, and whole.

That was what he needed her to be.

That was what he'd sacrifice anything for.

Because she was his.

His to have.

His to protect.

His to love.

With another press of his lips to her brow, he slipped from the bed. He placed a blanket over her, letting his palm linger on her stomach.

He didn't belong here. Not anymore.

He quickly scrawled a note on some scratch paper, leaving it on the nightstand. Then bent to kiss her temple one last time.

"I can't keep all my promises, kitten," he whispered against her skin. "I can't come back for you, but I need you to keep yours. I need you to try to be happy, and I promise to keep you both safe."

Another soft kiss.

Then he left to make his way to the Underground and back to the people he now belonged with.

PART TWO
SACRIFICE DEMANDS

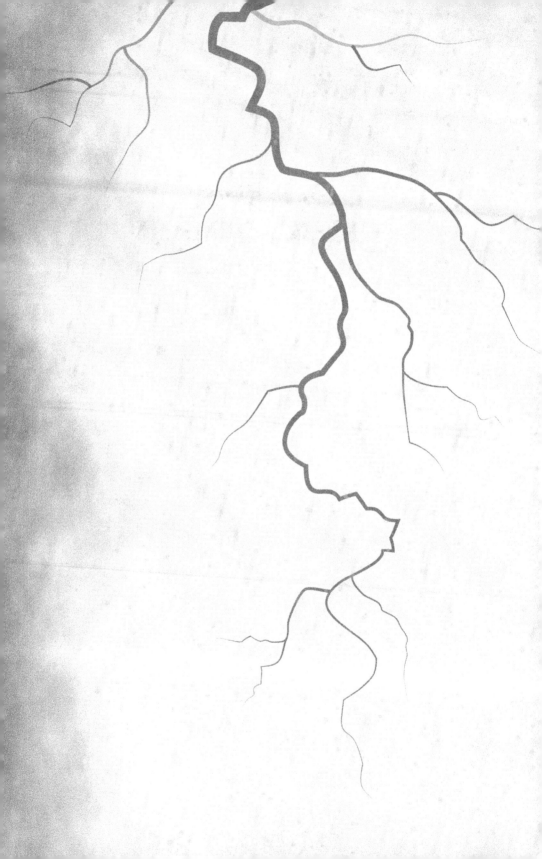

25

TESSA

"Tessa, stop," Theon rasped, blood seeping from beneath his hand where it was pressed to his side.

Tessa stood over him with a gold dagger in her hand, and she twirled it between her fingers.

"Tessa," Theon tried again. "It doesn't—"

"Have to be this way?" she interrupted. "You mean it should be me on the ground preparing to cross the Veil?"

"No, Tessa. I—"

But he was cut off by a shuddering breath that turned into a cough and was followed by curses.

"Fuck," he muttered, lifting his palm to look at his wound before immediately applying pressure again. "I wish Luka was here."

She smiled, and she could tell by the look on Theon's face the smile looked as wicked as it felt. "He's..."

That smile faltered a little. Where was Luka?

She looked around, expecting to see him standing off to the side, watching. That was where he'd been the last few times she'd had visions. But he wasn't here.

Thunder cracked, pulling her back to the male on his knees before her, trying to push to his feet.

"You're fulfilling the prophecy if you do this, Tessa."

She whirled to the source of the voice, seeing Tristyn on the ground nearby, light binding his hands and ankles.

"It's what they want. Don't you see?" the male pressed now that he had her attention. "You will be the—"

"You had plenty of chances to tell me what you know," she said, power flaring through the light that held him and making him wince as it coursed through his being. "And even when you did tell me, it was shrouded in half-truths and motivations that only served you."

"No—" he gasped out, but she was already turning back to Theon.

Until another voice had her spinning once more.

Axel stood there, Katya tucked behind him. She peered out, amber eyes wide with fear but also determination.

"A prophecy can mean so many things," Axel said, his tone calm and even. "It can mean whatever you want it to mean. Just like your fate. You can define what it looks like. Just like we did."

"It's not the same," Tessa said sharply.

"You're right," came yet another voice. This one was complete power and all-encompassing. No one appeared this time, but she knew the voice. She'd spoken to the same in a mirror. "It is not the same. The fates and destinies of Fae and Legacy are of no worry to you, but the fates of those with power can alter the course of history. You hold that power. And if you fail?"

He didn't need to say it.

If she failed, she was stuck in Devram forever. Alone in a realm to be used and caged. Someone would find a way to do so eventually.

Correct the balance.

That was what she had to do.

And if the entire realm happened to be the cost of that, she would smile as she stepped on the ashes when she was finally free of it.

"Tessa—" Axel was saying, but she cut him off.

"No," she snapped. "This world had millenniums to fix this. You all failed. That's why I was sent here."

"Is it?" Tristyn cut in. "I know you've spoken to Xan. What did he tell you?"

"Lies," she hissed. "Only more lies."

"You know that's not true," he insisted.

"Stop!" she cried, a hand driving into her loose hair and tugging on the ends. "You constantly lie to us. Half-truths and pretty words. You can't control chaos."

"No, but chaos can be balanced," Theon cut in.

She lurched forward, gripping his throat, and he let her.

"I'll take your fury, little storm. I'll take all your wrath and all your vengeance, but I will not accept that you are the cost for the balance," he rasped out around her hold.

"I will not be the cost. You will be," she sneered.

"You're wrong, Tessa. We were wrong. I was wrong. So very wrong." Her fingers squeezed, her power flickering around them and sinking into him, but he managed to get out on a breath, "Where is Luka, Tessa?"

"He's mine," she snarled. "He was always meant to be mine. Auryon said so herself."

"You killed Auryon," Theon gasped out, and his words startled her enough that she released him and stumbled back.

His darkness swarmed around his wound. Trying to heal him. Trying to save him while he gulped down several deep lungfuls of air.

A pointless effort, but she'd let him waste that power of his. It wasn't as if she needed him as a Source anyway.

"I didn't kill Auryon," she gritted out.

"Your Hunters did," Theon amended. "At your command."

"Because she was trying to keep me from my destiny."

Theon shook his head, damp hair from the misting clouds swaying with the movement. "I'm so incredibly sorry, Tessa."

She shot forward once more, gripping his hair and yanking his head back. The tip of her dagger pressed beneath his chin. "Your apologies are too late. They fall on deaf ears."

"I know, Tessa, but it changes nothing of how I feel for you."

"Stop it," she snarled as she felt his emotions flood down the bond.

She waited.

Because she should be feeling Luka right now too.

Where was Luka?

Three of them.

It was supposed to be the three of them bound to one another.

Connected in a way that was never meant to be, but couldn't possibly be any other way.

Unless sacrifices were made.

Oh, gods.

Unless sacrifices were made.

"Where is Luka?" she whispered, releasing Theon and stepping back.

Theon's face was full of anguish. "I think you know the answer to that, little storm."

Wind swept through the clearing, stirring dead grass and scorched earth from a battle that had left hundreds dead. Fae and Legacy alike had fought in a war that should have been reserved for the gods.

Too many sacrifices had already been made.

Corbin.

Lange.

Auryon.

Cienna.

But not Luka.

Not Luka.

Not Luka.

Axel was here.

Katya was here.

Everyone who should have cared had betrayed her.

But not Luka.

If this world took him from her, any mercy she might have found in her soul died with him.

Thunder rumbled at the thought, the sky breaking open and raining its own wrath to the ground.

"It doesn't have to be like this, little storm," Theon tried again.

But it did.

If Luka was dead, it was because she had failed in her purpose. Somewhere along the line, she had failed. Failed Achaz. Failed the Fates. Failed her parents. Failed him, *and he had paid the cost.*

"We don't have a choice," she said hollowly, echoing words he'd said to her so often in her dreams. "It's more than a bond, and it cannot be."

Emerald eyes fell closed, acceptance filling features she had once thought she could love.

For so long she had wished for death, and now, in this moment, if they would both be gone, she found herself wishing for it again. But more than that, she felt the need to avenge them. She'd found something to fight for, and then she was forced to sacrifice it. And now? Now she felt nothing but the fury that had consumed her.

"You're wrong," Tristyn rasped, trying to inch closer across the earth that had quickly turned to mud. "Have you learned nothing over these past months? We've tried, Tessa. We've brought you aid—"

"Once again to seek your own ends," she replied listlessly.

"To save you," Theon said, clearly trying to keep her attention on him. His hair was plastered to his brow now, rain mixing with the steady stream of blood from his wound. "I tried to change it. I did everything I could."

"But destiny beckons and sacrifice demands," she said, crouching before Theon once more. "Those that came to this world unbidden learned that truth. We've all learned that truth."

"*Their queen will seek her vengeance, Tessa. Make no mistake.*"

"*I'm counting on it.*"

"*Her vengeance will know no bounds.*"

"*Then she will know my wrath, just as you have.*"

"*And I'd ask for it again and again if it is all you will let me have, clever tempest,*" Theon replied, a shaky hand coming up to cup her cheek. "*But I understand we are out of time. Once again, I'm out of time.*"

She got a little lost in dark emerald eyes and black hair. In a small dimple and lips she'd kissed more times than she could count. Then she was kissing him. Deep and lovely, just like it always should have been.

"*I'm sorry I failed you, little storm,*" Theon said, when they broke apart, sorrow filling in his features. "*I tried. I tried to save you.*"

"*I understand,*" she whispered. "*I'm sorry I couldn't give you all of me. Every piece of me.*"

And she sank that gold dagger into his chest.

"*But only one can be left standing when Chaos comes to reign.*"

26

THEON

He shifted in his seat, finding the chair far more comfortable than he'd anticipated. Although he should have expected such a thing. The rulers of the realm wouldn't have settled for anything less. Of course the seats on the dais at the Tribunal building were luxurious, while the benches everyone else sat on were hard and uncomfortable.

The side door opened, and the Achaz Lord and the Serafina Lady appeared with their Sources. They each moved to their seats, the other Ladies already here and settled. Rordan sat back, crossing one leg over the other and folding his hands across his chest as his gaze fell on Theon.

"Heir St. Orcas. How kind of you to grace us with your presence," Rordan said tightly. He held Theon's stare, clearly waiting for something. An apology? An explanation?

He'd get neither.

His father might be a fucking bastard, but he'd made sure Theon was more than prepared to hold his own among these people.

Sitting back in his own chair, his legs sprawled wide in a casual fuck-you as he leaned an elbow on the armrest. "I had no choice in the matter," Theon said calmly. "Apparently while I've been busy tending to the power transition in my kingdom, you have let the Sirana Villas become a graveyard."

Rordan went eerily still. "Are you suggesting I had something to do with that?"

"Of course not," Theon said. "But the Villas are in your kingdom. They are your responsibility to keep safe just as the other kingdoms keep the Estates safe, and we keep the Underground confined and controlled. The Villas are your territory."

The room fell silent.

There was no audience today. The benches were empty. No heirs or nobles. Only the rulers and their Sources. Theon didn't even have an advisor with him. He would have brought Axel, if only for appearance's sake, but his brother had disappeared, leaving only a fucking note. When he'd learned of his leaving, Theon hadn't said a word. He'd gotten in a vehicle, driven to the banks of the Wynfell River where everything always seemed to go wrong, and unleashed everything.

His wrath.

His frustration.

His desperation.

His sorrow.

His despair.

His darkness had coated the ground, seeping into everything. Surrounding vegetation withered as life seeped from its leaves and roots. The earth turned grey and desolate. His vision was nothing but black, obscuring everything from the stars and the sky, to the earth and the water.

He didn't know how long he stood there, his power pouring out of him and the world dying around him. But when his vision finally cleared, the waters before him?

They were as dark and as black as the Night Waters in the eastern part of Arius Kingdom. The entirety of the Wynfell River was black, and he didn't know what to make of that.

But now he sat here, alone in a room full of people who clearly didn't want him in this seat, trying to figure out how and where he was going to fit into everything.

Tension filled the air after his last response to Rordan, the Lord's stare boring into him as Theon held his own. Gold mist floated around the Lord, and Theon let wisps of darkness appear in answer.

When Rordan said nothing in response, Theon said, "At least tell me you have suspects? A lead? Some type of information as to what happened there?"

"You mean *who* happened there," the Celeste Lady cut in with a sneer.

"Who?" Theon repeated.

"Yes, who," she snapped. "Let's not play coy. We all know it was your Source."

"Who I've been told is no longer mine. She was taken from me," Theon said, gesturing to the Achaz Lord.

"But she is still bonded to you as a Source, is she not?" the Falein Lady asked.

"Seeing as I do not have a new Source at my side, that is clearly the case."

"Yet you bear a new Mark," the Anala Lady said with a pointed glance to his right hand where Tessa had drawn the Achaz symbol.

He knew he should still be outraged by it, but it was a piece of her she could never have back. It might be the only piece of her she'd ever freely give him, so he didn't despise the marking on his hand like he should, even if it was a rival kingdom's symbol.

Theon shrugged, flexing his right hand. "We had a disagreement. She can be...unpredictable."

"That girl is more than unpredictable. She is *uncontrollable*," the Celeste Lady said. "Despite promises being made that she would be kept under control."

And that pointed statement was spoken directly to Rordan.

"I am handling it," Rordan retorted.

"And how is that going?" Theon asked, steepling a finger along his temple now.

"That is no longer your concern," the Achaz Lord sneered.

"I think it is all of our concern," the Falein Lady interjected. "Was she responsible for the Villas, Rordan?"

"It was a misunderstanding."

"A misunderstanding?" the Anala Lady asked. "Please explain that."

Rordan took a breath, visibly collecting himself before he straightened. Light crackled at the tips of his fingers as he gripped the ends of the armrests. "I went to visit Desiray for my usual monthly meeting. Tessa asked to accompany me as she had obviously never been to the Villas before. While hesitant, I agreed. If we want her to continue to be accommodating, she needs to be given some freedoms. I arranged for Larissa to give her a tour, but she..."

He paused, clearly searching for the right words, so Theon supplied them for him.

"But she had an agenda of her own?"

The gold rings in his eyes flared, and Rordan glared at Theon. "It was a miscalculation on my part."

"Then *you* are accepting responsibility for what happened in the Sirana Villas?" Theon asked, taking a page from Luka's book and sounding bored as fuck.

The room fell silent again, all eyes pinned on the Achaz Lord. "That is not what I am saying," he ground out.

"Then the girl needs to be locked up until she can be controlled," the Serafina Lady cut in, and that had Theon arching a brow in surprise. Achaz and Serafina were *always* a united front.

"And if she can't be controlled, she needs to be eliminated," the Celeste Lady added.

Theon couldn't hide his huff of amusement.

"Nothing about this matter is funny," the Celeste Lady snapped.

"Agreed," Theon replied. "But both of those suggestions are pointless. She will not allow either thing to happen."

"She cannot overpower a united front of the six kingdoms."

"Do we know what she is truly capable of?" the Anala Lady asked, and her question wasn't directed at Rordan but at Theon.

"If the Revelation Decree is to be taken as the omen it is, she will be the downfall of Devram," the Celeste Lady answered instead. "We have been preparing for this for centuries, and instead of dealing with the threat, you have welcomed her into your home, Rordan."

"Because having control over her makes him more powerful than the rest of us," the Anala Lady said calmly.

"That is not the motivation here," Rordan retorted. "Having her on our side is better for the realm as a whole. She cannot destroy the realm if she is working with us."

"But she can destroy the Arius Kingdom, right?" Theon cut in. "Let's not pretend that isn't a motivation from the rest of you."

"We do not wish for the Arius Kingdom to be destroyed," the Serafina Lady scoffed. "That is absurd."

Theon clicked his tongue. "There's no need for pretenses here, Maya."

Her silver irises flared at the informal address. "And *you* are not yet a Lord, Theon. Be grateful we are even letting you sit in on this meeting."

"Grateful? When I arrived I was admonished for not being present more. Now you are telling me I should be grateful to even be here. Which is it?"

"That does need to be addressed," the Anala Lady interjected. "When do we declare Theon the Arius Lord?"

"When there is proof Valter is dead," the Serafina Lady snapped.

"How long do we wait for such proof before we take matters into our own hands?"

Theon had to hide his surprise. He hadn't expected this to be discussed at this meeting. The Sirana Villas and Tessa, yes. His Lordship status? Not at all.

"Do you have any leads as to his whereabouts?" the Falein Lady inquired, her eyes on Theon.

"I have theories, but every attempt to prove them has failed, so I cannot confirm any of them," Theon answered carefully.

"And what are these theories?"

"He either fled, believing as I do that the rest of you wish for the downfall of our kingdom, and is in hiding. He is being held captive somewhere." His eyes slid to Rordan for the briefest of moments at that. "Or he is truly dead."

How he wished that were true.

"Who would be holding him captive?" the Falein Lady asked.

"Let's not pretend my father doesn't have enemies," Theon said flatly.

"And let's not pretend his own offspring wouldn't take an opportunity to steal his seat from under him," the Serafina Lady interjected.

"So what if I would?" Theon asked with a shrug. "You are telling me you didn't scheme and plot against your mother for that seat, Maya? We are immortal. If only death can relinquish a seat, tell me how your mother passed?" Her stare was pure malice as she glared at him, her lips pressed into a thin line. "But if I had killed him, I would be presenting his corpse to you to avoid this very conversation," he added.

"I think we can all agree that as long as he remains bonded to Tessalyn in a Source capacity, he cannot be instated as the Arius Lord," the Falein Lady said, forever the voice of logic and reason.

But didn't that just fuck him over? Because the only way to sever a Source bond was the death of one of the parties. He certainly wasn't going to let Tessa be killed, nor was he planning on dying anytime soon.

"So Arius Kingdom will just continue to be treated as less than?" Theon argued, sitting forward. "*This* is why I spend my time with my people instead of attending these ridiculous affairs."

"Ridiculous affairs?" Rordan snarled. "This is why Arius Kingdom has been shunned for decades. Your entire bloodline is arrogant enough to believe you are above the laws and rules. That covenants and agreements are beneath you, even if they are for the wellbeing of the worlds as a whole. You are no better than the god you descend from."

And at that, the entire room fell silent once more. Everyone was tense, power flickering in their eyes while it lingered at the fingertips of the Fae of the room. A part of Theon wondered if this was how these meetings always went. If it was, he could somewhat understand how his father had become such a hard and hateful male. You had to be ruthless to survive this and fight for your kingdom. The unified front presented to the realm was only a show. Behind the scenes, it was each kingdom grabbing as much power as they could. It had always been a fragile thing, and now it was cracking.

All because of Tessa.

Control the uncontrollable or to fury they *all* lose.

"I think we all need you to expound on that statement," the Anala Lady finally said, toying with a flame in her palm.

"What is there to explain?" Rordan said, shifting in his seat as he gripped the armrests tighter.

"Your words make it sound as though you have a personal vendetta against Arius himself," she answered calmly. "If that is the case, we can only assume said vendetta gives you underlying motives."

"Why would I have a personal vendetta against Arius? That is not even a possibility. The gods cannot interfere here."

"The gods cannot *come* here," the Falein Lady corrected.

"If anyone is harboring a secret vendetta, I would look at the Anala Kingdom. They are the ones who do not let others enter and keep the fire Fae from everyone else," he countered.

The Anala Lady arched a manicured brow, her red-gold hair shimmering like the flames she wielded. "Have you ever been denied a visit, Rordan?"

"No, but the requirements for such a visit are rather absurd."

"I fiercely protect what is mine to care for," she said matter-of-factly. "It is no fault of mine if you do not have such care for your own kingdom."

"Choose your next words carefully, Kyra," Rordan said in a low tone.

The fire in her palm expanded. "My words are always chosen with purpose, Rordan."

"Let's take a minute and focus on what we need to accomplish today," the Falein Lady cut in. "What are we going to do about the Sirana Villas?"

"And the girl?" the Celeste Lady cut in.

"And what of the missing Fae?" the Serafina Lady added on. "Those assets must be recovered, Rordan."

"Not to mention this is still a Selection year," the Celeste Lady said.

"Enough!" Rordan barked. "We have handled crises before. We will do it again. First things first, we need to put our people at ease. They are already anxious with the sporadic attacks on Legacy, even if it was kept to the Arius line until now."

Theon held his tongue at that comment, waiting to see where the Lord went with this.

"We hold the Sirana Gala as planned," Rordan continued. "We invite more than the nobles, make it a grand affair. A remembrance and tribute to those who were lost, and reassure everyone we are taking these matters seriously and handling it."

"I think we also use this as an opportunity to appoint a new noble to rule in Rosebell," the Falein Lady added. "Do we have anyone in mind?"

"I have a few ideas," Rordan said.

"As do I," the Anala Lady said.

"I as well," the Celeste Lady chimed in.

Rordan was visibly annoyed. "Fine. We submit names and meet a week before the gala to decide."

Everyone nodded in agreement.

"As for the missing Fae," Rordan continued. "The most valuable had Tracking Marks. The issue is that all the people who had the corresponding Marks to track them were also killed."

"Every single one?" Theon couldn't help but ask.

"Yes," Rordan said tightly.

"You are telling me you didn't have a single person outside of the Villas with this Mark in case something like this happened?"

A few seconds ticked by before the Achaz Lord gritted out, "Obviously not."

"By the gods," Theon muttered, swiping a hand over his mouth.

Granted, there were only three of them connected to Tessa's Tracking Mark but that was because he didn't trust anyone else. Out of six kingdoms, there wasn't *one* person outside of the Villas to trust with this Mark? Although, when he thought about it, the issue was likely they couldn't agree on who that one person should be, just like it would be hours of discussion to agree on a new leader of the Villas.

"Then how are we going to find them?" the Serafina Lady demanded.

"We can ask the priestesses to see if they can come up with something," Rordan said.

"Or we ask the Shifters for aid," the Anala Lady said.

"The Shifters? You cannot be serious," the Serafina Lady scoffed.

"They are excellent trackers."

"And there is a reason they are in the Underground."

"They are also notoriously difficult to work with," Rordan cut in.

"But if the interim leader of the kingdom that governs the Underground approached them, surely they would have to fall into line," the Anala Lady said, still playing with the fire in her palm.

He felt all eyes land on him, and he sighed. "Kylian and Giselle are indeed hard to work with."

"Are you saying you do not have control over a section of your kingdom?" Rordan asked with a smirk.

Theon shrugged. "They're all still breathing, which is more than you can say for a section of yours."

A streak of light erupted from the Lord's palm, spearing for Theon, who managed to get a shield of darkness in place a second before the powers connected. It was still enough to make his chair slide backwards several feet though.

"What the fuck?" Theon demanded, already on his feet. His power pooled, snapping and straining for vengeance. Rordan was on his feet too, ire lining every part of his features.

And then a wall of fire erupted between them.

When it receded, the Anala Lady still held a large ball of flame in her hand. "If either of you throw one more attack, you will be feeling my flames instead of just looking at them."

Tension blanketed the room, the Sources having all stepped in front of their Masters, ready to protect and defend them. Although, the Anala Lady's Source stood at her side rather than in front of her.

"Things always get so heated in these meetings," the Falein Lady sighed. "And always between your two kingdoms."

"I wouldn't know," Theon ground out.

"Exactly," Rordan spat, taking his seat once more as he straightened his suit. "You are too young and inexperienced. Too inexperienced to be running your mouth about things you know nothing of."

"Isn't it my job to know these things now?"

"Not until you are officially declared the Arius Lord."

With another dramatic sigh, the Falein Lady said, "The missing Fae must be found. There is no reason not to have both the priestesses and the Shifters aiding us. Offer the Shifters an incentive to find them first if you must."

Right.

An incentive to the Shifters.

Theon already knew what their price would be. He was already sporting the Bargain Mark for it, despite having found Axel.

"Weekly updates from each of you on this matter would be appreciated," the Anala Lady added.

"Fine," Rordan agreed begrudgingly. "Anything else?"

A huff of disbelief came from the Celeste Lady. "Yes. What are we going to do about Tessalyn? And do not say you have her handled because you clearly do not. She was under more control when she was with Theon than she has been with you."

Theon couldn't help the dark smile that curled on his lips at that, and he settled back in his chair to watch how this played out.

"You want me to give her back to the Arius Kingdom?" Rordan demanded.

"At least Legacy weren't dying when she was with him," the Anala Lady said casually.

"I will get her under control."

Theon swallowed his chuckle. He'd said those same words once. More than once actually. He could tell the Achaz Lord exactly how that was going to go, but he kept quiet. This was something it seemed everyone needed to learn for themselves.

"Perhaps it is because she is separated from Theon?" the Anala Lady mused, her chin resting in her hand now. "We all know how the bond reacts when we are separated from our Sources for too long."

"You want me to, what? Give him *visitation* with her?" Rordan mocked.

"You could ask her if that is something she would like," Kyra replied with a small shrug.

"You are trying my last nerve this day, Kyra," he ground out.

"And you are failing in your promises, Rordan. You said you would control the girl. Keep her grounded. That she would be an asset to Devram. Instead, she has destroyed one of our greatest resources, not to mention centuries of research and knowledge," she retorted. "And yet you still expect us to believe you can control her? All the evidence suggests otherwise. In fact, all the evidence suggests she should be with Theon."

"She has Achaz power," Rordan spat, his magic appearing yet again. "She does not belong with Arius."

"I am willing, if the others agree, to give you one final chance with the girl," the Falein Lady interjected. "But one wrong move. One more death. One more issue, and she gets locked away until her fate can be agreed to."

It took a full minute before there was a murmured agreement from everyone else. Even Theon agreed with them. It wasn't as if they could turn her back over to him. She was the one to decide if and when she let him be in her presence.

Which was going to make this Sirana Gala an issue.

He'd have to speak to Luka and have him talk to her.

And he fucking hated that this was where they were at.

"Now is there anything else?" Rordan ground out.

When no one voiced any concerns, the Achaz Lord was the first to leave, his Source following him out of the room. The Ladies all lingered, and so did Theon because he needed to speak with the Anala Lady.

He hung back, waiting until she separated from the others before he approached her. "Kyra, can I have a word?"

She turned to him, her amber eyes bright as she looked him up and down. "I am running late for another engagement," she answered. "But you can make an appointment."

"It is about the Anala Estate," he said, falling into step beside her as she left the Tribunal room.

Her brow arched in a silent command for him to go on.

"A Fae we claimed was originally from there. And another, the fire Fae, was not..." He trailed off when fire flickered in her gaze at the words. She was clearly still upset by that.

"And your question?" she asked coldly.

"I would like to visit. Not just the Estate. The kingdom itself," he said, feeling awkward as fuck for some reason. She was intimidating.

"My office can make arrangements for that."

"Yes, but that takes weeks, if not months," he argued. "I was hoping as a soon-to-be fellow ruler in the realm, we could expedite the process and skip all the formalities."

They were outside the Tribunal building now, her Source beside her.

"Tell you what, Theon St. Orcas. Gain the trust of one who knows the secrets of the winds, and he can tell you how to enter my kingdom without the formalities."

"What does that mean?" Theon asked, a fire portal appearing behind Kyra.

"The Shifter Prince knows," she answered.

Then she was gone.

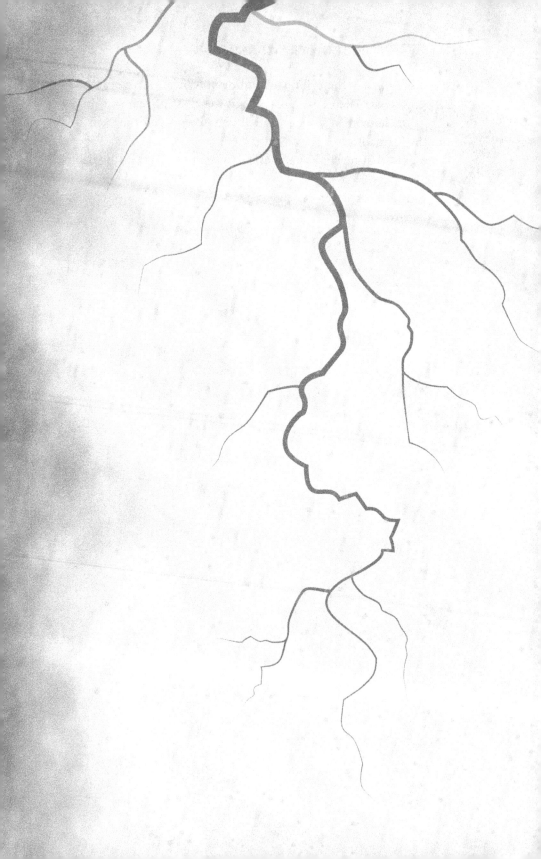

27

TESSA

"Think of where you want to go," Luka said.

Her eyes were closed, her breathing deep, but that command was ridiculous. Because where she wanted to go was anywhere but Devram, and it was not as if she could just *Travel* there. Then again, it wasn't as if she could Travel anywhere.

For the last hour, they had been doing this. Luka seemed determined to teach her to Travel, grumbling about how he shouldn't need to wear sunglasses every time she entered his room. She'd rolled her eyes, but humored him, letting him talk her through the basics of Traveling. Now, however, they were both getting frustrated because this was going nowhere. Or, more accurately, *she* was going nowhere.

"Can't we go back to training with our magic," she said, and yes, it was bordering on a whine.

"No," Luka said. "Focus."

"I am focusing."

"No, you're not."

"Yes, I am."

"Really? Then tell me where you're focusing on right now."

"Right now I'm focusing on the left side of your face because that's where I want to punch you," she snapped, opening her eyes and glaring at him.

And catching the barest hint of a smile before he quickly wiped it from his face.

"By the gods, I need to sit down," she gasped. "A smile from Luka Mors? I might faint."

"Shut up," he muttered.

"No, no," she insisted, plopping down onto the floor of the training arena. Nylah was across the room, curled up tight, but her eyes were always watching. "I need a moment. I'm in shock, and I want to remember this. Who knows when such a phenomenon will happen again."

"Tessa," he growled, crossing his arms where he stood over her. "Get up. You're wasting valuable training time."

She clicked her tongue, flopping onto her back. "No, *you're* wasting valuable training time trying to teach me to Travel. An ability we don't even know if I possess. Teach me to control my magic. Teach me to wield a sword. Teach me to kick someone's ass. My portals are fine."

"Your portals are going to blind me one day," he retorted. "More than that, how will you sneak into somewhere covertly when your portal is a beacon announcing your arrival?"

"Maybe I want them to know," she countered, stacking her hands on her stomach and staring up at him. "I want them to know when I am coming to end them. The fear is intoxicating. Empowering. Enthralling. Freeing."

Luka stared at her, his pupils having shifted and irises glowing a soft blue.

"What?" she asked.

"You are so vicious," he murmured, his voice all heat that she felt in her blood. Her bare toes curled at the sound, her stomach doing flip-flops that she tried to ignore.

She cleared her throat. "Can we just go back to our usual training?"

"No," he answered.

"Why not?"

"Because you're tired, and your power hasn't been refilled since your little escapade in the Sirana Villas."

"That's not true," she lied.

Luka's brows arched. "It's not? You haven't slept in my room since the night I found you in my bed, which you still haven't discussed, by the way. Since that is the case, I can only assume you're not sleeping well. Unless you've been going to Theon for such a thing, but I'm positive I would have felt that exchange down the bond, because you two don't know how to sleep beside each other without fighting and fucking."

Her mouth fell open at the insinuation. "That's not true," she admonished, pushing onto her elbows. "We slept beside each other plenty of times without fucking."

"Until the first time. After that? Don't lie to me, Tessa. I know what the two of you were doing long before you two realized I was part of the bond."

She glared up at him. "I haven't been going to see Theon."

"I know."

"Then why even suggest it?"

"Because it's an option if you don't want to sleep in my room. You need sleep, Tessa. I know you're powerful and can go for days without it, but that doesn't mean you should, especially when you're training."

She pursed her lips, her gaze darting to the side. She *was* tired. She hadn't let herself sleep in Luka's room since the night he'd held her. Mostly because he was a distraction from her purpose, and letting herself find comfort in others diverted her attention. It was easier to remember what she needed to do when she was alone. When she didn't let herself depend on others. The problem was, he was right. She slept like shit so far from one of her bonded, and when she did sleep, it was restless. She'd even tried drinking the tea that Rordan still had delivered to her room every night, but all that did was make her visions more intense. And while she might sleep, she was still exhausted when she woke.

"As for your power," Luka continued when she didn't speak. "I'm training you daily, Tessa. I can tell when it's weaker and a little off. You're also clever, and I know that you've figured out how to refill your power reserves. The question is why haven't you?"

She slid her gaze back to him. "I don't need blood."

"I assumed not," he said, his tone a touch softer, and to her surprise, he lowered to the ground beside her. She laid back once more, and he did the same, propping one of his hands behind his head.

"What are you doing?" she asked.

"I know you're not used to it, but this is called having a conversation."

"Oh my gods," she muttered, shoving at him with her foot.

She heard the small huff she could only assume was the closest he'd ever get to laughter. Turning her head, she asked, "What do you like to do for fun?"

He was clearly surprised by the question, and it took a minute before he said with a sigh. "It's been so long, I don't remember."

"Me too," she whispered.

She wasn't sure what to do when she felt his fingers graze over hers. Her breath stalled, her heart rate picking up, but he didn't do it again.

They lay like that for several minutes, and she was the one to speak again when she said, "I know this is going to sound a little insane, but just bear with me for a minute, okay?"

He muttered something under his breath that she couldn't hear, but then he said, "All right. Let's hear it."

"I have dreams or visions or whatever," she began, not even sure how to start this.

"I'm aware."

"And sometimes you are in them," she went on in a rush. "Not just as part of the visions, but *in* them. Like you're watching them with me, and a few times recently you've been interacting with them. Do you..."

Gods, she sounded more than a little mad.

When she didn't go on, Luka turned to look at her. "Tessa, if you're asking if I remember being pulled into your visions, the answer is yes. I didn't know if *you* remembered that."

"Wait, really?" she asked, pushing up to a sitting position to see him better.

Luka nodded. "The first time it happened, I didn't know what to think or do. But when it happened again, I started trying to figure out how and when it was going to happen."

"And?"

He shrugged. "The last time was when you slept in my room with me. The last time was also the first time someone didn't pull me out of it."

"What are you talking about?"

"The first time it happened, a female showed up. She asked how I got there."

"How *did* you get there?" Tessa asked.

He shrugged again, still lying on the ground. "No idea. She asked if you called me there, and then she shoved me out of the dream. Every time since then, she's shown up and shoved me out. Until the last time."

"The one with the dragons," Tessa clarified.

There was a small delay before he said, "Yeah. That one."

"And you don't know how you get in them?"

He sighed, pushing up to a sitting position and then getting to his feet. "No, but I can tell Theon about it. See if he knows anything."

She tipped her head back to see him. "Why would Theon know anything about this?"

Holding his hand out to her, he said, "Because Theon is very well read. He is a wealth of knowledge, both useful and frivolous." Slipping her hand into his, he pulled her to her feet. "If he doesn't know something about this, he will likely know where to look to find answers."

She knew all that. She'd seen him pore over books and scribble notes at all hours of the night. Luka was right. Theon would likely be the fastest way to get answers, but did she want him knowing about this? Then there was Lilura's warning that someone was messing with her visions, and she'd never seen this female that Luka was talking about. Rordan was being...different with her since the Sirana Villas, but could she trust Theon with this information?

Planting her hands on her hips, she blew stray hair out of her face. Luka was watching her, waiting for an answer, and when she didn't say anything, he said, "If there's one thing Theon knows how to do well, it's protect those he cares for, and you? You're at the top of that list."

She shook her head. "He'll do what *he* thinks is best for me. He could figure something out and keep it from me because he thinks it'll put me in danger to know. And don't tell me he won't because that's all he's done."

"That's fair," Luka conceded. "Both of you need to learn to trust other people."

"Trusting other people gives them power over you," she retorted.

"The ability to trust other people is a different kind of power, Tessa."

She glared back at him. "Then it is a power I do not want."

He shook his head, rubbing at his brow in obvious disappointment. With a sigh, he said, "We need to discuss the Sirana Gala."

"What about it?" she snapped.

"You need to give Theon permission to attend."

She barked a laugh. "What?"

"That stupid bargain he made with you," Luka said. "He can't be in the same space as you unless you allow it."

"I know that," she said, rolling her eyes. "I was asking about the Sirana Gala. They are still holding that?"

"Sounds like it," Luka answered. "Theon sent a message about it. They'll be announcing the new Rosebell overseer."

"They're just going to go on with their lives like nothing happened? Not even the Legacy mean anything to them?"

"What did you expect them to do, Tessa? Of course they are going to continue as normal. Otherwise their people will panic. If they see their leaders confident there is nothing to worry about, it puts them at ease."

"And Theon is okay with this?" she demanded.

Luka's head tilted as he studied her. "You have expectations of him?"

"Yes. I mean, no. I don't know."

"Yes, you do."

"No," she retorted, crossing her arms. "I don't. Are we done for today?"

"No," sounded a female voice, dark and chilling.

Nylah lifted her head a second before Auryon stepped from a swirl of ashes and smoke, her bow across her chest. Her black hair flowed around her, grey ashes among it like snowflakes. Her swirling eyes raked over Tessa, and ashy footprints were left in her wake as she prowled forward with a lethal grace that had Tessa tensing. She hadn't seen the female since Roan had nearly died, and she looked particularly murderous right now.

"Is something wrong? Is Roan all right?" Tessa asked, her entire chest seizing at the idea that something had happened. He'd been fine the last time she'd seen him. Still wounded, but recovering fine.

"Roan is well," the female said. "I suspect he will be up walking around in the next few days."

Relief flooded through her. One step closer to having him back at her side. Nylah was sitting up now, but she still stayed back. It was fine. Tessa didn't *need* her by her side, but Roan would have already been there.

"Then why are you here?" Luka asked, his irritation written all over his face.

"You should be asking where I have been," Auryon retorted, those mysterious eyes pinned on Tessa.

"Fine. Where have you been?" he amended.

"For days now, I have been tracking down all the Hunters you have summoned," she snarled, and she wasn't bothering to hide her ire at that. "You need to stop summoning them."

A smile curled on Tessa's lips as she said, "No."

"No?" Auryon repeated. "You summon them here and then do nothing to contain them."

"I do not wish to contain them."

Auryon took two steps towards her, violence glimmering, and before Tessa could call forth her power in answer, Luka was stepping in front of her.

Auryon stilled, a sneer curling on her lip as a dagger appeared amid a swirl of ashes. "I've been dealing with your kind long before you were born, dragonling," she said in a deathly calm tone.

"Perfect. Then you'll know that dragon fire is more powerful than your magic ashes," Luka retorted.

Tessa peeked around Luka to find the female staring at him, her fingers tightening around the dagger. The sound of Nylah shaking drew Tessa's attention, and she looked over to find the wolf stretching before she trotted over to Tessa's side.

"Temural would agree with me, you know," Auryon said, clearly speaking to the wolf, but Nylah just sat down beside Tessa, a low warning growl sounding. "Yes, yes, I know," she answered, rolling her eyes.

"Can you...communicate with them?" Tessa asked.

"We've discussed this," Auryon retorted. "I have known them for a long time. I raised them. You will eventually come to know the same."

"You raised them?" Tessa repeated in surprise.

Auryon nodded. "All the Huntresses aid in raising Temural's Trackers."

"How many Huntresses are there?"

She took a small step back. "There used to be twelve of us."

"Used to be?"

She nodded, the ire reappearing. "Yes. Used to be. Temural and Anala granted us our gifts in answer to the Hunters that Achaz created. We are some of the only ones that can kill them, and you continually summoning them is becoming an annoyance."

"So stop killing them," Tessa drawled.

"It is my purpose to kill them," Auryon shot back. "The sole purpose of a Hunter is to kill any being with Arius blood."

"And yet I still breathe."

Her smile was chilling. "For now."

"Are you threatening her?" Luka interjected.

"No," Auryon answered. "But if she believes they will not turn on her in time, she is more naive than I once believed. Stop summoning them, Tessalyn."

"I am not naïve," Tessa spat back.

"Stop summoning them," Auryon repeated. "If they make it to Arius Kingdom, you will not be able to control them."

"I do control them. They answer to me," she argued.

"They do not. They answer to Achaz."

"Who is not here."

Her head canted to the side. "Have you not spoken to him while in this realm?"

Luka whirled on her. "What?" he demanded.

"How can you possibly know that?" Tessa asked, ignoring his irate stare.

"You are not the only one who can move among wards undetected," Auryon replied. "Stop summoning them."

Then she was gone seconds before the door to the training room was thrown open. Rordan strode in, his Source and Dex at his side. Dagian and Sasha were a step behind. All of their faces were void of emotion, and Tessa immediately stiffened, stepping closer to Luka on instinct. Nylah's growl was loud, a warning to them both, as she stood, her hackles raised.

"Tessalyn," Rordan greeted tightly.

"Rordan," she replied in kind.

The Lord glanced at Luka dismissively before focusing on Tessa once more. "It appears the two of you are done with your training for the day?"

"Not yet," she answered.

"You are now," he said tersely, and her temper immediately ignited at the command. "I leave for a meeting in thirty minutes, and we need to discuss a few things before I go." He looked at Luka again. "You can go."

"Actually, he can't," Tessa cut in. "We are working on some things, so you can tell me your information and then we can continue."

"This isn't a negotiation, Tessa."

"I'm not negotiating," she replied sweetly.

The gold in his eyes flickered, his nostrils flaring. "After the events of the Sirana Villas, you need to be...looked after. For your own safety."

"Right. My safety," she repeated flatly.

"You will retain your freedom, but Dexter has been assigned to be with you any time you leave the premises. It would be preferable if he was with you most of the time as extra security," Rordan said.

"I don't think that's necessary," Tessa said evenly. "Luka can do that. He is more powerful than a *Fae*."

"Luka is not bound to this kingdom," Rordan ground out.

"Surely my wolves are more than enough security," she tried again, gesturing to Nylah.

"Dexter has been assigned this role, Tessalyn," he said, his tone saying she wasn't to argue further, and her eyes narrowed as the light around her wrists started winding up her arms.

"Just to clarify, you are assigning a *Fae* to protect her should something happen?" Luka interrupted.

"I was unaware you were part of this conversation," Rordan replied sharply.

"No," Tessa interjected. "He is not assigning him to protect me. He is assigning him to watch me and report back."

"Be glad that is all I am doing, Tessalyn," Rordan growled, stepping closer. Luka stepped closer to her too, but Rordan didn't seem to care. "I spent hours with the other rulers yesterday persuading them that harsher measures were not needed. You should be thanking me."

He said nothing else as he swept from the room, his son going with him, and then it was her and Luka and Dex, who was glaring at Luka.

Dex was better than a Legacy guard, she supposed. She'd slipped away from Dex on numerous occasions. The problem was that Dex wasn't Fae. She was more than certain he was one of these light guardians that Xan had told her of, but if that was the case, who did he steal his power from?

Maybe this wouldn't be so bad. She could try to get more information out of him. When she irritated him enough, he slipped at times and told her things he didn't mean to reveal.

Finally Dex's attention slid to her, his dark eyes looking her up and down. "You look tired, Tessie."

"I'm not," she retorted.

"I'll tell Elowyn to increase your tea. Have you been drinking it?"

Gritting her teeth, she held Dex's gaze as she said down the bond, *Luka?*

He didn't flinch. Not even a twitch of his brow at her speaking to him, but she knew he was listening. Knew they likely both were.

Ask Theon to look into the visions.

28

LUKA

This is why Tessa needed to learn to Travel, Luka thought to himself.

He had stepped from the air directly into the study at the Arius manor, and Theon hadn't even noticed. There was no bright light alerting him to his presence. The wards allowed him passage, and Theon was so engrossed in whatever he was reading on his laptop, he hadn't realized he was here.

It was surreal really. To see him sitting at that desk. Something they'd worked so hard for. Talked at length about. Dreamed about the day it was him there instead of Valter. And even if Theon hadn't officially been given the Arius Lord title yet, there was no one who could take it from him. He was the most powerful Arius Legacy. The St. Orcas line had made sure of it with all their careful Matches over the centuries.

"Lordship looks good on you," Luka said.

Darkness appeared, hovering around Theon as he lurched to his feet.

"You fucker," Theon muttered, closing the laptop.

His magic lingered, not because of any threat, but because he needed to let it breathe. It wasn't uncommon for him to let his magic free while they sat around late at night planning.

"What are you doing here?" Theon asked, rounding the desk.

Luka met him halfway across the space, the two of them embracing, and fuck, it felt good. Axel would have given them shit, but he was going to hug his best friend after all this fuckery.

Theon stepped back as he said, "She's not with you."

Luka could hear the disappointment in that statement. "I think she would have come with me, if anything just to see Roan, but the Achaz Lord has her under watch at all times right now after the destruction at the Villas."

"So it's true? She did that?"

"She hasn't admitted it outright to me, but yeah. I'm certain it was her," Luka answered. "I'm sure you felt her that night too."

Theon hummed an acknowledgement, sliding his hands into his pockets. "She knows you're here, though?"

"She does," Luka answered. "Actually, she sent me here."

Theon arched a brow. "She sent you here? For what?"

"We're trying to figure something out, but first tell me what's been going on here."

He listened while Theon filled him in on his trip to the Underground with Tristyn Blackheart of all people, his meeting with the Shifters, and Axel showing up and nearly killing Kat.

"He really left?" Luka asked when Theon finished telling him about Axel's note.

"According to the note he left, yeah," Theon sighed.

"Cienna could be wrong. He didn't think to wait to make sure?"

"He's too worried about hurting Katya."

Luka could understand that, but he also understood how *hard* it was to stay away from someone you felt drawn to. Would that change if this twin flame bond no longer existed between them? Luka didn't know, but Cienna had been wrong before.

"How is Kat?" he asked.

Theon shoved a hand through his hair. "Not well. She stays in her room when she's not at her required classes."

"That's not any different than before."

"She's not well," Theon said again. "Some of it could still be recovering from the attack by Axel, but she stays curled in bed. She's hardly eaten anything since we came back from the Underground."

"Does she even need to continue the classes? Do Lange and Corbin, for that matter? They seem kind of pointless seeing as they've already been claimed," Luka said.

"Do they *need* to? Probably not. Does it keep up appearances and play nice with the other kingdoms? Yes," Theon answered.

"Valid point."

"Give me an update on this bargain you made with Rordan," Theon said.

Luka shrugged, crossing his arms. "Not much to say. I gave him the ring. Never seen him wear the thing. I'll watch for a chance to steal it back. He's never asked me anything about my lineage, and—"

"But if he does, you now have a potential relative to worry about," Theon interrupted.

Well, fuck. He hadn't thought of that.

"And if he starts getting aggressive with Tessa, you won't be able to do anything about it," Theon added.

That son of a bitch.

"I've been training Tessa," Luka said.

"Not long enough to hold her own against a Lord," Theon countered.

"Point taken," Luka conceded. "Which brings me to why I'm here."

He gave Theon a quick run down of being pulled into Tessa's visions and what had been said in the last one about someone altering them.

Scratching his jaw, Theon said, "Cienna would be the best person to ask about that."

"You don't know anything? Never came across something in all that reading you do?" Luka said, a little mockery creeping into his tone.

Theon flipped him his middle finger, and gods, it felt *good* to be with his friend again.

"Cienna comes to check in on Katya every day, but she was already here today," Theon said. He pulled Axel's mirror from his pocket, turning it over in his hand. "I've never figured out how to use this thing the way Axel did. Cienna shows up when she wants to."

"I can try to come back tomorrow," Luka said, not loving that idea. "I don't like to leave her alone too long now that Rordan has someone babysitting her."

"Who's guarding her?"

"I don't know that guarding is the word I'd use," Luka said flatly. "But it's that Fae from her Estate. Dex."

"A *Fae*? He has a Fae guarding her. What the fuck is he going to do?"

"I said the same thing."

Theon swiped a hand down his face. "Rordan isn't a stupid male. He has a purpose with this."

"Which is why I don't like leaving her alone with him," Luka agreed. "This afternoon, however, she was being fitted for her gala dress."

"So she is going?" Theon asked.

Luka nodded. "But she agreed to your attendance."

Theon huffed a laugh. "Never, in all my immortal days, did I think I'd be asking permission from my Source to attend a gala."

"Does she draw from you?" Luka asked, because how the fuck was she filling her power wells?

She didn't need blood. It wasn't sleep and sustenance like the Fae. He may have told her he noticed that her power was weaker, but not enough to matter. It never seemed to deplete to a point where she would be in danger of running out. In fact, the only time that ever seemed to be something she'd need to worry about was when she wasn't in control and her magic had consumed her.

"No," Theon said. "If anything, she just plays with my power. Showing me she can. Or uses it against me." He paused for a moment before he said carefully, "You know, there is someone else we could ask about her power and the visions."

"Gia?" Luka asked.

Theon shook his head. "Razik and Eliza. Razik spends more time in books than I do."

Luka was fairly certain he stopped breathing for a few seconds.

Theon looked at his watch. "In fact, I'm supposed to be down in the dining room with them now. Razik needed more space to spread books around, so they emerged from their room this morning and took over that space."

Like a fool, Luka just stared at his friend.

"I understand if you don't want to, but he knows a lot of history that Devram has forgotten or never knew at all. He also knows things pertaining to Tessa," Theon went on.

"Such as?" Luka asked tightly.

"He basically confirmed the Revelation Decree is indeed a prophecy. Referred to her as the one who was never meant to exist."

"He sounds like a dick," he grumbled.

"He is," Theon replied.

Finally, Luka asked the question that had been burning in his mind from the moment he'd first laid eyes on the male. "Has he asked anything about our relations?"

"Not to me," Theon said. "And I understand if you'd rather not see him. I can ask him myself and let you know if he has any insight."

Did he want to see him? A part of him was desperate to talk to him. For most of his years, he'd thought he was the only Sargon Legacy left.

Then to learn there are not only more, but he has a potential *blood* relation? Not to mention the last vision he was in with Tessa suggested there were more dragon Shifters in the realms than he'd been led to believe, and he did want to know more about that. To know he wasn't as alone as he'd once thought.

But another part of him didn't want to talk to the male at all, and Luka knew it was a deep-rooted fear of rejection. It was the same reason he'd always been so determined to prove himself worthy of the blood that ran in his veins. What if this encounter led to him finding out it wasn't enough? That *he* wasn't enough?

Theon was silent, and with anyone else, this might have turned awkward. This had always been them though. Together for as long as he could remember. Inseparable. Sneaking into each other's rooms at night. When they were younger, it was to finish a board game or watch a movie when they should have been in bed. As they got older, it was to research and plan.

In the end, he wished he could say the choice he made was entirely for Tessa. That he wanted to talk to Razik for Tessa's sake. Help her figure out the visions because that was what was needed to keep her safe. But godsdammit, he wanted to talk to the male too. He finds out he has a potential blood relative in another realm and he doesn't even *ask* about it?

"Let's go," was all Luka said, and Theon nodded, leading the way out of the study.

They fell into step beside each other as they had thousands of times before, but it all felt wrong without Axel here.

"I still can't believe he just left," Luka said. "He didn't talk to you at all?"

Theon shook his head. "He was worried about being left alone with her. He told me, but I had a meeting. I would have blown it off, but I've been trying to get into the Anala Kingdom. I still need to build relations, and—"

"You don't need to explain yourself to me," Luka cut in.

"When you're back, everything will be different," Theon said.

When he was back.

Luka mulled over those words. He hadn't wanted to go to Tessa in the first place, but now...

Now he wasn't sure he could leave her either.

What a fucking mess.

They strode into the dining room to find Razik and the female sitting at the long table. Theon hadn't been kidding. There were books covering every inch of the surface. Some were stacked five or six high. Several were open, and the two of them were seated side by side. Neither of them looked up when they entered.

"We're hoping you might be able to help us with something," Theon said, and at least the female looked up at that.

Her grey eyes moved from Theon to Luka, where they lingered. She shifted, and Luka could only assume she'd kicked Razik under the table because he slowly lifted his head to peer at her.

"You know I love your excessively violent tendencies, *mai dragocen*," he said, his voice low and heated. "But we are not alone."

She rolled her eyes. "I'm aware. Are you?" she asked with a pointed look at Luka.

Razik took the hint and finally deigned to acknowledge them. Sapphire eyes that mirrored his own slid from him to Theon with hardly a glance before he went back to his book.

That was it?

"Raz," Eliza said, reaching over and closing the book.

They clearly had some sort of conversation down their bond that Theon had explained to him because a moment later, Razik turned in his chair to face them fully.

"How many years are you?" he asked, pinning Luka with a dominant stare.

"Twenty-nine," Luka replied in his usual bored tone. "How old are you?"

"Twenty-nine?" Eliza repeated, her eyes going wide while Razik continued to stare at him. "That's it?"

She had reached up, curling her fingers around Razik's arm where it was resting on the back of her chair.

"Were you born here?" Razik asked tightly.

"I don't think so, but all my memories are from here," Luka answered.

"And your parents?" Eliza asked, Razik tensing at the question.

"Died when I was young. I scarcely remember them."

Eliza tipped her head back to see Razik. "That doesn't mean—"

"Your father. What was his name?" Razik cut in.

Luka crossed his arms, holding his stare. "You first."

"By the gods, this isn't a pissing match between the two of you," Eliza grumbled. "Just tell him, Raz."

"My *father's* name is Tybalt Greybane," Razik said tightly, and something in Luka's chest fell at that. Until he added, "But the male who sired me is named Xan."

"You are sure?" Luka asked in disbelief.

"Am I sure of the name of the male who didn't want me and left me with my uncle in another world, never to be heard from again? Yes, I'm sure," he said.

Luka didn't know what to say to that. He had a handful of memories he could latch onto when it came to his parents, but a heartless male who didn't care was not one of them.

"And your mother?" Luka asked, his mouth dry as he waited for this answer. Half-siblings for certain, but full-blooded?

Razik's fingers flexed on the back of the chair, his tone tight and forced when he answered, "Aiyana."

"Maybe we should sit," Theon suggested.

Luka moved forward mechanically, sinking into a chair down the table from Razik and Eliza. A full-blooded sibling. He had an older brother.

"How old are you?" Luka asked again.

"Much older than you," Razik retorted.

"Centuries older," Eliza supplied.

"Centuries?" Theon repeated.

The Fae nodded.

"I am assuming by the way the blood drained from your face that those were the names of your parents as well," Eliza said.

Luka nodded, and she looked at Razik.

Who was just staring at him.

"Raz, you need to say something," she hissed under her breath.

"Why?" he countered.

"Because you just learned the answer to a question you've been brooding over for weeks."

Well, it was good to know he hadn't been the only one.

"Does it matter?" Razik said, and Luka flinched internally.

"Did you just ask if it *matters*?" Theon interrupted. "You learn the two of you are related, most likely brothers, and you ask if it matters?"

"We clearly had very different upbringings, and I learned long ago blood relations mean nothing," Razik answered, sounding completely indifferent to Luka's very existence.

Luka?

He saw Theon stiffen out of the corner of his eye as her voice echoed down their bond.

Are you all righ...? Luka asked, ready to Travel if necessary.

Are you? she countered.

Theon was staring at him now, and he shifted under the scrutiny.

I'm fine, Temptress.

She didn't say anything else, but he could feel her, as if she were sending her presence down the bond to him.

Luka cleared his throat. "He's right. It doesn't really matter."

"But—" Theon started.

"Do you know how someone could tamper with a vision?" Luka interrupted. If it didn't matter to Razik, it didn't need to matter to him.

"That's a question for a Witch," Razik said flatly.

"I'm aware," Luka drawled. "But Cienna is unavailable right now, and I'm short on time. I'm being pulled into Tessa's visions—"

"How?" Razik interrupted.

"I don't know," Luka gritted out, becoming irritated with the male. "But the last time we were in one, we were warned that someone was altering her visions."

"Warned by who? And where were you?"

He glanced at Theon before he answered, "A female named Lilura."

"Come again," Theon said, his surprise evident.

Luka nodded. "She knows Tristyn. They're involved somehow, but that's not the point. The point is she told us there was someone altering Tessa's visions."

"And where is she?" Razik repeated. "In this vision."

Luka shrugged. "Does that really matter?"

Razik sat back in his chair, his arm still slung around the back of Eliza's. "How do you know *she's* not the one altering the visions?"

That was a fair point.

"I guess we don't, but Tessa had clearly seen her before," Luka answered. He debated whether or not to tell them the next part. This guy had been a dick from the moment they'd stepped into this room, but curiosity got the better of him. "Lilura wasn't the only one in the vision."

Razik had pulled a book toward him, flipping pages as he muttered, "Well don't keep us in suspense."

This fucker.

"Someone in the vision knew you. Thought I *was* you," Luka ground out.

That had Razik slowly lifting his head, and it took all of Luka's self-control not to send him a satisfied smirk.

"Who?" Razik demanded.

"Never said her name. But she could shift fully into a dragon. Said the last time she saw you, the two of you had barely started walking," Luka answered. "Purple hair. Nearly crimson eyes."

Eliza turned to Razik with a questioning look. "Raz?"

The male's eyes were narrowed, studying Luka who held his stare without backing down. "You were in the sky," Razik said.

Luka nodded. "It seemed to be a floating island of some sort. There were others in the distance. And another dragon she went to...deal with. Her words."

"Razik," Eliza snapped in irritation. "Who is she?"

"Her name is Saylor. She's a cousin from another line of Sargon if it was truly her," he answered. "But she's not someone who could alter a vision."

"And where were they?" Theon asked.

"Nordrir," Razik answered. "Only now it's known as The Requiem."

"I don't know what that means," Theon said, his brow furrowing as he tried to follow all the new information being laid before them.

"Nordrir is Razik's home world," Eliza said. "All the dragons' home world actually. But they were hunted. Many who survived left the realm and went into hiding."

"Why is Tessa having visions of there?" Razik asked.

Luka stared at him in confusion. "Why would I know that?"

"You were in her vision."

"That I came to ask *you* about. I don't even know how I'm getting into her dreams or visions or whatever the fuck they are," he retorted.

Razik sat up straighter. "Whatever the fuck they are. What if they're exactly that?"

"Once again, no one understands your random revelations without an explanation, Raz," Eliza sighed, and Luka held in his huff of amusement. How many times had he said something similar to Theon?

"She is the granddaughter of Arius, right? Like Scarlett," Razik said.

Eliza nodded. "Because Scarlett is a direct descendant, she is more powerful. She has gifts of Arius, Serafina, *and* Saylah. What are Tessa's gifts?"

"She favors her Achaz gifts," Luka said, rubbing at his jaw.

"And her father is Temural, so we'd need to interchange the gifts from Saylah with the gifts from him," Theon added, that thread of excitement creeping into his voice. It always did when they are on the verge of uncovering something important.

"Saylah is the goddess of night and shadows. The shadows come from Arius and were passed down to Saylah," Eliza said.

Theon shook his head. "Arius and Serafina. I've never seen her use any of their gifts. Luka's right. She leans on her Achaz magic. She despises her Arius lineage."

"But the lightning and weather? That isn't any of them," Razik said, hand smoothing along his jaw in thought.

"This is stupid. How are we once again back to trying to figure out her lineage?" Luka asked.

"Do we know her Achaz line?" Eliza asked.

"All we know for sure is there is Witch blood in there somewhere. Texts suggest Achaz had a child with one of Zinta's daughters. I think we can safely assume Tessa came from that," Theon answered.

"But you just said her father is Temural," Eliza mused. "So Tessa is not the product of a child from Achaz and Zinta's daughter."

"She's too young anyway," Razik said, shaking his head. "Grand-daughter, however..."

"Granddaughter of two of the most powerful gods to exist?" Luka said. "You're fucking with me."

"It fits," Theon said, pulling on the back of his neck. "And it'd technically be the granddaughter of *three* of the most powerful. Serafina is a First Goddess."

"Let's say this is true, what is her mother then? A goddess?" Luka asked.

"Cienna did say her mother may as well be one," Theon supplied.

"Then what the fuck is Tessa?" Luka said

Theon and Luka both turned to Razik in question.

"Another pain in my ass," the male grumbled, pushing his hand through his hair. He exhaled a harsh breath, a trace of smoke furling. "I don't know what she'd be. If Achaz had a child with a daughter of Zinta, it would depend on the daughter's lineage. Who did Zinta have a child with?"

"Has she had visions of other places too?" Eliza asked.

"I only recently started being pulled into them," Luka answered. "All of them have been in Devram except the last one. But that doesn't mean she hasn't had visions in other places. She doesn't understand them. I think they are driving her a little mad."

"I think at this point we need to meet her," Eliza said. "Formally. Not just watching her lose control of her power."

The males all tensed at that idea.

"She's under too much scrutiny right now," Luka finally said. "It'll take a while to configure that."

"But we'll try," Theon said. "Until then, we try to figure out her gifts and visions. You've been training her, Luka. Is there any other type of magic you've seen?"

Luka shook his head. "We can't even figure out how she fills her reserves. It's like they can't run out."

"Everyone can run out of power," Razik said.

"Hers weakens some, but even then, it's still powerful," Luka said. "She doesn't need blood. She doesn't appear to need a Source, and she doesn't have a Guardian to draw from. Every time I've seen her use it, it's like she gets stronger, not weaker."

"Because she's not supposed to exist," Razik said plainly, and those few words made both Theon and Luka snarl in a low warning.

Eliza looked between them, her head tipping to the side as she studied them, but she didn't say anything.

"Get upset about it, but it doesn't change the fact," Razik said. "It upsets the balance having beginnings and endings in one being. I can imagine, because of this, her magic works differently than the rest of us. Likely different from the gods, the Legacy, the Fae. Unique because she is the only one of her kind." He got to his feet, looking down at Eliza. "You need to eat."

"I'm not..." she sighed. "Why do you always know I'm hungry before I do?"

"Afterwards, we should see if Katya will lend us that book she found the twin flame information in," he said, completely ignoring Theon and Luka now. "These books are useless," he added, gesturing to the ones strewn all over the table. "They're all from when Devram was created. Nothing of recent history exists in them."

"There is some place else we can go," Theon said suddenly. "It's a vast library system in catacombs. We need special permission from the Falein Lady to go there."

Razik stared at him flatly. "And you're just bringing this up now because...?"

"I've been busy," Theon retorted. "And it's not as if we can simply *go* there. I'll need to get documents forged for you two, and Eliza will have to...act accordingly."

Eliza scowled at them, but Razik bent down to speak low into her ear. Not low enough they didn't hear him though.

"I know you can follow instructions when it's worth your while, *mai dragocen*."

"And how will this be worth my while?" she hissed.

Razik straightened, taking her hand and tugging her to her feet. "We can discuss that tonight over *dinner*."

The look Eliza sent him was all heat and fire, and Luka averted his eyes because this was definitely something intimate between the two.

"Set up the visit to this library," Razik said then. "I'll see if I can find anything on visions, but if you think of anything else that might be useful, send a message."

Then he and Eliza disappeared—Traveled—out of the room.

Theon and Luka sat there in silence until Theon spoke the obvious.

"You have a brother."

"Yep," Luka said.

And that brother didn't seem to give a single fuck.

29

AXEL

Axel followed the male in front of him down a passage in Bree's home at the House of Four. It'd taken him three days to get back here. An entire day of driving from the portal station in Dark Haven had gotten him to Arius House, where he'd waited until well into the night to sneak into the sprawling house. He hadn't wanted to run into his mother, but he'd wanted to gather a few of his things. Some extra clothing. His favorite chaosphere sweatshirt. Extra earbuds. He'd been in and out in less than an hour, but then he'd had to drive another two days to the Underground. It was a trip he'd made numerous times before, but he'd always had a driver. It took him longer to navigate all the mountain passes on his own.

And during the day.

Because even with sunglasses on, the sun hurt his eyes.

The drive had been torturous in other ways though. The entire way he'd thought of Kat and their child. Had she told Theon yet? Was Eliza holding her hair back when she got sick? Was she eating? Was she healed enough for him to take more blood from her?

No!

He wasn't going there again. He'd make sure of it. It was why he'd left. To keep her safe from himself.

But wouldn't he go to that place again? He was going to be a Night Child. A vampyre. His world would revolve around blood, yet the idea of drinking from anyone else was as appealing as finding himself on the losing end of his father's wrath.

Once the transition was complete, it would get better.

At least that was what he had told himself over and over again, mile after mile. He just needed to get through these next two weeks of agony.

It'd taken another few hours to make his way to the Underground Districts and then to the House of Four. The guards at the entrance didn't question him, which meant Bree was expecting him. That was confirmed when the male leading him through the passages now had met him at the door and only said, "Come with me."

They finally stopped outside a set of large towering iron doors, and Axel had to wonder how they'd gotten them in here. The male pushed the doors open, standing aside and gesturing for Axel to go through. Hesitantly, he took a few steps and then paused as he looked around. It was some kind of vault or armory. Perhaps both.

Weapons of all kinds were along the walls. Swords. Daggers. Bows and arrows. Spears and whips. Even some weapons he didn't recognize. But stacked on the floor were chests full of coin, gold, silver, and all manner of jewels and jewelry. This was a room Luka's dragon dick would get hard over.

He wandered farther into the room, his hands in the pockets of his jeans. He didn't dare touch anything. This was new territory for him. Before he'd been their superior, although he'd rarely needed to pull rank with anyone in the Underground. But soon enough, he'd be one of them, and he had no doubt there would be more than one person lining up to prove they were stronger and more powerful than the fallen Arius Heir.

And the clan leader he was here to see was going to be one of the first in line.

He rounded a corner to find Bree. Her back was to him, her long black hair loose. She wasn't wearing her usual red dress. Instead, she was wearing a red skirt that reached the floor with deep slits up the side. Her black top left her back exposed, and when she turned, it barely covered her chest.

She was holding a sword in her hand, and by the gods, it was a beautiful weapon. The hilt was gleaming gold, intricately designed with several rubies inlaid. The blade itself appeared black at first, but as Bree moved, the light caught on the steel, revealing it to be a deep crimson red. With a skill that only came from years and years of practice, Bree swung the sword, spinning with the movement. Her skirt flared out around her, and Axel had to admit it was impressive she could move like that in heels that tall.

He stood several feet away, waiting for her to acknowledge him. Was this to be his life now? He didn't know, but he needed to figure it out, and that started with learning to control the bloodlust. It could obviously be done. Bree certainly didn't appear to have a need to maul every Fae that came near her. The problem was neither did he. He'd almost prefer that over only wanting *Kat's* blood.

She sheathed the sword before placing it carefully inside a case that sat atop a table. Snapping it closed, she replaced a lock that was clearly enchanted as it glowed beneath her fingers.

"That's a lot of protection for a sword," Axel said, unable to just stand there any longer.

She smiled as she ran her fingers along the top of the case. "What one person covets, another treasures," she replied. Honey-colored eyes trailed along his body, a slight frown appearing on her full lips. "What are you wearing?"

"Travel clothes," he answered.

Leaning a hip against the table, she asked, "How did it go?"

"As expected," Axel replied, a bite to his tone. "You set me up, Bree."

"I did no such thing, darling," she cooed. "I promised to find her for you, and I did."

"You knew what would happen," he argued.

"I showed you I deliver on my promises," she said sharply, pushing off the table. Her heels clicked on the stone floor as she came toward him, and when she reached up to brush his hair back, he jerked his head out of reach. With a pout, she chided, "And this is the thanks I receive? It's rude, Axel." When she reached again, he let her run her fingertips along his jaw, and she smiled. "Much better."

Axel grabbed her wrist, pulling her hand from his face. "I didn't come back here for this, Bree."

Her eyes narrowed. "Then what *did* you come back here for?"

"I…have nowhere else to go."

"And you think insulting me is wise in this instance?"

"I didn't intend to insult you," he replied quickly. "I simply need some time to adjust before we discuss…all of that. I do not think that is an unreasonable request in this instance."

The words appeared to placate her as her shoulders relaxed. "Of course. It's been so long for me, I forget that the transition can be rather jarring."

"Exactly," Axel said. "And I haven't fully...turned."

He nearly choked on the word. Maybe Cienna was wrong. Maybe two weeks from now he would still have his shadows. He wasn't using his magic, keeping his power wells full as long as he could, because for some insane reason he thought if he didn't use them, it would keep the inevitable from happening.

But he knew Cienna wasn't wrong. He'd been too close to crossing that line for a while now. He'd taken so much blood from Katya. More than enough to trigger the curse. Axel had thought it'd be an instantaneous thing. Slowly turning was far worse. As much as he'd hated coming back here, he didn't know where else to go. He hadn't been lying when he said he had nowhere else to turn. At least here they would understand what was happening and be able to answer his questions.

Linking her arm through his, Bree said, "Come join us for dinner. Relax. Get to know everyone."

He let her lead him from the vault room and back along the passages, trying to memorize the halls they were taking.

"Of course, I'll have a much more comfortable room prepared for you," Bree was saying.

"Thank you, Bree," Axel said. "I appreciate it."

They strolled into the dining hall, still arm-in-arm, and Axel quickly slid his Arius heir mask into place when he found Mansel and Julius already seated. There were a few others. The male who had led him to Bree upon arrival. Another male and two females. Bree didn't introduce anyone as she led him to the end of the table, gesturing for him to take a seat to her right while she sat at the head of the table.

Plates of potatoes and barely seared meat were placed in front of them. The vampyres were also all given a crystal glass of blood.

Including him.

Axel stared at the red liquid. Dark and thick. He didn't want it. Didn't *need* it.

Maybe Cienna was wrong after all.

"Anything you can share with us from your brief visit to the kingdoms?" Bree asked, slicing into her food.

"My...what?" Axel asked, distracted and still staring at the blood.

"Your trip outside the Underground. What news do you bring back with you?" she answered, waiting expectantly.

Finally tearing his eyes from the glass, he looked at her. "I don't have any news."

She clicked her tongue. "You were gone for nearly a week and have no news from the outside? Not even a weather report?"

"It's winter," Axel said, picking up his cutlery. "So snowy and grey."

"Not the weather I was referring to," Bree said casually before turning to Julius. "And you?"

"Nothing as big as the Sirana Villas massacre," the male replied. Rather than blood, his crystal glass held wine.

"Those fools," Bree scoffed. "But it works out well for us, I suppose."

"Agreed," Julius said.

Theon had filled him in with the barest of details about the Sirana Villas, but he didn't know how much had made its way down here yet. They likely knew more than he did.

"How do the murders at the Villas work out well for you?" Axel asked, cutting into his meat, red juices running all over his plate.

"For *us*," Bree corrected, picking up her glass of blood and taking a sip. "The more they kill off themselves, the less work for us when it's time to make our move. Let them tear themselves apart."

"Right," Axel muttered, eyeing his meat and opting for the potatoes instead.

"A shame, though," Mansel said. "Losing all those Fae and mixed lines."

Bree sighed. "There is no news as to their whereabouts?"

"None," Julius answered. "It's like they simply disappeared."

"How do dozens of Fae just disappear?" one of the other vampyres down the table asked.

"The mystery everyone is trying to figure out," Bree answered. "Although I would like to find them first. Tell our clan if anyone finds them before the rest of the realm, they'll be rewarded handsomely with a permanent position within the House and at this table."

The four vampyres all went still, glancing between themselves before the male said carefully, "But you only allow four of us seats at this table."

"Then I suppose one of you better be the ones to find them if you don't want to lose your position, hmm?" she mused, swirling the blood in her glass.

"Yes, your grace," he answered, the four of them all standing. They left their half-eaten plates on the table, quickly filing from the room.

"There are plenty of empty chairs," Axel commented. There were at least a dozen seats down the table. "Why only allow four?"

"It keeps the competition among themselves rather than letting them entertain the idea they might be able to come for *my* position," she said nonchalantly. "The same principle applies to the kingdoms. Let them fight among themselves, weaken their own defenses. Then we can come in and take it all."

"And why do you want to find the missing Fae first?"

"Why wouldn't we?" Bree countered. "The Legacy have kept the Fae so caged for years, they've forgotten their own power. If they came together?"

"They couldn't overpower the Legacy," Axel argued.

Bree laughed. "Child, so much can be accomplished when pushed to your limits. The Fae have been wronged since the inception of this realm, and with the mixed bloodlines? It would not be an easy victory, and there is no telling who would win such a war. But a Legacy victory is certainly not inevitable."

"Truly if we can find a few of the mixed, it would give us a significant advantage," Julius said.

"For so long that operation was rumors we could never substantiate," Bree replied conversationally. "Until you, Mansel."

"Glad I could be of service," he replied. "Participation in the program certainly wasn't a hardship."

Bree hummed. "I'm sure not, but you do not know if it was successful?"

Mansel shook his head. "They never tell us, and Valter never let it slip. But she was conspicuously kept out of sight for several months some time after."

Axel was having trouble following all of this, but he didn't want to seem too eager for information either. Forcing himself to take a bite of meat, he said, "My father kept his secrets close and his motives closer."

"The motive in this was more than obvious," Bree said with a dismissive wave of her hand. "If successful, he'll take the child for his next Source."

"What child?" Axel asked, trying to keep the panic from his tone. There is no way they could know about Kat.

Bree held her glass out, the blood gone, and let it be refilled with wine. "Surely the rumors swirl in the kingdoms as they do here. About what the Villas are truly for?"

"I know what they are for," Axel said tightly. He'd been there a few times with his father, and while he'd never taken part in the activities there, his father sure as fuck had. So had Theon and Luka, although the partners he saw them take to private rooms were always Legacy with an enchanted ring on meaning that was likely very consensual. But of course he knew about the forced breeding that went on in the upper levels of the Villas.

"And the rumors of the hidden villas?" Bree asked before taking a healthy gulp of her wine.

"What hidden villas?"

"Axel, darling," she chided. "You expect me to believe an heir of a kingdom does not know of the hidden villas?" When he just blinked in confusion, she tsked under her breath as she took another drink. "The hidden villas are where they cross Fae and Legacy, sweet one."

"That's forbidden," he said immediately.

Her head tilted, silky, dark hair slipping over her shoulder. "That's what they want you to believe, isn't it? I have found the most ridiculous sounding rumors tend to carry the most truth. Ask Mansel."

Axel's gaze slid to the Legacy across the table from him, and the smirk on his face told Axel he wasn't going to like anything he was about to learn.

"Well?" Axel demanded when Mansel continued to stare back at him. "Speak."

"You are out of your element, little heir," Mansel sneered.

And then he was choking on shadows as Axel's power leapt across the table, slamming into the male and shoving his chair back from the table. "And you forget your place," Axel snarled. "You think just because you are down here and in *her* house, you are more than I am? I am still above you, and the Underground is still my domain."

"For now," Mansel choked out.

His shadows tightened, Mansel's eyes bulging a little as Axel picked up his glass of blood and took the smallest of sips. It tasted nothing like her. This was lukewarm and salty. A water Fae no doubt, and it made him want to spit out the small sip he'd swallowed.

"And even when I cannot control the shadows that are keeping you from breathing, I will still be stronger than you, Mansel. I will still be more than you in every possible way. Wouldn't you agree?"

The male was glaring at him, but he finally gave a sharp jerk of his chin and Axel released him. Perhaps it was a waste of his power, but fuck had it been worth it. He glanced over at Bree to find her eyes glittering with delight, and that satisfaction faltered. This was exactly why she wanted him at her side.

Mansel's hands were clenched into tight fists where he still sat a few feet away from the table. When Axel's shadows started drifting towards him again, he gritted out, "The hidden villas are where Fae and Legacy bloodlines are crossed in an attempt to create stronger Fae."

"And what happens to the young?" Axel demanded.

"Depends on if they were a request or not."

"A request?"

Mansel nodded. "The rulers request certain...combinations. To add to their defenses or to replace a Source. If they're powerful enough, they are used to further the research."

Further the research.

What in the actual fuck?

"And you were part of this?" Axel asked sharply.

When Mansel's eyes flicked to Bree, Axel turned to her as well.

"He was," Bree said. "With Valter's Source. As he mentioned, we do not know if the results were favorable, but suspicions are they were."

"You are telling me Eviana has a child? That *you* sired?" Axel asked, looking back at Mansel.

His smirk was back. "That darling Fae does whatever Valter tells her to do, like the good little Source she is. It took a while to get her under control, but we did it. Would have done the same for Theon's Source if he hadn't been so godsdamn territorial."

"What happens to the rest of them?" Axel asked, ignoring Mansel. "The other half-Fae, half-Legacy young that are born?"

Bree shrugged. "We don't know because it's all rumors and whispers. If they're not powerful enough, it is said they are killed. If they are a coveted combination, the rulers work something out."

But what if it was an heir's child?

That was all Axel could think about as he listened to Bree, Julius, and Mansel continue to discuss the Villas. When it was discovered that Kat's child was an Arius Legacy crossed with a fire Fae, she and the child would be killed. If it was after he was born...

The mere thought of what could happen had him swallow the bile trying to crawl up his throat. He'd been in such a panic to protect Katya, he hadn't weighed all this. It wasn't Theon's job to protect her and their child. It was his. He should have brought her with him. But then who would protect her from *him*?

"And once you turn completely, you will pledge loyalty to the house, correct, Axel?" Bree was saying, drawing him back to the conversation.

"What was that?" Axel asked.

Her smile was pointed. "I assume by coming back here, you have agreed to pledge loyalty to my clan, yes?"

"As I said before, I think I need to take things a little at a time with this while I adjust."

Her features darkened. "I found her for you, Axel. My only request was repayment of that favor."

"You did find her, but—"

"I'm surprised he is not more distraught," Julius cut in, those icy eyes studying him. "Over her death," he added. "The way you acted that day in the dungeons, one would have thought you'd be beside yourself with her death on your hands."

"Hush, Julius," Bree chided. "He is moving forward, not looking back. It is better she is gone. It would have distracted us all from our goals, and that would have had to be taken care of."

All the pieces clicked into place at those words. She had let him go. Had unlocked his door and let him go find her, assuming he would be so overcome with bloodlust and mania that he would kill her. He likely would have if Theon and Tristyn hadn't been there, but they all assumed she was dead.

What if *they* learned of the child?

Your job in this is to keep her safe and protected when she is vulnerable.

Cienna had known even then. Had tried to tell him. Katya would not be safe anywhere. Neither was their child, but they had a chance if he was with them. No one would fight for them like he would. Sacrifice for them. Bleed for them. Kill for them.

Because they were his to have.

His to protect.

His to love.

He didn't need a fucking bond to choose them.

30

EVIANA

This was the most comfortable bed she'd ever lain on. Probably because she wasn't being forced to share it with someone. It was small, only big enough for one, and that was what made it so comfortable. No groping hands. Fully clothed. No dicks. Or cunts, for that matter. Just this bed and solitude.

Eviana had been in this room for weeks now, but there was a window that let in sunlight. She was given three meals a day. Clothing that actually covered her. What would Valter think if he saw her in these loose sweatpants and an oversized sweater that went up to her chin? No cleavage or defined ass to stare at? The horror.

She smiled to herself at the thought. No, she quite liked these arrangements. Her own space with her own bed. She didn't even mind the bands on her wrists that kept her from her magic. No expectations or demands of her time, her attention, her body. Just blissful silence.

Except for the incessant yammering of Valter down their Source bond.

Sighing, she rolled over onto her stomach as she listened to him curse Tessalyn for the tenth time in the last hour.

Do they still have you in shackles? She keeps telling me you are being taken care of, he asked down the bond.

Eviana looked down at the bands. She wouldn't call them shackles, but she'd learned long ago to let the male live with his delusions. Being sweet and accommodating made him let his guard down.

Yes, my Lord, she answered, kicking her feet up and stretching her arms. *They tell me nothing.*

It wasn't a lie. No one ever spoke to her. A Legacy delivered her meals without a word. The room wasn't a prison cell, but it certainly wasn't a luxurious suite either.

When I get out of here, you and I will take our revenge in flesh and blood, Valter snarled down the bond.

Sounds perfect, my Lord.

And by the gods, did it ever.

Only she dreamed of vengeance against *him.* For forcing her to do all manner of things with all manner of people. *To* all manner of people.

For forcing her to become the monster she was.

For forcing her to bring something innocent and perfect into this damned world.

For forcing her to love.

For forcing her to care.

He knew what he was doing, and she knew what he had planned.

A knock on the door had her getting to her feet. It was too early for dinner. She'd been served her midday meal only an hour ago. Standing in the middle of the room, she slipped into the role she'd been playing for decades now. Hands clasped. Eyes on the floor. Ready to serve.

Good and demure.

The perfect Source.

She was under no delusions it would keep her safe. She was a Lord's Source. Eventually they would come for her. Try different methods to get her to spill her master's secrets. Truly, she was surprised they hadn't already done so.

The door opened, and bare feet stepped in. It had her head snapping up as she found Tessalyn Ausra standing in the small space, the door closing behind her. The last Source Mark was in place on her hand. Her golden hair was loose around her shoulders, and she wore a cream dress, the hem stained with dirt because the female never wore shoes unless she was forced to. And as she looked into those bright violet eyes, Eviana recognized the mania staring back at her.

"Hello, Eviana," Tessa said, an eerie ring to her voice that had Eviana taking a step back.

"Tessalyn," she said carefully. "I cannot tell you anything. The bond forbids it."

"I'm aware," the female said, taking in the space. "Are you comfortable here?"

"The space is more than enough."

"But you would be more comfortable with him?"

It was a loaded question, and she wasn't sure how to answer it. Was she trying to get information out of her? Did she think she could trick her? Stupid girl. She'd been doing this far too long. She'd learned the secret to survival and that was to not care.

About anything.

Not even oneself.

Until Valter had forced her to care about someone.

"I find the space suitable," Eviana finally answered.

The light around Tessa's wrists flickered with energy, and it had her own magic shifting where it was trapped beneath her skin.

"So you do keep secrets from your Master," Tessa said, her head canting to the side.

"I don't know what you speak of."

The female hummed a response. "Did you hear news of the Sirana Villas?"

Wrath and fury immediately filled her, and she swallowed down the emotions. "What of them?"

"There was a massacre," she said simply, but the wicked smile that tilted at the corner of her mouth said more than enough.

"And you still breathe?" Eviana asked, taking a single step closer.

"I do," Tessa answered, making her way to the sofa and dramatically plopping down. "Let's chat, Eviana."

She stilled, debating what to do. The conversation could be kept from Valter. Her Master was too arrogant to realize she'd long ago learned how to keep him out of her head and block the bond. She simply made sure he was always feeling *something*. Right now, she was making sure he felt the unease of what this conversation could be, but the thrill of it? The downright *glee* at hearing of murders at the Villas? She made sure he wasn't feeling an ounce of that.

"My loyalty is to him," Eviana said carefully.

"Of course," Tessa replied.

What is going on, Eve?

Ugh. She hated when he called her that. That and 'my flower.' She supposed they could be considered affectionate names except that Valter was the opposite of affectionate in every way.

Is someone hurting you? They assured me you were not being harmed, he went on as if he actually cared about anything other than power.

I am well, my Lord, she answered, still staring at Tessa across the room. *Only discomfort from being so far from you,* she added, soothing his ego.

She didn't listen to his false reassurances, letting them be background chatter as she sat on the end of the bed. When a flare of light appeared, it had her flinching and turning away, and when she turned back, Tessa held a bottle of wine and two glasses.

"Drink?" the female asked.

When was the last time Valter had let her have alcohol?

Probably the time he'd given her to the overseer of Raven Harbor for a night as part of the Match Contract arrangements between Theon and Felicity. He always said it was to help ease the discomfort of the bond at them being separated. She didn't care. She let them do whatever they wanted to her. The alcohol just let her dissociate even more, for a little while at least.

It was the same when Valter told her to kill someone.

Or fuck someone.

Or torture someone.

It was the same whether she was eating or sleeping, serving or guarding.

She'd stolen for Valter. Tormented his own children. Maimed and murdered. Crawled across glass and danced across ashes. All to prove her loyalty and keep *her* safe.

Tessa poured the two glasses of wine, setting one aside before holding the second out to her. Eviana took it, but didn't take a drink. All her instincts were on high alert. Was this a test? A trap? Would failure result in a punishment?

"Don't be nervous," Tessa said, a look of pity crossing her face.

"I'm never nervous," Eviana said flatly.

"Never?"

"No. I've seen and heard too much to let anything make me nervous."

"Fair enough."

The seconds turned to minutes, the two of them sitting in silence, and Eviana couldn't help but wonder why she was here. What was this accomplishing? What was her motive?

"Are you lonely in here?" Tessa finally asked, sipping on her wine.

"No," Eviana answered immediately. "I enjoy the solitude."

"That's understandable," Tessa mused, tapping a nail on her glass. "But you've been with him for decades, right? Is it different without him now?"

"Of course it is different. What kind of question is that?"

Tessa arched a brow. "You are a little more outspoken when he is not here."

Eviana didn't reply to that, the glass of wine in her hand beginning to bead with condensation.

"You can drink that. I didn't poison it," Tessa drawled.

"Does Theon know you are here?"

She smiled again, and it was a chilling thing. "He's no longer my master."

"That's not possible," Eviana said, watching for the lie. "Only death can sever a Source bond."

"That is what they say," Tessa sighed. "And perhaps if it were a real Source bond, that would be the case. As it stands, we are still bonded, but it's broken. Everything is broken. We're all broken."

She sounded more mad the longer she sat here.

"What do you want? I already told you I can tell you nothing," Eviana said tightly.

"I told you I wanted someone to chat with. Dex follows me everywhere right now."

"Then where is he?"

Tessa shrugged. "I have a little more freedom within the palace walls. I told him I was going to take a nap."

"You live at the Achaz palace now?"

"Live here? I don't know," she mused before draining her glass. "But I'm staying here for now. Similar to you, I suppose. I just have more freedom."

"No one is free in Devram."

"No one? Rordan seems pretty free. The Ladies seem to do as they please."

Eviana shook her head. "They are the most trapped of all. They must always be looking over their shoulder. Someone is always waiting to kill them." Then she added, "Or imprison them."

Tessa hummed, pouring more wine into her glass. "And where do you fall on that scale?"

"What do you mean?"

"Would you save them or kill them?"

"I am bound to save my master," she answered without thought.

"Bound to, yes. But if you had the choice?"

"I don't."

Tessa nodded, tapping her nail again. "How much time did you spend at the Villas?"

"Whatever was required of me."

Resting her chin in her hand, she mused, "Have you been there since your daughter was born?"

"I don't have a daughter."

"No? Your name was on the file. A female. Nine years. Currently at the Serafina Estate?" Tessa asked, a knowing look in her eye.

Is that where she was? Valter would never tell her. Only used her as a threat whenever Eviana even thought about defying him. Everything she did was to keep that child from harm, and now she'd been told where she was.

And judging by the look on Tessa's face, the female knew exactly what she was doing. A clever thing then. A little insane, but who wasn't in Devram?

"I do not have a child," Eviana said carefully, letting Valter hear this part of the conversation. He'd made it clear if she ever admitted to it, her daughter would be dead within an hour.

So loyal, my flower, he praised down the bond.

She rolled her eyes, and Tessa huffed a laugh.

They fell into silence again until finally Tessa got to her feet, stretching her arms above her head. "Well, this was delightful," she said, tapping her now empty glass and setting it beside the wine bottle that was still half-full. She wasn't going to...leave that here, was she? "I find your company far better than most."

What a bizarre statement. They'd hardly spoken.

Tessa was reaching for the door handle when Eviana said, "The Villas. Was everyone killed?"

"Just the full-blooded Legacy," she answered, turning to face her.

"How would they know that?"

Tessa shrugged, but lightning flickered between her fingers. "No idea."

"And they were all killed?"

"Every last one of them within the walls at the time."

"Desiray?"

"I'm told her death was particularly merciless," Tessa answered, nothing but fury glittering in her eyes.

"And Mansel?" she couldn't help but ask.

Tessa frowned. "I know who that is to you, but I could not tell you if he was there that night. I do not know him."

Disappointment churned in her chest at that, but that was fine. It would be nice if he'd died, but he wasn't her concern. Her concern would forever be the child with turquoise eyes and auburn hair. Eventually she'd have her vengeance, but not until she was beyond sure that child would be safe from the fallout.

"Tessa," Eviana called out when she reached for the door handle again.

"Yes?" she asked, looking over her shoulder.

"I hope precautions are being taken," Eviana said, holding her stare. "To protect the Legacy."

"Of course," Tessa said with a wicked grin. "We're making sure everyone is prepared for what might come. We want to be sure everyone understands others might be sent to help. To ensure everyone can recognize ally from enemy."

"I enjoyed our chat," Eviana said, tipping her still full wineglass towards her.

"I'll have to make them a habit," she replied with a wink.

And then she was breezing through the door, a male glaring at her on the other side. Tessa didn't acknowledge him. Just left him to trail after her. That was all she saw before the door was shut once more, the enchantments that kept her confined slipping into place.

But Tessalyn was not what she was expecting.

That was what she pondered as she stood near the small window and sipped the wine. The window wasn't nearly large enough for anyone to climb in and out of, but she could see the surrounding vegetation. It had her magic writhing to be used. So much plant life within reach. She could conjure her own, sure, but it was much less draining to use the resources around her.

To ensure everyone can recognize ally from enemy.

She didn't give two fucks about which side anyone was on. Her only care was protecting that child. She didn't care whose blood was spilled or in what manner. She'd played the roles required of her and fucked whoever she needed to for information. She'd shoved stakes into backs and sliced blades across throats. She'd burned things to the ground, along with everyone inside, and let others take the fall.

Because one day she'd have vengeance.

One day she'd have more than that.

Eviana picked up the bottle of wine, pouring all of it into her glass. It overflowed, spilling onto the floor and soaking into the rug. A red stain on all the white in here.

She didn't care about Tessa's vendetta or what her plans were, but if she was offering a way out of here *without* Valter? She'd take it. It didn't matter what she had to do, she'd do it all.

Who tried to get information out of you, Eve?

One of Rordan's spies, she answered, sipping from the overflowing wineglass. It was enough of a half-truth to bypass the many bargains and oaths he'd forced her to agree to over the years.

And? he pressed.

Your secrets are safe with me, my Lord. Always.

That's my beautiful flower.

Eviana smiled, picking up the empty wine bottle and carrying it into the small bathroom. There was hardly room to move in it. Big enough for a toilet, pedestal sink, and shower so tiny she could scarcely fit in the thing. Turning the water on to mask the sound, she smashed the wine bottle against the side of the sink. She still held the neck of the bottle, jagged pieces of glass now protruding from the end of it. She set it carefully in the sink before grabbing a hand towel. Humming to herself, she started picking up the glass shards from the floor and wrapping them in the towel. Then she took it and slid it all the way under the bed.

Just to be prepared for whatever may come.

She flopped back down on the bed, lifting her wrist and studying the dark band on it. It'd been a long time since she'd been forced to wear these. Valter never let her be defenseless. His beautiful flower was far too important to him and his plans.

Too bad his flower was more poison than beauty.

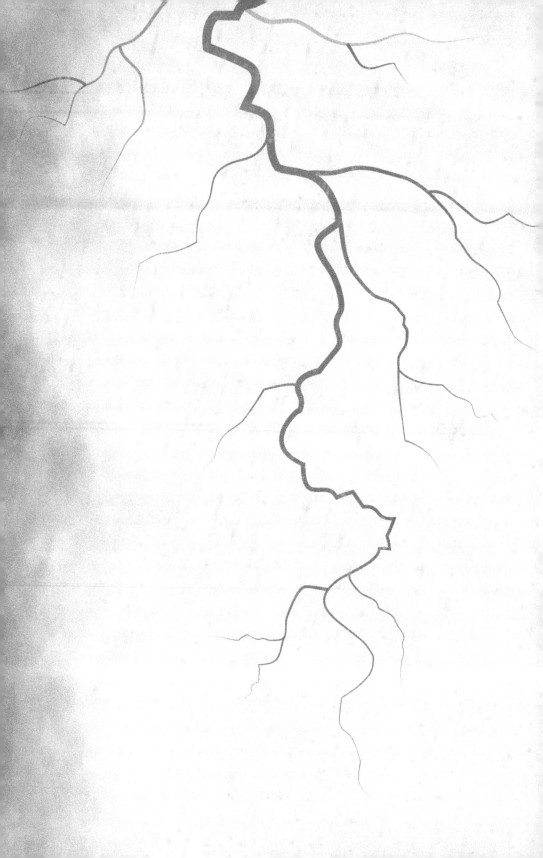

31

TESSA

"By the gods, Dex. I'm going to bathe. You're not following me into the bathroom," Tessa snapped when he trailed her into her rooms.

After she'd lied about napping and instead gone to see Eviana a few days ago, Dex rarely let her out of his sight. She hadn't been able to go to Luka's room to sleep, let alone sneak off anywhere else. Rordan hadn't been lying when he'd said Dex was to watch over her, but that was supposed to be whenever they left the palace. Not inside of it. This was no different from when Theon wouldn't leave her be, but at least Theon came with orgasms.

Wait. No. She was not going to sit here and think about how being at Arius House with him was better than *this*.

"Then I'll get Oralia," Dex argued. "She can sit in there with you."

"What do you think I'm going to do in the bath, Dexter? You won't let me go find a mortal, so I have to take care of things myself," she spat.

"Tessa, the last time you said you were going off to fuck someone, you killed two Legacy. Then you went back a few days later and desecrated the Villas."

"There is no proof of any of that," she groused.

"Proof or not, this is your own fault. You created this mess, and once again, I'm cleaning it up."

Her power slammed into him, sending him flying across the room and into the wall. Sliding down the wall, he cursed, rubbing the back of his head. Tessa stalked forward, and he tipped his head back to look up at her.

"I didn't ask you to *clean up* anything," she said, her voice too calm. "You took that role on yourself. You always have because for some reason you took it upon yourself to make me your responsibility." She tipped her head to the side, holding his dark stare. "But that's not true either, is it?"

"What are you talking about, Tessa?" he sighed, his arm dropping to his side. "I know you suffered a lot in the Arius Kingdom, but did he really drive us this far apart? You think I've been working against you?"

She huffed a humorless laugh. A part of her had hoped his wings would appear with that small attack, or perhaps some hint of the power he'd stolen. He hadn't even used his supposed air magic to catch himself. That was something he was supposed to be proficient at by now.

"*You* did this to us, Dexter," she hissed, pointing a finger at him. "You did this to us every time you spoke down to me and made me feel like an uncontrollable mess. You did this to us when you held me down under the guise of 'fixing my mess' instead of letting me stand back up. You continue to do this to us with every lie that spills from your lips and secret you keep from me."

His dark eyes were wide at her outburst, but now they filled with ire. "What lies have I told you, Tessa?" he demanded, getting to his feet so quickly, she stumbled back a few steps.

"What lies haven't you told?" she countered.

"Everything I have done is to keep you safe and coddled," he sneered. "Everything I have done is to prepare you to be what you were always meant to be."

"By keeping *everything* from me!" she cried. "By letting me think I was worthless and unwanted. By letting me believe I was a mess and everything I did was wrong. Even now, you sit here and berate me, tell me how you have to fix things for me yet again."

"Because I do!" he bellowed. "I've been fixing your shit long before you even knew who I was."

And there it was.

The slip-up she'd been waiting for, and he knew it too.

Her smile was pure hatred as she looked up at him. "Tell me again about how you haven't been lying to me," she said in a tone too soft and lethal.

"To protect you," he snarled.

She barked another joyless laugh. "Now you sound just like Theon, only he never pretended he was anything other than what he is."

Light flared, a portal appearing behind her.

"Tessa, you can't leave without me," Dex said, lurching forward, but her power slammed into him again. He hit the wall harder this time, frames rattling with the impact. "The Achaz Lord—"

"Is not my master," she sneered, stepping backwards through the portal.

She turned, taking in the gardens behind Arius House. She was just down the path from the stables and the kennels, and all she wanted to do right now was to sit with Roan. Her shields were in place, blocking the bond so Luka and Theon wouldn't know where she was unless they used the Tracking Mark.

Still in her training clothes, they stuck to her with the chill air. For once, she was wearing boots as she made her way down the path. She'd take them off once she found Roan.

Rounding the corner that would take her into the kennels, she went utterly still. Beyond the kennels was an open field that led up into the mountains. She knew that field. She'd run through it the day she'd tried to run from Theon what felt like a lifetime ago. But Theon stood there, two of his hounds prancing around him, while Roan sat off to the side watching. Her wolf turned to her, but she shook her head as she darted behind a nearby tree. Keeping out of sight, she crept closer, unsure what she would do if either of the hounds spotted her, but they seemed to be busy with their master.

Finally reaching the kennels, she edged along the building until she could peer around the corner. Not only could she see better from here, but she could hear what Theon was saying too.

"Let Rigel get this one, Kacela," he was chiding.

Tessa expected him to throw a ball or stick, and he did. Sort of. His darkness converged, an inky orb in the air by his shoulder, and then a ball shot out of the magic, sailing off into the distance. Rigel yipped excitedly as he took off, Kacela giving a disgruntled whine from where she sat beside Theon.

He crouched beside her, scratching behind her ears.

"We all know you're the best," he consoled. "Let's just give him this one, yeah?"

She whined again, leaning into his hand before she leapt, knocking him onto his ass. Theon landed with an *oomph* and a muttered curse, and

Tessa swallowed her laugh before it could give her away. The hound's front paws were on his chest, her tail wagging as he used his magic to tease her. Wisps of black playfully tugged on her tail, her belly, her ear. She yipped, snapping at the magic, and Theon...*laughed* while he played with her. It was another minute before Rigel reappeared with the ball, dropping it at his feet. Kacela sat back, allowing Theon to sit up and praise the other hound for retrieving the ball. He didn't get up though. He sat there with his knees bent, elbows resting atop them as he stared out across the field. What was he doing?

Kacela drew closer, nudging at his elbow before she tucked her head under his arm and sat beside him. A steadfast companion. The same way her wolves were with her. Tessa watched while the two sat, Rigel lying at his side. A soft whine came from Kacela, and Theon sighed.

"I don't know when we'll get to hunt again," he said, as if the hound had spoken to him. "You could track down Axel, but he made his choice. I can only protect him for so long, even if it feels wrong to let him do this."

Had he spoken to Axel? Seen him? Tessa had given him information, but had he acted on it? Luka hadn't said anything to her, but then again, why would he?

Kacela gave another low whimper, and Theon huffed a bitter laugh. "I'm out of time for everything these days. Too many new responsibilities and worries. Even hardly sleeping, I don't have enough time in the day. I'm out of time to help Axel. I'm out of time to help my kingdom. I'm out of time with her."

Sighing again, he patted the hound's head before he pushed to his feet, swiping up the ball as he went. He made his way to where Roan was lying down now, and the wolf raised his head at his approach.

"What do you say, Roan?" Theon asked, tossing the ball in the air a few times. "You going to try today?"

The wolf stared back at him, glowing eyes unblinking.

"I'd love to give her news other than the same old, same old," Theon added. "You don't even have to run. Just walk and get it."

Roan's eyes flicked to where Tessa was lurking, then back to Theon before the wolf stiffly got to his feet. Tears welled in her eyes as the wolf limped forward, moving slowly.

"That a boy," Theon praised softly. He looked at the ball, but then a swirl of darkness had it disappearing. "You know what? Let's just walk a little, yeah?"

Roan huffed a sound, and Theon reached out as though he was going to pet him but then thought better of it, shoving his hands into the pockets of his jacket. He looked so different out here with the hounds. He was in jeans, something he never wore. His boots crunched on the frozen grass while they walked, Kacela and Rigel trotting over to join them where they made their way across the empty field. Theon kicked large rocks and sticks out of Roan's way as they approached, and Tessa felt her chest doing something it definitely should not be doing.

He didn't need to be out here in the cold looking after her wolf. He didn't need to be tending to him himself. There were people he paid to do that, yet here he was. Taking time he was just telling Kacela he didn't have to walk with her wolf.

"She's going to be proud of you, you know," Theon said to Roan as they continued their slow path. "She'll get that smile on her face that she never lets anyone see. It'll be a real one. She doesn't do it often, so you better burn it into your memory when you see her again. It's the most beautiful thing you'll ever see, and I hope I'm there to witness it. Selfish, I know."

Tessa swallowed thickly, reaching up to swipe her fingertips under her eyes as she stepped back. Moving as fast as she dared, she went back the way she came until she was far enough away that the light from her portal wouldn't give her away, but she needed to leave because she was feeling too many things.

Stepping back into her room, she gasped as emotions assaulted her, and she didn't know what to do with them. She'd never had to deal with them. Never *wanted* to. This is when she found alcohol with the others or sneaked out to find a mortal to occupy her. This is when she shut down, shoved everything down so deep she was nothing. Just an empty shell. It hurt less than feeling, and all she'd ever wanted was to not fucking hurt all the godsdamn time.

Dex was gone, thank... Not the gods, because fuck them. The Fates? No! Fuck them too and their fucking purpose for her. Fuck sacrifices and demands. Fuck beginnings and endings, and fuck all these gods-damn fucking feelings!

Her hands were in her hair, tugging on the ends. Anything to keep her grounded, but there was nothing but fury and confusion, madness and desperation.

Tessa? Tessa, what is going on? Luka demanded down the bond.

At the same time, Theon's voice sounded. *Little storm? Tell us what to do.*

Tell them what to do? As if they were hers to command. No. That was another trick. Another choice of pretty words to calm her, tame her.

She needed...to breathe, but she couldn't get air down.

Luka, go to her now! Theon ordered.

She needs to feel these things, Theon, Luka argued. *If she doesn't want—*

She doesn't need to feel them alone, Theon cut in. *And I can't go there. Luka, now!*

Then he was there, standing before her, and Tessa glared at him. "I don't want you here just because he told you to come."

He was staying back, glowing sapphire eyes watching her. "Tell me what happened, Tessa."

"No," she snapped, the light around her wrists spiraling out from her. Reaching for him yet recoiling at the same time. "Just go, Luka."

Tell him what you need, Tessa, came Theon's command down the bond, and gods, *that* was what she needed right now. Someone to tell her what to do so she didn't have to think. Didn't have to feel. But Luka wouldn't do that. He'd told her if that was what she needed to go to Theon, and she couldn't do that either. She was stuck. Trapped. Only this wasn't a cage someone else had put her in. It was one of her own making.

"Tessa, just take a breath," Luka coaxed. "Just one. That's all you need to do right now."

One breath.

She could do that.

Until the door flew open and Dex stormed in.

"What the fuck are you doing in here?" he sneered at Luka.

"She asked me to come," he answered, and that was a lie, but she didn't care. Of the two of them, there was only one she didn't want to see right now.

"What are *you* doing in here?" she demanded of Dex, her power switching paths. It had been tentatively reaching for Luka. Now it was snapping out at Dex, making him lurch back.

"By the gods, Tessa. Haven't we had enough dramatics today? I brought you tea from Elowyn," Dex said, his displeasure with all of this clear.

"Tea?" Luka repeated. "It's midday."

But Tessa didn't care. That tea made her tired. Let her sleep. And in sleep she didn't have to feel.

She lurched forward, taking the tea from his hand and taking a healthy sip. It burned her tongue and throat on the way down, but she didn't notice as she took another gulp.

"Tessa, stop!" Luka said, trying to take the cup from her, but she was already tipping it up and draining the entire thing.

Then her world was spinning.

The cup slipped from her hand, the porcelain shattering as it hit the ground. She stumbled, tiny shards cutting up the bottom of her feet. She didn't feel them as she started to drop to her knees. Large hands caught her, scooping her up and holding her against a broad chest.

"What did you give her?" Luka snarled.

"She didn't give me a chance to say that Elowyn increased the ingredients," Dex said. "She drank it too fast."

"What is it going to do to her?"

"She'll just sleep. Deeply," Dex said, sounding unconcerned. "She'll be fine."

"She is anything but fine," Luka retorted. "Get out."

"You can't kick me out," Dex said, and Tessa watched him straighten to his full height. "I was assigned to watch her. You get out."

"I am not going anywhere."

The words were laced with a deep growl she felt rumble in his chest. Looking up, there was a trace of smoke, and she tried to push away from him.

"Just put me down. I'll be fine," she murmured.

"I am not going anywhere," Luka repeated, carrying her to the bed. He held her while he toed off his shoes before he gently laid her atop the blankets. She started to protest when he climbed onto the bed beside her until Theon's voice echoed in her mind.

Let him take care of you, Tessa. For once, just let someone care for you.

Do you wish it was you instead of him? she asked, sleep clawing at her and dragging her down.

Desperately.

Then there was nothing but blessed darkness.

And she loved it there.

The dead lay all around her, the rain turning to a faint sprinkle as the storm slowed.

"This way, Tessalyn."

She turned, finding Rordan gesturing for her to follow him into the Pantheon. Hesitant, she took a step, her bare feet squelching on a mixture of rain, mud, and blood. When she slipped and nearly fell, a hand caught her elbow. She looked up to find Dagian there, his features passive as always. Sasha was at his side, her face ashen as she dutifully followed her master.

Rordan led them down passages, and Tessa realized where he was taking them. To the center of the Pantheon where there was a mirror. The same mirror where she'd once spoken to Achaz. When they filed into the chamber, she paused, finding Dex, Oralia, and Brecken already there. All of them with feathered wings arching over their shoulders, the colors varying. They stood with their hands clasped behind their backs, as if they were warriors waiting for their commander. Several of her Hunters drifted around the chamber as well, an excited buzzing filling the air.

"Come here, Tessalyn," Rordan said, motioning her closer.

When she didn't immediately move, Dagian tugged on her arm. She tripped over her own feet this time, catching her balance as she came to a stop beside Rordan.

"Call him," the Achaz Lord instructed.

Her brows knit together. "Call who?"

"You know who," he said. "You did well. You fulfilled your purpose here. Not a drop of Arius blood still breathes in this realm."

"I still breathe," she argued.

He waved her off. "You are the exception, and now that they are gone, he can come here."

She was even more confused now. "He can't come here. The gods cannot come here."

"There is no one to stop him anymore. Call him, Tessalyn," Rordan ordered again.

When she still didn't move, one of her Hunters glided forward, extending a hand. "Allow me, my grace."

She lifted a hand, and in a flash, a dagger was slashed across her palm. The Hunter tugged her forward as she dug in her heels.

"No! Wait!" she cried. This wasn't right. Something felt wrong.

"This is your purpose, child," Rordan chastised. "Everything has been leading up to this moment."

The Hunter forced her bloody palm to the Achaz symbol, but as he released *her, she slid her hand down. Blood covered more than one symbol, and the Hunter hissed in dismay.*

"You call more than the Light King," the Hunter breathed. "He will be unhappy."

The mirror was swirling with darkness and light, fire and shadows. It took a minute, but then Achaz was there. Golden eyes peered down at her, a chilling smile curling on his lips.

"Well done, granddaughter," he praised, his deep voice washing over her. His eyes left her, fixing on something over her shoulder. "They are all dead?"

"Only she remains," a Hunter answered.

Looking behind her, she found everyone in the room was on a knee. The same way the Fae had to kneel in the presence of a Legacy.

"And only she can let me in," Achaz answered, drawing her gaze back to the mirror. "Captain, proceed."

She didn't see who shoved her forward. She tried. Gods, did she try to twist around and see, but one hand held her firmly by the back of neck, shoving her towards the mirror, while the other was gripping her wrist, forcing her hand to the mirror.

"No!" she screamed, her power flaring, but little happened. She tried again. Where were Roan and Nylah? Why was her power so weak if they'd just killed hundreds? It should be fully replenished. She should be at her strongest.

She kicked out when they got close enough, planting her feet on the glass and pushing back, but it was no use. With a grunt of effort, her still bloody palm landed on the glass. Directly atop the reflection of Achaz's bleeding hand.

Sparks of gold and silver skittered across the smooth surface, and Achaz's smile grew. "I am told you nearly failed in your purpose," he said, pacing back and forth as the mirror continued to crack. "I am told you nearly chose a bond that would have—" His head snapped up, eyes going wide. "What are you doing here?"

Tessa didn't know who he was speaking to, his attention diverted to someone in the room with him on the other side of the mirror.

"Who released you?" he demanded.

A melodic laughter that was tinged with madness echoed into the chamber. The Hunters all hissed in unison, and she heard Oralia's high-pitched voice say, "She will ruin everything!"

"I was summoned," a female said, and Tessa strained, as if she could see further into his side of the mirror if she only had the right angle.

"That shouldn't matter," Achaz spat.

"Ah, but it does," she said, a shadow falling across Achaz's features when she

crept closer. "Because all magic comes with a cost, including unlocking a realm. It's all about balance, right, Father?"

Father?

Tessa scrambled forward, both her hands feeling along the glass that continued to crack beneath her fingers. She knew. She knew in her soul that was her mother. Right there. Just out of sight, out of reach.

"He does not want you to know of this yet," a female voice hissed into her ear, and then Tessa was being yanked away from the mirror, away from the chamber, and out of the dream all together.

32

LUKA

"Why is she still sleeping?" Luka demanded.

Dex sat in an armchair across the room where he'd been sitting for the last six hours, eyes never leaving where Luka was with Tessa. She'd hardly moved. Only curled into him whenever he shifted on the bed when his ass or legs started to go numb. Six hours without so much as a soft sigh or whimper was more than worrying considering he knew how she normally slept. Even when she'd been recovering from the Markings, she'd moved more than this. He'd watched over her and Theon enough while they'd slept to know that even in that agony she still made soft sounds every once in a while, and her brow pinched when she moved in sleep, as if the movement itself were annoying her.

More than any of that though, he couldn't *feel* her. Neither could Theon. He'd tried calling Luka multiple times before he'd finally spoken down the bond. Maybe the connection between them was useful after all so he could let Theon know he couldn't speak with the fucker across the room watching him.

"I said the tea was more concentrated. She was the impulsive one who drank it all before I could inform her of that," Dex said.

"And you plan to sit here all day? You have nothing else to do?" Luka asked flatly.

"*She* is my assignment," the male replied. When Luka only held his stare, he added with a sneer, "I know what she is to you too."

What the fuck did that mean? He couldn't possibly know about the three-way bond. Only Axel knew about that outside of the three of them. And probably Cienna, but not because anyone told her. Hadn't Lilura said that same thing though?

I know what she is to you, Son of Xan.

But she had thought he was Razik, so that didn't explain anything. His brother might have been able to shed some light on the matter if he'd bothered to give a damn. Which he didn't.

"It wasn't something we were expecting, but we're dealing with it," Dex continued as if someone had asked him to go on. In reality, it seemed the male just liked to hear himself talk, and Luka wondered how he and Tessa had ever been as close as she claimed they once were.

"Dealing with what?" Luka asked.

Dex only gave him a mocking smile. Now he decided to stop running his mouth.

Silence fell in the room, and for the next two hours, that was all there was. Glares between the two males. Tessa hardly moved, let alone made a sound. The tension was so thick he could feel it.

Still nothing? Theon asked down the bond.

No, Luka answered. *And her babysitter won't fucking leave.*

Ignore him, Theon replied. *That's what I always did.*

You never ignored him, he said dryly. *You'd become irrationally jealous.*

Like you are right now?

I'm not jealous. I'm annoyed. There's a big difference.

A thread of amusement flickered down the bond. This was fucking weird. He didn't want to be feeling Theon down this thing.

He won't leave, and I don't trust him enough to leave her alone with him to even go to the bathroom, Luka added.

And they call me overprotective, Theon muttered.

The last time I left her alone with him, she had some kind of emotional breakdown, and now she won't wake up.

She'll wake up, Luka. I think everyone there would be a lot more panicked if they didn't believe that to be the case.

He was probably right, but when had Theon become the logical one in their friendship? Then again, he'd always been logical, just not when it came to Tessa. Now Luka sat here wondering when he'd become just as irrational when it came to her.

Long ago if he was being honest with himself.

But when she does wake up, make sure she drinks plenty of water and eats something decent, Theon added.

And there he was. It almost made him smile. If only Tessa understood his neurotic tendencies when it came to the ones he felt were his responsibility.

He was about to say something in response when the door to the room banged open. It had him pulling Tessa tighter into him, and she buried her face in his chest. It had to be instinctual because she didn't make a sound.

A female stormed into the room, her raven hair half up with gold ivy threaded through it. Tall and lithe, her gold dress was stark against her pale skin. Luka didn't need her to turn around to know her eyes were violet or that she would be beautiful in a haunting sort of way. He even knew what her voice was going to sound like before she spoke.

"What part of don't let her drink it all at once did you not understand?" the female hissed to Dex.

Dex's eyes were narrowed, but he'd lurched to his feet. His voice was tight and barely controlled when he said, "You know how impulsive she can be, but we are not alone."

The female turned, her attention snagging on Luka. "*You,*" she spat. She turned back to Dex. "I made adjustments for the other, but this is something different."

"I know what this is," Dex snapped in reply, grabbing the female's upper arm and dragging her from the room. The door banged shut behind them, leaving him alone with Tessa for the first time in hours.

Not knowing how long he had, he gently pried her from his chest. "Tessa? I need you to wake up, baby girl," he said softly, but her breathing didn't even change. "Come on, my light," he pressed. "Something. *Anything* to let me know you're all right."

He wasn't expecting it when her eyes snapped open, glowing violet irises streaked with gold connecting to his, and gods, the *pull* to her. He felt his eyes shift, knew they were glowing as brightly as hers.

"Come see," she lilted in a voice that was not her own. It was eerie and chilling. The voice she spoke in when she was lost to her magic. "Walk my dreams," she whispered, before her eyes fluttered closed once more.

And he was pulled into nothing.

Blinking, he looked around, trying to figure out where they were. The waters here were dark, shimmering black under the dying sun. He only knew of waters like that in the Night Waters in Arius Kingdom. What were they doing so deep in the kingdom?

The snarling of wolves had him turning to find Nylah and Roan deep in a fight. In fact, down the bank, there was more than a fight happening. Robed figures were battling against translucent ones. The Augury and Tessa's Hunters. And in the middle of the fray, he could make out Tessa and Theon. He was swinging his short swords with the lethal grace and skill he'd honed for more than a decade. His power surrounded him, darker and thicker than the waters as he shoved a sword through an Augury member while swiping with the other. But the Hunters? Gods, the Hunters were feasting. Their excitement was palpable as they cut through people with their gold weapons.

And Tessa?

She was beautiful with her own weapon, but she hadn't been trained as long. She was working on instinct. Her grip on her sword was all wrong, but she compensated with her power. Lightning flickered, striking the ground sporadically as thunder rumbled above them. Theon was trying to shield her while she let her power free to protect them both.

Luka wasn't sure what he was seeing, but he was running, yelling at them that he was coming. Neither seemed to hear him. No one seemed to be able to see him either. The Hunters glided past him. The Augury didn't acknowledge him, but as he drew closer, he could hear Tessa and Theon.

"He will come, Tessa. Just keep fighting," Theon ordered, his sword never ceasing its movements.

Tessa shook her head as she lifted a hand, power arcing from her palm and bringing an Augury member to the ground with a scream of agony. "He will not," she panted, spinning to take on another. "He is too angry. He will not forgive—"

"He will," Theon snarled, cutting off whatever she was going to say. "He will come because we are his as much as he is ours."

"You need to call Eliza and Razik," she said, shaking her head. She was drawing up more power, her entire body glowing as gold and silver embers swirled around her. "He will not come, Theon. My betrayal was too deep."

"Whatever you did— Tessa, move!"

Theon dropped one of his swords, reaching for her and yanking her to him as an Augury member got too close, but he hadn't seen the other one coming from the opposite direction. A moment before a blade met Theon's side, Tessa's hand connected with the person's throat, and before he could scream, black webbing erupted all along his skin. She released him, and as he sank to the ground, her power flared even brighter.

That was when the Night Children appeared.

As fast and strong as any Legacy, they were vicious and skilled. They were blurs as they moved; even the Hunters had trouble keeping up with them.

"There are too many!" Tessa cried. "We can't fight them all, Theon."

"We can, Tessa! Luka will come!" Theon replied, having retrieved his dropped sword. Darkness rolled from him like a wave, shrouding several vampyres. When it receded, they lay dead on the ground.

"He won't, Theon," she argued, turning to him. "He's too—"

But her words turned into a garbled mess as blood bubbled from her mouth. When she'd turned to speak to Theon, a Night Child had struck. A sword with a crimson blade and a gold hilt had been shoved through her back. As she dropped to her knees, the vampyre pulled it out.

Theon bellowed a roar, dropping down to Tessa and pulling her close. His magic lashed out, wrapping around the vampyre and dragging them closer. "You can't kill her with a sword, but I will make you wish for death for even thinking you could achieve it."

Hood still in place, Luka couldn't see who spoke, but they laughed. "It may take seven of those blades to kill a god, but only one should be needed for her."

His head twisted to the side at an unnatural angle. Luka heard the crack from where he stood as Theon's magic broke his neck before ripping the entire being in half.

"No!" Theon cried as death rained around them. "No, no, no! Where the fuck is Luka?"

"I told you... He won't..." Tessa tried, but she trailed off.

Blood dripped from the corner of her mouth, and Theon held her closer, his magic wrapping around her while she clung to him.

"I'm here!" Luka yelled, but no one heard him.

And no one else came when a Hunter sank a gold blade into Theon's back.

It was the only vision he was pulled into while Tessa slept nearly two entire days. When he'd come out of that vision, Dex and the female had been there. She had appeared furious, leaving the room before he'd had a chance to reorient himself. Dex had just sat back in the chair, but he hadn't stayed. For whatever reason, he'd left that night. He came back every hour on the hour, but he never stayed. He never asked if she'd woken. Never said a single word.

With Dex no longer hovering, they could have gone back to using their phones to communicate, but he and Theon had continued to use the bond. They were both hoping that by using it, it might call to Tessa and wake her. That maybe she'd be drawn to their voices, but it had yet to work.

Luka hadn't slept. Not for a single minute. Every time he closed his eyes, all he could see was the vision she'd pulled him into. Why would he not show up? Especially if both she *and* Theon were in danger. It went against the Guardian bond, and it went against... He didn't know what it was with Tessa. Even if he was supposed to have been her Guardian, there shouldn't be this draw or pull. That was not how it worked. Or maybe it was, and he just didn't know it because he'd been alone in this realm for twenty-five fucking years, the only one of his kind, and when another finally did show up, he was a godsdamn prick.

"Luka?"

He looked down, startled. Her eyes were open—not glowing, thank Sargon—and she was staring up at him. He could feel a faint worry down the bond, and that had *him* worried because there was no way she had the inclination to be blocking the bond right now.

"Are you all right?" she whispered.

"Why wouldn't I be all right?" he asked, shifting so he could see her better.

"You were feeling..."

She trailed off, and he jumped in before she could go on. "I'm fine, my light. Are *you* all right?"

She blinked slowly, as if the action took too much energy.

"I'm tired. And thirsty," she rasped.

Fuck. There wasn't any water in here.

I told you to have water ready for her, Theon chided down the bond.

Luka rolled his eyes, but when he looked back at Tessa, hers were closed again.

"Tessa, he's right. You should drink something. Eat. Move around a little," Luka said.

She hummed an acknowledgment, but that was it. Which wasn't

going to work for him. He threw the blankets back, letting the cool air hit her skin and watching it pebble, but she still didn't move.

"Up, Tessa," he said, slipping from the bed himself.

Give her a minute. She always needs a minute, Theon said. *Get her some water. And grab your phone.*

Cursing him—and letting him hear it—Luka swiped his phone off the nightstand and made his way to the bathroom to fill a glass with water. He was shutting the tap off when his phone vibrated with an incoming call.

"What?" he growled into the phone.

"How is she?" Theon asked immediately.

"Thirsty apparently."

"Fuck off with the mood, Luka," Theon snapped.

He sighed, setting the glass on the vanity and turning to lean against it. "I don't know how she is," he answered. "We're in the same situation here, Theon. I can't feel her, just like you can't."

"But you can *see* her," Theon said, and Luka could hear the thin veil of desperation. "How does she look?"

"I don't know because I had to go get her water," he said dryly.

"Can you not be an asshole for the time being?"

Luka sighed again, rubbing at his brow. "Sorry. It has been...an intense few days. It's different from the Markings. We had known what to expect. This was...not that."

"Yeah, you've felt...off," Theon said carefully.

He debated saying anything about this, but if he couldn't talk to his best friend, then who could he talk to? If he couldn't confide in Theon, then he truly was alone.

"She pulled me into a vision, and it was... I don't know how she handles seeing that kind of stuff all the time," Luka finally said. "And this vision? It's all I see when I close my eyes now. I haven't been able to talk about it with her, but she woke up for a few seconds before she pulled me in."

"Pulled you in?" Theon repeated. "Explain that."

"She said something along the lines of 'come see.' Then she closed her eyes, and I was in her vision," Luka answered.

He knew Theon was pacing on the other end of the line, could practically see him trying to put all the pieces together.

"Her visions are actually why I called," Theon said. "We got passes for Ekayan Island. Today."

"Today?" Luka repeated. "Today when?"

"This afternoon. You, me, Razik, Eliza, and Katya. I also got one for Tessa."

"How'd you manage that?"

"Oh, you know. Accruing debts and owing favors," Theon said. He paused before he asked, "Do you think she'll go?"

Luka could hear the thread of hope in his voice, and it had him swiping up the water glass and heading back to the bedroom. "I'm sure she will *want* to go, but I don't think I'll be able to get her away."

He paused mid-step when he entered the bedroom. Tessa had rolled over, facing the bathroom door now, and her eyes were open, watching him. She hadn't reached for the blankets. Still in the training clothes from days ago, the only thing he'd removed was her boots.

"See what you can do," Theon said. "We have a portal scheduled from the Acropolis station at high noon."

"Yeah, I'll let you know," he said before he hung up and set his phone aside.

The two stared at each other for several seconds before Luka held up the glass of water. "I'm going to need you to sit up and show me you can move."

"I rolled over," she rasped.

"I didn't see it."

"You're worse than Theon."

"I think you like it."

Her brow pinched. "Like it?"

"Yes," he answered, closing the distance between them so he stood directly beside her. She rolled onto her back to see him better, and something in him breathed a sigh of relief at seeing her just fucking move. "I think you like being taken care of."

"I don't need anyone to take care of me," she said, and he knew she meant for it to sound strong and snappy, but it came out tired and resigned.

"I agree," he said, holding out a hand. "You don't *need* it, but a part of you doesn't mind it. Having someone care." Before she could argue, he added, "I feel the same way when someone cares enough to take care of me. Even if it's just making sure I've eaten something decent in a day, because yes, Theon gets annoying about that with me at times too."

She opened her mouth to say something, but then closed it as she reached for his hand. He helped her into a sitting position, watching her wince when she slid her legs over the side of the bed. They were likely more than stiff after not moving for nearly two days. When she was situated, he handed her the water, watching her throat bob with each swallow. She drained the entire glass before he took it back.

"How long?" she asked, her voice clearer now that she'd had something to drink.

He knew what she was asking. How long she'd been asleep.

"Two days," he answered.

Her fingers curled into the edge of the mattress, the light around her wrists not as bright as it usually was. He could tell she was lost in her own thoughts, probably thinking about all the visions she'd had during those hours.

"I was talking to Theon," he offered, setting the glass aside.

"I know."

"We didn't want you to be overwhelmed upon waking."

She nodded, looking anywhere but at him.

"We weren't keeping anything from you, Tessa. In fact, he's trying to include you."

She huffed a disbelieving sound.

"I asked him to look into how I am being pulled into your visions, and he made some kind of deal with the Falein Lady for an afternoon at the Ekayan Catacombs," Luka went on. "He secured a pass for you as well."

That had her gaze sliding back to him. "She would never allow that right now. I am too much of a threat. I'm too *uncontrollable*. That's why— Where is Dex?"

"Which brings me to another thing we need to discuss," Luka said. "There is a priestess here. Dark hair. Violet eyes."

"You are describing half the priestesses in the realm, Luka," Tessa said dryly, gingerly setting her feet on the floor as if testing the feeling.

"But this one was upset. She was scolding Dex for letting you drink all the tea at once when she'd told him not to let you."

Tessa shrugged. "That was probably Elowyn."

"She is also the one pulling me out of your visions."

"What? How?" Tessa asked.

"I don't know, but I recognized her as soon as she stepped into this room. She is the same one," Luka said, instinctively moving forward when Tessa made to stand. His arm went around her waist, steadying her, until she nodded that she was fine to be on her own.

"That doesn't make any sense," she said.

"None of this makes any sense. Which is why we want to go see what we can find in the catacombs," Luka said, letting her get a few steps ahead of him before he followed.

"An afternoon won't be enough time. The catacombs are expansive," Tessa said.

"We take what we can get when it comes to the Ekayan Island," Luka answered. Then he hesitated before adding, "And what we could get was this afternoon."

She turned to him, leaning against the doorway into the bathroom. "*This* afternoon?"

He nodded, and she fixed her gaze on something past him.

"I know you're still not feeling well, and then we have to worry about Dexter," Luka said. "But he got you a pass. Know that he orchestrated this and paid a high cost even knowing you likely wouldn't be able to join."

She nodded once. "And where is Dex?"

"He comes and checks on you every hour." Glancing at the clock, he added, "I expect him in the next few minutes."

She nodded again. "And you will still go?"

"Not if you ask me to stay."

Her eyes met his then, studying and searching. "But you wish to go," she finally said.

"We are the ones being directly affected. I am the one being pulled into your visions. I think it would be best if one of us was present for the research," he agreed.

"You can do whatever you wish," she said. "You are not mine, nor am I your responsibility."

The dragon in his soul snapped to attention at those words, and Luka felt like she'd physically punched him. Which was stupid. Because she was right with both of those things.

The door opened before he could decide how to respond to that, Dex striding into the room. Luka recognized the flash of relief in his eyes at finding her awake and out of bed.

"Tessie," he said, pushing past Luka to stand in front of her. "How are you feeling?"

Tessa glared up at him, only saying, "I'm going to shower," before she went into the bathroom, slamming the door in Dex's face.

And Luka smiled in satisfaction.

Dex turned to him, a sneer on his lip. "Has she said much?"

"Only that you're a dick," Luka said flatly.

Dex gave him a derisive look before moving to the armchair and taking a seat to wait for Tessa. "All of you are smug assholes until you realize you're not invincible."

"I never said I was invincible," Luka retorted.

"Overconfident. All of you," Dex repeated.

Luka didn't have time to argue about trivial shit with him. Instead he said down the bond, *Tessa? Do you want me to stay?*

Go, she answered. *We need the information.*

We.

She'd said we, and that was…progress.

Reach out if you need anything, he said.

I know.

And don't drink any more of that tea. Not a drop.

She didn't respond, and when he left her room, something in him recoiled at the action. Because whether or not it made sense, he *did* feel like she was his responsibility.

And whether or not she knew it—whether or not he wanted to acknowledge it—a part of him also knew he was hers. He just didn't understand why.

33
THEON

He checked his watch, then his phone again. Luka only had a few minutes to get here. The portal would wait. That wasn't the issue. The issue was they needed every possible second in those catacombs. Last time they'd had an entire day. This time, the Falein Lady had begrudgingly only agreed to an afternoon, and if Tessa showed, she had to put bands on. Not the same bands everyone else would be wearing that would only suppress their magic, but the stone bands that would cut her off from her power. He hadn't told Luka that, but he also didn't expect her to show up either.

Tension bled out of him when he spotted Luka striding through the foyer. Unlike when he'd shown up at the manor a few weeks ago, he was dressed for business in his suit and tie. His hair was tied back, stoic and unreadable expression in place.

"Cutting it close," Theon said, handing over the documents for the Fae, disappointed not to see Tessa with him, even though this was exactly what he'd been expecting. He could feel her though, as if she was gifting them this small glimpse of her emotions to be able to keep tabs on her when they couldn't physically be with her. He couldn't hear her thoughts, but just being able to feel her was something, even if right now she was more conflicted than anything.

"You already know why I'm cutting it close," Luka answered, looking through the papers. "Where'd you get these?"

"Used Axel's guy," Theon answered.

"Tucker?"

"Yep."

"And for the electronic records?" Luka asked, tucking the documents inside his suit jacket.

"Corbin took care of that for us," Theon said, leading the way to where he'd left the others in a secluded area of the station. He needed them out of the public eye as much as possible.

Luka nodded. "And Kat? She was feeling up to this?"

Theon hesitated. "I needed her to come with us. She knows the Ekayan Island better than we do, especially the catacombs."

Luka nodded again, understanding exactly what he was saying. He'd had to order her to come with them. It truly hadn't taken much, but he hadn't given the female the choice either. Eliza's constant glares told him exactly what she thought about that. To be honest, Theon was more than a little worried about how this was going to go with Razik and Eliza. Eliza was one thing, but Razik not treating her like a Fae was expected to be treated here was a whole other worry. He'd observed them long enough now to know there was no way he was going to outright disrespect her.

And then there was the obvious tension between Razik and Luka that immediately thickened when they came into sight.

"Tessa didn't come?" Eliza asked when they drew closer, and Theon sighed, rubbing at his brow.

Thankfully they were tucked far enough back into the secluded nook of the station that no one overheard them. "You can't do that, Eliza. We discussed expected behavior," Theon said.

Her brows arched. "Expected behavior?"

"Yes," Theon snapped, because they really did not have time for this. "You cannot speak to a Legacy unless spoken to."

"You were serious about that?"

"I was serious about everything I told you," he retorted. "Why would I say it if I wasn't serious about it?" When she only glared at him, he added, "Just follow Katya's lead. Can you handle that?"

"She'll handle more than that if you continue to speak to her that way," Razik said lazily.

"And you," Theon said, turning to him. "I know she's your twin flame, but if you treat her as anything other than a Fae, it *will* draw unwanted attention. We need this time in the libraries. We will not get another chance."

"And I suppose I'm to follow *your* lead?" he drawled.

"No," Theon said, the corner of his mouth turning up in a small smirk at his startled reaction. "You are to follow *Luka's* lead because the moment we step out there, I am the Arius Lord."

He didn't give either of them a chance to respond. He was done wasting time.

"They'll follow behind us," he heard Luka say, and a moment later Luka was at his side. Razik fell into step as well, and Theon hated it because that was Axel's spot. Maybe they'd find something in the catacombs to help with that mess too.

"Place your palm here and conjure power," said the Legacy when they reached the security platform. Reading his screen after Theon did so, he said, "Passage for six was granted by Lady Farhan. Is that correct?"

"Yes," Theon answered impatiently. "But there are only five present today."

"Documentation for the Fae," he ordered, holding out his hand.

Luka handed over the identification documents for Katya and Eliza. Theon wasn't nearly as worried about this part as he was about Razik having to have his power scanned. Corbin not only had to hack the network to plant fake documentation, but it had to be extensive. Name. Background. Education. Residence. But not even that was what caused Theon to hold his breath when Razik placed his hand on the scanner. They'd told him to conjure the smallest amount of fire with the intention of passing him off as an Anala Legacy. It wasn't uncommon for Legacy to be contracted to work in other kingdoms, and that was the plan here. The trick was making sure it only detected the flame and not the dragon fire part of it, but it wasn't as if Razik could separate the two.

The Legacy's brow furrowed for a moment while he studied the screen before his gaze flicked to Theon. He opened his mouth to say something, but Theon let his darkness free to writhe around him. Tendrils crept along the floor while wisps of the same swirled in his eyes. The Legacy swallowed thickly, his attention going from Theon to Luka before going back to Razik.

"Everything looks fine," the Legacy finally said. "There must have been a slight glitch in the system."

Theon only nodded once before striding past the platform to the portals.

A half hour later, Katya was leading them through the shelves of the catacombs. They were in the same building as before, but they were in a different section. They paired off, Katya staying with Razik and Eliza while Theon and Luka went down another few rows.

"How is Tessa?" Theon asked while they studied the books on the shelves.

"You can feel her as well as I can, Theon," Luka muttered.

"Yes, but how did she *look*?"

"Tired."

Theon bit down on his sarcastic retort. He needed to focus on the task at hand, and yet all he could think about was her.

Forcing his thoughts elsewhere, he grabbed a few books, not even sure what they were. "I'll meet you back at the table," he said before heading to the agreed upon space tucked back in a corner. It was a place they were least likely to be disturbed.

Shedding his suit jacket, he rolled his sleeves up to his elbows before he took a seat. If anything could distract him from Tessa it would be getting lost in history and theories. He hardly noticed when the others joined him, and soon the table was stacked with heavy tomes, ancient scrolls, and so many books they had to set some on the floor. Kat warned them against that, but Theon had made the executive decision to risk the wrath of the scholars.

This was nothing like the last time they were here. No one spoke. Part of it was the time crunch they were on, but the bigger part was the massive standoff going on between Luka and Razik. He was sure Eliza and Razik were speaking down their bond rather than to the rest of them, and Kat was quiet and withdrawn, dutifully turning pages and making notes on the paper she'd secured for them. Theon knew they'd all be checked after their last trip here, and he knew their movements were being monitored far more closely this time too. Theon also gave her any texts that needed translating because she was more proficient at it than he was.

More than once he had to force himself to stop reading after getting caught up in information that didn't pertain to what they were looking for. Witches. Prophecies. Visions. That was their main focus, but he skimmed anything having to do with the gods, particularly the Firsts and the Sister Goddesses, which is what had him finally breaking the silence.

"How long after Devram was created did Serafina betray Achaz?" he asked.

Everyone looked up from their texts. Well, everyone except Katya.

"I don't know how long ago that was," Razik answered, immediately going back to his book.

But Eliza said, "What do you mean Serafina betrayed Achaz?"

"When Devram was created, Serafina was Matched with Achaz."

"Matched," she repeated. "That is similar to a betrothal, correct?"

"It was a sensitive arrangement," Katya murmured, still not looking up from her own reading. "The Firsts were not supposed to create children together. The Fates decreed it would upset the balance too much."

"And it did," Luka said. "Who's to say Arius and Serafina only have two children?"

"I'm not concerned about that so much as I am about what convinced Serafina that she should choose Arius instead of Achaz," Theon said, trying to sound nonchalant about it, but clearly failing as Luka sat back in his chair.

"Her visions, Theon," he said. "That's what we need to be focusing on."

"I'm aware."

"Are you?"

"Yes," Theon snapped. "But they are part of her lineage. There might be something there."

"If you're going to look into the gods and goddesses, look at Zinta," Luka retorted, going back to his own book. "And figure out who or what the sorceress is."

"What did you just say?" Eliza asked, her head snapping up and eyes going wide.

Razik had also looked up, and in a rare show of emotion, a look of alarm crossed his features.

Clearly confused, Luka said, "I told him to look into Zinta."

"No, you said something about a sorceress," Eliza said.

"That's what Lilura said to Tessa," Luka said. "There is a sorceress altering your visions."

"A sorceress or *the* sorceress?" Eliza said, sounding slightly hysterical.

"Does it matter?"

"Yes, it does!"

"Calm down, *mai dragocen*," Razik murmured, his hand soothing down her hair. "We do not wish to draw attention."

"If it is—"

"We don't know," Razik interrupted. He turned to Luka. "What were her exact words?"

"Exactly that. 'There is a sorceress altering your visions,'" Luka replied.

"Could there be more than one?" Eliza asked, looking up at her twin flame, and Theon looked around to make sure no one was here to witness any of these interactions.

Razik rubbed his jaw in thought. "I don't see why there couldn't be."

"For once I wish Cyrus was here," Eliza grumbled.

Razik chuckled at that. "I'm telling him you said that when we return."

Eliza shot him an unimpressed glare.

"Can one of you fill us in?" Theon asked, more than annoyed. "We have limited time the way it is."

"There is a being imprisoned in our realm," Eliza said. "She has been imprisoned there for centuries. She is extremely dangerous and is known for making deals with others by twisting and wording the terms to her advantage. If she gets access to one's blood, she can use it not only for blood magic but to get into their mind. She's used it to alter memories to the point that one doesn't know what was real and what wasn't."

Luka sat up straighter. "She can alter memories?"

"Which is not the same as altering visions," Razik said.

"Thanks for pointing out the obvious," Luka retorted dryly.

"You seemed excited for no reason."

"Altering memories can't be that different from altering visions," Luka drawled.

"She had a spell book," Eliza cut in. "Descendants of the Witch goddesses can create new Marks. Her book was full of them along with potions, spells, and other enchantments."

"Had?" Theon asked, getting stuck on that one word.

"Scarlett stole it," Eliza said. "Then returned it. Then tricked her into giving it back."

Of course that insane female had played a deadly game with a dangerous sorceress.

"But could she affect Tessa from another world?" Theon asked.

"Again, altering memories is not the same as altering visions," Razik said.

"But if there was another sorceress..." Kat said. She trailed off as she stood. "I'll be back."

"Should I...?" Luka asked, looking to Theon.

"Yes," Theon answered.

Luka immediately stood, following the female. Not because she needed to be watched, but because Theon knew exactly what a Legacy was capable of with an unaccompanied Fae.

Turning back to the others, he said, "You're really not going to discuss the fact that the two of you are brothers?"

Eliza looked between them, while Razik stared back at Theon. And gods, the look was the same as Luka. Unreadable except for the clear annoyance.

"I don't think it's your business," Razik said coldly.

"I think it is," Theon retorted. "Because while you may be his blooded brother, I *chose* him as my family. We have been through everything together. For twenty-five years, he has believed he was the last of his kind. Then you show up here, not only a Sargon Legacy but a brother, and don't give two fucks?"

"We had very different upbringings. The male he knew clearly cared about him, but couldn't give two fucks about me," Razik said, returning to his book.

"And that's not Luka's fault, you prick," Theon shot back.

That had Razik looking up again before he sat back in his chair and crossed his arms. "And what will it matter in the end, Arius Lordling?"

"What does that mean?"

"You want us to get to know each other and become close when I am not going to *stay* here?" Razik asked. "Us forming some kind of relationship isn't going to matter in the end."

Eliza was silent, her head down and acting the part of a submissive Fae for once, but Theon knew she wasn't reading the book in front of her. She was listening to every word, and now he was annoyed with her too. She obviously had sway over the male, and she was going to say nothing?

"Forget it," Theon said, going back to his own research.

Nothing else was said until Luka and Katya returned. She looked a touch more like herself, that excitement Theon recognized buzzing faintly around her, even if her amber eyes were still too dull.

Setting a large tome on the table, she flipped it open. It was in an ancient language, but one that Razik clearly knew as she turned the book so he could see it better. Theon recognized some words, but not enough to read it proficiently. It would take him a little time to translate it.

"What is this?" Razik asked, scanning the page.

"A book from another building," Luka said. "It's why it took us so long."

Theon glanced up at him. "They let you take this from another building?"

"Not exactly," Luka said. "But Katya insisted it was important, so we may have Traveled."

"Because it *is* important," Razik murmured, fully engrossed in the book now. "Have you read all this, Kat?"

"Not in its entirety, but you mentioning a sorceress made me remember," she said. Coming around the table, she sidled in between Theon and Razik where they were bent over the book. Pointing at a paragraph, she said, "Here. But this word isn't the same."

"Eliza, do we know Gehenna's lineage?" Razik asked, still reading.

"Gehenna is the Sorceress in our realm," Eliza clarified, having sat back in her chair to let Razik do his thing. "She is one of Zinta's daughters."

"One of?" Theon asked.

"The gods are thousands and thousands of years old. You think they only have one child each?" Razik muttered.

"Sorin learned that Gehenna only calls herself the sorceress," Eliza cut in. "But among the gods, Zinta is known as the Sorceress, and Taika is known as—"

"The Enchantress," Razik cut in. "And according to this, some worlds refer to their descendants as such, particularly the most powerful ones."

"So it could be Zinta affecting her visions?" Katya asked, pushing curls from her face.

"She can't come here," Razik said.

"No, but would she have to come here to alter visions? It's already been proven that just because the gods can't come here doesn't mean they can't meddle," Theon argued.

"But with all the Zinta Legacy here, there could logically be one powerful enough to be referred to as a sorceress," Kat cut in. "Especially with the way Matches are arranged."

"That's true," Theon said, trying to translate more. "Do we think all their descendants have these spell books?"

"The Witches in our world have spell books," Eliza supplied. "Particularly the most powerful ones."

"We need to take this book with us," Razik murmured.

"We *cannot* steal a book from here," Kat said in horror.

"She's right. We can't take books from the Ekayan Island," Theon said. "The sentries here have permission to kill someone on site for even trying."

"Okay, but there are two dragons in this room," Eliza said. Turning to Luka, she added, "Don't you steal shit? Razik steals bowls all the time."

"I do *not* steal bowls," Razik growled. Then he added with a grumble, "This book is much larger than a bowl."

Eliza rolled her eyes as Theon said, "That does have a familiar *ring* to it."

Luka sent him an unimpressed glare while Eliza turned to Razik. "How old do you think this book is?"

"Don't do that," Razik snarled.

Running her finger along a page, Eliza's voice turned sensual. "It seems *really* old. Centuries and centuries. Maybe even from before Devram's time. That'd make it incredibly *valuable*, right?"

"I swear to the Fates, Eliza," Razik growled again.

"You're just going to leave this *incredibly valuable* book down here? Where no one appreciates it?" she went on.

"That's not true—" Katya started, but Theon slipped a hand over her mouth to stall the words. He knew exactly what Eliza was doing, and they needed to let this play out. To be honest, he was surprised Luka hadn't—

The book slammed shut before Luka was pulling it across the table and slipping it under his arm.

"I was reading that," Razik said in a dangerous tone that had Theon's magic churning in his soul.

"And I'm stealing it," Luka said. "That will make it *mine*."

Razik's eyes narrowed, but Eliza burst out laughing. When Razik's glare swung to her, she smirked, "You had your chance."

Pushing his hand away, Katya said in a hushed whisper, "You can't steal that book, Luka. There are wards and enchantments everywhere here. You'll surely be caught."

"Yet you are the one who insisted I Travel it to this building," Luka countered, his hold on the book tight. He eyed his brother as though he thought Razik would take it from his hands.

"He has a point," Theon said.

Kat whirled to him. "You are not seriously going to let him steal a book, Theon," she hissed. "You will never be allowed back on this island. None of us will be."

A little shocked at her tone, Theon said carefully, "They won't be able to prove it was us, and we can return it when we're done."

"And if we are caught?" she demanded.

By the gods, he'd never seen her this worked up.

"I'll handle it," he said.

"*You* will be fine," she retorted. "Luka will be fine. Razik and Eliza will be fine because they are not from here. But me and— *I* will not be afforded the same consideration."

There were unshed tears shining in her eyes. Theon hadn't known her long, but he knew she wasn't usually the emotional type.

"You think I will not protect you?" he asked, bending to peer up into her eyes.

"The Legacy sacrifice Fae all the time," she retorted. "Tell me you haven't done so in the past."

"That was different."

"How?"

"Because..."

Theon wasn't sure how to explain this. She was right. He'd sacrificed others to get what he wanted. Not just Fae. Anyone who got in the way. Anything to prove to his father he was what he needed to be to avoid suspicion. He did what needed to be done, and he did so without remorse. This should be no different, but it was.

"We can make a blood oath," he finally said. "I'll swear to keep you from harm and protect you."

Her brow pinched. "I don't want a blood oath from you, Theon," Kat replied. "This isn't about what you can give me. It's about the reality of this realm. They will seek retribution, and I am the one who will suffer."

"I swear that won't happen," he argued.

"If we are caught, they will arrest all of us. A Tribunal Hearing will be held. You can't be killed because you're the Arius Heir or Lord or what-ever," Kat said, speaking rapidly while two tears slipped free. "Luka and Razik won't be killed because they're both Legacy. Eliza is Razik's twin flame, and he will have her gone from this world before anyone could even entertain the idea of killing her. That leaves me. To punish you and your kingdom for the betrayal of your agreement in coming here, they will take me from your kingdom and kill me. A coveted fire Fae whose twin flame *left her here* with no one to care."

All the mirth from a few moments ago was gone. Theon wasn't entirely sure what he was doing, but he reached out and pulled Katya into his chest, holding her tight. It wasn't anything more than what he hoped was something comforting. He used to do the same for Axel when they were younger.

She was sobbing, his shirt dampening with her tears where she cried against his chest. He smoothed a hand down her hair, and he looked up, meeting Luka's gaze and saying only, "The book stays."

Hours later, when the sun had set and they were back at the estate, Theon knocked softly on Kat's door. She appeared a moment later, swollen eyes telling him she'd been crying all over again.

"Yes? What can I do for you?" she asked.

"Can I come in?" Theon said.

"Of course," she said, stepping back and pulling the door wider for him to enter. She closed it behind him as she said, "I apologize for not being dressed properly. I didn't know—"

"It's fine, Katya," he interrupted. "I only wanted to check on you after earlier today."

A faint blush crept across her cheeks. "I also apologize for my behavior and for speaking to you in such a manner," she murmured, hands clasped in front of her and eyes on the floor.

"I know everything with Axel has been difficult for you," Theon said. "I'm working on a way to fix this."

She nodded, still avoiding his gaze. "Is he why you did it?"

Confused, Theon asked, "What?"

"Axel," she clarified, finally looking at him. "Is he why you agreed to leave the book behind? You believe he would be upset with you because you think I am someone he cares for?"

"You *are* someone Axel cares for. It's why he left," Theon said.

"You don't leave someone you care for," she said, her tone hardening. "There is nothing logical in that statement."

"We do leave if it means the safety of someone we love," Theon countered. "But to answer your question, no, I did not do that for Axel."

"Then why?"

"I guess..." Theon pulled on the back of his neck. "We've spent a lot of time together these past months. Researching and trying to find Axel. I consider you— I mean, I hope we are some kind of..."

"Friends," she finished for him. "You consider us friends."

Did he? Was that what this was? For so long, it had just been him and Luka and Axel. Everyone else was someone to be used to further his own agenda, or someone who wanted to use him to further theirs.

"Yes," he finally answered. "I think I do."

She smiled softly. "In that case, thank you, Theon. Can you wait here a moment?"

He nodded, and she made her way to the nightstand. When she returned, she held a book in her hand. The same one where they'd found information about the twin flame bond.

"Can you give this to Razik?" she asked. "I'm sure he is upset about not stealing the other book from the Ekayan Island. He will be able to decipher things faster than I will. I only request that I get it back when you have finished with it."

"Of course," Theon said, taking the book from her. "Do you need anything else tonight?"

She smiled again. "No, I think I just need some rest."

"If you need anything, though, know that Axel didn't leave you alone."

Her smile faltered. "I appreciate that, Theon."

"You know where to find me," he added.

"Yes, thank you," she whispered.

He left her alone in her room, not wanting to make it any more awkward. Stopping at Razik and Eliza's room, he knocked and waited. It was Razik who answered. Theon said nothing, only held up the book Kat had given to him. Razik didn't say anything either. He only stepped to the side to allow him entry.

"Eliza has retired for the evening," Razik said, shutting the door behind them.

"That's fine. I was checking on Katya, and she said we could borrow this," Theon replied, holding out the book.

Razik took it, flipping through the pages. "It has information not readily found here."

"I figured," Theon said, helping himself to the alcohol cart in the room. "Want one?"

Razik grunted an agreement, and Theon poured another glass before carrying one over to him. He took a seat in an armchair while Razik took the sofa. Placing the book on the low table, he continued to flip through it while sipping on his drink. Theon grabbed another book, doing the same. It wasn't like he'd get any sleep anyway. The moment Luka had Traveled and returned to Tessa, her shield had been back in place. At least he'd given Luka an update on Roan to deliver to her.

"So you and Eliza share a Source bond and a twin flame bond," Theon said after a good hour had passed.

"Yes," Razik said, not looking up from the page he was reading.

"Essentially that is the same as our Source Marks, no?"

That had the male slowly raising his head. "Outside of the fact that such Marks are forced upon the Fae here, they are altered from their original intention. There is a cost for that. You don't mess with blood magic, and yet that's all Devram appears to have done."

"I can agree with that statement," Theon said. "But could others have done the same somewhere else? With other bonds?"

"Other bonds?" Razik repeated.

"You can't tell me there aren't other types of bonds," Theon said. "In all the realms and among all the stars, there's *nothing* else? Only two?"

Razik sat back, rubbing at his jaw. "That's a good point."

"You've never come across anything in all your reading?"

"Have you?" Razik countered.

"No, but clearly my resources are not nearly as extensive as yours," Theon replied.

"There are soulmates," Razik said. "A bond between kindred souls that is completely platonic. They are people who understand each other on a deeper level, but there is no romantic attraction. The intimacy is deeper than friendship. Soul deep. Scarlett has such a thing with her Guardian and another in our world, and I have one with her brother."

"Then that would not be me and Tessa," Theon said.

"You are trying to figure out something between you and Tessa?"

"I know we cannot be twin flames, but we were drawn to each other before she bore a Mark. Luka was too, but none of the bonds we've discussed can be that," Theon said.

"Perhaps it is simply a strong attraction," Razik suggested.

"It has to be more than that."

"It has to be, or you wish it to be?"

More like he *needed* it to be, but he didn't want to admit that aloud.

"She hated the Legacy even before I claimed her as my Source," Theon said. "A strong attraction doesn't explain that. It doesn't explain why I was drawn to her from the moment I saw a photo of her. Same with Luka."

"Luka is drawn to her?" Razik asked.

Theon nodded, standing to refill his drink. "He hasn't outright said it to me, but his shields have slipped a few times. And more than that, I know him well enough to see the signs."

"And you are okay with that?"

Theon didn't answer right away, ice clinking as he dropped it into his glass before he tipped the alcohol bottle up. "We have shared partners in the past a few times, but that was only a physical thing. This is more than that."

"And you are okay with that?" Razik repeated.

Theon turned to look at him, sipping on his drink. He wasn't completely sure how he'd ended up in this conversation with the male, but he found it was nice to have someone to talk to with Luka and Axel both gone.

"I don't know," he finally admitted.

Razik picked up the book once more. "So you wish to know about another bond so you can substantiate your claim to her over his?"

"What? No, that's not..."

But was that it? He was looking for something to explain the draw to her, yes. Maybe even try to convince her it truly was more than a bond like he'd always said, but what if Luka claimed the same? Luka was loyal to a fault, but Theon knew the more time he spent with her, the harder that pull was to resist. What if Luka decided to stop resisting? Would he be okay with that in the end?

"I will see what I can find on other types of bonds," Razik said after a few minutes of silence. "As well as what we can find about Tessa's visions."

"It's too bad we cannot speak to this Sorceress in your world," Theon mused.

Razik's laugh was humorless. "Even if we could, her cost would be steep. I do not know that anyone will ever make a bargain with her again."

"Again?"

"It was necessary, but costly," Razik replied. "But we are discounting an obvious resource here. Why are we not asking Cienna and Tristyn about this?"

"They are careful about what they reveal," Theon replied. "They worry about tempting the Fates, and always say we must ask the right questions."

"Then we best be figuring out what those questions are. We are running out of time," Razik said, returning to his reading, which Theon had come to learn was his way of saying he was done with the conversation.

But he was wrong.

They weren't running out of time. They were already working on borrowed time, and Fate would come collecting soon.

34
AXEL

He sat up straight on the small bed. Fully clothed, he yanked the earbuds from his ears so he could focus fully on the Tracking Mark. For four days he'd been at this inn waiting for Tessa to show up at the Acropolis, and finally she was here.

Axel had left the Underground the morning after his dinner with Bree, telling her he had some loose ends to take care of in the kingdoms while he still could. She'd seemed a little suspicious, but ultimately hadn't objected. Even if she had, he was still an Arius Heir for a little while longer. He didn't want to burden Theon with protecting Kat. It was his own responsibility. Theon had enough to worry about, and while he knew Theon would never feel threatened by the life growing in Kat's belly, an irrational overprotective part of him didn't want him to know yet. If his father ever found out, he would certainly have the child killed. Theon needed an heir before Axel would be allowed to have one, and even then, that heir could never be half Fae. He'd contemplated Luka, but again, he was Theon's advisor. Tristyn was an option, he supposed. Cienna clearly already knew, but Kat and Tessa were friends. Surely Tessa would want to make sure she was safe. Surely she would help him get her out of the Arius manor house somehow without the others knowing.

That was what he was counting on anyway.

Slipping on his sweatshirt, he pulled the hood up to shield his eyes from the sun. It wasn't even sunny out, but the daylight in general made his eyes hurt when he was in it too long. He slid on sneakers and left his room, taking the stairs down to the tavern on the first floor. None of the patrons paid him any attention as he made his way out to the streets. He wasn't technically *in* the Acropolis. This was a rundown area on the outskirts, and it was perfect for keeping a low profile.

Keeping to the shadows, he followed the pull of the Tracking Mark into the heart of the city, and that was where he found her being escorted into one of the finer dining establishments. Well, fuck. He certainly wasn't dressed for that restaurant, and even if he was, she was with those Fae that had been claimed by the Achaz Kingdom. Dex and that female. What was her name? Olive? Orleen? It didn't really matter, but he'd need to get her away from them if he had any hope of speaking to her.

Making his way to the alleys, he found the door to the kitchen of the restaurant. Knocking a few times, he waited until a haggard-looking cook pulled it open.

"We don't give handouts," he snapped, already shutting the door, but Axel was there with his shadows, sending them down his throat. Muffling the man's startled cry, he pushed inside, kicking the door shut behind him. He yanked the hood of his sweatshirt back, letting his magic drift across his irises.

"You know who I am, yes?" Axel hissed.

The male nodded, eyes wide.

"Then kindly forget you saw me here," he added, stepping back and pulling his magic with him.

"Of course, my lord," the male said, eyes on the ground. "My apologies."

"Accepted but not needed," Axel replied. "Now, where would I find the sound system for the restaurant?"

"The...what?" the male asked, wiping his hands on his apron.

"The music that plays in the background while people eat," Axel explained impatiently.

"I don't know, my lord," he stammered. "The main office maybe?"

"And where would I find that?"

The male gave vague directions, and Axel decided it would probably be easier to find it on his own at this point. The cook did tell him about the side passages the staff used, though, which was helpful in moving about unseen. In the end, the office wasn't too hard to find, and even better, it was conveniently empty. More than that, it came with a one-way window that overlooked the dining room. Flicking the lock behind him, he stood at the window, searching until he found Tessa seated at a table near the back. Dex and the two other Fae were with her, but there was another male there too. Axel immediately recognized him. A relation of some sort to Rordan, he was an Achaz Legacy. His father oversaw a seaside city, Astown Port, in the south of Achaz Kingdom where the Wynfell River met the Asning Sea.

The male's blond hair was dark with brown undertones. He was tall and thin, and for the life of him, Axel couldn't recall his name. Theon would know it, and Axel *should* know it. He watched them for a minute. The male was speaking, his gaze fixed on Tessa. She was sipping on a glass of wine, her back to the window.

Moving to the sound system, he pulled up the current music selection before syncing his phone. Corbin had taught him a few tricks in their short time together, and he moved back to the window to watch Tessa as he clicked the first song on a playlist he'd created just for her.

He saw her stiffen and her head tilt as the new music drifted into the room. A few other patrons looked around as well, but for the most part, no one seemed to notice. He let the song play for thirty seconds before clicking on the next. After thirty seconds, he moved to the next. On the fifth song, he watched Tessa set her napkin on the table and excuse herself, likely to use the restroom. Dex said something to her, but ultimately she left the table alone.

Perfect.

Being sure to disconnect his phone, he let the original music resume as he rushed from the room and down the stairs. He ducked into a restroom. Male or female, he didn't pay attention. He made sure it was empty, and then he waited by the door for the Tracking Mark to tell him where she was. When he felt her right on the other side, he yanked the door open and pulled her inside.

Then he was yelping a curse as shocks rippled through his body.

"By the gods, baby doll," he muttered. "It's me."

"Axel?" she said, staring at him in disbelief. "What are you doing here?"

"Came to talk to you," he replied, taking her in.

Her golden hair was pulled back into a sleek ponytail, while her cream dress was fitted down to the lace sleeves that covered her arms. Not enough to block out the bands of light though. Violet eyes were watching with flecks of grey and gold that peeked through.

"About what?" she asked. "They told me you were missing."

"I was," he admitted.

"Where were you?"

"Locked up somewhere."

Understanding flickered in her eyes. "Then how did you escape?"

"I was kind of...let go, in a way," he answered, sliding his hands into the front pocket of his sweatshirt.

"Let go," she repeated, her suspicion evident.

"It's kind of a long story, but I came to you for your help."

"My help?" she scoffed. "Have you spoken to Theon?"

"Yes. He filled me in on some things, but he didn't have time to catch me up on all the details," Axel said, pulling out his phone to check the time.

She hummed in response, leaning against the locked bathroom door. "What did he tell you about me?"

"That you had left. Went to Achaz Kingdom. That he sent Luka with you so you wouldn't be alone," Axel replied. "That you have my father locked up somewhere. Thank you for that, by the way, even if that was the reason I couldn't be located. Except that..." He trailed off as something occurred to him. "*You* could have found me, Tessa."

"I tortured your father for information and passed it along," she said icily.

"But the Tracking Mark. You could have found me the same way I found you," Axel said.

She blinked, her features void of any emotion.

"After everything... You didn't care?" he asked, beginning to realize this had been a huge mistake.

"I passed along information so they could find you," she repeated.

"But they didn't find me," he said, his voice rising. "I found *them*. I nearly— You did nothing."

"I did more than was required of me to begin with," she snapped.

"Fuck you, Tessa," Axel snarled, trying to keep his shadows in check. "I was going mad. I almost killed Katya. You could have prevented all of that."

"I could have done nothing at all," she argued.

"Instead, you did the bare minimum. Congratulations," he sneered.

"After everything, I owe you nothing," she retorted, pushing off the door and prowling towards him. Light echoed each step, a trail of gold mist left in her wake. "I don't owe anyone anything, least of all the bloodline I am destined to kill."

"What?"

She smirked. It was cold and unfeeling. "Theon didn't tell you that part? I vowed to destroy all the Arius blood in Devram."

"You're fucking with me," Axel said, unwilling to believe that.

"It's my purpose," she recited.

"Then what are you waiting for?" he demanded, spreading his arms out wide. "I'm right here, Tessa."

Her smirk faltered before she recovered, her mask slipping back into place. "All in good time," she simpered. "Still want my help?"

Axel huffed a laugh of disbelief, his arms falling to his sides. "I know the Fates dealt you a shitty hand, Tessa," he said. "But that doesn't mean you have to be a shitty person because of it."

She stepped back from him in shock. "This isn't about me, Axel."

"Sure seems like it is," he replied, striding past her. "If you're not going to kill me now, I'll be on my way." He paused before he unlocked the door. "But the help was for Kat, not me."

"For Kat?" she repeated, lurching forward. "What's wrong with Kat?"

"Guess it doesn't matter, does it?" he answered, before he pulled the door open and left her behind.

He rushed around the room, stuffing various items into two overnight bags. Mainly Kat's stuff. He had plenty of things at the Underground penthouse for himself. She would need things. And the baby. No, wait. They had time to prepare for that.

Going into the bathroom, he studied all the hair products before swiping them all into the bag with one fell swoop. Admittedly, he should have made sure they were all sealed properly, but he was in too much of a hurry. He'd bought some extra blood from a dealer at the inn he'd been staying at, and he was praying to any god that would listen that would be enough. It had tasted terrible, but if it kept him from lunging for her the second she walked through the door, it will have been worth it.

He was just coming out of the bathroom to grab one of the soft blankets she preferred when the door opened. Amber eyes locked onto him as she pushed the door shut behind her, and she never slowed, crossing the room to him.

"Kat, I—"

But he never got to finish what he was going to say. Not as her palm went across his cheek, the crack reverberating through the room. He slowly turned back to her, shock rippling through him, and he found flames flickering in her eyes.

"What are you doing here, Axel?" Kat demanded, and there was nothing soft or demure about her right now.

"Okay, you're angry. That's understandable in this situation," Axel started, the side of his face burning.

"Answer the question," she hissed. "What are you doing here?"

"I came for you," he said, holding up one of the bags he still held.

"You left."

"I know, but not because—"

"I told you how I felt. Told you I believe you are my twin flame. Told you I am carrying your child. You said you were happy. You agreed. And then you fucking left," she cried, her hands slamming into his chest and shoving.

Axel stumbled back, his chest burning now, and he looked down to find two perfect handprints burned through his sweatshirt down to his flesh.

"I did it to protect you," he insisted, dropping the bag and taking a step towards her.

"Then why are you here, Axel?" she asked again.

"I thought you'd be safer without me. *Both* of you," he said. "I... Cienna showed up to check on you, and she told me the reason Eliza couldn't give me the twin flame Mark was because I triggered the curse, Katya. When I took so much from you, I... I panicked and left. If I'm away from you, I can't be a danger to you."

"You're not answering my question," Kat said, the fire still burning in her eyes. "If that's the case, then why are you here?"

"Because I realized no one will protect you both like I will," he said, throwing his hands in the air in frustration. "I made a mistake, Kat. I'm here to rectify it."

"For four days, you have been in the Acropolis, Axel. Yet you just came here now?" she countered.

Well, fuck.

"How do you know how long I've been here?" he asked.

"Because I still bear my twin flame Mark," she snapped, holding up her hand. "It allows me to feel you, find you."

"Kat, I'm sorry. I'm so sorry—"

"No," she interrupted, shaking her head. "You don't get to apologize to me. For the first time ever, you treated me like just another Fae when you left me."

"No, Kat. No, that's not—"

"For the first time ever, you made me feel like I was beneath you," she went on, and that fire in her eyes banked as tears filled them, spilling over. "You walked away as if I was something you could simply discard when I was no longer useful to you."

"No, kitten," Axel snarled, taking her face in his hands and swiping at her wet cheeks with his thumbs. "I left because if I ever hurt you like I did before, I would not be able to live with myself. But what if there's a next time, and there's no one to stop me? What if I kill you? What if this child is born, and *then* it happens? That's why I left, Katya. Because I would rather live a life without you, knowing you are healthy and whole, than live a life where I endanger you just by existing."

"I am not whole without you!" she cried, more tears falling. "Do you understand that? Because I do not. It is not logical, but you being away these past weeks? Axel, it felt like a part of me was dying a little more every day."

"Kat, I'm sorry," he murmured, pulling her into his chest. Her salty tears stung as they soaked into the burns, but he'd live every day in agony to never see her like this again. "I'm sorry, kitten. I'm so fucking sorry," he murmured over and over into her hair.

For the next several minutes, he just held her, and she clung to him, her sobs eventually lessening. He waited until she pulled back, letting her take whatever she needed.

Taking her face in his hands again, he waited until she brought her eyes to his. "I'm sorry, Katya. Please know that."

She nodded before dropping her eyes and stepping back from him. His hands fell to his sides as she said, "What are you doing here, Axel?"

"I told you. I came back for you," he answered.

"So you can leave me somewhere else?"

"No," he said instantly. "No, Kat. I came to take you back with me."

"Back where?"

"To the Underground."

She went silent, and he shifted under her scrutiny when she just... stared at him.

After a full minute, he said, "I need you to say something, Kat."

"You want to take me to the Underground," she repeated.

"Yes."

"To stay with you."

"Yes."

"In the Underground."

"Yes."

"Stop saying yes," she snapped.

He forced himself to swallow his laugh at her irritation. "I will need to stay there while I...adjust to things, and it's the only place I'll be able to keep you both safe. Even once I have things under control, I can't say that I'll ever be welcome anywhere else. All Legacy who succumb to the curse are banished to live there." Then he said words that nearly gutted him to speak. "So if you'd rather not come with me and stay here, I'll understand."

She rolled her lips while she got her thoughts in order before she said, "I have lived these last weeks without you, and they were miserable, Axel. But if you are only moving me from place to place and not planning to stay with me, I want to stay here. Where there are people I can depend on."

"I swear to you, Kat. Never again," he insisted.

"But how can I believe you?" she asked. "You sat with me on that bed. Told me we'd figure things out together, and then you left. And I..."

"Katya, I need you to understand something," he said, taking a single step forward. "Love to me is defined as safety, and I know loving someone as protecting them. It's fucked up, and I know it's not how the whole love thing is supposed to work, but that's how I've known love. And this thing between us? I don't understand it either, but I know that I love you. I was loving you when I sent you with Tristyn, and I was loving you when I left you here. I know I need to learn to love you differently. Normally maybe? Whatever it is, I'll do it. If you're telling me that loving you means we're together no matter what, then that's what I'll do. Tell me how to love you, kitten, because I'll pluck stars from the sky and walk through your flames. And when I've turned, and this bond we never got to have has faded, I'll still choose you. I'll still love you, and it will mean even more because we're choosing it. We're not being drawn to each other by some bond gifted by the Fates."

More tears were tracking down her face as she stared at him. He didn't know what he was supposed to do in this situation, so he stood there, waiting. He didn't move when she closed the distance between them. Not until she reached up and slid a hand around the back of his neck, pulling him down to meet her lips. Then he was gathering her close and taking control of that kiss. Her mouth parted easily, and he chased her tongue with his own. His fingers tangled in her curls, and her warmth was seeping into his chilled skin. A perfect balance.

He forced himself to pull back first, dropping small kisses on her cheeks, her nose, her brow. "Does this mean we're done fighting?"

She huffed a laugh. "Yes, Axel. It means we're done fighting."

His lips brushed her temple. "And you're coming with me?"

"Yes," she whispered.

"Do you feel up for leaving now? You are not too tired?"

"I'll be fine."

"We just need to take a portal. Then you can sleep on the drive. It'll be a few days to get to the Underground," he said.

She smiled softly. "Okay."

"I grabbed some of your things, but if there's anything I missed, there's room in the bags," he added.

"All right," she murmured. "I just want to change."

"Of course."

Katya pulled some clothes from a dresser before heading for the bathroom, but she stopped just outside. "Axel?"

"Yes, kitten?"

"I do not wish for a normal love," she said. "And I choose you too. I choose us, even if our days are spent without light."

"Good thing you can make some for us, kitten," he replied, his soul feeling lighter than it had in months. "You and me."

Her hand went to her stomach. "You and us."

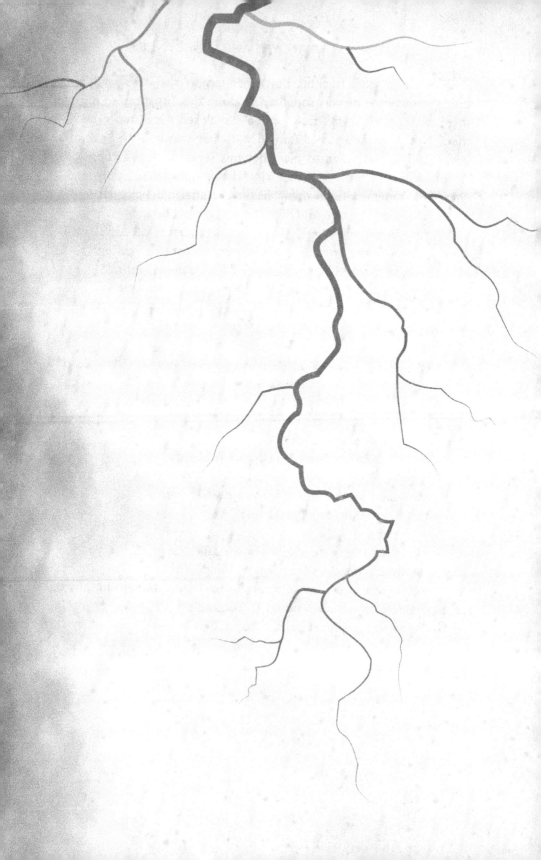

35
TESSA

Propped against her headboard, Tessa turned the phone over and over in her hands. She hadn't powered it on. In fact, ever since Theon had given it back to her, it had sat in the back of her nightstand drawer. Out of sight, out of mind type of thing. Except now it wasn't out of mind. Ever since Axel had tracked her down at that restaurant a few days ago, she'd been thinking about it.

The help was for Kat. Not me.

She wanted to ask Luka what was going on with Kat, but she couldn't. That would show she cared, and she couldn't care. Caring led to feelings, and feelings were a distraction from her purpose, but this was *Kat*. She wasn't a Legacy. She was as innocent as the Fae had been at the Villas, so what did Axel need her help with?

That was what had her digging the phone out and debating whether or not to turn it on. Would Axel even answer if she called now? Or would she have messages waiting for her from when he was trying to get in contact with her?

Her thumb hovered over the power button, and she glanced over to the seating area where Dex was sound asleep in an armchair. He stayed in here every night, and it was annoying. However, he also rarely slept, and she wondered how his kind refilled their power. If they stole a Fae power, did it refill in the same manner as the Fae? Something to ponder another night, she supposed.

Her thoughts returned to the phone, and she was just about to turn it on when movement caught her eye. Luka stood in her ensuite, his stare boring into her. She'd felt him on the other side of her shields, asking her to lower them. He felt different from Theon. Theon was dark and possessive, always intense and anxious. Luka was dark and possessive too, but in a different way. A way she couldn't explain. Where Theon was intense and anxious, Luka was a solid presence. Calm and stoic, but intense and commanding all the same.

A balance she didn't understand, but some days she desperately wished she did.

Luka tapped the side of his head, and she rolled her eyes, lowering her shields.

About godsdamn time, Luka grumbled down the bond.

If you're solely here to complain, you can leave, she retorted flippantly.

His eyes narrowed. *Get your ass in here.*

She arched a brow, but quietly slipped from the bed. Tucking the phone into the back of the nightstand again, she made her way to the bathroom, closing the door behind her.

"What?" she whispered, crossing her arms

He looked her up and down, gaze lingering on her bare legs in her short sleep shorts.

"Dex is sleeping?" Luka asked, finally bringing his eyes to hers.

"Yes, but I don't know for how long."

A rare half-smile curled on his lips. "I may have made sure he drank some of your tea tonight."

Her mouth dropped open because that was...brilliant.

"Why?" Tessa asked.

"Because Theon may have found some information about your visions. I'm going there now and thought you might want to tag along," he answered.

"He did?" she asked, excitement bubbling.

Luka nodded. "If I take you with, you are agreeing to be in the same space as Theon."

"Obviously," she drawled.

"And it's not just him. Razik and Eliza will be there too."

"The one that looks like you?"

Luka nodded. "It sounds like he's my brother."

"Like a *real* brother?"

"As opposed to a fake one?" Luka countered.

Tessa brought her hand dramatically to her chest. "By the gods, he jokes."

"Shut up, temptress," he muttered.

Then he looped his arm around her waist, pulling her into him, and her entire body forgot how to function. She hadn't been expecting that, but she was fairly certain her heart stopped for a few seconds at the same time she forgot how to properly breathe.

Before she could come to her senses, she was standing in a different room. She immediately recognized it as Luka's. The warm and earthy decor. Trinket boxes everywhere that she was betting held rings. Random empty frames scattered throughout the room and adorning the walls.

"Do you want different clothes?" Luka asked, bringing her back to herself.

"What?"

He was smirking now. "Do you want different clothes?"

She looked down at her night clothes. "I'm not bothered by them. Are you?"

"No. I'm only bothered that others will see you in them."

"Like Theon?"

"No," he scoffed. "I'm well aware he's already seen everything, and even if he hadn't..."

She waited, but he didn't continue. "Even if he hadn't what?"

Luka only shrugged before he disappeared into his closet.

What the fuck did that mean?

He returned with a hooded sweatshirt and tossed it to her. Scowling, she held it up and then said, "Absolutely not."

"It's a sweatshirt, Tessa."

"It's a *Firewings* sweatshirt, Luka," she retorted.

"That you've worn before."

"And once was enough."

"It'll do the job for tonight."

A hand on her hip, she asked, "And what job is that? Making me sick?"

"No. It will cover your nipples," he replied casually, heading for the door. "Let's go."

She looked down to find her nipples indeed peaked against her thin top, and she cursed under her breath as she pulled the sweatshirt on. "Now it looks like I'm not wearing *anything* underneath it," she grumbled, stalking over to him. Of course it was huge on her and hung nearly to her knees.

"But at least what you *are* wearing is Firewings apparel," he returned, pulling the door open for her.

She glared, flipping him her middle finger as she passed. "Are we going to Theon's rooms?"

"Actually, we have one stop to make first," Luka said, falling into step beside her.

"Kat?" she asked hopefully.

Luka glanced down at her. "No. She is not here."

"What do you mean she is not here?"

"Apparently she left with Axel." Before she could ask, he added, "None of us know much."

He stopped outside another room, knocking twice, and a moment later, the door opened, sky-blue eyes connecting with hers.

"Lange," she breathed, launching herself at him.

He chuckled as he caught her. "Hey, Tessa."

"Where's Corbin?" she asked when he set her back on her feet.

Lange looked over his shoulder into the darkened room. "He's not feeling the greatest."

"What's wrong?" she asked, trying to peer past him.

"A headache or something," Lange said. "Anyway, what are you doing here?"

A headache? Fae rarely got sick, let alone suffer from ailments like a headache.

"Theon has some information for us, I guess," she said absent-mindedly, her thoughts still on Corbin.

"He'll be okay, Tessa," Lange said gently. "Just needs some rest."

She nodded again, worrying her bottom lip as she looked up at him. "And you? You're good?"

He smiled. "Yes, Tessa. It's actually not so bad here. Comfortable rooms. Food. Protection."

"Those are basic necessities, Lange," she deadpanned.

"And they're provided for us here and more," he replied, crossing his arms and leaning against the doorjamb. "There aren't any added expectations. It's like we can just…live. We have privacy. We can be together." He shrugged again. "I don't think we'll get that in another kingdom. I know we'll be expected to contribute and all, but it's different from what I thought it'd be."

They wouldn't be getting that at all if Valter were still ruling. But that also meant that Theon was giving them that little bit of freedom.

And she was going to take that all away when she came to fulfill her purpose.

Clearing her throat softly, she offered him a weak smile. "I'm glad to hear that."

"And you?" he asked, everything about his demeanor was kind, like it always had been. "You coming back soon?"

"I don't really think I belong here anymore," she answered, almost inaudibly.

"We didn't think we belonged here," Lange replied. "Things change. The winds shift." He shrugged again. "New beginnings. A genesis and a new dawn."

She laughed. "You've started speaking nonsense in your time here," she teased.

He bent and pressed a kiss to her cheek. "I'll let Corbin know you missed him. Stop by again, yeah?"

"Yeah," she said faintly. "I'll do that."

Lange backed away, the door closing, and she turned to find Luka leaning against the opposite wall. She'd forgotten he was even there.

"Thank you for that," she said softly.

He only nodded and pushed off the wall, leading her down the hall once again. As they descended the stairs, she heard voices coming from the dining room, and they followed them. Books were everywhere on the table, Theon and two others seated around them. Theon was on his feet before she stepped a single foot into the room.

"Tessa," he breathed, heated emerald eyes sweeping over her. "Did you see Lange and Corbin? I told Luka to take you there first."

"You did?" she asked, glancing up at Luka for a moment. "I mean, yes, I did."

"Good," he said, slipping his hands into his pants pockets.

Still in dress pants, the top few buttons of his shirt were undone. His tie was draped over the back of his chair, and his sleeves were rolled back. He'd definitely been running his hands through his hair, and of course, he still had shoes on.

Clearing his throat, he said, "This is Razik Greybane and his...mate, Eliza."

"We sort of met already," Tessa said, stepping farther into the room.

"If we could keep the destruction to a minimum tonight, that'd be great," Razik muttered, not looking up from his book.

At least not until Tessa said, "You are Luka's brother?"

That had his head snapping up. "You are very blunt."

"I've found it's the best way to get information from your kind," she said casually, her fingers brushing over books as she moved along the table. She knew without looking that both Luka and Theon had their eyes fixed on her, and she ignored the way that was making her feel.

"My kind," Razik repeated deadpan.

"Mhmm," she hummed, flipping open a book. "Sargon Legacy. Speaking of, how far down the Sargon line are you?"

"What?" Razik asked tightly.

Tessa gestured to Theon. "Theon is so far removed from Arius, it's really just a fancy title at this point."

"Careful, beautiful," came an icy warning, and gods, it sent chills up her spine.

"Just stating facts," she replied, managing to keep her voice casual. Looking back at Razik, she said, "Well?"

She recognized the look on his face. Broody. Annoyed. It was a mirror of Luka's usual expression.

"Well, what?" Razik asked, a growl in those two words.

She huffed a dramatic sigh. "You know my cousin, yes?"

"Unfortunately. You appear to have the same flare for unnecessary dramatics that they do," he retorted.

"Razik," Eliza hissed, elbowing him hard.

"They?" Tessa asked, her head tilting at the word.

"Scarlett has a brother," Razik said tightly.

"Interesting," she murmured. "Anyway, you were saying?"

"I wasn't saying anything."

"By Anala," Eliza interrupted, clearly exasperated. "His father was one of Sargon's sons."

"One of?" Theon asked sharply, but Tessa was looking at Luka. Who was staring back at Razik. His features were taut, and Tessa was worried he was going to crack a molar. It was all she needed to see to know Razik hadn't told him this.

But all this meant that Xan was Sargon's son, making Luka the grandchild of a god. Not of Firsts like she was, but the direct descendant of a god nonetheless. Which made so much sense. It explained why Luka was stronger than other Legacy. How he could train her and help her manage her power. He wouldn't be as powerful as her, but more powerful than any Legacy in Devram.

"Sargon had seven children," Razik said, sitting back in his chair and crossing his arms. "Each of those children comprises one of his seven bloodlines."

"Greybane and Mors," Theon clarified.

"Are two of those lines," Razik confirmed.

"And your mother?" Tessa asked.

"A shifter," he answered. "It is why we can isolate the shifts."

"What does that mean?"

Razik sighed as though this was the most inconvenient conversation he'd ever had. "Sargon can isolate the shift like we can. Just wings or eyes, for example. He can do that because he is a god. Some of his children, however, cannot. Some are either in their human forms or their dragon forms. All or nothing, so to speak. Because our mother was a dragon shifter and not a mortal, we can isolate our shift."

"How fascinating," Tessa said, dropping into a chair and propping her chin on a fist. Drumming the fingers of her other hand, the bands around her wrists flared slightly.

"You are unnerving," Razik said frankly as she studied him.

Her smile was pure wildness when she replied, "I like it that way."

He gave her a sardonic smile. "Let's talk about *your* lineage."

"What of it?"

"Luka told us of your visions," Theon cut in, drawing her attention to him. "How he has been getting pulled into them."

She listened while he filled her in on their trip to the Ekayan Island. Luka had told her much of this already, but the brief refresher was nice.

"So what does all this mean for me?" Tessa asked, flicking through pages of notes.

"That you are not supposed to exist," Razik said.

Theon and Luka both rumbled a sound, and Tessa dragged her eyes to the male across the table.

"If she can be blunt, so can I," he said, completely unfazed. "It was not meant to be an insult. It is simply a fact. You are the combination of four powerful bloodlines. Two of those lines were never meant to cross. It makes sense that crossing those powers would alter others."

"What do you mean alter powers?" Tessa asked, sitting back in her chair and drumming her fingers again.

"The gifts from the Achaz line and Zinta line are clear," Theon explained. "But that is only half your heritage, Tessa. You have Arius and Serafina gifts as well."

"I'm aware," she replied coldly.

"Are you? Because you never use them."

"That you know of."

Theon smiled, something razor sharp. "I don't think you are always aware when you are using them either, clever tempest."

She stayed silent, waiting for him to continue, but it was Razik who spoke.

"Arius and Serafina had two children together: Saylah and Temural. But Saylah and Temural's gifts are simply extensions of Arius and Serafina's," Razik said. "Saylah is the goddess of night and shadows, which are extensions of Arius's gifts of death, darkness, and endings and Serafina's gifts of dreams."

"And Temural?" Tessa asked.

"I admittedly do not know him as well."

Her brow arched. "You *know* Saylah?"

"Better than I'd like to," Razik muttered. "But Temural is the god of the wild and untamed. Both could conceivably come from Arius and Serafina's gifts, which brings us to *your* gifts."

"Have you ever had visions when you aren't sleeping?" Theon asked.

Tessa's brow furrowed. "No. That's why I always thought they were dreams."

"Exactly," Theon said, and she almost smiled at the excited note that had entered his voice. "The visions of your Zinta bloodline merged with the dreams of the Serafina bloodline."

"And we think that because...?" Luka asked, having taken a seat between her and Theon.

"Because one of Serafina's gifts is being able to walk among dreams," Razik said. "But because the powers were altered in Tessa's case, she is pulling others in to walk *her* dreams. Or in this case, her visions."

The room fell silent as they let all this sink in. Tessa had to admit in some ways it made sense, but in others, it still didn't.

"Then why is it only Luka?" she asked. "Why did I never pull Theon or Axel into a vision? Or anyone else, for that matter?"

"Because you trust Luka the most," Theon said, his emerald eyes already on her when she met his stare. "You feel safest with him. When was the first time this happened?"

"After the Tribunal Hearing," Luka said. "She didn't trust me then. She wasn't even speaking to me."

"But you showed up," Theon said. "And you'd been showing up before that. You'd found her by the river after everything with Felicity. You'd been training her. You found her when the Augury attacked. You bought her the fucking flip-flops."

Tessa blinked as she stared at Theon, seeing a side of him she'd never noticed before. He was more observant than she gave him credit for, and...

There was a reason he'd sent Luka to her. Not to watch her or report her movements. But because he was right. Some part of her had trusted Luka, even if she'd still harbored suspicions. Even if she still had reservations now.

She swallowed thickly, tearing her gaze from his when Eliza said, "The only thing we haven't been able to piece together is your Arius gifts."

But Tessa knew exactly what gifts she'd received from her paternal grandfather. It was the way her light took life from others. It was what fed her magic, made it stronger.

Because life always fed death.

Life must give, and death must take.

"And where the weather manipulation comes from," Razik added.

"No, but I have a theory on that," Theon said, bringing all their attention back to him. "I think it has something to do with your mother. The only piece of all this that we don't know."

"Right," Tessa murmured, lost in her own thoughts, because she knew where to find those answers.

She glanced at Luka, who was staring at his brother.

She cleared her throat, turning to Eliza. "You are a fire Fae? Like Katya?"

Startled at the change in subject, Eliza said, "Yes and no. My father was a fire Fae. My mother was earth."

"Was?" Tessa asked.

Eliza smiled darkly. "Another killed them. I killed him."

"Sounds satisfying."

"It was," she replied.

Turning back to Theon, she asked, "Luka said Katya left?"

Theon nodded, darkness drifting across his eyes. "Apparently with Axel."

"And you don't know where they went?"

Theon and Luka exchanged a glance before Theon said. "We're assuming the Underground. Axel..." He pushed out a harsh breath, pulling on the back of his neck. "He's transitioning into a Night Child."

Tessa stared back at him, blinking several times before she said slowly, "I don't understand. Axel is going to be a vampyre?"

"Yes," Theon answered.

"And he took Kat with him? How is that safe?"

But he'd come to her. Axel had come to her to ask for her help, and she'd sent him away.

When no one answered, she said, "So Axel won't be a Legacy anymore?"

"No," Theon answered tightly.

She didn't expect the flood of relief that coursed through her. She wasn't supposed to care, but she did. She cared that she wasn't going to have to kill Axel. Gods, she *cared*.

"He'll take precautions to not hurt Katya," Theon said, mistaking her sudden rush of emotions for worry.

Tessa nodded. She believed that. He'd come to her for help, and she'd dismissed him.

"And I'll figure out a way to bring them both home," Theon added.

She didn't reply because in the end she still had to kill him. In the end, there wouldn't be a home to bring them back to.

Because while they were her villains, she was theirs.

It took her a minute to realize that Luka had Traveled them back to *his* room and not hers when they went back to Faven. He dropped her hand and went into his ensuite without a word. She stared after him, unsure of what was happening. He hadn't spoken much at the Arius manor, especially after learning he was a grandchild of Sargon. It had mainly been Theon and Razik tossing around theories and history with occasional insight from Eliza. Tessa had listened to every word, absorbing it all.

You are not supposed to exist.

Those had been Razik's words, and they'd stung. She'd been told her entire life she was wrong. An inconvenience. Wild and reckless and difficult.

Not supposed to exist.

Just like Arius and Serafina weren't supposed to have children.

But if that was the case, and Serafina was to be with Achaz, was that not the same plan? Would that not also have upset the very same balance? Would Arius then have the same vendetta against Achaz?

None of it added up.

She wandered to the dresser along the wall, pulling open the top drawer. She'd expected to find socks or underwear, not...rings.

Rings being corralled in place by an empty picture frame.

She picked up one of the rings. It was simple. A solid silver band. Nothing special.

Replacing it, she picked up another. This one was more intricate. Fine detailing was etched into the bronze band with tiny red rubies interspersed.

The frame itself was nothing special either. Ivory and gold. Like everything else in the Faven Palace.

She closed the drawer when she heard the bathroom door open, and she turned to find Luka leaning in the doorway. He'd changed into loose pants, and he was shirtless.

His eyes narrowed when he found her near the dresser. "What are you doing?"

"Wondering why you brought me back here instead of my room," she replied, leaning back on her elbows where they rested on the dresser. His gaze roamed over her, but when he didn't say anything, she found herself saying, "Do you want to talk about it?"

His eyes snapped back to hers. "Talk about what?"

"Being the grandchild of a god."

"No," he growled immediately.

"Then what do you want?"

His hair was down, the strands falling to his shoulders. It was rare to see it completely down like that, and she suddenly wanted to run her fingers through it. That was always comforting to her.

And why was she thinking of a way to comfort him right now?

But his gaze was fixed on her bare legs again, and she suddenly knew exactly what he was looking for.

A distraction.

He didn't want to think about Razik or his heritage right now. He didn't want to contemplate being the grandchild of a god or what that could mean. He wanted to think about anything but that. Get lost in something that wasn't their wretched reality.

One of her hands dropped to her side where she toyed with the hem of the sweatshirt. Because for whatever reason, she wanted to be the one to make him feel better. She wanted to be the distraction.

"You have to ask for it," she said, her voice sultry.

"Ask for what?" Luka replied, but she watched his pupils shift to vertical slits. Watching his eyes glowing softly only spurred her on.

"I owe you," she said. "But I'm not going to make such a *hard* decision for you. You need to ask for what you want."

Recognition of his own words flashed across his features, and a small, cold sneer curled on his lips. "And if I asked you to crawl across the floor and beg sweetly from your knees?"

"This is about what you need right now," she retorted. She watched him swallow down whatever he was going to say next, and when he didn't speak, she added, "Thank you, by the way."

"For what?"

"Taking me with you tonight. I know you didn't have to."

"That was Theon."

She arched a brow. "Really?"

"Yes. He told me to ask you if you wanted to be included."

"So I should be thanking him? Asking *him* what he wants?"

"No," Luka growled.

She smirked, and he straightened to his full height. All dominance and predatory, and something inside of her lifted its head to meet the challenge. She knew her eyes were glowing to match his, and every part of her wanted this as much as he did now.

Her head tilted as she watched him. "Are you worried about Theon finding out? Is that why you won't ask for it?"

Luka didn't say a word, and she knew that was exactly what was stopping him.

And she didn't give a fuck.

If it pissed Theon off, good. He deserved every bit of it.

But if Theon approved...

Gods, the very idea made her entire body *hot*. Desire coursed through her, and fuck it.

She was wild and impulsive and uncontrollable. May as well lean into it.

Theon? she asked down the bond, a disapproving rumble coming from Luka across the room. But the dragon didn't move. Didn't tell her to stop.

Tessa? Are you all right? came Theon's reply.

I am, she replied. *But Luka isn't.*

What happened? he demanded.

She held Luka's stare the entire time when she answered, *He wants me to crawl across the floor and beg him sweetly from my knees, but he's afraid you'll disapprove.*

The silence down the bond was deafening, and she watched the taut tendons in Luka's neck while they both waited to see what Theon was going to say next. It didn't matter to her. If Theon said no, she'd let him feel every bit of her emotions as she openly defied him. And if Theon said yes… Well, she'd let him feel every bit of her desire then too, knowing exactly what it would be doing to him hundreds of miles away.

And what do you think about that, little storm? Theon finally asked, and she couldn't decipher the emotions that accompanied those words.

Will you hate it, and wish it was you? she retorted.

Always, he answered. *But is the only reason you're debating it to punish me?*

Luka's eyes narrowed at that question, and she knew he wanted that answer as much as Theon did.

No, she replied.

It was one word, but the feral want that flooded down the bond made her press her thighs together beneath Luka's sweatshirt.

Then on your knees, clever tempest, Theon answered. *But Tessa?*

Yes? And her voice was breathy even down the bond.

Only him. If anyone else touches what is mine, death will be a mercy.

She ignored that comment, still focused on Luka across the room, as she dragged his sweatshirt over her head and let it drop to the floor beside her.

Then she slowly sank to her knees.

I'm not there, but I feel Luka, little storm. Gods, you must look stunning, Theon said, and the praise… She knew what this was. Theon valued control. He knew she wanted this. Knew Luka wanted this. And the only way he could give it to them was to still be involved. Still have *some* type of control over all this. And while she didn't care, Luka clearly did. Luka's loyalty was both a blessing and a curse to him, so she let Theon have this. Not for him, but for Luka.

For Luka who came for her again and again. For teaching her to defend herself. For believing she was worth it. For not demanding her trust, but earning it slowly over time. For letting her rage, but also insisting she learn control. For understanding that sometimes she needed someone else to take control, but that she also needed to learn to take it for herself. For letting *her* make that choice. For taking her to Theon when Roan was dying. For coaxing her through the dark and cramped tunnels of the Underground.

For the fucking flip-flops.

Her eyes stayed on his as she crawled across the floor, and she could feel him. Wild yet controlled. Untamed yet steady. Impulsive yet restrained.

She stopped directly in front of him, sitting back on her heels and looking up into glowing sapphire eyes. His hand trembled as he lifted it, fingers caressing her cheek.

"Ask me."

It was a whispered command, and she watched his throat bob. She'd never felt more powerful as she watched him watch her. She didn't have to do this. No master was forcing her to her knees. No one was ordering her. She wanted to do this, and knowing Luka wanted her for no other reason than because she was who she was? Gods, this wasn't a thank you for taking her with tonight. This was thanking him for always accepting her as she was while simultaneously encouraging her to never settle.

He swallowed again, his fingers trailing along her jaw before his thumb brushed over her bottom lip. "Have you done this for Theon?"

She shook her head. "He wishes."

Luka's chuckle was dark. "I bet he does, temptress." His thumb brushed over her lip again. "I want that bratty mouth of yours around my cock, baby girl."

Her smile was all sin as she slid her palms up his thighs, and it grew when she felt his entire body shudder under her touch. This power was more intoxicating than the rush of knowing people feared her. When she reached the band of his pants, she watched his stomach cave as she dipped her hand inside and pulled out his cock.

She couldn't help but compare him to Theon. Theon was longer, but Luka was thicker. Already hard, it jutted up, and she gave it a couple of slow strokes before she leaned forward and swirled her tongue around the tip. The bead of precum was salty, and she felt his sharp inhale in her core. Then she sank forward in a wet-hot glide. The sharp inhale became a groaned curse, and she smiled around him when his hand slipped into her hair.

She didn't stop, letting him hit the back of her throat where she lingered. It wasn't until she was feeling light-headed from the lack of oxygen that she pulled back just enough to get some air. Then she took him even deeper, hollowing her cheeks and sucking hard.

"Fucking Sargon," Luka spat, his fingers tightening in her hair. They alternated between massaging along the back of her head and fisting to the point of pain. It was barely controlled restraint, and gods, she wanted to take that from him too. Have him completely undone and at her mercy.

She looked up to find his jaw slack, and she swallowed around him, his eyes rolling back. Then he thrust forward, down her throat, and she let him. Because this wasn't him taking what he wanted. This was her giving it freely.

"Gods, you can be such a good girl when you're not being a brat," he rasped out on ragged breaths, thrusting into her mouth again and again.

What does she look like? came Theon's strained voice down the bond.

Like a fucking goddess, Luka answered. *Her mouth was made for this.*

She pitched forward, meeting his thrust this time, and the barked "Fuck!" as she gripped the backs of his thighs to hold herself deep on him had her clenching her own thighs together.

"Godsdammit," he rasped out, tugging on her hair to pull her back.

Tessa gasped, feeling the wetness on her face as her eyes watered. The look in his eyes was nothing but awe and wonder. He wrapped her hair around his fist, hauling her mouth back to his cock. Her wet gasps mixed with his soft, grunted praises until she felt him swelling in her mouth.

His release hit her tongue as a tight, guttural sound filled the room. She tried to sink deeper, but his grip was holding her back, keeping her from burying him in the back of her throat.

Don't swallow, little storm. Not yet, Theon commanded as Luka finished emptying himself onto her tongue.

Are you touching yourself, Theon? she taunted.

Beautiful, I just came all over my stomach knowing what you are doing to Luka.

Luka was breathing hard when his grip loosened on her hair, his cock slipping from her lips.

Show him, Tessa, Theon ordered.

Her eyes widened, but the hungry look on Luka's face told her this was something he craved. Theon clearly knew that.

Sitting back on her heels once more, Tessa opened her mouth and stuck out her tongue, letting him see his release sitting there. Then, holding his stare the entire time, she closed her jaw and swallowed.

Before she knew what was happening, Luka hauled her up. Her feet left the ground, wrapping around his waist, and his mouth crashed into hers. Something about him licking into her mouth and tasting himself made her even hotter, and she pressed herself to his chest, just wanting to feel him. She wasn't seeking release or looking for anything in return for what she'd just done for him. Because there was freedom in being able to choose to give this to him.

Her choice.

Him looking at her with that rapture in his eyes, seeing her as someone worthy for simply existing? Tonight, that was more than enough.

"Stay with me tonight," she breathed into his mouth. "It's a lonely club being the grandchild of gods, but we don't have to be alone anymore."

He kissed her again. "I'm not supposed to want you like this," he murmured. "But I don't think I care anymore."

"Please stop caring," she whispered.

"We should go to your rooms so Dex doesn't lose his shit when he wakes."

She nodded, resting her head against his chest, her legs still wound tightly around his waist as he Traveled them.

She didn't have to be alone anymore.

36
EVIANA

Curled in the chair she'd dragged over to the window, she stared out at the falling snow. As much as she hated it, there was an odd comfort in being seated here. Some sort of normalcy that allowed her to simply...be. With Valter, that chair by the window meant she wasn't needed. There were no commands to follow or orders to carry out. Whenever he'd told her to go to her chair, a part of her would breathe a sigh of relief. Even if the respite was only for a minute. It was the singular thing she'd ever really considered her own.

Not even her flesh and blood was her own.

Eviana tipped her head back, letting her eyes fall closed. She slipped her hand in beside the cushion, feeling a large shard of the wine bottle she'd stashed there. Obviously it was still there. No one else had been in this room to take it, but she obsessively checked multiple times a day to make sure. And the one in the small dresser. The small pieces she'd carefully and painstakingly pressed into a thin shirt. It would do some damage if raked down bare flesh. There was the neck of the wine bottle under her bed, and the wineglasses themselves she'd hidden in the back of the small bathroom cabinet.

I am wasting away down here, my flower, came Valter's voice down the bond.

She didn't bother opening her eyes. Every time she was enjoying her solitude, he reminded her she was never truly alone.

They are not feeding you, my Lord?

Nothing of sustenance.

He meant nothing grand and fancy. He was likely receiving the food she was often served. Plain chicken and rice. Baked fish and vegetables. Not premium cuts of meat with expensive aged alcohol. It was the symbolism of it all for him, but to her, food was food.

Hopefully we will see each other soon, she consoled.

I have asked every day.

Thank you, my Lord.

He continued to ramble about the condition of the cell he was being held in, and she ran her finger over the smooth, flat side of the glass until she reached the edge. She pressed the tip of her finger to the jagged point. She felt nothing as she dragged her finger along it before lifting her hand to peer at the cut. Blood welled, running down her finger to her palm and dripping onto the pristine white chair. How much more blood would there be if she was dragging that piece of glass across Valter's throat?

And she'd say "Thank you, my Lord" as she watched him panic, unable to breathe. Unable to scream for help.

She frowned.

She couldn't do any of that until she made sure he was cut off from his magic. Otherwise it was pointless.

Which was annoying, but she had time.

Not as much as she used to have, but she had time.

A knock sounded, and Eviana found herself smiling. Not a big smile. Just the faintest tilt of her lips. Tessa had a specific knock. This was only her third time coming to see her, but she already recognized the sound. It was softer than a male knock, and there was a...buzzing to it. A vibrating energy. She didn't bother getting out of the chair this time, only lifted her head to watch the female breeze through the door.

The first thing she noticed was that Tessa's hair was pulled back today. It was half up with two combs. They were beautiful, if not a bit flashy. A silver crescent moon with black antlers on either side of them. The second thing she noticed was that Tessa was barefoot. That wasn't surprising. What had been surprising was the last time she'd shown up here, she'd been wearing boots. Tall black boots that laced up the front and had buckles on the sides, and they'd seemed a touch too big for her. She'd taken them off by the door before settling into the same chair as before, pouring herself a glass of wine from the new bottle she'd brought.

She'd conveniently forgotten to take those boots with her when she left, and even more coincidentally, they fit Eviana perfectly. Now those boots were hidden beneath a stack of blankets neatly folded at the end of the bed.

Tessa's hands were full, a pastry box in one hand and a wine bottle in the other. Placing everything down on the small end table, she pulled wineglasses from a swirl of magic before opening the pastry box and plucking out a doughnut with chocolate frosting.

"Want one?" Tessa asked, nudging the box an inch closer.

Eviana blinked at the sweets. Valter rarely allowed her such a thing. A piece of chocolate cake as a Winter Solstice gift. Desserts at special events, but that was it. She never really minded. Food was sustenance. Something needed to fuel her power. That was it. Some tasted better than others, but all of it served a purpose.

"How did you sneak away today?" Eviana asked, still in her chair and ignoring the pastries. She wouldn't drink the wine until after Tessa left either.

Tessa's smirk was all delighted mischief as she set the doughnut aside and said, "I've found dragons to be bigger than angels."

That was...a bizarre statement. The girl was full of those.

"Which dragon?" Eviana asked.

Tessa paused with her glass halfway to her lips. "What do you mean which dragon?"

Valter had told her Tessa had been visiting Xan, and she seemed far too clever not to have put it together yet.

When Eviana only held her stare, Tessa slowly set her glass aside, sitting up straighter. "Of course you know he's down there. Valter truly tells you everything, doesn't he?"

"Not everything," Eviana answered.

"Right. Your daughter," she said, sitting back once more and swiping up her glass, taking a healthy sip. Her nail tapped against the glass as she contemplated something or other. Then she said, "Do you know Lange and Corbin?"

"Two of the Fae Theon claimed early this Selection," Eviana said. "Valter was upset for a short period of time."

He'd been particularly rough with her that night. She'd still had bruises on her hips the next morning. Normally those healed within hours, but those had taken nearly two days.

Tessa set her glass aside again, pulling the combs from her hair and laying them on the sofa beside her. Running her fingers through the strands, she tugged on the ends a little as she said, "They are friends of mine. It is why he claimed them."

Eviana nodded.

"But I'm guessing after Valter looked into their information, he wasn't quite so upset anymore?" she added.

"I cannot tell you my Master's secrets," Eviana answered, letting Valter hear the words.

They are questioning you again? Valter demanded.

They are trying, but they never succeed.

Good, Eve. Very good.

She sighed, propping her chin in her hand while she watched Tessa. She hadn't worked out what these visits were for. Tessa truly appeared to come just to chat.

And leave her things.

"I know you can't betray Valter," Tessa said, picking up her wine once more. "I would never ask that of you knowing how he enjoys... correcting behavior."

She knew nothing.

She'd never experienced Valter's sick pleasure of inflicting pain in the name of punishment and correction. Theon had always shielded her. She'd always had someone who cared about her. Eviana could tell it was more than a Source bond the minute Theon brought her home to Arius House. The moment he'd tried to make a strike against his father at the mere mention of sharing Tessa. She'd had her vines wrapped around him, holding him hostage. She'd whispered to him how he was going to want to believe that Tessa loved him too when she finally gave in. He may have locked the girl in a wine cellar, but he would never dream of handing Tessa over to Julius and Mansel. He would have never let another carve into her flesh. Would never let another impregnate her and then tie her down while that babe was taken from her the moment she took her first breath.

He wouldn't use an innocent child to keep her in line.

"Can you speak of Cressida?" Tessa asked, snapping Eviana back to the present.

"What of her?" Eviana replied.

Tessa shrugged. "I rarely saw her with Valter outside of dinners. What does she do all day at Arius House?"

"You want to know of her daily activities?"

"I never see Rordan's wife either," Tessa said with a shrug.

"Their wives are matches for breeding children."

"I know *that*," she said. "But surely they must do something else?"

"I was always at Valter's side. I know little of Cressida's daily activities."

Tessa only hummed at that, taking another bite of her doughnut. "You've known Theon and Axel their entire lives, right?"

"Yes."

"And Luka?"

"His father was one of Valter's advisors for a short period of time."

"Interesting," Tessa mused.

"To some people, yes."

"How old is Valter anyway? I don't think he's as old as I believed."

"Why would you believe any different?" Eviana asked.

"Because I saw your file. I know how old you are, and if you were tagged to be his Source from a young age, he would still be in his first century of life," Tessa answered.

Eviana smirked. "So clever, yet so naïve."

"What does that mean?" Tessa asked, immediately defensive.

"Theon and Axel wouldn't know any better, I suppose. But I was not Valter's first Source."

Tessa's eyes widened. "His first Source died?"

"Yes."

"How?"

Eviana slipped her hand beside the cushion again, feeling the slice of the glass on her palm. "I don't know."

Tessa went quiet, and Eviana left her with her thoughts as she got lost in her own.

The first time she'd ever seen Valter, she'd been six years. She'd lived at the Celeste Estate. Mother Cordelia had even been her Estate Mother, just like Tessa. Eviana had never been allowed to be near the other children, and she'd never understood it. Not until decades later. Instead of sharing a room with several other females, she had a room with only one other. That female was also claimed for the Arius Kingdom during their Selection

Year, although Eviana never saw her again. When the others would be sent outside to play, she was given books to study and read. Her assessments were harsher right from the beginning. Even her attire had been different.

But when she was six years, seated at her own small table in the dining hall, a male had walked in. The entire hall had fallen silent. He was tall. Handsome. Hazel eyes and black hair. Power emanated from him, but he wasn't who had snagged her attention. It was the female Fae a step behind him. Her icy blonde hair was pin straight, and her eyes were the color of a clear sky. She was beautiful, and Eviana had immediately been enamored with her. Valter's gaze had slid over everyone, lingering on Eviana for what felt like a full minute before Mother Cordelia had led him through the hall.

She didn't see him again for ten years. Then his visits became more frequent, but he didn't speak to her until she was nineteen years. Her Selection Year would be when she was twenty. The female that followed him everywhere appeared more and more haunted each time Eviana saw her. Three months before the Selection Year was to begin, she disappeared all together. Two months before, she learned Valter planned to Select her as a replacement. One month before, she had a "trial run" with Valter. The night before her Emerging Ceremony was the night she was introduced to Mansel and Julius.

That was the night she gave in to the life the Fates had given her.

That was the night she died inside.

Became nothing but a vessel.

That was the night she stopped feeling anything.

That was the night it didn't matter what sins stained her name.

And the day that child was ripped away from her was the day she'd been reborn with a singular purpose.

"The Sirana Gala is next week," Tessa said, filling the silence.

"A frivolous night," Eviana replied. "Surely you are expected to fetch a fair sum."

"What?" Tessa asked with a frown.

Eviana rolled her eyes. The girl truly was naïve. "Sirana is the goddess of love and fertility, but the Legacy use it as an excuse for orgies and debauchery. The Sources are traditionally offered up for one night to the highest bidder. Then again, you are not a normal Source, so perhaps you will be spared such theatrics."

Tessa's wineglass slipped from her fingers, shattering on the floor as lightning flickered in her eyes. "The Lords and Ladies are all right with this?"

Eviana scoffed. "More coin for their accounts and securing coveted alliances? Yes. They are more than fine with the arrangements. Whose idea do you think it was? Offer something that is otherwise inaccessible, and the wealthy covet it as much as they covet riches. Lengthy contracts are agreed to, of course."

"Of course," Tessa parroted, clearly outraged by all of this.

Which was odd.

She'd been a part of the kingdom politics for months now. Why was any of this surprising to her?

"It is also when Match contracts are routinely announced for the year," Eviana added.

Tessa frowned. "Theon's was announced months ago."

"Because he is an heir, and Valter was proving a point. But it will still be acknowledged at the Gala."

"Right," Tessa murmured, drumming her fingers on the armrest of her chair.

"Theon was always different," Eviana said.

Tessa's fingers paused their rhythm. "What?"

"Theon," Eviana repeated. "Valter tried to mold him into a replica of himself, but Theon always resisted. I found it pointless, but he persisted."

"Are you trying to tell me that beneath it all, he is good?" Tessa asked doubtfully.

"No," Eviana scoffed. "There are no good Legacy in Devram. Only ones that try to justify their transgressions and balance them out with the occasional, almost decent, deed."

Tessa stood abruptly, careful to avoid the shards of glass at her feet. "Sorry about that. I will send someone to clean it."

"No need," Eviana answered.

"Is there anything you'd like me to try to bring you next time?"

"Next time?"

"Unless you wish me to stop visiting," Tessa added.

"You can do whatever you wish," Eviana said. "You are the one with freedom."

"What would you do if you had the same?"

"I don't."

Tessa nodded. "Lange and Corbin are quite trustworthy."

So many random things from her mouth.

"Until next time, Eviana," she all but sang before she left, the door clicking shut behind her.

Idly, Eviana wondered what Luka thought of her coming here. None of them cared for her, not that she could blame them. She'd inflicted Valter's wrath on them more times than she could count. Or she'd sat in her chair and watched, doing nothing. That was the difference between her and Theon, she supposed. While Theon tried to justify his sins, she simply didn't.

Interesting that Tessa had asked of Cressida though. The female must have slipped up to garner such attention.

Eviana uncoiled from her chair, the fresh cut on her palm still tender. The one on her finger was healing. Crossing the room, she picked up one of the hair combs. It was beautiful. The ends of the crescent moon were pointed, and the tips of the antlers were sharp enough to stab with.

Clever, cunning girl.

Picking up the other comb, she lifted the cushion of the chair and slid one beneath it. Then she wound her long hair up and used the other comb to secure it.

Truth be told, she would be a little disappointed if Tessa stopped coming to visit now. Disappointed but she'd move on. The female was providing her useful updates and information that she could potentially use later, and she was providing the same. She'd be lying if she said she wasn't doing so solely to lure her back here. And fine, the wine wasn't terrible.

Swiping up the bottle, she didn't bother with the other wineglass this time. She drank straight from the bottle when she went back to her chair and settled in.

The first time she'd laid eyes on Valter she'd been six years.

Three years ago, Valter had gone to the Serafina Estate and left her behind.

When Tessa had told her that was where *she* was, the pieces had all clicked into place.

Fifteen years.

That was how long she had before her Selection Year. To most immortals, fifteen years were nothing, but her immortal life suddenly had a countdown.

And she'd be damned if she crossed the Veil before Valter did.

She'd be damned if she crossed the Veil before that child was safe from any Legacy.

Because there were no good Legacy in Devram. Only those who tried to justify their transgressions and balance them out with the occasional, almost decent, deed. She had no such compunction. Whenever she found freedom, she'd leave more than a blood trail in her wake.

She'd leave her wrath.

37
THEON

"What's our story about Axel?" Luka asked as they strode up the stairs of the Pantheon to the Grand Hall where the Sirana Gala was being held.

"Same as the Selection Opening, I suppose," Theon answered, adjusting his bowtie. This was one of the few events that he wore a tuxedo for. The Sirana Gala and Match Ceremonies. That was about it. Selection events only required a suit, and that was his everyday attire.

"Don't you think we should vary the story a little?" Luka asked as they reached the third floor, the throng of people milling about becoming thicker.

"Saying he is taking care of some matters in the Underground is plausible," Theon argued. "And if we're keeping up appearances, it fits the best."

Keeping up appearances.

That was what they were doing now. It was why Luka was at his side. It was why they'd be meeting his mother inside the hall at their designated table, and it was why he stopped to register for an auction number before he entered the hall. He'd never once bid on anything being offered, but again, they needed to keep up appearances. He'd have to bid on *something* to contribute to the new Sirana Villas, which is what the Gala was always for. Funds collected went to supporting the Villas, and this year, they needed more funds than ever to rebuild after Tessa's *alleged* destruction. He didn't give two fucks if the Sirana Villas were rebuilt. He just wanted the people in his kingdom to live in peace. If that meant keeping up appearances and forging advantageous alliances, then that was what he would do.

He and Luka wove their way through the crowd, people parting for an heir. They were handed flutes of champagne along the way. Theon hated the stuff, but he took a drink anyway. Tradition and all that. The tables were always arranged the same, but when the round table with seating for eight came into view, he paused, and his eyes narrowed. He knew his mother would be here. That was a given. What he was not expecting was to see Felicity Davers seated at their table, chatting casually with her.

That scene had him knocking back the entire flute of champagne. He signaled for a Fae waiter to bring him whiskey instead, Luka taking the empty flute from him and passing them off to another waiter.

"What the fuck is she doing here?" Theon hissed.

"She *is* your Match. The contract still stands," Luka supplied. "She didn't say anything to you about this?"

She probably would have if he ever took her calls.

His mother spotted him then, her smile wide. Felicity looked up, smiling as well, and Theon clenched his jaw. There was no denying she was beautiful. Her shiny brown hair was pulled up in an elegant twist, her brown eyes sweeping over him. She wore a classy black and silver gown. Arius Kingdom colors. She looked every part the Match of the Arius Heir, and once again, he had to keep up appearances.

He closed the distance to their table just as the waiter brought his new glass of liquor. Glass in one hand, he bent to kiss Cressida on the cheek.

"Mother," he greeted tightly before turning to his Match. "Miss Davers."

"Felicity is more than fine, your grace," Felicity said as she stood and bowed to Theon.

He smiled tightly, leaning in to press a small kiss to her cheek as she stood.

"I know you have been so busy these last weeks with your father absent," she said softly, waiting to reclaim her seat until Theon had taken his. "Has there been any luck in locating him or your brother?"

"No," he answered sharply.

"If there is anything I can do to help, you know to simply say the word, right?" Felicity asked, her hand landing lightly on his forearm.

He looked down at it. Her touch was all wrong, and it made him want to throw her hand off him. At that moment though, the Serafina Lady appeared with her husband.

"Theon," she greeted with a mocking lilt. "So glad you could tear yourself away from your busy schedule to join us."

His smile was sharp as he stood to speak with her, his mother and Felicity standing as well. "Lady Isleen, you look beautiful this evening," he replied.

Her smile was as mocking as her words before her silver eyes slid to his mother. "Cressida. Lovely to see you as always. I am so sorry to hear Valter's whereabouts are still unknown."

Cressida's smile was as sharp as Theon's. "I have never underestimated him before. I wouldn't start now."

Lady Isleen only returned the smile before her gaze moved on to Felicity with interest. "And you must be Theon's Match."

"Felicity Davers," Theon said. "Felicity, meet Lady Maya Isleen and her husband, Tovin."

"It is a pleasure, my lady," Felicity replied immediately, bowing her head.

Then she stepped forward and interlaced her fingers with Theon's.

It took every ounce of self-control not to rip his hand out of hers.

"I look forward to seeing much more of both of you," the Serafina Lady said before taking her leave.

Theon understood the double meaning. He was expected to be in attendance at more Devram meetings and events. In short, he was expected to perform all the duties of a Lord without the actual title.

Felicity's other hand came to his forearm as she leaned into him, and the muscle in his jaw ticked.

"I'll get you another one of those," Luka muttered, taking his empty liquor glass from his hand.

He didn't even remember drinking that.

Luka disappeared into the crowd, but before Theon could take his seat again, his mother was chiding him. "Go around and introduce Felicity to the others, Theon. This is important."

"How is any of this important?" Theon retorted.

Cressida's eyes widened. "All of this is important. Not just rebuilding those Villas, but maintaining our alliances. Honestly Theon, I thought your father had prepared you better for this role." She swiped up her flute of champagne. "Our entire way of life is at stake. It is your job as an acting Lord to help maintain that. And *she*," she went on with a pointed look at Felicity, "is here to help with that. It is her role as your Match."

Theon wasn't entirely sure what to say. This was the most his mother had ever spoken about the politics of Devram, but he suddenly realized she'd been paying far more attention than he'd thought.

"The Celeste Lady is across the room. Start there," Cressida said before she was off to greet others she knew.

He looked down at Felicity. The female smiled nervously up at him.

"I am here to make your life easier, Theon," she said in a low whisper. "Whatever you need of me."

What he needed was for her to stop fucking touching him, but that clearly wasn't an option tonight. He gave her a tight smile, adjusting his arm so she could slide her hand to the crook of his elbow, before leading her over to the Celeste Lady and her husband. Luka appeared a few minutes later, handing off another drink and keeping close. Theon tried to stay focused on the conversations he was holding as they moved about the room, but Felicity never stopped touching him. She was always holding his hand or brushing her fingers along his arm. The wrongness of it all kept him thoroughly distracted, which is why he didn't realize it when Tristyn Blackheart joined them. Probably because the male had stopped using his infamous glamours as of late. Ever since Tessa's power had emerged, he hadn't been nearly as preoccupied with keeping his identity a secret.

Tristyn hadn't so much joined them, as he had come over to speak into Luka's ear. Luka's emotions spiked down the bond, his entire body tensing, but before Theon could ask, the air in the room changed. It became charged with energy, and he didn't need the bond to know something powerful was approaching. Not something, but someone.

What he wasn't expecting was her arm to be looped through another's.

That wasn't Rordan or Dex. That wasn't Dagian or Brecken.

That was Liam Vance.

The male was an Achaz Legacy, a distant nephew of Rordan, and his family oversaw the seaside city of Astown Port. Tall and thin, his blond hair was dark with brown undertones making it look muddy next to Tessa's shining golden hair. His brown eyes were ringed in gold, and right now those eyes were dancing with arrogance at the attention he was receiving with Tessa on his arm. Nevermind none of the attention was for him. It was all for her in that dress.

That fucking dress.

Intricate floral detailing was strategically woven among the sheer bodice that hugged her upper body. With open shoulder details and quarter sleeves, the back was open as she turned to someone who said her name. The rest of her sleek skirt draped to the floor in panels with a sweeping train that glimmered as the light hit it. He knew her heels had to be at least six inches, and he knew part of the reason she was still clutching his arm was so she didn't fall in the things.

"I just found out," Luka said, his eyes flicking to Felicity.

"Found out what?" Theon ground out.

Felicity's hand fluttered down his back in what he was sure she thought was a soothing motion, and Luka looked pointedly at her, telling Theon whatever he wanted to say couldn't be said in front of her. If they used the bond, Tessa would hear, and Theon wasn't sure if this was news she should hear right now either.

Liam and Tessa followed Rordan to their table on the opposite end of the room from his own. Theon didn't care about mingling anymore. He only wanted another drink and to eat. To get this godsdamn night over with.

He was staring at her—as if he could do anything else when she was in the room—so he knew the moment she finally looked at him. Violet eyes connected with his before they slid to Felicity and narrowed. The only thing he felt down the bond was Tessa reinforcing her shields.

There was nothing they could do but return to their own table when it was signaled dinner was ready to be served. Fae pulled their chairs out for them, and Felicity's fingers brushed along the back of his hand while they sat.

The soup course was served, and as was customary, a Sirana Legacy stepped up onto the dais to announce the year's Match Contracts. With it being a Selection Year, the list was considerably shorter than most years. Theon was the only heir with a contract announced, which wasn't surprising. Selection years were always quieter. The kingdoms were focused on the new Fae they would be choosing from at the end of the year, and since no Match Ceremonies could be completed during the year, the rest of the Legacy took their time with the required paperwork.

He couldn't help but look over at Tessa when his contract was announced, only to see Liam with his arm draped along the back of her chair. Tessa didn't seem happy about it, but she didn't seem *unhappy* either. Her elbow was propped on the table, her chin in her palm. She looked bored, which was a dangerous thing for her. It was when she got into trouble. He knew that better than anyone.

"We have one final Match to announce," the female said from the dais. Theon had stopped listening, eating his soup mechanically. "While we normally only announce official contracts, Lord Jove felt it would be in the best interest of everyone to share that another contract is close to being reached."

You need to keep your cool until we know what's really going on, Luka said down the bond.

Tessa's head turned slowly to them, violet eyes narrowing from across the room as she listened in.

Why would I care about an Achaz Match Contract? Theon asked.

Luka's gaze was fixed on Tessa too, and whatever he saw there, had him speaking to her directly. *Baby girl, you need to keep yourself under control too.*

Her lips thinned, and she returned her attention to the Sirana Legacy who was speaking again. "Lord Jove expects this contract to be signed in the next few days, so he felt comfortable announcing the Match of Liam Vance, Achaz Legacy, and Tessalyn Ausra, Achaz Legacy."

The uproar from the Ladies was immediate, and Tessa's head whipped to Rordan. The light on her wrists was flaring so brightly, Theon had to look away. When he turned back, that light was winding up her arms. The Lord was both incredibly stupid and utterly brilliant to announce that pairing here. The Ladies wouldn't make a huge scene here, despite their initial outrage, and Tessa was already on her last chance with everyone. If she lost her shit here, it would only confirm to the Ladies she needed to be dealt with. This was proving to *everyone* that the Achaz Lord still had control.

Over everything.

Tessa sat back in her seat, a glare Theon had been on the receiving end more than once was directed at Liam when he leaned in to speak to her. Theon could see her eyes glowing brightly from across the room. Her shields had slipped, and he could feel her working to keep herself under control. All those times he'd berated her for not controlling herself, and she had been doing her best. Just like now. Only now he could *feel* it all. Every bit of the turmoil and the restraint and the *fury*.

We'll fix this, little storm, he tried to console down the bond.

You and Felicity? she sneered in return.

His hand tightened around his liquor glass as he leaned back for the wait staff to replace his soup bowl with his main meal.

Glad to hear your snark, beautiful.

The light around her arms sparked, and Luka was kicking him under the table.

Don't fucking antagonize her right now, he chided.

But gods, this was the most she'd spoken to him in weeks, and she very rarely spoke to him down the bond unless *she* was antagonizing *him*. He'd do almost anything to keep hearing her voice.

But her shields were already back up, the moment gone. Now he was in an even worse mood that was not helped when Felicity shifted closer, leaning in to speak.

Her hand once again landed on his arm when she said in a low voice, "I take it Tessa did not inform you of this development?"

"Tessa didn't know," he retorted.

She frowned. "Are you sure? I have seen them together more than once."

Theon slowly turned to her, every muscle in his body going rigid. Was that Tessa's real issue? That it had been revealed before she was ready? That she had wanted to use this secret to her advantage, and now that had been blown? The more he thought about it, the more it made sense.

Picking up his cutlery to cut into his steak, he said, "Where have you seen them?"

Luka had shifted, clearly listening in on the conversation. Why hadn't Luka told him about any of this? Probably because Theon had told him not to tell him anything. He was just doing as he'd asked, and now here he was, blindsided.

"Most recently at a luncheon together," Felicity answered, finally not touching him as she worked on her own meal.

The absence of her touch had some part of him relaxing, able to think more clearly. "Were they alone?" Theon asked.

"No. There are always Fae with them."

"Dex," Luka whispered under his breath.

"What does it matter?" his mother cut in, also apparently listening in on the conversation. "As soon as this messy bond is taken care of, you can claim a new Source, she can go to Achaz Kingdom where she belongs, and you can start focusing on the things that matter."

"Like kingdom politics?" he all but sneered.

"Like finding your brother," she retorted with a sharp smile.

Theon ground his molars. He hadn't figured out how to break it to his mother that her favored son was not only becoming a vampyre but likely wouldn't be back any time soon. He still hadn't figured out how to track him down, let alone what he was going to say to him to convince him he could still live at home, even as a Night Child. There was no way in all the realms he was going to banish him to the Underground, especially when their father was the very reason he was facing this fate.

The rest of the dinner conversation was short and tense. While they ate dessert, Rordan announced the new overseer of Rosebell and shared what was being done to rebuild the villas and increase security so something like this never happened again. New wards. Tighter protection measures. All things that wouldn't matter for someone like Tessa. The entire time he spoke, Theon refused to look at her table. Refused to see Liam with his arm around her shoulders. Refused to acknowledge her at all.

After dessert was finished, the floor was cleared, leaving only the six tables for the ruling families. Everyone else would be made to mill about or use the sparse seating set up along the perimeter of the room. But there was no ignoring her when the newly announced Match pairs were instructed to take the dance floor. Tradition mandated they open the dance portion of the evening by sharing the first dance.

He held Felicity stiffly, but she didn't seem to care. Not as she pressed herself against his chest, one of her hands gently slipping around to cup the back of his neck. Her fingers toyed with the short strands at his nape as they moved.

"I know you are upset by the events of the evening, Theon," she said quietly. "Tell me what I can do to help?"

"Nothing," he said flatly.

"I'm trying here," she insisted. "But I need you to guide me. I want to be the perfect Match for you. I want to be a wife you'll be glad to have at your side, but you need to teach me, Theon."

Teach her.

Isn't this exactly what he'd told Tessa he wanted? Just do as she was told. Listen and obey. Here was a female laying all that at his feet, offering up that very behavior, and he didn't want it. All he wanted was her wildness and her impulsiveness. He wanted to be challenged just enough. He wanted to take care of someone not because she needed it, but because she *didn't*.

Gods, how had everything become so godsdamn fucked?

The song ended, and before he could extricate himself from Felicity, Tristyn was there.

"May I dance with the Arius Lord's Match?" Tristyn asked, the question poised to Theon. His gaze flicked to the side almost imperceptibly, but Theon saw it. He followed the look to see Tana, the Anala Heir, intercepting Liam and Tessa.

"Of course," Theon said, handing Felicity over.

Tessa was just reaching the edge of the dance floor when he caught up to her. He grabbed her hand, pulling her back and spinning her around.

He anticipated the shocks that assaulted him, knowing he had startled her, but the bond was vibrating just as violently at touching her after going so long without.

"What are you doing?" she hissed, but she didn't fight. She let him pull her back onto the dance floor, and there was no stiffness in his hold this time. She settled into him like she belonged there, a hand smoothing up his chest before reaching to slide around the nape of his neck. Her thumb brushed up and down along his throat, and he wondered if she even realized she was doing that. The back of her dress dipped low, giving him access to bare flesh where his hand sat on the small of her back, while his other clutched hers to his chest.

"Dancing with my Source," Theon said simply.

"You mean I'm dancing with *my* Source," she retorted.

He arched a brow. "Are you claiming me, little storm?"

"No," she guffawed.

"But you are claiming *Liam?*"

Her eyes snapped to his, lightning flickering among the grey and violet. "I hardly know him."

"Yet you're about to agree to a Match Contract?"

Her lips pressed together, and her gaze slid to something over his shoulder. She moved imperceptibly closer, as if seeking him out for comfort.

Still holding her hand, he extended a finger to touch her chin, bringing her eyes back to his. "Tessa, are you not going into this contract willingly?"

"Did you go into your contract with Felicity willingly?" she countered.

"No, beautiful. I did it to save you."

"You keep saying that," she said. "But—" She cut herself off, shaking her head a little as if trying to clear her thoughts. "Can we not do this tonight?"

"Do what?"

"Fight."

"You promised it would always be a battle," he said, pulling her even closer, eliminating any ounce of space between them.

"It is," she murmured, more to herself than him. "Just not the battle I was anticipating."

She fell silent, and he could have pushed her, but gods, he just wanted to enjoy holding her. The gods-only-knew when she was ever going to allow such a thing again.

He bent down so his lips brushed the shell of her ear when he whispered, "You look stunning tonight, Tessa."

He could swear a soft cry came from her, but her brow was pressed to his shoulder. The bond. She was soaking it up as much as he was.

"Come home," he murmured. "Please, Tessa. Just...come home. We'll fix all of this. Figure it out. I'll—"

"Can a mother interrupt to dance with her son?"

Theon looked up to find Cressida waiting expectantly, Tessa's head snapping up at the intrusion.

"Of course," she said, all her softness bleeding away, but Theon caught the glimmer in her eyes. The thin pools of silver that he watched her blink away as she let her light swirl around her like a golden mist. It called to his darkness, and he let it go, wisps of dark rushing out to greet her.

Then she turned and walked away from him.

Again.

"Mother," Theon said, not bothering to hide his displeasure as the next song started.

"You need to stay away from her," Cressida hissed, not hiding her own displeasure either.

"She is my Source."

"But she is not supposed to be," she snapped. "And when this is all taken care of, you need to be ready to move on."

"When this is all taken care of?" Theon repeated.

"You know what I mean. When you fix all this."

"Right," he muttered, certain that wasn't what she'd meant at all.

He was kept on the dance floor for the next three songs, finally getting a reprieve when it was announced the auction would begin soon.

That was when he saw her slipping out a side door. If he had to guess, it was the same side door she'd slipped out of on the night of the opening Selection Ceremony. He followed, because at this point, he'd follow her anywhere.

Stepping into the hall, his suspicions were confirmed, which meant he knew exactly where to find her. He didn't need the bond or a Tracking Mark. His footfalls echoed down the deserted hallway until he came to an alcove.

And tucked back into its shadows, he found a female. There was no chocolate in her hand this night. Only two tear tracks down her face that she quickly wiped away.

"We're meant to destroy each other," she whispered, the words pained and agonized.

"Then destroy me, little storm."

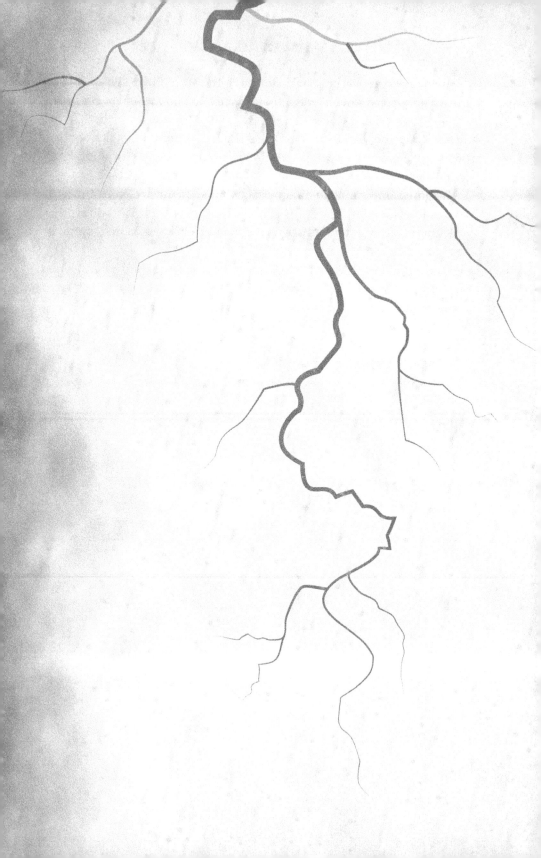

38
TESSA

Then destroy me, little storm.

She stared at him as his words echoed in her mind. Destroy him. It was what she was supposed to do. Her purpose. Her ticket out of this world for the rest of her immortal years. She wasn't a Fae or a Legacy. She didn't belong here. But she wasn't a goddess or a deity. She was...alone. Even if Luka was similar to her, he had a place here. She still didn't. She belonged nowhere.

And then Rordan had pulled that shit with Liam. Gods. She'd suspected he was going to push for this after the second time he'd arranged a luncheon for them, but to announce it tonight? In front of everyone? In front of Theon? That shouldn't matter to her. It *didn't* matter to her. What did matter to her was being used as a power display before the realms.

Everyone only wanted her for her power.

To take from her.

Use her.

Theon was silent where he stood, blocking the alcove from view. His emerald eyes searched her, waiting for her to make the next move.

"What do you want from me?" she rasped, because at this point, she honestly didn't know. Not anymore.

"Whatever you'll give me, Tessa."

"Nothing," she spat. "I only want to take. Just like this realm, the worlds, the stars, only want to take from me."

"Perfect, little storm, because I'll give you anything you want."

As it always was with them, she didn't know who moved first. She only knew she was pulling his mouth to hers while he was pushing her up against the wall. The cool stone of the Pantheon pressed into her back in perfect contrast to her heated skin and Theon's hot mouth. Kissing Luka was willingly giving him a piece of her. Kissing Theon was willingly letting him *possess* her, and that was exactly what he did.

His tongue prodded at the seam of her lips, demanding access, and she let him in, needing the distraction from this night. He knew what she needed, and Luka clearly knew she needed to let someone else have control tonight. Knew that tonight she didn't want to ask for anything. She just *needed*.

As though he was aware of everything happening in this alcove, Luka's voice drifted down the bond. *I'm watching the doors to the hall.*

Even with that reassurance, she felt Theon's dark magic wrap around them. The shadows she was tucked back into deepened just as Theon deepened the kiss. Tongues tangled for dominance, but she didn't know why she was trying to fight. The bond was elated. Her magic was elated. Her entire being was elated. Because she needed them both, and gods, she wished she understood why. But like Razik had said, she wasn't supposed to exist. Everything was altered because of her crossed bloodlines. Wouldn't it make sense that what *this* was would be different from the rest of the realms too?

His tongue became rough, the kiss turning sharp and fast. It was all teeth and demand, and a small part of her screamed at giving him this. After everything he had done, she shouldn't be letting him have any piece of her, but that was just it. He *wasn't* demanding or forcing this. He'd waited for her, and she'd let herself fall into him, knowing the pleasure he would give her. Knowing that he would take care of her. Knowing she didn't need to worry about this one simple thing. In this alcove, it was okay to simply exist.

Theon's hand slipped to the back of her neck, the grip tight and possessive, and she nipped his bottom lip, feeling his groan all the way down to her core.

"I've missed you, little storm," he gasped into her mouth, forcing her to swallow the words.

"I still have to destroy you," she rasped, her head falling back. It hit the wall, but his hand was already sliding up from her neck, creating a buffer between her and the stone. His fingers curled into her hair, ruining the sleek updo it had painstakingly been wound into that night, but she was too lost to her emotions to notice.

With a small tug, he tilted her head back more and to the side, making room for him as he kissed down her neck, sucking and biting the tender skin. This was absolutely going to leave a mark. He knew it. She knew it. And a thrill went through her at the idea of openly defying every fucking thing Devram stood for. At saying fuck you to all their traditions. At shoving their power plays and politics up their asses. She just never thought she'd be doing all that with Theon.

His tongue swirled over the raw spot he'd left behind, a whimper coming from her mouth.

"Shh," he soothed. "I always know what you need, tempest."

Then his mouth was back on hers, any lingering thoughts disappearing as the hand gripping her hip slid up. He palmed her breast through her dress, and she suddenly hated that there was anything between their skin. She knew what those hands could do, which is why her breath hitched when he slid it back down. His fingers traced the delicate design of the corset top, leaving a branding trail of heat and need down her side, and when he started gathering the skirt of her dress, she couldn't stop the pleased moan that came from her.

She felt him smile against her mouth as he broke the kiss, sliding his lips to her ear. "I know Luka is watching the doors and my magic is creating a barrier, but you still need to be quiet, Tessa."

But when his fingers finally slipped beneath her dress and found the bare skin of her thigh, it was his breathing that stuttered. And when those fingers dragged up and were met with wet heat, he was the one groaning. "No undergarments, little storm?"

"This dress isn't made to be worn with undergarments. Lines would show," she panted.

"You and these fucking dresses will be my destruction," he murmured.

Tessa held her breath, waiting to see what he was going to do next, the tension so thick between them, she could taste it. Holding her stare, his thumb slid along her entrance again, gathering her slickness before moving up to circle her clit. Her whimper was almost pained.

"You know what I want to hear, Tessa," he said, his voice a dark rumble she felt vibrate through her.

She shook her head in refusal.

A soft, dark smile curled on his lips. "One day you will say it."

"How can you still possibly believe that?" she gasped when he circled his thumb again.

"Because it's more than a bond."

Then she was crying out as he sank two fingers inside her, but it was quickly muffled by his hand sliding over her mouth. "I love hearing you, beautiful, but we have to keep it down."

She tried to glare, but couldn't muster it as he pumped his fingers in and out again. Her eyes rolled back, pleasure coursing through her, and she rocked into him, seeking more. Her magic thrashing to reach for him, the bond was intensifying everything.

"I will never tire of watching you take what you want from me," he murmured, something akin to awe shining in his eyes.

"More pretty words," she breathed.

"When will you realize I never lie to you?" The addition of a third finger kept her from answering as his hand muffled another cry. "I've come to collect what is mine. Give it to me, Tessa."

She shattered around him, giving him exactly what he'd demanded from her. No thinking. No plotting. No secrets. Just pure pleasure. Just pure existing.

When she came down from her high, her brow was pressed to his chest, and he tilted her chin up to claim her mouth once more. He acted as if he thought he'd never get to do this again.

Maybe he was right.

"You're my source," she panted against his lips.

"Are you finally claiming me as yours, beautiful?" he asked between the small kisses he was peppering along her jaw.

She shook her head. "You're my source of everything I hate."

He went utterly still, pulling back to peer at her. "Tessa, I—"

But he stopped when she pressed a finger to his lips to silence him.

"You are my source of everything I hate about this realm, but you are also my source of the things I crave. You are the source of what broke me, but you are also the source of what saved me. You are the source of my fury, but you are also the source of every dark desire. You are the source of what I have become, but you are also a source of complete acceptance of who that person is. You are the source of my own self-discovery, and how twisted is that, Theon?" she demanded, his emerald eyes staring back at her with a mixture of shock and tenderness. "How wrong is it that you are the source of everything that has happened these last weeks, months—that I loathe you so deeply in my soul—yet here I am?" Her power flared, lighting up the alcove where his darkness swirled around them. He sucked in a sharp breath at their magic mingling. "How wrong is it that I am light, and yet I crave the dark?"

"Because you are light and dark, Tessa," he said, resolve sounding in each word. "You need both to have balance."

"I do not understand how I can hate someone so much and still want them," she went on. "You are the source of every confusing thought and frustrating want."

"The bond makes things—"

"It's more than a bond," she interrupted, her frustration climbing as she said those words, knowing they would damn her. Her next words were a whisper. "It's always been more than a bond."

She heard his sharp inhale of breath a second before he was gripping the back of her thighs and lifting her off her feet. Her legs wrapped around his waist as he rocked into the cradle of her hips. His cock strained against his pants, pressing to her center, and she moaned into his neck.

"I don't understand it," she said, the words raw and agonized. "I don't understand any of it."

"I know, Tessa," he murmured. "I'm trying to find the answers for you."

"You mean for you," she panted when he rocked into her again.

"No, little storm. I mean exactly what I said. For *you*."

"Why?"

"Because I know you want them. Need them. And I will always give you what you need," he answered, easily holding her up with one hand while the other reached up to smooth a strand of hair out of her face.

It didn't matter. She lurched forward again, her mouth taking his this time. He groaned into her while her hands slid along his arms, his chest, his torso. Anywhere she could touch. Her fingers brushed over the cool metal of his belt buckle, and she started trying to unfasten it. It was seconds before she let out a frustrated growl and tiny sparks of energy went flying.

"Easy, beautiful," he murmured. "Let's not have that power flaring so close to sensitive areas."

She couldn't help her huff of laughter, but when he lowered her to her feet, that huff turned into a discontented whine that she should have been embarrassed about.

Theon made quick work of his belt, unbuttoning his pants and lowering his zipper before bunching up the skirt of her dress again. Within seconds, he had her hoisted up once more, and she nearly sighed when he rocked against her bare center.

She wished she was touching bare flesh as her hand slid down his chest again before it slipped into his undergarments and wrapped around his length. She pulled out his cock, lightly scraping her nails along it and relishing his muttered curse. Her lineage made her one of the most powerful beings in Devram, but this? Having the source of so much...*everything* at her mercy? Having control over him with the mere touch of her hand? The barest brush of her lips? *That* made her feel more powerful than anything. Taking power back from someone who had taken so much from her. A part of her recognized that was twisted and wrong, and it made her just as terrible as him. A bigger part of her didn't care. Because she had become his villain, and he still kept coming back for her. Again and again and again.

Just like he'd promised.

"Please, Theon," she whispered, knowing exactly what the begging was going to get her.

He groaned again, sliding the head of his cock through her wetness before thrusting inside her with one smooth movement. Her head tipped back, and it was only then that she realized his magic was cushioning her back against the wall.

No.

Not just his magic.

His shadow wings had formed and were wrapped around them. Feathers of swirling darkness kept the stone wall from digging into her back as she clung to his shoulders. Last time she'd taken her pleasure from him; this time, she would let him give it to her.

And he did.

Each thrust had her climbing higher. The thought of him losing control with her, for her and only her, had her dropping her brow to his shoulder to muffle her cries. She let him have this, have her. She knew he wondered when she would let him have her like this again, but the truth was, *she* didn't know if they'd ever have this again. Because he had Felicity, and she was supposed to have Liam.

"Stay with me, Tessa," he rasped into her ear, each word a guttural grunt.

He sank into her again, adjusting his hold on her to hit a spot just right that had her sucking in a breath.

"That's it," he urged. "You know I'll always give you what you need. At least in this one thing, you trust me."

She knew he hadn't meant to say those thoughts aloud, but he was right. She knew when she needed to get lost to pleasure and not think about anything, she could go to him. She'd known he would follow her out here. Known he would find her. Because he would always find her.

And when his darkness reached out and caressed her, scraping along her throat, her breasts, her thighs, she let her magic out too. Felt the light latch onto the dark. Felt all of it shudder around her. Or maybe that was his body. Her head tipped back once more, and he was there, his mouth capturing hers and swallowing her cry as she came. He followed her into pleasure. If there had been any doubt about where they'd slipped off to, there wouldn't be now. Their scents were inter-twined. Their magic.

Every part of them.

He dropped his head to the crook of her neck, still holding her up as he worked to steady his breathing. After a minute or two, he slowly lowered her to the ground, setting her onto shaky legs.

"Are you all right?" he asked, peering at her with concern.

Tessa nodded, her hands slipping from him. She pulled them behind her back, leaning against them as he tucked himself away before moving to retrieve her shoes. He dropped to a knee before her, gently taking her foot and placing it into a shoe, buckling the strap around her ankle.

You two need to finish up. Felicity keeps glancing towards the hall, and Rordan is not happy right now, came Luka's warning.

"Still not mine," Tessa whispered, running her fingers through Theon's hair as he reached for her other shoe.

He stilled, looking up at her. "I am yours, Tessa. Every piece of me."

Her smile was grim. "No, Theon. You are hers."

"I will never be hers," he retorted, and she watched his entire body tense while he finished buckling her other shoe before pushing back to his full height.

"Even the villains and the monsters fall to fate," she said.

He took her face in his hands. "If there is anything I have learned about my Arius bloodline these last months, it is that we do not much care for fate, little storm." He bent, brushing his lips across hers before he added, "And you are just as much death as you are life. Denying it is only harming you, beautiful." One more light kiss to her temple. "I'll go back first. Come back when you're ready."

She didn't.

She made her way to the same balcony Luka had found her on the night of the Selection Ceremony, and she stayed there until someone finally came to take her back to Faven.

She ran her hands through her hair now that it was fully down. Her fingers tangled in the ends as she tugged on them, feeling the burn in her scalp. She didn't even realize that Luka had appeared in her room until he spoke.

"Tessa?"

She whirled around, light filled with gold and silver embers swirling around her. "What?"

He looked her up and down, concern etched into his features. "You've been back for nearly an hour, and you haven't changed. You still have your shoes on."

She looked down at her dress, pulling up her skirt to peer at her feet that were indeed still in heels. Had she truly been back in Faven for an entire hour?

Luka had changed out of his tuxedo and into loose pants and a short-sleeve shirt that clung to every muscle. Just like muscles she'd traced through fabric mere hours ago.

No!

No, no, no.

She tugged on her hair again as she turned away from him, pacing across the floor.

It was another few seconds before he growled, "Tessa, stop."

But there was no stopping. Because she hadn't been confused before tonight. Well, not *this* confused. She'd had firm control over this gods-damn bond. Shoved all the unnecessary burdens of it so deep, they'd become background noise. She was an expert at repressing feelings, and that was what she'd needed to do to focus on her purpose. Do what needs to be done and show no remorse. That was what villains did. That was what—

"Tessa, stop."

The words were gentler this time, and they were accompanied by words just as soft down the bond.

Breathe, little storm.

She took a shuddering breath, but any tension that was ebbing from her body stopped abruptly when the door was thrown open. Oralia strode in, her features pinched with displeasure and annoyance.

"What is he doing in here, Tessa?" she asked, her hands on her hips as she glared at Luka.

"Where is Dex?" Tessa asked instead.

"The Achaz Lord wanted to discuss some things with him after your display at the gala this evening," she answered with a pointed look. "So I was sent to stay with you tonight."

"Get out."

Oralia clicked her tongue in annoyance. "You did this, Tessa. Once again, Dex is trying to fix—"

But she was cut off by Tessa's hand wrapping around her throat and squeezing. A glow emitted from between her fingers as her power appeared, Oralia gasping under her hold. The female's hands came up, clawing at Tessa's wrist, but Tessa only smiled.

"Dexter does not need to fix anything, and I do not require anyone to watch me anymore. *That* is what you can report back to Rordan," Tessa said, an icy calm settling over her.

She loosened her grip just enough to let Oralia splutter, "The Achaz Lord wants someone with you at all times."

"You can tell him that after what *he* pulled tonight, if he wants to come to detain me, he can certainly try. But unless he comes here himself, there will be no one else watching my every move," Tessa replied. "Get. Out."

Energy spiked from her fingertips at the same time she let her magic sink into Oralia, taking and feeding. The female's supposed Fae power of water never appeared, and Tessa waited, hoping whatever magic she'd stolen would show itself. After several seconds of nothing, Tessa released her with a shove.

"This is your fate," Oralia sneered, pressing a hand to her throat.

"And you're about to alter yours if you don't get the fuck out of my rooms," Tessa replied, one of the bands at her wrist winding down her fingers before unfurling into a whip.

Oralia scurried from the room, the door slamming shut behind her, and Tessa sank to the floor. She reached for the heels, unbuckling them before throwing them across the space. Then she flopped onto her back, stacking her hands on her stomach.

She started when sapphire eyes peered down at her. She'd forgotten Luka was in here.

"Are you planning on changing tonight? Or are you sleeping in that dress?"

"I need a minute," she answered, suddenly exhausted by the events and emotions of the last few hours.

Luka nodded, disappearing from her line of sight, and she closed her eyes. It felt like mere seconds had passed when Luka spoke again.

"It's been ten minutes, baby girl. Let's get you changed."

Her eyes fluttered open to find him crouched beside her, a shirt in his hand. He pulled her to her feet, handing over the clothing before he unzipped the side zipper on her dress. She made her way to the bathroom to change, wash the makeup from her face, and brush her teeth. Then she crawled into bed where he was already waiting for her.

"Do you want to talk about tonight?" he asked, his fingers combing through her hair.

"Theon and I fucked in an alcove."

"I'm aware."

"Am I..."

"Are you what?" Luka asked when she trailed off.

"I don't know how to feel. About anything. None of this... I don't..." She trailed off again.

"You have to face it some time, Tessa."

"I don't know how."

"Which parts?"

"All of it," she whispered. "What I am. My purpose. What I should do. How I should do it. Devram. My lineage. This power I never asked for. Dex. Oralia. Brecken. Tristyn. Axel and Kat. Lange and Corbin. Rordan. Valter. Eviana. Me. I don't know how to face myself," she finally admitted. "I am wild and untamed. I am uncontrollable. I am utter chaos."

His hand never stopped moving through her hair while she spoke, but when she fell silent, Luka said, "It helps to talk things through with someone you trust, but you have said so yourself, you trust no one. Take things one at a time. You cannot simply ignore them and seek out distractions. Not anymore. Chaos or not, you still control your path."

"Salvation or destruction," she murmured, eyes growing heavy.

"And Theon and I? We'll wait."

"Both of you?"

"Yes."

"And you are all right with that?"

"Yes."

"What if it *is* both of you?"

She felt his smile as he pressed his lips to the top of her head. "We'll wait for you to figure it out."

Her hair whipped around her as she clung to the horse's mane, her thighs squeezing tight. Nylah and Roan ran with them, somehow keeping pace with the horse. She had no idea how to ride a horse. She'd only been on one with Theon, but the horse had shown up when she'd been desperate. One of Theon's own prized stallions. With no saddle or bridle, he'd lowered beside her so she could climb on. Then he was up and racing, her only option to cling to his mane, but the horse seemed to know she didn't know what she was doing.

"No one is coming to save you this time, Tessalyn," a dark voice echoed around her. "You killed them all, just as I needed you to."

A voice she knew.

Achaz.

He was here.

"Faster, Eyal," she urged, and as if the horse could understand her, he raced onward over the rocky terrain.

Her wolves were growling and snapping as Hunters descended, no longer answering to her. Her magic flared, lashing out, but it wasn't nearly as strong as it should be. When had death last taken?

She screamed when Eyal skidded to an abrupt halt, his hooves kicking up rocks that skittered over the edge of the cliff they'd come to. He turned, facing the way they'd come. Nylah and Roan planted themselves in front of them as the Hunters formed a half circle, trapping them all. Then they were dropping to a knee a moment before golden light flared so brightly, Tessa had to look away. She blinked several times as the light faded, her grandfather standing before her.

His smile was too wide and cunning while he looked up at her. "You did well, granddaughter."

"You promised to tell me who my mother is at the end of this. Where is she?" Tessa asked, lifting her chin.

"I did," he agreed. "Akira is in my home world where she belongs."

"You promised to take me to her."

"No, child," he said, slowly shaking his head. "I promised to take you from this world. I never said where or how."

Eyal backed up at the words, his hooves causing rocks to skitter over the edge of the cliff.

"You used me," Tessa said, her soul breaking all over again. Always something to be used, never loved.

"You have fulfilled your purpose, Tessa," Achaz said calmly. "All that's left is to correct the balance."

"Correct the balance," she repeated, her fingers tightening in Eyal's mane.

"You cannot continue to exist."

"I am your granddaughter!" she cried.

"You are also theirs."

Nylah and Roan snarled, snapping their massive jaws, and Achaz glared.

"These mutts of your father's cannot save you here."

Her father.

Half light. Half dark.

"You cannot outrun fate," Achaz chided with mock sympathy, power surging around him brighter than the sun.

She glanced over her shoulder, staring out over the dark cavern, before she turned back to Achaz. "Perhaps not," she agreed. "But I can alter it."

Eyal turned faster than a horse should be able to, leaping into the air. Nylah and Roan followed.

And they fell into the dark.

39
AXEL

"Kitten, what are you doing?"

Kat looked up from where she was on her knees, scrubbing the kitchen floor.

"I spilled a glass of orange juice," she answered, huffing a curl from her face.

"So you decided to scrub the entire floor?" Axel asked in confusion.

She looked around. "No one else is here to do it."

"But...why are *you* doing it?"

Her brows knitted. "I just told you there is no one else here to do it. You don't want staff here, and there isn't a need for it. It's only the two of us."

He took a few steps into the room, careful not to step where she'd already cleaned. "But you're pregnant."

"I'm aware," she muttered, returning to her scrubbing. "I knew before you did."

He swallowed his amusement at her obvious irritation, but it quickly faded as he watched her work around her swollen stomach. He'd come down here for a reason. Fresh from the shower, his hair was still damp, but he'd gone out and stocked up on blood after he'd gotten Kat settled in the penthouse.

In the next blink, he was crouched beside her, his hand halting her movements. She rocked back, nearly knocking over the bucket of water next to her.

"By the gods, Axel," she snapped.

"Sorry," he muttered.

He hadn't meant to move that quickly. It was just...starting to happen. Fae and Legacy were fast, but Night Children were faster. They were blurs when they moved. Legacy could do that, but vampyres could sustain that speed for prolonged periods of time.

He gently took the scrub brush from her hand.

"You don't need to do that, Axel," she said.

"Neither do you."

"Do you even know how to..."

"Clean a floor?" Axel asked with a laugh. "I think I can manage it, kitten."

"I truly don't mind," she insisted. "I need something to do."

"Go read some books. Please don't clean the floor."

"That's not..." She reached for the scrub brush, but Axel pulled it out of her reach. "Tell me, Kat." When she remained silent, he tenderly took her chin and tipped her face up. "I know I'm not the expert on how normal relationships are supposed to go, but I think if we're going to do this thing, we have to talk to each other. It's only logical."

"Shut up," she sighed, but the corner of her mouth tipped up in a small smile.

He couldn't resist leaning in to brush his mouth against hers. So much freedom to just *be* with her here.

"Tell me, kitten," he murmured against her lips.

She sighed again. "I need to feel useful. We were trained to serve. It was a purpose, and to just sit around doesn't feel right."

"You don't need to serve anyone. That's the beauty of the Underground. You can create a new purpose."

"I think it will just take me a little time to adjust."

He tucked her hair behind her ear, tracing the slight arch. "I can understand that. I think we're both facing that right now. But it was always useful when you read books. Your knowledge helped immensely."

"Maybe," she said. "Like I said, we just need time to adjust to... everything."

"Great. You go start adjusting on the sofa. With a book," Axel said.

"We can't leave the floor like this," she argued, gesturing to the kitchen floor full of soap suds.

"I'll take care of it."

"But you're a Legacy," she blurted.

A sharp sensation went through his chest at the words. "Not for much longer," he replied, trying to make the words sound light and joking. It was how he'd always survived. Music and nonchalance until he figured how to deal with something, but he didn't know how to deal with this. How to deal with no longer having his shadows. How to deal with not belonging with his family anymore. How to deal with a child. How to deal with *loving* someone who wasn't a brother. Maybe Kat was on to something with this whole scrubbing-the-floor thing. It was certainly something to keep him busy.

"I didn't mean to make you upset," Kat said when silent seconds ticked by.

"You didn't, kitten," he sighed. "As we've both said repeatedly in the last ten minutes, we simply need time to adjust."

She nodded as she stood, shifting on her feet and worrying her bottom lip. He knew what she was going to say when she opened her mouth, and he stopped her before she could.

"Go rest, Katya. I'll finish this."

The words were harsher than he'd intended, more command than request, and because it was so ingrained in her, she didn't argue. He knew it was pure habit when she bowed her head before quickly leaving the room.

"Fuck," Axel cursed, throwing the scrub brush across the room. It hit the wall with a loud smack, water and soap suds flying everywhere.

He sat back, elbows resting on his bent knees as he shoved his fingers into his hair.

He wasn't sure if any amount of time would allow him to adjust to this.

A few hours later, Axel found her on the sofa in the living room. She wasn't reading anything. Instead, she was curled into one end, clearly lost in thought. Her amber eyes immediately met his. Whether she heard him coming or felt him, he didn't know.

"So this orange juice..." he started, watching the crease form in her brow. "Are we out?"

"Yes," she sighed. "I spilled the last of it."

He'd figured as much. He'd done more than clean the kitchen floor and scrubbed that room spotless, letting himself get lost to the mindless tasks to avoid thinking about the fuckery his life had become. It probably wasn't up to anyone's standards, but for his first time cleaning a room, he was pretty fucking proud of it.

During all that avoidance cleaning, however, he'd found the empty orange juice container. The same juice Kat was drinking several glasses of every day since they'd come here. He was fairly certain she was drinking more orange juice than eating peanut butter at this point. He was also certain the sudden cleaning of the kitchen floor was in large part due to being upset about spilling the last of that orange juice.

Axel crossed the room, taking a seat next to her. Lifting her legs, she draped them over his lap as she twisted to see him better. Her hand landed on her swollen stomach that was more than obvious now. Admittedly, Axel didn't know much about pregnancy. It wasn't something he thought he'd be dealing with for several decades. But he knew Fae and Legacy pregnancies were shorter than mortal ones by about a month or so, the magic in their blood helping the babes grow faster. But it also made the pregnancy harder on the females with so much extra magic in *their* body too. He knew there were cravings and amplified emotions. He knew he was now responsible to protect her at all costs, and at the end of this, a tiny little life would be his to guard too.

An entirely new life.

That was terrifying.

"I can get you more orange juice, Kat," he said softly, tracing a line along her calf. His gaze was still fixed on her hand where it splayed across her stomach.

"Can we go get it?"

"I can have it delivered. I know—"

"I know you know people, Axel," she interrupted. "I just wanted to go... I don't know. Walk around, maybe?"

"You know why we can't," he said. "That Mark Eliza gave you has long since worn off, and even if it hadn't, it's getting pretty hard to hide."

She looked away from him when she said, "I know."

"And I'm too recognizable," he added.

"What does that matter?" she argued. "You are still royalty here."

"Yes, but—"

He hadn't told her yet. He hadn't filled her in on Bree and the vampyre's requests and plans. He'd been too concerned with getting her back here safely and keeping her protected. Too focused on keeping them secluded so word didn't get out that she was pregnant. Everyone knew about the fire Fae the Arius Kingdom had acquired. She was more than recognizable now, and with everything he'd put her through these last months, he hadn't wanted to add to that burden. Because he'd been raised that to love someone was to protect them at all costs, even if it meant keeping secrets, but he supposed this was another thing he needed to adjust to. The whole Theon and Tessa debacle had proven that.

"Axel?" Kat pushed.

He rubbed at the back of his neck. "There are some things you don't know."

"I understand if it is not my place to know," she answered.

His brows knitted together because he didn't like the sound of that at all.

"That's not..." He cleared his throat. "There are things I haven't told you about my time being held captive."

"By your father?"

"By one of the Night Child coven leaders."

There was a small gasp as Kat pushed herself up into a sitting position to see him better. "What are you talking about?"

"No one else knows," he said, watching his fingers brush up and down her warm skin. "Her name is Bree DelaCrux. She is the oldest of the four coven leaders that rule the Night Children."

"I thought the Arius Lord ruled the Underground?"

"We do. Or he does, but the Underground has always been its own sort of kingdom. The five districts are ruled by different beings. It has its own balance. A balance I've learned to navigate, but when I am no longer an Arius Legacy? My position here will change. There are plenty of people who will welcome the opportunity to take out the former spare heir," Axel said.

"That's not what you are," Kat said gently.

"It is," Axel answered plainly. "I made peace with that fact long ago. My father always wanted me here. Theon to rule above and me to rule below."

"That can't be true," she insisted.

He finally turned to look at her. "The Arius Kingdom is called wicked and cruel for a reason, kitten. No one knows that better than the Arius Lord's own children."

"But— That can't—" Her hand rubbed over her stomach. "You're his son."

He knew what she was thinking. How could a father do that to his child? Because he couldn't imagine doing a single thing to harm that babe in her belly.

"Anyway, Mansel and Julius betrayed my father and have aligned themselves with Bree. They took me from the place my father had me hidden away and brought me to her, where she continued with the same torture. Only her motives were different. My father wanted submission; Bree desires an alliance."

"An alliance?" Kat repeated in confusion. "She wants to rule the entire Underground?"

"Not exactly. She wants to rule all of Devram, and she offered me a spot at her side," he answered.

The silence in the room was so loud he finally looked at her again. She was staring back at him, but he knew it wasn't shock so much as it was her running through logic and reason.

"It's a calculated move," she finally said. "But no one would accept a Night Child as a ruler of Devram. The Legacy are far more powerful."

"She believes they will destroy themselves over Tessa, and she might not be wrong. I was only back a short time, but the peace out there is strained and fragile. It won't take much to push everyone over the edge. A war among the kingdoms would be destruction," he replied.

"Then she would rule a broken realm."

"In a way, I suppose," he agreed. "But she has her own agenda. With the focus of the Lords and Ladies elsewhere, she wants to take over the Underground. Then, when Devram is broken, there will be no one to stand against her when she comes in."

"With the whole of the Underground behind her," Kat said in understanding.

Axel nodded. "All the mistreated and forgotten of the realm. Everyone banished for whatever reason."

"And she wants you at her side."

"Yes," Axel said. Swallowing thickly, he added, "She...*helped* me find you in the end, but she believes I killed you."

Kat lurched back. "Why would she care?"

"I think...she knew," he said. "I think she knows about this twin flame bond. I think she knows what we are."

"How could she possibly know?"

"I don't think she's from Devram," he admitted. "She's one of the oldest beings in the realm. Honestly? I think she's been here from the beginning."

Kat's brows arched in disbelief. "Since the realm was created?"

"I know it sounds insane," he said. "But the way she spoke and the things she knows..." He shrugged. "The point is, when I...left you last time, I went back to her. Not *to* her," he added in a rush as Kat's eyes went wide. "But I didn't know where else to go. I don't know where I belong anymore. I'll be one of them, and it seemed...logical, I guess. When I came back for you, I told her I had some things to take care of before I could fully commit to her and her House. She can't know I'm back yet, and she certainly can't know about you."

"So you brought me to the Underground? Where, if I am discovered, we will both be killed?" she asked slowly. "How is this any safer than staying in the Arius Kingdom?"

"It's not really for you," Axel admitted. "It's easier for me to get blood. It's safer for me to be around you in the Underground."

Kat nodded, but she didn't respond. He gave her time to process everything, his fingers still moving along her soft skin. Letting his shadows out, he wondered how much longer he'd have them to toy with, and he sucked in a breath when she let tendrils of flames tangle with them. He reveled in it, cherished it, knowing in mere days it would likely all be gone. They'd never feel these pieces of themselves act as one again. They'd never get to have something that was supposed to be fated for them.

Fate could fuck off.

Finally, after several minutes, she said, "I understand everything you've told me. I understand your reasoning, but Axel, I can't just stay in this penthouse day after day. I don't need to leave the Underground, but I do need to leave this space. We'll both go mad."

"I just need more time, kitten," he said. "We need to get safeguards in place, and—"

"From what I've gathered, there are no such things as safeguards in the Underground. Or Devram, for that matter," Kat interrupted.

She wasn't wrong, but that didn't mean he couldn't try.

"I still have my power," she went on. "And while you might not have your magic anymore, you will still be of the Arius bloodline. You'll be powerful in other ways, Axel. You've spent years in the Underground. You are constantly telling me you have connections and know people."

"It's not the same," he said, shaking his head. "I know you don't understand—"

"Don't do that," she snapped. "I *do* understand. It's *you* who doesn't. I know you see certain behaviors as ingrained into the Fae, but the Legacy are the same. You are all so indoctrinated with the way things are, you don't realize that they *could* be different."

"I don't know what you want me to say, Katya," he said, meeting her stare once more.

There was a warmth there he wasn't expecting, along with something else he couldn't place. Some type of unwavering belief in him maybe? He wouldn't know because no one had ever looked at him like that before.

"You say you don't know where you belong anymore, but there's a freedom in that, Axel," she said softly, reaching up to cup his cheek. "You gave me a freedom when you let me be more than another Fae bound to your kingdom. I know it's strange. I know it's hard to know what to do with that. I'm still trying to figure it out too, but you get to decide where you belong now. You get to make a new path."

She took his hand then, placing it on her stomach.

"And maybe that new path will lead to a world where we don't have to hide."

Cienna had said it would take a week or two for the curse to take everything from him. She'd been wrong. It had taken three.

Three weeks of slowly feeling his shadows slip from his grasp. Three weeks of drinking more and more blood every day. Three weeks of exercising self-control when Katya walked into a room.

These last few days had been torturous. Her blood had called to him as much as her power. He'd ordered extra stores, was more than prepared, but none of it smelled like jasmine and citrus, spices and heat. None of it smelled like her, and the urge to take grew stronger with each passing day.

But despite his agony, despite the gnawing hunger and the desperation to take from her, the rations he'd secured were doing their job. They were allowing him to stay in control. They were keeping him from attacking her as she sat beside him, a damp cloth pressed to his brow.

There was a sadness in her eyes, and her heart was racing too fast. That couldn't be good for her or the babe.

"You don't need to be here for this," he whispered.

His entire body hurt.

Curled in a ball, sweat beaded on his brow as he shivered from chills that wracked his body, and Axel idly wondered if this was what a fever was like. He'd heard of such a thing, but he was sure he'd never experienced one. This couldn't be a fever though. He was fairly certain that was when the body temperature got too high, and he was freezing. But he was also sweating. None of that seemed right.

Theon would know. Theon knew everything with all that stupid, useless knowledge. His nose had always been in a book. In fact, Axel couldn't remember a time Theon didn't have a book in hand. Granted, he was five years younger, but it still remained that his earliest memories of his brother included books. The asshole had never deigned to join in chaosphere games with him and Luka, and Theon never let him go into his room or touch his things. One time, Axel had found his tablet left somewhere. He'd opened it and tried to figure out the password. He hadn't known it would lock up after so many attempts.

He learned later that Theon had been punished for that, taking the blame. It was the first time he'd associated safety with love. Theon loved him, and therefore did whatever he could to keep him safe and protected. It was how he'd been taught to love, and it was how Axel had learned to love.

Kat's smile was soft and sad. "I do."

"I'd rather you not, just in case."

"We've already had this argument. Multiple times," she chided. "I'm not going anywhere. I don't believe you will hurt me."

"I know that, but—"

"Tristyn will be here any minute," she cut in.

He nodded, and gods, even that small action hurt.

They'd sent a message to the male a week ago, asking him to be on standby for this. It was the only way he'd let Katya stay in the room when he finally transitioned from a Legacy to a Night Child.

As though he'd heard his name, the male walked into the room, features grim.

"Axel. Kat," he greeted. Placing a small bag on a table, he shucked off his leather jacket and tossed it across a chair. "Cienna sent supplies. Just in case."

"Where is she?" Axel rasped.

"She is tending to other matters at the moment," he answered. "She will come if we call, but she doesn't think she'll be needed."

Axel rolled his eyes, not wanting to deal with her prophetic ways in this moment.

"Any news to report?" Axel asked.

Tristyn arched a brow. "That's what you want to talk about right now?"

"Anything to keep my mind elsewhere," Axel muttered.

Tristyn sighed. "Everything has been unusually quiet since the Sirana Gala. It has everyone on edge."

Axel nodded, but that was about all he could do.

The male offered nothing else, instead turning to Kat. "Have you eaten today? I can hear your stomach and your heart rate."

"I have," she answered. "I don't...feel right."

Alarm spread through Axel at those words. "What? Why didn't you say anything?"

She glanced at Tristyn before focusing on the bedding beneath them.

"You didn't tell him," Tristyn said.

"Tell me what?" Axel demanded.

"He doesn't need to know. He's dealing with enough," Kat cut in.

"That's not how this works, kitten," Axel said, shaking his head and grimacing. All he could feel were the dregs of his power. Every instinct in him was telling him to fill those reserves, to make sure he wasn't defenseless, to take back his power. It was making it hard to focus on anything else with the familiar mania creeping closer, but he could sure as fuck focus on something that would affect Kat.

"Tell me," he ordered Tristyn.

The male didn't hesitate, despite Kat's protests. "When you change fully, the bond between the two of you will die."

"The twin flame bond," Axel clarified.

Tristyn nodded. "She will feel it."

Axel lurched up, ignoring the pain that assaulted him. "What does that mean?"

"She will feel the bond being ripped from her soul," he answered. "You will too. It will make the change even more agonizing, but because she took the Mark to find you, it will be intensified for her."

"Because that piece of her soul she offered up will die too," Axel said in horrified understanding. He turned to Kat, taking her face in his trembling and clammy hands. "I am so sorry."

It was all he could say. All he could do.

"It was worth it to find you," she replied.

"No, kitten. I wasn't worth this at all," he said, full of sorrow. "But I will do everything in my power to repay you for your sacrifice."

"Someday you will see what I see, Axel," she said. "You will see that you are more than a spare heir, more than a bloodline, more than what your father has led you to believe. Someday you will see yourself as I see you."

He opened his mouth to reply, but the words stalled in his throat as everything inside of him screamed for blood. He knew this feeling well. Knew it was the craving demanding, and this was more intense than it'd ever been. Dark mist swirled around him as the last of his shadows were ripped from his soul. The next sound that came from his mouth was raw agony, a bellow of pain so severe he wished Arius would come for him. All he could smell was blood. All he *wanted* was blood. Nothing else mattered.

Until his eyes fell on her.

On the way she was curled into herself, swallowing her own screams of despair.

Tristyn was there, hovering over him and waiting to intervene. He seemed to know not to touch him right now. Axel was certain if he did, he'd snap and someone would end up dead. Him. Tristyn. He didn't know.

"Kat," he rasped, reaching for her, but she jerked back from his touch.

His heart shattered at the action. It was worse than everything else he was feeling.

"Give her a minute," Tristyn tried. "Drink this."

He extended a bottle of blood, sympathy lining every part of him.

"When will it stop?" Axel demanded.

"When the change is complete."

"How is it not?" He lifted a hand, his muscles and bones screaming at the movement. Another wave of torture surged through him, his jaw and gums burning. He'd meant to show Tristyn he had nothing left, that his shadows and power were gone. That he was nothing anymore, but instead he was given more anguish, drawing another bellow from his soul.

It mixed with Kat's cries, a symphony of torment that would haunt him for the rest of his days. But her cries also drew his attention, particularly to her throat. Suddenly, all he could hear was her heartbeat, fast and strong. He could practically *see* her veins fluttering with warm blood. The power he was craving was right there for the taking.

A bottle was shoved in his face, but that wasn't what he wanted. One sniff told him it wasn't as powerful. It wasn't fresh. It wasn't fire.

"Fuck," a male muttered as Axel surged forward for the defenseless Fae in front of him. He could swear his canines lengthened. Perfect. That would make his strike more precise.

His fangs didn't sink into warm flesh of fire, but it was powerful blood that flooded his mouth.

It still wasn't what he wanted most, even if it was enough to satiate the need. The power he drank was soothing and mighty, a sense of peace and calming coming over him. But more than that were flashes of images he didn't recognize.

A female with red-brown hair and violet eyes.

Another female with dark skin that glowed with a silver aura and raven black hair floating around her.

A kiss beneath the moonlight.

Swords clashing.

A panther prowling.

"That's enough," Tristyn growled, yanking his arm back. Axel's fangs tore his flesh, but the male didn't seem to care. "She needs you."

Clarity settled over him as he realized what had happened. That Tristyn had intervened, given him his own blood so he didn't take from Kat.

"I can't," Axel rasped. This was all too fresh, too new. He didn't trust himself yet.

"I won't go anywhere, but she needs you," Tristyn repeated, stepping out of the way.

Kat was still curled into herself, her curls matted to her brow. Her entire body trembled, and tears streamed down her face.

"Is it over?" Axel asked. He needed to be sure before he reached for her.

"Yes," Tristyn said. "The effects will linger a bit longer, but the change itself is complete. And the bond you two shared is…"

He didn't need to finish that statement. He could see the back of her left hand where a black Mark no longer showed, faded into nothing.

Axel crawled across the bed, reaching for her, but she shrank back from him again.

She may as well have twisted a dagger in his chest.

"Kitten, let me help," he whispered.

"You can't. The bond is dead. You can't help," she gasped. "It hurts. It hurts so much, and I—"

She broke off as a sob escaped her. It was enough to make him ignore her protests, and he pulled her into his chest. She may have told him he couldn't help, but she still buried her face in his chest, clinging to him. He could hear every beat of her heart. Could hear the blood rushing through her body. More than that, he could hear the babe, his heartbeat strong and steady. The babe was fine. Katya may not be. He may not be. But their child was fine. He just needed to fix the rest.

He leaned back enough to tilt her chin up, swiping a tear away with his thumb. "I still choose you, Katya. Bond or not, I still choose you."

Another small sob came from her, and she reached up with shaky fingers. He felt them brush along his cheeks, gathering the dampness. Then she showed him her fingertips, faint red glimmering there.

"Your tears are red," Kat whispered.

"And yours are heartbreaking," he replied, pressing a kiss to her temple before he pulled her back into his chest.

"I'll be in the other room if you need me," Tristyn said, slipping from the room. The door clicked softly behind him.

For once, Axel wasn't worried about hurting her. He knew in his soul that in this moment, he wouldn't attack her or try to take from her. In this moment, it was just them and their brokenness, but they were together. That's what they'd promised each other.

So they sat in their heartbreak and cried.

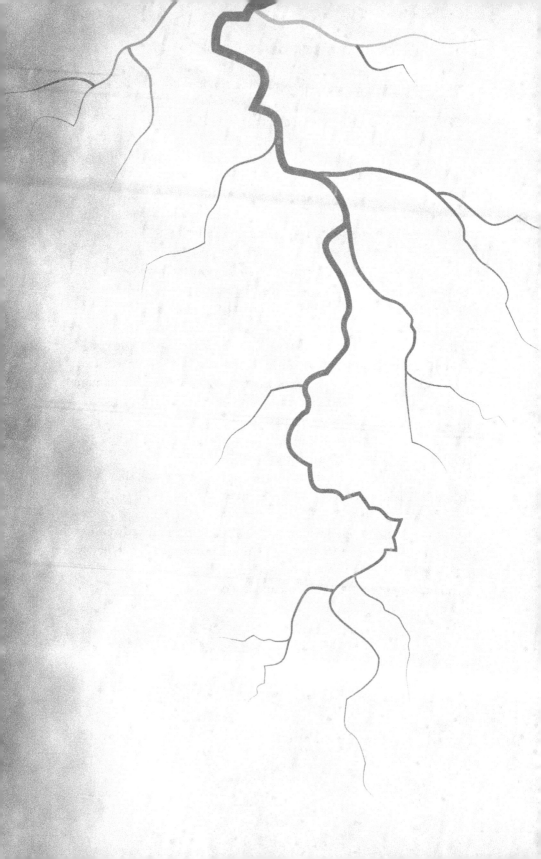

40

TESSA

"A word, Tessalyn," Rordan said when she pushed away from the breakfast table.

Surprise coursed through her, but she didn't let it show. She'd been waiting for this moment for weeks now. Really since the Sirana Gala. Ever since she'd kicked Oralia out of her rooms and told her to tell Rordan and Dex that she would no longer tolerate someone monitoring her every move. Ever since Luka had started spending nearly every night in her rooms rather than his own. She simply slept better when he was near. She felt more in control of herself and her situation. Still restless. Still wild, but...

Honestly, she couldn't really explain it, but she'd been waiting for the other shoe to drop at her defiance. It looked like today was going to be that day.

"She will meet you in the training arena," the Achaz Lord added, effectively dismissing Luka.

Luka held her stare for a long moment until she nodded.

I don't like this, he growled down the bond.

I can handle him.

Luka turned, leaving the room, but she knew she was going to get an earful at training. She wasn't sure when she'd started answering to him about her decisions, but she was almost looking forward to the argument. Which was perverse, but he always lost a little of his own steadfast control when they argued. As if some part of her was able to claw its way through all that dragon broodiness.

Okay, she *liked* the fact that she could make him lose that control.

Just like she liked that she could bring Theon to his knees.

"Sit back down," Rordan said when the door closed fully behind Luka.

The only other person who remained was his Source, dutifully seated next to him. If her visits with Eviana had taught her anything, it was that maybe her Source bond with Theon wasn't as odd as it had seemed to everyone. Now she wondered if any of them truly embraced the bond or if they gave in purely for survival's sake.

Or perhaps they simply got tired of fighting and gave up. The gods knew she'd tried that.

She thought about saying something snarky to start this conversation off, but she'd learned that letting someone else start often revealed more of their true motives. So instead, she sat back down, crossing one leg over the other, and waited.

Rordan studied her with those blue eyes ringed with gold, his features giving nothing away. A part of her expected some sort of a subtle display of power to show her he was in control, but she wasn't surprised when he didn't do that either. He'd moved beyond physical displays of power. He'd proven as much when he'd announced that fucking Match Contract to Liam. She'd done the same when she'd shoved Oralia and Dex from her rooms. It was his move now, and she was more than a little curious about how it would play out.

"We have several matters that need to be discussed," Rordan finally said, sitting straighter and adjusting his shirt cuffs before he reached for a leather-bound book sitting on the table beside him.

"And this needs to be done now?" Tessa asked. "This is my usual training time."

"I have other matters to tend to this afternoon, and my time is more valuable than yours," he replied.

Tessa arched a brow.

"Don't act offended," he chided, flipping open the book. Tessa realized then it was a journal of some sort. "After training, you spend your time indulging in frivolous explorations and other nonsense. I have meetings and commitments."

"And what should I be spending my time on?" she asked, tapping a single nail on the table.

He placed the pen he'd just used to jot something down in the crease of the open book, a square black ring on his finger gobbling up the light.

A ring she recognized.

Where had he gotten it?

"I'm glad you asked," he said, folding his hands and placing them on the table before him. "You can start by fulfilling your purpose."

That had her gaze snapping to his.

"What is that supposed to mean?"

"I told you before that freedom wasn't free, and it was time to start paying. What have you done since then? What have you done since you learned what Achaz requires of you?"

"I do not answer to Achaz," she spat.

"Wrong, child," he retorted. "We *all* answer to Achaz. He is the ruler of the gods. It is why I rule Devram."

"What does Achaz care? He cannot come here," she countered.

But Rordan tsked, his eyes doing a thing that could almost be classified as an eye roll. "We're done with games, Tessalyn. I know you spoke to him. I know what he told you. Do you not wish to leave this realm? Have you grown complacent and comfortable with a dragon in your bed and an Arius Legacy at your beck and call?"

She couldn't hide her shock this time, jerking back in her chair. "How do you know any of that?"

"I know all of your movements, Tessa. Every breath you take and move you make. I lost track of you once. I certainly would not allow it to happen again," he said. Picking up his pen, he continued, "Now it is time to move forward. Things have grown quiet. The ruling Ladies have settled down. You need to make a visit to Arius Kingdom."

"And do what?"

"What you were fucking born to do," he answered, any trace of warmth and kindness he'd once shown her now gone. "And when you return tonight, Liam will be here to join us for dinner. I will be sure to have extra vials and quills available."

"Absolutely not," she balked at the implication. Match Contracts were signed in blood. "What happened to the freedom you promised me?"

Rordan stood, buttoning his suit coat. "You haven't held up your end of our deal. Why should I hold up mine?"

Lurching to her feet, the chair skidded across the floor, a shrill screech sounding. "I will go to Arius Kingdom today, but I will not dine with Liam."

The Lord paused the gathering of his things, his head tilting as he studied her. "I was unaware we were bargaining now."

"It's not a bargain," she replied quickly. "But I will deliver today."

"Not some trivial Arius death," Rordan warned.

"I understand."

Rordan continued to gather his things, everything disappearing in a burst of light.

"Do not disappoint me, Tessa. To be clear, this is a test. Failure is not an option."

He swept from the room, his words still ringing in the air between them.

Failure is not an option.

Words that had haunted her.

Words that Mother Cordelia had said to her.

Words that Theon had said to her.

She sank back into her chair, wondering how she was going to get out of this.

She'd waited until she knew Theon was gone. He wouldn't feel her cross the wards of the estate manor, but she didn't want to accidentally run into him either. Technically, she was keeping her word. The various kingdom manors were just outside the Acropolis, each in their own territory. So in all actuality, she *was* in Arius Kingdom, just as she'd told Rordan she would do. She still wasn't sure what she was going to do to fulfill his order of providing a suitable Arius death, and she'd skipped training because of it. Her mental shields were up, blocking Luka. He was going to be furious.

Moving quickly and quietly, she stopped outside a door, knocking softly. She knew they were here because while she'd seen Theon leave, she hadn't seen them leave.

The door opened, sky-blue eyes staring back at her.

"Tessa?" Lange said in surprise. "I had a feeling I was going to see you today, but I didn't quite believe it."

"Hi, Lange," she said, surging into him.

He huffed a laugh, catching her and pulling her into a hug. "Everything all right?"

"Yeah, I just..."

Needed to talk to someone that wasn't involved in all this mess.

Lange stepped to the side, letting her pass. The curtains were open, letting natural light bathe the room. She hadn't been expecting the small suite they had. There was a little sitting area with a fireplace and television and a door leading to what she assumed was a bedroom.

"Is Corbin feeling better?" she asked.

Lange gave her a warm smile. "He'll be out in a minute, and you can see for yourself."

"How come you aren't at your classes?"

"The instructors are all gone today. Assessments at the Estates," Lange answered.

"Oh," was all she could think to say as she looked around their space. Small but homey. Little pieces of them scattered throughout. Something stirred in her soul, and she knew it for what it was: jealousy. She was jealous that they had this little haven of solitude to simply exist without expectations. Sure, they had responsibilities, but in this space, it was just them.

"Are you sure you're all right?" Lange asked.

But before she could answer, Corbin appeared, striding through the bedroom door. He seemed a little pale, his hair longer than the last time she'd seen him, and she could swear he was a little thinner.

"Corbin," she breathed, closing the distance between them and relishing the feel of his arms coming around her.

"Hey, there," he said around a soft chuckle. She looked up to find him exchanging a look of concern with Lange.

"Are you feeling better?" Tessa asked, extracting herself from him and swallowing the emotion clogging her throat. "You were ill the last time I was here."

"Lange mentioned you stopped by," he said. "I'm sorry I missed you."

"What was wrong?"

"Just a headache and some body aches."

She frowned. Fae rarely got sick, let alone with something as minor as a headache. "Did a Healer see to you?"

"I'm fine," Corbin said. "How are *you*?"

"Fine," she parroted, and Lange barked a laugh.

"Well played, Tess," he said, flopping onto the sofa. "Take a seat and tell us what you've been up to."

Tessa perched on the edge of a chair while Corbin moved behind the sofa. His fingers brushed along Lange's arm stretched across the back of the furniture. "I'm grabbing water. Need one?"

Lange shook his head before focusing on Tessa again. Once Corbin was back and settled beside Lange, they both looked at her expectantly.

"Theon is really treating you well?" she asked.

"I already told you this," Lange said. "We have food and shelter. A little bit of freedom and the protection of the Arius Heir. Even if we weren't bound to the kingdom, I don't know that we'd find something better anywhere else."

Tessa nodded, worrying her bottom lip as she looked around some more.

"Is the Achaz Lord treating *you* well?" Corbin asked, his tone low and soothing.

"I can take care of myself," she answered immediately.

"We never said you couldn't," he replied. When she didn't say anything else for several seconds, he added, "You know you can talk to us, right? I know we're not Dex, but—"

"I don't trust Dex," she interrupted. "And you shouldn't either. Don't tell him anything if you see him. Or Oralia."

Lange's eyes were wide in disbelief. "But you and Dex are... Well, you just are."

"And Brecken," she added. "I'm not sure about him yet, but don't trust him either."

"Tessa, what is going on?" Corbin asked, leaning forward, his arms braced on his knees.

"So much. Too much," she murmured.

She shouldn't have come here. They were happy and safe. She shouldn't involve them in this. All her friends had ever wanted was to find some place to be together, and they had that here. They had that here because of *Theon*, of all people.

She shouldn't have come here.

She said as much as she lurched to her feet. "I'm sorry," she murmured. "I need to go."

"Tessa, wait," Lange said, somehow already standing in front of the door when she turned to it. She hadn't even seen him move. "You can tell us, Tess."

"I can't involve you," she said. "You deserve to be happy."

"So do you," Lange insisted, taking her shoulders in his hands. "We all do."

"We all do," she repeated, more to herself than to him. Her eyes snapped up then, meeting sky-blue ones. "If things... You trust me?"

"I do," he said, and she could hear the sincerity in those two words. "If it wasn't for you, we wouldn't be together. We wouldn't have this place, this security. We owe you, Tessa."

"You don't owe me anything," she said. "But I would ask..."

"Anything," Corbin said, coming up beside them, his hands in his pockets as he studied her.

"I think something big is coming. There is a Fae being held captive in Faven, and if the kingdoms suddenly find themselves at odds with each other, I need you to free her," Tessa said.

"How would we possibly do that?" Lange asked.

"Just...if you find you are able, don't leave her behind. That's what I'll ask of you."

"Who is she?" Corbin asked.

"Eviana."

He took a step back. "The Arius Lord's Source?"

Tessa nodded. "No harm will come to you. Valter is locked up. He cannot be freed."

"But she can?"

"Maybe? If the right things happen at the right time with people in the right places," she said, knowing she sounded insane.

But something was coming. Soon. She could feel it in her bones, as if it was a vision trying to form, but couldn't quite make it to the surface. Suddenly, she wished she was sleeping. Then that vision could find her. She could know what was coming. Prepare for it.

"Tessa?" Lange said gently. "You're kind of scaring us, sweetheart."

Her smile was weak and wobbly. "It was good to see you both. I miss you."

"Tessa, we—"

"I have to go," she said, pushing past them and practically stumbling into the hall. She heard them call after her, but she was stepping through a light portal in the next breath. She didn't even realize where she was going until she turned to find the rushing river.

The black rushing river.

The waters of Wynfell were dark and foreboding as they flowed, chunks of ice getting caught along the sides in the current. Spring was coming, but it hadn't been enough to completely thaw the river yet. There were still clumps of frozen snow in the trees. The banks were still frozen mud. She wasn't sure how or why she'd ended up here, but she sucked in a lungful of fresh air. The clouds were few and far between today; the sun shining down and warming her face as she tipped it up to the sky. Seeing Lange and Corbin had been good for her soul. Now she just needed to figure out how to appease Rordan. Maybe going to dinner with Liam wouldn't be the worst thing in the end, but he'd made it clear the Match Contract was the purpose. With the power plays lately, she could only assume Rordan had a plan to coerce her into signing the damned thing too.

Stepping closer to the water, she watched the darkness churn. She knew of the Night Waters in the Arius Kingdom. Those waters were black as night too, and she'd heard the Wynfell River had fallen to the same. What no one could figure out was how or why.

"After all that time I invested in trying to teach you, you never did learn to control yourself, did you?"

Every part of her body stiffened, her blood turning to ice. As if in slow motion, Tessa turned to face Mother Cordelia.

The Estate Mother looked down at her as she'd done her entire life, blue eyes full of disdain. Her hair was back in the tight bun as always. The only difference today was that she was in the black cloak of the Augury. She hadn't bothered with a mask.

But those gathered behind her had.

Pearlescent masks stared back at her, more and more filing in, but one in particular stepped to Mother Cordelia's side, silent as they watched on.

"Where have you been hiding?" Tessa asked, her head tilting as she watched the Estate Mother.

"Hiding?" Cordelia scoffed. "I haven't been hiding, child. Simply... reassessing our strategy."

"Our? Who leads you now with Valter gone?"

Cordelia clicked her tongue. "We all know he isn't *gone*, Tessalyn."

"If you know where he is, you should let the Arius Heir know. He has been searching for him," Tessa said with faux sweetness.

"He has been doing no such thing," said the figure beside Cordelia, a cold sneer to her tone.

Her.

A female.

A voice Tessa should recognize.

Her power was already winding up her arms, sensing that it was going to get to feast. It was in a frenzy, her body buzzing with energy. Her veins crackled with it, the magic straining and reaching in anticipation of being set free.

But then everything in her froze with shock as the female removed her mask, and the emerald green eyes of Cressida stared back at her.

"You?" Tessa gasped.

Truly, she should have known. Valter was the leader of the Augury. His wife being part of it shouldn't have come as the shock that it was, but she had always seemed so...distanced from everything. Too preoccupied with societal standards and trends to care about the politics of the realm. A female who had won a Match Contract to elevate her status in exchange for having children with the Arius Lord.

"My son has done everything *but* search for his father," Cressida said, tossing her mask to the side. "Since you came into his life, he has forsaken all his responsibilities. He has tossed everything he was raised for and trained to be to the side."

There was nothing here of the dramatic mother who had cried about her sons going to the Acropolis for Selection Year. Any traces of the submissive wife of the Arius Lord were gone. This female was power and grace, and Tessa realized then that she actually didn't know what Legacy line she descended from. She didn't know what kind of power to expect from her.

But her surprise and distraction had left her wide open for Mother Cordelia to strike.

She gasped as the air was ripped from her lungs while a gust of wind simultaneously knocked her to her knees. It brought back too many memories, too much pain, paralyzing her as the females advanced, the Augury following their lead. Once again, Tessa found herself in the center of a circle of cloaked figures.

"I am actually not overly upset about Theon not looking for his father," Cressida confessed while Tessa continued to struggle for air. "I am more upset about his nonchalance with finding his brother, but he's always so focused on *you*."

Cressida grabbed her chin with that final word, nails digging into her jaw.

"A mother has to do what is best for her children, you know," she went on. "Sometimes that means doing something that hurts now but will be better for them in the end. I'll admit you have given me a challenge, forced my creativity into new territory. Every time I think it will be enough, you somehow still survive. The last time you were on the banks of this river, I thought for sure I had you, but you have new... pets."

Her wolves.

Well, Nylah at least.

Why wasn't she here yet?

Better yet, why the fuck wasn't she fighting back?

She was stronger than Mother Cordelia. And even if she wasn't more powerful, Luka had taught her more than enough to fight back against her. Maybe not all the Augury members, but she didn't need to be on her knees in front of *her*.

With a dark grin, she stopped struggling, letting her power rise to the surface. The power wrapped around her throat shuddered as her light sank its claws into it, draining it of life. As it did so, she was gasping down a breath. And another. And another. She let her power feast. Let it fester. Let it pool around her, gold and silver sparks floating among the magic.

"You can't defeat us all," Cressida chided as Mother Cordelia struggled to yank her magic free.

"Are you sure about that?" Tessa asked, her voice icy and eerie.

"This is precisely why you were never meant to be," she answered. "You will be the death of Devram if death does not find you first."

"Death has found me, and I have bound him to me," Tessa answered, lifting a hand to show her the Arius Mark that adorned the back of it.

Cressida's lip curled. "I had never been more disappointed in him than that day."

"That day?" Tessa asked, sending a surge of energy through her power just as Mother Cordelia thought she'd freed herself. The Estate Mother cried out in pain, and Tessa's smile grew.

"Yes, that day," Cressida answered.

"But no one knew..."

But some had known. Some had known all along what she was. Valter had thought she'd been lost, but Rordan had known. Dex had known. There were pieces she hadn't been able to put together yet. Like why Dex had waited so long to show up, or why Rordan kept saying he'd lost track of her for a time. But Cordelia had said she had been sent there. That she'd been instructed to keep her hidden.

Rordan had done this. From the very beginning, it had been him, and if Cressida knew then…

"You are aiding the Achaz Lord," Tessa said in utter shock. "But you are married to the Arius Lord."

"Don't act so surprised, Tessalyn," she cooed mockingly. "Nith Legacy are known for their creativity, and yet we are still always underestimated. Theon didn't get much of that gift from me. He is cunning and smart enough, but he likes things in their boxes. Black and white. Light and dark. But Axel? He may command shadows, but he sees the world in color. Don't you think?"

Tessa didn't know what to think anymore.

"But you made this so easy, my dear," she went on.

Gods, she certainly liked to talk. She had always chattered at the dinner table too, but it had been mindless nonsense. Apparently, Tessa should have paid more attention.

"Everyone talks about how wild and reckless you are, but you're also predictable. You always come to this same spot when you're searching for answers," Cressida said.

Tessa blinked, so taken aback by the truth of the statement, her control of her magic slipped, freeing Mother Cordelia.

And they didn't let the opportunity go to waste.

The Augury converged, several powers attacking her at once. Vines snapped out, snaking around her limbs. Winds blew, and air was pulled from her lungs. Tendrils of water reached from the river, creating an icy cage and trapping her in the center of it all. There was light and shadow from the weaker Achaz and Arius Legacy. This was so much power. She couldn't fight it on her own. Even if she let her magic have control, she didn't know if it would be enough against all of them, but she wasn't going down without fighting. Not again.

Never again.

Tipping her head back, she screamed to the sky in fury. The sun was gone, dark clouds having rolled in. They burst open, rain mixing with the icy waters the Anahita Legacy were controlling. She focused on one arm. She just needed one hand free to spill a drop of blood. Her Hunters would come, and everyone here would wish they were dead.

She'd grant that wish with wrath and golden blades.

With another cry of rage, light radiated out from her so forcefully, those closest to her were thrown back. It gave her just enough time to pull a dagger and slice her palm.

"No!" Cressida cried from where she was pushing up onto her knees. "Not yet!"

But she was far too late as the blade slid across Tessa's palm, drops of red splattering at her feet.

"You're all dead," Tessa said darkly as the first of her Hunters appeared.

"You called, your—" the Hunter started, but then he stopped as another gust of wind swirled around them courtesy of the Sefarina Legacy.

The Hunter's head tilted too far to the side, and he inhaled deeply before a wide and terrifying grin filled his pale face.

"We are here to serve, your grace," he said, a feral thread of excitement ringing in his already haunting tone.

Despite them all looking the same, Tessa knew this was the same Hunter that always appeared first. This was the Hunter who had served her. He was the one who had brought her Valter and Arlo. He was the leader of the others in whatever hierarchy was granted among their kind.

"Kill them all," Tessa said, her gaze locking with Mother Cordelia's as she spoke the words.

The Estate Mother's face was taut with disapproval, but for the first time in her life, Tessa saw apprehension fill her features too. Yet even with that, she didn't seem nearly as concerned as she should be with death a breath away.

"We will eliminate the threats," he replied, more and more Hunters appearing.

The Legacy could do nothing as golden blades were drawn, but this was nothing like the last attack. Many of the Augury members *weren't* fighting. In fact, only a handful were panicking. As the Hunters made their way through the crowds. They didn't kill them all like she'd instructed. Instead, they almost seemed to be...*selective* about the ones they drove those gold swords into.

Cressida and Mother Cordelia came closer, the leader of the Hunters stepping in front of Tessa, but Cressida just waved him off.

"I know the rules," she scoffed, a vindictive smile on her full lips as she stared at Tessa. "Rordan will be thrilled she is finally fulfilling her purpose."

"What are you—" Tessa started, but she was cut off by the howling that filled the air.

Not one wolf, but two.

Nylah *and* Roan.

Her heart both soared and stuttered. She still smiled when they appeared though, dark and light fur jumping into the fray. The Augury members who hadn't appeared fearful before did now, more power appearing and flying through the air.

Tessa called her own magic back to the surface, but a piece of her also hesitated. The last time Roan had come to protect her in an attack, he had nearly been killed because of her. What if it happened again? What if she lost control and this time they were too late to save him?

She froze, her palms glowing and gold mist undulating around her. Luka hadn't prepared her for *this*. In all her training, no one had told her what to do when your actions could *kill* someone you loved. Because that was what this was. She *loved* those wolves. They were hers, and she was theirs, and where the fuck *was* Luka? Theon? Her shields had slipped long ago. She could feel them, so surely they could feel her.

I need you both. Now! she cried down the bond, fear and dread taking over as she continued to watch her Hunters selectively take life.

We know. We're trying, Theon said, anger and panic coloring his words.

What do you mean you're trying?

Keep fighting, Tessa. We'll be there, Luka replied.

But Roan is here, and I—

Fuck! Theon snapped.

Where are you? Tessa demanded.

But there was no response, only their own emotions of fury and wrath and...fear? She'd never felt that from them before. Where were they?

A scream from an Augury member drew her attention, faint black shadows fading as the Hunter withdrew his blade from his chest. An Arius Legacy then.

"What have you done?"

Tessa turned just in time to see three arrows fly from Auryon's bow where she now prowled around her. The Hunter who had been guarding her snarled at Auryon's appearance, his lip curling back.

"Huntress," he hissed. "We've been waiting for you."

Auryon's smile was razor sharp as she nocked two arrows, letting them fly before Tessa could blink.

The Hunter had already disappeared.

Auryon let out a shrill whistle, and a moment later, Nylah and Roan leapt from the melee.

"Find the females," was all Auryon said, all while releasing two more rounds of arrows.

The wolves were gone once more, taking down Augury members as they moved and somehow avoiding the Hunters at the same time. Then again, the Hunters truly weren't focused on them as much as they were on certain Legacy.

Arius Legacy.

It was their purpose. It was *her* purpose. She wanted them all dead. If they were slaughtering *all* the Augury members, she wouldn't have cared, but this was...not what she had told them to do.

The thought seemed to flip a switch in her soul, fury bubbling up at being disobeyed. "Stop!" she cried, rushing toward the nearest Hunter. Her hand went through him, so she reached for his blade instead. Her fingers wrapped around it, and she hissed as it sliced into her flesh, more blood dripping to the ground.

Summoning only more Hunters.

Stumbling back, she pulled her hand to her chest, trying to staunch the bleeding.

"What is happening?" she cried, turning to Auryon, who shoved an arrow into a Hunter's chest before nocking it and directing the same into another.

"You assumed you had control over something you do not understand!" Auryon seethed. "I told you to stop summoning them. I told you to never summon them *here.*"

"I didn't know—"

"You *did* know," Auryon snapped, shoving a handful of arrows at her. "I told you. Repeatedly. We've all tried to tell you that the path you are on only leads to destruction, and now you will witness it. The least you can do is try to diminish the damage. If you won't use your power, use those."

Tessa stared down at the arrows in her hand. This was her fault. She understood that. Some dark, sadistic part of her didn't care. They could all die. Devram could waste away, and she wouldn't give two fucks.

But not with Nylah and Roan still here.

And there will still be innocents.

And she hadn't survived so much just to die with the rest of them when she'd been promised freedom from this realm.

But that freedom would come on *her* terms. Not those of a lord or a god.

Auryon glanced over at her, a look of satisfaction flashing in her eyes at whatever she saw. "There she is," the Huntress said in approval. "The fury of your mother. Use it."

And Tessa did.

She stalked forward, moving only on instinct. It was how the wild and untamed survived; it only made sense that such instincts were innate for her too. She sank into fury as she drove those arrows into the chests of Augury members and Hunters alike. She didn't care. One wanted her dead; the other had tricked her and used her. Both had preyed on her, and she took her vengeance in flesh.

For the next few minutes, sounds of life and death filled the air. Shouts of defiance and screams of agony. Growls of determination and pleas for mercy. A song that she knew in her soul because it was who she was. She knew all the steps to this dance.

Her magic thrashed in her veins, begging and pleading to take and take and take, but she couldn't do it. Not with Roan so close. She knew it made her weak, but every time she came close to summoning any of her magic, fear locked it down tight. She had something to fight for now, yes, but she also had something to protect.

"Dammit," she muttered when she was down to her last arrow.

Frowning, she wiped the bloody tip on her pants while she looked around for Auryon. She'd been so lost to the song that she hadn't kept track of everything around her. She wasn't a warrior like Luka or a trained Huntress like Auryon. She just...*was*, so she hadn't noticed that they weren't exactly winning this battle. It was messy and chaotic. She wasn't sure why she thought bloodshed would be anything other than that. She'd taken enough lives these past months to know there was nothing clean or organized about it.

But this was Hunters against...select Augury. Augury against her and the wolves. Wolves against the Augury. Auryon against Augury and Hunters, and her against everyone too. It wasn't enough. There was no way, and certainly not without her power.

Ashes and smoke swirled to her right, Auryon stepping from them. Her wicked features were sharp and hard, and she looked exhausted.

"Cordelia and Cressida have disappeared. Again," she said, slightly breathless.

Tessa couldn't help the lightning that sparked around her at that statement.

"We need to get you out of here. Nylah and Roan are clearing a path," Auryon continued, sending an arrow flying. Tessa was fairly certain she hadn't even *looked* when she let it go. "We can take you to—"

Her eyes went wide, and it was the first time Tessa had ever seen them still. The ash and smoke that usually swirled in them was frozen, and Auryon's features twisted into feral rage. Tessa didn't understand what was happening. Not until the female spun, and instead of arrows in her hands, two daggers appeared, the blades narrowing into wicked points.

A Hunter stood behind her, and before Tessa could blink, Auryon shoved both daggers into the Hunter's gut, somehow cutting the being completely in half. Gold blood sprayed as he dissipated.

And Auryon sank to the ground.

"Auryon!" Tessa screamed, dropping down beside her. "No! No, no, no!"

There was no way this was happening again.

Auryon looked up at her with those too still eyes. Eyes that should be swirling in an unnatural way. She still looked fierce and wicked. The same way she'd looked every time she'd appeared to protect Tessa. To stand between her and whatever this fucking realm was trying to do to her. Whether on her father's orders or her own volition, all Auryon had ever done was protect her.

"You're fine?" Tessa said, studying her for any grimace of pain. Nylah and Roan had appeared, circling them and keeping everyone else back, but they couldn't hold out much longer.

Luka! Theon! Now!

It was a desperate scream down the bond, and she felt them both still and shudder at the anguish.

End this! Theon snarled.

Tessa didn't know what they were dealing with, but gods, she'd never wanted to see his arrogant face more than she did right now.

Her eyes were frantically searching Auryon, trying to find a wound, any sign of blood, but there was nothing.

"You're not hurt? I don't understand," Tessa said, her hands hovering over the female's body trying to figure out what they should do.

"There will be no undoing this," Auryon said, her voice somehow strong and fading at the same time. "Just as my arrows and blades are death for the Hunters, their blades bring the same to a Huntress."

"But there's no blood. You weren't stabbed," Tessa said, confusion and panic squeezing her chest so tightly she couldn't breathe. "You're fine. I'll make a portal. You just need to get up and go through with me. We'll figure the rest out. We'll— What are you doing?"

Auryon's hand had closed around the grip of her bow that she was now shoving towards Tessa. "You need to take this."

Tessa shook her head, only then realizing her cheeks were wet. Everything was wet. The ground. Her clothing. Cloaks and fur. She was crying, and so was the sky.

"It is your birthright," Auryon said, shoving the bow at her again.

"No," Tessa said, shaking her head again so violently her hair whipped around her with the denial.

"Tessalyn!" Auryon snapped. "You are wild *and* fury, light *and* dark. Once lost, you were found. The only one who hasn't realized that is *you*."

"I don't understand," Tessa said, throwing out a hand and letting light flare when several Augury members broke through the fray.

She scarcely heard their screams as her power ripped away their life force.

And Auryon *smiled* up at her. "It is in your blood. The life you seek. What you desperately want. Many have sacrificed to give you a choice, Tessalyn. The costs have been great because of love for *you*. You only need to accept that you are worthy of such a thing, then take what is yours to claim."

This time, the female's arm trembled when she lifted the bow to Tessa.

"Slice your palm and grip the bow in blood. Speak the words of the Huntresses to bind it to you," Auryon said before reciting words in an old language. She coughed then. Tessa wished there was blood. It would all feel more real. This was like a cruel joke with no wounds and no agony. "And when you see your father, tell him I never served out of purpose or duty, but out of honor and friendship. Tell him—" She sucked in a sharp breath. "Tell him thank you for allowing me the privilege."

"Auryon, stop." The words were a whispered sob, and she didn't understand it. She wasn't close to this female. Yes, she had guarded and protected her, but she didn't *know* her. This shouldn't shred her soul like it was doing.

A swirl of smoke and ashes had her rocking back in shock, and the sound that ripped from her throat was echoed by thunder. Because when the smoke and ashes waned, there was nothing left but two ashy footprints and a bow.

Movement caught her eye, and Tessa looked up from her knees, her gaze connecting with white eyes.

The Hunter.

Their leader.

And his smile was one of victory.

Before Tessa could move, an arm wrapped around her waist. She tensed for the briefest of moments before she recognized the touch, the chaos in her veins calming a fraction.

"I'm taking you somewhere safe, but he is there," came Luka's gruff voice in her ear. "Tell me you are fine with that."

She nodded once, scrambling to grab Auryon's bow. In the next breath, she was tugged through a rip in the air.

But not without vowing to destroy the very beings she'd summoned here.

41

LUKA

He kept her held tight to him, her back to his chest, when they stepped from the air. Her heart rate was still fast, her emotions too wild and chaotic. They had lessened some when he'd finally been able to get to her. There was no doubt this had all been a meticulously planned setup. The thing they hadn't been able to sit down and figure out yet was why and who.

"Nylah and Roan," she gasped out, her breaths as rapid as her heartbeat. Her inhales too short as if she couldn't remember how to breathe.

"Were already making a run for it. They will be fine. They are somehow always fine," Luka said. "I need you to take a breath, baby girl."

She shook her head, the movement violent and erratic as she tried to break from his hold. What the fuck had happened there? And why was she holding a bow?

"Tessa, just—" Luka started.

"Tessa, stop."

The command rang out in the space. An order from someone who was used to being obeyed.

An order from a ruling Lord.

Her head whipped to the side where Theon stood, emerald eyes narrowed on them.

"I don't take orders from *you*," she sneered. "Not anymore."

A dark smirk curled on one corner of his mouth. "Beautiful, you took orders from me just a few weeks ago when you crawled across the floor."

"Only because I knew it would hurt you to know I was sucking off your best friend when I never did that for you," she snarled back.

Theon shrugged, slipping his hands into his pockets as he rocked back on his heels. "I've always said I'll take whatever you're willing to give me, and I got off to all the lust flooding down the bond between the two of you. There was nothing painful about that, clever tempest."

Tessa tsked in annoyance, rolling her eyes.

But it had worked.

Theon's words, his voice, had made her still in Luka's arms. His continued taunting had held her focus. Instead of manic thrashing, she was looking around the room, but Luka could feel her. She was focused entirely on Theon. He might be an overprotective, controlling bastard, but Tessa also needed that sometimes. And thank all the gods and fates if Theon was finally figuring out *when* she needed it, and when he needed to back the fuck off.

Maybe.

Hopefully.

Something to worry about in the future. Right now, it was working for them. Her heart rate was slowing. Her breaths were coming more evenly, tension bleeding out of her muscles as she started to relax in his hold. He still didn't let up, not sure if she was in control of herself. Or that power.

"Where are we?" she finally asked.

Theon glanced at Luka, his smirk turning into one of amusement. "Luka's super secret cave."

"Fuck off," Luka growled, but Tessa was twisting in his arms to look up at him.

"What is he talking about?" she asked.

"I have a place in Arius Kingdom," Luka grumbled.

"Right. Your smaller estate. Near Arius House," she said.

"Yes. In the mountains."

"*In* the mountains," Theon emphasized.

"Stop talking," she snapped at Theon before turning back to Luka. She didn't say anything. Just stared at him, waiting.

Luka sighed. "It's a cave."

"A cave," she deadpanned.

He nodded, his grip slowly loosening as she took in the space once more. This time, her eyes roved slowly, sweeping over the walls adorned with various frames and shelves with odds and ends. The smooth floors with plush rugs and low leather sofas. The high-end kitchen and table with seating for six. The fireplace and overstuffed chairs. Everything in warm, earthy tones. The passageways that led to other areas of his space.

His.

All of this was his.

His chest was tight as he watched her, the dragon in him peering out and waiting.

"This isn't like caves in the Underground," she finally said, her fingers doing this odd twitching thing at her sides.

"We're not in the Underground," Luka said gruffly.

"Same mountains," she countered with a shrug.

"Yes," he bristled. "But not the *same.*"

"Careful, beautiful," Theon cautioned, silencing his phone when an incoming call rang through. "He gets sensitive about things that are *his.*"

"Would you shut up?" Luka growled.

Tessa glanced between them while she wandered across the room, running her hand along the smooth wall. "And why are we in a cave?"

All the tentative playfulness evaporated at her words.

"Only a handful of people know about it," Theon answered. "It's a safe haven for you until we can figure out what happened."

"For me?" Tessa repeated, turning to face them fully. "Why do I need a safe haven?"

"Why don't you tell us what happened today?" Theon replied, silencing his phone when it rang again.

Her eyes immediately flared, bright and violet, and the bands around her wrists sparked with energy.

"*Your mother* is what happened today," she spat.

Theon reared back. "My mother? What does she have to do with anything?"

The humorless sound that came from Tessa was pure derisiveness. "She is in league with Rordan."

"Impossible. She's married to the Arius Lord," Theon argued.

"She planned this entire day!" she cried, hands diving into her hair.

Luka knew what was coming before she started the pacing. The sparks of light that followed her steps. The tugging at the ends of her hair. Knew the next words she spoke were going to be seemingly nonsensical, and they needed to listen carefully if they had any hope of figuring out what the fuck had happened today.

"She lured us there," Tessa said, still gripping the bow in her hand. "With them. With her. He did this. Him and the light guardians."

"The Augury," Luka clarified, keeping his tone calm yet forceful.

"And her," she answered with a nod, still pacing, her eyes wild and scanning the room.

"Who, Tessa?"

"Mother Cordelia," she hissed as though the words were venom.

"Cordelia was there? You saw her?" Theon demanded, taking a few steps towards her but stopping when her feet lifted an inch off the ground.

"Where were you?" she demanded. "You said you'd always come, and you *didn't*. You *lied* to me."

She may as well have hit him. That was how Theon looked as he stared at Tessa, his face pale. "We couldn't—"

Then he was cursing when his phone rang yet again.

Pulling it from his pocket, he answered with a barked, "What?"

His eyes went wide, darkness pooling at his feet. "What do you mean?" Silence while he listened. "Where are they now?" Silence. "We can't do that." Silence. "That won't stop them." Silence. "I'll be right there."

He hung up, slipping his phone back into his pocket as he crossed the room. He paid no mind when Tessa's power flared again, taking her face in his hands. "I did not lie to you, Tessa. Do you understand me? Luka will explain everything, and I'll be back as soon as I can. You will be safe here."

"Don't bother," she sneered.

He sighed, and Luka could feel his internal conflict down the bond. It felt like he was being torn in two directions. Stay here like he wanted to, or go because it was his responsibility.

He dropped his hands and turned to Luka. "I need you to Travel me to Dark Haven."

"Dark Haven? Why?" Luka asked.

"The city is under attack. Hundreds are already dead."

"What? By who?"

With another glance at Tessa, he answered. "Hunters."

"I'll go with—" Luka started, but Theon shook his head.

"You know someone needs to be with her. Guarding her."

"You are ordering this *again*?" Luka demanded. "I was *born* to fight in wars like this, Theon. Don't you get that? This is a godsdamn *war*!"

"And she is what everyone is after!" Theon roared back. "That is why I am tasking *you* with guarding her."

"I am *your* Guardian," Luka countered. "Not hers."

"Maybe not her Guardian, but you're her *something*, Luka," Theon said. "Take me to Dark Haven, and then come back here and figure it the fuck out. I think it's the only way we're going to survive this anymore."

Tessa had fallen quiet, feet back on the ground. Her violet gaze flicked back and forth between them while they argued.

"If there are Hunters involved, we need to find Auryon," Luka finally said.

"She's dead," Tessa supplied.

"What do you mean she's dead?"

"I mean a Hunter killed her. This was hers," Tessa said, helplessly lifting the bow she still held.

"I told you we should have brought Razik and Eliza here," Theon said. "They've dealt with the Hunters before. Or at least Razik has."

"And I told *you* he is *not* coming to my cave," Luka growled. "I'll take you to them. They can go with you to Dark Haven."

"Fine. We don't have time to debate this anymore," Theon said. Then he added, "Luka will be right back, Tessa. Less than a minute."

"Don't touch anything," Luka muttered.

She was still flipping him off when he grabbed Theon's arm and Traveled him directly into Razik and Eliza's room at the Arius manor. His brother glanced up from whatever the fuck he was doing, but didn't say a word. Eliza sighed, resting her chin in her hand and waiting for an explanation.

"There are Hunters in Dark Haven," Luka said. "Don't let Theon get killed."

They were both lurching to their feet, but he was already Traveling back to his cave to find Tessa still standing where he'd left her. She said nothing when he reappeared. Just stood there, holding that godsdamn bow in her hand.

Luka waited, unsure of what she was going to say or do. He never knew with her, and it drove him mad. She might be calm and collected, ready to have a civil conversation. Or she might lose her ever-loving mind and start ripping things apart with her power. It was always one extreme or the other.

He wasn't expecting her to lift the bow up after nearly five minutes of silence and say, "I don't know how to use this."

"What do you need to use it for?" Luka asked, watching her carefully.

"Auryon said it was my birthright to have it. I don't know. I don't understand." She trailed off, her bottom lip disappearing between her teeth. "I know you don't want me here, but—"

"I know you don't want to be here," he interrupted. When she sent him a perplexed look, he clarified, "In Arius Kingdom."

Although, she hadn't said much about the cave either, and she'd basically said it was just like being in the Underground. Which she loathed. So he supposed she'd said all she needed to about what she thought about the space he'd spent hundreds of hours and an exorbitant amount of coin to make it feel like anything *but* a hole in the side of a mountain.

"You were with Theon?" she asked, still not moving. "That was why you didn't come?"

There was a clear accusation in the question, but he also heard the undercurrent of hurt. They'd spent every night sleeping beside each other these last weeks, ever since she'd been on her knees before him. Ever since she'd given him something she didn't have to. It was more than her "sucking him off," as she'd so eloquently put it to Theon. Or it had been more to him. He thought it had been for her too. Thought he'd made it clear, but apparently not if it was just another means of torture for Theon.

"You didn't show up for training," he started.

"Don't start with that," she sneered.

"Would you just listen?" he retorted. She huffed, moving to cross her arms before realizing she still held the bow. She looked around, trying to decide where to set it down.

"For fuck's sake," he muttered, closing the distance between them and taking it from her.

He made sure not to yank it from her hands, gently easing it from her grasp. It was obviously important to her, despite the fact he was certain she hadn't been close to Auryon.

After carefully laying it across the dining table, he returned, keeping distance between them again. Her fingers were curling into the hem of her shirt as she worked to keep herself grounded, splatters of red and gold marring her clothing and skin.

"Are you hurt?" he asked suddenly. He couldn't believe neither he nor

Theon hadn't asked that immediately. They would have felt it down the bond if she had been hurt, but they usually still asked for peace of mind.

Tessa shook her head. "They tried to hurt us. The others tricked us." Right on cue, her hands flew into her hair. "They *used* us."

"Look at me, Tessa," he ordered, violet irises immediately snapping to his. "Stay right here, okay? Stay with me, and focus on my words." She nodded slowly before he continued. "You didn't show up for training, but Dex had delivered a message that said you would be gone all day due to whatever Rordan had discussed with you. I wasn't pleased, but I know this is a delicate balance between you, me, and the Achaz Lord right now, so I didn't argue. It turned out I would have had to cancel training anyway because while I was making my way back to the palace, Theon called. There had been an emergency Tribunal Hearing called to discuss the fate of Arius Kingdom with Valter still unaccounted for. Theon was required to be there, obviously. You can't go to those meetings alone. You've seen them. They would all be against him. Axel is gone. I am still his advisor. You left, but I didn't."

Tessa nodded, and he thought it was in understanding of what he was saying until she said, "I am merely your responsibility. He is your family. I understand that."

Luka was certain the look on his face was the same that Theon had sported when she'd accused him of lying to her. It felt like she'd hit him harder than she ever could. No, it felt like she'd punched him with the weight of her power behind it.

And the dragon beneath his skin had had enough.

She stumbled back as a gasp of surprise fell from her lips when his wings appeared, shredding through his shirt. He was prowling towards her, and with each step he took, she took another back until she was pressing against the wall.

He didn't stop until his boots were touching the tips of hers. His wings flaring behind him, he planted one palm above her head and gripped her chin with the other, forcing her face up to meet his gaze.

"What are you doing?" she snarled, but there was a breathiness to it that made his dragon rumble in satisfaction.

"Making sure you are looking at me," he answered. She rolled her godsdamn eyes, but she didn't look away. "Do you truly think I have spent these last months in the fucking Achaz Kingdom out of *responsibility?*"

"I know you don't want to be there," she retorted. "I know you'd rather be here. With Theon. You didn't want to go there."

"You're right. I didn't."

The slice of pain that flashed across her eyes was gone in the next blink, but the pang of hurt down the bond lingered.

He loosened his grip on her chin, instead cupping her jaw. "My place is in Arius Kingdom with Theon and Axel," he went on, not letting her turn away at the words. "But it isn't home unless you are there with us."

"Please don't give me pretty words right now," she said, her tone so defeated it made his chest hurt.

"If you would fucking listen for once, you'd know they aren't just pretty words, baby girl," he chided. "Do you know how jealous I was when Theon Selected you?"

That had her eyes flying wide. "What?"

He gave her a knowing look. "We'd gathered all this godsdamn information about so many Fae, but you... Godsdammit, Tessa. It was always *you*. For both of us, and he may be a brother to me, but I hated that he was the one who would get to have you. For the years leading up to the Selection Ceremony, I forced myself to be indifferent, but I couldn't help trying to convince him to Select someone else. I constantly told him you weren't the one for this. Not because I had any inkling you weren't Fae or were the grandchild of the most powerful gods, but because dragons are jealous creatures, temptress. If I couldn't have you, I didn't want anyone else to have you either."

"You didn't even know me," she whispered.

"I know," he growled in frustration. "That's what made it so godsdamn ridiculous. Because I shouldn't have cared. I shouldn't have cared about the stormy grey eyes in a photograph that stared up at me on the screen of a tablet. I shouldn't have cared that you wanted flip-flops. I shouldn't have cared that you didn't know how to defend yourself. I shouldn't have cared because you were supposed to be his, but I did care because some part of me claimed you as mine from the moment I saw your photo."

"But you're too loyal," she said in quiet acceptance. "And he is your family."

"He is my family," he agreed. "But you? You are my light."

"You said yourself you are his Guardian, not mine," she said, so much hope in those guarded words.

His hand slid along her jaw, slipping into the golden hair she so often abused. "Baby girl, I've always been yours. I just didn't understand it."

She surged onto her toes, her mouth crashing into his. Gods, he wanted to drown in her and never come up for air. He didn't need to breathe if she was finally accepting what he had to offer. His entire life he'd been constantly trying to prove himself worthy of his place in the Arius Kingdom household. Worthy of being part of the St. Orcas family. Worthy of his bloodline. But when she kissed him, all he cared about was being worthy of *her*. If *she* accepted him, none of the rest of it mattered.

Something in his soul slipped into place at the thought. A piece that he'd been trying to find for nearly three decades. Trying to belong when he didn't quite fit in anywhere else. Searching for something and never knowing what exactly that something was.

Finally giving himself permission to understand it had always been her.

Luka gathered her up, lifting her off the ground and feeling her legs wrap around his waist as his tongue slicked over hers. A low whimper sounded, and everything in him became a frenzy of desire and possession. Because she needed something, and he could give it to her.

His mouth never stopped exploring hers when he Traveled them to his bedroom, not bothering with walking through the passage. He didn't have time for that right now. Didn't want to navigate around furniture and knickknacks.

They were both breathing hard, one of his hands tracing along the waist of her pants. Her shirt was short enough that it raised up, letting his fingers graze bare skin. The single touch had her pressing herself into him even more, both of them hungry and desperate. Sliding an arm under her ass to keep her balanced, he slid his other hand under her shirt because the small indulgent touches he'd allowed himself in the past weren't going to be enough. Not anymore. Never again.

He found her breasts, snarling at the sports bra that blocked his access, and a choked laugh came from her.

Until he all but dropped her onto the mattress.

"Luka!" she barked, glaring up at him with lightning sparking in her eyes.

"I want you naked," he growled, watching the flush that crept up her chest, her neck, her face. Another growl sounded when his gaze slid down her body. "Why the fuck are you wearing boots?"

She tipped her head back as she spouted, "*You* insist I wear them for training. Which is where I was supposed to go. Instead, I was shoving arrows into people and painting myself in their blood."

"Gods, I love it when you're vicious," he said, his voice nothing but gravel. Dropping to his knees, he removed her boots in record time. He dragged her pants down her legs, undergarments with them, before he reached up and made quick work of her shirt and sports bra.

With a not-so-gentle shove, he pushed her onto her back. His mattress was on the floor here as it was in his various rooms at the manors, and he could stare down at her from his knees. He still towered over her small frame splayed out before him. Naked in his nest of blankets and pillows. Completely at his mercy and squirming under his gaze.

"What are you doing?" she asked, an uncertainty in her tone he didn't like.

"Looking," he answered immediately. "Looking at a goddess. So let me look."

"It's weird," she murmured, squirming some more.

He clicked his tongue. "You paraded around naked all the time, never bothered."

"I did not," she cried in outrage.

"Bare skin always on display. You were a tease, temptress," he chided. "You made me so godsdamn crazy, I couldn't be around you sometimes."

"Wait," she said, pushing up onto her elbows to see him better. "Is that why you were so scarce all the time when I first came to Arius House?"

He nodded, letting his eyes slowly roam down her body. Starting at the top of her head with that golden hair he'd had wrapped around his fist while he'd thrust into a mouth that drove him half mad. Down her delicate throat to her perfect round breasts, her nipples rigid peaks just waiting for him to suck on them. Down her rib cage, her stomach, her hips to where her creamy thighs pressed together.

A rumble sounded from his chest, his palms landing on her knees and nudging them. "Spread your legs, temptress. Let me see you."

"You and Theon have dirty mouths," she said, her voice sultry and erotic as she dropped her knees to the sides and spread herself wide for him.

All for him.

His tongue darted out, wetting his lips as he stared at her. "You love our mouths," he replied distractedly. "I can only imagine what you'll do when we're both worshipping you."

He felt her heart stutter down the bond. Heard her sharp inhale. "Do you... The two of you... Do that?"

His gaze flicked to hers, finding her eyes heavy-lidded and full of heated lust at the idea.

And he smirked.

"You like the sound of that, don't you, temptress?" he crooned, sliding his palms up the inside of her thighs. She gasped as he climbed higher. "Both of us on our knees before you, giving you pleasure. *Serving* you. Letting you take whatever you want."

"Oh, gods," she cried when he ran two fingers along her cunt, finding her soaked.

"Such a good girl," he murmured, her back arching at the small touch.

Then he lowered his lips, planting a long, open-mouthed kiss to her center. He was going to devour her. There was no other option when he finally tasted her, the dragon in him snarling in satisfaction but also pushing him to take more. He knew what the dragon wanted. Knew he wouldn't be satisfied until he'd fucked her properly and claimed what was always meant to be his.

She whimpered when he licked a hot path to her clit, a hand driving into his hair. Then there was a frustrated growl as she yanked the band out of the strands. Luka chuckled against her skin while his tongue continued to toy with her, one of his fingers making its way back to her entrance.

"Ask me for it," he murmured against her skin, huffing another laugh when she shoved at him with her foot.

"Don't be an ass right now," she whined.

But he just lifted his mouth from her cunt, instead planting small kisses along her thighs.

"Luka," she cried in frustration.

His answer was a nip to her flesh. "Wouldn't you rather wait to come until I'm fucking you?"

She shook her head against the mattress, hair flying around her. "No," she panted. "I want both."

"So greedy," he mocked, slipping a finger inside of her. Her moan morphed into a gasp when he added a second finger. Then it became unintelligible sounds when he returned his mouth to her clit, laving at the sensitive nerves. It didn't take long for her thighs to lock around his head as pleasure rolled through her, his tongue lapping it all up.

She was still gasping for air, her body trembling, when Luka stood. Hooded eyes tracked his every movement when he pulled the remains of his shirt from his body and tossed it aside. He watched her gaze skate over his chest and down his torso, lingering where he thumbed the button of his pants.

"What are you doing?" he mocked.

"Looking," she tossed back, her eyes dragging back up his abdomen. Suddenly, she sat up, shifting onto all fours and crawling closer.

"Fuck me, temptress," he growled. "What the fuck are you doing?"

"*Looking*," she said again.

She came to the end of the bed, reaching out and tugging him closer by the waist of his pants as she sat up on her knees. Her eyes darted over his shoulder, and he suddenly realized *what* she was studying so hard.

"You can touch them," he said, his stomach sinking in when her fingers glided along the ridges of his abdomen.

Her eyes widened. "What?"

He gently took her wrist, bringing one wing around them. Guiding her hand, he said, "You can touch them."

Far more careful than she needed to be, she skated a single fingertip along the edge of the wing. It could barely be classified as a touch.

"*Touch* it, baby girl," he said, engulfing her hand with his and pressing her palm flat against his wing.

He watched her face as she marveled at the cool, leathery appendage beneath her fingers, feeling a shiver go down his spine as she moved her hand. A sound rumbled from him that couldn't quite be called a growl.

She stilled, peering up at him from beneath thick lashes. "Do they get in the way?"

His brows knit together. "Did they get in the way of me feasting on your cunt?"

Her cheeks flushed. "You can't just say things like that, Luka."

"Tessa, your mouth is just as dirty," he replied, stepping closer because he couldn't handle so much space between them. He bent, brushing his lips along hers and letting his wing graze her bare back. "But to answer your question, no. I'm used to them, I suppose. They are a part of me."

She nodded, her eyes glazing over when he bent to kiss her again. "Now can I fuck you?" he murmured against her lips.

"Only if you say please," she crooned back.

He huffed a laugh before shucking off his pants and easing her back down on the bed. Crawling over top of her, his mouth found hers again, tongue dipping out to lick along her lips. Working himself between her legs, she gasped into his mouth as he lined himself up with her, the head of his cock grazing her opening.

Eventually this would turn into fast and chaotic fucking, but this part? The first time he was finally, *finally*, going to claim her, he was going to take his time with this part. He lifted up to watch her as he slowly eased inside her warm heat, his eyes nearly rolling back in his head.

"Fuck," he spat, sinking in another inch. "You feel— *Gods*."

Her laugh was more of a soft keen as he pushed in a little more. "I'm not fragile, Luka. You can actually *fuck* me."

"I know," he rasped. "I will. Just— Fuck," he cursed again, his entire body quivering when he finally seated himself fully. Her hands came up, nails stroking along his biceps. His gaze got caught up in violet eyes glowing with specks of gold. Her smile was softer than he'd ever seen it as she bit her lip, clearly debating if she should say something, and panic blossomed in his chest. If she was suddenly changing her mind, he didn't think he could handle it. He'd stop, obviously, but she was *his*. The dragon in him would never see it any other way. Just like Theon would never see it any other way. Not now that he was inside her, even if he hadn't completely fucked and claimed her yet.

"Are you all right?" he asked, every ounce of self-control keeping him from going feral to keep her.

She nodded, her nails making another pass. "I was just thinking that if you've always been mine, maybe some part of me has always been yours in a way too. We just never understood it because we're all so... broken."

She wasn't wrong. They were all so broken, all so irreparably fucked up, that no one knew how to properly love anything. No one knew what a healthy partnership looked like. It was all status elevation, power struggles, and dominance in Devram. Who could you take the most from while giving the least amount in return. It was obsessively protecting and clinging to illusions of freedom while trying to secure a place to make sure you belonged. There was no fucking balance. There never had been. Not in Devram.

"We just don't have to be broken alone anymore," he replied, pushing stray hair off her brow.

"Never alone again," she agreed.

He started off slow, pulling out and easing back inside her. Feeling her inner muscles clench and try to keep him inside with each pass.

"Gods, you are greedy," he murmured, dragging his mouth along her collarbone and down to a breast.

"I call it knowing what I want," she gasped as he sucked a nipple into his mouth.

"And what do you want?" he asked against her flesh.

"You," she said on a breath, and those words undid him. Gods, those words of her accepting him for what he was?

Anything slow and measured about this was gone.

He sat up on his knees, ignoring her protesting whine at the loss of heat, but from this vantage, he could see himself lodged inside of her. The sight of it was erotic, but the sight of it also satisfied something primal.

His hands curled around the fronts of her thighs, and he flexed his hips, thrusting in and out. He watched himself fuck her, claim her, take her for his own.

"You like watching?" she asked in a tone that told him *she* liked him watching.

"Do I like watching my cock inside of you?" he asked with a huff of disbelief. "Yeah, temptress. I like watching how well your cunt takes my cock."

Her hips rose, seeking more. "Okay, well, do you think you could stop admiring your outstanding fucking skills and actually *do* the fucking?" she panted.

He paused, his cock halfway out of her.

"That bratty mouth of yours," he snarled, slamming back into her and smirking at the gasp that punched from her chest. "Like that?"

"Yes," she breathed when he did it again. "Just like that."

Luka coiled forward, his body covering hers as she clawed at his back, his arms, his shoulders. Anywhere she could touch. His hips moved faster, giving her what she'd asked for. The change of angle made his pelvis scrape against her clit with every deep plunge of his length, her whimpers and moans driving him on.

He didn't need to ask if she was close, feeling her core start to spasm around him, and he didn't slow, sliding his palms under her ass to lift her a little higher. She shuddered in his hold, her entire body vibrating with her orgasm as her magic flared, her skin glowing.

But the flare of power also called to his own, black flames rushing to the surface and licking along her bare flesh, drawing out her pleasure as another cry fell from her lips. The sound of it shoved him into his own release, his head dropping as he groaned hoarsely into her neck. His cock jerked, emptying into her, and his dragon was finally satisfied... for now.

Gods, he almost wanted to go again now that he'd had her.

Her breathing was still uneven when her trembling fingers drifted through his hair.

"Luka?"

He hummed an acknowledgment.

"If I... Would you still..."

He sat up, internally mourning when his cock slipped out of her. "Tell me, Tessa."

She wouldn't look at him when she said in a rush, "If I fulfill my purpose, will I still be yours?"

He stared down at her. At this female who had been a pain in his ass from the moment he'd laid eyes on her. At the cautious hope that lingered in her violet eyes, fully prepared to accept his rejection because she'd been rejected her entire life.

Knowing the words would mean more to her than any declaration of feeling or love, Luka said, "My loyalty is to you, Tessa."

Two tears immediately slipped from her eyes as she rose up, her arms wrapping around his neck and hauling him back to her.

It was hours later when she was resting against his chest, her fingers toying with the fine hair there while she drifted in and out of sleep, that he realized he hadn't blocked the bond. In all the chaos and heat of the moment, it hadn't occurred to him once. Even when they'd spoken of him, he hadn't thought to shield his friend from this.

Theon had felt all of it.

Every whispered word and conflicting thought.

And his friend hadn't said a single word.

42

EVIANA

"You need to hurry it up," sounded a whisper from beyond the door.

"You need to shut up," came a hissed retort.

Eviana sat in her chair, head tilted as she watched the door. Her hand slid down the side of the cushion, a shard of glass there should she need it.

When she'd heard the scuffling start, she had perked up, thinking it was Tessa. She hadn't seen her in a while. The last time she was here, she'd suddenly become too warm in the room, shedding a long coat. It had looked ridiculous on her. She was so short, the hem of it reached nearly to Tessa's ankles. But on her? It reached mid-calf.

Eviana had slipped it on after she'd left. The inside, along with the hood and cuffs, were lined with some kind of grey fur, looking elegant against the black fabric. This was a coat Cressida would wear. Extravagant and frivolous, but it *was* warm.

She'd turned the thing inside out, planning to slice pockets into the interior, only to find them already there. Seven of them. Only one of them contained anything though: a single piece of paper with a seven-digit code on it. She had no idea what it meant, but she'd slipped it back into the pocket before sliding one of the hair combs into another. Two of her makeshift weapons filled two of the pockets. She stored food in another. She'd left the final two open, folding the coat up. It looked like a small blanket draped across the back of her chair.

"For the love of Sefarina, Cor, get the fucking door open," came the first voice again.

"Lange, I love you. But if you don't shut the fuck up, I'm causing a scene just to get us caught so I can have two godsdamn minutes of quiet," came a snarled retort.

Then a laugh. "You've gotten more domineering since—"

A click had the door opening, and two Fae rushed inside before closing the door behind them. The two seemed to breathe a collective sigh of relief before spotting her near the window.

It was the one with the hair so blond it was white that stepped forward. She knew who they were—likely knew more than they did about who they were—but she didn't speak. Always let them speak first. Let them ramble a little. See what they reveal.

"Eviana, right?" Lange said, shifting awkwardly on his feet when she continued to stare at him. "We were, uh, sent to…help you?"

She arched a brow. "Why are you asking me a question? I do not know why you are here."

"That's fair," he murmured. "You're just…a Source."

Her smile was tight and joyless. "And you are a Fae serving the same kingdom, so what are you doing outside of it?"

Lange glanced over his shoulder at Corbin before he said simply, "Tessa sent us."

"Tessa," Eviana repeated.

Lange nodded. "Yeah. Theon's Source. Kind of. Or she was, but isn't now. I think?"

"I know who Tessa is," she replied coolly.

"Okay…" He pulled on the back of his neck. "Because she kind of made it sound like you'd *want* us to come get you."

"Listen, we're working on limited time the way it is," Corbin cut in, stepping up behind Lange. "Tristyn gave us ten minutes maximum, and we used too many of them getting through the security to your room."

"Tristyn Blackheart is here?" Eviana asked.

That was interesting.

"Yes," Corbin said. "Cienna said this would work if everything was timed perfectly."

"The Witch?"

That was even more surprising.

Corbin muttered a curse under his breath. "Yes. The Witch. The

Witch who told us our timing had to be perfect, and we are close to testing her warning. Do you want out of here or not?"

"To go where?"

"Back to the Arius manor for now," Lange answered.

"Without my master?"

"That's the plan."

"He will remain locked up?"

"We're not going to free him," Lange replied.

Keeping her features expressionless, she reached out down the bond. *Are you well, my Lord?*

Am I well? he snarled. *No, I am not well, Eviana.*

She winced internally. He was angry. Something must have happened. It explained why he'd been so quiet these last hours. He always got too quiet when he was angry. He let it brew and fester until he could take it out on someone or something.

Usually her.

Is there something I can do from here? she asked, the knowledge that he couldn't touch her right now the only reason she did so. If she were in the same room as him, she would have remained quiet and still in her chair, not daring to breathe.

Yes, Eviana, he snapped. *You can do what is expected of you and serve your Master. Get me out of here.*

Tell me what to do, my Lord.

You know what to do. Kill whomever you must. Fuck whomever you must. Do and sacrifice whatever is necessary. My kingdom is at stake.

Lange and Corbin were staring at her, clearly unsure of what to do.

Corbin pulled a small phone from his pocket, glancing at it before he said, "We need to go right now. You need to decide."

"I just need to gather a few things," she replied.

"There isn't time," Corbin insisted.

She ignored him, moving to pull the boots from their hiding place. Slipping them on, she grabbed the coat, unfolding it while she made her way to the bathroom and twisted her hair up, sliding the other comb into it. Lange and Corbin were fidgeting by the door, growing more anxious by the second.

She dropped to her knees, reaching under the bed.

"Fuck," she heard Corbin whisper. "Someone is out there now. We ran out of time."

Eviana stood, the broken neck of the wine bottle in her hand.

"Should we call Tristyn?" Lange asked.

"I could, but— Wait!" Corbin cried.

But she didn't.

Eviana strode by them, pulling open the unlocked door.

"What the fu—" the guard started, and then he was gurgling. Bright red bubbled from his lips and dripped down his neck from where she'd shoved the jagged end of the wine bottle into it.

"That...won't kill him," Lange said weakly. "He'll heal too quickly."

Eviana smiled, and he shrank back into Corbin. "Not if there are too many wounds and a severed spinal cord."

It took a matter of seconds for her to stab in strategic places. *Creative* places Mansel had shown her. The harder part was sawing a broken wine bottle through a spinal cord. It took some muscles she hadn't had to use since being locked in that room. When she was done, she pushed back to her feet with a frown. It was messy. Valter would reprimand her for that if he was here.

But he wasn't.

She shrugged, slipping the wine bottle into an outer pocket of her coat. "What is the plan for leaving?"

Corbin and Lange stared back at her. She recognized the looks of shock and terror. She'd seen them enough in her years.

"We're, uh, meeting Tristyn one floor up," Corbin answered, placing himself between her and Lange.

Interesting, but not entirely surprising considering who they were.

"Is he there yet?" she asked, directing her question to Lange.

"Why would I know that?" he countered. She only stared back at him expectantly. It was a few more seconds before he said, "He is probably waiting for us?"

It was good enough for her, and she stepped to the side to let them lead the way. She'd been in that room for weeks. She certainly didn't remember her way around the Faven Palace. The few times she'd been here with Valter, they'd always been led from the entry to either the dining room or a study.

Rival kingdoms and such nonsense.

Sure enough, Tristyn was waiting for them, a look of disapproval on his handsome face. Whether it was from their tardiness or the blood splattered across her, she didn't know, nor did she care.

"What now?" she asked.

He glanced at Corbin and Lange. "Any issues we need to deal with?"

"I think we should just get out of here," Lange said, eyeing her in a way that told her he was questioning whether they should even bring her along.

"If you leave me here, I will be forced to try to free him," she said in response to his unasked question.

"Tessa asked us to do this. We owe her this," Corbin said. When Lange sent him a glare, he added, "I never said it was a good idea. She rarely has those."

Tristyn huffed a laugh at that. "You'd be surprised how wrong you are in that statement."

He reached out a hand, placing it on Lange's shoulder. Lange reached for Corbin, who stretched out a hand to her.

"We all have to be touching," Lange explained.

She hesitated only a moment before placing her fingers in his palm. Not because she trusted these fools. Not in the slightest.

But because she knew what to do.

Kill whomever she must.

Fuck whomever she must.

Do and sacrifice whatever was necessary.

Not for a kingdom or for her master.

But for a little girl named Priya.

"Should we take those bands off?" the Fae with the red-gold hair asked.

"No!" Corbin and Lange both shouted in unison.

The female huffed, crossing her arms with a glare.

"I think we should hold off on that until Theon returns," Tristyn said, everyone in the room seeming to relax at his words.

Eviana observed him, trying to figure out how he fit in here. The male had always been elusive, known for his glamours and technology. He had never once taken a meeting with Valter. Or if he had, not in this form. With the ease with which everyone was conversing with him, she was inclined to believe this was not only his natural form, but that they knew him well.

She was standing in the living room of the Arius manor, a place she'd been thousands of times. They always stayed here during Selection Years and whenever Valter had business in the Acropolis that required an extended stay. Her hands were clasped in front of her as she watched the five others in this room debate. They'd introduced her to the newcomers, but no one had volunteered where they had come from and what they were doing in her master's house.

Or why the male looked so similar to Luka Mors.

"So what do we do with her?" Razik asked, before he growled a curse when Eliza elbowed him in the ribs.

"She is standing right there," the female chided. "Don't speak about her as if she isn't." Then she rounded on the others. "*And* she should have the same rights as the rest of you. She deserves to have those bands taken off. It can drive us mad to be separated from our power like that for long periods of time."

Eviana almost huffed a laugh. She would have if she could feel anything. The truth was she'd gone mad long ago.

"We can't," Tristyn said, rubbing at his temple. "She is the Source of Valter. If she is free to access her power, he could instruct her to use it against us."

Eve? Where are you? Did they move you? The bond is stretched far too thin, came his voice down the bond, and now she was the one rubbing at her temple.

She couldn't lie to him, but she didn't have to tell him exactly where she was.

They did move me, my Lord, she answered. *I fear it is quite a distance from you.*

What are their plans?

I do not know yet.

Relay any information you gather.

Of course, my Lord.

As if being separated from you for weeks wasn't enough, now they have taken us farther apart. On whose orders?

I am unaware of the orders, my Lord.

Find out! came the barked command.

I will share what I learn.

"Are you all right?"

She looked up, all of them staring at her, but Eliza's grey eyes held concern. Eviana's head cocked to the side, and her...whatever he was to her, clearly didn't like what her face did because he stepped in front of the female.

Eliza clicked her tongue in annoyance. "If the bond is the issue, then we find a way to block it."

"There is no way to fully block a bond," Tristyn said, exasperated. "Just as there is no way to sever the bond without a death."

Eliza's lip curled in a mocking smile. "Scarlett did it."

"Impossible," Tristyn said, shaking his head.

"Not impossible," Eliza countered. "She blocked her twin flame bond and then ended up getting captured. It set off a whole series of events, but the point is, she did it. Why can't we do it for Eviana?"

"You can block the bond?" Eviana repeated, and everyone turned to her.

They were the first words she'd spoken since they'd appeared here. Traveled through the very air. She didn't know how long she would be able to keep that secret, but if the bond could truly be blocked... Well, that would be convenient. More convenient than death to sever the thing, she supposed.

"That was her twin flame bond," Razik was saying. "This...*thing* they've created is more than that."

"Yes, but it blocked *everything*," Eliza argued. "Including her Guardian bond."

"That still doesn't account for the Source bond that is woven into those," Razik countered, gesturing to the Marks on her hands. "You know as well as anyone we don't mess around with blood magic."

"But it is possible?" Eviana interrupted.

"Can you not block the bond with mental shields?" Razik asked, watching her with familiar eyes.

"I *can*," she answered. "To protect myself from those who would harm a Lord's Source, but that does not block the ability to feel one's physical presence."

The male rubbed at his chin. "I see."

"Where did Scarlett find such a Mark?" Tristyn asked. Then he added, "Corbin, can I see that tablet I gave you?"

The Fae handed over the tech, Tristyn unlocking it before tapping numerous things on the screen.

"She has a book," Eliza answered. "A spellbook."

Tristyn looked up. "Where'd she get that?"

"She stole it."

"From a Witch?" he demanded. "They kill for such a slight."

"It's not a Witch that will ever kill that female," Razik grumbled, stepping back a step before Eliza could elbow him again.

"She stole it from a being imprisoned in our land," Eliza supplied. "The point is, it can be done."

"But not to the same capacity," Razik argued.

She rounded on him, fire sparking in her eyes. A fire Fae then. Even more interesting.

"Are you suggesting that we leave an innocent Fae locked in bands that suppress her magic and keep her bound in some sadistic mockery of a bond she was forced into?" Eliza demanded. "She should have a choice. She had a curse forced on her, and she should have a fucking choice, Razik."

Something pained crossed the male's face, and Eviana watched him pull her into his chest. "This is not the same thing, *mai dragocen*," he murmured into her hair.

"Isn't it?" she demanded. "Not the same outcome, but still something forced on her. Something that took a choice away from her."

Her head cocked to the side as she took in the exchange. She had seen several Source bonds over her years, and none of them looked like that. Surely she chose her bond with Razik, but she wasn't wrong with the way she spoke either. She was still trying to work out where they came from that a Legacy and Fae were together so freely. Or maybe they weren't so free? And that was why everything about them was so secretive?

Either way, none of it mattered. If the bond could truly be blocked, it would make her tasks insurmountably easier. No incessant voice in her head. No dealing with his emotions. No way for him to track her down.

She remained quiet while Razik continued to console Eliza. Lange had plopped down on the sofa, and Corbin was hovering over Tristyn's shoulder, watching him work on the tablet.

"Why not use the other code?" Corbin asked.

"Because that one leaves a trace," Tristyn answered. "When you add these extra digits and symbols, it scrambles everything further. It becomes untraceable."

"Nothing is untraceable," Corbin argued.

"It is when we can shift the energy and power," Tristyn said. "Watch."

Seconds later, Corbin's hazel eyes lit up with excitement. "That's amazing. You can access anything from anywhere."

Tristyn nodded. "It takes longer with certain devices, but it's why I gave you one of my own. I can navigate it faster."

Fingers swiping quickly, he flipped the tablet over, showing the screen to Eliza and Razik. "You're talking about this Mark, right?"

Extricating herself from Razik's arms, Eliza peered at the screen. "Is that a spellbook inside there?"

Tristyn chuckled. "No. I do not keep a spellbook in here, but I do have a database of Marks and such."

Eliza studied the image for a moment longer before saying, "I never got a good look at Scarlett's Mark. It was...a complicated situation."

"Her bond obviously isn't still blocked," Tristyn mused, flipping the screen back to him and studying the Mark more. "What was the cost?"

"It blocked *everything*," Eliza answered. "Any and all bonds, including the one with her Guardian, and to reverse it, she had to let her power drain away to nothing."

"We're forgetting that she is not Fae," Razik said. "Who's to say the Mark will be the same for a Fae versus a Legacy."

"That wouldn't be an issue," Eviana interrupted.

They all turned to her. She stood in the same place, still and with her hands clasped.

"Why wouldn't that be an issue?" Tristyn asked slowly.

"Because I am not a pure-blooded Fae."

"Then...what are you?" Eliza asked.

"My mother was a Silas Legacy."

"But..." Eliza trailed off, the look of horror on her face morphing into anger.

Eviana only smirked. "The Marks are not the only things perverse and altered in Devram. They like to...experiment. It is how advancements are made."

"Not all advancements," Tristyn cut in, an angry red flush to his cheeks. "Things like that were never done at Lilura Inquest."

Eviana shrugged. "The point is, if the Mark requires more than Fae blood to be successful, it is an unnecessary worry."

"There are costs with blood magic," Razik started.

"Then I will pay them."

"But it might not be you," he argued. "It will affect any bond you have. Could affect anyone connected to you."

"Like who?" she asked.

"That's the thing," he retorted, sounding annoyed. "We can't know.

Magic is still magic. We don't know all the secrets of it, despite our best efforts. It's like the realm and the stars. It's like trying to make sense of Chaos."

"I will take the risk."

"But—"

"Razik, it's her choice," Eliza interrupted.

"And if that choice leads to death?"

"Death hasn't had mercy on me for decades. He won't start now," Eviana cut in. "But if you do not do this, you may as well return me to Faven. Eventually, I will be forced to betray everything I have seen here."

She'd betray them all anyway in the end, but they would learn that in time.

"If the Mark can block the bond, it would buy us time," Tristyn said.

"Shouldn't we consult Theon before we do this?" Corbin asked.

"Are we loyal to Tessa or Theon?"

They all turned to Lange where he was casually lounging. His platinum blond hair had fallen into his eyes, one arm stretched along the back of the sofa.

"What does that mean?" Corbin asked.

"Tessa asked us to free her. Not Theon," Lange went on. "Knowing Tessa, I would imagine she meant freeing her from more than a room. Like a genesis."

Tristyn's brow furrowed. "What are you talking about?"

At the same time, Corbin said tightly, "Lange, not now."

A third voice rang out among the sudden chaos.

"What did you just say?" Razik asked.

Lange blinked, looking confused. "I'm...not sure."

Eliza looked up at Razik, but he was already striding from the room. "Do what you want. I need to look into something."

"Is that normal?" Tristyn asked Eliza.

"Unfortunately. It's annoying," she muttered. Turning to face Eviana fully, she gave her a small smile that Eviana did not return. "I think the choice should be yours."

"I already said I would take the Mark," Eviana replied curtly, wondering why they were having the same conversation over and over. This was like sitting in a room with the Lords and Ladies. They once debated what kind of bread to serve at the Selection Closing for three days. Someone just needed to make a decision so they could all move forward one way or another.

There was a burst of flames, Eliza pulling a scion from them, and Eviana's brow arched. "You can bestow Marks? I thought you were a Fae, not a priestess."

"It's complicated," she said, motioning for Tristyn to turn the screen back to her.

"They have to be drawn precisely," he warned.

"I'm aware," the female drawled, moving closer to her. "Where would you like it?

Unclasping her hands, she looked down. A Mark on the back of each. Three identifying Marks on her inner wrist. Maybe not somewhere quite so obvious though.

Unbuttoning the coat she still wore, she slipped it off, laying it carefully across a chair. Then she reached up and pulled aside the collar of her shirt, baring the back of her shoulder.

"Here," she said.

"You are sure?" Eliza asked.

"I wouldn't say it if I weren't."

Eliza nodded, not questioning her again before she got to work. It took only minutes, Eviana scarcely feeling the burn of the scion against her flesh as she focused on the bond, wondering if this would truly work.

Eve?

She sighed internally. *My Lord?*

What is happening?

I do not know what you mean.

You feel faint. Are they moving you again?

No, my Lord. I am in the same place as before.

Then what— happening— Eviana?

For the first time in a long time, she smiled.

Yes, my Lord?

What is... They doing... kill them... Now!

"Almost done," Eliza murmured.

She couldn't remember the last time she'd truly smiled.

Goodbye, my Lord.

Eviana!

It was a cry of rage and panic rather than any type of mourning at losing her. He was losing power, not her.

But she couldn't feel him. She could feel...

Nothing.

There was no voice rattling around in her mind.

No commands or orders.

No feelings.

Just blessed silence.

"I hope you understand that we still need to keep you locked up for now," Tristyn said tentatively.

"You cannot be serious!" Eliza cried in outrage.

"I compromised on the Mark. I cannot compromise on this until we speak to Theon," he replied in a tone that said he wouldn't budge on this. "There is too much happening right now. Too much unknown with Dark Haven and the rest of the kingdom."

Eviana didn't care. They could lock her up. It was fine.

"Can I have some paper and a pen?" she asked.

"Yes," Eliza answered immediately, going to secure the items.

They led her down the stairs, and she already knew where they were going. There were a few small cells in the basement. She wasn't surprised to pass Ford sitting along the wall in one of them. His gaze followed her.

The sound of the bars clanging shut behind her didn't bother her. Neither did the uncomfortable cot that Eliza promised to bring down extra blankets for. She waited until the footfalls faded. She waited until there was nothing but still quiet.

Then she sat on the floor, smoothing out the paper, and started to plan.

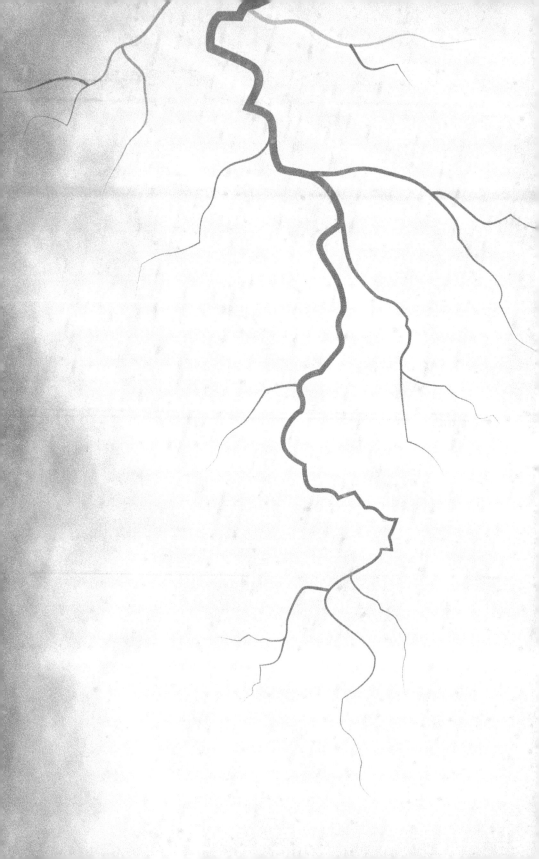

43
TESSA

"I'll let her know. Let me know if you can get away for an hour tonight," Luka was saying, his phone pressed between his ear and shoulder as he cut something at the kitchen counter. "I know that," he added, before grabbing the phone and tossing it aside.

Tessa didn't know how he'd managed to make this place not feel like a cave, but it suited him. The decor was similar to his spaces at the Arius holdings. The mattress on the floor with too many pillows and blankets. The leather sofas and large overstuffed chairs.

And all the frames.

So many fucking frames of all sizes.

She was surprised she hadn't found drawers full of rings in this place.

He even had running water here. It was impressive, and she'd been grateful as the water had rained down on her after all the sex.

The *really* good sex.

That had been going on for a few days while she'd been hiding from the rest of the world.

The only other person she'd had sex with like *that* was Theon. It'd been different, but equally intense, and *gods*. Just thinking about any of it —Luka, Theon, both of them—had her pressing her thighs together.

She looked up to find Luka smirking at her, still chopping whatever he was preparing in the kitchen. She huffed, crossing her arms. For the last few days, she'd hardly worn clothing, slipping on one of Luka's shirts if needed. When she'd come out of the bathroom this time though, she'd found a set of neatly folded clothes waiting for her. A fitted long-sleeve black top and pants.

Training clothes.

She hadn't bothered with the socks or boots, and she'd left her hair down to dry around her shoulders.

This whole thing suddenly felt awkward. One would think she'd learned how to navigate this after Theon. It had been awkward with him too. Again, the same, but different, and it was all so fucking confusing. Because she was drawn to Luka in ways she couldn't explain, but wasn't she drawn to Theon in the same way, but different?

The same, but different.

None of it made any sense, and trying to figure it all out was driving her mad. Because her visions were showing her one thing, and her feelings were leading her down another path, and what was she supposed to do with any of it?

"Tessa, stop," came a soft command, and she stilled at his voice.

Her hands were in her wet hair, and at some point she'd started pacing. Her power was flaring too, the bands on her wrists lighting up the space.

"How long are we staying here?" she asked, looking up at a large onyx frame. There was nothing in it. It was like he'd framed a section of the wall.

The sound of the chopping paused for the briefest of moments, but she felt something akin to…disappointment down the bond. Which was odd. She turned to watch him, his attention focused on the ingredients on the counter.

"For a while," he answered tightly. "I was finally given information. I'll explain while you eat."

"Eat what?"

"Food," he drawled, swiping up a bowl before making his way towards her. He stopped by one of the sofas, while she stayed planted by the wall. Luka sighed, setting down the bowl on an end table. "Out with it."

"Out with what?" she asked.

"What is causing this spike of uncertainty and confusion down the bond."

"It's nothing."

"Tessa."

The way he said her name told her exactly how much he believed that statement.

"Who were you talking to?" she asked instead.

But he shook his head, crossing his arms. "You already know the answer to that. We'll talk about it after we sort out whatever this is."

"What do you want me to say?"

He huffed in annoyance. "I want you to tell me whatever it is you're thinking about."

"You can hear my thoughts."

"Only the ones you want us to," he countered. "Just say it."

"I don't know what to say," she snapped, sufficiently irritated. "I don't know what to do in this situation. When I've fucked around in the past, I was gone as soon as it was over. It never mattered. Not until—"

She snapped her mouth shut, pressing her lips into a thin line.

"Not until Theon," he finished for her.

"Yes. Not until him. And we're so fucked up ourselves that was a whole other thing to unpack and deal with."

"Did you? Deal with it?" he prodded.

"What do you think?" she drawled.

"That you use sex as avoidance, and when it was more than that, you didn't know *how* to deal with it. When feelings were attached, you couldn't use your usual avoidance methods," he answered.

"Fuck off with your introspective bullshit, Luka," she said. "The only thing I felt for Theon was hate."

He hummed in response.

"What is that supposed to mean?"

"Love and hate are equally intense emotions."

"I do *not* love him," she spat.

"But you do feel something more than hate."

"I—" A sound of frustration clawed up her throat. "I don't know. I don't know what any of this is. And how can I feel something for him after what we did? Is it always awkward when feelings are involved?"

Her face screwed up at the thought. If that was the case, she didn't understand why people enjoyed sex when it wasn't cut and dry and without feeling.

A sigh came from Luka as he closed the distance between them. Her arms dropped to her sides when he took her face in his hands, bending down to brush a kiss to her brow. "It is only awkward because you do not know how to accept that someone cares for you simply because you exist."

"Everyone wants something, Luka. Don't be naïve," she scoffed. "This is Devram."

"Answer this then: did you only fuck me to avoid something?"

She lurched back. "What? No!"

"Did you just use me for your own pleasure?"

"No."

"Then...you want something from me?" he asked, and she saw his lips twitch as he fought his smirk.

"No," she snapped.

"No?" he repeated, leaning in to brush his lips along the shell of her ear. "But you just said everyone wants something, so you must want something from me. If it's not avoidance or pleasure, then..."

He trailed off, moving lower and kissing below her ear.

"And what about Theon?" she blurted. "You suddenly do not care that he thinks I am his? That I hate the male you are sworn to guard? That he and I were always meant to destroy one another?"

Luka pulled back, just far enough to look into her eyes. Tucking her hair behind her ear, he brushed another kiss to her lips before he said, "I won't deny it will take time to navigate everything, but this is new for all of us. Nothing says it needs to be decided and figured out today."

"Right. So when you were speaking to him a few minutes ago, the two of you just avoided the topic?"

"For now," he agreed.

"You know why that is, right?"

Luka arched a brow, waiting for her to go on.

"Because this is *awkward*."

Then she was squealing as Luka scooped her up and deposited her on the sofa before sinking down beside her.

"Was that necessary?" she demanded.

"Yes," he answered. "That conversation was going around in circles. We needed to break the cycle, and you need to eat."

He grabbed the bowl from the end table, placing it in her lap. She looked down to find yogurt with berries, granola, and honey.

Her nose wrinkled. "Did Theon send this?"

"He may have let me know there were supplies gathered. I Traveled and grabbed them while you were in the shower," Luka answered.

She stirred the yogurt. It actually sounded really good, and she was starving.

"Did you eat?" she asked.

He nodded. "I waited to make yours until I heard the shower shut off."

Taking a bite, she said, "What did Theon want?"

All the lightheartedness drained from him. "Tell me again what happened by the river."

That fucking river.

She was never going there again.

In between bites of yogurt, she told him everything that had happened. The argument with Rordan in the morning. The Augury and the Hunters. Cressida and Mother Cordelia. Auryon dying. She'd already told him all this, the two of them trying to piece things together with limited information while waiting for word from Theon.

She glanced over to where the bow still sat on the dining table, dark and ominous in the space, and fell silent as she finished speaking. Luka hadn't stopped touching her the entire time. Toying with her hair. Brushing his fingers along her arm, her leg. Listening to her and watching her eat. She only managed a few bites in between words.

"We couldn't get to you because an emergency Tribunal meeting was called," Luka said. "With everything that's happened since, and with what you just told me, it just confirms it was all a setup."

"For what?" she asked in confusion. "And what has happened?"

"We're not entirely sure. Theon was summoned to another Tribunal meeting in a few days to discuss the crisis in Arius Kingdom, particularly Dark Haven."

Tessa swallowed thickly, suddenly not hungry. When she said nothing to that, Luka went on.

"Dark Haven had to be evacuated, but we lost hundreds," he said solemnly. "Males, females, children. It didn't matter. They all had Arius blood."

"Because that's what they were created for," she whispered. "To hunt down Arius descendants."

Auryon had told her. She'd warned her not to summon them inside the boundaries of Arius Kingdom, but she had panicked. She was under attack, and they were severely outnumbered. She'd had no choice. Almost as if—

"It *was* planned," she said suddenly, her gaze snapping to Luka.

"Explain, baby girl," he encouraged, as if he'd expected her to be the one to figure this out.

But her brow furrowed at his words. "Why did you stop calling me little one?"

He blinked at the odd question, twirling her hair around a finger again. "Little one was what I called you when I needed to remind myself you weren't mine. Or that's what it was supposed to do. It was a code only I understood. It worked for a little while, but by the end..." He trailed off, then sighed. "When I realized it wasn't working anymore, I stopped using it, I guess."

She nodded, mulling that over. "I still don't know what this is."

"Neither do I, but we don't have to figure it out alone, right?"

She nodded again, stirring her yogurt just to have something to do with her hands. Clearing her throat, she said, "Anyway, Rordan was angry with me. Told me I was taking too long to fulfill my purpose, and I needed to start showing some effort. He told me I needed to prove I still understood my purpose, so I went to Arius Kingdom. I went to see Lange and Corbin while I tried to figure out what to do."

"What did he want you to do?" Luka asked.

"Kill a prominent Arius Legacy. To prove myself to the cause, but I..."

"You couldn't do it," he breathed, and Tessa looked up to find him staring intently at her.

She braced herself, knowing this wasn't going to be the answer he wanted. "I would have done it," she said. "I still will do it, but I want it to be on my terms. When I'm ready. Not his."

It was Luka's turn to remain silent, so she went on. This was...nice. Sharing information. Working things out together. Not learning things when someone else deemed it necessary. Maybe her loyalty *was* wavering.

"But Cressida is aiding Rordan," she said. "Valter was leading the Augury; Cressida was obviously a part of that. She's been reporting movements back to Rordan for decades. It's the only explanation. When I was attacked by Night Children, when Roan was injured, she had set that all up."

"Theon did mention she had seemed upset by all of that," Luka said, rubbing at his jaw. "Dex is working against you then?"

"Dexter has been working against me from the beginning," she said derisively. "It has always been one big long game for them and Rordan."

"Them?"

"Rordan. Dex. Oralia. I'm unsure about Brecken, but he is still one of the light guardians," she replied.

"A light guardian? You said that phrase before."

She nodded, scooping up another bite. "Xan said they are basically the counterpart to you."

It took her a moment to realize Luka had gone so still she could swear he wasn't breathing.

"What?" she asked in confusion.

"What did you just say?"

"I said that light guardians are your counterparts. Arius and Sargon created Guardians. Achaz got mad and created light guardians in answer," she explained.

"And *who* told you that?"

His tone was too calm. Too dark. Too deadly.

And in that moment, she felt the blood drain from her face.

Oh, gods.

The bowl slipped from her hands to the floor, yogurt and berries spilling onto the rug.

"Luka, I—"

Her hair was still wound around one of his thick fingers, and she could feel him vibrating with fury. "Who. The fuck. Told you that, Tessa."

She swallowed, the yogurt threatening to come back up. "Just let me explain—"

"Say it!" he yelled, and she flinched back, her hair slipping from his hold.

"Xan," she whispered. And to make sure there was no doubt, she added, "Your father told me."

Luka pushed to his feet, and she scrambled after him, keeping her distance as his eyes shifted and his wings tore free. She could see him trembling from where she stood, and she was certain he was fighting a full shift.

"Let me explain," she tried again.

He'd never looked at her the way he did in that moment. His lip curled back, baring his teeth, as he snarled. "Explain it to me, Tessa. Explain to me how you've spoken to my godsdamn father and didn't say a fucking word to me. Where is he?"

She swallowed again. "I discovered him by accident."

"Where is he?" he growled again.

Tessa took a few more steps away from him before she said, "In Faven. In the cells beneath the palace."

"When?"

"When what?" she asked, only because she didn't want to answer the wrong question and make him more upset.

"When did you— How did you say it? *Accidentally* discover him?"

"Luka, please—" But she snapped her mouth shut at the look he sent her.

What is happening over there? Theon demanded down the bond, and she couldn't blame him. Luka's emotions were all over the place. She couldn't separate the fury from the hurt from the wrath of the betrayal. But in all of that, she knew the adoration he'd looked at her with just moments ago was no longer there.

"You are not speaking to him right now," Luka said, stalking towards her. "You are speaking to me."

She moved back with each step forward he took. At one point, her feet tangled in the rug, but he never stretched out a hand to catch her or help her. When her back hit a wall, there was nowhere else for her to go.

"When?" he growled.

She exhaled through her nose, her eyes falling closed. She knew this answer was going to ruin everything, and it was entirely her own fault.

"No," he growled. "Look me in the eye when you tell me how you've played me this entire fucking time."

She took another deep breath, trying to swallow down her tears, but they spilled over, tracking down her face. "Days after I left Theon."

He reared back as if she'd hit him with a bolt of her power. And the look on his face? Gods, it shattered her. The pieces she'd been trying to hold together slipped through her fingers. She thought Theon had broken her? This realm? No, she had destroyed herself because there was no coming back from this. She knew it in her bones.

"I have been... This whole time?" he demanded, and she wasn't quite sure what he was asking.

She thought he was going to start pacing. He'd taken a few steps, but then he whirled, lunging for her again. She didn't struggle in the slightest when his large hand wrapped around her throat.

She wished he would squeeze.

She wished he would summon his flames and burn her. It would hurt less than watching him learn all of this. Than watching the consequences of her own actions.

Wild.

Reckless.

Uncontrollable.

That was what she had been.

"For weeks I have been in the same place as my *father*. Who I have thought was dead for nearly twenty-five years," he yelled, his breath hot on her face. "For twenty-five years, I have thought I was alone. The last of my kind. I have been trying to— You said nothing. Fucking nothing!"

"I'm sorry," she rasped.

He was still holding her in place by the throat, but he suddenly yanked his hand back as though *she* had burned *him*.

"No, you're not," he spat. "You have had so many opportunities to bring this up. The first day I came to you. Any of the days you've slept beside me. Any of the times we were training. When I found out I had a fucking brother. Any godsdamn time, Tessa!"

She didn't move. Not because she thought he would hurt her. He wouldn't physically harm her. Deep down she knew that, but she'd never feared physical punishment. It was being shoved into a small, dark place. Into a cupboard or a wine cellar.

Being thrown into the dark.

Sure, she could make her own light, but that didn't eclipse the loneliness.

She didn't dare breathe because she was terrified that the slightest movement would remind him she was still here, and that he would make her leave the only place she'd ever felt wanted.

Accepted.

Loved.

The only place that had almost felt like home.

"Instead, you used me," he snarled, and she didn't deny it.

She had done that. So determined to have her vengeance, she'd become everything she'd hated about Devram. It was the only way to survive in a realm full of villains. You had to become one.

"Are you going to say anything?" he bellowed.

But what was there to say to this?

His palms landed on either side of her head, flat against the wall as he bent to peer into her face. "Tell me, Tessa. Look me in the face and tell me how you fucking used me. All this time you've sneered about me only being here because Theon sent me, when you've been using me. Using Theon. Probably using my own godsdamn father."

"You can't mean that!" she gasped, finally finding her voice.

"You said yourself everyone wants something, right?" he sneered. "Did you get what you wanted from me?"

"I did not ask you to stay!" she cried. "Not right away. You did that, Luka Mors. Not me."

He scoffed, the sound so full of derision it made her flinch again. "Well? Did you get what you wanted from me then?"

"It was never like that," she pleaded. "Not with you. Not in the end. I still have a purpose, and he is still an ally of Arius, not Achaz. I couldn't free him, and he..."

"He what?" Luka barked.

"He knows my father. My mother. He knows so much," she said, nearly in a whisper. "He was a link to something I was desperate for. He kept me company when no one wanted me."

Something that could only be described as a dragon's growl ripped from him, his palms slamming into the wall again. "If you would ever fucking listen to any of us—me, Theon, Axel—you would know that isn't true. Theon has wanted you from the beginning. Not to use you. He's wanted *you*. It's all he's ever wanted. I had to give you a pet name to remind myself *not* to want you. We've loved you far longer than even we realize."

She shook her head, the tears streaming now. "None of you know how to love."

"Or maybe you just don't know how to let yourself *be* loved."

He pushed off the wall when she didn't respond to that. Turning his back to her, he said, "You wanted to be a monster? Congratulations, Tessa. You succeeded."

He was moving towards a passage she hadn't been down, walking away from her.

"Wait!" she cried, taking a single step. "Where are you going?"

"Away from you."

"What am I supposed to do?"

"Go home, Tessa," he snarled. "You never wanted to be here anyway."

"I don't have a home," she said, the words nearly a sob.

"It sure as fuck isn't here."

She stumbled, her back hitting the wall as something tugged at her naval. A pull she'd only felt with Luka, but it was how she knew what it was.

She didn't look back as she stepped through a rip in the air and Traveled from Luka's cave.

He didn't want her anyway.

In the end, she had become her own villain.

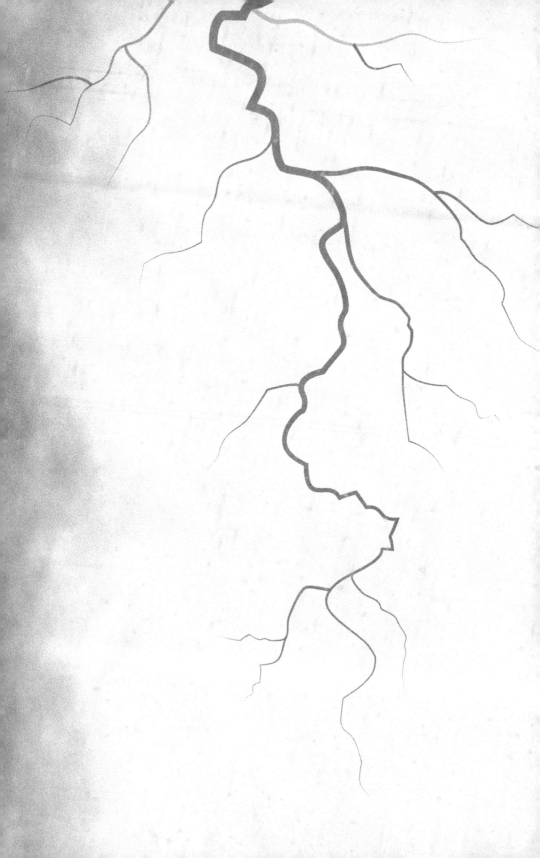

44

TESSA

She didn't know how Traveling worked, but she somehow managed to get herself back to the Achaz capital. Not the palace exactly, but at least it was Faven.

At least she was out of Arius Kingdom.

She made her way through the city, not missing the sentinels that started following her from a distance. It didn't surprise her. She'd been expecting this. Expecting to be watched and monitored after instigating a massacre, then disappearing for a few days.

Nylah and Roan eventually appeared too, sticking close to her sides. Her fingers wound into soft fur, seeking comfort that she knew she wouldn't find there. They were her companions, yes, but they weren't her comfort. They weren't her solace.

They weren't home.

The walk back to the palace took over an hour, and when she finally got there, Nylah stayed outside, prowling the perimeter. Roan, however, followed her up to her rooms, a faithful friend she'd missed terribly.

The sentinels that had trailed her through the city stopped at the gates, a new set of guards taking over. They didn't bother hiding it. Shutting the door to her rooms behind her, three of them stayed outside. Stupid, really. They all knew she could make portals. Having guards outside her rooms seemed pointless.

Or it would be if she wasn't so broken.

If she wasn't back in a place she'd tried so hard to claw her way out of. She thought she'd made it too. More powerful than anyone else. Someone people feared as much as they feared Theon. A villain. A monster. Forcing dark to bow so light could rule.

All of it as fleeting as her visions.

Instead of clawing her way out, she'd only dug a tunnel to another pit of torment. This place was arguably worse. She'd experienced what it felt like to have people fight for her. Gotten a taste of people wanting her, and still she'd pushed them away. Still she'd created a mess.

Or maybe you just don't know how to let yourself be loved.

Truer words had never been spoken.

She changed out of the black training clothes, sliding on cream, loose, linen pants and a white top. She braided her hair over her shoulder before she crawled onto her bed to wait. They would come for her soon enough.

Roan leapt onto the bed beside her, turning in a few circles before settling down, and she scratched behind his ears.

"I'm sorry we lost her," Tessa whispered. "I know you were close."

Roan whined, lifting his head to nuzzle into her hand. She let the pain of losing Auryon wash over her. Another loss and hurt that Luka had soothed away now raw and painful.

She didn't know why she did it, but she reached into the nightstand drawer, finding the phone Theon had given her.

But that was a lie.

She knew exactly why she did it as she powered on the device. She watched it blink to life, waiting as it loaded and tipping her head back against the headboard. Her eyes fell closed, and she inhaled deeply, then regretted it. Luka had been sleeping in here with her, and there were still traces of his scent in the air.

The phone in her hand suddenly started vibrating, ping after ping sounding loud in the silence. Message after message poured in, and she stared down at the phone, her mouth dropping open. More than a hundred messages were being downloaded to the thing. What in the realms?

With a trembling hand, she thumbed open the text threads, gasping at what she found. Save for a few messages from Axel when he had been trying to track her down, every single message was from Theon. She scrolled up to the first, finding the date it had been sent—the day after she had left him on his knees. There was a text every single day since, sometimes two.

Scrolling back to the top, she clicked open the first.

Theon: I understand the hate. Today, I hate you too.

A bark of laughter escaped her. Probably not the reaction he'd envisioned when he sent that, but wasn't that what she'd wanted? Him to feel what he'd done to her? Have a taste of her wrath and vengeance?
She clicked on the message sent the next day.

Theon: But I'll still come for you.

The next.

Theon: I said I'll still come for you, but I know you don't want that. Luka is coming. I've told him not to tell me anything. He's loyal. He'll follow the order. You can trust him, little storm.

A sob hitched in her throat. She opened the next one.

Theon: Axel is missing. I know you don't have your phone, and this is pointless, but... Fuck.

She scrolled down, opening one a few days later.

Theon: Somehow I have to search for Axel and run a kingdom. I thought I was prepared for this. Turns out I wasn't prepared for anything.

Tessa scrolled down more.

Theon: You were here today, beautiful. I'm still healing from your attack, but for the record, you never need to be armed around me.

A tear rolled down her cheek as she scrolled down a little more and opened another.

Theon: I know Luka is giving you updates, but I'll send them here as well, just in case you actually turn on your phone. Roan is being constantly monitored. The recovery will take a while, but they think he'll make a full recovery.

Theon: No real update today. Nothing has changed, but he hasn't gotten worse, so we'll count it as a good day.

Theon: He opened his eyes today, beautiful. I wish you would have been here to see it.

Tears were streaming down her face now as she scrolled through several before clicking on another.

Theon: I started taking Roan outside with me when I visit my hounds. I tried to convince him to play fetch. He didn't seem impressed.

She barked another laugh, looking over at her wolf and plunging her hand into his fur again. Returning to the phone, she scrolled some more, opening one from a few weeks ago.

Theon: I know I told you, but I need to say it again. You looked stunning tonight, Tessa.

She smiled through her tears as she scrolled some more, opening the one he'd sent a few days ago.

Theon: I've never lied to you, Tessa. Withheld information? Yes. Hurt you? Yes. But I've never lied to you.

She scrolled to the last one. The one sent this morning.

Theon: I want you to know that despite all of this, I'll still come for you.

The phone slipped from her hand, plopping onto the mattress. He couldn't mean that. She'd unleashed beings specifically created to kill his people. They *had* killed his people. *Hundreds* of them. To say he would still come for her after everything she had done? Impossible. This betrayal was arguably worse than keeping Luka's father from him, and she knew that was unforgivable. The deaths of hundreds?

If being a villain required no remorse, she wasn't one because she had caused the deaths of innocents and she felt every bit of that guilt. She was exactly the monster Luka had called her.

She swiped the phone back up, tapping out a reply. Then her thumb hovered over the send button for the next hour. She was still debating sending the message when her door opened.

Roan growled, but she hushed him with a pat to the head. Dex stood there, dark eyes hard. His lips pressed into a thin line as he stared at her before he slipped a hand into his pocket and pulled out two bands.

She didn't even fight it.

She let him slip the bands onto her wrists and watched the light that wound around them die out.

"I have to take you to the Pantheon. They will hold you there until they decide," Dex explained.

Tessa only nodded.

Then he pulled a ring from his pocket. She'd seen ones like it among Theon's things. A solid black band, and she gasped when Dex grabbed her wrist, forcing the ring onto her pointer finger. The bands may have separated her from her magic, but she could take them off. This ring was not the same. She could feel it digging its claws into her power. Feel her magic thrashing in her soul.

She lifted horrified eyes to Dex. "What are you doing?"

"You did this, Tessa," he said, taking her elbow and leading her from the room. Roan leapt down, keeping pace beside them. "We'll get what we need from you one way or another."

"What does that mean?" she demanded, trying to dig her feet into the smooth floor, but Dex just dragged her along.

"It means you just had to do as you were told. Now, we'll take what we're owed."

45

AXEL

Axel checked his watch again before returning to cleaning the windows.

Yep. That was what his life had come to. Cleaning. Because it kept him busy and let him free-fall into avoiding...everything. Currently, it was keeping him busy while he waited for a delivery of blood and groceries. He knew Kat was getting restless, and he wouldn't be able to keep her convinced they needed to stay indoors for much longer.

Indoors?

Was he really going to call it outside when they were still in a giant cavern?

Realizing the pointlessness of that internal debate, he turned up the music that was playing throughout the first floor of the penthouse. He moved to the next window, spraying it with some cleaner he'd found in a supply closet before wiping it down. It left smudges behind. Maybe it wasn't supposed to be used on glass?

He was working on the third window, when the music suddenly shut off. Spinning, he found Kat holding his phone. She looked exhausted.

He frowned. "I thought you were resting?"

"It's hard to sleep when you keep turning the music up," she replied, stifling a yawn as she held the phone out to him.

He took it, noting the time yet again. The guy he'd hired to bring their supplies was over an hour late. He'd paid far too much for him to be this tardy with things.

"Sorry," he murmured to Kat, setting the cleaning supplies aside. "Just trying to...kill some time."

"By cleaning?" she asked, eyeing the bottle of cleaner.

He shrugged. "Not sure what else to do."

"We could leave the penthouse, you know," she said, crossing her arms.

Yeah, he'd walked right into that one.

Sighing, he ran a hand down his face. "Kitten..."

"Don't *kitten* me," she argued. "I didn't let you bring me here just to hide me away."

"That's exactly why I brought you here," he deadpanned.

"It is not," she scoffed.

He reached out, gripping her hips and pulling her towards him. "What if it is?" He pressed a kiss to her jaw. "What if the real reason I brought you here is to hide you away from the rest of this depraved world so I could keep you all to myself?"

"Stop," she said around a laugh as he peppered kisses down the column of her throat.

"I would do that, you know," he murmured against her skin. "If I thought for one minute you'd let me."

"You would not," she said, her arms coming around his neck as he dropped his brow to hers. "But Axel, I *need* to get out of this space. Even if we just walk around the Charter District for fifteen minutes."

He sighed again, brushing his lips across her brow before releasing her. "I know, kitten. I know I'm being paranoid, but—"

A notification sounded near the door. Cell service was shit down here, but they did have a speaker system installed connecting them to the lobby downstairs.

"Hold that thought," he said, pressing another kiss to her cheek before moving to the screen.

Pressing the button, he said, "Yes?"

"There's a delivery here for you. Can I send them up?"

"Yes," he answered.

It was about fucking time.

"You don't have to look so imposing," Kat said, coming up behind him.

"Yes, I do," he replied. "I paid for a service, and he failed to deliver based on the terms set up. You shouldn't even be out here for this."

It was her turn to sigh, but as the lift doors opened with a soft *ding*, he was shoving her behind him. Because it wasn't the common thief he'd hired to bring him blood and food.

It was Bree DelaCrux.

"Axel, darling," she greeted as she stepped into the room, a bag dangling from her manicured hands. "Rumors are swirling that you've returned, and I thought I would come visit."

"Bree," he said carefully, and he felt Katya stiffen behind him. It was part of the reason he'd said her name. So Kat would realize the severity of this situation. "You could have just sent a note."

Her red-painted lips turned down in a pout. "I could have," she agreed. "But I was under the impression that you would be returning to me when you returned to the Underground. Instead, I learned that you have been wasting away here. Surely, you have completely turned by now?"

"I have," he answered, because there was no point in denying it.

Just like he knew he'd eventually have to let Kat leave this space, he'd known he would eventually have to face Bree too. He'd just been trying to form a decent plan. This wasn't his greatest strength. Theon and Luka were the planners and strategizers. He was the "people person." The one who got along with everyone and could smooth things over. He just had no idea how he was going to smooth *this* over with the coven leader.

"I didn't realize you'd taken on an extra job," he said, nodding to the bag she still held.

She laughed, a melodic thing, as she made her way through the living area, setting the bag on a small table. One look told him it was the groceries he'd ordered. One look also told him the rations of blood he'd ordered were not included.

"I figured I was coming all this way, I may as well save someone else the trip," Bree replied.

"How benevolent of you."

"I thought so," she agreed.

She turned to face him again, leaning her ass against the arm of the sofa. Somehow she looked immensely out of place here, which was ridiculous because his father had the penthouse decorated in the finest luxuries coin could buy.

"I see you've already found a vessel," she said when he continued to stare at her.

"A what?"

"A vessel, darling," she drawled. "A warm blood supply always at your disposal."

"That is *not* what she is," he balked before he could stop himself. He recognized the mistake immediately when a dark smile formed on Bree's lips.

"Fae and powerful," she said. "I can smell it on her. If we were at my House, I could take her from you."

"Except you are in *my* house," he snarled. "And if you lay a single finger on her, it will be the last thing you do."

"So protective," she crooned, clearly not phased. Then her features morphed into something dark and deadly. "No one has been able to kill me for millenniums. You will not succeed where others have failed." She pushed off the sofa, her heels clicking on the floor as she circled them. "Vessels are the equivalent of a Source for you, I suppose. Only we do not limit them to the ruling coven leaders. Any Night Child can have one if they choose to." She smiled then, her fangs on full display. "The hunt and claiming is half the fun."

"What is the other half?" Axel asked dryly.

"Fighting to keep them," she added with a shrug of her slender shoulder. "It is not uncommon for others to try to steal a more powerful vessel for themselves. Even down here, power decides fate. You know this, darling. It's why you are in such a predicament."

"I was unaware I was facing any such thing," he replied, turning to keep Kat behind him as Bree continued to circle.

"With your Arius magic, you were one of the most powerful to walk the Underground. The power itself conjured respect and fear, but now?" She pouted again. "What are you now, darling?"

"He is still an Arius Heir," Kat snapped. "He still demands the same."

Bree's head tilted, a pleased curl of her lips. "An Arius Legacy with no power? That's not how things work down here, poppet."

"Don't speak to her," Axel snarled.

The smile disappeared instantly, replaced by an icy glare. "*You* do not speak to *me* in such a manner, Axel. Kindly remember whose House you agreed to pledge allegiance to."

"I never agreed to that," he argued. "I told you I needed time to figure things out."

Her eyes narrowed. "I do not play games, Axel St. Orcas."

He barked a humorless laugh. "I think you do, Bree. Is that not what you were doing when you *found* someone for me? Playing games? Playing *me?*"

Something sparked in her honey-colored eyes, and he couldn't decide what it was. Intrigue? Understanding? Disappointment?

"Where did you say you found her?" she asked, moving to try to get a better look at Kat.

"I didn't," Axel growled.

"And am I correct in understanding you are no longer honoring your agreement to pledge allegiance to my House?"

"That agreement was never made."

Bree hissed. An honest-to-the-gods hiss of fury came from the female. "You owe me, Axel St. Orcas. I let you leave in good faith and only asked that you repay the favor."

"I *owe* you?" he scoffed in outrage. "You preyed on me when I was at my most vulnerable. You saved me only to torture me yourself. Then you 'let me go' assuming I would kill her."

"But you didn't, did you?" Bree said, her eyes fixed over his shoulder. "Instead, you brought her back with you. Tell me, how did you manage such a feat? You should have been consumed with blood lust, even if she was your fated."

"I did nearly kill her," he sneered. "If Theon hadn't been there, I would have."

"Let's meet her properly then," Bree snarled. "Let me meet the thing you are throwing away everything for."

Before he could stop her, Kat stepped to his side, her chin held high as she stared back at Bree. Part of him wanted to shove her back and ask her what the fuck she was thinking. The other part of him was so gods-damn proud of her for showing no fear in the face of someone they should definitely be fearing. If there was a fragile peace among the king-doms of Devram, that fragile peace was mirrored among the Districts of the Underground. There was no doubt in his mind where this was going to lead, and he was going to need Theon's help to deal with it. But without Tessa, without a Source to make his power supremely unmatched, would it be enough? If Bree managed to unite the Under-ground, he wasn't sure Theon alone would be enough to bring them all to heel.

The look of shock on Bree's face quickly morphed into something smug and sinister. "Perhaps not a vessel for blood, but clearly still a vessel," she said, her hungry gaze fixed on Kat's swollen stomach.

Kat's hand landed on her belly protectively as she shrank into Axel's side, his arm slipping around her waist.

"Stop referring to her as that," Axel said darkly, baring his own fangs.

Her eyes roamed over Kat some more. "Based on how far along she appears, I assume that babe came to be before you turned?"

"Obviously," he replied coldly. "The Night Children cannot create young."

There was an icy lilt of laughter. "My dear little heir, why would you ever think such a thing?" Before he could question her further on that statement, she mused, "I should have known you wouldn't kill her. I thought you were beyond the bond when you couldn't even recall her name."

Axel sprang forward, that speed he'd acquired propelling him in the blink of an eye. His hand wrapped around Bree's slender throat, and the vampyre's eyes went wide as he slammed her against the wall. In the back of his mind, he knew he shouldn't be able to. Bree was stronger than him, but he was too furious to process that in the moment.

"Let me be *very* clear, Bree," he snarled. "The only reason Katya isn't dead is because Theon was there to stop me. If I had killed her, it would not have accomplished what you think it would have. You think I was crazed from bloodlust? I would have been *feral* learning I had killed her. Then to learn I had killed my *son* on top of that? And that *you* were the cause? There is nowhere you could have gone to hide from me. I would have hunted you down across the stars."

He released her, slowly taking a few steps back.

Her glare was all predator as she smoothed down the red fabric of her dress. "You are creating an enemy, young heir." Her head cocked, and a sadistic smile formed. "Then again, you aren't really an heir anymore, are you?"

His returned smile was just as sadistic. "Oh, I think I am. Not the heir I thought I was, but the heir I was always meant to be."

"Do tell," she purred.

He stepped forward again, still towering over her, even in her heels. "The Underground is *mine*, Bree. All of it. *This* is my kingdom. Always has been. If you want it, you'll go through me."

"Careful, darling, you're about to start a war."

He bared his fangs. "You started it the moment you sent me to kill my wife." Bree blinked at the words. "Get out of my house, Bree. I'll summon you when you're needed."

He turned his back on her, making his way back to Katya, who was staring back at him. He had to give her credit. She didn't let an ounce of confusion show at his statement. Instead, she held her head high. A solid presence at his side.

A perfect balance.

Fire and shadows. The only difference was he'd rule in the shadowed lands of the Underground rather than control the shadows themselves.

He'd leave that to his son.

"You're creating enemies, Axel," Bree said, cold and deadly.

"I create new enemies every day," he sneered. "It's just good business. Now *get out*."

"I think you will find it's not as easy as you believe to keep a kingdom that was never yours," Bree said, sauntering to the lift. Then she added, "After all, control can be an illusion as much as it can be fleeting."

He let her have the last word, holding her stare the entire time until the lift doors closed and he heard it descending.

Then his hands drove into his hair as he started pacing. That had *not* been the plan.

"Um, Axel?" Kat asked tentatively.

"Yes, kitten?" he asked distractedly.

"You called me your wife."

He stopped mid-step, turning to face her. "Yeah. I guess I did."

"But...we're not that."

"We should be," he grumbled, resuming his pacing.

A strangled laugh came from her. "What?"

Then he was standing in front of her, and she lurched back.

"Stop doing that," she admonished, her hand at her chest.

"Sorry," he said in a rush, taking her face in his hands. "But I said we should be. You should be my wife."

"Axel, I... How would that even work? It wouldn't be a Match Contract because that's between two Legacy," she said, her brow furrowing in thought. "And the few Fae that are granted a union have to have it anointed by a priestess."

She had a point. Fae had to petition for unions, prove it wouldn't interfere with their duties to their kingdom, and get approval from whichever noble they answered to. In some cases, that was the ruling Lord or Lady themselves.

His father had never granted such a petition. Pen and Caris were proof enough of that.

He pressed a quick kiss to her cheek. "Grab your shoes, kitten. We're going out."

"Out?" she repeated, a note of excitement in her tone. "You mean we can leave the penthouse?"

"We were hiding out, and our secrets were just revealed. Doesn't make much sense to stay hidden anymore," he answered. "Besides, I'll be damned if Bree thinks I'm hiding from *her* now."

There was a small smile playing on her lips when he looked over his shoulder after sliding on his own shoes. He quirked a brow. "Something to say, kitten?"

She shook her head, but that smile still tilted as she went upstairs to get her shoes. He didn't know what it was for, but he liked seeing it on her.

And *wife* sounded pretty damn good.

"Are you doing all right?" Axel asked, looking down at Kat where she strolled beside him.

They'd had to go to the Apothecary District to see a Witch. He'd been recognized, and when they'd ducked into a small shop of a Witch he knew, the female had smiled. Or, as close to a smile as Witches come. It was more of this tight-lipped press of lips as she said, "Cienna sent word you might be coming."

In the end, it hadn't taken much to get a union anointed, mainly because of who he was. Even in the Underground unions had to be petitioned and approved, but who was going to deny his own request when he was one of those who did the approving?

Now they both sported Union Marks on their hands. It was something usually reserved for Legacy Matches, but Axel was done pandering to traditions and outdated laws. The fact he'd married a Fae was proof enough of that, but just to drive the point home, he had the Union Marks bestowed. Now he wanted to take her to the Apparel District to secure rings too. He wanted any and every possible way to stake his claim.

As if the babe growing in her belly wasn't enough.

"I'm fine, Axel," Kat answered. "It feels good to be out and about. Thank you."

"Please don't thank me for this," he replied, guiding her around a corner.

"But I will thank you for this," she insisted. "If we were still in the kingdoms, do you think I would be calling you husband right now?"

He tugged her into his side, pressing a kiss to the top of her head. "Such a logical statement," he teased.

"Shut up," she muttered, peering up at him.

And his heart skipped a beat.

He pulled her to a stop and took her face in his hands, searching those amber eyes.

"Axel, what in the name of Anala are you doing? We're in the middle of the street," she chastised.

"I know, but—" He looked back and forth between her eyes, his chest tightening at what he found. "Shadows," he whispered.

"What?"

"There are shadows drifting in your eyes. Like mine would do," he explained, watching the black wisps.

"What are you talking about?" Katya said, sounding alarmed.

"Just...look," he said, pulling her into a clothing shop of the Apparel District. The bell of the door rang out, and he found the nearest mirror, positioning her in front of it.

He heard the small gasp when she saw them. "He's been moving more lately," she murmured, still staring at her reflection. "Getting bigger and stronger. I feel it in my own power."

"You need to rest more," he said immediately.

"When did you become a pregnancy expert?"

"I'm not. It just seems logical," he countered. Then he frowned. "We should have Cienna or Gia visit at least weekly though, especially at this point. I mean, isn't the babe coming soon?"

Kat laughed. "Yes, Axel. If by soon you mean a few months, then yes. But it is probably a good idea to have them visiting weekly at this point. Only because we've never done this before."

"Deal, kitten. I'll send word when we get back," he replied.

He dropped a few coins for the shop owner on their way out as an apology for the disturbance before making their way to a jeweler.

"Do we really need rings?" Kat asked. "I think even the Marks were unnecessary."

"It's all necessary," he replied, holding the shop door open for her. "But I also need to get rations here."

"Rations?" she asked, taking in the shop of accessories.

Axel nodded. "It's the Underground, kitten. I can find contraband anywhere." He led her to a glass case. "Stick to the rings on the left side."

"Why?" she asked, eyeing the gems and precious metals on the right.

"The ones on the right are cursed," he said simply, pressing another chaste kiss to her cheek before wandering to an opposite counter. A Fae male appeared, his face dropping when he saw Axel.

"Heir St. Orcas," he said, nervously wiping his hands on a towel. "What can I do for you?"

"Nolan," Axel greeted. "I'm in the market for some rings." The male visibly relaxed until Axel added, "And some rations."

"I'm, uh, out," the male said, avoiding eye contact. "But I can show you some rings."

He made to step around Axel, but Axel moved in front of him. "In all my years, you've never been out, Nolan. Are you saying I should visit Turner instead?"

"Yes," the male snapped.

"That's an additional trip I don't have time for today."

"I said I'm out," Nolan answered.

"Prove it."

The male's eyes went wide. "You can check my coolers, sir. I don't have any. I was cleaned out earlier today. I'm guessing so was Turner. We all were."

A sinking feeling filled his gut. "Explain that," he demanded, his tone icy with threat.

Nolan swallowed again. "I have suppliers just like you, sir."

"And?"

"And they came through and took all the stores. If you want blood, you have to go to the Dispensary District. Said they wouldn't be supplying anywhere else anymore."

"Who took them all?" Axel snarled.

"B-Bree DelaCrux and some of her coven," Nolan said, visibly trembling.

That fucking bitch.

46

THEON

Standing on the front steps of the Tribunal Building, he read through the information again while he waited for Luka. Razik had sent this information via his magic, and fine. Theon could admit using that method seemed more practical than sending this via email. Especially with the fact that if this information got out, it would cause chaos.

Well, *more* chaos.

Because he was about to walk into a storm of pandemonium.

With a swirl of darkness, he sent the paper to a pocket realm to study again later when he was with Razik. The male had given him the barest details. Just enough to make sense, but he still had questions.

So many questions.

But right now, he had to focus. He pulled his phone out, finding no missed calls or messages. Was Luka seriously not going to show for this? He knew something had happened between him and Tessa, but he hadn't heard from Luka since then. The male wasn't answering calls, had blocked the bond, and had seemingly disappeared. He was likely at his cave, but Theon didn't have the luxury or the time to fly up there right now.

So he settled for sending him a message.

Theon: We're having it out after this, fucker. I cannot believe you're sending me into this alone. This is not just about her, and you know it. Get your head out of your ass, and do what needs to be done.

Sliding his phone back into his pocket, he straightened his suit jacket and made his way into the Tribunal Building. He didn't bother with the entrances that were reserved for the ruling Lords and Ladies meant to keep them always separate and above everyone else. Instead, he walked straight into the hearing room, striding down the main aisle and making his way to the dais where the Anala and Falein Ladies were already waiting on their thrones.

They weren't here to discuss his kingdom. Not this time. Or not directly, he supposed. They were here to decide Tessa's fate after the massacre, all the blame landing on her shoulders despite his belief she was setup. She had still summoned the Hunters. This was still a direct result of her actions, and he didn't think even the Achaz Lord would be able to stay the Ladies' judgment this time.

He stared out across the empty hearing room. There would be no one else in these proceedings today. No heirs or nobility. Just the rulers and their Sources. Another disadvantage for Theon since he didn't have one, and another reason he'd wanted Luka here. His gaze fell on the table where he'd sat mere months ago, Axel at his side, as they'd argued his case to keep Tessa as his.

So much had changed in the span of a few heartbeats.

Theon took his seat, feeling strange sitting in his father's chair. After everything, it still didn't feel right. He'd been trained for this. His entire life, everything he'd done, all the blood and betrayal and brutality, had been for this. It had all been so he could sit in this fucking seat.

And it didn't feel right.

He sat casually though, not letting his discomfort show. Legs spread and elbow on the armrest with a finger steepled along his temple, he didn't bother to acknowledge the other three rulers when they entered. He only followed their path with his gaze. They all took their seats, Rordan sitting straight and tall. Before he could say anything, the Celeste Lady spoke.

"Where is she?" Lady Candra demanded.

"She is where we agreed she should be housed until her fate is decided," Rordan said, sounding as though he was already exhausted by this conversation that was sure to last for hours.

"She should be here," the Anala Lady said. "This hearing is about her, after all."

"After what she has done, she gets no say in her own fate," the Serafina Lady snapped. Her silver glare fixed on Theon. "*You* should be outraged more than anyone, Arius Heir."

Theon held her stare for a full five seconds, the room going quiet, before he said, "It is my understanding the Augury attacked her yet again. Are we now doling out punishments for defending ourselves? Is that not what our entire realm is built upon? Proving who is the most powerful?"

"Hundreds of your people died," the Celeste Lady cut in. "If you are this cavalier about it, I question whether you are fit to be the Arius Lord."

If only she knew he questioned the same as of late.

But he said, "Losses that could have been avoided if we could get the fucking Augury under control. How many times do they have to come after Tessa before we do something?"

"The Augury is a myth," scoffed the Celeste Lady.

"Tell that to the souls of the dead," Theon deadpanned.

"You cannot possibly still be defending the girl after all of this," the Serafina Lady said.

"*Tessa* did not ask for any of this," he retorted, sitting up straighter. "She was chosen against her will to be a Source. Then, when it was discovered she wasn't Fae at all, a hearing was held to determine her fate. She has never had a say in any matter. None of the Fae ever have."

The Ladies stared back at him, and it was the Falein Lady who said, "What are you saying, Heir St. Orcas?"

"I'm saying maybe it's not Tessa or the Augury that led to this. Maybe it's this whole godsdamn system."

The Serafina Lady straightened. "It is how things have been done since the creation of the realm. The gods decreed it."

"The gods don't come here. They don't give two fucks what we're doing thousands of years later," he retorted.

"Let's all take a moment," Lord Jove interrupted, his voice ringing out above the arguing. When everyone fell quiet, he continued. "I know you are new to this, Theon, but it has long been the responsibility of the ruling Lords and Ladies to uphold the laws and traditions of Devram."

"And you were all around when these so-called laws and traditions were decreed by the gods?" Theon asked.

"Of course not," he scoffed.

"Then how do we know? How do we know what the gods decreed before they abandoned us all here?"

"It has been passed down from the Lords and Ladies before us," Rordan replied coldly, his eyes narrowing. "Are you suggesting we should shun those who came before us and the gods who gave us every-thing we have?"

"I am saying it is foolish to expect an entire realm to continue to operate in the same way for thousands of years without any advance-ments or changes," Theon said, a sneer curling on his lip. "But that's not entirely what has happened either, is it?"

"Whatever do you mean?" asked the Anala Lady, but when Theon swung his gaze to her, he could swear she was fighting a pleased smile.

"Yes," drawled the Serafina Lady. "Please expound on such a state-ment as if you have the experience to speak about anything. You are a child."

"Do I have experience in withholding information for my own personal gain to try to manipulate people into doing and being what I want? To make sure I keep control and power?" Theon countered. "Not only do I have that, but I've been on the receiving end of it my entire life. It is why I believed it to be normal. It's what I was taught, and all I'd ever known. But that was all by design, right?"

Lady Isleen sat back in her seat dramatically, as if affronted, but Theon pushed on.

"But to answer Lady Aithne's question, I think the Lords and Ladies over the years *have* changed and adapted over time, but those advance-ments were as manipulated as everything else in Devram. All of those advancements were instituted to widen the divide between not only the Legacy and Fae, but also among the Legacy themselves. The mortals have been left alone because they could never challenge beings of power, but the Fae?" He chuckled derisively. "They could pose an issue if not kept under control, right?"

"That is enough," Rordan snarled, but Theon had seen the Sources in the room shifting on their feet, cutting glances at each other. "We are not here to discuss how Devram has evolved or been ruled in the past, and we are certainly not here to discuss how it will be run in the future. We are here to discuss the fate of Tessalyn."

"Death is the only fate I will accept in this matter," the Celeste Lady replied sharply.

"That seems a bit foolish, Luna," Rordan scoffed.

"It is anything but," she all but squawked. "The girl has been nothing but a menace since her power was awakened. Even before, her records state how she was a constant nuisance at her estate during her formative years. She has been given numerous chances only to prove time and again she cannot control herself. She continues to fight, and the people of Devram continue to fall. We gave *you* the chance to prove you could control the uncontrollable, and you have failed in that regard as well, Rordan. This is the only viable option I see moving forward, or Devram as we know it will fall."

"Do I not have her under control at this very moment?" Rordan demanded, light flickering around him, a golden mist swirling at his feet. "She is locked up at the Pantheon. You know the manner of beings those cells hold. She is under control there until an understanding can be reached. She is already responding favorably and has signed a Match Contract she was previously resistant to. She is wild, yes, but it just means she is taking a little longer to understand her place in this world."

"You mean her place in *your* kingdom?" the Serafina Lady asked. "You know well how upset we all were by your revelation at the Sirana Gala, Rordan. You expect us to be fine with you having that kind of power in your kingdom? Breeding it into your bloodline? I think not. I agree with Luna. Death is the only acceptable answer at this point."

"Death is the logical answer," the Falein Lady chimed in. "It would alleviate the most problems with one simple action."

"Simple?" Theon cut in. "We all know how difficult it is to kill a Fae, let alone a Legacy. You think it will be simple to kill *her*?"

"Dragons are difficult to kill, and we seem to have accomplished that fairly successfully," the Serafina Lady said with a mocking smile.

"Obviously not," Theon replied, his smile all teeth as he accepted what she was admitting to.

"Your kingdom keeping the existence of one a secret from the rest of us is not the victory you think it is," she replied coldly. "It only deepens the mistrust already sown in the events that led to their extermination in the first place."

"I wonder," Theon mused, holding her silver stare. "What will you do when you learn Serafina rejected her Match with Achaz and joined Arius?"

"How *dare* you speak such blasphemy," she cried in outrage.

But Theon only smiled. "So much time separated from the gods. While the other realms were free to advance and grow, Devram was left to rot. They made it look pretty with all the technology of the times, with the *gifts* of Fae and mortals to serve, but it's never been a gift to their legacy. It's always been a curse, and we have only warped that curse over time."

"That is enough!" Lady Isleen cried, her hands slamming onto the arms of her chair. "I call for a vote. Those in favor of sentencing Tessalyn Ausra to death, voice your agreement."

Three feminine voices rang out: Serafina, Celeste, and Falein.

"Your motion fails," Rordan said, his words full of power.

"Then we will find a way around it," she sneered. "We always do."

"Remember the cost of treason and failure, Maya," he replied darkly, the threat clear. "The Arius and Sargon Legacy played this game once before and lost."

Her smile was as sharp as his tone. "Perhaps you should remember that dreams born in the dark become nightmares."

The Achaz Lord's eyes narrowed on her. On this steadfast alliance that was cracking before Theon's eyes.

"Perhaps a short recess is in order," Rordan gritted out after a long, tense moment.

"Agreed," the Anala Lady said, immediately standing and striding from the room.

Theon followed suit, only he made his way outside and pulled his phone from his pocket. There was still no reply from Luka, but that wasn't what he was checking for anyway.

Opening his contacts, he clicked on a name and brought his phone to his ear as the call rang through.

"What, St. Orcas?" came the sharp answer.

"They're holding her in the cells in the Pantheon. Do you know where those are?"

There was a long pause before, "They are in the center."

"Fuck," Theon muttered, carving a hand through his hair. "You don't happen to have any tech that could get us past the Keeper, do you, Blackheart?"

"Getting past the Keeper won't be the issue," Tristyn replied. "It's the cell she's in that will be the problem. I'll need a few days."

"She doesn't have a few days," he bit out.

"I'll do what I can as fast as I can. Meet me there in two days at high noon. If I can do it sooner, I'll let you know."

"Not if," Theon snapped. "Make it happen sooner, Blackheart. Meet me there at sundown."

He hung up on the male, and Theon yelled a curse, startling two Fae passing by on the street. They practically ran to get around the corner, and he only then realized his darkness was undulating around him.

Hours.

He needed to stall this ridiculous hearing and outcome for the rest of the day, and he already knew how to do that. There were cracks among the kingdoms. Fragile alliances on the verge of breaking.

He needed them to shatter.

47
LUKA

Theon: We're having it out after this, fucker. I cannot believe you're sending me into this alone. This is not just about her, and you know it. Get your head out of your ass, and do what needs to be done.

Ignoring yet another message from Theon, Luka shut his phone off before sending it to a pocket realm. He didn't want to risk losing the thing with what he was about to do.

Dressed in black pants and a fitted long-sleeve black shirt, he tied his hair up before Traveling from his cave to the Arius manor. He didn't keep it down when he made his way up the stairs and down a hallway. Bypassing his own room, he went straight to a set of guest rooms. He didn't even bother to knock before he threw open the door.

Flames of black and orange greeted him, but he'd suspected as much, a shield of his own in place. When all the flames died down, Eliza stood there with a beautiful sword in hand, while Razik glared at him with glowing sapphire eyes, the pupils shifted to vertical slits.

"What is wrong with you?" Eliza demanded, lowering her sword.

"I need your help," Luka answered.

The female looked him up and down. "You look like you're about to do something stupid. Or dangerous. Or both."

"Both," he confirmed.

Looking up at Razik, she said, "We're helping him."

"We don't even know what he's doing," Razik countered.

"I don't care. I'm *bored*, Razik," she said. "I haven't stabbed anything for weeks."

"You sound like Scarlett," the male grumbled.

"I need to get out of this house. I need to do something other than research in books—"

"You love books."

"You know what I mean, Raz," she retorted. "We were sent here to help, and all we've been able to do is skirt around truths and confirm theories when they finally figure shit out. I need to *do* something."

Luka understood that feeling. From the moment he'd learned his father was alive, he'd been driven by a need to *do* something. Raiding Theon's books, he'd found everything he could about the Faven Palace and sat down to write any details he could remember about the time he'd spent there these last months. Tessa had said he was in cells, but he'd never come across them. He had, however, been keeping tabs on Tessa. She might have been blocking the bond, but she couldn't block that Tracking Mark Theon had put on her. He'd taken a page from Theon's book and used the thing to always know where she was.

It was how he'd tracked her down in that hallway on one of his first days there when everyone was looking for her. She'd seemingly appeared out of nowhere, Roan at her side, but as he'd watched her more and more over the coming weeks, she went to the same place more than once. Spent extended periods of time there.

He was a link to something I was desperate for. He kept me company when no one wanted me.

Those had been her words, and it had all clicked into place. There was an entrance to some sort of dungeon down that hall. They just needed to find it.

He waited while Razik and Eliza disappeared into their bedroom, becoming increasingly impatient with each minute that passed. While he waited, he wandered around their rooms. Various pieces of their lives were scattered about. Although he couldn't really say scattered. The room was remarkably neat for two people that rarely left it. The things that were left lying around appeared to be hers. A lone dagger here. Discarded shirt there. Ties for her braids collected in a small porcelain bowl. Luka preferred trinket tins for his hair ties, but this bowl was black, the light glinting off of it.

Swiping it up, he dumped out the hair ties before sending it to a pocket realm to retrieve later.

Moving to the table, he looked over books and notes. His brow furrowed as he read some of the hastily scrawled words. Something about the Fates and bonds. A genesis bond. That term was circled multiple times.

"We're ready," Eliza announced, and Luka turned to find her in black pants and some kind of white tunic. She had what appeared to be leather armor strapped to her arms, legs, and along her torso with numerous weapons sheathed...everywhere. Her hair was braided in a plait, and the hilt of her sword peeked over her shoulder. Razik wore black pants and boots, along with a loose black tunic.

"Based on your tight-fitting clothing, I'm assuming you don't anticipate needing to shift or summon your wings?" the male asked, sounding annoyed.

Luka shrugged. "It'll rip easy enough if I do."

"Wasteful," Razik scoffed.

"I'll buy you new clothes if you get blood on yours," he tossed back.

A growl rumbled from his brother, his lip curling, but Eliza stepped between them, practically bouncing on her toes. "You two can have a brawl later. Right now, let's go—" She paused, frowning. "You should probably fill us in a little."

"We're going to rescue someone being held in the Faven dungeons," Luka answered.

"Rescue mission. Great. Let's go," Eliza said, grabbing Luka's hand while simultaneously intertwining her fingers with Razik's.

Luka didn't let them ask any more questions, Traveling them to the very hall he needed. The wards would recognize him since he'd been staying here. These two, however, could pose a problem. Wandering through the halls didn't seem like the wisest of options, so he settled for the hall Tessa always emerged in.

"There is a hidden entrance here somewhere," he said, already inspecting the walls. "We need to find it."

"Are you sure it's hidden?" Razik asked.

He paused, looking over his shoulder. "I guess not. Why?"

"Have you checked all these doors?" he said instead, gesturing down the hall.

There were a few small doors he assumed were storage closets. He would assume if it was an entrance to a place prisoners were being held, there would be guards.

Or wards.

They wouldn't need guards if there were wards, and Tessa wouldn't have any difficulties getting around them because of who she was. The direct descendant of gods explained why she could always cross wards without issue. They weren't designed to detect beings like her. They were, however, designed to sense Legacy and Fae.

"You overlook the obvious," Razik said, less than impressed as he wrenched open a door down the hall.

"What do we do about the wards?" Eliza asked, coming up beside her mate as Luka approached.

Beyond the door was a set of stairs leading down, sconces lit by Achaz magic lining the walls.

"I don't know," Luka admitted.

"You don't have a plan for the wards?" Razik demanded. "Did you plan this out at all?"

"It was kind of hard to plan when I didn't know what we were going to find," he shot back.

"What good is rescuing this person if we can't get them out of here? More than that, how do you propose getting them out of the cell? I'm assuming it's more than wards keeping them imprisoned."

"You'd be right."

They all turned, the three of them drawing weapons, only to find Cienna standing there. As she approached, she slipped a hand into a hidden pocket of the suit she wore, producing three vials.

"Drink," she instructed, passing one to each of them.

Luka didn't question the Witch, downing the contents of the vial in a single gulp, but Razik and Eliza studied the liquid, holding the vials up to the light.

"What is it?" Eliza asked.

"A potion to let you pass the wards. It will only last for an hour at most. We must be fast," Cienna explained.

"We?" Luka asked.

"I have seen this play out many different ways over the decades. The only times you are successful is when I am along to aid you," she replied, brushing past them and walking through the doorway.

She didn't wait as she descended the stairs, and Luka shot his brother a look before he followed. He heard their footsteps behind him a moment later, and within minutes they'd reached the base of the stairs. Panes of glass lined the walls, and Luka peered into one, finding the cell empty. He reached out, pressing a palm to the smooth surface, then yanked it back with a curse as light speared into his being.

"The fuck?" he muttered, shaking his hand to ward off the sting. Then he went still when he saw who was in the next cell.

Valter.

Hazel eyes zeroed in on him, and the Lord lurched to his feet, stopping just short of the glass. He looked...terrible. The linen pants and top hung off of him, showcasing how much weight he'd lost. He had bands on his wrists keeping him separated from his magic. A cot and a bucket to piss in were all he had in his cell. His hair was long and a full beard had grown in.

"It's about fucking time," Valter snarled, his voice hoarse from disuse. "Did you bring Eviana?"

Luka didn't know what to say. It was surreal to see him in there. The bane of his existence for so long. The tormenter of his chosen brothers. The male who had forced him to take life after life after life.

He wished Theon and Axel were here to witness this moment.

"Luka!" he snapped. "Get me..."

But he trailed off as Razik and Eliza came to his side, and then he was cursing when Cienna appeared.

"You traitorous bitch," he rasped. "I see he rescinded the death order as the acting Lord."

"Did you know?" Luka asked, but a part of him already knew the answer. Handing his father over to Rordan was absolutely something the male would do. Force Luka to become completely dependent on him and his *charity*. Force him to be grateful for a place in his home. At his side.

Valter obviously understood what he was asking, his lip curling into a disgusted sneer. "I gave you everything."

Luka nodded slowly. "Including misery and regrets."

The male tsked, his gaze sweeping over Razik once more. "Who is this?"

"None of your concern," he answered.

"Are you going to free me?" he demanded, nearly slamming his palms to the glass again.

"Sure," Luka said. "In about twenty-five years."

He turned his back on the male as he screamed curses after him. His heart beat faster with every step down the corridor. Then his chest seized, and Luka momentarily forgot how to breathe when he saw him. There were no shackles. Only a collar of white stone at his throat. There was scarcely enough room for movement. He'd been given the same accommodations as Valter, and all Luka could think was *twenty-five years.*

His father had been here for twenty-five years, and he hadn't known.

He could feel Razik and Eliza beside him, but he couldn't look at them. Had no idea if his brother had figured it out yet. He couldn't tear his eyes away from his father.

The male's eyes had gone wide, bouncing back and forth between him and Razik. He opened his mouth, then closed it, as though he couldn't find the words.

Then Cienna appeared at his other side, and his father's gaze slid to her.

"Cienna Blackheart," he said, something akin to relief filling his features.

"Xan Mors," she returned in kind.

"It is finally time," his father said, and Luka could swear there were tears glimmering.

Cienna nodded. "If you can convince him."

Xan's eyes went wide, and his gaze skipped over Luka, swinging to Razik. "*Him?*"

"What is happening here?" Luka asked. "We are running on very limited time."

"There was a prophecy given when I arrived here with you and Tessa," his father answered, but his eyes were still fixed on Razik. "When a son learned truth, a genesis would commence. That's when my imprisonment would end. I just always assumed it was when *you* learned I still lived, not that…"

He trailed off, staring at Razik, and Luka shifted, a jealous sensation creeping up. He *was* the one who had learned the truth. *He* was the one who had planned all this. *He* was the one who had come to get him out of this place, and all his father could do was stare at Razik. The one who wanted nothing to do with either of them.

"How do we get him out?" Luka asked, turning away from him and facing Cienna.

"There are powerful enchantments here, and that stone around his throat prevents him from not only accessing his magic but shifting as well," she answered.

Horror washed over him. "He's been unable to access his magic or other form for twenty-five years?"

Cienna didn't answer. Instead, she said, "Your time is slipping away."

"Then what do we need to do?" he asked again.

"Dragon fire is one of the most powerful gifts in existence," she said. "But Achaz knows this. The enchantments here are designed to withstand any gifts of Arius and Sargon— dragon fire, starfire, and otherwise."

"That is not helping," Luka gritted out.

"It needs more. It needs something not recognized in Devram."

"Spit it out," Razik growled, his glowing eyes fixed on Xan's stare.

"Raz—" Eliza tried.

But the male suddenly rounded, glowering at Luka. "Is this why you brought me here without saying a fucking word? To use me to get him out?"

"I knew I'd need help," Luka admitted. "You've wanted nothing to do with me since you learned of our relation, and I assumed it'd be the same for him. But did I know how we were going to accomplish this? No. Do I know you're well read and knowledgeable in several areas? Yes. And that is ultimately why I asked you to join me."

"I'm sure it is," the male sneered.

"Fuck you, Razik," Luka said, finally reaching his breaking point. "I don't have time to debate motives with you. Either help or leave, and I'll figure it out myself."

"Or end up in the cell next to him."

"Like you'd give a single fuck if I did."

"Razik," Eliza said, drawing his attention back to her. "Just because you help here doesn't mean you have to do anything else. No one is expecting anything else from you, and even if they are, you helping here? That's all it is. It is not an offering of anything else."

The male clenched his jaw, and Luka knew he was fighting a shift.

"After this, we can leave if you wish," she added. "We do not have to stay."

Razik said nothing, but they clearly communicated down their bond because Eliza turned to the rest of them. "How can we help?"

"You are his?" Xan asked, pulling everyone's attention back to him.

"Yes," she answered immediately.

"His chosen inevitable?"

Eliza frowned. "If you are asking if I am his source, the answer is yes. If you are asking if I am his twin flame, the answer is also yes."

"That is not what I was asking, but the confirmation will suffice," he answered.

"Someone just tell us what the fuck to do," Razik snarled.

"You can combine your gifts," Xan answered. "Not as a source, but as—"

"Twin flames," Eliza finished. She looked up at Razik. "Scarlett and Sorin do this all the time."

"It's not the same," he argued.

"How is it not?"

"We both have flames. They're just different."

"So we combine them, and make them more powerful," she answered. "Or you absorb my magic into yours, and twist it all into dragon fire."

"We have minutes left at this point. For the love of Sargon, do *something*," Luka cut in.

And they did.

Black flames appeared at the same time as flames of red and orange and hottest blues. They tangled together, winding and twisting, until something burst from the center of it. One would expect a dragon, but it wasn't. It was a giant bird of dark flames, his eyes the bluest of fire, while its wings and tail were tipped in oranges and reds.

Razik yanked Eliza back with an arm around her waist as the bird let out a shrill call before soaring above them. Luka ducked, feeling the heat blaze down the back of his neck.

"What is that?" he barked.

Cienna was standing tall, watching the flaming bird. "A dark phoenix," she answered. "Anala favored phoenixes. Interesting that is what their magic chose to form."

"Yeah. Interesting," Luka muttered. This was anything but *interesting*. It was going to announce their fucking presence.

The bird circled again, seemingly with no sense of purpose.

"Control the fucking thing!" he yelled at Razik.

His brother met his gaze with glowing eyes, flipping him off before focusing on the magic. Eliza straightened, doing the same, minus the vulgar gesture. Luka didn't know what they did, but the bird made a sharp turn before diving. It pulled up a second before colliding with the glass of the cell, its wing brushing along the length. Luka watched as the glass cracked, spider-webbing in red and orange. Then he was throwing himself in front of Cienna as the window exploded.

His own flames burst forth, surrounding him and the Witch as it incinerated the glass shards raining down around them. Luka peered through the falling ashes, then he cursed. The flames hadn't only incinerated the glass in front of Xan's cell, but *every* cell down here.

Luka rushed forward into his father's cell, glass that hadn't been burned to ash crunching under his boots. His father hadn't been spared either, cuts and burns marring his skin and clothes. Luka winced, reminding himself he would heal once they got that collar off of him. He didn't know how they were going to manage that. All he cared about right now, though, was severing the chain connected to the wall. They could remove the shackle once they were out of here and safe.

"The chains?" he asked, avoiding looking at his father as he studied the silver links.

"Not the same, but dragon fire will not work," Xan answered.

Luka nodded, once again finding himself useless as he stepped aside so Razik and Eliza could approach.

"You do it, *mai dragocen*," Razik said, keeping a healthy distance away, but he sent a small tendril of black flames to her. She wound her own magic around it, producing only the smallest amount, before carefully twisting their joined magic around the chain. It sparked, heating to a glowing orange, then red, then blue before it snapped apart.

Razik didn't move, but Luka did, extending a hand to pull his father to his feet. His hand wrapped around his forearm, his touch far too cool for a dragon. He stumbled on his feet, as if he hadn't stood in ages. Maybe he hadn't. But surely he'd bathed recently, and his clothes didn't look aged. They seemed relatively fresh, and there wasn't an odor like he was sure he'd find with Valter.

Shit.

Valter.

His cell would be open too.

"Are you steady?" Luka asked, gaze darting down the hall.

"Yes," his father answered. "I will be slow though. I apologize."

He whipped his head to look at him. "Don't fucking apologize."

The answering smile was a grim one. "I fear I have much to apologize for, Luka. To you and your brother."

"Our time is up," Cienna said. Luka had no idea where she got it, but the Witch was holding a blade, twirling the hilt in her hand.

"We can't Travel out of here," Razik said. "I just tried."

"So we need to get back to the main hallway," Luka replied, throwing an arm around his father's waist to take some of his weight.

Razik's eyes grazed over them, but he didn't offer any assistance. If that was how he was going to be, then he would need to take on the responsibility of getting them out safely.

"Either help our father or lead the way," Luka said. "But expect company."

Razik's smile was sharp. "Eliza's been dying to spill some blood."

"I have not," she scoffed, but that was excitement in her eyes as she drew her sword.

"Where did you get that?" Xan asked, eyes wide and fixed on her blade.

She smirked at Razik. "I was faster than a dragon and won it."

"By mere seconds," he snarled.

"It's still *mine*," she tossed back.

"If I take out more guards in the next few minutes, I get to use it in the next fight," Razik said, sauntering past her and drawing a blade from his magic.

"Deal," she replied eagerly, darting past him.

Luka watched, more than a little confused at the interaction, but the clamor of feet told him guards were nearly here. He'd have to contemplate his brother's relationship later.

His father hadn't been wrong. He was slow moving, and Luka felt like he was dragging him along. Cienna kept pace on his other side. It hadn't escaped him she would have known Xan was down here this entire time. She hadn't said a word either, but the betrayal didn't hit the way it had with Tessa. He had expected something like this from Cienna. She had always spoken in riddles. For all he knew, she'd dropped hints, and he'd just never understood them. But Tessa?

After these past months? After the slow building of trust and breaking down of walls? After finally giving in and accepting he was part of something unconventional but not caring because it meant he could still have her? After all of that, for her to not say a fucking word?

"I'm ahead by two," came Eliza's voice.

"One," Razik growled, his flame-wrapped sword plunging into the gut of a sentinel. The dragon fire spread, turning the Legacy to ash.

"Luka!"

He paused at the gasped snarl, turning to face Valter.

"You will take me with you," the Lord said, limping forward. And yep. He definitely smelled.

Luka stepped back, taking his father with him. "You've lied to me. For years. You're lucky I'm not taking my time with your death right now."

"As if you'd dare after all I have done for you," the Lord scoffed, hazel eyes landing on Xan. "We all made sacrifices for the good of Devram. Isn't that right, Xan?"

"Do *not* speak to him," Luka snarled.

"Make a choice, young warlord," Cienna cautioned. "If you stay for vengeance, we may not walk out of here, even if you make it quick."

"As much as I wish I could, his death isn't mine to take," Luka answered. "He's wronged my brothers far more than he's wronged me."

"Glad to see you still have some sense," Valter said, foolishly attempting to straighten his shirt. "Let's go."

"I never said I was taking you with me," Luka deadpanned. "I'll leave you here for Rordan to find."

"You can't do—"

But a wall of flames erupted, a curse sounding from Valter as Luka turned his back on him. He could have killed him. Maybe he should have. But Tessa had left him alive for a reason.

She always had her fucking reasons.

He couldn't think about her right now. Right now, his focus needed to be on his father; so they made their way down the corridor, Razik and Eliza taking down any guards that crossed their paths. Eliza was a whirlwind of flame, her red-gold braid flying with every precise turn and strike. There was no doubt she was skilled as she threw a dagger before turning and plunging her sword into another. Razik followed her almost lazily, as if he trusted her to hold her own. If anything, it appeared he was letting her have her fun while still making sure he kept up with the sadistic competition between the two of them.

The Fates must have been on their side because they made it to the corridor, everyone Traveling out the moment they crossed the threshold. Luka helped his father lower onto a sofa, the male groaning.

"I haven't had cushion under my ass in decades," Xan sighed, sinking into the fabric.

Luka couldn't help his chuckle. "What do you need? Food? Water? Something for the cuts and burns until we can remove that collar?"

"Liquor," Xan said. "Valter's good shit."

Luka nodded, leaving to retrieve just that, and when he came back, Razik and Eliza were having a heated conversation on the other side of the room. Blood was splattered across her white top, blending in with her black clothing. She still held her sword, gesturing wildly with it.

"Put that away while we argue," Razik muttered, eyeing the blade.

She sent him a dry look before sheathing her blade.

"I brought glasses for all of us," Luka said, holding up the bottle and stack of shot glasses.

"See? Now we get alcohol," Eliza said, gesturing in Luka's direction.

"There is alcohol in our rooms, *mai dragocen*," he gritted out.

"Your *dragocen*?" Xan said, nodding stiffly in thanks when Luka handed him a glass before pouring the amber liquid into it. His father knocked it back, careful not to disturb that stone collar too much, before immediately holding the glass out for a refill. "You have completed the proving ritual?"

Razik's jaw clenched again, hard eyes sweeping over them.

"*Dragocen* is a word from our home world," Xan tried again.

"I'm aware," Razik growled.

"And you know what it means?"

Razik looked visibly affronted. "Yes, no thanks to you."

"What Razik means to say," Eliza cut in, "is that we have not completed the Trials yet."

But Xan shook his head. "You are blessed by the gods and Fates to have a twin flame bond, but that is not the same."

"What do you mean?" Eliza asked, taking a few steps closer until Razik's hand shot out and tugged her to a stop.

"What does *dragocen* mean?" Luka asked.

"It is an ancient language from the Beginning," Razik replied, his tone pure arrogance. "Dragons hoard treasure. Their most valuable is called *dragocen*. *Mai* is a claiming. My most valued treasure."

Luka looked at their father, who was sipping on his second glass of liquor. "That is true, but it is more than that."

"By all means, enlighten us," Razik drawled.

Xan's lips twitched as though he was fighting a smirk. He'd already picked up on his son's love of knowledge and was using it to pull him into a conversation.

Luka finally poured his own drink, settling into a chair. He still couldn't believe he was sharing a drink with his father.

"*Dragocen* is from an ancient language, but it refers to a bond that emerged with the Beings of Chaos," he answered. "It is the bond the twin flame was modeled after when the gods created it as a gift to their children and the Fae who fill their magic."

"Modeled after," Eliza repeated, shrugging out of Razik's hold.

Xan nodded. "I haven't had the pleasure of meeting you."

"You don't need to," Razik snapped.

She sighed. "Eliza. My name is Eliza."

Xan's smile was warm. "I've only witnessed your interactions with Razik for an hour or so, but I can tell you are his inevitable."

"That is the second time you've said that," Luka said.

"At its core, it is what a *dragocen* bond is," Xan explained. "An inevitable bond."

Eliza stiffened. "You mean a forced bond?"

"No," Xan said. "A bond can always be rejected. But if the proving ritual is done and accepted, it becomes inevitable."

"What is a proving ritual?" she asked.

"I am assuming my son sacrificed greatly for you," Xan said, his tone softening. "Perhaps nearly died? Proving he values you above all else?"

Eliza swallowed, looking over her shoulder at Razik.

It was the only answer that was needed.

"You will complete your twin flame Trials," Xan said. "But you are his *dragocen*. A bond not created by gods or designed by the Fates, but born of the stars and chaos. A pull that cannot be denied? That appeared when you both needed it most? Am I correct?"

Eliza shifted on her feet, her hands pulled into her sleeves and curling around the ends. Razik said nothing, staring coldly at his father.

"We thought it was just the twin flame bond," Eliza said quietly, and it was only when she spoke that Razik broke his stare.

He stepped forward, wrapping his arm around her and pulling her into his chest. "It changes nothing."

"I didn't intend for it to," Xan replied. "I only meant for you to properly understand." Then his sapphire eyes landed on Luka. "Both of you."

"If this is a bond of all the Chaos beings, then why is it called *dragocen*?" Razik demanded.

"That is simply what the dragons call it. Each of the Beings of Chaos call it something different, just as each being has adapted to it differently. Dragons become obsessively protective, guarding their chosen as the treasure they are. But in the end, it is the same. A chosen inevitable."

"That is a contradiction," Eliza said.

"That, my dear, is Chaos," Xan replied.

"I must go," Cienna said, striding back into the room. Luka didn't know where she'd gone. He'd forgotten she was even here. "With Valter free, my movements must be guarded."

Fuck. He'd forgotten about that.

"We have time," Luka said. "His first move will be to find Eviana. She's locked up in Faven. He won't leave without her."

"But she's not," Eliza said.

Luka's brow furrowed. "Yes, she is. Tessa would often visit her there."

"She's locked up, but not there," Eliza replied.

"She's in the cells beneath this house," Razik supplied.

"What?" Luka demanded, shooting to his feet. "The bond will lead him straight here."

"We blocked it," Eliza said quickly. "With a Mark. He will not be able to track her. We have experience with this."

"What are we supposed to do with her?"

Razik shrugged. "Ask Tessa. She sent Lange and Corbin to free her."

Ask Tessa.

As if that was some simple task.

A chosen inevitable.

Eliza was right. It was a contradiction.

But what if he didn't want to choose it anymore?

48

EVIANA

Head tipped back against the wall, Eviana reveled in the utter silence. Not in the surroundings. No, she could hear Ford shuffling around his cell. He'd tried to talk to her the first day, but had finally given up after she'd repeatedly ignored him. The sound of footfalls above them was a dull thumping here and there, and the sound of water in the pipes was a constant lullaby. But in her head? That was blissfully quiet.

Still, she heard the footsteps on the stairs, cracking an eye open. From what she could gather, Theon had cleaned out all the staff. Smart really. They were all loyal to Valter and would report any and all movements back to him. Even their beloved Pen and Caris betrayed Theon and Axel at various points. Denying the Arius Lord was simply never an option. It explained why Ford was down here and everyone else had presumably been reassigned to different duties. Food was delivered at various times, but it wasn't a consistent schedule like it had been in Faven.

She was still a little taken aback when it wasn't Lange and Corbin or even Razik and Eliza who appeared in front of her cell. Instead, she was staring into the sapphire eyes of Luka Mors.

"Show me the Mark," he said roughly, crossing his arms as he waited.

Without a word, she tugged the collar of her shirt to the side, twisting so he could see the blocking Mark. When she turned back to meet his stare once more, he asked, "Why did you take it?"

Her head tilted. "I suppose for the same reason you pledged your allegiance to Theon rather than Valter."

"But you have been his Source for decades."

"Have you not been forced to do unsavory things over the years? Or was it of your own volition that you took lives and inflicted pain?" she countered.

He was quiet for a few moments before he said, "We can't trust you."

"Then don't."

"That is hardly helpful," he scoffed.

She said nothing. Only held his stare and waited to see what he would do next.

Finally, he pulled a key from his pocket, slipping it into the lock before pressing a palm to the door. Recognizing his magical signature, it unlocked. He slid it to the side and gestured for her to follow him. She'd been here a few days now, and she assumed this was about being allowed to bathe. When she was led to the dining room, her curiosity grew.

"Take a seat," Luka said, sinking into one of his own.

Eviana scanned the room, taking them all in. It took effort to keep her surprise from showing when she found Xan at the table. It had been some time since she'd seen him. She'd known Valter had betrayed him, of course. She'd helped set it all up, so this was an interesting turn of events. He still wore the collar around his throat that kept him from his magic and from shifting, and she idly wondered how they planned to remove it.

"You truly cannot communicate with him?" Luka asked.

Her hands folded in her lap, she answered, "Will you believe my answer either way?"

His stare was icy, but he didn't respond.

"I already told you," Eliza cut in. "We have experience with this Mark. The only way it will stop working is if her power is allowed to completely drain."

"Did you ever see him in Faven?" Luka asked.

"No," she answered, her attention now fixed out the window. The sun was setting, not that she could see much of it through the clouds that had gathered. New life was starting to show though. Small buds on trees and glimpses of green in the yard. It made her magic thrum where it was locked away.

"But you could speak with him?" he pressed.

"Yes."

"And?"

Finally, she met his gaze once more. "The bond may be blocked, but I still cannot tell his secrets. It appears you are more than capable of unearthing them yourself," she added, her eyes flicking to Xan.

"Hello, Eviana," the male said coldly.

She didn't bother replying.

Luka rubbed at his temple with his forefinger, his elbow resting on the table. "We know he's going to come for her first now that he's free."

"What do you mean he is free?" she demanded, turning to Luka so quickly, her chair scraped on the floor.

He eyed her with suspicion. "When we freed Xan, we inadvertently freed everyone in the cells. Assuming he found his way out, I mean. We left him there."

She swallowed thickly, getting herself under control.

"Obviously he is going to want to find you. Does he have a Tracking Mark on you?"

"Why would he do that if there is a bond in place that allows for the same?" she asked.

"You'd be surprised," he muttered. Then louder, he said, "The point is, when he doesn't find you in Faven—"

"He knows I was moved," she interrupted. "I was not given the blocking Mark until I was here. He felt the bond being stretched and knew I was taken a great distance from him."

"Great," Luka said dryly. "All the more reason to believe this is going to be one of his first stops while he tries to track you down. We need to move you somewhere else." He looked at Xan. "Do you recall any holdings that wouldn't be obvious?"

"Much has changed during my time of imprisonment, Luka," he answered. "I suspect where he prefers to do business has as well. She would be your greatest source of information, but we cannot trust her."

"What did you and Tessa discuss when she'd visit you?" Luka asked suddenly.

"We drank wine. Or rather, she did. She can talk. A lot," she replied.

The male's brow furrowed. "She doesn't talk a lot."

"She does when given the opportunity."

Luka's glare was harsh. "And what will you do if Valter finds you?"

"What can I do?" she countered. "I am bound to him."

"Then you would return to him?" he clarified.

"You speak as if I have a choice to do anything else."

His finger steepled along his temple now, he contemplated that before saying, "That is a valid statement." He sighed. "Theon might know of a lesser-known holding, but he's in a Tribunal Hearing all day today. I don't think we'll be lucky enough to have that much time, especially if Valter figures out how to get those bands off."

"There is a place outside of Raven Harbor," Eviana said tentatively.

"I know of it," Luka replied.

"Valter does not enjoy going there. Says the city smells like fish."

"Why are you telling me this?"

"I am offering a suggestion," she replied. "A show of good faith, perhaps."

"We've already established we cannot trust you," he said.

"Believe what you will, but I do not desire to see him. He will be angry, and you know well how he expels such emotions," she answered.

She watched the male as he clearly debated what to do. One of his first real tests at being Theon's advisor and being forced to make a decision without consulting him first. Valter had never trusted anyone with such a role. He had close nobles like Julius and Mansel—had others who were trying to claw their way into such a position—but they were all disposable to him in the end. Theon, Luka, and Axel had forged something different. She'd watched it grow over the years, and while it allowed them to share burdens, it also created exploitable weaknesses.

"I can't leave you there by yourself," he said, rubbing a hand along his jaw. "Eliza and Razik are needed here, and Xan is not in any condition to monitor you."

She waited, letting him come to the conclusion on his own.

"I suppose as long as you are in bands, I could leave Corbin and Lange with you," he went on. "It won't be for long. Just until I can talk to Theon." His gaze bored into hers. "But I swear to the gods, Eviana, if you fuck with them or betray us, the only place you'll be going is the Underground."

As if that was any type of threat to her.

"May I retrieve things from my cell before we go?" she asked instead.

"What things?"

"A coat that Tessa gave me and a book I was reading."

"If Eliza and Razik will escort you while I speak with Corbin and Lange," he agreed.

Ten minutes later, they were gathered in the living room. Apparently Razik could Travel like Tristyn, and they were pulled through the air and stepping into a three-story brick manor. It was decorated as lavishly as any of Valter's other properties, and she stood with her hands clasped in front of her while Luka laid down a set of rules she paid no attention to.

The sun was setting fully when the male's phone rang, and he pulled it from his pocket to silence it. Seconds later, a message came through, and Luka cursed.

"I need to go...deal with something," he said. Looking at the Fae males, he asked, "You two can handle this?"

Lange rubbed at the back of his neck. "I mean, we don't really have a choice, right?"

"You are the two who went to retrieve her," Luka argued.

"Well, yeah. At Tessa's request. We didn't realize we would be *responsible* for her," he said, clearly uneasy about this entire situation.

He really should be.

"You have a phone. Contact me if you need anything," Luka said. "Whatever you do, don't take her bands off, and you'll remain more powerful than her."

Even without the bands, that was likely true, but no one needed to know that.

"I'll check in," Luka added.

"It'll be fine, Lange," Corbin said.

"I don't think we have the same definition of that word," he muttered.

Luka clearly didn't like this either, but whatever message he'd received had obviously made him feel like he had little choice.

"I'll check in," he said again before Razik Traveled them out.

She turned to the Fae, a hand slipping into her coat pocket and pulling out the extra comb that matched the one in her hair. The pair eyed her uneasily.

"You came from the Anala Estate originally, right?" she asked, watching Corbin's reaction.

"Uh, yeah," he said, a divot appearing between his brows.

Eviana nodded. "Lady Aithne has lots of secrets tucked away. What was her Estate like?"

"Similar to the others," Corbin answered.

"No need to lie," she tsked, toying with the comb. "We all have secrets. There's no denying that." She moved to the window, watching twilight settle over the Night Waters. Valter always had to have his grand homes just outside of the cities. Always separating himself from his people. "Can either of you drive?" she asked.

"No," Lange answered immediately.

"I suppose it's never too late to learn though, right?"

"Listen, I don't know what you're trying to imply, but we're not going anywhere," Corbin said. "Luka said to stay here, and that's what we're going to do until we're told otherwise."

"Spoken like a Fae."

"Because that's what we are," he shot back. "And while I understand our experience in the Arius Kingdom differs vastly from yours, we have it pretty good here. We're not going to do anything to jeopardize that."

Eviana smiled, something dark and promising. "I'm happy to hear that because if one of you doesn't learn to drive, the pretty good life you've grown attached to will cease to exist."

"What the fuck are you talking about?" Lange said. "All we have to do is call Luka and tell him—"

"You won't," she answered, sliding the second comb into her hair.

"I'll bite," he drawled. "Why won't we?"

"Because I know what you both are, and if that gets out, you'll undoubtedly never see each other again."

They stared at her, neither of them seeming to breathe.

"We're Fae," Corbin said slowly.

She sent a knowing look. "You're as Fae as I am," she agreed. "Which means not entirely. You even less than him."

"We don't know what you're talking about," Lange said, but his face had paled.

"I'm sure you've done well hiding the signs. Survival instincts and all that," she said, making her way out of the living room and down a hall. They followed just like she knew they would, and she led them up a small set of stairs before entering Valter's study.

She moved to the desk, pulling open the top drawer on the right and lifting the false bottom. A dagger sat there, the blade so black it absorbed the light.

A blade capable of killing a Fae or Legacy if you knew where to strike.

Valter had taught her where.

She supposed that was one thing she could actually thank him for.

Turning to the males, she held out her hand. "I'll take that phone."

"The fuck you will," Lange scoffed.

"You forget I have spent decades with the rulers of this realm," she said, her tone filled with venom as she darted forward. They weren't expecting it, and her dagger was at Corbin's throat before either of them could blink. "I know their secrets. In the time it would take your call to Luka to connect, I will have already killed your lover. While you were panicking, I will have alerted the Serafina Lady that you can hear the winds."

Lange's eyes went wide. "What does that even mean?"

But Eviana only smiled. "Make your choice. I don't have time to waste."

"What choice?" Corbin balked, holding out the phone to her. "You're essentially blackmailing us."

"This is Devram," she said casually, stepping back and lowering the blade as she slipped the phone into her coat pocket. "I don't know why you'd expect anything different."

"We freed you!" Lange cried in outrage.

She shrugged. "That was your mistake."

"And what, exactly, is the plan? Where are we supposed to go?"

"To the Serafina Estate. Why do you think I suggested this location? It will be the easiest place to cross the border."

"You planned all this?" Corbin said in shock.

But she'd planned more than this.

She'd planned wrath and vengeance.

"Tessa won't like this," Lange said.

"My loyalty is not to Tessa," she replied.

"It is to the *Serafina Kingdom*?" he said. "How is that possible?"

"I am loyal to no one but what I seek there," she answered, turning from them and heading for the door.

"Which is what?" Corbin demanded. "Maybe we can help another way."

"There is no other way," she replied, moving back down the stairs and heading for the door that would lead to the garage.

"We will be caught, and then we will all pay the price," Corbin argued.

"Then make sure we don't get caught," she answered.

"This is madness," he said, but a thread of acceptance was creeping into his tone.

Perhaps he was right. Perhaps this *was* madness. But madness would be needed to carry this out. She truly did not care if she died in the process, nor did she care who went down with her.

If this was madness, it was the only gift Devram had ever given her.

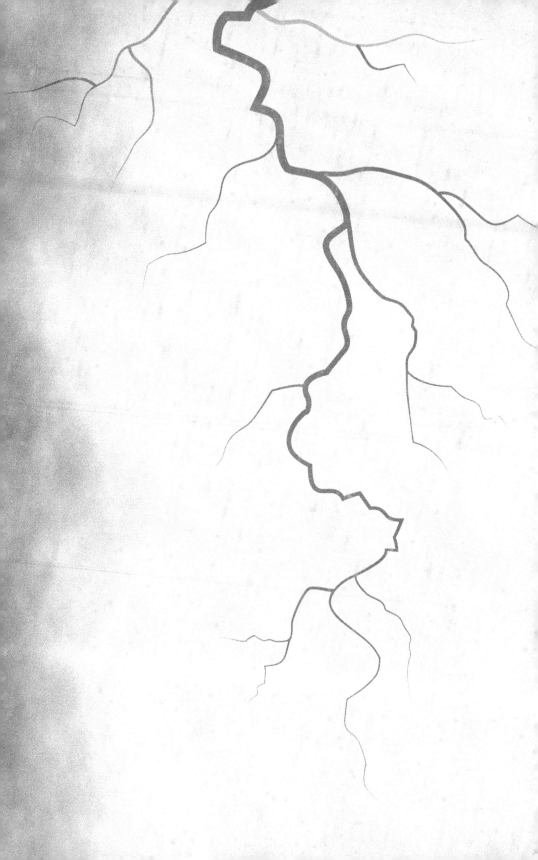

49
TESSA

T he wall of the cell was smooth beneath her fingertips as she moved along the perimeter, dragging her fingers. The bands on her wrists bit into her skin, but the ring? Gods, the fucking ring was trying to sink into her power, and her magic was fighting back. It was a constant war within her being, the chaos driving her half-crazy.

Or fully?

Maybe Theon had been wrong this whole time. Maybe the only way to survive in a realm full of monsters and villains wasn't by becoming one, but by giving in to the mania.

Humming a song from Axel's playlist, she made another pass. Her bare feet left prints on the dusty floor of the cell. She could feel it humming with power. Not just any kind of power though. This was more than Fae or even Legacy. This was the power of the gods.

This was Chaos.

The very essence of it was infused into this cell. It called to her as if it was a part of her. So much power in one soul. Something so small was never meant to hold something so mighty.

She didn't hear them approach, too lost to the call of it all, but she heard *his* voice.

"Tessa?"

It was tentative. Uncertain. So unlike him.

She turned to find the Heir of Death staring back at her. Could those emerald eyes see what lay in the center of her being? Could they see the chaos and the depravity? The sacrifices and the betrayal? The apathy and the hunger?

"No, but I can feel it all," he answered as if she'd spoken the thoughts aloud.

She lurched forward, wrapping her fingers around the bars. "Does it call to you too? Do you understand it? Because I don't, Theon, and I'm trying. I'm trying to understand."

"I'm starting to understand, beautiful," he said gently. "I'm starting to understand all of it."

"Then you can help?"

"I can help," he agreed.

Relief flooded through her, and it was only then she noticed the other figure in a cloak. The hood was down, revealing his face. His russet eyes had a sage glow to them.

"Keepers of the realm," she sang. "You and your sister. Both. Together and separate. So many faces. So many *secrets*."

"What is wrong with her?" Theon demanded, turning to Tristyn.

"We were all so worried about her siding with Achaz, we missed the obvious," he said. "Even Cienna missed it."

"Missed what?"

"Dark must bow and light must rule, but Chaos does not choose."

"Control the uncontrollable, or to fury they both lose," Tessa sang, dancing back from the bars. "Life must give and Death must take, but Fate requires more. So much more." She sprang forward again, practically climbing the bars. "Fate requires balance."

"Tessa, stop," Theon said, his voice an order and a small piece of her settled at the tone. "We're going to get you out of here, and then we'll figure out the rest. All right?"

A wicked smile curled on her lips. "Destiny beckons, and sacrifice demands."

"I know, clever tempest. I understand what's demanded."

"Who will be left standing when Chaos comes to reign?" she recited, her smile growing wider.

"Get her out of there, Blackheart," Theon growled. "*Now*."

"I'm working on it," he snapped. "I told you this would normally take a few days. These cells were designed to contain gods."

"Why would you ever need to contain gods?" Theon demanded. "They can't come here."

"Yet," Tristyn gritted out. "Now shut up and let me work. Keep her talking so she doesn't fall any deeper."

Tessa pressed her face to the bars, feeling the magic of them seep into her. She knew her eyes were glowing, could *feel* them doing so.

"He knows things," she whispered loudly.

"Yeah?" Theon said, taking a step closer. "What does he know, little storm?"

"He knows the female in the land in the sky."

He hummed in response, and it did something to her. Her eyes dipped to his mouth. "I know things too," she murmured.

He stepped closer. Leaning in, his whispered words brushed against her lips. "What do you know?"

"That I am wrong. An imbalance," she said, suddenly stepping back. Dragging her hand along the bars, a metal rasp echoed in the chamber as she began pacing back and forth. "Too wild. Too reckless. Too uncontrollable. Control the uncontrollable, but it takes more than one." She paused, looking over her shoulder. "It takes two. I'm not meant to exist. We break all the rules, all the bonds. All the visions and dreams, dreams and visions. Balance and no balance. It's all the same. Sanity and madness. Where's the line?"

"Tessa, I need you to stay with me a little longer. I need—"

She darted forward once more, her grip on the bars so tight her knuckles turned white. "We were always meant to destroy one another, but how do you destroy death when you want to drown in the darkness?"

"Blackheart," Theon barked. "We are out of time."

"I know. I know," he answered. He'd been muttering and drawing symbols and Marks on the ground. He pushed to his feet to face Theon. "Here's the thing: this area of the Pantheon is designed to keep things *in*. That is what we keep. Everything about it is designed that way."

"By who?" Theon demanded. "Surely you weren't here when Devram was created."

"No," he agreed. "But others were. Cienna and I are not the only Keepers. There have been others over the millenniums. Some have faded; others still live. One now leads the Apothecary District in the Underground. The point is, on the rare occasion something makes its way into Devram, a Keeper is here to meet it. Cienna and I were no exception. Neither were Xan and Luka when they brought Tessa."

"What does any of this have to do with getting her out of here?" Theon asked.

Tessa was listening, but she was also restless. She started wandering the perimeter of the room again. No windows. She couldn't see the sky.

"Because everything about it is designed to keep her *in*," Tristyn said in exasperation. "It's designed to contain gods. It is why technology is not allowed in the Pantheon. It is too unpredictable, and we don't know what those who make it through are capable of. We give them less to manipulate. I can get her out of that cell, but doing this quick and dirty is going to trigger other enchantments."

"Such as?" Theon asked.

Tristyn sighed. "You already know we can't Travel in or out of this part of the Pantheon. But if I break her out of that cell, she won't be able to Travel at all until I can properly figure out how to break the enchantment."

"She doesn't need to Travel. You can Travel us," Theon argued.

Tristyn shook his head. "You don't understand. It is an enchantment to slow someone down. If someone comes through, the enchantments are designed to hold them until their intentions can be established."

"Then how did Dex get through?" Tessa asked.

Tristyn's gaze slid to her. "You know the answer to that, wild fury. The Achaz Lord."

"He is not a Keeper," she said, her head canting to the side, and she ran her fingers through her hair, tugging on the ends.

"Correct," was all he said. Turning back to Theon, he added, "What I am saying is, if we get her out right now, you need to be prepared to *walk* out of here with her. Walk to your territory, and even then—"

"Half the rulers of the realm want her dead," Theon said. "Leaving her here for them to try is not an option, even if they are fighting among themselves right now."

"Then be prepared," Tristyn said. Turning to Tessa, he gestured to her. "I need some blood, wild fury."

"My blood summons those who serve Achaz," she said. Not a warning or apprehension. Just a statement of what was.

"Your blood can summon many," he countered. "We don't have time to debate this though. I need you to trust me."

"You used me," she hissed, her hands curling into fists. "For your own gain. I did not forget."

"I won't deny I have my own motives," he replied. "But that doesn't mean I do not care. I can have motives and still care. It does not have to be one or the other."

"It doesn't?" she asked in confusion, creeping forward.

He shook his head, a mischievous smile on his lips. "And when this is over, there's some lull-leaf and pizza with our name on it."

"Pretty words and promises don't work with me, Keeper of Lies and Deceit," she said, her answering smile dark.

"A blood vow then," he said, the dagger he was holding gliding across his palm.

"A what?"

"A blood vow is a promise. An agreement made between two people. If either party breaks it, the results are unfavorable," Theon replied.

"Isn't that what the Fae do when they are Selected by their Kingdom?"

That muscle feathered in his jaw. "Yeah. That's exactly what they are forced to do."

Her gaze swung back to Tristyn. "Why would you do this?"

"To prove you can trust me," he answered, gesturing for her hand once more. "A slice across the palm, and we merge our blood."

She hesitated for a moment, glancing at Theon. He nodded in encouragement, and she wondered when she'd started looking to him for such a thing.

Finally, she stuck her hand between the bars, the slice of the blade stinging against her flesh. Tristin took her bloody palm in his, russet eyes holding hers.

"I vow and swear my loyalty to you, Tessalyn Ausra, Daughter of Wild and Fury," he said.

A flare of white light emitted from their palms, and Tessa felt the vow settle in the depths of her being. Even the magic battling in her soul paused.

Then Tristyn was swiping a finger through her open wound before stooping and smearing it across all the Marks he'd drawn on the ground. He stood once more, the dagger in hand.

"I need to slice both palms, and you need to grip the bars," he said. She offered her hands without preamble, and the male turned to Theon. "Are you ready?"

Theon only nodded, stoic and steadfast.

Another stinging bite of pain, and Tessa wrapped her hands around the bars. They flared, gold and silver ashes swirling around the bars—

around *her*—and then the gate of the cell was swinging open. Theon was tugging her out before she'd even processed everything, and she sank into his chest as he stroked her hair.

His darkness wrapped around her, and the war in her soul calmed. Not completely, but enough that she could think clearly. She pulled back to look up at him, realizing once again it wasn't his darkness, but his dark wings.

"You came for me," she whispered.

"I told you I will always find you," he answered. "I have some things to tell you, but it would be better if we get somewhere safe first. Is that all right with you?"

A choice.

He was…giving her a choice.

She swallowed thickly, nodding her head.

Turning to Tristyn, he said, "Give her your cloak."

"Disguise her as a Keeper?" Tristyn asked, already pulling the garment from his body. "Brilliant."

Within seconds she was swathed in fabric that was far too big for her, but they'd make do. The three of them walked side by side through the passages. They met no one until they reached the main foyer. Tessa tensed, but Theon moved ahead of them, darkness trailing his footsteps.

"Dagian," he greeted.

The Achaz Heir looked from Theon to her, then back. "I assume that's her," he replied.

"The Keeper?" Theon asked. "No one knows their true identity."

"I am supposed to alert my father whenever someone emerged with her," Dagian said, ignoring the ruse. When Theon stayed quiet, only holding his stare, he added, "I was hoping it would be you that got to her first."

"And why is that?" Theon asked, dropping the pretense. Tessa stepped closer, itching to stretch out a hand to touch him.

"Because I know you'll do what needs to be done," he answered. "Let them pass, Sasha."

The Fae nodded, stepping to the side. Tessa hadn't even seen her emerge to block their path.

"I don't know what this is," Theon started.

"It is the start of a genesis," he answered.

Theon didn't move for several seconds, then he reached behind him, grabbing her hand and pulling her to his side. Together, they walked out of the Pantheon, Tristyn at their side.

"Can you put a glamour on her?" Theon asked as they discarded the cloak in the shadows.

Tristyn shook his head. "The enchantments won't allow it."

Theon said nothing else. They couldn't run. They didn't want to draw attention to themselves. Theon led them down side streets, keeping to alleys and using his darkness to mask them whenever possible. It wasn't until they were crossing into Arius Kingdom, the river coming into view, that she dug in her heels.

"They are waiting for us," she said, trying to tug Theon to a stop.

He paused, looking over his shoulder. "What do you mean?"

"This..." She looked around frantically, taking in the now dark waters of the Wynfell River shimmering in the twilight of the dying sun.

Theon was suddenly filling her vision, taking her face in his hands. "Tell me, little storm."

His touch grounded her, and she forced herself to hold his stare. "I have seen this. The Augury and Hunters. They are waiting for us." Her voice caught in her throat as tears welled. "Luka does not come to help."

"He will come," Theon said resolutely, as if there was no other option, but Tessa knew. She had seen this before. She already knew what was going to happen.

He would not come. Her betrayal had been too deep.

"Look at me, Tessa," Theon said. She hadn't realized she'd looked away. He dropped his hands from her face, pulling the bands from her wrists, then the ring. Her power flared, her skin glowing. "We are going to fight," he went on, beginning to pull daggers from swirls of black. "He has been training you, and you, Tessalyn? You are the most powerful being in Devram. No one decides your fate but you. Do you understand me?"

She stared at him, unsure of what to say. There was another swirl of black, and then he extended a gold dagger to her. The same one she had left in the study months ago.

"He's right," Tristyn said, and she turned to find him pulling weapons from his own magic. "You are wild and fury. Lean into it, Tessa. Let instinct guide you."

She shook her head, her mouth drying out as she clutched the hilt of the dagger. "The last time I... Roan almost *died* because of me!"

"I'm here, Tessa," Theon said, his darkness covering him like armor. "I'll help you control it. Can you trust me to do that?"

"I... I don't know," she answered honestly.

He nodded. "Okay. I'll work with that."

She didn't know what that meant, but then he pulled his two short swords, and gods. He *looked* like the god of death. Darkness drifted across his emerald eyes. His dark hair stirred in the wind as his wings stretched wide behind him. He held the swords as if they were extensions of him, and his power swarmed around him.

And her power wanted it all. Tendrils of light reached for it, winding into his darkness.

"That's it, Tessa," he coaxed. "Let them play. Let them become familiar."

She cocked her head, her breathing coming faster as he let her power explore and take.

Then his darkness bit back, and she gasped.

He smiled. Dark and wicked.

"Someone they fear as much as me," Theon said, and her gaze snapped back to his.

Maybe...

Maybe the villain had fallen in love with the monster in the end.

With a shuddering breath, she reached into her magic, her skin glowing brighter as her light wound around her in the way Theon's darkness clung to him.

"That's my girl," he praised. "Whatever you do, no matter what happens, do not stop fighting. Luka will come."

"He won't," she insisted.

"Until it comes to pass, the future can always change," he replied. "Let's go."

Theon led the way, Tristyn falling back and staying on her right while the river rushed along to her left. It wasn't until they crested a small hill that they saw them. Dozens of Augury members assembled in their cloaks and masks. Hunters hovered among them, and she knew none of those Augury members were Arius Legacy. They would have already been killed.

"Your mother is likely down there," she said to Theon as they faced them down.

"Then she will die with the rest," he said coldly. He looked down at her. "If Cordelia is here, will you let me kill her for you?"

Tessa blinked, her chest doing something it definitely shouldn't be doing at the idea of murder on her behalf.

"Yes," she breathed.

He bent, his arm wrapping around her waist and hauling her into him. His mouth landed hard on hers. His tongue licked at her lips, demanding access, and she let him in, taking from this kiss as greedily as her magic took from his power.

She didn't have time to think about what any of it meant. Not as the Augury and Hunters surged forward. They stood their ground, letting them expend their energy.

When she felt Theon tug on her magic, she looked up at him. "Trust me and trust yourself," he said, somehow looking at her like they weren't about to fight for their lives.

She nodded slowly, and then she closed her eyes. Drowning out the din and cries of rage. She let her own fury flood to the surface, growing and festering, and she felt his darkness there, providing a stability she'd never known.

Thunder crashed, and she opened her eyes to watch lightning strike directly into the center of the fray.

"Yes, Tessa!" Tristyn cried.

The howling of her wolves sounded seconds before Nylah and Roan prowled from the surrounding foliage. They made it to her side at the same time the Augury and Hunters met them. Then all that existed was weapons clashing and powers colliding.

She sank into her power, light arcing and striking. Her power feasted, only strengthening her.

A Hunter advanced, his white eyes peering at her. "I cannot kill you, your grace," he said in that voice that gripped her bones. "But I have orders to detain you."

"You can try," she growled in response. Then it was *her* tugging on Theon's magic. Light and dark wound around her dagger, life *and* death, and she sank it into the Hunter's chest. His wail rang out before he drifted away on the winds, nothing left but wisps of pale, translucent ashes.

"How did you do that?" Tristyn demanded, shoving his weapon through the neck of an Augury member.

"I don't know," she admitted. "But I'll do it again."

She bent, picking up the sword the Hunter had left behind.

"We'll guard you, Tessa," Theon said, falling into step on her other side. "Take what you need."

It felt wrong. Not Theon, but Tristyn. That was not how this was supposed to be. Someone else was supposed to be there. She still felt off balance, but she gritted her teeth. She'd done this. Now she had to face the consequences of her own actions.

Roan and Nylah had her front and back, and Theon's and Tristyn's magic swirled around her, leaving her to focus on her power. It was all instinct at this point. Even Luka's training had become part instinct. Her power sparked and flared as she swung her sword. Theon was a dark god beside her, his short swords cutting enemies down in quick succession. She could feel Tristyn's power working too, lulling their enemies into a sense of calm and keeping them at bay until someone could end their lives.

But she wasn't naïve. It was the five of them versus Legacy and Hunters nearly impossible to kill. They couldn't win. Not on their own.

"He will come, Tessa. Just keep fighting," Theon ordered, his sword never ceasing its movements. He'd clearly heard her thoughts.

Tessa shook her head as she lifted a hand, power arcing from her palm and bringing an Augury member to the ground with a scream of agony. "He will not," she panted, spinning to take on another. "He is too angry. He will not forgive—"

"He will," Theon snarled, cutting off whatever she was going to say. "He will come because we are his as much as he is ours."

"You need to call Eliza and Razik," she said. She was drawing up more power, her entire body glowing as gold and silver embers swirled around her. "He will not come, Theon. My betrayal was too deep."

"Whatever you did— Tessa, move!"

Theon dropped one of his swords, reaching for her and yanking her into his side as an Augury member got too close. But he hadn't seen the other one coming from the other side.

A moment before a blade met Theon's side, Tessa's hand connected with the person's throat, and before he could scream, black webbing erupted all along his skin as she pulled Theon's power into her and used it. She released the Augury member, and when he sank to the ground, her power flared even brighter.

Then Tristyn was cursing, and she turned, a gasp falling from her lips.

Because those were Night Children. Dozens and dozens of them.

"What are they doing out of the Underground?" Theon snarled, his eyes wholly black now as his power swirled.

As fast and strong as any Legacy, the vampyres were blurs as they moved. Even the Hunters were having trouble keeping up with them.

"There are too many!" Tessa cried. "We can't fight them all, Theon."

"We can, Tessa! Luka will come!" Theon replied, having retrieved his dropped sword. Darkness rolled from him like a wave, shrouding several vampyres. When it receded, they were dead on the ground.

"He won't, Theon," she argued, turning to him. "He's too—"

But her words turned into a garbled mess as pain seared through her spine. Blood bubbled from her mouth when she tried to speak again. She dropped to her knees, screaming as something was ripped from her back. She saw the vampyre from her periphery holding a sword dripping with blood.

Her blood.

Her magic was already swelling, working to heal the wound, but each breath burned in her chest.

Theon bellowed a roar, dropping down beside her and pulling her close. His magic lashed out, wrapping around the vampyre and dragging them closer. "You can't kill her with a sword, but I will make you wish for death for even thinking you could achieve it."

But the vampyre laughed. "It may take seven of those blades to kill a god, but only one should be needed for her."

Luka heard the crack from where he stood as Theon's magic broke his neck. His head twisted to the side at an unnatural angle before the entire being was ripped in half.

"No," Theon said as death continued to rain around them. "No, no, no! Where the fuck is Luka?"

"I told you... He won't..." Tessa tried, but she trailed off. She couldn't talk and breathe around her magic clamoring to heal her.

She felt the blood drip from the corner of her mouth as Theon held her. His magic wrapped around her, and she clung to him. Unable to get the words out. Unable to tell him she'd be fine.

Unable to scream a warning as a Hunter approached.

She scrambled, trying to draw her magic to the surface, but she was still struggling to breathe and focus and—

And the Hunter sank a gold blade into Theon's back.

And still Luka did not come.

50

THEON

His entire body seized, but still he did not release her. He clutched Tessa tightly to him, fighting to keep his magic around her, protecting her. He knew without looking it was one of those fucking golden blades. It had to be. There were few things that could pierce his magic so easily. If these beings were designed to hunt down Arius blood, it only made sense their weapons were immune to Arius magic.

"Theon," Tessa gasped. "Are you—"

"I will be fine," he soothed. "But we need to get out of here. Blackheart!"

Tristyn was there, fighting alongside the wolves with a skill that could only come with experience. Decades, possibly centuries, of experience. Any being that came near him met its end. Well, other than the Hunters, but they were dispersing for whatever reason.

"We can't Travel her," Tristyn yelled back. "I told you this."

Luka still had the bond blocked. He couldn't reach him, but surely he could feel their pain. Tessa's terror. His own rage. Even without the bond, the male was still his godsdamn Guardian. Where the fuck was he?

Not knowing what else to do, he pulled his phone from his pocket. "Then you Travel somewhere safe, and call Luka. Tell him... Tell him whatever you have to."

Because he refused to lie to her. He never had, and he refused to accept that Luka was forcing this to be his first.

And he refused to let her die. He refused to let this be her end, a prophecy playing out exactly as everyone said it would because it had been manipulated from the very beginning. Devram had tried to shield themselves from it, and instead, they had brought about the very end they feared. He finally understood why Cienna and Tristyn were so fearful to speak of the future. He finally understood why the Witches never wished to tempt Fate.

Because when you tried to learn the secrets of the Fates, everything changed.

One could go mad trying to stay ahead of the visions, constantly seeking new prophecies and omens, and still destinies would alter. In the end, nothing was inevitable. The only certainty among the stars was that fate was a culmination of choices made over days, months, and years.

"Are you sure?" Tristyn asked, while Tessa was shaking her head in refusal. The male was already tapping out something on the phone while the wolves continued to hold the line.

"We need...him to stay," Tessa gasped, but at least she was getting words out now.

"If he does not go get help, we will not survive this, and—"

He was cut off by the roar that ripped through the air, yet Tessa's sob of relief was still somehow louder. Everything stilled, all eyes going to the night sky, where not one, but two, dragons soared. One let loose another roar of rage, black flames blotting out the emerging stars, and then the Augury scattered. The Hunters hissed in outrage, disappearing into the air, while the vampyres followed the Legacy.

It did not matter.

Not as two dragons dove, dragon fire calling forth screams of agony before silencing them just as quickly. They left nothing behind but ash, and within minutes, the world around them was quiet.

One of the dragons landed beside them, the ground trembling at the impact. The other soared over the trees. Theon assumed it was going to search for stragglers who were attempting to escape.

Sapphire eyes were pinned on them before his snout was sniffing first her wound, then his.

"Yeah, you dick," Theon snarled. "We're hurt. Took you long enough."

Luka huffed, his shields crumbling. Guilt and regret barreled into

Theon down the bond, but as quickly as Luka had lowered his shields, Tessa was putting hers back up.

In a dull flash of light, Luka shifted. He reached for them, but Tristyn spoke first.

"She can't be Traveled right now. There are enchantments in place," he explained.

"Then what the fuck are we supposed to do?" Luka demanded, eyeing Tessa whose face was buried in Theon's chest.

Funny how this was something he'd craved from the moment he'd claimed her, and now he was trying to figure out how to fix...whatever the fuck they were. All of them. This whole godsdamn mess.

"Ideally, I'd take her to the Underground, but there's no way we can make it there without magic," Theon said, his body starting to not feel right. It felt...too heavy. Shaking his head and trying to clear his thoughts, he said, "The manor? It's closest."

"Except your father is free," Luka said grimly. "He'll be looking for Eviana, and that's one of the first places he'll go."

"Why?"

"It's a long story to tell when we're in a secure location."

His hold on Tessa loosened some, and not by choice. The world around him was going in and out of focus.

"Back to the..." he tried, but his arms fell to his sides. Tristyn lunged to grab Tessa while Luka reached for him.

"What the fuck? Theon? What's happening?" the dragon demanded.

Fuck if he knew. He just knew he was exhausted. So was his magic. He felt it slowly falling into slumber. Maybe he just needed some rest to recover. Every part of him liked that idea. Blinking was becoming increasingly difficult.

"Move," came a growled voice before another set of sapphire eyes was staring down at him. He sounded annoyed when he asked, "He was stabbed with a Hunter's blade?"

"In the back," Tristyn answered, sounding far away. Or maybe underwater? But that didn't make any sense unless he'd moved to the river...

"This is going to be unpleasant," the male said.

And then Theon was burning.

Everywhere.

His arms. His legs. His insides. All of it was on fire, and he couldn't go anywhere. He was being pressed into the hard ground, being burned alive. Thrashing, he tried to cry out, but his throat was on fire too. There was nothing but heat and excruciating pain as his lungs, his veins, his *blood* were ignited and scorched. It didn't stop as it ravaged his body from his feet to his fingers to his scalp. No part of him was granted mercy from the agony.

After what felt like hours, it all stopped. The sky was still dark. Luka still stood over him, and Tessa—

He lurched upright.

"Tessa?"

"I'm here," she said, and he found her still with Tristyn. Her eyes were wide, and those were tear tracks down her face. Had she been crying...for him?

"What the fuck was that?" Luka demanded.

He turned to find his friend glowering at his brother. Everything was still moving in slow motion, and he was *hot*. His clothes clung to him, drenched in sweat.

"He was stabbed with a Hunter's blade," Razik answered. "It is poison. Not to kill Arius blood but to paralyze. There is no antidote. There are only two ways to remove the poison. One way is burning it from the body with dragon fire."

"I know that," Luka growled. "I did the same for Kat once."

"Then why did you ask? Better yet, why didn't you act?"

Smoke appeared on Luka's exhale. "What is the other?" he gritted out.

"Persuading a Hunter to suck it out from the throat. It's not easily done," Razik answered.

"That's..." Luka trailed off, clearly disturbed.

But Theon was starting to think more clearly. "Tessa was stabbed. Before I was."

Everyone turned to her, but she was sitting up on her own. Still wide-eyed, but she appeared relatively fine.

"My magic healed me," she supplied. "Or still is. I'm not fully fine yet, but I don't think I need...that. A Night Child stabbed me. The Hunters are forbidden to harm me."

"Can you walk?" Luka asked, turning back to Theon.

"Maybe? Where are we going to go?" he answered.

"Back to the Pantheon," Tristyn said.

"There is no way we simply walk back into the Pantheon," Theon said, testing the mobility of his limbs.

"There is a hidden way. Once inside, we can go back to the center and decide our next moves. I think it's our only option right now."

So they went back the way they'd come, far worse for wear now. Tristyn stayed at Tessa's side, where she remained silent and withdrawn. Roan was on her other side while Nylah prowled ahead of her. Razik and Luka flanked Theon. No one spoke while they made their way back into the Acropolis. Theon was used to making sure he was seen, his power announcing his arrival. Sneaking down dirty alleys and trying to blend in was not an easy feat.

Finally, Tristyn drew a Mark in blood on a wall, and they all ducked inside. Tessa was tense in front of them, her movements stiff, but she didn't stop as they moved through the narrow winding passages. It was another twenty minutes before they all emptied into a large circular chamber. Theon immediately recognized the mirror on the opposite side. It was the same as the one in the Underground. What he hadn't expected to find was Eliza and another male with a white stone collar around his throat.

A male that looked an awful lot like—

"It's my father," was all Luka said. "Tell me what the fuck happened."

"You mean what the fuck happened while you were busy brooding and ignoring all my attempts at communication?" Theon shot back.

"Gods, you're pissy when you nearly die," Luka muttered.

"He didn't nearly die," Razik said, crossing the room to Eliza. "He was slowly becoming paralyzed."

"No one asked you," Luka retorted.

"You did," Razik deadpanned. "After I stopped the poison from spreading."

"You freed him?"

Those were Tessa's soft words as she stared at Xan, the male looking back at her almost with a fondness.

"Yes, and freed Valter in the process," Luka replied. "We need to come up with a plan—"

"Actually, we don't," Theon cut in, leaning against the wall.

"What do you mean we don't?"

But his gaze was fixed on Tessa, who was staring back at him. "You asked me if I understand what is happening, and I didn't until recently. Or maybe..." He sighed, swiping a hand down his face as he prepared to do this. "Maybe I just refused to accept it." For the first time ever, he watched hope flicker in her violet eyes. "The decree was never about ruling Devram; it was about saving it."

Immediately, that hope disappeared, everything about her hardening.

"Saving Devram," she repeated. "You mean what the Augury believes?"

Theon nodded. "They are not wrong, Tessa."

"They believe my very existence will be the end of Devram unless I am killed," she deadpanned.

"And they are correct," he said again.

"Theon, what the fuck are you talking about?" Luka cut in, watching Tessa, who was dutifully avoiding eye contact with the male.

"The balance," Theon said. "In all things there must be balance, and when the balance is left uncorrected for too long, the Fates are forced to intervene."

"I don't understand," Eliza said, stepping forward. "The Fates *don't* interfere. They often refuse to, letting natural consequences follow actions."

"Until they are forced to," Razik interrupted. "If the imbalance becomes too great and threatens the realms, they step in. Ultimately, that is their purpose. To make sure the balance is not allowed to tip too far to one side."

"What, exactly, are you saying?" Tessa asked, her power vibrating around her.

Theon held her stare when he said, "We're saying the Revelation Decree was a warning for Devram. If the balance is not corrected, Chaos will reign and the realms will fall. Time has run out. There are signs everywhere. The kingdoms are about to go to war with each other. Lines are being drawn, and old allies are betraying one another. Even the Underground is seemingly in disarray. The Night Children are not supposed to be in the kingdoms. The Fates will come for you, Tessa."

"So you are...going to hand me over to the Augury? To the Fates?" she demanded, gold and silver sparks floating around her, drifting through her hair. "After all of this, all of your promises about keeping me, you are just going to give me up?"

He smiled then, a soft thing he'd only ever give to her. "No, beautiful. I am going to give up Devram."

"Theon," Luka cut in. "I need you to spell this out. What exactly is the plan here?"

"The Fates will come here seeking Tessa, but when they get here, she will be gone," Theon answered.

"Gone?" Luka repeated. "Gone where?"

He turned to Razik and Eliza. "You are going to take her to Scarlett. I understand a goddess hid in your world for over a thousand years. That should be plenty of time to figure out a way to save her."

"She can't go there," Razik said. "Scarlett will not allow such a harbinger into our world so soon. Not because she does not care, but because she will not subject the people of Halaya to such danger. We are still recovering from a war we barely survived."

"But she can take her somewhere else? World walk her to another realm to stay hidden for the time being while a solid plan is formed?" Theon pushed.

"We can make sure that is done," Eliza agreed, stepping closer to Razik's side.

Turning back to Luka, who was staring at him in disbelief, Theon said, "When the Fates come here and cannot find her, they will destroy Devram, assuming she is being hidden here. It will take some time for them to figure out she still lives, just as it has taken time for them to find her here. This will buy her more time."

"Destroy Devram?" Tessa said, her tone betraying her confusion. "But...you will still be here? Luka? Axel?"

He pushed off the altar, crossing the room and taking her face in his hands. "Luka will go with you, Tessa." She was shaking her head, but he still cupped her cheeks. Swallowing his own emotions, he said, "He was always supposed to be yours, right? When I am gone, he can become your Guardian. The way it was always meant to be. Yeah?"

"No!" she spluttered. "You are condemning an entire world to death, Theon. There are innocent Fae and mortals here. There are... No!"

He couldn't keep himself from pressing his lips to hers, soft and tender. A way they'd never kissed. This was an entirely new battle of acceptance and denial.

Pulling back just enough to look into her violet eyes, he said, "Tessalyn Ausra, I would sacrifice all the realms and all the stars for you. You are perfectly wild. Perfectly untamed. You were not made to be caged, nor were you made to be a sacrifice for a realm that does not deserve such a gift. You were made to live in the light. Go live, little storm."

She was crying, her tears slipping beneath his fingers, and he swiped them away with his thumbs. But that was not sorrow in her eyes.

It was fury.

"You *lied* to me," she seethed. "You told me you would always find me, and now you are *leaving* me?"

"I will find you in the After, Tessa. I'll be waiting for you. You will forever be mine."

"No," she said, shaking her head in refusal. His hands slipped from her face. "No," she repeated. "You don't get to just *decide* this, Theon."

He turned to Razik. "You know how to call Scarlett?"

"Yes," he answered. "We will work out where to hide them."

Theon turned to Luka, who was still staring at him. Summoning a half tilt of his lips, he said, "It is the last order I'll ever give you."

"You're really doing this? Condemning an entire realm?" Luka demanded.

"To save her from something she never asked for? Never deserved to be shoved into? Yeah, Luka, and I'm trusting you to take care of her," he answered. "Make sure she leaves."

The two stared at each other a moment longer before Luka was pulling him into a hug. "You don't have to do this."

"I do," Theon answered. "I've finally accepted that I have run out of time."

Stepping back from his chosen brother, he turned to Tessa once more. She was pacing, her hands in her hair, and he caught her wrist, tugging her into him. "Be happy, little storm."

"No," she said, still shaking her head.

He reached up, brushing hair back from her face and taking her all in. The violet eyes with gold and grey peeking through. The golden hair. The light winding up her arms and making her skin glow. He leaned in, pressing a kiss to her brow, before cupping her cheek.

"Be happy," he repeated. "But more than that, be *free*, Tessa."

"You lied to me!" she cried again, shoving at his chest while simultaneously clutching at his shirt. "You lied to me, and I hate you for it!"

"I know, little storm," he said, holding her close a second longer. "But know that I am yours. Every piece of me."

Then Luka was behind her, wrapping an arm around her waist. He easily picked her up off the ground, gently pulling her backwards and away from him. She thrashed in his arms. Tears of wrath were streaming down her face while her cries of fury echoed off the stone walls.

With one last look at the ones he loved most in this world, Theon turned and walked out of the chamber, doing the one thing he'd sworn he would never do.

He let her go.

CHAOS DOES NOT CHOOSE

She toyed with the storm in her palm, the orb of energy crackling with gold and violet light. Silver and gold sparks flitted throughout.

So much Chaos in the palm of her hand.

With a dark smile, she tossed the orb up, watching it swell and grow. It soared higher, seeping into the clouds until thunder rumbled. The sky lit up with the same strikes of violet and gold, and a moment later, it began to rain. Big, fat drops that splattered against her face as she leaned against the balcony railing looking across the vastness below.

"I have asked you to stop doing that," came a voice full of power. A voice that often sparked fear. A voice others might fall to their knee for. A voice people *worshipped*.

A voice that made her dark smile only grow to one of wicked delight.

"One cannot deny their nature. After all, my father *creates*. Naturally, I do the same," she replied, turning to face him.

Blue eyes with brilliant flecks of gold glared back at her. His golden hair was tied back, but a few strands had fallen free and fell into his face. At least he'd tamped down on the gold mist that usually followed him around.

Of course, that was self-preservation when he came here. Her magic would lose control if he let his own power linger.

And she would let her magic have its way.

"Yes, let's talk about your *creation*, Akira," Achaz sneered, keeping a healthy distance from her.

Adopting a faux innocence, she replied, "Whatever do you mean?"

"She deflects her purpose just like you did."

"My purpose?" she questioned, moving along the railing and dragging her fingers along the stone while the rain continued to fall around them.

Her father narrowed his eyes.

She laughed, climbing onto the railing. One foot in front of the other. Heel to toe. Balance, balance, balance. There was no such thing. In all the realms. Across the stars. Only Chaos.

So much Chaos.

"I do so enjoy riddles," she quipped, the railing slick beneath her bare feet as she moved. "Would you like to hear one?"

"No," he snapped.

"That's disappointing."

"What is disappointing is you being too weak to control the gifts you were given."

Akira's head tilted. Others might feel the sting of his barbed words, but she only cackled. "You did create such a mess, didn't you? Thinking you could control Chaos." She clicked her tongue in disapproval. "Power does drive us mad, though, doesn't it?"

"Akira," he growled, his power flickering around him.

Her magic snapped to attention, lightning crackling around her as gold and silver embers flared.

"You chastise me for not having control, and yet you..." She sank down onto the railing, hooking her knees over it and hanging upside down. "You have no control, do you?"

"Akira, stop this," Achaz ordered, and she felt him step closer.

So foolish.

She stretched her arms, toying with her hair where it hung in the air, swaying in the wind.

"Power can drive us mad though, can't it?" she murmured. "We're drawn to it. Crave it. *Sacrifice* for it. It wants us, and we want it, and what are we to do?"

In a flash, she pulled herself back up, once again balancing on the railing. "You cage me up here. Wards and enchantments." Her lip curled up at the words.

"For your own safety," Achaz gritted out.

Her head canted to the side. "Do you think that is what they tell my mother as well?"

"Gehenna did her duty," he retorted.

"Yes, yes. Lay on her back and spread her legs. Gave her power so you could take what is not yours," she sang, pushing onto her toes and spinning, her arms out at her sides.

"And what of you, daughter?" Achaz sneered. "Did you not do the same?"

She leapt from the railing, each step echoed with energy that skittered along the balcony, charging the air around them. "I am the daughter of creation and magic. *You* made me more. I wasn't enough for you."

"I wanted to give you more," he retorted.

"And you did," she purred, circling him. "You created *Fury*."

"Akira—"

She shot forward, pressing a finger to his lips. "Shh," she hushed. "You are not the calm to my storm. You took him from me. Then you took her. You created this. Sparked every bit of it. You thought you would use this against me?" The laugh that fell from her lips was pure mania. "Did you know I could see forward in time? A gift from my mother." She practically floated backwards from him. "Would you like me to tell you a story?"

"No," he barked.

"Too bad. You have no control here," she sang, the rain falling harder now.

"I have no control here?" he retorted. "I am not the one trapped in this tower, Akira."

She held up her hand. A silver band encompassed her pointer finger, a large, black onyx stone in the center. "Not for much longer," she returned, her power thrumming at the idea of freedom.

"I can never let you free," Achaz said, the words laced with power and dominance. "You are too..."

"Impulsive? Reckless? Uncontrollable?" she offered.

"You refuse to let me help you."

"Help me?" she scoffed. "Father, you only wish to use me."

"No, I—"

She lurched forward, power in her palms, and Achaz caught her wrists, halting her a moment before her hands landed on his chest. "If you wished to help me, you wouldn't have separated him from me. The only one who understands is wild and untamed. The only one who helps me control Chaos."

"I can have Anala come back. I know I've waited too long to send her to you—"

"No, no, no!" She cried, shaking her head and her eyes falling closed. "We can harm her, and she is a friend. Taika understands, but she is busy. I need him. Only wild and untamed, and you—" Her eyes flew open, hard and merciless. "*You* took him from me."

"And you created something that should not exist with him," Achaz snarled.

Akira tipped her head back and laughed, the sound getting lost in the rumble of the sky. She yanked her wrists free of her father and slowly walked backwards from him until she reached the railing. Dragging her fingers along the surface, she let the rain and the thunder and the storm ground her.

"In all things, there must be balance. Beginnings and endings. Light and dark. Fire and shadows. The sky, the sea, the realms. The worlds are no different. Beings emerged from the Chaos to create such a thing," she sang, holding his gaze the entire time. "Beings of Chaos. More than one, but there was one who wasn't satisfied. Never satisfied."

"Akira—"

A bolt of lightning arced from her palm, slamming into a shield of pure light, but she heard his muttered curse.

"Do *not* interrupt my story," she said coldly. Clearing her throat, she continued. "Never satisfied and consumed by vengeance, he created out of revenge. But he upset the balance more than Arius. More than Serafina. He brought his creation to the Source of Chaos, and he took. He took what was not his to have and created something just as strong as the gods and the Fates, the dragons and the angels." Moving along the railing once more, her fingers dragging with every step, she said, "And so the Chaos drove her mad. Chaos is uncontrollable, and she became the same. But he tried, didn't he? He tried to control her, not realizing he had created one just as powerful as him. She was not a god, nor was she a Fate. She was not born of the Chaos, but *created* from it. He realized too late that she would be the one to ruin his everything."

Achaz was staring back at her when she finally turned to face him fully once more. Light wound up her arms while gold and silver embers floated around her. Lightning flashed in her eyes, and the sky echoed in kind.

He was a god, but she was a Fury.

Uncontrollable wrath fueled by Chaos itself.

And her daughter?

She was so much more.

She was wild and fury. Light and dark. Beginnings and endings.

But while she was created from vengeance and Chaos, her daughter was created with all that and more. Her daughter was created out of something pure and selfless. Out of acceptance and understanding. Out of something unconditional and unbreakable. Out of something inevitable and uncontrollable.

If she could find the same, she would know peace. She would be what she was created to be.

Salvation and destruction.

"It will take more than you and a child to ruin what I have built," Achaz said, power flickering in his eyes, but nowhere else. "And if you continue down this path, it is destruction for all of you. Give me your ring, and let me save her. For you. I will bring her to you, and—"

Akira laughed. "I will not cage her, and he will come for me."

"Temural cannot come here."

She brushed a fingertip over the black stone in her ring. "He will always come for me."

"Not this time, daughter. I will never allow it."

"Then I wonder," she mused.

When she didn't continue, Achaz gritted out, "Wonder what?"

"A Being of Chaos playing with things he shouldn't. What will you do when Chaos comes to reign?"

Because he was a god, but she was a Fury.

And her daughter?

She was Chaos.

BONUS CHAPTER

Need more from the new Arius Lord? Who doesn't? Learn all about how Theon was feeling while Tessa and Luka were at the cave in this bonus chapter.

You can find it on my website at https://www.melissakroehrich.com under Book Extras.

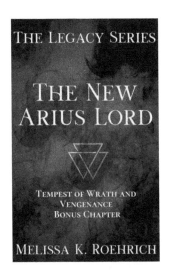

A NOTE FROM MELISSA

Book three!

When I say I have been waiting to write this book since I started writing this series, it isn't an understatement. Devram is messy and raw, and I don't think it's really all that much different from our own world. We grow up being taught to believe certain ideals, and many times it takes harsh realities and hitting rock bottom to make us question those things. We always have a choice on where to go. There are forever crossroads that alter fate and destiny.

We always have the choice to call bullshit on fate.

My characters are flawed, as we all are, and I hope that even in the depravity of Devram, you see the faint flicker of hope. I hope you know that you are worth fighting for, and that you can break generational cycles. I hope you know you are strong enough to get back up one more time. I hope you know that you don't have to have everything figured out right now. And I hope you know that your past does not define you. There are consequences for actions, yes, but you get to decide how to move forward from here.

We have one more book to go. Writing the last book in a series is always so bittersweet, but I promise I'll put my everything into it. These babies deserve nothing less.

Until next time, let them underestimate you... Then prove them wrong.

XO- Melissa

ACKNOWLEDGMENTS

This wouldn't be my life without **you, the reader**. You do so much in my world without realizing your impact. The messages and comments, passion and excitement. It all fuels my soul and pushes me to keep going on the hard days. Thank you.

To my Book Slut Besties: **Brit Irvin, Sara Abel, and Tracey Goodson**, we did it! We made it through another book. Every time, we sit back and wonder how we made it here yet again, and every time, I know I couldn't have done it without you.

To my dearest Bestie in the entire world, **Miranda Lyn**: I remember writing some of these first chapters with you while we were at murder house. Thank you for hours of talking out plot. Thank you for believing in me. Thank you for helping me get to the finish line. It may have taken nearly four decades to find each other, but you're my soulmate and there's no going back now.

To **Sarah Mori** and **The Realm Studios**, for every single damn thing you do, thank you. For the constant encouragement and love, for the laughs and the friendship. Thank you.

To my beta readers, **Ashley Nolan and Rachel Betancourt**, thank you for the spirals that end up being nothing and all the laughs, reactions, and love. I adore you both. To my editor, **Megan Visger**, you make me and my writing better. If I could find a way to bond you to me forever, I'd do it. Just saying. To **Covers by Jules**, whose covers are utter perfection. To my audiobook narrators, **Laura Horowitz and Christian Leatherman**, you are two of my favorite people, and I cannot thank you enough for being so damn amazing. To my agent, **Katie Shea Boutillier** and the Donald Maass Literary Agency, thank you for all your words of wisdom and expertise. The relief I have knowing you are in my corner is invaluable.

To my **ARC/Street Team**, your love and enthusiasm are unmatched.

I am so honored you continue to choose to be part of my team. Thank you.

To **my boys**— You don't have to have life figured out anytime soon. The world will wait for you, and I cannot wait to see how you shake things up.

To **my husband**— Thank you for indulging in my constant Chaos. I love you.

ABOUT THE AUTHOR

Melissa K. Roehrich is a dark fantasy romance author living her best life in the Middle-of-Nowhere, North Dakota. She resides on a hobby farm where she homeschools her three boys with her husband. They have four dogs, several barn cats, and chickens. When she's not writing or reading, she's probably watching reruns of *How I Met Your Mother* or *Gilmore Girls* while trying to convince her husband they need to add goats to the farm. She loves coffee and traveling and dreams of owning a dragon someday.

Scan the QR code for links to social media and other ways to stay connected!

Printed in the USA
CPSIA information can be obtained
at www.ICGtesting.com
LVHW092242161124
796641LV00012B/491/J